Married to Murder

(A novel)

By

Caleb Lott

Kindle Direct Publishing

Though inspired in part by true events, the following is a work of fiction. Any similarities to any actual persons, places, events, or circumstances are purely coincidental and is in no way any representation of any actual persons, places, events, or circumstances; and if it seems so, it is purely in the mind of the reader.

To Marilyn

Flee fornication.

> I Corinthians 6:18
> Holy Bible
> King James Version

Prologue

One winter night, when I was about four years old, on the occasion of one of my family's twice-yearly excursions to visit relatives in the country, my mother awakened me out of a sound sleep, wrapped me in a thick blanket, and carried me outside into the freezing air. In the dark, we carefully negotiated the steps off the tall porch into the yard in front of my grandfather's weathered old house that sat on a hill near a dirt and gravel road two miles from the paved highway.

As we made our way across the yard to a lighted driveway, I could see a knot of men standing at the rear of a pickup truck. Among them were my uncle and a couple of my father's in-laws. They were standing around a buck deer that was strung up by his foreheels; tied to the lowest hanging limb of a mature oak tree next to the gravel drive.

Wide eyed and shivering, I watched as the men made an incision on the animal's forehead and began the process of removing the hide. They pulled the pelt down off the front quarters and the back, and then cut into the belly. As I watched, I felt no shock, no empathetic pain for the animal, no feeling whatsoever.

I looked on silently until the meat was divided, the head and rack were presented to the shooter, and the carcass was abandoned in a field not far from the house; a gift for the nocturnal omnivores that roamed the woods on my grandfather's eighty acre parcel. Afterwards, I went back to bed and off to sleep, very quickly.

A couple of years later, when I was six, at my maternal family home in upstate Mississippi, I was ushered by my mother to the bedside of my grandmother who was in her last moments before succumbing to cancer. As I stood, posed next to her bed, even *I* could see that the woman was unconscious and very unaware of my presence.

The room was cool and dry, and one lone, very dim light bulb in the corner illuminated the space. My mother took my hand and laid it in her mother's palm. Then she spoke loudly several times in an effort get the dying woman's attention.

"Mama, it's Henry. It's Henry, Mama. He's here."

After a couple of minutes, when there had been no response, I was commanded out of the house and into the front yard, where my father and I leaned on the fender of our family's 1962 Mercury and waited. A couple of hours later, my mother and her siblings exited the home, sniffing, and announced that my grandmother had expired.

Once again, I was either too young or, rather unbelievably, too calloused to feel any pain or grief. My grandmother was, and then she was not. I knew her, but, frankly, her passing affected me little.

I didn't know what those two incidents meant – then. Now, I do.

Chapter 1

The 1990's

It took close to a year to close the Zoe Woods case; and nearly two to finally get it completely resolved at trial. Will, my partner, a very outspoken and opinionated man, said that it would never be solved, especially after we saw what kind of person she was. But then she died, and he said we had a chance.

It was not that we couldn't have made the case with her alive, but early on we found out that she was 'slow.' By that I mean she had an IQ somewhere around seventy-five or eighty – barely walking around sense, Will said – and it would have been difficult trying to get a jury to make sense of anything that she had to say on the witness stand. So, when we got the call that she was dead, it made our work a whole lot easier – we thought.

Will – Sergeant William John Eubanks, called 'Snuffy' all of his life by everyone who knew him, except me – had over twenty years experience in death and homicide investigation and had seen just about all the pitfalls there are in making a murder case. He hadn't seen everything, but he'd seen a lot, and he knew that putting a mentally challenged person in front of a group of average citizens who otherwise knew nothing about a case like this – and she would *have* to testify or everyone would wonder why – and asking them to decipher what she had to say, would be next to impossible.

I was inclined to agree with him. I had once watched another stunted victim on the witness stand. When she was asked to identify the perpetrator who had raped and stabbed her, she pointed at the defendant. When asked how she knew it was him, she said that a local television newsman had told her so. It seemed that the station had aired the perpetrator's mugshot at the time of his arrest, and our victim thought the anchor person was talking to her, telling *her* that he was the guilty party. Needless to say, we lost the case, and, frankly, we were never quite sure that the woman understood that she had been wronged.

I say all that to say that we had an uphill battle from the beginning, which was, for me, when I was called to work at a little after five AM on a Saturday morning in late February, the 20th to be exact, to investigate the serious assault of a woman found off Lauderdale Road in Theodore, Alabama, a small bedroom community five or so miles southwest of Mobile.

The Sheriff's radio dispatcher told me by telephone that an ambulance, while on its way to pick up a heart patient on Dauphin Island, had spotted the woman lying on a short, dirt trail off the north side of the road. The EMTs had dispatched another ambulance to the Island and then had stopped to check on the woman.

A deputy had been sent to locate the crime scene and was standing by. I was to report to the Emergency Room at Springdale Hospital.

The dispatcher told me that the woman had been found that morning at about four but that the hospital had just gotten around to calling. I said, that was fine, was she dead? The dispatcher said, no, that they were working on her in the ER and that at the moment she was stable. I said, okay, I would be there within thirty minutes.

I got up and rubbed my face. The heater in my studio apartment was set on 72 degrees, but I was cold. I showered; brushed my teeth; and dressed in khaki pants, a white, long sleeved polo shirt with the Metro Sheriff's Office badge embroidered over the left breast, and chukka boots. I wore one pistol on my right hip and another on my

14

left ankle; and after making sure I had a steno pad and a pen, I set out.

The weather was freezing. An icy wind was blowing from the south, off the Gulf of Mexico; and though my feet were cold, the lining of my black, all-weather jacket managed to keep out the bluster reasonably well.

At that time of the morning, in winter, the sun has not yet arisen, and it's the darkest time of the night. As I sat in the car warming the engine, loneliness and anxiety began to creep over me. They were familiar feelings; feelings of doubt and angst, as if I was walking into a situation that I couldn't handle, to a problem that I couldn't solve, into a tunnel with no light at the end of it. I felt like I was rocketing into outer space on a trip to nowhere.

See, I didn't view cases the way that other detectives did. They saw crime as a puzzle to solve; kind of a game to play. They enjoyed the challenge and the uncertainty. I didn't. To them it was fun. To me a case was more like a disease from which I had to be cured, an affliction to throw off. Unlike my peers, I considered it hard work, and when one of my cases went unsolved, I took it personally, and I saw myself as an incompetent failure. In some ways, I was dead from the illness. It was a wonder that with such a poor outlook I was able to survive, much less succeed.

It was odd that I was even in this line of work. I hadn't started out to be a policeman, much less a detective. I had wanted to be a salesman, but the economy, and the times, dictated to me another path, and I was just making the best of it. Soon, I was typecast, and the work had so damaged my personality that I was fit for nothing else. My father once told me that, somehow, we all just kind of fall into the work that we're supposed to do, and really, after that, we're stuck with it. I've often wondered if that was true, and just how rich I could have become doing something else . . . but, I digress.

It took fifteen minutes to melt the ice from the windshield, but once underway, I made good time in almost

15

non-existent traffic. I live about ten minutes from the hospital. I made it in seven.

Springdale Hospital was a two hundred bed infirmary located on Darby Drive about a half mile north of US 90 – called the Blue Star Parkway by locals – a mile or so east of the Mobile city limit sign. It sprawled over a twenty or thirty-acre campus and was the newest facility of its type in the city.

I turned my government vehicle out of the darkness and into the emergency room parking lot at about half past five. The lights made the area as bright as day, and their brilliance was a welcome sight. They made me feel as if I was still in a world with which I was familiar, one with which I could cope, and not some strange, foreign land where I was a peculiar alien with an impossible task.

The ER doors were at the head of a circular driveway on the east side of the campus. An ambulance was parked against the curb near the door with its lights on and its diesel engine idling.

Inside, the Emergency Treatment Department consisted of a waiting room, six curtained examination rooms, and a doctor's office. The admissions counter was inside the ER proper and was separated from the waiting area by a magnetic door.

Becky was the recorder that morning. She was a twenty-something blonde with a full figure hidden under pink scrubs. Her most outstanding feature was a mouthful of sparkling, straight, white teeth. She knew it, so she smiled often. She recognized me from the two earlier times that we had spoken.

"Just coming on?" I said.

"Yep." She yawned and buzzed me in, past the magnetic lock.

"I heard you guys're having a pretty big morning around here."

16

She nodded toward the back of the examination area. "Oh, you mean her? Yeah, it's been kinda busy. I heard the night shift say she'd coded twice already."

"You know anything about her?"

"Just that the ambulance guys were going to get a cardiac case down on the Island and they saw a pack'a dogs standing around something on the side of the road. They stopped to see what it was, and it turned out to be a body." She made a face. "Yuk."

"Well, that was certainly an odd thing for *them* to do; stopping to see what the dogs were looking at, I mean. It looks like they would've had their minds on getting to the heart attack patient."

She shrugged. "I don't know about that, but can you imagine a pack of dogs standing around you sniffing and licking; maybe waiting for you to die? Ewwww. That's like from a horror movie or somethin'."

"Any idea who this person is?"

She looked down at some papers on her desk. "Uh, no. Just, India 43."

'India 43' was a hospital designation given to the woman when she came through the front door without a name. Like 'Shotgun 12' or 'Africa 76,' there was no rhyme or reason to the label. It was just a noun and a number given to her so that at the most vulnerable time in her life she would have an identity and not remain a nameless lump of humanity on a table.

I looked toward the rear of the room. "Alright if I go on back?"

She smiled again. "Sure. Stop back by before you leave."

If she was coming on to me, I was glad, but I couldn't tell because she was always friendly, and she smiled very broadly at everyone. I smiled back, walked past her, and took a deep breath.

To me the emergency room is a study in contrasts. It's the intersection of injury and healing; the place where the sterile setting of therapy meets the soiled environment of the outside world. It smells of cleaning fluid, but also of sweat, body odor, and waste. The linens and towels are spotless, yet there always seem to be bloody gauze and wrapping papers on the floor. The lights inside are brighter than outside, yet not as intense; they're somehow softened, muted.

I walked three steps forward and looked around the room. My eyes started at the front, immediately to my left, and began to scan down the examination spaces until I found activity. My eyes stopped at the theatre farthest from the door. The mesh curtain, on a runner in the ceiling, was about half open, and I could see a small knot of people standing around a table. I walked that direction.

When I got within five feet, I paused. There were three individuals, a male and two females, standing around a body lying supine on an examination table. The male was tall with sandy hair and a round face. One of the women had wedge cut, dark hair. She was husky and had a pale complexion. And I could tell by the white coat that the other female was wearing that she was the doctor.

A step closer and I could see that the person on the table was a naked female. The overhead light was pulled to within four feet of her body, and I could see her dirty feet. There were bloody towels and sponges, as well as paper wrappers that had previously contained tubes, bandages, and other sterile articles, strewn about on the floor.

The woman wearing the coat must have heard me because she looked up. I recognized her as Julia Harris, the ER doctor. She didn't smile, but she wasn't frowning either.

"Hey," she said.

Though I had responded to several of her cases, she never called me by name. Doctors are like that.

"Good morning, Doctor Harris." I peered into the space. "Can I take a look?"

She turned aside. "Sure, come on in. We've got her stabilized right now, but she was in a bad way earlier."

Taking a couple of steps forward, my eyes ran over the naked woman from crown to foot. The female nurse, whose ID badge identified her as 'CHARLOTTE,' shot me a dirty look, after which she got a towel and laid it across the woman's groin, thereby concealing her genitalia.

I wondered what that was all about. The last thing this victim could possibly be worried about was her modesty. As I began to picture in my mind the glimpse that I had gotten of the woman's pudenda, I thought of the naked women of all ages and races that I'd seen in the course of my work. This one seemed no different from the rest.

"So, what's up, Doc?" I said.

Harris was a glamour girl who appeared badly miscast as a physician. She was about forty-five, five-two, with muscular legs and shoulders and tiny hands and feet. Her olive complexion was unblemished, and her medium length-hair was streaked with blonde highlights, parted in the middle, and puffed with hairspray.

But the most noticeable thing about her was her wardrobe. She eschewed the scrubs that nurses and other employees wore. Every time I'd ever seen her, under her personalized, white lab coat, she'd always worn a dress – usually some garish frock with a psychedelic design – and abnormally high heels; stilettos, I think they're called. Costume earrings hung from her lobes, and it was not unusual for her, when she was not working on a patient, to have several bracelets on her wrists and more than one necklace around her neck.

Harris was married to a psychiatrist whom she'd met at the hospital; and she only worked at the ER one weekend a month, just, as she had once told me, to keep her license up and her hand in. She no doubt wanted to maintain a viable income stream when the divorce that was inevitably going to happen finally came to pass. The shrink was her third husband.

"Well, it looks as if this poor girl had her throat cut," Harris said as she pulled off her rubber gloves. She looked down at her dress to see if it was stained.

"We've been able to stop the hemorrhaging, but her pressure is still pretty low." She looked down at her patient with brows raised. "She coded twice; once in the ambulance, and once here."

I nodded toward the victim. "Is that the way she came in?"

"Yes. Well, except for a shirt and a bra."

"You'd think she would have died of exposure."

"It's certainly cold enough, her body temperature was eighty-nine; but oddly, that's probably what saved her. It slowed her heart rate down, probably stanched the bleeding, and generally kept her unconscious until someone could find her."

I looked closely at the bizarre gash in the woman's neck. It went from ear to ear.

"That laceration her only wound?"

"I'm not sure, but I think so. We haven't had time to go over all of her." She looked back around at the shelf behind her and pulled a clean pair of gloves from an open box.

Once protected, Harris started at the woman's head and began a full body exam. She ran her hands all over her skull; looked into her ears and eyes, down her mouth, then felt her ribs. Harris removed the towel from the unconscious woman's groin and using two fingers spread apart her vaginal lips.

"Well," she said. "This is exciting."

I watched as she pulled at the corner of a piece of cloth. What looked to be a pair of women's underpants unfolded from inside her vagina. Stuffed in by force, the tightly packed cloth emerged slowly.

"Is that what I think it is?" I said.

She unfolded the garment and held it up. "Sure is. See here?" She found the label on the back of the waistband. "Vassarette."

I shook my head in disgust. Charlotte the nurse, the one who had tried to protect the woman's decorum, had a sick look on her face; and the male nurse, who had not spoken, finally did.

"Man, that had to hurt."

I chuckled in spite of myself then wiped the smile off my face after I got another dirty look from Charlotte.

"Would you complete a rape kit, Doctor?"

"Sure." Harris nodded and gave the appropriate directions to Charlotte.

A rape kit, consisting of vaginal swabs, pubic combings, and just a good going over of a woman's privates by the doctor, is about the only way to really make a rape case these days. With women giving sex away often enough, allegations of sexual assault always turn out to be a 'he said/she said,' proposition. And, unless a doctor looks at a woman, documents her injuries, and is able to wipe some sperm out from inside her, it's hard to convince a jury of rape. We were lucky in this case. Our victim had been in no condition to cleanse herself of any evidence, including the lingerie.

I stood and watched as the doctor and both nurses continued the examination. Charlotte waited until they were finished and was just about to wash the woman down when I stopped her.

"Wait, wait. Let me take a few photos . . . just in case."

She looked at the doctor, who nodded affirmatively. I turned and walked out of the ER at a brisk clip. When I got to my car, I took a thirty-five millimeter camera from its case in the trunk and was back at the victim's bedside within three minutes.

Standing over the unconscious woman, I snapped photos of her face and neck; then I worked my way down to

21

her legs and feet. Before they put them in paper bags and turned them over to me, I also got a few shots of her shirt and brassiere, as well as the blood-soaked underpants that had started out white but were now pink.

When I finished, I turned back to Harris. She was washing her hands and preparing to get back to her office, where she no doubt really wanted to be, to dictate her report.

"Why do these nights always have to happen when I'm here?"

She spoke rhetorically, knowing full well that when she worked the twenty-four hour period starting at six PM on Friday and ending at six PM Saturday that she would see more than her share of violent cases. I waited for her to dry her hands before I spoke.

"So, Doc, what are her chances?"

"What do you mean?" she said. Her tone was playful, not accusatory. "She's been healed." She smiled broadly and threw out her hands.

I chuckled. "No, really."

Harris took a deep breath and exhaled. "Well, the only real problem is infection, and possibly some brain damage. We just don't know how much blood she lost and for how long. Truthfully, she could code again at any moment."

"Did you notice any damage to her vocal folds?" I said with an eye on one day talking to her and trying to get her to answer back.

"You know, that's a question for the surgeon who'll operate on her. I really didn't take the time to notice much in there. I think, well, I'm sure, there was some muscle damage and also some injury to her esophagus." She paused and looked back toward the woman pensively. "She's really lucky, you know."

"I'm glad one of us is."

Chapter 2

I spent the next few minutes making notes for a police report and getting the nurse to examine the woman's body for any scars, marks, tattoos, amputations, or deformities, or anything else that might help identify her. I looked at her face. It appeared as if she was sleeping peacefully.

She was a white woman, about thirty, with dark brown, almost black hair that was straight and parted in the middle. Her face was plain, save for a mole on her right mandible. There was a small chip off the canine on the right side of her lower bridge, an injury that all present agreed occurred prior to the assault.

The stitches that closed her neck were merely bastings, just something temporary until she could get to the operating room. She would need a plastic surgeon to return her to some semblance of a normal appearance. Oddly, there was only one small bruise on her face, a quarter-sized contusion below her right eye.

She was a small breasted woman whose weight was proportionate to her height. Her pasty complexion was by and large unblemished, but dirty from her ordeal. Her nails were cut short, but filed and buffed. She was about 5'4" and a hundred and ten pounds; all in all, an average-sized female whose appearance said that she didn't spend a lot of money on herself, probably because she didn't have it to spend.

I looked at the male nurse whose badge pegged him as 'Rusty.' He looked bored.

"Rusty, did her labs come back yet?"

"Yeah, I think the doctor's got'em." He paused. "Lots'a alcohol, no drugs; .22, I think."

"That's what I was lookin' for."

I went back to my note taking and tried to think of what else I needed to do right at that moment. A mental checklist materialized in my head: clothes, photos, injuries. All that was left was to interview the ambulance attendants. With any luck they'd still be at the hospital.

The two paramedics, a male and a female from City Ambulance Unit number 41, were in the hospital's cafeteria eating breakfast. The expansive dining hall was almost deserted. They were seated in the corner closest to the exit that led back to the ER.

"Mind if I join you guys?" I said smiling.

They looked up at me, and I could see the suspicion in their eyes until they spotted the embroidered badge on my shirt and the notebook in my hand.

"Sure," the male said as he looked up from a plate of eggs, toast and bacon. His left fist completely encircled a glass of orange juice.

He was brown haired, not a day over thirty, and he had the look of a weightlifter. I made him a veteran. His white polo shirt had the 'City' logo on the left breast, and there was an EMT patch on his left sleeve. Underneath the shirt, he wore a thick white sweatshirt.

"Henry Faulkner, Sheriff's Office."

"Bill Thomas."

I nodded at the female who had looked up from her bowl of cereal and was smiling. She was a blonde with a round face and rosy cheeks. Her pudgy figure was clothed identically to Thomas. She swallowed and spoke.

"Sylvia Marshall."

"Are you the two that brought in the woman from Lauderdale Road?"

They both nodded while continuing to eat. After I opened up my notebook, I looked at the woman first. She'd have more to say, and in greater detail.

"You guys get off at seven?"

They nodded again. Marshall took a bite of toast.

24

"Can you tell me what happened?"

Marshall emptied her mouth and took a drink of water. "Well, we was on our way down to Dauphin Island to pick up a cardiac patient, and we were comin' down Lauderdale Road. Billy was drivin'. We were headin' to'ards 193, doing about forty-five, I guess."

"Can I stop you for just a minute? You weren't running code?"

"Oh, no. See, there were medics on scene down there, and they were looking after the old man. It was called in as a heart attack, but it was really just an arrhythmia, I think." She looked over at Thomas.

"Once we got underway," he said, "we talked to the medics down there by radio and found out it wasn't that serious; they just wanted him to go to the hospital as a precaution. His doctor just wanted to be on the safe side."

I looked back at Marshall. "So, you were going forty-five . . ."

She nodded. "Right. So, we're drivin' along and Billy says, 'Hey, I think I saw something.' So he slowed down and turned around in the road, and we come back; and we saw these dogs, there must have been six'r eight of'em, just kinda' millin' around with their heads down, on this dirt road."

"A dirt road?"

"Well, a dirt trail, really."

"It's a farm access road off Lauderdale," Thomas said. "I bet it ain't a quarter mile long; just leads up into a field – a soybean field, I think."

"Whereabouts is it?"

"'Bout halfway between Bellingrath and Rangeline; on the north side."

"So," Marshall continued, "we drove up there and the dogs scattered, and when Bill turned on the spotlight, we could see a woman layin' there."

"Anybody else around?"

She shook her head. "Nope. Just the dogs."

25

"How'd she look?"

Thomas spoke up. "She had on a shirt that was pulled open, and her bra had been cut open in front; but nothin' else."

"No shoes?"

"None that I could see," Thomas said.

"No pants, either?"

Both of them shook their heads.

I wrote quickly. "And what time was this?"

Thomas looked at his watch. "About three thirty, quarter to four."

"Okay, so you found the woman . . ."

"And we got out and checked her for a pulse," Marshall said. "Well, Billy said he found a faint one, so we got out some blankets to get her warm."

"What do you think the temperature was out there?"

Thomas shrugged. "I bet it wadn't much over thirty. It was cold, now."

"When did you call it in?"

"Sylvia radioed the office that we were gonna have to stop on the call to the Island, and that they should get another truck to go down there."

"Anyway," Marshall said, "so we got her on a gurney and got it in the back, and then got underway; and Bill's checkin' her all along, and he says, 'uh oh, she's codin'." She looked at Thomas. "We was about halfway up Rangeline, I think. So, I pulled over and jumped in back with him, and we start workin' on her; and we brought her back."

Marshall smiled as if extremely proud of herself. The two had saved a life. It was my guess that all they had done was delay the inevitable. The girl would probably be dead soon.

"So, we started up again and brought her here. I guess you know the rest," Thomas said.

"Well," I shook my head and chuckled, "not yet."

After we concluded our conversation, I walked back to the ER. I wanted to get another look at the woman, but she'd already been moved to a room. I sat down at a desk next to Becky and cleaned up my notes.

"So," she said, "any leads?"

"Not yet." I paused. "Got any ideas?"

She nodded and smiled. "The husband did it."

Chapter 3

My next stop was the crime scene. I left the hospital, drove south on Alabama Highway 193, and when it dead ended into Lauderdale Road, I turned west. In five minutes, I spotted a Sheriff's Department patrol car parked on the side of the road with the engine running.

The sun had risen to clear skies. The temperature was still down, and it wasn't expected to get much over forty, but, except for the cold, the forecast was for a beautiful day.

I stopped my vehicle behind the marked car and got out. Ice crunched under my feet as I walked forward. When I got to the driver's door, I was surprised to find a female deputy behind the wheel. She looked around at me and then got out.

"Hey," I said. "What's goin' on?"

Her name tape identified her as, M. CRENSHAW. She was tall, but her solid build made her look very fit. Her brown hair was pulled back in a ponytail, and she wore no makeup. She looked feminine, but not ladylike.

"Are you Detective Faulkner?" Her voice was an alto, but clear, not hoarse.

"Yeah. Which way to the scene?"

"Well, best as I can figure, it's up this little trail." She pointed north.

I nodded that direction. "Let's go."

We walked side by side, eyes to the ground. The sand was very fine, and very dry, so I didn't expect to see footprints. There were, however, some hard places where there appeared to be tire tracks. The tracks I saw looked thinner than the ambulance tires. I had no reason to believe it was our suspect's vehicle, but on the off chance that it was, I turned to Crenshaw.

"Go ahead and tell the dispatcher to contact Roy Rogers." Rogers was the Identification Division supervisor.

She nodded and removed the portable radio from her Sam Browne belt. When some other radio traffic died, she made the call.

I looked around. "Let's fan out a little and see if we can find out where she was when the EMTs found her. We're looking for a lotta blood and some clothes."

About thirty feet from the paved road, Crenshaw veered to the right side of the trail, and I to the left. I walked up and down, then back and forth, in a grid search. The ground was alternately firm and loose. A few sprigs of grass mixed in with the silt made up the landscape.

In three minutes, Crenshaw spoke up. "I think I've got something."

I walked to where she was and stood over a brown, low cut, leather shoe. It looked to have blood on the toe, and it looked expensive.

"Good. Just mark it."

By the time we finished, Crenshaw had located both shoes, a pair of socks, and some bloody jeans. I found the location where she was cut; across the road from the clothing. It appeared as if her assailant had cut her throat, then took off her clothes and flung them over to the other side of the trail.

"You got any crime scene tape in your car?" I said.

"Yeah."

"Well, get it and let's find a way to rope off this area." I paused. "And, be careful and don't step on any prints out here."

Crenshaw left and in minutes returned with a roll of barrier tape emblazoned with the words, 'POLICE LINE, DO NOT CROSS.' We managed to find enough dead stalks of whatever grew in the field in the spring and summer to tie the tape in a large square.

I made notes and tried to stay warm, while Crenshaw waited in her car. It had been thirty minutes since the call had gone out for Rogers. I hoped it wouldn't be much longer. He only lived three or four miles away.

In ten minutes, a Ford SUV with opaquely-tinted windows parked behind my black, county-issue Crown Victoria. A short Hispanic, who was not Roy Rogers, got out and walked towards me. He was wearing a departmental-issue brown jumpsuit with patches, and black boots.

Chuck Hernandez was one of the department's newest ID officers and had recently transferred over from the Patrol Division. His big smile and white teeth made his complexion seem even darker.

"Detective Faulkner?" He had no accent.

"Good morning. Roy not comin'?"

"He sent me along also. I'm supposed to get the photography done."

29

"Okay, well, here's what we got. A woman, who we've been unable to identify as of yet, somehow found herself out on this dirt road this morning with her throat cut. A couple of EMTs picked her up and took her to the hospital. She's still alive right now, but it don't look too good."

Crenshaw, who had gotten out of her car and joined us up the road, stood by and looked at Hernandez. I thought I caught a glint in her eye.

"Deputy Crenshaw here will show you what we found and where." I waved an arm. "Just do that voodoo that you guys do, and let me know what you find."

He smiled then turned to Crenshaw. "All right, show me what ya got."

She smiled at him. It looked like love to me. I turned toward my car.

Chapter 4

In twenty minutes, I was pulling into my parking space at the Metro Sheriff's Department's Administration building on Western America Circle in Mobile. I had just enough time to get the paperwork done before lunch. While at the office, I could also check the missing person reports to find out if anyone had reported our anonymous victim absent from her home, or anywhere else.

The Sheriff of Mobile County is required to keep an office in the Mobile County Courthouse, however, about ten years previous the county had built a new building to house the courts, as well as all the other city and county offices, and, since they didn't want the Sheriff around, they called it the Mobile Judicial Complex and kept him out. He was so offended that he moved his whole department, lock, stock, and handcuffs into a nine story, steel, office building near the intersection of Airport Boulevard and Interstate 65 and billed the county for the move and the rent. Then he started working behind the scenes getting the state legislature to pass a bill making it the Metro Sheriff's Department, and in five years he had total law enforcement authority in the county. Each municipality still had its own agency and its own chief, but they all answered to the Sheriff.

The Major Crimes Bureau was located on the seventh floor, two floors below the Sheriff and just above Property Crimes and Vice and Narcotics. Our office, mine and Will's, was located in the northeast corner of the building. There were offices on every wall and several cubicles in the center. Three interrogation rooms were located on the north side. Each one was outfitted with a tape recorder and a one-way mirror. The boss was Captain Linus Askew.

On the way in, I stopped on the first floor at the Records Division to look for a report on my victim. There was only one person on duty that weekend, and when I knocked on the door, she was in the back eating a biscuit.

"Hey," the woman said after she opened the top of one of those Dutch doors.

Patty was a pudgy, thirty year old with dishwater blonde hair, a porcelain complexion, and a needle nose.

"What can I do you for?"

"Hey, yourself. Any missing persons cases come in from the night shift? I'm looking for a white female with brown hair; about 5'4", 110 pounds."

"Hmmm, that sounds a lot like me?"

She was 110 pounds in her dreams. "Why, that's silly," I said. "We know where you are."

She giggled. "Well, let's just see."

At her desk, she picked up an inch thick stack of reports and thumbed through the first ten or fifteen. "These

31

are the ones that came in this morning." She shook her head. "No missing persons."

"Okay, just give me a call if ya see one; and also call the city police and see if they've gotten anything." I left her and caught the elevator up to my office.

In some ways, I loved working weekends. The solitude allowed me to get twice as much work done; and the fact that none of the supervisors were around didn't hurt either. Most importantly, I could run things with complete autonomy, and there's something good about the feeling of being in absolute control; though I knew I wasn't.

I slid into my chair, opened my notebook, and began writing about the mysterious woman with the nasty slice to her throat and the underpants in her vagina. As I retold the story on paper, it didn't sound nearly as serious as it most certainly was. There was no way that I could reduce to words on a page the act of being taken to a field and assaulted the way that she had been.

The way I had it figured was that this woman was probably with a man, somewhere, drinking; either a bar or at a house. My guess was that, given her alcohol level, she wasn't necessarily kidnapped. She could easily have been talked into leaving, or even suggested it herself. The first question to answer was whether or not she knew the man. As far as I was concerned, it could go either way.

The lacerated throat might indicate that he was trying to silence a witness that knew him and could identify him. But if he was, why not make sure the job was done? No, it was more likely that this wound indicated anger; the injury was inflicted because something made him mad. I say him, because I didn't really believe that a woman had committed this crime – although it wasn't out of the question. And the panties inside her made it a sex crime. Probably, they both drank too much, then when she did or said something to set him off, he lost his temper. That's the trouble with women and alcohol. Sometimes, it makes'em grow a pair that they don't always know what to do with.

Two hours later I'd finished my report and had my lunch. On my way back in, I stopped and checked to see if the crime scene people were back. Inside their outer office, I assaulted the punch bell on the counter. Hernandez responded in a minute.

"Hey. Is Rogers in the back?"

"Sure, come on in."

He disengaged the lock, and I walked to the back office in the northeast corner. I stood in the threshold and looked out a huge picture window that overlooked the entire Airport and I-65 intersection.

"What are you doing?" I said as I walked in.

Roy Rogers was seated in an overstuffed leather chair behind a large oaken desk. He was a short, stocky man with sandy hair and big ears. He also had a thin mustache that reminded you of Boston Blackie.

There were shelves on two of the walls and certificates and diplomas on the other two. A large table outfitted with a microscope and one of those extended arm magnifying glasses was next to the door.

"Mr. Faulkner. I see you made it in out of the cold. Anything new?"

"Not unless you've got it."

He leaned back in his chair. "Well, we looked and we looked and we looked. And then we picked up what we looked at."

"Did you find any prints; shoe or tire or something?"

"Oh, yeah. We found a shoe print."

"Well, did you cast it? What is it they call it, a 'moulage'?"

"Yeah, well, we were going to, but we didn't want to make a big moulage out of it."

I smiled because I got the joke.

He continued. "We got a tire track, and we got a shoe print. It looks like some type of athletic shoe. There's a wear pattern and at least one cut. If you get an exemplar, I think we can match it."

"What about a tire impression?"

He shook his head. "No. Well, I mean, there were plenty of tire prints out there, but most of them looked like they belonged to the ambulance. But there was one print that was different; the tire was almost completely bald. Not even a little bit'a tread. It'd be tough to match it."

I nodded. "Anything on her clothes?"

"No. Just regular stock clothing, nothing unique; could've come from WalMart or Kmart any one of the other marts."

"Have you gone over'em yet?"

"Not yet. I'll probably get to it on Monday. Oh, wait, Monday's a holiday. It may be Tuesday. Your victim's still alive, right? Maybe you can get some information from her before then."

"She's still living, right now. But I gotta look at her, and I don't have a good feeling about her chances."

"Well, we'll get to it when we can. I'll try to get a report up to you in a few days."

I nodded again. I only hoped she could hang on until then.

"So, how'd your boy Hernandez get on with Ms Crenshaw out there? They were pretty lovey dovey when I left," I said.

"I had to wet'em down with a hose. I thought she was gonna give birth."

Back in my office, the phone was ringing. It was the dispatcher. I sat down at my desk and took out a pen.

"The hospital called." The voice was that of Cindy, the sexiest-sounding of all the dispatchers.

"And?"

"And they said that mystery woman was out of surgery and awake. They said you could have a few minutes with her if you want."

"Okay. I'll take a run out there."

"Was she pretty bad?"

"Well, I've seen worse, but let's just say she's not gonna be singin' opera for a while."

"What's that supposed to mean?"

"It means she'll have a little trouble swallowin' her food; she'll have to buy a big supply of turtlenecks; she almost lost her head." I paused. "What I gotta do, paint a picture?"

"Ewwwwww."

"Bye."

Chapter 5

In thirty minutes, I was walking into the lobby of Springdale Hospital and heading toward the silver haired volunteer wearing a pink smock. I asked her where I could find Surgical Intensive Care, and she told me that it was on the fourth floor of the 'C' Building, the building on the far west side of the campus. I was to take the elevator to the fifth floor, walk the hall over the courtyard, and go down two flights. Then I had to walk a long hall and take another elevator to the fourth floor. The nurse's station would be straight ahead.

I was leaning over the counter of the round desk in the middle of a large ward in ten minutes. The station was designed so that the nurses could monitor all of the rooms at once, but only one nurse was manning the post.

"Yes, ma'am, my name is Faulkner, with the Metro Sheriff's Department."

I presented my shiny, six-pointed gold star, and the young, brown-haired nurse leaned forward to examine it. She smiled.

"She's over in 414. She was awake when I went in there ten minutes ago."

"Can she talk?"

"Not really. She just grunts, but if you ask her a question, she can respond."

I nodded. "I don't suppose there's anyone in there with her."

"Nope. Do you know who she is yet?"

I shook my head. "Still lookin'."

With that I turned toward her room. Intensive care rooms have sliding glass doors, and the one in Room 414 was open, but a white mesh curtain was pulled across the threshold. I walked up to the corner and peeked inside.

The woman that was lying on the bed bore little resemblance to the one I had seen in the ER. Her hair was hidden in a surgical cover, there was a small tube in her mouth, and her face was puffy and swollen. A thick bandage covered her neck, and sheets and a comforter were pulled up to the top of her torso, almost to her chin.

I walked over to the side of the bed. This was the part of the job that I hated the most. I could deal with the crime, but unfortunately, I just wasn't good at having sympathy for the ones who were suffering as a result of it.

"Ma'am. Can you hear me?"

The woman opened her eyes. They were gray, and they looked tired and slightly fearful. I pulled out my badge case and showed her my star.

"I'm with the Metro Sheriff's Office. I'd like to talk to you. Is that okay?"

She stared at me with a blank look; the look of someone lost and confused.

"If you can, nod for 'yes', and shake for 'no.' Can you do that?"

She stared. I decided just to jump into it.

"Do you know who hurt you?"

She stared.

"Do you know his name?"

Her lips began to move. I leaned forward to hear her whisper.

"Bur."

She spoke in a breathy voice that with the tube in her mouth was barely audible. It came out almost without the initial 'b' sound. 'Bur.'

"Are you trying to say 'Burt?'"

"Bur."

"Are you cold? I'll get the nurse."

"Bur."

I was frustrated. "What's your name?"

I leaned forward. She said, "O E," in a whisper.

"Joey?"

"O E."

I was getting increasingly frustrated. "I'm sorry, I don't understand. Is his name Burton, or Bert, or something like that?"

She closed her eyes and turned away, toward the window. I knew I'd lost her.

"Okay, well, I'll come back later and check on you. You get better now." I smiled weakly as I backed away and turned toward the exit.

Out at the nurse's station, I stopped to make notes: the date, time, 'O E,' and the syllable or word 'bur.' I had no idea what any of it meant and was sure I wouldn't until she could tell me.

"How'd it go?"

The same young, brown-haired nurse, whose name tag identified her as 'Cassie,' smiled and leaned toward me. I got the signal. I smiled back.

"Well, not so good. She can't talk very well, and I didn't know what she was trying to say when she did talk. We'll just have to wait."

"What do you do now?"

"Go back to the office, check the missing reports, and see if the evidence techs have come up with anything. Other than that, there's not much to do."

37

She nodded. I could tell she wanted to say more, but she was at a loss. Well, today was not the day to help her. I said my goodbyes, gave her my card, and told her to call me when 'O E' got the tube out of her mouth.

Chapter 6

The next morning, I came to the office early. If there was anything new on my case, I wanted to run it down.

Before I left on Saturday, I called the Captain and filled him in on how things were progressing. He suggested that I check the missing person cases at the City Police Department. I told him I thought that was a good idea, why didn't I think of it? He also told me to call Will.

I couldn't get Will on Saturday afternoon, but I left him a message, and he called me on Sunday. I told him what I had. He didn't sound happy.

"Hey. I couldn't get you yesterday," I said.

"Yeah, I been workin' on my motor."

Will had a World War II-vintage Harley-Davidson that he was restoring. It was parked at a storage shed on the west side of town, and sometimes Will would spend whole days there working on it; even sleeping on the floor.

"Captain said call you about this case. So, I did." I paused. "Sorry."

"Shit. That old man don't know shit about nothin'. I'm sure you're doin' everything that can be done, Son. Are you not?"

Will, who was nearly twenty-five years my senior, called me 'Son' when he was either pensive, or condescending. Sometimes he called me 'boy.' I learned to live with it.

"I've done everything I know to do, Will."

"Well, sometimes that's just all you can do, Son."

I heard him cough on the other end. He had a very deep, bass voice, and when he coughed it sounded like a lion's roar.

Will had a very 'down to earth' way of looking at things. He had learned after many years in police work that justice had a way of rising, like cream, to the top. If it didn't, it certainly wasn't his fault. He taught me that we, as a team, were in no way responsible for finding out who the perpetrators of homicides were. The people responsible for crimes and their solutions were the community as a whole.

He'd worked for three sheriffs, but only the current one had given him a title: Sheriff's Homicide Investigator. He was a Vietnam veteran and a graduate of the Southern Police Institute, spending the three months in Louisville studying Death Investigation. He'd been at police work for over thirty years, homicide for twenty; and had a hand in putting ten men on death row.

Will was a tall man (6'5") who weighed a solid two hundred and fifty pounds. He had an olive complexion and brown hair that was parted on the right side and thinning on top. Will – I didn't call him Snuffy; I have a thing about nicknames – had very large bones. I used to tell him that his size and build helped him bear the stress of homicide cases better than most people, including me. He had a Roman nose, and a square jaw, and at 55 or so – he never told me his exact age – he was just beginning to show his years, mostly around his brown eyes. He had huge hands and big thick fingers, and if he got a grip on someone, they were seldom able to break free.

He got his nickname at birth. His father looked at him lying in his mother's arms and noticed that his bottom lip was pooched out. He said that it made the child look as if he was dipping smokeless tobacco, or snuff. Will was 'Snuffy' from that day forward.

Will used to say: 'Son, these dead bodies was here long before me and you came, and they'll be here long after we're gone; so don't let'em worry you so much.' I tried to take his advice to heart, but I just couldn't. Once I got on it, my personality wouldn't let me leave a case alone.

In our little operation, Will asked most of the questions, and I kept all the notes. When he finished talking to a witness, he'd look over at me and ask if I had anything. I usually had one or two questions; questions I used to clarify a point made earlier. Oftentimes, they brought to mind another thread for him to pull. I did all the report writing, ninety per cent of the driving, and, unless it was personal, most of the telephoning.

We were on call twenty-four hours a day, seven days a week, and rarely missed an unnatural death case, whether it was a homicide, suicide, or accident. It was exhausting. Each case carried with it its own stressors. The only reason we both might not respond to a case was if one of us couldn't be reached; the case wasn't a murder; or there was no doubt about the cause and manner and it was just a matter of mopping up the paperwork.

"How's she look?" Will said, asking about the woman in the hospital.

"Well, she's gonna have a pretty ugly scar when it's all over, if she lives."

"You don't think she's gonna make it?"

"I don't know. The hospital seems to think she'll get better; of course, that's how they make their money. But I've got my doubts. She had kind of a hopeless look in her eye, kinda vacant; plus, she coded twice – on the way to the hospital and at the ER."

"Which hospital is she in?"

"Springdale."

"Well, no wonder, Son. That place's got a reputation. It's like the roach motel."

I'd heard that before. Most of the deputies said that if they ever got shot, they wanted to be taken downtown to the trauma center instead of out to Springdale, even though it was usually much closer.

"Okay," he said. "What do you have on this thing?"

"Well, we've got half a shoe print; we've got some bald tire prints that may or may not belong to the suspect vehicle; we've got her clothes that the evidence people haven't gone over yet; and we've got what she told me . . ."

"Which was?"

". . . which was the word, or name, or something: 'bur.'"

"'Bur'? What the fuck does that mean? Was she cold?"

"That's what I thought."

"She say anything else?"

"When I asked her name, she said, 'O-E.'"

He paused on the other end. "Joey, Chloe?"

"Could be. After that she shut down and went back to sleep."

"Well, shit, Son. That don't help."

I chuckled. "I agree."

He paused on the other end. "Okay, look. I'm gonna come on in. Just stay at the office 'til I get there."

The fact that he was coming to work didn't surprise me. Deep down, Will loved a puzzle. His overtime would total out to about thirty-six dollars an hour, and he was almost too expensive to summon. But he worked autonomously, and if he wanted in on a case, the higher ups normally didn't keep him away.

"Got it."

I hung up the phone glad that he was going to respond; two heads being better, and all that. But more than that, if he was there, it took a huge amount of stress off me.

Will arrived at ten. I was in the office writing up the final report of my visit to the hospital when he walked in and sat down with a thud, at his desk, directly across from me.

Our office was about twelve by twelve. Our desks were front to front, against the wall opposite the window, next to the door. We both could look out windows on two

41

walls, but Will had the better view. He didn't know it, but sometimes when he wasn't there, I sat at his desk to write and make phone calls. The other two walls were bare, save for a calendar. Two large, gray filing cabinets sat in a vacant corner. Will showed up in a pair of slacks and a white dress shirt that looked as if it had been worn last Friday – a day that now seemed as if it was a week ago. His black Oxford shoes were unshined and untied, and he had on one of those green and orange, reversible bomber jackets. Will was not known as a snappy dresser. He hated ties. He always said that he couldn't understand why he had to come to work with a rope around his neck.

But it had not always been so. I was told that twenty-five years ago, when he was younger and newly installed in the Detective Division, Will was always attired at the height of style. It was as if he had seen so much death, and the slab to which he himself was destined, that what he wore, to him, was no longer a priority.

"Anything new?" he said.

"Not yet. I've just been cleaning up the paperwork. I was thinking of taking a run back out to the hospital. What do you think?"

"Has her condition changed? If it hadn't changed, there ain't no need to go, Son. We'd just be talkin' to a woman who's still got a mouthful'a tubes."

He was right. But absent anything from the Records Section about a missing person, either with our department or the city police, there was really nothing left to do.

"Let's try to do something with what she told you. When you asked her name, what did she say?"

"She said 'O-E.'"

"Okay. What name does that sound like to you? I make it Chloe, or Joey, or Zoe."

I agreed. "I guess we could call the radio room and let them put a white female, first names 'Zoe' and 'Chloe' into the machine and see if they can get something. They're not very common names; couldn't be too many of 'em, especially around here."

"Make the call."

In a minute I had Betty, the most veteran of our dispatchers, on the phone. "Run these names through the driver's license data base," I said. "First name, 'Zoe'; white female; age about 25 to 40." She could have been younger, but not by much. "Go ahead and look for one with a Mobile County address. She may be from somewhere else, but we don't know it yet. When you finish, do the same with 'Chloe'."

"Is that all you have?" Betty said.

"That's it for now. Just run 'em and see what comes up. It's a shot in the dark, I know."

"Okay. With just a first name, you're prob'ly right. I'll call you back."

I hung up and looked at Will. He was leaned back in his chair with his feet up on the corner of his desk, his hands clasped behind his head, and his eyes closed. He called it his thinking position.

"Did I tell you about her underpants?" I said.

His eyes shot open, and he turned to look at me. "No."

"Well, when she got to the ER and they examined her, they found her underpants stuffed up in her vagina."

He nodded. "Anybody else know that?"

"Just the people at the hospital. I'm sure it's in the medical record, but I haven't told anyone."

He turned away and closed his eyes again. "Good. Keep that quiet. Don't even tell Linus. And keep it out of the reports for now. Maybe we can hold onto that for a while; at least until we can lay hands on somebody."

About that time, the phone on my desk rang. It was Betty.

"Henry, we only got one locally. A 'Zoe Woods' has a non-driver's ID in Alabama."

"You got an address?"

"3500 A Lewis Circle, off Michigan, in Mobile." She also supplied a date of birth, April fourth; and the physical description matched.

I hung up and relayed the information to Will. He opened his eyes long enough to acknowledge me.

"All right. Let's take a ride down there and see if that's her. Then we'll go eat lunch."

Chapter 7

We made the trip to Michigan Avenue in twenty minutes. Lewis Circle ran through a Section 8 housing complex, part of the DC Tatum Project. The homes were all single-story duplexes; brick with wood trim, including lattice work around the porches. This part of the complex had recently been renovated and landscaped, and it shamed the rest of the neighborhood.

The apartment was in the crook of the circle, in the northeast corner, within eyeshot of the Duval Street and Michigan Avenue intersection. The area seemed deserted.

At the front door, I knocked. Country music – George Jones – played softly in the background. In thirty seconds, the music stopped and the door opened.

"Hey," a man said.

He was a tall man, over six feet, and very thin. His hair was sandy and thin also, and a long thin nose protruded from his angular face.

I said thin, but that was an understatement. His chest was concave, almost as if he had Marfan Syndrome. Even the fingers off his bony hands were long and skinny.

"Hey," I said. "We're with the Metro Sheriff's Office." I showed him my badge. "Could we talk to you for a minute?"

"I ain't done nothin' wrong, have I?"

"You ain't done nothin' wrong, Buddy," Will said. "We just wanna see if you've got some information about a case we're workin' on."

The man nodded and bladed himself in the doorway, which is to say that he turned to the side and became almost invisible. We walked in.

"Find a place to sit if you can," he said. "I ain't much of a housekeeper, and my ole lady ain't here."

We picked our way over and around furniture and boxes in the small living space. There was an old couch on the south wall under a window. I planted myself on the end, near a lamp. Will found a folding lawn chair next to the television. The thin man moved slowly and without animation to a kitchen chair that he removed from that room.

Will began, as he always did. "Buddy, my name's Eubanks, and this is Mr. Faulkner. What's your name?"

"Albert Neal Jr., sir," he said. His voice was as country as his music.

"Do you happen to know a woman name Zoe Woods?"

"She's my wife."

"Legal or common law?"

"Common law.

"How long ya'll been together?"

"'Bout four or five years."

"Do you know where she is right now?"

He looked at the floor as if he didn't understand the question. Will continued.

"When's the last time you seen her?"

"I don't know. A couple'a days ago, I guess. She left here going up to The Society, on the corner."

45

The Society Lounge was a red neck bar on Duval Street about half a block west of Michigan. It was unusual in that it was a white bar in a neighborhood that was predominately black.

"Was that in the mornin' or the evenin'?" Will said.

"Uh, 'bout dinner on Friday."

"And you ain't seen her since?"

He shook his head. "No. What's this about?"

Will looked at me. "We've got a woman at the hospital, Buddy. She's been bad hurt, and she's unable to talk. We have reason to believe that it might be Zoe Woods. You gotta picture of her?"

"Yeah, ah, I thank so. Let me look." He rose and headed for what was probably the bedroom. His movements were only slightly more energetic now.

In a minute he was back with one of those Polaroid instant photographs. He handed it to Will who passed it immediately to me. I looked at an image that bore the same pale features and dark almost black hair as those of the woman at the hospital. I handed it back to Will.

"It looks like her," I said. "Does she have a chipped tooth?"

"Yeah, one down here, on the bottom." He pointed to his lower canine on the left side.

"And a mole?"

"Yeah, on her jaw."

"Mr. Neal, looks like your wife might be in Springdale Hospital. You need to contact'em and see about her."

"How'd she get hurt?" Neal said.

"We don't know, yet. You say she left the house goin' to The Society?" Will said.

He nodded. "She goes over there a lot. She's gotta lotta friends there."

"You don't go with her?"

"Sometimes."

Will looked at me. "You got anything?"

46

I nodded. "Mr. Neal, how is your wife?" He looked at me curiously. "I mean, is she ill, or something?"

"Oh, no. She's . . . well, she's just a little slow, I guess you'd call it. You know, she didn't go far in school, and it, it just takes her a little time to do things."

"Is she mentally ill?"

He shrugged. "I don't think so. She's just a little slow."

She was retarded, I could tell. The way her eyes looked at me in the hospital. I looked at Will.

"How can we get in touch with you during the day, Buddy?" Will said.

"Here."

"You're not workin'?"

"I'm tryin' to get on disability, for my heart." He pointed to his chest.

Will nodded. I knew what he was thinking: another free loader. He didn't have much use for people who didn't or wouldn't work.

Will asked about Zoe's family – mother and father up in Citronelle; her job – Tyndall's Poultry plant in Mobile; and her friends – all at The Society."

"What does she do at the chicken plant?"

"She's a washer; and she plucks some, too. When the chickens come down the line, after they been kilt and plucked, she washes 'em."

Will rose from his seat. "You mind if we take a look around, Buddy?"

Neal stood up also. "Ah, no, ah, go ahead."

With that Will stalked off toward the back of the apartment, out of our sight. I told Neal to sit down, that he'd be back in a minute, and I continued talking to him about nothing in particular. He seemed not to know the difference.

Will was back in five minutes. He shook his head at me.

47

I spoke to Neal. "Are you going to the hospital today?"

He nodded. "Right. Sure. I'm going right on out there."

He started to get up. I was beginning to think he was little dim, himself.

I rose also. "She's in Surgical ICU. Here's my card. Call us and let us know for sure about Zoe."

Will and I said our goodbyes and left. In the car, I looked at him. He rubbed his face with both hands.

"Well, shit, Son. How the fuck we gonna make a case with a crazy girl?" He said.

I chuckled. "He seemed a little touched his self, didn't he?"

"We got to get out there and see if she's able to talk before he gets her all confused. No tellin' what she's liable to say after he gets through with her."

I nodded then turned the vehicle toward the interstate and west to the hospital.

In thirty minutes, we were on the intensive care floor and walking into room 414. Zoe Woods was awake and looking out the window. The bandage had been removed from her throat and the tube from her mouth. The nurses told us we could only see her for about five minutes. She apparently wasn't doing so well.

Will spoke to me. "You know her, you talk to her."

I walked up to the side of the bed. "Hey, Zoe? Remember me?"

The ghastliness of the wound on her neck was startling. She looked back at me with tired and unanimated eyes. Then she cocked her face to one side like the RCA Victor dog. I heard Will mutter something under his breath.

"Can you talk any better, Zoe?"

I got the same confused look. Her breathing was shallow.

"Can you tell me who it was that hurt you?"

48

Her brows went up. "Bird." Her voice was a whisper.

"Are you saying, 'bird'?"

She nodded.

"Was his name, Bird?"

"Bird."

I looked at Will. He shook his head.

"Can you tell me anything about what happened to you?"

She just looked at me and said nothing. Then she turned her head to the window.

I walked around to the other side of the bed. "Who hurt you, Zoe?"

She turned her head the other way. The interview was over.

"Okay, well, you get well soon, now. We'll come back to see you a little later."

We turned toward the door just as the nurse was coming in. I stopped her.

"Is she okay?"

"She's developed an infection. Her temperature's elevated." She put her lips together and made a sad face.

"Prognosis?"

"You'll have to talk to her doctor. He's the only one that can say." She walked past me and up to Zoe Woods' bedside.

Will and I stopped in the hall. I knew what he was going to say, and it wouldn't be complimentary of our only witness.

"Shit, Son. What the fuck does that mean, 'bird'?"

"I don't know. But, hey, you came up with her name. You can probably figure out what 'bird' means. I've got confidence in you." I smiled.

He looked at me. "Fuck you."

I laughed, and we left.

Chapter 8

The next day was a holiday; one of those obscure Alabama ones that celebrated some aspect of the Confederacy. I was scheduled to work. Will was not, but he came in anyway. We had a couple of leads on the case now, and though it was not a murder, the threat that it soon would be lingered.

We were sitting in the office trying to decide what to do first when the phone rang. It was the dispatcher.

"We need you to run on a case," she said.

I got a sick feeling in the pit of my stomach. I always got one when a call came in.

"What is it?" I said.

"The paramedics called. They've got a dead baby over off Theodore-Dawes Road."

I went from apprehension to a state of calm depression. There would be weeping, and maybe even some yelling and name-calling, but the chances of the case being a homicide were probably slim. At the very least, whatever I spotted on the scene that might indicate murder would have to be confirmed by the medical examiner. He would have the final say. This trip would be just to pick up the evidence and take a few statements.

She told me the address. It was in an apartment complex near the dog track, and it would take about thirty minutes to get there, and probably another hour and a half to do what needed to be done. I wouldn't be back to the office before lunch.

When I hung up, Will looked at me. "What'chu got?"

"Dead baby."

"You need me?"

"I don't think so. Can I call you if I do?"

"Yeah. I'll stay here and make a few calls on this other thing."

Will didn't like dead baby cases either.

True to my estimate, I arrived at the apartment in question in twenty-seven minutes. The complex was a rundown community consisting of about fifteen three-story, wood buildings with stucco siding. The cars in the lot were mostly late models, but just about all were dusty, and a sizeable number had dents and scratches. The scene was upstairs on the third floor of the second building on the right, building 'B'.

I stopped behind one of three marked patrol cars, a paramedic truck belonging to the City Fire Department, and a City Ambulance. When I got to apartment 10B, I found Deputy W.E. White at the front door.

White, a tall, thin officer with slicked back, blonde hair, was called 'We-We' by everybody in the department but me – including the Sheriff. He carried a chrome plated, six-inch Colt Python revolver and relished riding in lower class neighborhoods. There he could police the way he wanted and not worry too much about objections. Complaints from poor people who spend most if not all of their money on drugs and alcohol weren't usually paid much heed.

"Detective Faulkner. Glad you could make it."

"Willard. Trouble?"

"Not right now. We kind'a got'em all calmed down. They was hysterical earlier."

"Who's inside?"

"The Sergeant, Meg Crenshaw, the paramedics – who were packing up to leave a couple of minutes ago – and, I think, two ambulance attendants." He paused as I wrote the names down. "The coroner's people are on the way."

I nodded. "Okay, let's take a look."

Inside what seemed to be an abnormally warm room, Sergeant Terry Scarborough looked up and nodded. He was a middle-aged man with a bald head and a thin build who stood against the far wall, next to a couch. Two women

51

sat on the piece. The younger one was overweight, and the other, a bleached blonde, was only slightly thinner. Both were sniffing. The young woman held a handkerchief, winding it tightly around her fingers.

Scarborough motioned me away from the mourners. We walked across the room and partially down a hallway, stopping in front of the bathroom door. He spoke in low tones.

"We just got'em calmed down."

"What's up?"

"Looks like a six month old male. Mama put him to bed last night about ten, and when she went to get him in the morning, he wadn't breathin'."

"Who all was home?"

"Just mama and grandmama; the two in there on the couch."

I looked around. "Is it hot in here, or is it just me?"

He looked up. "It does feel a little balmy."

I nodded. "The paramedics back there?"

"In the bedroom. I don't know where the ambulance people went."

I nodded toward the women. "Okay, just try to keep'em calm until I can get in there to talk to'em. Crenshaw in the bedroom?"

"Yeah."

"When the coroner's man gets here, send him on back. I want to get this baby outta here as soon as possible."

"Right."

The apartment appeared to be about a thousand or maybe eleven hundred square feet. At the end of the hall, the door on the left was closed. I knocked softly. Crenshaw opened it.

"Hey."

"Hey, yourself," I said.

I entered the room and stopped. Two firemedics stood on either end of a crib. One was a tall man with a black mustache, the other a female with short brown hair. Both were silent.

"Anything amiss?" I said.

The male shook his head. "No. Looks like just plain old crib death. Nobody knows why it happens or how to stop it."

Looking around, I could see that it was a child's room for sure; with stuffed animals on the floor near a playpen, stacks of Pampers over in the corner, and a mobile hanging from the ceiling over the bed. The walls were blue, and the carpet was tan.

"Well, I know why this happened. It's just too hot in here. This baby probably got overheated." I paused. "Any idea what the temperature is?"

Both the medics shook their heads. Crenshaw shrugged. I looked around for the thermostat, but figured it must be out in the hall.

"If you guys need to go, take off. I'll be here until the coroner's man comes."

They nodded, picked up their drug cases and prepared to depart. The male, who was the last one out the door, handed me a copy of the run sheet as he shook his head and ducked into the hall.

"Wonder what's up with him?" I said to Crenshaw after the door closed.

"I don't know. Could be he just doesn't like dead babies."

"Well, heck, who does? You'd think that by now he'd be used to'em."

Making notes is my passion. I looked around the room and began to record on paper what it all looked like. I drew a small diagram, including an estimate of dimensions, and penciled in the room's furnishings.

"Who's doing the report? You or Willard?"

Crenshaw looked at me quizzically. "Who's Willard? Oh. You mean, We-We? He is. I'm just here to deal with the mother and grandmother."

"Shouldn't you be in there with them?"

"Oh, they said they were fine. Besides, I'd rather be in here, learning."

Laying my notebook on a small table next to the closet, I pulled a pair of rubber gloves from my hip pocket. At the side of the crib, I bent low and looked at the child. He was wearing a pair of light blue pajamas; onesies, I think they're called. They're the kind with feet in them. A pacifier lay near his head, and a thin blanket was wadded up at his feet. The bed was devoid of stuffed animals or any other toys.

The crib was normal-sized, with side rails, about thirty inches high. The slats down each side were about two or three inches apart. The head and foot pieces were solid and featured paintings of unicorns and angels. There did not appear to be any way that the child could have gotten between the slats and strangled himself.

The baby was about twenty-five inches long and looked to weigh about fifteen or so pounds. He was lying supine with his head turned to the right. His sleep shirt was open and patches were visible where the paramedics had apparently used an EKG in an attempt to locate a pulse.

The child's lips were blue, and his face was ashen. Without moving him, I looked closer and inhaled deeply, trying to determine if his mother had given him a nip of whiskey to make him sleep – an old country home remedy that had been known to backfire and kill infants. I lifted up his top lip and looked at the frenulum to see if it was torn. It was intact. I lifted up one of his eyelids and looked for petechial hemorrhaging. I saw none, only a kind of cloudy lifelessness. Finally, I lifted his chin and examined his neck for signs of strangulation. It was clean.

I stood up straight and backed off. Until the coroner arrived, I decided not to delve any further. I looked at Crenshaw.

"Learn anything?"

"Yeah. Lots. You think he was murdered?" she said.

"Got no reason to believe it."

At that moment, there was a knock at the door. Crenshaw reached for the knob and opened it. Danny Leftwich was standing there with a ballistic nylon bag over his shoulder.

"Mr. Leftwich," I said, "glad you could make it."

He froze. "Is that a crack about how long it took me to get here? 'Cause there was a wreck out on the interstate. Traffic's backed up to the interchange."

"Okay, okay. Calm down. Do you know Deputy Crenshaw?" I said nodding her direction.

"I do not, but I'm glad to, now." He smiled and shook her hand.

Leftwich was a forty year old medical school dropout from Las Vegas who ended up in Mobile after spending Memorial Day at a Jimmy Buffet concert in nearby Orange Beach. Oddly, he loved the humidity so much that he decided to move here permanently. He was an intellectual who had determined that he didn't want the stress of being a doctor, but he still had a yen to work with the human body, and he thought that playing with the dead might somehow scratch that itch.

He was over six feet tall with brown hair and wire rimmed glasses. He had a square jaw and was very muscular, and if his job had been anything other than picking up dead bodies and taking them to the morgue, he'd've probably had his pick of women.

Leftwich dropped his bag and took out a metal clipboard. He looked over at the baby.

"Now, what's this little shaver's name?" he said.

I looked down at the run sheet. "Ahhhh, it looks like Jason Alex Myers; born September ninth of last year."

"Have you filled out the 'book' yet?"

The 'book' to which he was referring was an eight page, front and back, checklist designed to cover every aspect of the death of an infant. It was called the 'book' because of its length, and because the information taken from it was destined to be part of a grant-funded research project for some doctor in the northeast who'd probably never touched a dead baby, but who would no doubt get rich turning the information into a large volume about what causes infants to die.

"Nope. I'll leave that to you. Just take a look at him, and while you're getting him ready for the ambulance, I'll go talk to the mother."

"Sieg heil," he said clicking his heels.

I smirked. "Don't be a smart ass."

Leftwich smiled at Crenshaw and put down his clipboard. After photographing the child, he too pulled on rubber gloves. He did everything I had done, and, in addition, he pulled off the baby's pajamas and went over every inch of him with a magnifying glass. He looked at his genitals and with two hands – grabbing an arm and a leg on one side – he flipped the baby over and looked up his anus.

"While you're there, would you take a body temperature for me?"

"Sure."

Leftwich reached into his bag and produced a thermometer encased in a silver tube. He removed the glass instrument and inserted it into the boy's rectum, then looked at his watch. Crenshaw stood against the wall with eyes wide and mouth agape.

In three minutes, Leftwich pulled out the utensil and wiped it with a sponge. He looked and squinted.

"Looks like ninety-five." He looked up. "Wow, that's still pretty high."

"You got an ambient thermometer?"

"Yeah."

"Why don't you set it up and let's find out how hot is in here."

He did so, and after five minutes of small talk, he announced that the room temperature was eighty-three degrees. In my mind, at least, this case was solved.

"Okay," I said, "you see anything to indicate murder here?"

"Nope. If you're going to talk to the women, go ahead and do it so you can be gone when it's my turn."

I nodded and turned to Crenshaw. "If you can tear yourself away from Danny boy here, go outside and tell the ambulance people to go. I'm guessing that Mr. Leftwich is going to ride this child to the morgue in his car."

"I'll take him," Leftwich confirmed. He'd wrap the child in a large sheet thereby making him an indistinguishable bundle.

Gathering my notebook and disposing of my gloves, I braced myself to go to the living room and meet the parent of the dead baby boy. It was a conversation I wasn't anxious to have.

At the front of the apartment, I found the room deserted except for the younger of the two women.

"Ma'am, my name is Faulkner. I'm with the Metro Sheriff's Department. Can you tell me what happened to your child?" I sat down in a club chair near the door.

Monica Alyce Myers – middle name pronounced 'A-leece' – was barely seventeen years old. She was five feet two, with blue eyes and rosy cheeks, and it appeared as if she weighed in at somewhere in the neighborhood of one hundred and seventy-five pounds. I used to not be good at gauging the weight of females until Will told me to take my best guess and then drop it twenty pounds to account for the lack of a woman's bone density and muscle mass. In this case, it was obvious that Monica Myers had gained a considerable amount of heft during her pregnancy and had not yet shed it.

Crenshaw returned from the front door and sat down on the couch next to Myers, thereby displacing the young woman's mother. The deputy tried to do her best sympathetic public servant routine.

"Well, he was kind'a fussy last night, so I put him to bed early," she said. Her sobs had quieted, but I could tell that they were just below the surface.

"And we went to bed a little later, Mama and me. We set up late to watch TV. When I went in to get him up this morning, to change his diaper and all, he wadn't movin'." Tears began to pool in the corners of her eyes.

"Had he been sick or ill in any way?"

She shook her head.

"Has he been taking anything? Drugs or medicine, or something?"

She shook her head again. "No. He hadn't been sick."

I decided to get right to it. I looked around the room. "I was just noticing that it's a little warm in here. Do you normally keep the apartment at this temperature?"

She looked around herself. "Sure, well, I'm mean, Mama likes it warmer." Her brows went up.

"How did you put him down?"

She looked at me questioningly.

"You know, on his back? Stomach? What?"

"Oh. I always put him down on his back. He seems to fall asleep easier that way."

At that moment, we heard a toilet flush, and Monica Myers's mother reappeared from down the hall. She was fifty-something with skin that hung from her arms, neck, and jowls. Her hair had been dyed blonde – a really bad job – but splotches of gray could still be seen on her temples and at her front hairline.

I turned and introduced myself, and Monica Myers identified her mother. She took a seat in a club chair across the room from us.

"This is my mother, Eileen Rogers."

"You live here, Ms Rogers?" I said.

"Yes. She keeps Jason when I go to work," Monica Myers spoke up.

"And where do you work?"

58

"Down at the Circle G."

"Cashier?"

"Yes, sir."

There were a thousand questions I could ask. Was he a full-term pregnancy? Do you or did you smoke? Any history of SIDs in your family? But I decided to ask about the boy's father.

"What's the child's father's name?"

"Oh, uh, Tim, Tim Myers."

"He live here?"

She shook her head. "Well, yeah. Well, not now. He's workin' offshore."

"Everything okay with you two?"

"Yeah, I guess." She seemed a bit confused by the question.

At that point, a new line of questioning hit me. "When he's gone, off shore I mean, do you let your son sleep with you?"

"Well, yeah, sometimes."

"Did he sleep with you last night?"

She looked at the floor. "Well, yeah, when we went to bed, I checked on him. He still wadn't asleep, so I put him in the bed with me until he dropped off."

"How did he get in the bed where he is now?"

"I put him there."

"When?"

"I don't know, about two, I guess." She paused. "What's this all about?"

As if she didn't know. Anytime an infant sleeps in the bed with its mother, there's a danger of a rollover homicide. Coroners and medical examiners will rarely identify it as such, but it happens more than anyone would care to believe. In this case, Monica Myers was a large enough person so that she could have rolled over on her child, suffocated him, then rolled back over and never been the wiser. If she moved him to his own bed before he got cold and rigor set in, then she wouldn't have noticed his death until the next morning; even if he wasn't breathing.

I'd heard about all I wanted to hear. My initial assessment had been dead wrong, but I could tell by how she was acting, her body language, that she had a pretty good suspicion of what she had done. The autopsy would tell us if there was a reason to confront her about it. If the child had a couple of broken ribs, for instance, we'd have to come back out and question her again. If there was no sign of trauma, chances are the case would be classified as a natural death, with SIDS as the cause.

I rose and turned to Crenshaw. She looked confused and just a little bored.

"Stay with Ms Myers until Danny gets in here, then you can go; unless he needs you for something else."

She nodded. I gathered my belongings and left.

It took forty-five minutes to get back to the office. On the way, I stopped to relieve myself and purchase a peach milk shake from one of the chain fast food restaurants. It was shortly after noon, and Will had undoubtedly eaten already.

Upstairs, I found him in our office, in his thinking position. There was a yellow, legal-sized writing pad on the desk in front of him, and I could tell he had been making notes. I couldn't tell if they were about the case, or about what motorcycle parts he was going to have to order next. When I entered the room and threw my notebook on the desk, his eyes opened, and he sat up straight.

"Boy, what the fuck you been doin'?"

"Man, I been lookin' at dead babies."

He rubbed his eyes with the heels of both hands. "Oh, yeah. What happened to that one?"

I sat down in my chair and shrugged. "Well, I don't know for sure, but I think his mama rolled over on him and killed him. He was in the bed with her for most of the night. She put him in his bed at two. The lividity and temperature all look like he was dead by then."

60

"Well, shit, Son. Ain't no coroner in the world got balls enough to tell a woman she rolled over on her baby and killed it. You might as well write this one up as a crib death."

That's what I liked about Will. He could always be counted on to speak plainly.

"It's a problem as old as the Bible, but nobody wants to admit it exists. Mamas ought not sleep with their young'uns 'til they get old enough to wake up and tell'em to get their fat asses off of'em." He paused. "How big was she?"

"The mother? Probably about one sixty-five, one seventy, and not too tall."

He nodded and leaned back. "Yep. That's what happened."

I looked around the office. "Anything going on here?"

He looked down at his desk. "Just makin' some notes."

"About our case?"

"Yeah, sure; about our case. I gotta 'do' list here. When you get through fuckin' off, we can get some'a this shit done."

I grinned and shook my head. "Well, I'm here now. What'chu got?"

He picked up his legal pad and studied it. "I think we need to get down to this lounge and see who this crazy bitch was drinkin' with. Maybe we can begin to piece together her last couple'a hours. How drunk was she?"

".22. You think he was drinkin', too?"

"Well, shit, Son. You know he was. That's the only way he'd'a gotten in the car with that crazy broad; or got her in the car with him."

I chuckled, something I did frequently while working with Will.

I picked up my notebook. "Let's go."

61

Chapter 9

It took thirty minutes to get to The Society Lounge. I took the long way, down Airport Boulevard to the Loop, then on Government to Michigan Avenue. It was about a mile and a half to the Duval Street intersection.

On the way, at about Airport and Sage, I noticed an older woman out walking her dog. She looked to be about sixty with gray hair – the woman, not the dog – and wearing a red jogging suit. The dog was a Doberman Pinscher. My guess was it weighed over a hundred and forty pounds. I pointed at the two.

"Look at that," I said. Will turned his head and stared.

"If that dog bolts," I continued, "there's no way she could stop it. It'd kill her if she didn't let go of that leash."

"That big dog means nobody's gonna fuck with her, Son."

As we sat at the stoplight, the dog walked up to a telephone pole, sniffed the grass around the base, and then urinated.

I looked at Will. "Wonder why a dog always stops to smell another dog's urine?"

It was something I did often, comment on strange occurrences in nature. Assuming it would be humorous, I really just wanted to get Will's take on them. Lately, he'd just been giving me a pat answer.

He studied the scene carefully. "God only knows why, Son. God only knows."

Fifteen minutes later we drove inside a chain link fence that surrounded the parking lot of The Society Lounge and stopped our vehicle near the front door. The lot was covered over with oyster shells, not unlike many lots in Mobile. It was a convenient use for a plentiful resource.

The building was made of cinderblocks that were once red but had long since faded to pink. There were no windows. A ten foot tall, board fence enclosed a small space on the west side of the building that served as a 'patio' for patrons who wanted to exit the smoky interior and do their drinking and laughing and hooking up under the stars, most often in the summer.

The dingy, gray-colored front door was flanked with warnings: '*Be twenty-one, or be gone!*' and '*No guns allowed. Violators will be prosecuted.*' The words were painted in black and written in a professional, cursive script.

The sun shone brightly outside as we opened the door and walked into the dark interior. It took a minute for my eyes to adjust, but when they did, I could see that the interior was just as unimpressive as the exterior.

The board floor looked recently swept, but it felt as if it would crack with the next step. Nineteen fifties-era metal dining tables and chairs with white upholstery were broadcast about the main room; with two or three pushed away into one corner, near the old Rockola jukebox, in order to create some semblance of a dance floor.

The bar was to our right. A short stocky man with brown hair and a big belly was washing glasses – a not altogether expected sight – and setting them upside down on a towel, on the bar next to the beer taps.

The bartender wiped his hands on his white t-shirt as we walked toward him. Apprehension painted his face, and he looked as if he was about to drop everything and run into the kitchen and out the back door – if there was a kitchen and if there was a back door. I thought I saw him twitch.

I was hoping he would speak freely considering there was no one else in the building, and once he found out we weren't there to rob him. As we got to the bar, I laid my notebook down and took out a ball point pen. Will spoke.

"We're from the Sheriff's Office, Buddy. My name's Eubanks and this here is Detective Faulkner."

"Oh, okay. How you folks doin'? I'm Larry."

Larry relaxed noticeably and spoke with an accent that I didn't recognize. His voice was mid-ranged and tinged with nasality.

"You the owner?" Will said.

"Yeah. Yeah, I am."

"Well, we wanna ask you about a woman that was in here last Friday night. Her name was, uh . . ." He looked at me.

"Zoe Woods," I said. Will repeated it.

"Zoe? What about her?"

"You know her?"

"Well, yeah. She's a regular; lives across Duval Street, over in the apartments. She's over here about every night."

"It looks like she hooked up with an old boy in here, and he took her out and cut her." Will was matter of fact in his tone and his description.

"No shit? I hadn't heard that."

"We was wonderin' if you knew who she was drinkin' with that night?"

"Well, let me see."

He looked away as if trying to remember. If he said 'no,' I wasn't prepared to believe him.

"She was with a man with jet black hair. I remember that 'cause they was drinkin' Black Russians."

I didn't know much about mixed drinks, but I knew a Black Russian. It was a pretty powerful after dinner cocktail made with vodka and coffee liqueur. It would only take about two, perhaps three at the outside, of them to get a woman Zoe Woods' size completely smashed.

"Remember anything else about him?"

"Well, coal black hair, dark complexion, not too tall; I remember he parted his hair on the right. Every hair was

64

plastered down in place. It looked like he used Brylcreem or Vitalis, or somethin'."

I wrote fast. Will continued.

"You know his name?"

He shook his head. "No. First timer."

"What was he wearing?"

"Looked like a flannel shirt, with a union suit on underneath; jeans; some boots."

So much for the athletic shoe print found at the scene.

"What kind'a boots?"

"Ah, I guess you'd call'em motorcycle boots. You know, the kind that guys wear when they ride; with the buckle on the side."

"You know where he works, or lives?"

"Nope. Can't help'ya."

"How about his car?"

He shook his head. "No. First time in. I didn't notice when he got here, nor when he left; and hadn't seen him since."

I got the feeling that he was being mostly truthful. He spoke calmly and continued working on his glasses.

Will looked at me. "You got anything?"

I looked up from my notebook at Larry. "You say you know Zoe pretty good?"

"Yeah. You know, she's kinda slow. I mean, she talks normal and everything, but she's kinda slow on the uptake." He shook his head. "She wouldn't see it if somebody was out to hurt her."

"So, what kinda drunk was she?"

He raised his eyebrows. "Oh, well, now, when she gets tight, she's kinda sarcastic; pretty quick to speak her mind." He paused. "You know how women are, always startin' shit for somebody else to finish."

"Ever start a fight?"

"Oh, no. Nothin' physical; maybe an argument, or somethin'."

"Kind of a mean drunk?"

"That's right."

I nodded then wrote. "What's your last name, Larry?"

"Flynn."

He supplied me with a DOB that I was pretty sure was bogus, and a phone number and an address that I was pretty sure weren't. I looked back at Will.

"Who was Zoe Woods's best friend, if you know?" he said.

"I guess that'd have to be Gretta. She usually sits over there." He nodded his head toward a table next to the dance floor. "They're kind of alike. I mean, Gretta's a little dense, too."

"You know where she lives?"

"Over on Stewart Avenue. It's about the third house down on the right, I think."

"She come around pretty often?"

"Every night. She and Zoe are kinda like fixtures around here. They don't work for me, but they show up, talk to the men, and I let'em hustle drinks. As long as they don't hook or try to roll nobody, I let'em hang around." He shrugged. "I mean, you know." He shrugged. "Where they both gonna go?"

I could see his point. A couple of kooky broads would tend to give the place a little color. Wonder what were the odds of the two of them finding each other as friends?

"Can you remember anybody else that might'a been here last Friday night?"

He looked away again and shut his eyes as if to think. "Well, let's see, Sis was here – she's my waitress – Gretta was here; and Jerry Painter; Linc; and Wes; and, uh, the black haired guy. I think that's about it. There was a couple'a women with the men."

"You got any last names?" I said.

66

"Well, Sis is Susy Weaver. Gretta, I think she told me once that her name was Margaret somethin' or other." He shook his head. "I don't know the women. They're just ladies that show up at night with the men. And the men, well, we don't use a lotta last names."

Will looked at me. I finished up my notes, after which I reached in my pocket and took out a business card.

"Well, Mr. Flynn, we 'preciate your cooperation," Will said. "We'll be back one night this week to try to locate some'a these folks. If you should happen to see the black haired man, give us a call."

Will watched as I handed Flynn the business card. Will never carried cards. He didn't want anyone calling him. He never carried a gun either. He said homicide detectives didn't carry guns; that people wouldn't talk candidly to men carrying firearms on their hips because everyone who saw them would know they were talking to the police. I understood his logic, but couldn't bring myself to go without some protection, so I carried a small nine millimeter semi-auto in a holster on my left ankle. I couldn't draw it fast, but I was sure it would help in a pinch.

Flynn took the card and stared at it. "I sure will. I sure will."

I had my doubts, but Will and I nodded and then turned and walked back out of the bar and into the bright sunlight of the early afternoon.

When we were in the car, I spoke. "That place is a regular 'Long Branch', hunh? Everybody's there, every night."

"Ever'body 'cept the bastard we're lookin' for."

I paused and smiled. "How about that, though? Two crazies, best friends."

"Son, you think it's funny, but you don't know how hard it's gonna be to make this case if we have to use either or both'a them bitches as witnesses."

"So, where to now?"

"Well, while we're down here, I guess we can run down Stewart Avenue and see if we can find this woman named 'Gretta.'"

I drove out onto to Duval Street while dodging the large potholes that pockmarked the lot. I turned west, went one block, then turned south on Stewart. Flynn had said that he thought she was in the third house on the right. I parked the car in front of a small brick cottage that looked as if it was built in the forties. We exited the car and walked up to the front door.

Will knocked as I prepared to show my badge. In one minute, an older woman answered the door. She stood behind the screen wearing a print housedress and an apron.

"Can I hep ya?" she said.

"Yes, ma'am. We're from the Sheriff's Office." Will said. "Is 'Gretta' available?"

The old woman looked at my badge and smacked her lips. She pushed open the screen partially.

"She ain't here now. I'm her mama. She had to go downtown to the doctor."

"And your name is?"

"Mildred. Mildred Jones."

"What's Gretta's last name?"

"It's Jones, too."

"Will she be back soon?"

She shook her head. "I don't 'spect her back 'fore about six. She'll catch the last bus outta town. She's at her head doctor."

"Head doctor?"

"Her psychiatrist."

"I see. Well, could you get her to call us?" Will looked at me for another card. I obliged.

"She done somethin'?"

"No. Not at all. We'd just like to ask about her friend Zoe," I said.

"Pshaw," the woman said. "That girl deserved everthang that happened to her."

68

"You know what happened to her?"

"I know she got her throat cut."

"How'd you know that?"

"Her old man told us."

"Did Gretta tell you who did it?" Will said.

"No. She just said Zoe was drinkin' Black Russians at the lounge up there."

"Why do you say she deserved it?"

"'Cause she don't do nothin' but hang out at that bar; drinkin' and lettin' them men grope her. She ought'a be ashamed."

I guess she didn't know that Zoe also held a job; which was apparently more than Gretta did.

"Okay, well, just give her our number and ask her to call us if you will." I said.

"I sure will. She should be back in a little while."

I could tell that Will had just about had enough. His tolerance for stupid and ignorant was normally pretty low anyway, and what he was hearing today hadn't done anything to raise the bar.

Back in the car, he was fit to be tied. "Son, we're running into some real winners in this thing." He looked at me. "I think even you could find you a wife amongst these crazy gals."

Though his face was deadpan, he was trying to be funny, and I knew it. Will was always telling me how to find a wife. He would point out that women jogging on the side of road were recently divorced and trying to get back in shape to find another man, and I should stop and introduce myself. He also counseled that what I needed was a woman with 'a good government job' – one who was building her own retirement plan. Failing that, I should look for a woman with three or four children who was drawing public assistance for all of them. Then I could 'lay up' and not have to work.

"I don't think so." I paused. "You want to hang around and wait on her?"

"Are you kiddin'? That bitch may not come home at all. If she really is seein' a psychiatrist today, when she gets back, she's liable to be so pumped full'a pills we couldn't get the truth out of her with a pair'a pliers." He looked at me. "No, let's call it a day. We know where we can find her if we need her."

Chapter 10

When I arrived at headquarters the next morning, I found Will walking toward our office holding a Styrofoam cup of coffee and blowing into it. When he saw me, he nodded toward our door.

"Good morning. Come on in," he said.

I walked into the office, dumped my notebook on the desk, and fell into my chair. Then I took two hands and rubbed my face, hard. I was exhausted, a condition that usually followed my having been called out over the weekend. It generally took me two or three days to get over each bout of overtime that began after I was awakened from out of a sound sleep.

We had knocked off at six the evening previous, after finishing up paperwork and briefing the night shift on the status of the case. The two night men, who came on at five and went home at two AM, were supposed to surveil the lounge and watch for a man with pitch black hair. They were also supposed to contact one of us if or when they heard from 'Gretta' Jones or the Springdale Hospital. We did not anticipate any change in Zoe Woods' condition; however, I had no illusions regarding the seriousness of her injuries. She had lost a lot of blood and had stopped breathing twice, so, in my mind at least, she was on borrowed time.

"What's up?" I said while yawning.

"We got a call from Margaret Jones' mama," Will said, "that the crazy girl from Stewart Avenue. She said come on by her house this mornin' and Gretta'd talk to us."

"Man, I don't feel like going nowhere. I'm waxed."

"Take your time, Son. You got time to get a cup before we go."

It was a nice thought, but I didn't drink coffee. The large amounts of caffeine made my heart skip a beat – and not in a good way. When I needed a pick me up, I usually settled for a twenty-ounce soft drink, with less caffeine, but more calories. It seemed to work well.

I shook my head. "No coffee. I'll stop by and get a drink from downstairs."

"Well, take your time. I gotta run in and see Linus." He sat his coffee cup down on the desk and ambled out of the office.

I leaned back in my chair and closed my eyes. It would have been very easy, right at that moment, to drop off to sleep, but a picture of the dead baby from Theodore kept popping into my head. The child's post mortem would be this morning and what had happened to him was bothering me. In fact, I had dreamt about it the night before.

Dead baby cases weren't hard for me in the same way that they were hard for other detectives. I had no children. But, at death scenes, I'm forced to manipulate their little bodies and examine them. There was something about performing that particular duty that stuck with me; looking in their eyes, down their throats, at their tiny fingers and toes, even at their genitals. For me, at least, it wasn't natural.

Will was back in ten minutes. When he walked in, he was slightly less amiable.

"That son of a bitch," he said as he picked up his coffee cup. "He wants us to go back out there to that hospital and try to interview that ole gal again. I told him she could barely talk." He shook his head and fell back into his chair.

"So, we'll do it. No big deal."

"It's easy for him to order people around. He don't never get his fat ass outta that chair in there." He took a deep breath and exhaled. "That's got to be the laziest man that ever shit between two shoes."

I couldn't figure out what had gotten under his skin. Perhaps it was having his judgment questioned about the handling of the case. Or, maybe it was the fact that we hadn't come up with anything as of yet. Maybe, it was because he just didn't think this case was solvable.

We were getting our things together when there was a knock at the open door. I looked up and saw Lonnie Zane standing in the threshold.

Zane was another of the Major Crimes detectives. He was a thin man with pale skin and a shock of black hair that fell across his forehead. He and Will had partnered in the past and were at one time considered the number one team, but, about three years ago, he had complained of severe bouts of stress and had ultimately suffered a slight heart attack. He had thereafter been moved down to second chair in the Bureau and was partnered with Scott Neely.

"Come in here and take a look at this, Snuffy. You gotta see this," Zane said.

Will sat his coffee cup back down, and I pulled myself up out of the chair. We both followed Zane across the large squad bay to the Bureau's media room, along the east wall. Inside, Neely was standing in front of a 24-inch television monitor. He had a smile on his face.

"Run it back, Scott. Show Snuffy," Zane said.

Neely was thirty-five, with a red face and a buzz cut. He wore a Fu Manchu mustache and walked with a slight limp, the result of a motorcycle accident that had never quite healed properly. He rolled the VHS player back to the beginning and then stepped back and adjusted the position of the holstered .45 caliber pistol on his left hip.

"This is funny," Neely said.

I found a standing position where I could see, next to Will. Zane sat on the edge of a stool to one side, and Neely stood on the other.

"What are we lookin' at here?" Will said.

"Yesterday afternoon, late, about four thirty, we got a call out to a house off Two Mile Road," Zane said. "The woman that called it in said that she had gotten a phone call from her ex, about noon, and he told her that he was gonna kill his self. She said that he'd made that statement several times in the past, usually when he was drunk, so she didn't pay much attention; 'cause it sounded like he was drunk this time, too. She said she tried to call him a little later in the afternoon, and when she couldn't get him, she picked up her daughter and went on out there. When they went in the house, they found him, and this." Zane motioned toward the video screen.

We watched in silence. The scene appeared to be a living or family room. There was a blue club chair right in the middle of the screen, and a small table next to it. On the table sat a lamp and one of those older model princess phones. The background was dark, but it looked as if there was a bookshelf behind the chair – kind of a Masterpiece Theatre effect.

In about two minutes an older man walked around from the rear of the camera and sat down in the chair. He had gray hair that was parted on the right and combed back. His face was brown and weathered, skin hung down over his eyelids, and he had a pretty sizeable wattle hanging off his neck. He wore a white dress shirt and dark trousers, and when he crossed his right leg over his left, his black oxford shoe and white sock were visible. He looked a little like Archie Bunker, in his living room, on his throne.

A Budweiser beer can was in his right hand, and he took a swig of it just after he sat down. There was a lit cigarette between the first two fingers of his left. After the

73

beer, he took a long drag, after which he coughed loudly and swirled the dislodged phlegm around inside his mouth.

When he'd gotten himself situated, he put the beer can down on the table, wiped his face with his hand, and spoke. His speech was slow and slurred.

"Baby, this is the last time you and me is gonna talk; or, I'm gonna talk to you, that is. You treated me like shit for thirty years. I tried to do the bes' I could by ya. I got'cha a house and a car; I went to work ever'day, baby, ever'day. I love you Denise . . ."

"That's his daughter," Neely said.

". . . and I tried to give you what you needed, but baby, you didn't 'preciate it bit; not none of it." He coughed again. *"So, I don't know what else to do. You run off and left me five years ago, and I ain't . . ."* He looked away as he appeared to choke off a sob. *"You been a real bitch, baby. I didn't do nothin' but love ya, and you treated me like shit.*

He paused. *"We was good together, Hon. 'Member when we used to go dancin' down at the Hall? Man . . ."* He shook his head and laughed until he coughed.

"I never looked at another woman. You said I did, but I didn't. You said I drank too much, but I didn't."

He reached over and picked up the beer can, toasted the camera, then took a long pull. Then he said, *"Ahhhhhhhhh,"* in that way that one does when he is satiated by liquid and the word scrapes the back of his throat. He shook the can to see if there was any left and then replaced it on the table.

"I'll tell you what else you said, baby. You always said I wadn't worth killin'." He took a deep breath and exhaled. *"Well, you was wrong."*

And, with that, he reached down on the seat between the cushion and the right arm of the chair and produced what appeared to be a .22 caliber revolver; a blue steel weapon with white grips. He held the gun in his right hand, pulled back the hammer with his thumb, put the muzzle to his right temple, and pulled the trigger.

The small 'pop' that was the gun's report was almost imperceptible. If you had not seen what he was doing, you wouldn't have known what had happened. His gun arm relaxed immediately and fell into his lap; and his head fell forward and then to the right, with his chin resting on his chest. The scene was completely quiet. The cigarette still burned in his left hand as it hung over the arm of the chair, the tendril of smoke from the fire end lazily rising toward the ceiling.

"Son of a bitch," Will said.

"Wait, wait," Zane said pointing at the screen. "Watch this."

We watched on. In a minute a small calico cat suddenly jumped into the dead man's lap and curled up with its head nestled against his abdomen. The animal shut its eyes and promptly went to sleep.

Neely chuckled. "Well, I guess he showed her."

Zane slapped his leg and laughed out loud in the way that only an experienced homicide detective can laugh; not a belly laugh, but an uncomfortable guffaw that kept him from crying.

I shook my head and looked at the floor. "Man, if we showed this movie at the high schools we'd have fifty suicides in a month."

"How's that?" Zane said.

"Well, look at it. He's sitting there in a comfortable chair. The gun sounds like a cap gun. He nods off to sleep, and afterwards the cat comes up and sits down in his lap. It doesn't really look like somebody just bought it. Does it?"

"Well, we just gotta make sure this doesn't fall into the wrong hands, don't we, Son," Will said.

Chapter 11

Back in our office, Will and I gathered our belongings, and we were on the road in fifteen minutes enroute to Margaret Jones' residence on Stewart Avenue. It was a nice day, with a temperature in the fifties.

As we turned off Duval onto Stewart, I could see a female sitting in a folding chair in the front yard. The brown haired girl was wearing jeans and a sweat shirt, but no shoes. A mangy dog was lying beside the chair, on the ground; ground that was primarily dirt with very little grass. Children's toys, including a yellow Tonka truck and some plastic, multi-colored Playskool playthings, lay strewn about the driveway; toys that I hadn't noticed the day before.

"Look at that. I bet this crazy bitch has two or three young'uns runnin' around somewhere," Will said.

He looked at me, and I smirked. Sometimes, I didn't quite know how to respond to him. He was right, of course. If her mental or psychological condition was what we thought, and the fact that she was seeing a psychiatrist was a pretty good indication that it was, she had no business giving birth or otherwise trying to raise children. Still, what was done was done, and somehow I believed that there were other things to be worried about.

"If she's as slow as they say, they might be her toys," I said.

We stopped the car on the street and got out. The young woman opened her closed eyes and put on a kind of a sheepish grin.

"Ya'll the police?"

"Yes, lady, we are," Will said. "Your name 'Gretta?'"

She nodded.

We stood in silence in front of her for a moment until a female voice from inside the house called out through the screen door. It was Mildred Jones, trying to be neighborly, even if her daughter did not have the sense to do so.

"Well, ask'em to come inside, Gretta."

"Ya'll wanna come inside?"

"Let's do that," Will said. "That way it's a little easier for Mr. Faulkner here to write."

She got up from the chair and the three of us trooped through the front door into the light and airish interior. Mildred Jones was standing at the head of the hallway wearing the same print dress as yesterday, and drying her hands on a dish towel.

"Ya'll want somethin' to drink?" she said.

"No, ma'am," Will said. "We just wanna talk to Gretta a minute, and then we'll be outta your way."

The three of us arranged ourselves on the couch and two chairs that were in the living room. I looked around. The room was spotless; no clutter and no sign of any children.

"Gretta, your first name is Margaret, is that right?" Will said.

"Uh, huh."

"What is your birthday?"

"I was born on the Fourth of July."

She smiled proudly as she supplied the year. How fortuitous for her that she had the name of a holiday to help her remember her nativity.

"Tell us what you know about Zoe."

She looked away out of the window. "Zoe?"

"Do you know Zoe?"

She looked at Will. I spoke up.

"Zoe from The Society; you see her down there sometimes."

"Yeah, I know Zoe."

This was going to be harder than either of us dreamed. I looked at Will.

"Do you remember the man that Zoe was drinkin' with last Friday night?" he said.

It was a smart move, getting right to the information we were seeking. The more this woman said, the more she disqualified herself as a witness. She was only going to be good for the information, and not the testimony, that she could provide; anonymous information.

"Do you remember the man? The black haired man?"

"Ohhhh. Yeah. Mikey. He drank Black Russians."

"Tell me about Mikey."

"Mikey? Yeah, he drank Black Russians."

"What's Mikey's last name?"

"I don't know."

"Where does he live?"

She looked out the window, as if her mind was wandering.

"Where does Mikey live?"

She looked back at Will. "I think he lives by the farm."

"What farm?"

"Where the birds are."

I could tell that Will was getting impatient. He looked over at me.

"Tell me about the birds," I said.

"A brown bird, in his car."

"There was a bird in Mikey's car?"

"Um, hmm; a brown bird."

"Was Mikey tall or short?"

"Short."

"Was he fat or thin?"

"Kinda fat. I don't know." I could tell she was getting frustrated also.

"What was Mikey wearing? What color was his shirt?"

"Plaid." Imagine her knowing the term 'plaid.'

"Was Mikey old or young?"

She looked at me and then at my pad. "Kinda old, kinda young."

78

"Who was you with the other night?" Will said.

She looked away. "I danced."

"With who?"

"With Mikey; with ever'body."

It was apparent that she had reached the point where she was only trying to please us. When witnesses – especially children, and Gretta was like a child – don't know what the answer is, they give you everything in hopes they'll stumble onto what they think you want to hear.

"Did you see his car?"

"It was red."

Aside from his full name, at that point, the vehicle description was going to be the biggest help to us. Pity she didn't know more about it.

I looked back at Will. He started to get up. At that point Mildred Jones came into the room.

"Ya'll gettin' anything out of her?" she said.

Will, not one to mince words, said, "Not much."

Mildred Jones sat down on the couch near her daughter. Will sat back down.

"Honey, do you remember the man that Zoe was with the other night?"

Gretta played with her hands and looked at her lap. It was plain that her relationship with her mother was not going to help us a bit. Gretta had no doubt been frustrating her mother for years.

"Tell these men, honey."

She shrugged her shoulders and remained silent.

Will rose again. "Look, we're gonna go. I don't think she knows any more than what she's said."

Gretta sat silently with a blank look on her face. Then she picked her nose with her pinky finger.

"Did she help you at all?"

I nodded. "A little."

Back in the car, Will was philosophical.

"Well, I guess we got out of her all we could: 'Mikey,' in a red car."

"You think she really remembers his name, or was she trying to please us?"

"She knew it. It was the only thing that crazy girl said with any forthrightness. That's his name."

"Too bad she won't be able to be a witness."

"Oh, fuck no. We can't let her get near a witness stand. If a jury heard her talk, they'd disregard anything she had to say."

I took a deep breath. "So, we know his name is Mikey; he drinks Black Russians; he's got black hair; he may be old, may be young; he may be fat, he may be thin; and he's got a bird in his red car."

"That part about the bird in the car's bullshit, Son. I don't know where that come from."

"Where to?"

"Back to the office. I need a cup'a coffee."

Chapter 12

I took the long way back to the office, down Government. Just as we passed Catherine Street, I heard Will's stomach growl.

I looked at him and grinned. "Hungry?"

"I could do with somethin'."

"What makes your stomach growl when it's hungry?"

"Only God knows, Son. Only God knows."

About that time, the police radio sounded.

"SO 21." That was Will's call sign.

He picked up the radio microphone and cleared his throat. "SO 21."

"Can you take a dead body on Lauderdale Road; believed to be a natural death."

He looked at me. "Well, shit."

"Yes, ma'am," he said over the microphone.

The dispatcher supplied us with the address, and Will wrote it down on the back of an envelope he had in his shirt pocket. We were lucky. Sometimes, Will didn't have a pen.

I went south on Dauphin Island Parkway, then west on Interstate 10 to the Rangeline Road exit. I turned the car south, and we were at the address on Lauderdale Road about twenty minutes after the radio had sounded.

We parked in front of a brick home with no garage that sat on a short rise on the south side of Lauderdale, not more than a half mile from the Bellingrath Road intersection; not too far from where Zoe Woods had been found. It was one of about a half dozen homes recently constructed on that side of the road, on a parcel of land lately sold by the estate of an elderly Theodore, Alabama, woman whose deceased husband had owned a large cotton concern.

Two marked patrol cars and an SUV were parked on the road in front of the home. Two other cars, one a pickup truck and the other a large sedan, were in the driveway. Will took a deep breath, lightly uttered an obscenity, and we exited the car.

At the front door, We We White let us in. Bobby Welch, a thin, chain-smoking deputy with a bald head and a mustache was standing in the living room writing a report. He looked up and smiled.

"How ya'll doin?" he said.

Welch had a pronounced southern drawl and a tattoo of a Confederate flag on his right forearm. He removed the cigarette from his lips and nodded toward the hallway to his left.

"She's back in the bedroom. Her husband found her."

81

Will and I stopped and stood in front of Welch. I looked around the room. The first thing that I noticed was that the place was immaculate. The second thing I noticed was that there was plastic all over the furniture. In fact, we were standing on paper towels that someone had laid down on top of the shag carpeting.

"What's goin' on?" I said to no one in particular.

Welch looked around and grinned. "Oh, you mean the plastic and shit? Well, her son says she's a neat freak; can't stand for anyone to come into the house and bring dirt. Wait'll you see the bathroom."

"What's her name?" I said preparing the write.

"Claire Bowden, sixty-six. She lives here with her husband. He and the son are sittin' out on the patio."

I looked up from my notepad. Will had walked into the kitchen and was looking around.

"Paramedics?"

"Come and gone. They left a strip. I'll attach it to the report."

"Coroner?"

"I called'em. They said they'd get somebody on the way."

I nodded. "Who's here from crime scene?"

"Hernandez is in the bedroom takin' pichurs. He hadn't long got here."

I nodded again. "Well, it sounds like you've got everything under control."

"We aim to please," Welch said, smiling through a discolored front tooth.

I glanced toward the kitchen. Will walked through the door and back into the living room. He had a paper towel in his hands and was wiping liquid off his fingers.

"What were you doing in there?" I said.

"Messin' up the place." He smiled impishly.

We walked down the hall, a short one covered in paper towels, and stopped at the second door on the left, the master bedroom. Hernandez was standing at the foot of the bed snapping photographs. He looked around and smiled.

"Come on in. Just don't step on the good rug."

I smiled. Will snorted. We both stopped to look at the woman lying across the foot of a large four-poster bed, posts that almost reached the ceiling. The room was sparsely furnished, yet clean as a whistle. It appeared as if the walls and ceiling had recently been painted. The carpet, what you could see of it, was spotless. The dresser and night table were covered with clear plastic, the kind that's over your clothes when they come back from the dry cleaners.

The woman wore a pink nightgown and looked her stated age of sixty-six. She had fine gray hair that was curled. Her fair skin showed off the varicose veins in her legs and the blue veins under the thin skin of her hands. Her long and thin fingers were wrinkled and weathered. She was lying prone, her legs straight, arms at her sides. She looked as if she had just laid down to take a nap.

"What's in the bathroom?" Will said.

"What? Oh, nothing," Hernandez said. "Just that she's got that covered up, too."

Will stalked that direction. I followed and stood in the threshold. The room was a sight. The face bowl and fixtures were sparkling underneath Saran wrap. The toilet tank was encased in a clear plastic johnny bonnet, and paper towels not only covered the toilet seat, they also lined the inside of the bowl above the waterline. The tub and the floor were similarly shrouded.

I made notes. Will perused the medicine cabinet.

"This woman was in prison," I said.

Will looked around. "Fuck, Son. She was a nut." He paused. "I wonder where her ole man goes to take a shit?"

When we walked back into the bedroom, Angie McDowell, the best looking of the three investigators for the Mobile County Medical Examiner, was there putting on rubber gloves and unpacking her camera. She looked up and smiled.

"I'm glad you're here," I said.

"Oh?"

"Yeah. Only a female could understand what we're lookin' at here."

McDowell looked around. She was thirty-ish; a short but stocky and strong woman with blonde hair pulled back in an abbreviated ponytail. Her flawless complexion was tanned, and her weight was proportionate to her height; another way of saying she had an hourglass figure. Her button nose sat over a generous mouth and straight white teeth. She looked as if she should be starring in one of those crime scene programs on television instead of doing the work for real.

"Well, sure. It's simple. She had new stuff, and she didn't want it messed up by dirty old men," she said.

"You think it's that simple?" I said.

Will didn't speak. He was married.

"Of course. Well, that's the way it started, anyway."

"But the paper towels; the cellophane."

She looked around again. "Want to make a bet?" She paused and looked at the three of us. "I bet you that this is the first home she's ever owned. I bet it's the first furniture she ever bought."

"It's a bet," I said. "I bet you lunch she's been under the care of a psychiatrist, or at least takes pills for Obsessive-Compulsive Disorder, or some such thing, and it's not merely a case of wanting to protect new stuff."

"You're on." She looked at me and smiled. Something told me she wanted to get to know me better.

Will coughed. "If you two are through, can we just take a look at this woman so we can get the fuck outta here?"

Angie smirked. She raised her camera and snapped three or four shots of the dead woman from various angles. Then she placed her camera back in her bag and walked toward the corpse. When she got next to the woman, she reached and took her by the arm and leg on her left side and in one motion flipped her over onto her back.

McDowell started at the woman's head, and slowly and methodically worked her way down her body looking for signs of trauma. She looked in her mouth, down her throat, in her ears, and deep into her eyes. Then she lifted up her nightgown and prepared to look at her genitalia.

"Everybody, hide your eyes," she said.

She took two fingers and spread the old woman's labia and then manipulated her way down for a look at her anus. When she finished, she stood up straight and took off her gloves.

"Well, I don't see anything to indicate that she has died from anything other than a natural death. Of course, the blood test will tell us for sure." She looked at me. "Have you guys gotten a medical history on her yet?"

I shook my head. "We were waitin' on you."

"Let's go."

McDowell, Will, and I left Hernandez with the body while we walked back through the living room, out the sliding glass doors, and onto the brick patio adjacent to the home.

Arthur Bowden and his son, Vincent, sat in lawn chairs looking straight ahead. The older man was seventy, nearly bald, with a thin build. His large nose and hanging ear lobes affirmed his age. He wore suit pants and a white button up shirt. Black oxfords sheathed his long, narrow feet.

Vincent Bowden looked about thirty-five. He had a full head of thick black hair. His tanned face was clean shaven, and he wore a light blue oxford shirt, suit pants, and a red tie.

Will took a seat beside the old man and introduced himself. McDowell and I stood under an overhang, out of the sun, and prepared to take notes. Wind rustled through the large oaks in the yard, and I heard a woodpecker beating its head against the hard wood.

"Mr. Bowden, tell me about your wife," Will said.

Arthur Bowden looked up. He spoke in low tones, the picture of a man whose spouse of many years – maybe not always the happiest of years – had left him. He had the confused look of someone who did not know what to do next.

"Me and Claire just moved into this house; it's the first one we ever owned, and she was real proud of it. I bought her all new furniture, and she was very protective of it." He paused and nodded toward the interior. "I guess you all could see that."

McDowell looked at me and stuck the very tip of her tongue past her teeth in that time-worn gesture of contempt. I raised my right eyebrow and continued to write.

"Yes, we did see that. Has your wife been ill?"

He took a deep breath and exhaled. "Well, no, not really. She had high blood pressure, and she had a heart attack about five years ago. But, other than that, she was in good health."

"What about her mental health?"

"Oh, that. She saw a psychiatrist once or twice. He had her takin' some pills."

"When did that start?"

"She began to act a little erratic just before we moved in here. She started havin' nightmares and nervous fits, I guess you'd call'em. Her heart'd start beatin' fast, and she couldn't get her breath. She'd get to where she couldn't sleep, or either she wanted to sleep all day."

I looked at McDowell and raised my lip in an almost imperceptible sneer. She saw me and wrinkled her nose.

"How long ago did you folks move in?"

"Two years ago." Vincent Bowden spoke up. His voice was deep and much stronger. "They lived in a trailer all their married life. Daddy did mechanic work, working on heavy equipment for a construction company, and we'd move around to be close to his job sites."

Will continued questioning Arthur Bowden about both his and his wife's movements that day. Claire Bowden was last seen at about ten AM when she said that she didn't feel well and was going to lie down. Arthur had fallen asleep in his easy chair – the only one in the house in which she would let him sit – and when he awoke, he went to the bedroom and found her unresponsive. He called his son first, then the paramedics.

As he talked, I was convinced that there was no murder here. Will finished up his interview and turned to me.

"You got anything?"

"Just one thing. Mr. Bowden, what was the psychiatrist's diagnosis?"

He turned his head. "Son?"

Vincent Bowden looked up. "I think he said that she was mildly schizophrenic and clinically depressed, with obsessive compulsive tendencies."

I jotted the words down and nodded at Will. "That's all I got."

When Will rose from his seat, Angie McDowell took his place. She would remain and gather information regarding the drugs that Claire Bowden took and the doctors that she had seen on a regular basis. For our part, Will and I stepped back into the house and spoke to the two deputies. White and Welch gathered around.

"One'a you guys can leave. When Hernandez and the coroner's girl finish up, call an ambulance and have the old lady sent to wherever the girl says." Will nodded toward the bedroom.

"Make sure that you put in the report that the woman had a previous heart attack and mark it to forward a copy to me. I'll want it if somethin' unusual comes back from the lab."

Both men nodded. Then Will and I left the home via the front door. When we got to the car, I spoke.

"Well, at least I came out of this a winner."

"You mean, bettin' with that young gal in there?"

"Sure. I figure it means I'm in line for lunch or dinner, or something."

"You mean you wanna fuck her?"

I smiled but said nothing.

"The way I see it, Son, she's the loser."

Chapter 13

Very late that afternoon, after an abbreviated lunch and some time catching up on overdue paperwork, we went back over to The Society Lounge to see if we could meet and interview the regular crowd there, and ask them about Zoe Woods.

Before we left, I contacted the hospital to check on her condition. The charge nurse on her floor told me that hospital rules wouldn't let her say much other than that Zoe was holdin' her own. She labeled her in 'stable but guarded' condition. She did mention that her husband had been in and out and also that her parents had been by her bedside for two days.

When we pulled into the parking lot of the lounge, at around five o'clock, there were four cars there. We parked at the far northwest corner because Will said he wanted to watch for a few minutes. Fifteen minutes later nothing had happened, so we locked the car doors and went inside.

Once again, we stood in the threshold and surveyed the room. To our right, Larry Flynn was still behind the bar. To our left, a man and a woman were slow dancing to *Rose Colored Glasses* on the jukebox. There were four other people, two male/female couples, sitting at separate tables near the bar. A red haired woman wearing jeans and a pullover shirt, who I guessed was a bar maid, was sitting on a stool close to the cash register.

Will walked that direction and spoke to Flynn. I hung by the door and looked around. If anyone tried to make a break for it, I was going to make an effort to keep them inside. But, as far as I was concerned, the bar maid was the person most likely to have *good* information.

When no one tried to escape, and while Will finished telling Flynn what we were doing, I walked toward the couple seated closest to the dance floor.

"Excuse me, sir, my name is Faulkner, and I'm with the Metro Sheriff's Office." I showed him my badge, and he looked at me with a guarded expression.

"I just wanna ask you about Zoe Woods. Do either of you know her?"

The man nodded. He was forty, with a balding head and a dark suntan.

His face softened just a little as I took a seat at the table. I could smell the liquor on his breath. The woman, a twenty something in jeans and a white sweater, leaned back and crossed her arms and legs.

"Were either of you here last Friday night?"

"I was," the man said. "I'm Linc, Lincoln Hayes, by the way. I was sorry to hear about Zoe."

"You saw the man she was with?"

"I did, but I didn't talk to him."

His voice was a little slurred. I began to wonder what kind of witness he'd make.

"Tell me about him," I said. The woman picked up a glass and sipped beer.

"He was about forty; not too tall, maybe five seven or eight; with kind of a stocky build. He was dark, and he had jet black hair."

"Kind of a dark brown?"

He shook his head. "Oh, no. It was black; real black, coal black. Dyed black, you know?"

I nodded. Will came over and pulled up a chair from the next table. He sat down but did not speak.

"Did you ever hear him talk?"

"No. He just talked to Zoe; bought her drinks. They had their heads together real close. I think they danced a couple of songs, too."

"Did they come in together, or did he meet her here?"

"You know, I'm not sure; seems like they was both here when I come in. I was s'posed to meet a woman here, but she never showed, so I didn't stay long." The woman at the table snorted.

"Did you recognize this guy? Had he been here before?"

He shook his head. "Nope. Never saw him before or since. We pretty much know ever'body that comes in here. He was new."

"What about a car?"

"I didn't see him get into a car."

"When you left, did you see a car in the parking lot that you didn't recognize?"

He thought a minute. I got the sense that he suddenly realized that he might have said too much and that if he had seen a car, he didn't want to say. He shook his head.

I looked over at Will to see if he had anything to ask while I made notes. Will sat with folded arms and shook his head.

"How about you, ma'am, did you see the man?" I said.

Lincoln Hayes spoke up before she could say anything. "She wadn't here. This is Lisa. She come with me tonight. She's new."

Hayes supplied us a name and address, and also a place of employment. I gave him a card and told him to call if he saw the man again. I nodded to him and the woman, who looked purposely disinterested.

90

"Okay, well, thanks for your cooperation."

Will and I both stood up and moved toward the couple who was dancing when we first came in, but who had since repaired to a table close to the juke box. This time, Will talked.

"Hey, we're with the Sheriff's Office, Buddy. I'm Eubanks and this is Mr. Faulkner. We wanted to ask you about Zoe."

The woman, a bleached blonde with a full figure and plenty of makeup, spoke first.

"Oh, sure. Sit down." Her tone was enthusiastic. "We heard what happened. I hope you guys catch that bastard."

"What is your name, ma'am?"

"Jeannie Pollard."

"Do you know who that was?"

"No. I saw her with him. That was on Thursday night, right?"

"Would'a been a Friday."

"Oh, well, maybe I'm not thinkin' about the same guy. The man I saw her with had sandy hair and a mustache; one of them kind that twirls up on the ends. He had on a kind of a salmon-colored shirt and some khaki pants. And, I remember his shoes, they was loafers with tassels; real shiny."

"Are you sure that was on Friday?"

"Well, let me see? I went to the grocery store on Thursday then I come here. And, Friday . . . yeah, I think I was here on Friday night."

She was talking so much that the man at the table couldn't get in a word, even though he was trying. Will looked over at him.

"Is that the way you remember it?"

He cleared his throat and took a cigarette out of a pack in his shirt pocket. The man was about fifty with a thick head of salt and pepper hair and a weathered face. He had a protruding belly, and his dark shirt just barely covered the expanse.

"Well, I wadn't here on Thursday. I was outta town. I drive a truck. And I was with you on Friday," he said looking at the woman. "And I don't remember the man that looked like what you just said, so you must'a seen him on Thursday."

"And you are?"

"My name? My name's Wes Hightower."

Jeannie Pollard looked at Hightower with raised eyebrows, like he was crazy. He raised his eyebrows back at her and snorted.

"I was outta town on Thursday, and I got the log books to prove it."

He looked over at Will and nodded, pleased with himself for being able to tell the woman where to get off.

"So, you were here on Friday. Did you see Zoe with a man?"

He took a swig of beer and then a puff. It was clear he was trying to think. "You know, I don't remember, really; seems like he was fat and kind'a old. I 'member he was drinking Black Russians 'cause he had hair black as the ace'a spades. I remember thinkin', 'wonder if Russians has hair that black.' He had on a red shirt, and . . . that's all I remember. It was a red shirt, though."

"Did it look like they was gettin' along?"

"You mean Zoe and the man?"

Will nodded. "Yeah."

"Oh, yeah. I mean, I guess. They was talkin' real close like. I couldn't hear what they was sayin', but they wadn't arguin' ner nothin'."

Will nodded again.

"Zoe was a mean drunk," Jeannie Pollard said. She had begun to feel left out and unimportant, so she had to jump in with something.

"Really?"

"Oh, yeah. When she got a few drinks in'er, she'd really let'cha have it."

"How so?"

"You know, just ridiculin' what you was wearin', how you looked; just bein' sarcastic, you know."

The word 'ridicule' seemed wholly out of place in her vernacular.

Will looked back at the man. "Did you see what kind of car he was in?"

"He was in a red car," Jeannie Pollard spoke up.

"Are you sure?"

She nodded. "I saw'em leave. It was an older model red car."

I was writing quickly. Will paused to let me catch up. He turned to the man again.

"Did you see his car?"

"You know, I didn't. I just remember his black hair and those Black Russian drinks."

I began to believe that these people and their whiskey sopped minds were going to be as useless in court as Gretta Jones would be; sandy hair, black hair; red shirt, salmon shirt; red car, no car. I wasn't sure who or what we could believe.

Hightower and Pollard both supplied contact information, although Hightower said that he was an over the road trucker who was gone three weeks out of four. We just happened to catch him on his week in Mobile, but he said that his dispatcher would always know how to find him. Pollard was a cashier at Naman's Food Store up on Broad Street every day, five days a week.

We left their table and wandered back toward the bar. I noticed that the other couple that was in the building had disappeared. My guess is that one or the other of them was wanted, and when they found out who we were, they decided to check out before we checked them out.

At the bar, Will took a stool next to 'Sis' the waitress. I stood just to his left, my pad and pen at the ready.

Susy Weaver was the only barmaid at The Society, having worked there for the past five years. She and Larry had grown up together, and when he left one of those dance clubs on the west side of town to start his own place, she came with him. I wondered if there was something going on between them.

Sis was not a beauty. Her henna-colored hair was short and frizzy, and she had big hands and thick, muscular arms and legs. She looked almost as if she had once been a man, but her high tinny voice ratified the fact that she was truly female. She was dressed in jeans and a pink, long sleeved, pullover shirt, with cross trainers on her feet.

"Sis," Will said, "you remember seein' the man that Zoe was with?"

She nodded and took a puff from her cigarette. "Yeah."

"Was his name Mikey?"

"Well, that's what she called him, but I don't know if that was his name."

"Why not?"

She chuckled. "'Cause Zoe never did call nobody by their right name. I guess it was 'cause she couldn't remember it. Half the time I was 'Loretta.' Heck, when she got a few in her, she couldn't remember her own name."

Sis laughed that raspy laugh of the chronic smoker and one who had spent too many nights in a bar without enough sleep.

"Tell me about him?"

"Well, he drank Black Russians. I 'member 'cause he asked me to put a tablespoon'a chocolate sauce in it." She paused and took a swig of a can of Sprite. "And, he had hair so black it was almost blue. It looked dyed, really. And he was new; never seen him in here before or since."

"Chocolate sauce?"

"Mmm hmm. I went and looked and found a bottle'a Hershey's in the 'fridge. He drank four or five

94

of'em. Zoe had a couple and some beer. She got all he had to spend."

"How so?"

"Oh, you know; drinks, music in the box. He even bought her a sandwich and some fries."

"I didn't know ya'll cooked in here."

"Well, we don't advertise it, but the reg'lars know. If you want somethin', I'll make you a sandwich and maybe some onion rings; just not a seven-course meal."

"Sis, does the name 'Byrd' mean anything to you?"

"You mean outta here?"

"Yeah."

She thought for a minute then shook her head. "No."

"Anybody ever bring a bird in here with'em?"

She chuckled. "Not that I ever saw."

"Did you see Zoe 'n' him leave?"

"No. I must'a been in the back, or in the ladies' room or somethin'. I don't remember'em leaving."

Will looked over at me. "How'd they get along?" I said.

"Well, they looked like they was doin' okay. Nobody raised their voice ner nothing. You better believe that if somethin' hadn't been goin' right, Zoe would'a said somethin'. She never kept her feelin's to herself."

"If he had tried to take her someplace against her will, she'd've raised a ruckus?"

"Ooo, you better believe it."

"We heard that Zoe could get a little contrary when she got a couple'a drinks in her."

"You mean was she a mean drunk?"

"Was she?"

"She could get pretty ugly when she got too much." She paused. "I tend to believe that she maybe liked this guy. She drank a lot, and while they was here, she never got outta hand."

"She could get outta hand?"

"Most folks just looked past her because she was slow, but a couple'a times she did get on the wrong side'a guys that didn't know her. She just comes in here to talk to the men and get'em to buy her drinks. She was just part of the local atmosphere, so to speak."

I looked around trying to think of what else to ask. "One more thing, there was another couple in here when we came in. They bugged out. What were their names?"

Sis looked left and right and spoke in low tones. She was comfortable telling what she saw, but she didn't necessarily want to implicate others as witnesses.

"That was Jerry Painter. I don't know who the girl was. That was the first time I saw her."

"Do you know how to get in touch with him?"

"He works at a car place over on Broad Street. I don't know how many there are, but you could prob'ly find him."

I looked back at Will and nodded, then turned toward a short hall and the men's toilet. When I opened the door, the smell nearly knocked me flat. I breathed through my mouth while I quickly pissed into a dirty urinal, and was back out the door and to the bar without washing my hands. Will looked up and saw me.

"Well, thank ya, Sis. You've been a help."

"I want'chu to catch this son of a bitch. If I can do anything else, now, you let me know." I slipped her a business card.

Outside in the car, Will cleared his throat. "Well, that was a fuckin' waste'a time. The only lead we had to this old boy's identity just got shot down 'cause our victim never calls anybody by their right name."

I laughed and smiled at him. "The more we find out about her, the crazier she gets."

Will nodded. "How dirty was the head?"

I looked at him and smiled. "They don't call it a shithouse for nothin'."

Chapter 14

The next morning, I met Will coming out of the Captain's office. He had a cup in one hand and a sheath of papers in the other. Downstairs, I closed our office door and fell into my chair. Will sat down and began looking through the papers.

"What's all that stuff?"

He looked up. "This is paperwork from the AG's office. They're retryin' the Carlton case. The people from Montgomery are gonna be down here on Friday mornin' for a meetin'."

The Carlton case was an old murder that happened close to fifteen years ago. John Carlton and a hired hit man came to Mobile to kill a young boy that they thought was responsible for the accidental death of Carlton's sister. After a six month long investigation, Will was able to build a case against Carlton and the hit man, both of whom were sentenced to death. They'd been fighting the chair ever since. This was to be the second retrial.

"What are the grounds this time?"

"Well, accordin' to this motion, apparently the prosecutor made 'inflammatory remarks to the jury' in his closin' summation."

"Imagine that."

Will shook his head. "That means I'll have to run around and hunt up all the fuckin' witnesses again, and gather up all the evidence again, and get all tied up in this shit again." He paused and looked at the paper. "It says here that they want me to ride up to Atmore and talk to Hankins."

97

Harold Walter Hankins was the hit man from Dallas that was arrested with Carlton. He was convicted of putting a shotgun to the back of a sixteen year old boy's head and pulling the trigger.

"What do they want you to do that for?"

"They want me to ask him if he wants to testify against Carlton."

I shrugged. "You know him. Any chance'a that?"

"Oh, fuck, no. Right now, he's on Death Row. No way he wants to give up his single cell and go back into population. He's gotta TV and a desk, and privacy. My guess is he'll just let his own case run its course and see what happens."

We sat in silence for two minutes. Then I took out a legal pad and started making a 'do list' to occupy my day.

Will looked my direction. "What'chu writin', Son?"

"I'm just trying to get my head together. It's a list of things to do on the Zoe Woods thing." I paused and looked up from the pad.

"The first thing we need to do is to run out and see her. The last time I talked to a nurse out there she told me that she was just 'holding her own.' The way she said it had kind of a bad ring."

"You're right. That don't sound good," Will said before taking a sip of coffee.

"I don't know. They repaired her throat, but there's always a chance of infection; and she did lose a lotta blood."

"Well, I'll tell you somethin', Son." His tone was somber. "We'd be better off, for our purposes, if that bitch'd die."

Thirty minutes later we were on the fourth floor of Springdale Hospital. We stood in front of the nurse's station and waited for the charge nurse to get back from her break. Will sipped his cup of coffee, and I chewed a stick of gum. It was nine o'clock.

In ten minutes, Ellen, a tall brunette wearing purple scrubs, whose ID card told us she was the manager for the part of floor that housed Zoe Woods, told us that we could go in after one of the nursing assistants finished giving Zoe a bath.

In ten more minutes a short, round female in scrubs exited Zoe Woods's room carrying a metal basin and soap. She was shaking her head.

"That po' girl just couldn't keep herself still. She was thrashin' 'round like a fish."

I looked back at Ellen. "Is that a good sign?"

She smirked. "Not necessarily. She might be delirious."

"Can we go in now?" Will said. He clearly did not want to be there.

She nodded. "Don't stay long, and try not to get her excited."

I pulled back the curtain, and we walked into the room. Zoe Woods lay on the bed with her eyes closed, apparently asleep. Her head was turned to her left, and I could see the Frankenstein-like stitches holding her neck together. The sight, even in its healing condition, was repulsive. There appeared to be well over fifty stitches, on the outside. No telling how many there were on the inside.

"Zoe?" I said.

She didn't respond. I called her name again.

She opened her eyes slightly and rolled her head my direction. I heard her make some type of guttural sound. It was as if she had regressed in her ability to speak.

"Can you talk this morning?"

"Unhhhhh."

"Can you say who cut you?"

"Unhhhhh."

I stood up straight and backed away, then looked at Will. He nodded toward the door, and we were two steps from walking out when an older man and woman came through the curtain and stopped.

"Who are you?" the woman said suspiciously.

She had graying hair, a round face, and a dumpy figure. Her tone was accusatory.

"I'm Detective Faulkner, and this is Sergeant Eubanks. We're with the Metro Sheriff's Department."

"Oh, I see. Well, I'm Robert Woods, and this is my wife, Evelyn. We're Zoe's parents," the man said.

He was about sixty with a bald head and horn-rimmed glasses. He wore a brown barn coat and khaki slacks.

"We're working on Zoe's case, and we just stopped by to see if she was able to give us anything that might help."

Robert Woods shook his head. "She hasn't spoken since we got here, two days ago. It's gotten worse in the past day and a half."

"Do you have any leads?" Evelyn Woods said.

I looked at Will. He spoke up.

"We know that she was in a bar on Friday night drinkin' with a black haired man. They apparently left together, but we haven't talked to anyone who saw her after that. We're still tryin' to get an ID and a vehicle description on this black haired man. Do you have any idea who he might be?"

Both of Zoe's parents shook their heads. "We don't see Zoe much. We live in Chunchula, almost to Citronelle. She moved out a couple of years ago, against our wishes." She paused. "She works over at the Tyndall Chicken Plant and hangs out at that bar near her home," Evelyn Woods said.

"How did you find out she was hurt?"

"That man that she lives with called us. He said that you had been by, and he told us she was in the hospital. He came to see her to make sure it was her, and then he called us." She paused and looked at her daughter. "I guess you know she's different."

I nodded. "That's what we've heard. What was her diagnosis?"

"She's classified as mildly retarded. Her working IQ is about 75. She can function alone, but she's not intelligent enough to make decisions wisely. She's . . ."

Her voice trailed away as she looked at her daughter and began to regret that she had let her get away.

Will spoke. "Did she ever talk about anyone at work, or anyone that she ever met in the neighborhood? Any of her social acquaintances, maybe?"

"You don't understand," Robert Woods said. "We were almost estranged. We rarely talked to her. She left home to be on her own; it was something that she wanted to do. She hardly ever called us. We didn't know where she was for the first couple of months."

"I guess all little birds wanna get outta the nest," Will said.

"Yes, but she was flying on only one wing."

I got personal information from Robert and Evelyn Woods, and the names and addresses of her siblings, one of whom lived in Mobile. Then I gave them my business card, and as we parted, they agreed to contact us when she was able to talk.

Outside in the car, Will was philosophical.

"Well, you gotta admire that the girl wanted to be on her own," he said.

"Not if she couldn't do it. Heck, she was a sittin' duck for anybody that wanted her. I'm surprised she lasted this long."

"They weren't gonna be able to hold onto her forever, Son. All she needed was some do-gooder lawyer to get her out of the house, and she'd'a been gone anyway."

"Well, you know who's really to blame in all this – aside from the old boy that did it," I said.

"Who's that?"

"Her old man, Neal. He shoulda' been lookin' out for her. He calls himself her husband, yet he lets her run the bars at night."

"Son, have you ever tried to tell a woman what she can and can't do? It's like talkin' to a fuckin' wall. The same stubbornness that took that girl away from home is the same stubbornness that put her in that hospital bed."

Twenty minutes later we were sitting in a corner booth at the Hereford Steakhouse on Airport Boulevard waiting for a waitress to bring us a menu. The Hereford featured a lunch special consisting of a cheap hamburger steak and baked potato for four ninety-five. The place was a favorite of Will's.

The police walkie-talkie that sat on the table in between us rattled on with the business of law enforcement in Mobile County while I sipped water from a clear glass, and Will worked on a tumbler of cow's milk.

The waitress, who looked to be college-aged and had a tattoo of a butterfly on the back of her right wrist, arrived to take our order about five minutes into our wait. Will spoke first.

"Lady, do you see a hamburger steak anywhere on here?"

She pointed to the lunch specials. "Right there. It comes with a baked potato and one other vegetable."

"I'll take a salad with Thousand Island dressin'."

"How would you like that cooked?"

"Medium well. And could you bring some ketchup?"

"Sure." She looked at me.

"I'll have the same, but bring Heniz 57. And I'll have a glass'a sweet tea."

While she was gone, we talked about the case; what we knew, what we didn't, who we needed to talk to, and who was a low priority to contact.

"I think we need to get over to that chicken plant," Will said. "This old gal don't make a huge number of friends outside'a work and that shit hole of a bar over there, and the man we're lookin' for apparently hasn't been seen in it before, so chances are that if he didn't just wander in over there, she might'a met him at work."

The waitress arrived with our two specials, and Will poured ketchup all over his. I shook the pepper shaker three times on the meat, poured a slightly less generous amount of steak sauce, and then dug in.

"Should we be considering the fact that this girl's old man might've taken her out there and tried to kill her?" I said. "After all, she is a barfly, with all that implies. Maybe this one time he got jealous."

Will chewed, and I could see him thinking. When he finished, he pointed his fork at me.

"I don't think that's right for a couple'a reasons, Son. For one, why does he suddenly fly off the handle and decide he wants to get rid of her? What sets him off? If he's jealous, he could'a killed her a long time 'fore now. Second, what's he got to gain? If the boy kills her, he loses money."

I raised my eyebrows.

"Oh, sure," he continued. "She prob'ly gets a check from the gov'ment, plus she brings home at least minimum wage from that chicken plant. He said it himself, 'he's *tryin*' to get disability.' He wouldn't kill her until he knew he could make up the income he'd be losin'." He paused. "Besides, I think the old boy is just too stupid to do it.

"And I'll tell you another thing. The panties up her snatch make it a sex crime. This ole boy might'a killed her, but he's got no reason to rape her like that. He's had her before."

"Maybe that's the reason we should consider him. Because what he did was dumb and out of the ordinary."

"Well, that's one way to look at it. But right now, we've got a suspect. Let's find him and eliminate him first." He paused. "If it'll make you feel better, when you get back to the office, see if Al's got a car, and we'll go by and take a look at it."

I nodded. About that time, the police radio squawked. "SO 21."

Will picked up the radio. "SO 21."

"10-21 (call) Ellen, at Springdale Hospital." The dispatcher supplied a telephone number.

I jotted down the number on a pad that I kept in my right hip pocket. I tore out the page and handed it to Will.

He took it and laid it on the table. "First things first, Son," he said as he forked in a piece of baked potato.

When we finished, Will found a telephone on our way out, near the cash register. I walked on to the car. He followed about three minutes later.

"Well, you'll never guess," he said.

"Do tell."

"Zoe Woods is dead."

"Marvelous."

Chapter 15

The next morning, I parked the county car in a space marked 'POLICE' in front of the Alabama Department of Forensic Investigation (ADFI). There were only two parking spaces for law enforcement at the Forensic Department, one up close, near the front door, and the other about twenty yards away. We got the one closest to the building.

Inside, I spoke to the woman behind a thick glass, and she directed me to sign in on the visitor's log. She slipped two visitor badges through the slot, and Will and I clipped them on.

104

The Department of Forensic Investigation was another name for the state's crime laboratory. A half dozen scientists joined three pathologists in providing evidence examination and autopsy services for the law enforcement agencies in the eight counties in southwest Alabama. In addition, one of the pathologists doubled as the Mobile County Coroner. He was backed up by investigators who took call and performed initial investigations of unexplained deaths.

We entered through magnetically locked double doors, walked down a short hall, then passed through another magnetic door into the autopsy suite, a large forty by fifty foot space with concrete walls and a tile floor. There was a stainless steel sink that ran the wall around half of the room, which, with four perpetually running commodes, created autopsy stations capable of handling the busiest of days in the district. Large lights extended down over each of the stations, and pan scales hung over the sink near each of the commodes. The space was brightly lit, but smelled of formaldehyde, feces, disinfectant, and death.

Inside, the room bustled with activity. I recognized the figure of Martin Goldberg as he stood next to the eviscerated torso of Zoe Woods. I could tell it was her by the stitches in her neck. Goldberg's gloved hands were covered in blood, and he was turning to place a human heart into the scale when he looked up and saw us.

"Hello, Snuffy." His tone was jovial.

He called out Will because the two had worked together on probably sixty or seventy murders since the red-haired doctor had come to Mobile, and they knew each other well.

Goldberg was a New York-born, Yale-educated transplant who was talked into coming south by a psychiatrist friend who had spent time in the Navy in Pensacola, Florida. The shrink had sold Goldberg on the mild winters, the beaches, and the low property taxes. It just so happened that at the time Mobile County needed a coroner – the state Forensic Department was just about to consolidate their operations to include a medical examiner locally – so when the county commissioners heard that he was available, they snapped him up and turned him over to the state to do double duty.

Goldberg tried his best to take all the murder cases in Mobile County. There weren't too many in the unincorporated areas; however the cities of Mobile and the much smaller, but more violent Prichard usually totaled out to about sixty or seventy a year, sometimes higher.

"Red. How you doin?" Will called the doctor, 'Red,' and Goldberg called Will, 'Snuffy.'

"Oh, I'm able to sit up and take nourishment. Another day above the weeds is a good day." He stopped what he was doing and leaned on the stainless steel autopsy table. "Mr. Faulkner, how are you doing?"

I looked at the body on the table whose face had been pulled off its skull. "Just fine, Doctor. Better'n her."

He nodded. "She came in yesterday afternoon about three. I held her over until today thinking you'd be here."

"After we talked to her yesterday, it seemed as if she went downhill pretty fast. Any cause yet?" I said.

"Esophageal infection."

"Esophageal infection?"

"Yep. It looks like there was a cut in her esophagus that didn't get repaired, and when she experienced some heartburn the other night – there's note of it in her chart – the acid seeped into her neck and got it infected."

"Manner?" Will said.

"Oh, homicide, of course. But for the cut throat there would have been no infection."

"Anything on the knife?"

He shook his head. "Could have been anything. My guess is a small pocket knife, maybe two or two and a half inches long. But, don't hold me to that."

"One long cut or a bunch of little ones?"

He looked down at the body. "I've got to look at it a little more closely, but, initially, it looks like one long one on each side; from ear to chin."

Will nodded. "Anything else?"

"Yeah. Was she mentally challenged?"

"She was."

"I thought so. She had a tumor; probably benign, but it was pressing on a part of the brain that has something to do with learning. I'm not really that up on it. I'll have to do some reading."

Will looked at me. "Well, shit, Son. Nothin' she told us is gonna be any good now. A defense lawyer'll tear it up." He paused. "I thought we was gonna be better off without her, but looks like that ain't gonna be true neither. This ole girl's reachin' back from the grave to fuck up our case."

I chuckled while looking down at my notes. Absent her death, I didn't think Will would be interested in this case at all. I saw that I was going to have to work hard to keep his attention.

"Well, she didn't tell us much. I don't think it'll hurt us too badly," I said.

Goldberg continued. "She would have probably died from it, anyway, even though it wasn't cancerous. Was she under the care of a psychiatrist?"

"Her mother said she'd been tested, but whether it was by a doctor, that I don't know," I said.

"I'll call her family and find out. A psychiatrist should have ordered a cranial exam."

"What about other injuries, Red?"

Goldberg picked up the scalpel and started cutting out her lungs. When he got the right one out, he turned and put it on the scale. One of the pathology technicians, a female named Shaquita, recorded the weight on the eraser board above the long sink and then took the organ out.

"Well, aside from her neck, she had a couple of defensive wounds on her hands; not too big, just nicks. My guess is she tried to fight him off until he started cutting, then the shock hit her, and she just relaxed. It might have been what saved her, for as long as it did, that is.

"And her pudenda was pretty badly mauled; lots of little tears in the labia. There was also quite a bit of hair pulled out." He looked down at her groin. "Was there a rape kit done?"

I nodded. "The morning she came into the ER."

"Well, you can be thankful for that."

"Not really," Will said. "It looks like she was raped with her panties; but keep that under your hat."

"Interesting. If he used a tool, it might be because he was impotent himself. Any suspects?"

"Just a couple of sketchy descriptions," I said.

"Well, you might look for someone older, less virile."

I looked at the floor. Truth was he didn't have to be old. It could'a been that this guy just got too much liquor in him, or he was too fat, or he was under too much stress. Any number of things can make a man go limp when the moment comes – even a young man.

"Could be," Will said. "Anything else?"

Goldberg, who was standing with a kidney in his hand, shook his head. "No, not that I can tell right now. Her chart'll have her blood alcohol on admission. I would suspect that it was pretty high."

"It was," I said. "But I'd be interested in whether or not she had any drugs in her."

"I'll look for that."

Will and I exchanged looks. I could think of nothing else to ask, and neither could he, so we said our goodbyes and left.

In the car, I spoke. "Well, except for that tumor thing, he didn't tell us anything we didn't already know, did he?"

"No, but knowing about her head was somethin' we needed to hear. It might explain that business about the

108

'bird,' or whatever the fuck it was that she was talkin' about. She might'a just been out of her head."

I backed the car out of the space and pointed it toward Mobile Street.

"Well, where to now?" I said.

"Let's take a run over to where she worked, that chicken plant. Like I said, she had to meet the old boy somewheres, and I don't think she met him at the bar."

Chapter 16

The Tyndall Poultry Company was a collection of four corrugated metal buildings located next the railroad tracks that ran diagonally through the middle of the midtown section known as 'the Loop'; so-called because it was where the streetcars that left downtown 'made the loop' and turned back east toward the center of the city – when streetcars ran, that is. The buildings were located, oddly enough, within three blocks of middle class cottages that were being bought as starter homes and renovated by yuppie couples who would quickly flip them and relocate to the much more stylish Spring Hill neighborhood; or maybe to the Garden District, which in Mobile was called Oakleigh.

Parking was on Williams Street, a block off Airport Boulevard. I put the car in the space marked 'VISITOR.'

Inside, in the front office, we spoke to the receptionist, a corpulent blonde with a bouffant hairdo and lots of makeup. The nameplate on her desk identified her as 'Bonnie.' She smiled broadly when I showed her my badge.

"Yes, sir. What can I do for you?" she said enthusiastically. Oddly, she was looking at Will.

"We'd like to talk to the Human Resources manager, lady," he said.

"Sure."

She picked up the phone and dialed a three digit extension, after which she spoke in low tones. When she hung up, she smiled, motioned us toward a door to our left, and said:

"Go to the end of the hall. It's the door on the right. Mr. Smoot."

We nodded and thanked her. The hall turned out to be paneled and about fifty feet long. There were unmarked doors on either side. When we got to the last door on the right, I knocked. A high pitched voice on the other side told us to come in.

"Are you Mr. Smoot?" Will said.

"Frank Smoot. How do you do?"

"Fine, sir." Will made the introductions.

Smoot sat up straight then motioned toward two chairs. The small office was paneled also. It was furnished with cheap, plain furniture and looked too understated for the director of human resources.

He was a round man of medium height, balding on top, wearing wire-rimmed glasses. His white shirt, blue necktie, and dark slacks were as plain as his office.

"We'd like to talk to you about one of your employees, Zoe Woods," Will said.

"Ms Woods? Well, she's not in. She's been out sick."

"Actually, she deceased yesterday."

"Oh, my. What? How?"

"Somebody killed her, sir. We'd rather not say any more than that."

He nodded. "Sure. How can I help?"

"We'd just like to interview her supervisor and maybe a couple'a other employees that worked beside her, if you have a room we could borrow."

"Sure, sure."

110

Looking down at a manila folder on his desk, he opened it and ran his finger down a list of names on the top sheet.

"Looks like she worked in the cleaning room . . . let's see . . . she worked for Tom Walston." He looked up with raised brows. "You don't suspect anyone around here, do you?"

"No. Not at this time, sir. Do you have any reason to believe that somebody from here killed her?"

"Well, uh, no. No."

"Well, we'll start with this Mr. Walston."

He nodded. "Okay. I'll call him."

In five minutes, we were sitting at a table in one of the rooms off the long hall when in walked a stocky man wearing a blue jumpsuit. His name was stitched in red cursive writing inside a white cloth oval, just above his left breast.

"How you fellas doin'?" he said. The look on his face was apprehensive.

"Fine, sir. Sit down, please," Will said.

Tom Walston settled into a metal chair at the end of the table, facing Will and me. The room looked as if it was made for interrogation. The walls were bare and the floor was tile, and there was no other furniture. I prepared to take notes.

"What's this all about?"

"We're with the Sheriff's Office, Buddy, and we want to ask you about Zoe Woods. I understand she worked in your section."

He nodded. "Yeah. Her old man called and said that she was gonna be out sick a few days." He paused. "She okay?"

"What kind of employee was she?"

"She was all right." He shrugged. "I mean, what we do's not rocket science. She was a little slow, but she got her share done."

"She plucked?"

111

"Sometimes. Mostly, she washed. The birds come to her hot, and she makes sure they're clean."

"She worked alone?"

"She's in a section with two other girls."

"No men?"

He shook his head. "No."

"Ever see her hangin' around any of the men here at work?"

He thought a moment. "No. She talks to the girls that work with her, but I never saw her with any guys."

Will looked at me. I looked at Walston.

"What kind of disposition did she have?"

"Disposition? You mean like personality? She's okay, I guess. She don't take change very well. I mean, try to change the routine a little, like if she don't expect somethin' to happen, and she can get kinda feisty."

"What do you mean? Cryin'? Angry?"

"No, just nervous. She'll start shakin', and she'll get a little defensive; make comments."

I made some notes. "You know anything about her social life? Her life away from work?"

"Oh, heck no. The only thing I know about Zoe is that she plucks and washes chickens; and every once in a while I have to keep on her to do that."

I looked back at Will. He cleared his throat.

"All right, Mr. Walston. I think that's all. I wonder if you'd send in those two women that she worked close to."

"I can send in one. Tammy. The other one, Myrtice, is out sick today; but, hey, if you've talked to one, you've talked to the other, really."

"Okay, well, Tammy then."

He rose from his seat but paused. "Is Zoe okay? Did she do something?"

Will and I looked at each other. There was really no reason to keep the facts from her supervisor. We just didn't want this Tammy woman to know that Zoe Woods was dead, at least not at first. Walston didn't fit the description of her assailant, and in the interest of humanity, I really didn't see the harm. Will spoke.

"Mr. Walston, Zoe's dead."

His face told of his shock. "How?"

"We're still lookin' into her case. We hope to know somethin' soon." He paused and looked at him. "You know of anyone who had a reason to kill her?"

Walston shook his head slowly. "No. She was harmless, really."

"Okay. Well, we hope you can keep that fact to yourself, for a little while."

He nodded slowly. "Sure," he said in a soft tone before turning and walking out the door.

Will rubbed his face. He was becoming more disenchanted with the case by the minute, I could tell. I hated it, because he was the leader of our little group. He had the experience, the knowledge, and the gut. Sometimes, you solve a case by your gut. You don't get a conviction with it because it's not what you feel, it's what you can prove that matters; but you can solve it. I thought gut feelings were your perception of non-verbal communication. Lonnie Zane said that your gut feelings were God talking to you.

It took five minutes for the woman to show up. When she walked in the door, I could see by her face that Walston's promise had lasted all of about thirty seconds.

"Have a seat, ma'am," Will said. "My name' Eubanks, and this is Mr. Faulkner, and we're from the Sheriff's Office. We'd like to ask you about Zoe Woods." He paused. "What is your full name, please?"

She sat down, adjusted her clothes, and wrung her hands. Then she cleared her throat. When she spoke, her voice was an alto, but not too loud.

"Tammy Harris. Tammy Lynn Harris."

Tammy Harris was thirty. She had a dumpy figure, and her dishwater blonde hair was covered over by a clear plastic cap. She wore blue coveralls and white shoe covers.

113

"Ms Harris, did Mr. Walston tell you why we're here?"

"He said Zoe was dead."

"That's right. What can you tell us about Zoe?"

She shrugged her shoulders. "Well, not much. We worked side by side on the line. We both plucked and washed chickens. She was a pretty nice person, most'a the time. We got along all right."

"Most of the time?"

"Yeah, you know. I don't think Zoe was none too bright. She was okay to talk to, but sometimes the slightest little thing would get her upset."

"Like what?"

"Well, you know, if the lunch bell was a minute late, or if the line sped up the least little bit, it just seemed to get her agitated. If you tried to talk to her to get her calmed down, she'd snap at'cha."

"Tell me about her away from work."

"Away from work? Well, I don't really know much about that. I know she hung out at some bar down off Michigan Avenue. Besides that, I really don't know nothin'."

"She ever talk about any men she knew? Or met?"

She shook her head slowly. "No, I can't think of any."

I spoke up. "How about her husband? How was their relationship?"

She turned her head my way. "I guess they got along. She never complained about'im. I don't think they was really married, anyway."

"Did you ever go to her bar with her?"

She shook her head again. "No. I don't do bars. I used to, but I don't no more; too many bad mornings after."

I didn't delve into it any further. Will picked up the conversation.

"How about men around here? Zoe ever express an interest in any men here on the job?"

"If she did, I never knew about it. You see, in our little section, we're kind of self-contained in a room. Me, Zoe, and Myrtice – uh, Myrtice Abercrombie – all take care of our line; the chickens comin' down our line. I think they put us all together 'cause we all speak English. Most of the other girls is Vietmanese," she said mispronouncing the word.

"How about Myrtice? She and Zoe get along?"

She chuckled. "'Bout like a cat and a dog. They usually didn't say two words to each other."

"What started that conflict?"

"Well, it wasn't over a man, if that's what you're thinkin'." She paused. "I don't know. I guess it was 'cause Myrtice didn't have a lotta patience with Zoe 'cause she was the way she was. She didn't like havin' to have to tell her twice or to make up her share'a the work."

I began to believe that Myrtice might be a good person to talk to when this lead about the black haired man ran out. The thought crossed my mind that he and Myrtice might have a connection; no reason, it just popped into my head.

"Do you know what happened to Zoe? We just heard she was in the hospital," Tammy Harris said.

"Zoe ran into some trouble with a date. Any ideas who that might'a been?" Will said.

She shook her head. "No. I don't think it was nobody around here."

Will and I exchanged looks. It was time to go. I wrote down personal information about Tammy Harris, and we said our thank yous. In two minutes she was gone.

We left the room, spoke to Smoot on our way out, told him that we'd be back to see Myrtice, and then nodded at Bonnie behind the front desk. Frankly, I was glad to be out of the chicken processing plant. It didn't smell really great in there, and the thought of Zoe Woods plucking a chicken tended to ruin my appetite.

115

After lunch, we returned to the office so I could catch up on paperwork. Will went upstairs and filled in the Captain about the case. Agnew never went out to a restaurant for lunch. He took an hour and a half to drive home to his ranch on the north side of the county and eat with his wife, and he was just getting back when we arrived. They went in the office and closed the door.

I went on to our office and was there when the Bureau secretary, Denise Allenbach, a thirty-something with straight brown hair and a thin build, came around collecting for flowers for one of the girls in the Civil Division who had just given birth. Denise was somewhat attractive – by that I mean to say she had a small nose and a clear complexion, and her waist was thinner than her hips – and had dated at least two of the deputies in the department. She was wearing a mini-skirt and tall heels, and she smiled at me as I looked up.

"You wanna give to Tina down in Civil? She had a little girl."

"What does she need money for? Is she broke?"

She smirked playfully. "We're buying flowers."

"That supposed to cheer her up?" I grinned. "Flowers ain't gonna make her feel any better when her daughter gets to be a teenager and starts hatin' her."

She snorted. "If you don't wanna give, just say so."

I reached back and pulled my wallet out of my left hip pocket. There were three, one dollar bills inside. I took out one and handed it to Denise.

"There. That should get her through high school and pay for her first semester in college."

Denise took the money and put it into a plain white envelope, then wrote my name on the outside.

"Where's Snuffy?"

"He's with the Captain. But don't count on gettin' anything from him. He never carries cash."

"Why not?"

"He wants to avoid having to give at the office."

116

She smirked again; something I think she did quite often. "I'll wait."

I went back to my typing, and Denise sat across from me, picking at her red, recently-polished nails.

"So," she said, "anything new on your case?"

"We're following up on several leads."

I gave her the line that I would give to the press if they asked. Truth was, since she took care of case file management for the Bureau, Denise knew as much about things as I did.

"Okay, if you don't want to talk about it." Her tone was exasperated.

"Well, there's nothing to tell, really, she went to a bar and hooked up with a guy who took her to the woods and cut her throat. That's it. She's the poster child for stupid."

"She didn't know the guy?"

"If she did, she didn't tell us." I paused and looked at her. "You know, there's a good lesson in this thing for you."

"Me? I don't run the bars; and I certainly don't hook up with men I just met." Her tone was indignant.

I smiled. "Just where do you meet your men?"

She raised her eyebrows and threw her chin in the air. "Never mind."

At that moment, Will walked into the room. He passed by Denise without speaking and sat down in his chair. His expression was deadpan.

"What'd the Captain say?"

He exhaled loudly and closed his eyes as if to imagine the conversation in his head.

"He said that apparently this murder had gone by under the radar, press-wise. He said that the Sheriff said he wanted to keep it that way. He wanted to know how close we were to juggin' somebody. I told him we had a couple'a leads, but we hadn't ID'd nobody yet. He said for us to do

117

our best and try to get somebody put in jail before the press got wind of it."

"That all?"

"That's all."

"What did you tell him?"

"I told him that we were following every lead, and I'd let him know when we had somethin' to report."

"No, really."

He opened his eyes. "That's what I told him."

I went back to my typing, and Will sat in silence. The room was quiet for about a minute, until Denise spoke up.

"Snuffy, do you want to contribute to some flowers for Tina down in civil. She just had a baby girl."

Will turned his head her direction but kept his eyes closed. "I'm sorry, dear, but I don't seem to have any cash on me."

I looked at Denise. "I told'ja."

She rose from her seat and wrinkled her nose at me. "Fine. You two scrooges just remember this whenever your wives are pregnant."

Will opened and closed his first two fingers in the universal sign for scissors. "I'm fixed."

Denise looked at me.

"I can't have children. I work in homicide. The stress makes me impotent."

"Pshaw."

"No, really. I've already had my semi-annual erection."

Denise turned for the door in a huff. "That's disgusting," she said as she slammed the office door on her way out.

Will looked at me. "You better quit sayin' that, Son. It's gonna come true."

"How do you know it hasn't?"

Chapter 17

A day or two went by. I heard from the Coroner's Office about the dead baby from Theodore. The diagnosis was Sudden Infant Death Syndrome with excessive heat as a contributing factor. No mention was made of the possibility of the boy's mother rolling over on him in her sleep. The toxicological screen wasn't finished so there wasn't a final report, but Goldberg related to me that he was satisfied that no homicide had occurred.

He also told me that Claire Bowden, the woman with the bad case of OCD, died from a heart attack.

"I saw the pictures of the house," Goldberg said.

"It was creepy, that's for sure. The woman had never had anything, and when she got it, she just didn't want to lose it."

"The only thing I can't figure out is why her husband tolerated it."

"I guess he loved her."

Will, starting Thursday, had to meet with the Attorney General's investigators and lawyers about the John Carlton case. I went with him over to the Circuit Clerk's office to round up the articles that had been offered into evidence in the first trial seventeen years ago, including a shotgun, a revolver, and some blood-spattered road maps, and brought them back to the office and stacked them up in the corner.

Meanwhile, I was in contact with Zoe Woods's mother and father by telephone and they filled me in on the times for both her wake and funeral. Will hated to go to things like that, so it was left to me to attend. I called Roy Rogers and asked him to dispatch a photographer to take pictures.

The next Monday afternoon, shortly after five, I arrived at the Haven of Rest Funeral Home located off Highway 45 in the Gulfcrest community. The building was red brick, and from the outside it looked like a four bedroom, four thousand square foot home. There were four white columns supporting the front porch, and the gravel parking lot looked as if it could accommodate maybe fifteen cars. A black Cadillac hearse sat under the covered driveway on the west side of the building.

Inside, the business looked like all funeral homes: plush. There was lots of crushed velvet, brocade upholstery, shag carpeting, and cherry wood furniture.

I entered the double doors in front and walked into the expansive lobby. A sign with those removable, white letters said that the Woods' wake was to the right, in Viewing Room B. I walked that way and stepped through the open door into a vacant room; vacant, that is, except for a mahogany casket and three or four arrangements of flowers, mostly roses and baby's breath, on the opposite end.

No one, not even family, was present. I looked all around then moved toward the open coffin. When I got within three feet, I heard talking behind me. I turned quickly and saw Robert and Evelyn Woods walking toward me.

Zoe's mother was wearing a simple black dress, heels, and one strand of pearls. She carried a wadded up handkerchief in her right hand. Robert Woods wore a black suit and a red tie. The toes of his black oxfords looked like glass.

"Detective Faulkner, thank you for coming," Evelyn Woods said.

"I'm sorry for your loss. Sergeant Eubanks sends his condolences, also."

Robert Woods looked at the obviously expensive coffin and shook his head. "She just had problems. Did the doctor tell you what he found?"

"He did." I nodded.

"We had no idea," Evelyn said. "We just thought she was 'touched.'"

"An autopsy is a very informative procedure. It can sometimes answer a lot of questions."

I looked around the room. "Anyone else show up yet?"

They both shook their heads. "We don't expect a lot of people; maybe those bar friends of hers, and that man she lived with," Robert said.

"Did you ever meet him?"

"Once or twice. She brought him up to the house one Christmas. He looked like a vagabond," Evelyn said.

"I take it you all didn't get along."

"Oh, I guess he was okay. Zoe liked him. We just thought he was with her because she could take care of him."

"But, her salary at the chicken plant; maybe some disability money?"

Robert shook his head. "No. Zoe came into a rather large trust when she turned twenty-one."

"How large?"

He looked at me hard. "Seven figures."

The words hit me solidly. The fact certainly shed a little more light on Albert Neal.

"Did Zoe leave a will?"

Robert nodded. "Certainly."

"What does Al get?"

"Absent a marriage license, nothing."

"Did he know that?"

"I don't think so."

I whistled. "There are probably a bunch'a lawyers in town that would like a crack at that will. You know, Al calls himself her, 'common law husband.' And, they've been together for quite a while. I'd be interested to know what he knows about it."

"It doesn't matter much to me what he knows. With her mental state, I'm told this will is airtight."

About that time, Larry Flynn and Sis from the bar walked through the door. I nodded their direction, excused myself to the Woods, and then made my way over to the door. As I stepped out into the hall, I saw the Woods retreat to one of two couches on either side of the room.

What Robert Woods had told me was intriguing. Suppose Al Neal knew about Zoe's financial condition, and the will. He would've either pressured her to get married, or he would have done his best to make sure he stayed on her good side. If he found out that he wasn't going to be able to hold onto her, he could kill her then take his chances in court trying to lay hands on her inheritance. If he didn't know about the will, he still had to keep her around to have access to whatever income she did have.

After having talked to him, my guess was that Neal didn't know anything about anything – including how much money Zoe had. He was just a deadbeat living with a woman who always had enough dough every month to pay the bills and buy beer. If she stayed with him, everything was rosy; if she didn't, well, he'd just go find a new way to make ends meet.

Outside, I stood on the end of the porch where I could see both the front and the side of the building and looked out at the darkening sky. The business was located in a rural area, with pasture land on either side – the east and west, as well as to the south, across the road. There was a nip in the air, from a slight breeze blowing out of the north. It was quiet and the only sounds were far off automobiles.

Headlights leapt into view from the east and got larger as a vehicle got closer. The large SUV turned into the gravel parking lot and the tires crunched as it made its way up the small hill toward the rear of the building.

In addition to the investigative angle, I was also mildly interested in who was going to show at this wake from a strictly sociological standpoint. Robert and Evelyn

Woods were obviously well off and a more conventional couple; but then there was Zoe and her collection of drunks and night crawlers that hung out at The Society. I smiled to myself as I thought of how it might be amusing to watch the two worlds collide.

It was obvious that Zoe was ripe for the taking by the 'other' life that the bar crowd represented. With her health problems and an apparent lack of will to resist, in my mind at least, she was doomed from the time she left home. There was no doubt in my mind that if she'd stayed with her family, she would still be alive.

I watched as some of Zoe's downtown friends exited the SUV and entered the building. The two men were dressed in clean pairs of jeans and pressed shirts, and the three women wore midi length dresses and heels. The women walked tentatively, taking the arms of the men, toward the front door; walking as if they didn't wear heels too often and were in danger of falling over.

It wasn't long afterward that a black Lincoln Continental also made its way into the parking lot. This had to be friends of the Woods family. An older man behind the wheel and a well-heeled, gray haired lady sat on the front seat and looked all around before they got out of the car. No doubt they had heard about Zoe's friends and were appropriately suspicious. Hernandez was directly behind them in a county vehicle.

I walked back inside to the viewing room, found a large club chair in the corner, and took a seat. I didn't expect a show, but at a funeral, you never knew what was going to happen.

Over the next hour, about ten or twenty assorted bar flies and drugstore cowboys, countered by older aged couples with blue and gray hair, wandered in and out of the room. Conspicuous by his absence was Al Neal.

The only fireworks that happened took place between two males from The Society; one a tall man with a duck ass haircut in a blue blazer that looked as if it had come

123

from the Rescue Mission Thrift store, and the other a shorter man with a large belly, blue jeans, and cowboy boots. Both were staggering drunk.

It was not apparent what they were arguing about, although I heard the words, 'she loves me,' a couple of times. I waited to see if an intervention was in order. Robert Woods stepped in between the two and with the help of another man in a suit, probably a funeral director, managed to push the two men outside where they yelled a little more and were eventually removed from the scene in a couple of pickup trucks.

I gave Hernandez the high sign, and he walked quickly out to the county vehicle for his camera. I watched through the window as he took several shots of the two men before they left. Later, I learned that they were arguing over the ownership of a stray dog.

After they were gone, I leaned back in the club chair and sat quietly thinking of the overtime I was earning. By the time the two hours was up, I was fighting to keep my eyes open.

The next morning, at eleven, I parked in the shell parking lot of the Second Baptist Church of Citronelle, Alabama. It was a sunny day with the same breeze out of the north.

The church was painted white and had a red roof. The windows on the sides were stained glass and depicted highlights in the life of Jesus: the Christ child in the manger, Christ healing a blind man, and the crucifixion. The sign out front indicated that the congregation had formed in 1910 and was a member of the Southern Baptist Convention. It looked like a very traditional rural house of worship containing an extremely conservative membership. The cemetery was on the west side of the lot.

Lucky for the congregation, Zoe's friends from the club would probably not be attending the funeral. It's pretty common knowledge that drunks, users, and other assorted sinners get a little queasy at funerals. It's generally thought that they can't stand to be reminded of the ultimate destination of their eternal souls. Anything that might suggest to them the hell to which they might very well be enroute is activity they normally want to avoid. Robert and Evelyn Woods could rest easy in the knowledge that all of Zoe's friends from The Society would either be mourning her loss alone or in the company of like-minded friends – probably over drinks.

As I stood just outside the chain link fence that surrounded the cemetery, Hernandez drove up in his county vehicle. I directed him to park in the back, mostly out of sight, just in case the man who killed Zoe decided to make an appearance. He nodded through the windshield and parked his unmarked SUV almost to the woodline on the north side of the property.

The pile of red dirt in the middle of the graveyard pointed out the location of Zoe's final rest. There was a blue tent over the site, and ten chairs were lined up in two rows of five next to the hole. The chairs had those velvet covers over the backs that were embroidered with the words 'Haven of Rest.'

I didn't know if there was to be anything more than a grave side service, so I walked over to the west side door and looked inside the church. The mahogany casket was sitting with the top open at the head of the middle aisle, on a gurney in front of the communion table. Four or five people, none of whom appeared to be our suspect, sat in the pews, spread out across the sanctuary. There was no sign of the Woods family.

As quietly as I could, I entered the building and made my way to the back pew. Hernandez walked in the front door, which was at the back of the room and took a seat, also on the back row, opposite me.

I gave him the high sign and sat back to wait. Two older couples walked in and sat down on the third row. Then, surprisingly, Larry Flynn and Susy Weaver stepped through the door and walked gingerly up the middle aisle.

They took seats two rows in front of me, and as they did Sis looked around and gave me a kind of a sheepish grin. She looked as if she didn't want to be there. My guess was that it was her idea to come – out of respect, she would say – and she was somehow able to talk Larry into taking her. But then, when she walked into the building, something came over her. Fear? Nerves? Larry looked like he had no use for churches or what they stood for, and he sat quietly looking at the floor. He may even have been drunk. Both were in their Sunday, or rather their Saturday night best.

In ten minutes, Robert and Evelyn Woods, along with an older, silver haired man who carried a Bible, walked into the chapel through a door to the right of the choir loft, a door that likely led to the church office. Noticeably absent were mourners who bore any resemblance to Zoe's siblings.

I could tell that Evelyn Woods had been crying; Robert, also. The pastor had a grim look on his face. He was of medium height with a bit of a paunch and hair that was combed straight back. Silver, wire rimmed glasses sat astride his nose and complimented his bluish-gray suit.

It surprised me that Zoe's brother and sisters weren't present. We had heard from Al Neal that Watson Woods lived in Birmingham, Harriet Thornton in Atlanta, and Laurie Woods-Tillman in Mobile. All had obviously not thought enough of their sister to even attend her funeral. I wondered about the family dynamics and even the mental states of the missing three.

Including the pastor, the family, and the police, there were fifteen grim faced souls in the room. Al Neal was absent.

The pastor took his place behind the pulpit, and the family sat down on the front row. They didn't look around to see who was in attendance.

"We are gathered here today to mourn the loss of Zoe Woods. This young woman was a special person . . ."

A polite way of saying that she was diminished.

". . . and lived life to the fullest. She was always smiling . . ."

Unless, of course, she was drunk. Then she tended to get a bit surly, I'd heard.

". . . and at an early age had decided to leave home and make her own way in the world."

Working at Tyndall's Chicken.

"She found her way to Mobile, and . . ."

To The Society Lounge, where she picked up men and talked them into buying her drinks.

His voice trailed off into the high ceiling and stained glass. There was nothing to see here. I gave Hernandez another sign, and the two of us rose and slipped out the front door.

Outside, we waited until we got to the parking lot before we spoke.

"For once, I wish somebody would tell the truth at a funeral," I said.

"If they did, it would probably cause a riot."

"Wouldn't that be a trip." I smiled and looked away.

"You want me to stay and take a picture of the crowd at the grave site?"

I shook my head. "No. I'm leaving. Whoever he is may show up later, but he won't be here today." I paused and looked around. "Go ahead and pack it in. I've got to go and find out why Zoe's old man skipped her funeral."

Chapter 18

The next morning, Will was still in consultation with the Attorney General's staff. They were holed up in a conference room on the second floor, off the Patrol Division ready room. After the day shift hit the streets at six, and before the second shift met at four, the second floor was largely deserted. I stopped in to see him, while on my way out to revisit Al Neal.

"Anything happen at the funeral?" Will said.

"No. It was pretty dead."

He nodded while not reacting to an old joke.

"Only one thing was amiss. Her old man didn't make an appearance."

"Really? Does he get along with the family?"

"Apparently, not too well. But it seems that Zoe wasn't as destitute as we originally thought."

"How much?"

"I don't know exactly, but it's in the millions. She got it when she turned twenty-one. Anyway, she had a will, and Al wasn't in line for any of it." I paused. "I'm on my way to see him about it."

Will nodded and looked away. "You know, I bet none'a that matters."

"How do you mean?"

"I mean, Al's too stupid to think that far ahead. My guess is he didn't even know about any money."

"You think?"

He nodded. "Just try to pin him down as best as you can about where he was when she got jumped. That's about all we can do. But I'd be surprised if he had anything to do with this."

I nodded. "Okay."

In twenty minutes, I was standing on the small stoop outside the threshold of the door of Al Neal's and the late Zoe Woods's apartment on Lewis Circle. The porch was concrete and small, and the wrought iron railing around it would serve to fence me in if he came out shooting – no matter how unlikely that particular scenario. I'd have to take a header over the rails to get out of harm's way.

128

I knocked twice and waited. The day was sunny but brisk. A north wind caused me to turn my back and huddle into my coat.

The door opened, and Al Neal stood behind the screen in his undershorts and a t-shirt. The smell of something cooking in the kitchen wafted through the doorway. It smelled a little like coffee, but for some reason I thought it wasn't. In the back of my mind, I quickly debated the wisdom letting Al Neal use a working stove.

"Al, you remember me?"

He looked at me as if he was confused. Then the light came on, and his eyes relaxed.

"Yeah, you're one of the sheriffs." He paused. "Zoe died, you know."

In a second, I knew Will was right. "Yeah, I know. You got a minute to talk?"

He stood aside, and I pulled open the screen. I crossed the threshold and immediately recognized the odd smell as burnt toast.

"You got somethin' cookin'?" I raised my nose and sniffed.

His eyes widened. "Oh, yeah. Shit."

He turned and took three long steps into the kitchen. He was back in a minute waving his arm back and forth in front of his face.

I had moved toward the chair in the corner and was preparing to sit when he took a seat in a cane rocker. I sat down when he did.

"I missed you at Zoe's funeral."

He looked confused. Man, how did these two find each other? How were they even able to exist?

"Oh, yeah. I didn't have a way."

"Do you have a car?"

"No."

I nodded. "Tell me, Al, I don't think I asked you where you were when Zoe was over at The Society; you know, the Friday night when she got hurt."

He looked at me blankly. "I think . . . I think I was here; watchin' TV."

"Remember what was on?"

"Uh, no. You know, the usual Friday night stuff."

"Did anyone come over?"

He looked up and thought. "No, I don't think so. I just watched some TV and went to bed."

This was hopeless. He didn't even have sense enough to know he needed an alibi.

"Did you order a pizza or anything?"

"No. I don't like pizza."

"Any calls?"

"I ain't got no phone."

I cleared my throat. "Al, did you ever know what Zoe did when she went to The Society?"

He thought for a minute. "She saw people and talked, I guess."

"She talked to other men, Al. She got them to buy her drinks." I paused for effect. "She maybe even had sex with'em."

He looked away as if hearing it all for the first time and wanting to wipe it out of his ear. I wasn't sure if he knew what it all meant, but he sure looked as if he did.

"Does hearing that make you mad, Al?"

"Zoe was a good person. She was my wife. She was good."

I wanted to see if any of this made him mad – mad enough to kill. So far, he hadn't shown me anything.

"You're right Al. Zoe was a good person. Did you know that Zoe had money?"

"Yeah, she worked at the chicken plant."

"No, I mean real money; lots of it."

He looked confused. "Well, yeah. Her check was three hundred dollars ever' two weeks."

I nodded at him. "You're right, Al." I paused and looked toward a short hall. "Al, you mind if I look at Zoe's bedroom?"

130

"There ain't but the one. It's mine too."

He rose, and I did also. We walked out of the living room, down a short hall, and into a bedroom that looked as if a cyclone had hit it. Clothes were everywhere. An unmade queen-sized bed sat in the middle of the room and took up most of the space. A bureau and a small night table upon which sat a short lamp were the only other pieces of furniture.

I didn't know what I was looking for, so I just walked over to the nightstand, pulled open the drawer, and looked inside. There was a dildo, a couple of condoms, a fashion magazine, and some hand lotion. It was good to know that Al and Zoe had an active sex life. I smiled to myself and turned away.

"Okay, I've seen enough."

We walked out of the room and back into the living space. I stopped next to the front door and turned to Al.

"Well, what are you gonna do for money, you know, now that Zoe's gone?"

He looked at me with that same blank look and said nothing.

"I mean, since Zoe was working and, of course, now she's not, and her not getting any disability anymore, and your disability not coming in yet. What are you gonna do for money?"

His eyes widened a little, as if it was the first time that he had thought of it all. It's funny how that the faculty that people who are mentally impeded are the most short on is foresight. They seem to only be able to live for the moment at hand.

"I don't know," he said.

I don't think he did.

Chapter 19

I spent the next week and a half looking for Jerry Painter, one of the witnesses at The Society the night of Zoe Woods's disappearance. At the garage where he worked they told me on three occasions that he was 'on vacation.' Sis, at the bar, told me she still hadn't found out where he lived, and the personal information on his very colorful rap sheet was two years old. His driver's license listed his address as a post office box, and he didn't have a vehicle registered in his name. It appeared as if he was hiding from me. My first instinct had been that he was wanted, and nothing had happened to change that opinion.

In the meantime, life went on. I got a subpoena for Circuit Court dated the middle of March. It was for an assault case on which I had worked about eight months previous.

The morning of the trial I made it downtown early. There was a parking lot dedicated strictly to government vehicles at the dead end of Royal Street, underneath the interstate, so I left my vehicle there and made the three-block walk to the courthouse in less than ten minutes. I still called it the courthouse, though the powers that be had christened it something else. It was a beautiful day; sunny, breezy, and with just a nip of a chill.

Entering on the east side, the side closest to Christ Episcopal Church, I strode across the building's expansive lobby, bypassed the metal detectors and the court police officers who manned them, and entered the elevator lobby. I looked good in a starched white shirt and blue blazer, and I felt good, having breakfasted at the Good Time Diner on Cottage Hill Road prior to my trip downtown.

Right at the end of last summer, on a Friday evening, I was called to the University Hospital to investigate a rather strange assault. An ambulance had responded to a house in west Mobile County to find that a

132

woman had thrown a pot of hot grits in the face of her husband.

When I got to the hospital, the nurse, an older woman in blue scrubs who'd seen it all, was painstakingly picking individual grits off of the morphine-sedated victim. He wasn't able to talk right then, however it was evident what had happened to him and who the culprit was. Hot food in the face is a uniquely domestic crime perpetrated ninety-nine per cent of the time by women.

There was one witness, a local private detective named MacArthur Penn, and he related to me what had happened. The victim was a black man with entirely too much pride, and he had refused to name his wife as his assailant. But with Penn's statement I was duty bound by Alabama's domestic violence statute to arrest and charge his wife as the aggressor. She freely confessed and said that she was angry that her husband had hired an investigator to follow her around.

She was charged with Assault 2nd degree. I recommended Assault 1st due to the fact that she was cooking grits at nine o'clock at night and for what other purpose could she have been doing that other than to use the mess as a weapon, a weapon that had produced permanent disfigurement. The charging DA, an alcoholic named Art Peterson, had refused due to the lack of seriousness of the injuries. I told him that he was crazy, that the man was mutilated for life and would forever have to walk around with a brown and white face that resembled a Jersey cow.

The case had wound its way through the system; first to a preliminary hearing where I laid out the evidence and the confession to the District Court Judge; then to the Grand Jury, where I gave the very same testimony to eighteen citizens. It seemed like an awful lot of trouble to put away a woman who was angry, had admitted what she had done, and said she just wanted to plead guilty anyway.

133

The case was to be prosecuted by Joyce Ritchie, an attractive thirty-something who had been with the DA's office for three years and had just recently been elevated to duty in Circuit Court, Alabama's highest local jurisdiction. We called it 'big boys' court.

On March 15th, I was waiting alone in Courtroom number 6200 when Ritchie walked in carrying a plastic tub of file folders. She was wearing a blue business tunic over a white blouse, and a navy skirt with matching pumps. Her blonde hair hung to her shoulders and was parted on the right side. The comb over in front hit her just above the left eyebrow, Veronica Lake-style.

Seated on the back pew, I was just to the left of the double doors, and she didn't notice me as she walked, or rather lumbered, with her heavy burden toward the prosecutor's table.

The court room looked like all other courtrooms. The wood benches and tables were a light brown, almost tan; or the color of a light caramel. There was no carpet and no wall ornamentation, save for a carving of Moses carrying the Ten Commandments down from Mt Sinai that was affixed to the wall above the judge's head.

I sat silently with my case file on the seat next to me and watched as Ritchie emptied the plastic tub of manila folders out onto the prosecutor's table. She was a good-looking woman who I knew to be recently divorced. She had a waist that was smaller than her hips and very muscular legs.

Shortly, she turned toward the rear and started walking that way. Her head jerked when her eyes fell on me.

She stopped at the end of the last row. "Sir, you should have made your presence known," she said in her best Scarlett O'Hara drawl.

"Why? Were you afraid I would see you pick your nose or something?"

"Don't be silly. But I might have had to get my panties out of my crack, and I wouldn't have wanted you to see that."

"That would have been an ugly sight."

"Well, it wouldn't have been *that* ugly. I can be very sexy when I'm readjusting."

"Hey, I'm from Missouri."

She wrinkled her nose and shook her head, after which she walked out the door and into the hall. I sat back in the pew and opened my case file.

There wasn't much in it. A couple of photographs of the victim's head, two or three of the scene inside the house, and a blow up of one of the pictures of the pot and the mess of grits on the living room floor. There were also two statements: one given by Penn, the PI; and the other, the confession by the victim. It was a bare bones file, for a bare bones case. I laid it down on the seat next to me and rubbed my eyes.

This was another part of the job that I hated. In my mind, the case was over when the investigation ended, when I had satisfied myself that the perpetrator had been identified. Juries were notoriously fickle and could be counted on to screw up about one case in ten; therefore, my peace of mind was satisfied by another standard. When I found out who broke the law, and could prove it, I was done.

In the middle of my musings, the courtroom door opened and the defendant's attorney, Joseph Gadowski entered. Gadowski was sixty with thinning, silver hair. He wore a gray suit and carried a black leather attaché, and he walked to the front without looking around. I watched him place the case on the defense table and open it.

The trial, of course, was still several hours from commencing. First, there would be a plea docket where defendants who wanted to, could, after properly being advised of their Constitutional rights about four or five times, allocute to the judge and go ahead and take their medicine.

After that, there was the motion docket where defense lawyers could attempt to persuade the judge to give their client even more advantages in a trial.

Only after all that housekeeping could a jury pool be introduced into the empty courtroom to be interviewed by the attorneys in my case. Each potential juror would be quizzed regarding his or her opinions on a variety of subjects, including: whether they had been victims of a crime; whether they had been a party in a divorce; what were their feelings regarding adultery and divorce; and, most offensively, whether or not the testimony of a police officer should be regarded as more or less truthful than that of anyone else.

I pondered the morning's time line and wondered if I could leave and get coffee. My cogitations were broken when Ritchie reentered the room.

We had spent the afternoon previous in her office going over my testimony, such as it was. I was to go on the stand first, followed by the victim.

Ritchie slid onto the pew next to me. I noticed when Gadowski turned and looked at us, then turned his attention back to his attaché case.

"I take it you've talked to the victim," I said.

"I talked to him, but I still don't know what he's going to say."

He was not obligated to testify against his wife; that is, he could not be compelled to do so. It was strictly his option.

"Can he be made to get on the stand?"

She raised her eyebrows and nodded. "Sure, but all he has to say is that he declines to testify against his wife, and he won't be up there long."

"He doesn't need to be. All he needs to do is to show the jury his face; and unless he's wearing a mask, well, mission accomplished." I paused. "Are you still going to put me on first?"

"You're my strongest witness; or the strongest one that I can count on." She paused. "You're not going to testify for her, are you?"

I chuckled. "No. But there might be a way to get her husband to. Just have a mirror handy and hold it in front of his face. Maybe he'll get religion."

She pursed her lips and nodded. "That's an idea. I'll get one from one of the ladies in the office. I bet Lucy has one."

Lucy Baxter was Ritchie's trial coordinator, a fancy term for a combination gopher and secretary. She was dark haired and young and working for the DA – a family friend – while waiting to retake the bar exam.

"If you're looking for your strongest witness," I said, "then that would be Mac Penn. He was there, and he works for the victim; and he's got some law enforcement experience."

"Yeah, but you know, I just don't know what juries think of PIs."

"What do you mean?"

"Well, you know. Rent-a-cops, peepers, gumshoes, even 'private dicks.' They didn't get those names for nothing."

I smiled at her, especially at the 'private dick' comment. "Well, they might not be deacons in the Baptist church, but with the way the economy is going, with crime going up and police forces not getting any larger, you better get prepared – and get juries prepared – to see a lot more of them."

"Maybe."

"No maybe about it."

She shrugged, rose, and walked toward the front. At the prosecution table, Gadowski walked over, and the two put their heads together. It wouldn't hurt my feelings if they were talking about a plea. A few people had walked in: three men in suits who looked like attorneys; a couple of kids with their pants down around the cheeks of their buttocks and hats all cockeyed on their heads; and one elderly woman with a print dress and a large handbag. She sat down on the second pew from the front, after which one of the men in suits walked over and began talking to her.

Five minutes later, an attractive, middle-aged brunette wearing a black dress entered the courtroom from the right side, the same side as the jury box, and took a seat on the judge's right, the gallery's left. She took out a pen and began to write things on a pad in front of her. I couldn't tell if it was one of the case files or the judge's calendar, but she looked intently at the page, and at one point even stuck out her tongue as she worked.

Slowly but surely, the courtroom began to fill up with various parties all seeking some sort of justice. I looked at the confusion and decided to go to the snack bar and get a cup of coffee. I rose, caught Joyce Ritchie's eye, and, with a nod, left out the double doors in the rear.

Downstairs, I walked across the lobby and through the glass doors of the coffee shop. I bought a large cup of coffee and creamed it heavily. I paid for it and a copy of the rag and took a seat at a table by the large picture window near the front door. I was half way through section A when Tommy Neill, the DA's chief investigator, walked in and sat down, smiling.

Tommy was a good investigator; by that I mean he could talk to anyone and people told him things. But he was hired because he could deliver certain parts of the county at election time. He was a politician, and he knew it, and politicians always made me a little uncomfortable. He was of medium height, with the beginnings of an alderman's belly and thinning hair. He always wore tailored suits, and this day was no different.

"Hey, what's goin' on?" Neill said smiling.

When people in our business smile at you, it usually means they want something. I wondered what he wanted.

138

"Nothin' much, Tommy. Just down here for a little assault case." I nodded at the file on the small table.

"Who's the assistant?"

"Joyce Ritchie."

"Good, good. She'll treat'cha right."

"Yeah. I've worked with'er before."

We sat in silence for a couple of uncomfortable seconds. He looked through the large window and around the lobby and then back at me.

"Look," he said, "are you working on the case of a woman out in the county who got her throat cut?"

"Sure am."

"Well, the other day, I took the grand jury over to the jail for the tour."

Part of the grand jury's duty was to tour the jail to ensure that it was being run humanely and prisoners were not being abused; at least, not openly.

"And," he continued, "one of the trusties stopped me and told me he had some information about a case."

I raised my eyebrow. "Who was he?"

"He said his name was Jerry Painter."

How stupid of me. I had looked for him everywhere but in jail.

"I been looking for that guy. What did he say?"

"He wanted to know about the case; who was workin' on it," he smiled, "was there a reward; things like that."

"Did he ask you about getting out?"

"He mentioned that he was certainly willing to trade his information for a reduction in his sentence."

"Which is?"

"He's serving six months for Indecent Exposure. I think he said he had close to five months to go."

"You know any details?"

"No. I didn't talk to him long. When I left, I called the city and they didn't know anything about the case. I figured you must."

139

"Well, thanks, Tommy. That's really a help. I'll get over and see him as soon as I can." I paused and looked him in the eye. "So, what can I do for you?"

He smiled slightly. "Absolutely nothing."

I smiled back. Then I got it. He didn't want anything. He was just piling up points.

Upstairs, I slipped into the back of the courtroom and replaced myself in my former seat. The room had thinned out a little. It appeared as if the judge was about halfway through the motions and plea docket. It was still a while before my trial would start.

As I settled back into my seat, I wanted to close my eyes, but I was afraid that if the bailiff or His Honor saw me, he'd think I was sleeping and find me in contempt; something that I'd seen happen once before.

The Honorable George Hartsfield was the jurist to whom it had fallen to judge the 'grits case.' Hartsfield was sixty. He had a thick shock of white hair that always appeared as if it had just been trimmed; as if he saw a barber every day after court. His jowly face and deep wrinkles caused him to bear a striking resemblance to John R. Rice. He always wore rumpled gray suits and walked with a stoop shouldered posture; and there was at times some question as to the adroitness of his faculties. But I liked him.

"Son, pull those pants up in my courtroom," his voice boomed from the bench. "Those pants are not designed to be worn around your knees."

"Yes, suh," the young boy said as he fumbled for his pants.

"And take off that hat."

The boy reached up and took off an Atlanta Braves cap and held it in his hand.

"You are charged with Burglary 3rd degree. It says here you broke into the Old Dutch Ice Cream Shoppe." He pronounced it with a long 'e' on the end. "How do you plead?"

140

The young boy lowered his head. "Guilty." His voice was so low it was almost inaudible, especially to the back of the room.

Judge Hartsfield looked down at the file. "Do you understand that you are pleading guilty to a crime for which you may be sentenced to prison?"

Fat chance. Property offenders rarely got jail time anywhere in Alabama.

"Yes, suh."

"Have you discussed this plea with your attorney?"

"He has, Your Honor." The person that spoke was a tall, thin, dark haired man with glasses. He wore a blue blazer, khaki slacks, and penny loafers; the standard issue uniform for new attorneys just out of either the University of Alabama or Cumberland law schools.

"You understand that you have the right to remain silent; that anything you say may be used against you; and that you have the right to confer with your attorney anytime you wish."

"Yes, suh."

The Judge looked down at the file. "What did you hope find inside the ice cream shop, son?"

The boy shuffled his feet and looked at the floor. "I 'on't know."

The Judge exhaled. "Well, I don't know what you were looking for either, but you sure have created a rocky road ahead for yourself."

About two people chuckled. The boy's attorney bowed his head. I looked at Joyce Ritchie. She was reaching for another file and was apparently not interested in the Judge's levity. As for everyone else in the audience, I'm sure his remark went right over their heads.

Hartsfield dispensed with the burglar's case by sentencing him to five years in the penitentiary with credit for time served, about two months; suspending the remainder of his sentence; and placing him on probation for that same period, probation that will require him to submit to weekly drug tests. He will also have to pay a one thousand dollar fine and reimburse the ice cream store for the damage he did breaking into their business – money he will no doubt have to steal in order to pay.

There was no doubt in my mind that the sentence Judge Hartsfield handed down would do absolutely nothing to deter this young kid from breaking into anything else. He was a thief, a full blown sociopath who took what he wanted when he wanted it. I'd seen dozens like him.

After the corrections officers had removed him – he first had to sign some papers to affect his release – the Judge's attention was caught by a gray haired female wearing a blue dress that entered the courtroom from the door leading to his chambers. I watched as she handed him a note. He opened it and read the contents. Then he looked up.

"Ladies and gentlemen, I have to leave the bench for a family emergency. The clerk will reschedule the cases and re-subpoena everyone."

With that, he banged his gavel, rose, followed the gray haired woman through the same door from which she had entered, and closed the door behind him. The courtroom came alive with voices. I stood up slowly and made my way down the center aisle to the prosecutor's table. Ritchie was busy packing up her case files.

When I got next to her, I stopped. "Know what that's all about?"

"I heard the clerk tell him that his wife fell and broke her hip."

I nodded. I guess that qualified as a family emergency.

"Well, I guess this thing is gonna to drag on for another two months."

Ritchie smiled. "Job security."

Chapter 20

It was ten o'clock by the time I got out of the courthouse and back to my car. I contemplated going back to the office, but decided to stop by and see Jerry Painter before I went west.

The Metro Jail had regular visiting hours for the public; however, police officers and other law enforcement personnel could see inmates at their leisure, just so long as their meals or their exercise periods were not interrupted. If convicts missed a meal, it was a lot of trouble for the jail staff to get them fed; and if they weren't fed, they could file a complaint, or, from the enterprising ones, a lawsuit. It was still far enough before noon that I could get into see Jerry Painter and still get out before his lunch hour.

I entered the front glass doors of the Metro Jail and signed the visitor's book. I told them who I wanted to see and was afterward directed back outside and around to the side entrance.

The Jail, called Metro because it was run by the Sheriff and serviced every jurisdiction in the county, was built in the late nineteen eighties and early nineties as part of a consent decree in a civil rights suit. Inmates had claimed that the old jail, which was built to serve five hundred inmates, but which routinely held eight hundred, with its overcrowding conditions, constituted cruel and unusual punishment. The new jail consisted of three, round, brick buildings of eight stories each and was, oddly enough, overcrowded the day it was opened.

I sat quietly in an attorney's room and waited for Jerry Painter to come down from upstairs. The space was about six by eight and was glass enclosed. It had a high ceiling and its one hard wall was painted a kind of a pink and tan hybrid; the product of a contractor who no doubt hadn't followed the building specifications correctly. There was a small table and two chairs inside, and the floor was tile.

My guess was that Jerry Painter was probably talking out of his ass, so to speak. Prisoners were always saying that they knew things that they really didn't know. It was a way of getting people to listen to them. In some ways, I couldn't blame them. If I was stuck in a jail cell somewhere with no one to talk to but a thug, I'd probably do or say just about anything I could to get someone with half a brain to come visit me. So, when you sat down with one of these guys you couldn't get too excited about what they were telling you. They all had some type of motivation for doing what they were doing, and being sociopaths by nature, that motivation was only to benefit them. I'd listen to Jerry Painter, but whether I'd hear him remained to be seen.

When he came into view, I recognized him from the previous night at The Society. He was of medium height and stockily built, and he had thick brown hair and a large nose that hooked on the end. Thick, stubby fingers issued from his solid hands, and he had a dark suntanned complexion. His brown, turd-colored jumpsuit told me he was a city prisoner. When he walked in, I said 'hello' and gestured to the other chair.

"Mr. Painter, my name is Faulkner. I'm with the Metro Sheriff's Office. I'm working on Zoe Woods's case – the woman whose throat was cut."

He nodded and his eyes got wide, as if he was surprised that Neill had told anyone; and further, that anyone had actually come.

"What are you in here for?"

He cleared his throat. "Ah, this woman said I took my dick out."

"What, were you two on a date or something?"

"No. See, I went out in the backyard to take a leak, and she said she saw me."

I opened my mouth and scratched my face in order to hide my smile. "So, did you do it?"

"Well, yeah. I had to take a piss. I can't help it if she likes to look."

I shook my head. "No. No, you can't." I paused. "Well, okay, I understand from Mr. Neill at the DA's office that you have some information about Zoe Woods."

"I do. But I need to get outta here."

"I understand that. Tell me who it was that killed Zoe and maybe I can help you."

"Oh, I don't know who killed her."

"Well, do you know where he is?"

He shook his head. "No, I don't know where he is."

I furrowed my brow. "Well, just what can you tell me?"

"I can tell you that the boy that she was drinking with at The Society that night was driving a red Nova."

"A red Nova?"

"Yeah. A red Chevy Nova"

"Is that it?"

"Well, I can identify him."

"Well, okay. Did you see his tag number?"

He shook his head. "No."

"What can you tell me about him?"

"He had jet black hair, and he talked with an accent."

"What kind'a accent? Spanish, Russian?"

"Oh, no. He spoke English. It was just from another part of the country."

"Could you tell where?"

"No. I never been around too much."

"Did you talk to him?"

"No. I just overheard him talkin' to Zoe." He paused. "You know, I liked her."

"What were they talkin' about?"

"You know, the usual stuff. He told her, 'you got nice tits, baby'; 'I gotta big dick'; things like that."

145

I wasn't getting much. "What can you tell me about the car?"

"Not much. It was a Nova; 'bout a 74 or 75, kinda beat up."

"Four door or two door?"

He looked at the ceiling. "Four door, I think."

"Anything special about it?"

"Not that I remember. But, see, if you just check the files for a Nova, I mean, there can't be too many of'em still on the road."

He was right about that. The only catch would be if it wasn't registered in Alabama, which might very well be the case. I didn't consider the conversation a total waste. He did confirm what one of the other witnesses had said about the suspect driving a red car. It was certainly plausible that none of them would be able to identify it as a Nova, it being something of a vintage automobile. Not everyone had seen a Nova, and Painter, being a garage monkey, would know one.

We talked for another ten minutes about all the things he didn't know about the black haired man. I looked at my watch and found that it was getting close to eleven.

"By the way, who was that woman you were with at the bar the night we came by?"

"Oh, that was Jenny." He shook his head. "She don't know nothin'. She's from outta town.

"Was she at the bar when Zoe was there?"

He shook his head again. "No. She wadn't in town."

"I'm gonna need her name anyway."

"Just Jenny, is all I know. I met her at the Honey for the Bears, downtown. I never seen her before, or since."

Honey for the Bears was a local red neck joint. "Okay, well, let's get you back to your block so you don't miss lunch." I rose from my seat.

He looked up with expectant eyes. "You think you're gonna be able to get me out?"

I looked at him and frowned. "For a red Chevy Nova? Are you kiddin'?"

146

He looked chagrinned.

"Hey, look on the bright side," I said. "Upstairs, you got a whole room full'a folks that haven't seen your package yet."

Back at the office, after putting away the department's paperwork on the grits case, I went up to my office and sat down. The most important thing on my mind was where to go eat lunch. Sleep was just about to overtake me when Will walked in the door.

"Welcome stranger. How goes the retrial?"

"Shit," he said as he took his seat opposite me. "Them sons of bitches couldn't pour piss out of a boot. They don't know the first thing about how to locate these people; how to interview'em to find out what it is they remember; or how to get'em to come to court."

"How close are you to getting through?"

"Well, the trial is next week. But we haven't found half the people we need to, yet."

"Oh, don't worry about it. It'll all come together. It always does."

He shook his head. "For ten cents I'd head shoot that John Carlton just to shut his ass up."

He leaned back, fell into his thinking position, and closed his eyes. We sat silently, like twins for five minutes.

Finally, Will looked up. "So, anything on the crazy girl case?"

I took a deep breath and exhaled. "Well, I had another talk with her old man. He said he was home at the time she came up missing, but he can't prove it. I took a look around the apartment, but didn't see anything more than what you did the other day; unless you missed the pink dildo.

"I found out from her parents that she had a stash, I guess I told you that. He says he didn't know anything about it. He says he doesn't know what he's going to do for money now."

147

"I don't think he had anything to do with this killin'."

"And, Hernandez and I went to her wake and funeral. Her old man didn't show, and neither did her brothers and sister. It was mostly her parent's friends. A couple of people from the bar came, including Sis and Larry."

"That's a little odd about her family. I bet they was jealous of her; mama and daddy havin' to dote on her, and her gettin' that money and all."

"Oh, and by the way, I was in court today and Tommy Neill put me on to an informant in jail; said he had some information about the case."

"Did it pan out?"

"Well, yes and no. It was Jerry Painter, the male half of the couple that ducked out on us the night we went to the bar. He said that our unsub was driving was a red, 74 or 75 Chevy Nova."

"You believe him?"

"I think so. He saw the man and ID'd his black hair. It confirms what we've heard about a red car; and this guy works in a garage, so he knows his cars. Hey, it's just crazy enough to be true; this guy drivin' a twenty-five year old beater."

"He know anything else about him?"

"That's the bad news part. He doesn't know his name or where he lives. But he can ID him; and he also said somethin' else."

Will looked at me, brows raised.

"He said he talked with an accent; not an overseas accent, but a somewhere else in America accent, like another part of the country."

Will closed his eyes again. "Hmm. New York, upper Midwest, Boston; thems the most recognizable accents.

"Well, there are couple of others: southern, tidewater."

"He'd know a southern accent."

"If he was telling the truth."

"I don't know. I think this guy'd prob'ly say anything to get outta jail. What's he in for?"

I smiled. "Indecent Exposure."

"Oh, shit."

After lunch, I went to the radio room and ran red Chevy Novas, 74 and 75 models, through the data base. There were about fifty still registered in Alabama, none in Mobile, and forty of them registered to men. I went back to my office to check driver's licenses and found that none of the male registrants had black hair; some brown, but none black.

I was becoming convinced that our man was not local; that he was either in town for a short period of time, or he had just moved to town. The quickest and easiest thing to do was to put out a BOLO on the red Nova and hope we stumbled upon it. It was such an odd car that, if it was around, it wouldn't be that hard to spot.

At four o'clock, I hung it up for the day. I felt as if I had accomplished nothing. Court had been postponed; Jerry Painter had been at least half a bust; and his information had not, so far at least, panned out.

I looked up 'Zoe' in the name book. Ironically, it meant 'life.'

Chapter 21

That evening, I was awakened at about eleven by a call from the office. The dispatcher said that, in case I didn't remember, I was on call, and I was needed at the K Bar Lounge on Airport Boulevard in State Line.

149

"What's the call?" I said.

"I understand there's been a pretty bad cutting," Mary, the dispatcher said.

"Suspect?"

I thought I could hear the smile in her voice. "In custody."

"Fantastic." I knew there was a smile in mine. "I'll be there in, oh, say, thirty minutes."

Fifteen minutes later, after dressing and a quick shower, I was on the road enroute to the K Bar. I took Airport Boulevard west, for about ten miles. The bar was on the right.

First opened in the mid-seventies by a Marine Corps sergeant recently returned from Vietnam and newly-separated from the service, the K-Bar – named for the edged weapon used by Marines – was a bar for serious drinkers. Bikers, rednecks, alkys, and out of towners who didn't know better were all welcome. The place had a couple of pool tables in the back, a shell parking lot on the outside, and no windows. The Marine sergeant had ultimately sold out to one of the locals, and the place had since become something of a community institution.

The building itself was located on a four or five acre tract with approximately two hundred feet of frontage along the highway. The actual building was about a hundred yards off the road, and the space in between the pavement and the front door was the parking lot. On this night there were only about three or four vehicles in the lot – excepting the county vehicles, of course – an unusually small crowd for a Thursday, the normal beginning of the bar weekend.

I arrived three minutes later than I said I would and stepped out into a mild and dry night. About ten or twelve patrons were standing up on the porch. Among them was Rassie, the bartender and owner, who had witnessed for me once before in a capital case involving a kid that was passing through and stopped long enough to murder a local homosexual man in a nearby motel room. Rassie was a large

150

ex-military type himself who was not afraid of anyone. I walked over to where he was standing.

"Evenin', Rassie. What's going on?"

He shook his head. "Some Cajun from Louisiana just got cut a new asshole."

"You see what happened?"

"Sure. Everybody saw it."

I threw a thumb toward the marked patrol car parked parallel to the highway. "That guy in the backseat the one that did it?"

He nodded. "Yeah. You know him. Simp Patridge."

I did know Stanley Simpson 'Simp' Patridge, a red haired psychopath who had been in trouble with the law for over half of his thirty years.

Patridge had grown up – and still lived – in Grand Bay, Alabama, about fifteen miles southwest of Mobile. He was an only child whose mother had nearly perished at his nativity. She recovered and in her subsequent barrenness doted heavily on the boy. Her affection led her and her husband to excuse every one of her son's legal indiscretions; from animal cruelty (setting the neighbor's cats on fire), to joyriding (he once took a stolen Porsche on a high speed chase), to arson (setting a barn ablaze in the middle of winter). They had bailed him out of jail, paid off his victims, and forked over thousands in fines and restitution to cover every one of his assaults, thefts, a multitude of traffic tickets, and all his vandalism, until they had almost spent themselves into bankruptcy.

I told Rassie I'd talk to him later, after which I walked out to the patrol car and looked in the rear window. Simp was sitting with his head back, eyes closed, and mouth wide open. He had no shirt and no shoes, and his blue jeans were stained with what looked like blood.

"Hey, Simp. You awake?"

I tapped on the glass. He didn't move.

151

Stepping away from the window, I looked around for the investigating deputy, and for someone else: the victim.

Deputy Barry Parsons was standing at the front of the patrol car with his foot on the bumper writing a report. I walked up to him, took my pen out of my pocket, and prepared to write, also. He looked up and smiled.

"Kind of unusual for you to be out this time'a night," he said smiling. His smile was always comical because he was missing two teeth – one upper, one lower – right in front.

"Only for blood." I nodded toward the backseat. "What happened here?"

Parsons laid his clipboard on the hood of the car and took a deep breath. "Well, you're not going to believe this one. Apparently, our victim, uh, Justin Daigle, a coonass that works at one of the gas plants down off DIP, was inside playin' pool when Simp walked in with a couple'a girls. Daigle looks across the room and says, 'Hey, buddy, no shirt, no shoes, no service'; kind'a makin' a joke, like. Well, asshole here flies off the handle, pulls out a hook bill knife and starts chasing this Daigle cat around the bar."

While he was talking, I was looking down at my pad and writing, and smiling. "Go on."

"Well, Daigle runs out the door with Simp two steps behind him. He makes two circles around the parking lot until finally dumbass here catches up to him and swipes the knife down his back."

"How bad was he hurt?"

"Well, he was only cut three ways: deep, wide, and continuous."

"Did you see him?"

"I got here just as he was leavin' in the ambulance. The cut starts at the top of his right shoulder, comes down, and ends up at the top of his ass crack."

I nodded and looked around. Another deputy, Glen Rush, was taking names and addresses from anyone standing around who would give them to him. If the man lived, I'd probably only need Rassie and the victim. If he died, I'd need all of them.

"Where'd you get him?" I said.

"He jumped in his truck, left the two girls here, and took off for home; that's his usual MO. We stopped him driving down Jensen Switch Road, about two miles off Airport. We towed his truck."

"Did you get the knife?"

He shook his head. "It wasn't on him or in his vehicle."

Oh, no. If it wasn't around the parking lot somewhere, then tomorrow we'd have to the get the dogs out and walk the side of the road for about four or five miles between here and where he was arrested in order to find it. That would take at least a half a day.

"Did Simp make a statement?"

"Yeah. He told me to, 'fuck off'; said he wanted a lawyer."

"Do you know where the victim is?"

"They said they were going to the Medical Center."

I continued writing. Rush was getting all their names, the victim was at the hospital, and the suspect would be on his way to jail shortly. All that was left was a few photos. I took the police radio off the hook that was attached to the dash in the front seat of Parsons' vehicle.

"SO 27."

"SO 27."

"Respond crime scene to this location."

"10-4."

I replaced the radio and stepped back out of the car. There was only one thing to do at that point. I walked to the edge of the lot where it met the highway and began walking back and forth across the width of it in what crime scene personnel call a 'line search.'

After about five trips, I spotted several drops of blood near a parked truck on the west side. I called and motioned to Parsons.

"This is where he was cut, I think. You got an evidence marker?"

"I'll get one from the car."

He was back in two minutes and sat the orange cone on the shells next to what looked like six or eight drops of blood. I continued my search until I found a pool of what looked like blood about six feet closer to the building. Parsons walked over and brought me another cone.

"When ID gets here, show'im these two spots and make sure he gets plenty'a photographs." I paused. "Do you see any need to keep Simp around here?"

Parsons shook his head. "Not really."

"Okay, get the tech to take a picture of'im, then get some paper bags and go on to jail. Book him for attempted murder, and tell the jail to take his clothes and give'em to you. Put'em in the bags, seal'em up, and make sure they get logged into the property room first chance you get. Just make sure they're in *paper* bags."

"You want me to take'em to the lab?"

I shook my head. "Not now. We can do that later. If this guy dies, we'll have to do it all. If he doesn't, we may not need'em."

Parsons nodded, and I watched him as he walked toward his vehicle and the sleeping man in the rear seat.

I stood in the middle of the parking lot and looked all four directions. It was getting late, and I was getting tired. Somehow, I didn't really know what I wanted to do next.

The whole thing was just so senseless. So a guy hollers at you and makes a joke, so what. Is that any reason to try to gut him like a fish? And, why even say anything to a dumb ass like Patridge anyway? It wasn't like they were gonna become friends.

On the porch and just to the right of the door, Rush was talking to Rassie. I walked that way to make sure I hadn't missed anything.

Rassie Ireland wore his gray hair in a buzz cut, and he had a short black mustache. I had talked with him at length on the occasions of previous cases in which had testified, and I had learned that he too had been in Vietnam, but in the Army instead of the Marines. His thick forearms and flat stomach said that even at his age he could still take a hill. He wore a long sleeve flannel shirt, jeans, and black boots. The large buckle on his belt indicated that he had once been a rodeo champion somewhere in Texas. There was a vertical scar on his right cheek.

I stood and listened while Rush copied down his vitals. As he did, something came to me.

Why would Simp be without shoes and a shirt? I mean, it was March, for Pete's sake. I thought about it and finally chalked it up to the man's crazy nature in general.

When Rush finished, I stepped up. "Tell me what happened, Rassie."

The big man cleared his throat. "Well, like I told this man here," nodding toward Rush, "everything was pretty quiet tonight. We had a really good crowd earlier in the evenin', but it had kinda slacked off. This Cajun fella – I mean, I guess he was Cajun, he said he was from Louisiana, and he sounded Cajun – come in by hisself and ordered a beer."

"You noticed him when he came in?"

"Sure, 'cause he was new. Well, he ordered a Bud in a bottle and then walked over to the juke box and put in some quarters." He looked up into the air. "He played Reba McIntire, and, uh, '*He Stopped Loving Her Today.*'"

I knew the song, a sad one by George Jones.

"Then he took a cue off the wall and racked'em up."

"He act like he knew anybody?"

155

He shook his head. "Nope; just drank his beer and started shootin' stick."

"Okay, what happened next?"

"Nothin'. The place was quiet. The few people that was here was just drinkin' and talkin'; real mellow like, you know?"

I nodded.

"Then, about thirty minutes later, shithead there," he nodded toward the patrol car, "busted in the door with a couple of girls talkin' loud and laughin'." Right then, Rassie looked over the parking lot. "I been lookin' for'em, but I don't see them girls around here now. Anyways, they come in, and he comes to the bar and gets beer for the two chicks. They take a seat, and he goes over toward the tables and leans against the wall – over near the juke box at the end of the bar."

"What was he doin'?"

"He wadn't doing nothin'. He was just starin'."

He was looking for a fight. I wrote as fast as I could.

"Then what?"

"Then the Cajun guy looks up and smiles at him. And he says, he says, 'Hey, Buddy. No shirt, no shoes, no service.' Well, ole dumb ass points at him and reaches into his right hip pocket and comes out with a knife. I reach for my bat and start from around the bar, but the Cajun guy starts runnin' 'round the table with Simp on his ass. Quicker than you can say 'Jack Shit,' they both hit the front door and was out in the parkin' lot. When I got to the door they was almost to the highway. Jackass was about two steps behind him and took a swipe at him when they got next to that truck. The dude ran about ten more feet then fell out." He paused. "I guess if he'd wanted to kill him he could have, but he just stood over him for a minute, and then he turned around and started walkin' to his truck."

"Did you see what he did with the knife?"

156

"No. I saw him swing his arm, so he may have thrown it under the truck."

I looked back at the vehicle. The evidence guys could get down on their hands and knees and look for it.

"Ever have any trouble with Simp before?"

"Oh, fuck yeah. He's come in here three or four times that I had to run him out; once for kicking the juke box and once for breakin' a beer bottle on the wall."

"He ever give you any trouble?"

"Nothin' but back sass. I mean, he always left, but he'd give me some lip first. I ain't afraid of'im. I'd knock the shit out of him, and he knows it."

"Did he say anything when he was chasing the Cajun around?"

"Not that I heard. He just chased him. He did have kind of a funny look on his face.

"Funny, 'ha ha' or funny, crazy?"

"Funny, crazy; like he meant to kill him, but then, when he had the chance, he couldn't pull the trigger."

Maybe Simp wasn't as out of it as he makes out. An assault charge he could beat, or buy his way out of. But murder was a crime against the state. No way was he going to just walk away from that.

I looked down at my pad and started cleaning up my notes. I shook my head as I wrote and thought about how we might really have old Simp by the stones this time. If we could get the Cajun to come back from Louisiana and testify, then we could get Simp to do some real jail time; five or ten years, maybe. Then, with any luck, somebody in prison would kill him.

Just as I looked up, Hernandez was getting out of his black SUV, near the edge of the parking lot. I took a step that direction when an important question suddenly occurred to me. I turned back toward the porch.

"Hey, Rassie. Is it a policy?"

He turned away from the two young women to whom he was starting to talk, and back toward me. "Is what a policy?"

"You know, the 'no shirt, no shoes,' thing. Is that your policy?"

He chuckled. "Oh, shit no. We'll serve anybody. We'll serve ya if you're nekkid."

Forty-five minutes later, I was at the Southwest Alabama Medical Center ER. I parked my car in the west side parking lot next to a black Porsche Boxter with a personalized tag that said, 'ERDOC.'

I walked through the automatic swinging doors while clipping my star to my belt. At the counter, I stood quietly while a large boned woman with brown hair talked on the telephone.

When she finished, I smiled. "Yes, ma'am, I'm Faulkner with the Metro Sheriff's Office. I'm looking for a man with a long cut down his back."

She made a face. "Oh, yeah. He's back in four." She nodded her head back over her left shoulder. "Domestic?"

"What? Oh, the case? You'd think so, but no. Just a bar fight."

"Oh."

She shuddered, and I smiled as I walked around the counter and toward the examining area.

Pulling back the curtain on Exam 4, I stepped inside. Things didn't look exactly like I thought they would. I guess I expected a group of people standing around, hovering over the patient.

A doctor I once dated told me she was on the hospital's 'trauma team,' a group of about six or eight interns that responded to emergencies and fluttered over and around a seriously injured patient, often one that was expected to die, and who was therefore a candidate for just about any and every procedure or therapy they could think of to try. That mental image always brought to my mind a flock of vultures.

Instead, there was a young male physician and an attractive female nurse standing by my victim, who was lying prone on a gurney with his bare back exposed. The doctor sat on a stool that was raised to its full height. He had a surgical mask over his face, and his rubber gloves were covered with blood.

The nurse, a blonde with a short, page boy haircut, wore green scrubs. Her gloves were cleaner. She fed the doctor sutures that he deftly used to close what looked like about a meter-long rip down the middle of the man's back. There were green sponges along either side of the length of the laceration, however, surprisingly, there was very little bleeding.

The doctor looked up. "Ah, you'll have to wait outside."

I showed him my star and walked on into the cubicle. I nodded toward the victim.

"Is he conscious?"

The doctor gave me a sour look, like I should obey his orders no matter who I was, then took a deep breath and exhaled in disgust. The nurse looked at me and smiled.

"He's kinda semi-comatose. We used a local, but he's in and out."

"Can I talk to him?"

She looked at the doctor. He nodded at her, and she stepped away from the bed so that I could stand next to the man's head. I took out my pen and opened up my pad.

"Mr. Daigle, can you hear me?"

"Unhhhh."

"Tell me what happened to you."

His face was half buried in the gurney so his speech was muffled, but I could make it out. I was pretty sure I knew what he was going to say anyway.

"Dat red headed sombitch cuth me."

"Did you know him before tonight?"

159

"No."

"Why did he do it?"

"I donth know. I thust told him, no thirt, and all that. I was justh joking."

"Did you ever hit him?"

"Thit, no."

"Did he say anything to you?"

He shook his head.

I cleared my throat. "Can I count on you to testify in court against him?"

"Are you fuckin' kiddin? Anythime, anywhere."

"All right. I'll let you rest. I'll come see you tomorrow. Okay?"

He didn't answer. I put a business card in his hand and stepped away from the bed so I could make a couple of notes in my book. I looked at his back and shook my head. This was one time when I wished I had seen a cutting victim on scene. The sight of Daigle's back half stitched together caused me to shiver. I looked at the doctor.

"What's his prognosis?"

He sat up straight. "Well, no major arteries were hit and the lacerations to the muscles are somewhat superficial, so, really, the outlook is pretty good. He's gonna be sore for a while, but, quite frankly, it looks a whole lot worse than what it is."

"You gonna admit him?"

He nodded. "Just for one night, maybe two; to make sure that he doesn't get an infection."

He went back to his suturing, and I made more notes. I had seen cuttings, but only one or two worse than this.

"How many so far?"

He stopped what he was doing again and surveyed the length of the laceration, from the man's right shoulder to the superior confluence of his two gluteus muscles. He took the back of his right wrist and wiped his forehead, and took another deep breath.

160

"Oh, probably about fifty."

"Headin' to. . ."

He shrugged. "Heading to about a hundred and twenty-five." He paused. "It's going to be a long night."

Chapter 22

It was three by the time I got home and eight when I got to the office the next morning. Will was sitting behind his desk blowing on a cup of coffee when I walked in. I yawned obnoxiously and plopped into my chair.

"What's up with you?" Will said.

"I got called out again last night."

He slurped some coffee and set the cup down. "Anything big?"

"Not really. Simp Patridge went crazy and cut a guy down his back, out at the K Bar."

"Kill him?"

I shook my head. "No, although today he probably wishes he was dead. He cut him from his shoulder to his butt."

Will snorted. "Aw, his mama and daddy'll just buy him out of it again."

"I don't think so. Not this time. The old boy that got cut was a coonass from over in Louisiana. He couldn't say much last night, but he seemed pretty mad."

"What kinda case you got?"

"Well, Rassie's gonna testify; and the victim. Roy Rogers called me this morning and told me his people found the knife under a truck in the parking lot. Simp's clothes have got blood on'em. And, the Cajun's got about a hundred

161

and twenty-five stitches. He'll make a devil of a good witness when he gets on the stand and takes off his shirt. I charged Simp with Attempted Murder, although I'd take a plea down to Assault 1st."

"How come?"

"Well, he had a chance to kill him and didn't take it. He threw the knife and ran."

"What brought it all on?"

"Just bar talk; a short temper; and, you know, Simp's crazy."

Will nodded. "Sounds like it's all wrapped up to me."

"Well, just about. I gotta sign a warrant and go back out to the hospital and get a better statement." I yawned again and shut my eyes.

"You about got your thing finished?" I said.

"We go to trial on Monday."

I nodded. "I've got to get back on that Zoe Woods case."

"Oh, that reminds me. Go see the Captain. He said that somethin' come in on that."

I opened my eyes and sat up in my chair. "Did he say what?"

"Just that it was a Crimestoppers tip."

"I'll go see him now."

The doors closed behind me as I stepped off the elevator and walked down the hall on the eighth floor – the Administrative Staff level. The Chief's – we called him 'Chief' for Chief of Detectives – door was closed, so I knocked twice. I was admitted by voice.

"Sit down," the old man said.

I parked in one of two chairs across the executive-sized desk from him. I always thought that the desk was much too large for the amount of work that the old man did.

In fact, the whole office was too big. It was almost as big as the Sheriff's. The paneled room looked to be about

162

sixteen by twenty. There were shelves on two of the four walls; shelves that were devoid of books but did contain a wide assortment of photographs of horses, fishing trophies, and a couple of stuffed critters that the Captain had shot while on a hunting trip to Montana. The desk was without papers or files and there was no evidence that a high level law enforcement supervisor inhabited the space.

Linus Agnew was seventy, a veteran of about forty-five years with the department. When the county, in the unincorporated areas at least, was much less populated, he was the only deputy who rode north of what's now called Airport Boulevard, the titular dividing line between north and south. He had the distinction of rising from deputy sheriff to captain and Chief of Detectives without ever having taken a civil service exam. Agnew was the consummate politician who always had an eye out for someone who could help him look good. He was loyal, until he saw a reason not to be, then he would cut anyone loose who threatened his situation, or at least couldn't enhance it. He had not, however, done anything to me – that I knew about.

He was dressed in a starched white shirt, dark slacks, and a pink tie. His horn-rimmed glasses sat down on his nose.

"I guess Snuffy told you about the lead that came in."

"Yes, sir."

He shoved a piece of paper across the desk at me then leaned back in his chair and put one hand halfway under the waistband of his trousers and left it there.

I picked up the sheet and read it. Then I looked up.

"How's that case coming?" he said.

"Well, we have a suspect and a vehicle description, but we've yet to put a name with him. We've interviewed most of the people that were in the bar that night, and we've talked to the people at her job. We went to the wake and the funeral. I've checked the vehicle through the state files, and

I'm in the process of running down their owners. Right now, it looks like it's just going to take a lotta leg work. Truthfully, I think the guy's not local."

He nodded. "Well, the girl's daddy has called the Sheriff. He's been askin' about the case."

"Yes, sir."

"You know, he's from up in Citronelle, or Chunchula, I think it is. He's a rich man who's kind of the unofficial mayor of that community up there. He told the Sheriff he'd like to see a little more progress on the case."

Something akin to anger, though not as intense, welled up in me, but just for a moment; until I realized that this case was political and there was nothing I could do about getting called on the carpet for it.

"Yes, sir," was all I said.

"Just take this lead and try to get on the others you have as soon as you can, and let's see if we can get this thing knocked out."

I nodded. "Yes, sir. You do understand the circumstances surrounding this case?"

He nodded. "You mean that the girl was retarded? Yeah, I know. Was she able to give you anything before she died?"

"Not really, no. Just some cryptic sounds. We haven't made any sense of 'em yet."

"Okay. Well, just do what you can."

I looked down at the paper in my hand. It said that a woman named 'Pearl' had called Crimestoppers and said that she needed to talk to the detectives working on Zoe Woods's case, that she had information. It also gave the woman's telephone number. I looked back at the Captain.

"Do we know anything about this 'Pearl'?"

"You know what I know, Henry."

"Yes, sir. Anything else?"

"Yeah, one other thing. The Sheriff has contacted the Governor, and the two have gotten together, and now there's a ten thousand dollar reward available for information."

I nodded and rose. "Yes, sir," I said, and I turned and walked out of the room.

It was going to be after lunch before I could get to work on the Captain's information. When I left his office, I went immediately down to Property. I checked to make sure that Simp Patridge's pants had been logged into evidence, and then I drove to the Medical Center to see Justin Daigle.

Daigle had been admitted to a room on the fourth floor. Unable to lie on his back, he was still face down when I found him. He was in immense pain, but he had slept some and was full of pills, so he was able to tell me a little more about what he remembered. His story did not differ from any of the others that I had heard thus far. I asked him if he could pick his assailant out of a photo lineup, and he said he didn't know, but he thought he could. I made a mental note not to let anyone show him any photos of Patridge.

Daigle was under sedation, but he was still angry. He told me that he was willing to let the justice system take its course, but if it didn't give him the desired result, he was going to kill Stanley Simpson Patridge.

I admonished him not to take the law into his own hands while secretly wishing that he would. It would certainly be no loss to the Metro Sheriff's Department, and I was sure that the community wouldn't mind one iota.

After I left the hospital, I drove by the jail. I learned that Patridge was being held under a fifty thousand dollar bond and was not going anywhere. Though he'd always asked for a lawyer in the past, I made a mental note to come back and let him tell me, 'fuck you,' in person, later, after he'd had a chance to get a little stir crazy.

Back at the office, I sat down at my desk and dialed the telephone number of the mysterious 'Pearl.' She answered on the third ring.

"Sister Pearl."

It was an interesting identification. "Yes, ma'am, this is Detective Faulkner with the Sheriff's Office. Are you the Pearl who has information about a homicide?"

"Yes. Yes, Detective Faulkner, I am."

Her voice was raspy and deep. She sounded as if she needed to clear her throat. I thought I knew who and what she was, but I decided to run with it anyway.

"I'd like to drop by and talk to you."

"Certainly, you may. I am on Three Notch Road, just past the Old Pascagoula Road intersection." She provided an address.

I knew the exact location that she was describing. "I'll be there in twenty minutes."

When I parked in front of Sister Pearl's, mine was the only vehicle in the small, shell-covered lot. The structure was barely larger than one of those metal storage buildings that Sears sells. It had a red shingled roof, green shutters, and a small eave that served as a porch over the yellow front door. There were two windows in front, on either side of the door, and a small sign hanging on the door jamb just to the left of the portal.

Sister Pearl
Knows all, sees all

Now, I have no respect for, no use for, and no time for psychics, and I was half tempted to restart my car and leave right then and there. However, the lead had been given to me by the Captain, and the chances were good that he would ask me how it panned out, so I decided to give her fifteen minutes.

I rang the buzzer on the facing, and the door opened in ten seconds. What was standing behind it made me step back.

She was about four and a half feet tall, and about three and a half feet wide. Her hair was gray, long and stringy. She wore a pink muumuu with no sleeves and two large pockets in front; and costume jewelry necklaces, about four of them of various colors, hung around her neck and wrists. Her flat feet were bare.

Her face told it all; all about the five thousand miles she'd lived. Three layers of make up almost glued her brown eyes shut. Her nose was a large hook bill, and her wide mouth was ringed by bright red lipstick. The lines on her face, lines that showed through the thick coat of powder, said she was at least sixty.

I didn't want to, but I accepted her invitation to come inside. She smiled. Surprisingly, her teeth were in reasonably good shape.

"Sister Pearl?"

"Yes. Come in. Have a seat at the table." Her voice sounded like Jean Carson.

I sat down across from her, feeling like Saul. I blinked and said a silent prayer that God wouldn't strike me dead.

My initial guess was that, for whatever reason, business was slow and she was looking for a way to get some traffic through the door. If she could somehow stumble onto some information that was pertinent to our case, then she could go to the press or otherwise get the word out that she had some insight and the people would come. Well, I wasn't going to help her any.

The room was dark. There were thick hangings of various colors on three of the walls and a dirty green carpet on the floor. I sat on a tan folding chair at a round table about four feet in diameter. There was a green and blue tapestry cloth that had gold fringe around the edges spread over the table. A hanging light with a green, cloth shade hung from the ceiling and fell to about four feet above the table.

"Did you know Zoe Woods?" I said.

"No."

"Do you know her family?"

"No."

I paused and exhaled loudly. "I understand you have information about her death."

"Yes," she said. "I had a dream. Many of my revelations come to me in my dreams."

She closed her eyes and took two deep breaths, as if transporting herself into some far off place where the spirits would tell her everything. She placed the palms of her hands on the table and wiggled her fingers.

"I see a large field." She opened her eyes. "Was she lying in a field?"

I shook my head. "Sorry, Pearl. You talk, I listen. That's how this works. No questions."

Her eyes shot open wide, and she froze. I could tell she didn't expect me to play hard to get.

"Of course, of course." She shut her eyes once again. "I see a man, a man with brown hair."

Her right eye opened slightly, ostensibly to see my reaction. I painted on my best poker face.

"He and Zoe are eating and drinking." She paused. "They are drinking . . . much whiskey."

"That's two strikes, Pearl. One more and I'm leaving."

"Quiet please."

She closed her eyes tightly and spread her fingers wide. Two, then three minutes went by before she spoke again.

"I see a car, a large car." She took a deep breath. "It is . . . it is white."

I rose quickly. "Have a nice day, Pearl," and walked out the front door.

Back at the office, I spent the rest of the afternoon writing police reports, both concerning the Patridge case as well as a supplement for Zoe Woods's file detailing my visit with Sister Pearl. I described her office in elaborate detail and put down our conversation almost word for word. What I wanted to know was just how she got word of the reward so fast.

When I finished writing it was four thirty, and the day was over. I leaned back in my chair and considered again, for about the fiftieth time, the Woods case.

Could it have been more than what it looked like? Could it have been more than just a woman and a man having a few drinks then having it all go bad? Was her money a part of it all? Was there an aspect of her life about which we did not know? Her siblings? Her parents? Her husband?

My head was spinning, and I shut my eyes. When I awoke it was seven PM.

Chapter 23

It wasn't until the month of May before we got another lead in the Woods case. I had spent the interim trying to run down all the red Chevy Novas in the state. By then, I was convinced that our suspect was from out of town.

I had also begun working on an informal psychological profile. We knew our killer was probably white. It stood to reason because she was in a white bar; she was last seen with a white man; and even then, in Mobile County, Alabama, the instances of interracial socialization were not that common.

Our suspect would not have an extensive criminal record; minor assaults mostly, and probably petty thefts. I based that theory on the fact that nothing about him said high class: the cheap used car, the low class hang-out, the damaged woman.

169

He also, I surmised, had a temper. The fact that a potential sex romp turned into a cut throat and panty rape indicated that this man could lose it pretty intensely, given the right impetus. That was another reason to believe that he had a record for assault.

I predicted that we would find our man in a boarding house, flop house motel, Section 8 apartment, or apartment adjacent to the home owned by an older person. If he was working, it would be in a factory or possibly even a farm. He would be a smoker, a drinker – but not very often to excess – and he might be slightly overweight. He would be born in another state, but in the south. He would be single, obviously, although there might have been a very, very short marriage in his past. He would have no military background, would have done poorly in school, and would likely have drifted through life.

I shared my theories with Will, and he just laughed. Will didn't go in for a lot of that sort of thing. He said that my profile matched about three or four million men, and I just needed to get out and find the guy that did it; and then we would all know who and what he was, and none of us would have to wonder and speculate.

Will had gotten a conviction in the Carlton retrial but this time the judge had sentenced him to life in prison without parole, instead of death. It was hoped by all concerned that the two defendants – especially Carlton – would sit back and chew their fat and let the system be. Will said, fat chance, that Carlton's do-gooder, New York lawyers had been stockpiling appeals, and just as fast as one was dealt with, another would be filed. He said that his lawyers were all commie anarchists anyway, and they were *trying* to flood the streets with criminals in order to bring the country down.

It was the first Thursday in May when we got the next clue in the Woods case. Will and I were in the office when we got a call from Sis, the waitress at The Society Lounge. She wanted to meet us. We made plans to see her at the Waffle Hut on Government Boulevard, near the interstate, at ten AM.

"Hey," she said, smiling as we entered.

She waved animatedly and motioned us toward a booth in the corner. She was wearing a yellow, short sleeved shirt and jeans, and her short hair was pulled back.

"How are you doing?" Will said as he slid in next to the woman. I took the other side, alone.

She shrugged. "Oh, you know; another day, another night at work."

"How's things at The Society?"

"Well, they haven't been the same since what happened to Zoe; not that she was any big thing, but, you know, ever'body's still kind'a thinkin' about it all. They will, too, until a new crowd starts comin' in."

"I understand," Will said.

"There's not much chance'a that, though. Mostly, kids go out to the west side, or downtown to Dauphin Street, and ever'body that comes over to us has been doin' it for a while now. We're not in a really great location, ya know. Larry wants to try some things to get some new people in."

"Like what?"

"Like a dance contest; line dancin', or somethin'; or maybe some slot machines, the kind that spit out drink coupons. Maybe even a mechanical bull."

"Sounds like he's gonna spend some money."

"I guess. I don't know where he's gonna get it, though."

There was a lull in the conversation as the waitress came over and took our order – a cup of coffee for Will, a glass of tea for me, nothing for Sis – so I produced my notebook and pen. Sis got the hint and reached for her purse.

"So, what I called you about," she opened the black handbag, reached in, and took out an envelope, "is this."

171

She handed it to Will. He opened it and looked inside.

"It's a two dollar bill," she said. "I didn't think about it 'til the other night when I was watchin' that crime scene show on TV, but the black haired man that was sittin' with Zoe tipped me with this two dollar bill – a silver certificate. Whenever I get some kinda unusual money, like two dollar bills or dollar coins, or even a silver dime or quarter, I always hold it out and buy it from the till. He had his hands on it. It might have his fingerprints."

Will looked inside the envelope and then up at Sis. "Well, sure. We'll take it and get it to the fingerprint boys." He handed the envelope to me.

"You think it's got somethin' on it?" she said looking at Will.

"I don't know, but we'll sure give it a look."

I licked the envelope, sealed it shut, and then wrote the date and time on the outside. Then I slid it over to Sis just as the waitress brought our drinks.

"Go ahead and initial it."

"I know. That way it'll keep the chain'a custody intact," she said as I tried to hide my smile.

"You watch a lotta them crime shows?" Will said.

"Well," she said as she wrote, "I didn't 'til Zoe got killed. Now, I don't know, I guess maybe it helps me understand things a little better. I watch the crime scene shows and that one with the lady coroner."

"Has Zoe's old man come into the bar at all?" Will said after blowing on his coffee.

She shook her head. "No. He never come very much anyway, but he hadn't been in since before that night." She paused. "The times that he did come he didn't sit with Zoe. He took a seat at the bar. If ya ask me, the man was kinda goofy."

"How so?"

"Well, Zoe would do her thing, you know, flittin' around the men and gettin'em to buy her drinks, and all the

172

while he'd just sit with a beer, actin' like it don't bother him."

"He never acted like he was jealous?"

She shook her head again. "Nope. He acted like he was too dumb to be jealous; like he didn't know what she was doin'."

"I don't know if we asked you this before, but do you ever remember Zoe leavin' with any other men? In the past, I mean, before that night?"

She looked up and closed her eyes. "No, I don't think so." Then she stopped. "Well, there was this one time it was a couple of years ago. She was drinkin' with a guy, and I remember'em walkin' out together. I don't know where they went, though."

"Did you ask her about it? The next night, I mean."

"Yeah, I asked her if she had a good time. She just said, 'yeah.'"

"You remember anything about this man?"

"Well, I don't know. I've usually got a pretty good memory for faces." She closed her eyes again. "Seems like he was kinda stocky, with dark hair. I do remember he had a big nose. His nose looked funny, like it kinda hooked on the end. It was weird lookin'."

"Anything else you can tell us about him?"

She shook her head. I took the last gulp from the glass of tea, and Will shoved his coffee cup toward the middle of the table.

"One more thing. You ever see Zoe with a knife?" Will said.

Sis shook her head. "No, not unless she carried it in her pocket. She didn't carry a pocket book. But, no, I never saw her pull one out."

I wrote. Will cleared his throat.

"Well, we sure do thank ya for hangin' onto this bill. We'll get it down to the lab boys and see if they can get anything off it. By the way, have you ever been fingerprinted?"

173

Her eyes shot open wide in surprise. "What'chu wanna know that for?"

"So we can compare'em to anything we find on the bill; for elimination purposes," I said.

"Oh, sure. Well, yeah, a few years ago I got a entertainer card. They should be on file from then."

I had to stifle another smile while imagining the muscular woman with the raspy voice and the frizzy hair dancing naked.

"Well, good," Will said. "We'll get those from over at the city police."

We rose from the booth and said our goodbyes. Back in the car, I chuckled.

"I know what you're thinkin'," Will said. "That bitch dancing nekked." He shivered as if he had just taken a bite of a lemon.

"Maybe she looked a lot better back then."

"It wouldn't matter. All she'd have to do is open her yap. That raspy voice of hers'd give me the limp dick right quick."

I chuckled. "One thing, though, she seemed awful nervous about the fact that we were asking about her prints."

"I noticed that, too." He paused and looked at me. "Do you think the guy she was talking about was Jerry Painter? The one that left with Zoe Woods, I mean. You've seen him."

"Well, I can't be sure. But it sounded an awful lot like him. Seems like she'd'a been able to identify him, though."

"Mister 'peter on parade.'"

"Right."

When we got back to the office, I dropped the two dollar bill off at the evidence office. Chuck Briley was there, and he took it and said he would treat it with ninhydrin spray. I gave him Susy Weaver's name and DOB and told him to compare whatever he found to her.

In my office, I called the jail to see if Painter was still incarcerated. He was, so Will and I decided to go talk to him right after lunch.

Jerry Painter had a toothpick in his mouth when he walked into the attorney's room. I wasn't aware that the jail was issuing toothpicks to prisoners after meals. It seemed to me that a small, sharp piece of wood might have some qualities as a weapon, but it had been a long time since I'd worked in the jail, and it was a cinch that I wasn't up on all the latest in correctional theory.

The idea that the behavior of a sociopath, or at least someone with sociopathic tendencies, could be rehabilitated enough to fit in with normal society had always been, to me, a little farfetched. There is just not anything in a jail that can change a man's heart enough to make him want to live within the law. When he's convicted, all you can really do is let him spend his full sentence inside and hope that he somehow grows out of whatever it was that made him start committing crimes to begin with.

Painter sat down with a smug look on his face, as if he thought we came back because we needed him and his information. He took his seat and folded his arms.

"Jerry," I said, "this is Will Eubanks of the Sheriff's Office. He's workin' with me on Zoe's case."

Will nodded, then reached across the table and relieved Painter of his toothpick. The quickness of his movement surprised Painter, and me too.

"I'll just take that," Will said.

Painter's eyes sprang open and his arms fell to his sides. He was too startled to retaliate.

"Buddy, I understand Mr. Faulkner came to see you a few weeks ago about Zoe Woods, is that right?"

Painter, clearly chastised, nodded but did not speak. I decided it would be best if I took over the questioning, at least in the beginning. I looked over at Will.

"Jerry, some new information has come to light, information that we need to get clarified."

He said nothing.

"We hear that you had a relationship with Zoe Woods. Is that true?"

His eyes opened up wide again. "Where'd you hear that?"

I was relieved. His non-denial implicated him strongly. "It doesn't matter where we heard it, is it true?"

He looked down and to the left. "We dated a couple'a times. That's all."

Will leaned back in his chair and listened. I was going to get him back into the conversation as soon as I could.

"Did the two'a you get it on?"

A smile began to creep across his lips, as though I should know better than to ask. "Hey, what can I say."

"So, tell me about it."

He shrugged. "What do you wanna know?"

"When did you start seeing her?"

"About ten months ago, 'fore the first of the year."

"How'd her old man feel about it?"

"I don't know. I don't guess he knew. Besides, it didn't bother me, and it shore didn't seem ta bother her."

"How many times did you and her go out?"

He shrugged. "Three or four, I guess."

I looked down at my notepad and tried to think of what to ask. Will spoke up.

"Was you at the club the night that Zoe was in there? That Friday night, I mean."

Painter looked down, as if trying to decide whether or not to lie. "Yeah, I was there."

"Was you with Zoe?"

He shook his head. "I seen her, and I tried to talk to her, but I wadn't there with her."

"Was you there when she got there?"

"Naw. She got there first. I think she lives just right around the corner. I come in after she did."

"Was she sittin' with somebody else?"

"She was sittin' with that black haired dude that drove the Nova; the one that I told'ja about." He nodded at me.

"Did you ever talk to him or her?"

He shook his head again. "Naw. I give her the high sign once or twice, but she ignored me."

"How'd that make you feel?"

He took a deep breath and exhaled. "Shit, man, she's just another split tail. They like buses, you know?"

"Did you follow her out?"

He shook his head. "No."

Will looked at me, then back at Painter. "Tell me everything you can about the man she was with."

He shut his eyes and looked up. I didn't have confidence in what he was about to tell us, but I readied my pen anyway.

"He had black hair – black as night; and not too tall. He was kinda big, I mean a little overweight."

"Ever seen the man before?"

"No."

"Ever seen him since?"

"Naw."

Will studied Painter's face. "Tell me about this car, this Nova."

"Well, you know, it was about a 74 or 75, faded red, four door. It had old tires on it, recaps, I think. It was nothin' special, just a car. It didn't look like the old boy drivin' it had kep' it up."

"When did you get a look at it?"

"When I walked outside; when I got ready to go."

"Is that when Zoe and the man left?"

"No. They was still inside."

"How'd you know it was his car?"

He paused for a minute. "Well, I don't know. I guess it was 'cause I knew all the other cars out there, and his was the one I didn't know." He shut his eyes. "Let's see, there was Larry's and Sissy's cars; mine; and Linc and Wes's. Yeah, his was the only one I didn't know, and I said to myself, 'that must be that dude's car.'"

"What time did you leave?"

"Oh, well, I don't know. It was late, though."

Will looked at me and then leaned in close to Painter.

"Listen, Jerry. Did you follow Zoe out and cut her throat?"

"No, sir. No, sir, I did not."

Will leaned back as I copied down his exact words. They might be important later. Will looked back at me in our silent code that said it was my time.

"Anything else you can remember about the black haired man? Tattoos maybe?"

He closed his eyes again. "You know, he might'a had somethin' on his arm. It wadn't a tattoo, though. It looked more like a burn or a birthmark, or somethin'."

Interesting, but it was unusual that Sis didn't notice it, what with her serving them drinks. She would have noticed a blemish, if it had been of any size or consequence. I looked over at Will. I could tell he was skeptical, too.

"How big was this mark?" Will said.

"Not too big; maybe as round as a silver dollar, but real prominent. I could see it from across the room."

We both leaned back. Now, Jerry Painter was making up stuff up; just saying what he thought we wanted to hear. It was time to stop.

"How long a sentence did you get on your case, Jerry?" I said.

"Six months." Rather than look chagrined or disgusted or one of any other of the other expected emotions, he looked proud.

"That's pretty stiff . . . if you'll pardon the expression," I said.

Will smiled, but the joke went over Jerry's head.

"Well, you see," he said, "it wasn't my first offense, and the judge said, 'a long sentence for a long dick.'" His expression indicated that at least in his mind it had actually happened.

Chapter 24

Out in the car, I slid behind the wheel. Will sat down with a thud.

"Well," I said, "what kind of witness do you think he'll make?"

Will chuckled. "Mister 'dick on display'?" He paused. "Well, let's just say we've got to do what we can to keep him off the stand."

I turned out of the parking lot and onto St. Emanuel Street heading back toward the office. "Well, he does confirm the black hair and the red car. We can use him for that."

"Well, sure. But if we find him, we've got the red car and the black hair, and we'll just use the other people. Maybe their records ain't so bad."

As I turned onto Government Street off Royal, the police radio came to life.

"Any unit in the vicinity, signal fifty at the Commerce Bank, Government and Espejo."

179

The call, airing over what Will called the 'bat channel' – the radio channel that simulcast to both the City Police and the Sheriff's Department in cases of emergency or serious incident – was for a bank robbery.

"That's just right down the street," I said.

"All units, be on the lookout for a silver, Ford Ranger pickup occupied by one black male."

We were just passing Broad Street, headed west, when Will pointed ahead. "There he is."

The truck was coming toward us at maybe sixty miles per hour, dangerously weaving in and out of early afternoon traffic, which was heavy, even on a Thursday.

Will saw it first, a hand extended from the driver's window. "Look out!"

I swerved to the right just as the truck passed, and I saw the puff of smoke that emitted from the muzzle of the gun at the end of the hand. The bullet hit the windshield and shattered it in a spider web pattern, but did not penetrate.

"Shit!" Will said.

After I made a U turn, I could barely see the truck, as it was at least a block ahead. Will reached and felt for the portable blue light on the floor board of the back seat. When he managed to get it, he plugged the cord into the cigarette lighter and set the device on the dash. Then he hit the siren function in the radio controls on the floor of the front seat. The blue light went round and round in front of the aluminum reflector, while the siren produced that mournful wail that I hate so much.

Meanwhile, I picked up the radio microphone and called in our circumstances and location. I was trying to talk and drive at the same time. Only a few of the cars ahead of us were pulling over to the right. We passed two damaged vehicles along way; vehicles no doubt struck by the silver pickup.

I caught up to within a half a block of the truck as it turned north on Royal Street. It weaved in and out of traffic and at one point careened up on a sidewalk just north of the old Battle House Hotel. Will took the microphone from me and called out our location.

When the truck reached Congress Street, it turned back west, taking the corner on two wheels. By that time, we had picked up an escort of three city police cars. I could hear sirens all around and knew that there were probably about twenty others in the area.

The silver Ford truck accelerated quickly and was a block ahead of us by the time we made the turn. He had busted the stop sign at St Joseph Street and Congress and appeared to be on his way west, but when he reached North Jackson Street, he did the unexpected.

He turned south on the one way street. It turned out to be an error from which he could not recover, for in the middle of the next intersection south, two Police patrol cars were parked broadside and had effectively blocked his way. The truck slowed down and hit the sidewalk on the west side of the street; and the driver jumped out without putting the car in park. It drove straight into and came to rest against one of two old growth oak trees just off the curb on that side.

The area in which he had stopped was called the De Tonti Square Historical Site, a nine square block locality containing homes of various architectural styles, as well as homes that had been turned into office space that were now occupied mostly by lawyers and architects. We could be pretty well assured that no civilians would be coming out into the street to get in the way.

I spotted our armed robber running west. He was of average height and weight, wearing a red, short-sleeved, pullover shirt and blue jeans. He was very dark, and from a distance I could see that he had a larger than stylish Afro haircut.

The block at which he had chosen to abandon his truck was for the most part vacant. On the Claiborne Street side, the next block over, there were two buildings that faced west, but no other structures. As Will and I slid to a stop

181

behind the truck, I could see three patrol cars on Claiborne, effectively blocking his flight.

"You gotta back up piece?" Will said.

"In the glove box."

Really, the gun in my car was my primary weapon. I kept it there because Will never carried a gun, and I wanted to plan for just such an eventuality as this.

Will pulled out the nine millimeter from the compartment and checked the magazine. I reached down and pulled my short barreled semi-auto from the holster on my ankle. Will called in our location as I slowly advanced toward the empty truck, my weapon at point shoulder.

Police officers had begun to fan out behind assorted types of cover on two of the three sides of the block. Someone, presumably a supervisor of some kind, had shown the good sense to keep the officers on the west side in their cars and out of the field of fire.

After I checked the interior of the truck – there was a paper bag on the seat, but no weapon visible – and turned off its engine, I slipped the truck's keys into my pocket. Will and I advanced toward the trees. He made a motion for me to stop. Will had military combat experience, so I deferred to his direction.

"Wait here. Let's try to get a bead on him first," he said.

I took up a position at the southernmost of two large oaks and peeked around the corner. Will stopped by the north side tree, and I saw him slowly scan the vacant lot. When he had gotten halfway across it, he stopped and pointed.

"There he is. Over in that hole."

'Hole' was a charitable description. From where I stood, it appeared to be little more than a foot or a foot and a half deep indentation in the earth. Our suspect was lying prone, as flat as he could in what was a poor attempt at concealing himself. The seat of his jeans was quite visible from our vantage point.

182

"Hey, man, this is the Sheriff's Department." Will shouted. "I see you over there. Throw out that gun and stand up."

The entire block got almost completely quiet. No one spoke as we waited for the man in the hole to answer.

His reply was not altogether unexpected. I watched from behind the cover of the tree as an arm extended from the hole and threw two shots our way. I heard the bullets whistle through the leaves above my head. A few broken twigs fell at my back.

His action seemed to incense Will. He took aim at the man in the hole and squeezed off two rounds in that direction. When he did, he started an onslaught from every police officer in the area. I looked to my left and saw at least fifteen officers barricaded behind patrol cars, some taking aim, the more young and inexperienced shooting wildly.

In about ten or fifteen seconds I heard someone yell, "Cease fire." It wasn't Will, so it must have been a police sergeant. The shooting stopped in a second.

"Ohhhhhhhhhhhhhh!" came a groan from the hole. I peeped around the tree and looked. Shortly, a gun came flying out.

"Can you stand up?" Will said loudly.

"No! Ahhhhhhhhh!"

"Just lay still, then."

Will motioned to me, and we both stepped out from behind the trees, weapons at low combat ready. We walked with short steps toward the hole. Out of the corner of my eye, I saw three uniformed officers walking our way, also.

When we reached the hole, the man was still prone, but now his arms were extended out to his sides so that his hands were visible. Will looked at him then motioned for one of the officers to come forward and handcuff him.

I looked at him also. Blood saturated the seat of his jeans.

"Where you hit, man?" I said.

"In my behind." His voice was a whimper.

I chuckled and looked at Will. He looked back at me.

"Look at that, Son," he said. "You shot his ass off."

Chapter 25

One week after the robbery, Roy Rogers sent me a report that detailed the fact that he found only one usable fingerprint on the two dollar bill submitted to us by Sis, Susy Weaver, and that was believed to have been handled by the black haired man. Rogers also put a note on it and said that he did find other ridge definition, although it was most likely from a palm. The note also said that the usable print did not belong to Sis.

May turned into June and I continued searching vehicle files, not only in Alabama, but in Mississippi and Florida, looking for '74 or '75 Chevy Novas, the vehicle that I believed was our only real and solid lead.

I also spent some time at the courthouse checking the backgrounds on all the players that we'd encountered thus far. Larry Flynn, the owner and bartender of The Society Lounge had a previous conviction for Disorderly Conduct – two in fact – when he was a young man, but was otherwise unblemished. It was a paltry record for someone who consorted so often with drunks, but he would have to be clean in order to hold a liquor license in the state. The thought occurred to me that he might have had something expunged from his record, and I made a note to check the Circuit and Probate Court records to see if any action had been taken to wash him out.

True to her word, Sis had once held an entertainer card in the city, albeit fifteen years ago. She also had three misdemeanor convictions for Theft of Property – most probably cases of skimming from the various lounges at which she had worked – and a couple of bad check convictions, but certainly nothing that would raise her to the level of murder suspect, or even conspirator.

Jerry Painter, well, what couldn't you say about him. He was a confirmed pervert. He had four previous convictions for Indecent Exposure – none, thankfully, to a child. I'm sure he knew that the state legislature was in the process of elevating the third IE conviction to a felony. My guess was that he would probably reform himself very quickly if that happened. He also had one conviction for Assault. I put that one on my list to check on also.

Lincoln Hayes, Wes Hightower, and the ladies of The Society were all unremarkable. All had convictions for alcohol related crimes, DUI mainly; all except Hayes who drove an eighteen wheeler. And all had driver's licenses that had been in the past or were at that moment suspended.

Robert and Evelyn Woods were clean. The other children, Zoe's siblings, were also legally unscarred. There was one in Mobile, but the other two were out of town and at that juncture, I saw no reason to make plans to visit them.

Zoe Woods's supervisor, Tom Walston, was clean, just a couple of traffic tickets. So was Tammy Harris, one of the girls with whom Zoe worked on the plucking line. But her other co-worker, Myrtice Abercrombie, about whom I had completely forgotten until I spotted her in my notes, had a past that was a bit more checkered.

It seems that Myrtice, who, according to her records, had spent at least some time in North Carolina, was a bit out of the ordinary. First, she held not only a passenger vehicle license, but also a commercial driver's license. Apparently, she had only been in Alabama for a short while as she had not yet had the licenses transferred into the state.

185

Second, her license said she was six feet one and a hundred and eighty-five pounds.

Also, Myrtice had done time. According to her package, she spent three years in prison in North Carolina for an ADW (assault with a deadly weapon) five years ago. I made a note of the contributing agency and called them.

"Yes, ma'am," I said speaking to a secretary in the Detective Division of the North Charlotte Police Department.

"I'm inquiring about a case that happened about six or eight years ago. The suspect was Myrtice Abercrombie. Do you think there might be anyone there that can give me some information about her?"

"Well, the only person that has been around here that long is Lieutenant Greenbaum. He's been in the Bureau for years. He's also the one with the best memory. I can let you talk to him. Hold on, and let me get the file, if I can find it."

She was gone for several minutes. Then, a man's voice came on the line. It was high pitched and very precise.

"This is Rufus Greenbaum."

"Yes, sir. My name is Faulkner. I'm with the Metro Sheriff's Office in Mobile, Alabama. I'm trying to get some information on an arrestee of yours, a Myrtice Abercrombie. You guys canned her for ADW about five years ago."

"Hmm. Myrtice Abercrombie. Yes, that was a domestic dispute that occurred on the outskirts of town."

"Stabbing or shooting?"

"A stabbing, as I recall."

"Who was the victim?"

"Ah, let's see, the file says that it was her boyfriend; a Michael Tolliver."

My ears pricked up as he said the name. "Do you have a physical description on him?"

"At that time? Looks like he was white male, brown hair, 5'8", and one thirty-five."

"Quite a bit smaller than she."

186

"Well, back then, she was not quite so large, herself."

Greenbaum filled me in on what he could. The investigator who worked the case had retired, and CID, he said, was staffed largely by younger officers.

He did say, however, that, according to the detective's notes, the two had fought for several years prior to the assault. They had once been married, but had divorced shortly before the incident. Tolliver had been stabbed in the chest and Abercrombie had been arrested without resistance. She had confessed freely.

"Was any motive stated?"

"Why, infidelity. What else?"

Later, I filled Will in on what I had learned. He agreed that Myrtice Abercrombie was someone with whom we needed to speak.

"So you think this Tolliver cat is the 'Mikey' that we're looking for?" he said.

"Well, I don't know. I've certainly got no reason to believe he is. There's no evidence to lead me to believe that our man is from North Carolina. I just know that she has a history of violence, and at this point we've got nothing else to go on."

Will studied her printout. "You got an address on her?"

"Just the one from the personnel office at Tyndall Poultry."

"Will she be at home today?"

"I called. Their office says it's her day off."

He rose from his chair. "Well, let's go."

It was a beautiful summer day, sunny with just enough of a breeze to make it comfortable, as we left midtown and drove toward Grand Bay, Alabama. Abercrombie's address put her in a mobile home park off Highway 188 about halfway between Grand Bay and Bayou La Batre.

The Bayou, as it was sometimes called, a fishing hamlet located at the shores of Mississippi Sound in the south part of the county, was famous for its prominent portrayal in the novel *Forrest Gump*. Grand Bay, however, was famous for watermelons, a truck stop, and the large amount of drug activity that was conducted on Highway 188 not far from the very trailer park to which we were enroute.

The Bayou Waters Mobile Home Park contained spaces for about two hundred units, but was inhabited by only about a third of that number. The streets within the park wound around in several figure eights that eventually emptied into two entrance/exits, and then out onto the highway. There was no rhyme or reason to the address numbering; most of the street signs had been knocked down, and only a few of the residences had numbers on them. The only way to find who you were looking for was to either know the park and the names of the streets, as Will did, or to know what type of vehicle you were looking for, and it happened to be parked out front.

The area was devoid of foliage, and, owing to the large number of hurricane level storms that had blown through the area in the past, there were precious few trees on the property. To say the park was cared for would have been an overstatement. It was clearly a money maker for the owner, who provided tenants electrical and water hookups and a space to put a 70 or eighty foot mobile home, but little else.

"What lot's she in?" Will said.

I looked down at my notebook as I navigated our vehicle past a weathered sign set in brick. "Looks like, Shore Drive, Lot 8."

"Turn right, up here," he said as he pointed ahead. I obeyed.

"It should be the about the fourth or fifth one on the right."

I piloted the car down the potholed path and slowly came to a stop in front of a faded green, sixty foot long mobile home with a white Ford parked out front. The structure was moldy in spots but appeared to be undamaged. The Ford had a South Carolina tag on the rear. I parked behind the vehicle and notified the radio operator of our location.

"Is there a warrant out for her?" Will said.

"None that I could find."

"Okay. Well, we'll see what she has to say."

I walked up two planks laid across four cinderblocks that served as steps to a wooden porch and bladed myself next to the door the best that I could with the space available. Will stood on the ground and looked up. I knocked twice.

Large feet attached to heavy legs lumbered to the door. The portal opened wide, and a mannish-looking woman who could only be Myrtice Abercrombie stood with her arms akimbo, as if daring us to speak to her.

"Ms Abercrombie?" I said.

"Who wants to know?"

Her voice was nothing like I imagined. It was high pitched and feminine. It was as if God had given her female and male hormones and the testosterone had given her a large frame, big bones, and muscle, while the estrogen had all settled in her voice box.

She had stringy, brown hair, a smooth face with fair skin, and piercing blue eyes. Her broad shoulders stretched out her white t-shirt, and her blue jeans were filled to the brim. Her bare feet were wide and flat.

I held out my star. "Metro Sheriff's Department, ma'am. We'd like to talk to you."

"About what?"

"Zoe Woods. We understand you worked with her."

She stood in silence for several seconds and eyed us both up and down. Then she took a deep breath and exhaled, opened the door wider, and motioned for us to come in. Will walked up the steps behind me, and we went into the comparatively dark interior of the woman's home.

The inside looked just as worn and weary as the outside, but the floor was uncluttered, the windows were clear, and the used furniture was surprisingly clean. There was a certain order to the room that I would have expected from a single woman living alone.

There's something inherently clean about a female. It has to do with the fact that the immune systems of children are weak and susceptible to disease, so the female of the species knows instinctively that the environment of the child must be kept as pristine as possible. You can almost always bet that a woman's home is going to be clean – cluttered, maybe – but clean, children or no.

Myrtice Abercrombie motioned toward a couch and two club chairs that took up most of the living space. Because the room was so dark, I couldn't tell much about the appointments, but I did see a portable television in the corner and a standing lamp at the end of the couch. The carpet was brown and worn, but there was no dust on any of the furniture.

Will took the seat on the end of the couch near the lamp. I sat down in one of the club chairs next to the window, so I could see to take notes.

"My name is Eubanks, Ms Abercrombie, and this is Mr. Faulkner. We interviewed the supervisor at the plant where you work, and he said that you knew Zoe Woods."

She cleared her throat and looked uncomfortably at the floor. "Well, we worked together on the line, if that's what'cha mean."

"I guess you know she's dead."

She nodded. "Yeah, I heard that."

"What can you tell us about Zoe?"

She took a deep breath and exhaled. "Well, there ain't much to tell, really. I guess you know she was kinda stupid. She made a lotta mistakes; like lettin' the chickens go by with feathers on 'em. I mean, we had a little thing going there. Tammy's pretty good, but Zoe, well, she was just slow, in more ways than one."

"So, the only thing you know about Zoe is what you saw of her at work?"

"Right."

"You know of any men that had the sweets for her? There at work, I mean."

She shook her head. "No, nobody at work there wanted Zoe, on account'a the fact that she wadn't none too bright. I never saw anybody hangin' around'er."

"You ever see anyone hangin' out with her away from work?"

"I told you, I never seen her away from work."

I wrote fast. Will's question went unanswered directly.

"When's the last time you saw her?"

She thought for a second. "I don't know. I guess it was the day before she got took off. We did our shift at the plant, then left."

"How did you hear what happened to her?"

"What, oh, ah, well, I guess Tammy told me."

"We heard that you and Zoe didn't get along."

"Oh, we got along alright. I just use'ta get put out with'er about her work. You know, we had a schedule, and she just slowed us down."

I took notes as fast as I could. Her Tidewater accent was unfamiliar to me, and I couldn't help smiling at her voice as she spoke.

Will asked her about The Society – she'd never been there; her social activities – bingo on the weekends, and a sometimes a little partying on Saturday night, but not in Mobile, and not with Zoe. He also asked how long she'd been in town.

"I've only been in town about a year. I come from Charlotte."

"What made you move down here?"

191

"Well, I had a little trouble up there a few years ago." She paused and looked away, then back at Will. "You guys can probably find out about it anyway, so I'll just tell ya. I done time."

"What for?"

"I stabbed my ex."

"What for?"

"I caught him cheatin' on me."

"But he was your 'ex'?"

"Yeah, well . . ."

"What was his name?"

"Mikey. Michael Tolliver."

"How much time did you do?"

"Three years, four months and thirty-six days."

"You and Mikey have any kids?"

She shook her head. "No."

"You ever see him?"

"I ain't seen him since I left Charlotte."

She blinked three times. It could have been a lie, but it could have been to hide tears. I let it slide.

"Your car's got a South Carolina tag on it."

"When I got outta prison, I spent some time down in Charleston. I wadn't there long."

Will looked over at me, and I shook my head. He looked back at Myrtice.

"All right, well then, the only thing left to ask is, where were you the Friday night when she was cut?"

She looked disgusted. "Playin' bingo up at the Masonic Lodge on Grand Bay-Wilmer Road, like ev'ry other Friday night. They got a sign-in book. You can check it out."

Will nodded at me, and I wrote. "Okay, well, we won't trouble you anymore."

We both rose and started toward the door. I looked around at Myrtice and spoke.

"Terrible about Zoe, huh? Guess she was just too slow."

She stared at me and said nothing.

192

"By the way, do you still love Mikey?"

"That son of a bitch?" After that assessment, she said nothing else.

In the car, I looked at Will. He had closed his eyes and was leaning back in the front seat basking in the warmth of the sun beaming in through the windshield.

"So, what do you think?" I said.

"I think she hates her ex-husband, and I think she didn't kill Zoe Woods."

"Well, I'll tell you what I'm thinking. I'm envisioning some jealousy thing going down here. I'm thinkin' this Mikey is the man we're looking for. And I'm thinkin' that Myrtice knows where he is and what he's done."

"That's sure a lotta thinkin', Son. First, if someone was jealous, why wasn't it Myrtice? She was a few years ago when she stabbed her old man. Second, she didn't kill Coo Coo, she's got an alibi, which, by the way, we need to check."

I paused. "Still, I think this Mikey's involved. And, hey, bingo was prob'ly over at midnight."

Back at the office, I took out a pad and pen and tried to make some sense of what I knew. Will was right. If the person who killed Zoe had jealousy as a motive, it would most likely be Myrtice, not Mikey; and she had an alibi. We'd stopped at the Masonic Hall on our way back to town to confirm it. All this was assuming somebody named 'Mikey' was involved. Zoe never called anyone by their right name.

Zoe Woods was dead. She was last seen with a black haired man who may or may not have been named 'Mikey.' They left The Society Lounge in what may or may not have been a red Nova. The next morning, she was found with her throat cut. This black haired man talked with a funny accent and drank Black Russians. That was all we knew for sure.

193

What we could speculate on was that a 'Mikey' had a relationship with a woman who lived here in Mobile; that the funny accent might very well have been mid-Atlantic or Tidewater; and that a man who had been stabbed with an edged weapon by a woman might be walking around nursing a healthy hatred for women in general.

I decided to narrow my search for the Nova to North Carolina. I also contacted their state police and ran a search for Michael Tolliver. With any luck he'd be in Carolina and we could lay hands on him if we needed him.

In the meantime, I decided to put a 'look out' on him with our department and the city police, just on the off chance that that he was in town, or coming through town. And, if we spread it around to the public that there was a reward out for information, hopefully we could get a bite. But nothing was going to happen in a hurry on this case.

Chapter 26

All the while, life went on. Simp Patridge pled not guilty at his arraignment after which the judge, who had some prior experience with him, appointed him an attorney – and not a very good one – from the local bar. My guess was that with all the legal problems that he had gone through, his mother and father were finally out of money.

After he got out of the hospital, the man that robbed the bank and took a shot at our car had been turned over the FBI for prosecution. He was indicted by the federal grand jury one week after he was arrested – they do things much quicker in the federal system, mostly because the case volume is considerably smaller.

The defendant, Alphonso Middleton, a small time punk who'd been arrested for bank robbery previously and had spent five years in the federal penitentiary for it, was treated for 37 gunshot wounds to his gluteus maximus. Fifteen of them were shotgun pellets. When he hobbled out of the hospital in a backless gown, the big dressing of gauze and cotton affixed to his buttocks made that part of his body appear three times its normal size. He looked like a baby that had just dumped a load in his Pampers.

I suspected that with his prior record, Middleton was institutionalized and wanted to be arrested. The shooting was just his insurance policy; an arrest in the federal system for a crime that involved a handgun or some type of violence would net him a few extra years in the joint.

The grits case was once again set over. The two parties had requested a jury trial in their divorce proceeding to determine the division of property, and I just happened to be in the courthouse that day. I met and talked with the private detective who was working for the husband at the time of the assault. MacArthur Penn was his name. He talked to me about the PI business.

"There's a certain amount of freedom associated with working for yourself," he said.

Penn was 6'2" and a muscular 190 pounds. He had brown hair and large bones, and he carried himself with an air of confidence and certainty.

"Is there enough business for a PI in this town?"

"Not really, no. The lawyers control most of it. When a client comes in and their attorney decides that they need an investigator, he takes the money that they would normally use for a PI and tells'em that he'll hire one. The lawyer tells'em that when a PI works for a client, that the information that he uncovers is not privileged, while if he works for the attorney, it is. That's all true, but unfortunately, some unscrupulous lawyers use that as a pretext to get all the money the client has."

"What about cases in which the court pays for an investigator?"

"Well, that's a bit trickier, for the lawyers, that is. It usually only happens in homicide defense cases that the court budgets for an investigator, and the attorney has to give a pretty strict accounting to the court on how he spends the money. But he somehow manages to keep what the investigator does to a minimum so he can keep some of the funds for the 'investigative' work that he does."

"So, how do you make it work?"

"Well, you have to get lucky. If you can hook up with a client on a sensational enough case – one that makes the news in some way and for some reason – you can begin to build a walk-in trade that circumvents the legal community. Usually, it's when a client is dissatisfied with the police. And, when someone comes to you, and they really want you, they can afford to pay – and pay pretty heavily."

I nodded. Private investigation was something that had crossed my mind for when I retired, or when the department had burnt me out so badly that I just couldn't stand to get up and come to work any longer.

Looking down at his business card, I studied the gold embossed printing. It certainly looked impressive.

"I've got an office over on Dauphin Street, in the entertainment district," he said smiling.

"Secretary?" I smiled too.

"Not yet."

"What kind of background do you have?"

"I was in Army intelligence; I spent time with the PD in homicide; and I was with the coroner, as an investigator, for four years."

"Sounds like you've been around."

"I've seen my share." He nodded and looked away wistfully leading me to believe that there was something behind his words.

196

"Well, I'll sure give it some thought," I said, knowing all along that I didn't have the faith in myself to go out on my own.

Chapter 27

The Fourth of July holiday rolled around, and that year it fell on the first Monday of the month. Both Will and I were off, but he was on call. I knew that if he got anything, he'd call me, so I hung around the house.

There's something about holidays that usually bring about the worst in people. Be it Christmas, Easter, Labor Day or whatever, when people get together on holidays, first the liquor flows and then the blood flows.

That's the way I had it figured when Will called me at about three o'clock that afternoon. He said we needed to get up to the Turnerville Airport and check on an accident.

Turnerville was more of a region than a town. Covering a ten or fifteen square mile area, it contained a volunteer fire department, a cemetery, a pretty nice park, and a few reasonably affluent homes. And, there was an airfield.

The Turnerville International Airport, derisively labeled so by the deputies that rode that area, and the more jealous residents of nearby Mt. Vernon, was actually a wide space in a pasture belonging to Vernon Duckworth, the unofficial mayor of Turnerville and one of the area's largest landowners. It was about six football fields long and a hundred yards wide, and sat on the north side of Duck Road, about three quarters of a mile south of Roberts Road, or County Road 63.

Duckworth always said that he built the airfield because it was meant to be. God wouldn't have opened up that perfect a piece of ground, he said, as flat as it was, unless He meant for planes to take off and land on it. Besides, if he didn't run the field, the drug dealers would just be using it anyway. This way, he could make money and keep out the riff raff besides.

The ground was as flat as a pancake and covered with a winter rye that Duckworth faithfully mowed and landscaped. He built what he called a control tower – actually an overgrown shooting house, the kind you'd find in the woods during deer season – on the south side of the field about halfway in between each end; and a metal hangar large enough to accommodate two single engine Cessnas. There was a two room, wooden office with a bathroom within twenty-five feet of the rear of the tower where Duckworth kept accounts, counseled drunken pilots, and took a nip himself when things were slow.

I picked Will up at the office, after which we motored north on Interstate 65 at a reasonable clip. Will said he wanted to get home in time to finish his bar-b-que. We made small talk until we turned off the interstate onto Celeste Road, about five miles from our destination.

"Do you know what happened up here?" I said.

"Not, really, no. But I understand it's ugly; something about a parachutist and a propeller."

When we turned off Duck Road onto the airport property, there were four county cars, an ambulance, and the coroner's wagon already there. I saw Roy Rogers standing near a plane that was sitting in the middle of the field. Vernon Duckworth was next to him. It was a beautiful day; blue skies, with only a few wispy cirrus clouds to the south.

The plane was unfamiliar to me. It had a wingspan of about seventy-five feet and was painted all white. There was a wide open door just aft of the starboard side wing; so that parachutists could load and exit as close to the pilot's compartment as possible. It looked as if it could hold fifteen passengers with chutes, but as I looked around, I could see only about twelve or thirteen guys who looked like they were there to take a dive, so to speak.

Vernon Duckworth was probably sixty-five. He was clean shaven, with silver white hair that formed a widow's peak just above his forehead. His face and arms were red from the sun, and he had a substantial beer belly. Will walked over to where Duckworth and Rogers were standing, and I made my way toward a sheet-enveloped lump almost directly under the plane's starboard engine. A deputy, whose name I could not call, and Angie McDowell were both standing next to what I presumed to be the body, taking notes.

"Detective," he said.

I nodded at him and then at McDowell. "Good to see you, Angie."

"Happy Fourth of July." She smiled broadly.

"And happy Fourth of July to you. I see the red and the white on the sheet, and I would suspect that this gentleman is pretty blue right now."

She chuckled. "Oh, please."

I looked around at the aircraft. "Either of you know what kinda plane this is?"

The deputy spoke up. "It's a deHavilland DHC-6-100. It's Canadian."

I nodded and knelt down. When I pulled back the blood-soaked sheet, I was surprised; surprised that what I saw was not as bad as I thought it was going to be.

The decedent was a male, white, with dark brown hair. He looked to be in his late teens or early twenties. His fair skin contrasted with his navy blue, short-sleeved shirt, dark blue nylon pants, and black boots. The freckles on his nose and a couple of pimples on his smooth face made him appear younger than what he really was, if that was possible. Someone had removed his parachute and tossed it about three feet away.

199

His injuries, at first glance, appeared to be minor. The hair on his head was matted with blood, but there were no other visible wounds. McDowell offered me gloves, and I took them.

When I pulled aside his hair, I could see that he had three or four long lacerations from front to back on the top of his scalp. They were deep and wide and looked almost as if someone had raked a trident over the top of his skull. The bone was visible but didn't appear to have been dented. If what I thought had happened did, then he no doubt had a pretty serious hematoma underneath, if not an outright skull fracture.

"You gotta name on this kid?" I said looking at the two at the same time.

"Tony Evans, 19, of Bay Minette," the deputy that I did not know said.

I nodded. "Is he blind?"

McDowell wrinkled her brow. "Not that we know of. Why would you say that?"

"Because it looks like he walked into the propeller."

I left the deputy and McDowell, who agreed to take custody of the parachute and have it looked at by a rigger from out at the Coast Guard base, and strode toward Will. Rogers was standing with his arms folded, watching Duckworth with an amused look on his face.

As I walked up, Will held out his hand and stopped Duckworth from speaking. The old man ceased in midsentence.

"Wait a minute," Will said. "Tell Detective Faulkner what you told us." Will turned to me. "You're not gonna believe this."

Duckworth smirked. "Well, like I was tellin' Mr. Rogers, these fellas here," he said motioning to a group of men standing near the hangar, "are the 'Bonzai Flyin' Club.' They're a skydivin' group from across the Bay. They come over here ever' so often for a mass jump."

"Why here?" Rogers said.

"'Cause my field is the largest and best kept." He looked at Rogers as if he should have known that already.

"Anyway, they formed a line on the left side of the plane so they could get in."

"How many were there?" I said.

"About ten or twelve, as many as are over there, now. Anyway," he looked disgusted at being interrupted again, "that dead boy over there was in the back of the line and apparently, he wanted to get to the front. If you go in first, you jump last. So, he walked to the head'a the line and tried to cut in." He paused, expecting a question. When none came, he continued. "When he got up there to the door, he just stepped in front of the lead guy. Well, they got into a shovin' match and the kid stumbled over into the prop." He shook his head. "It was kinda bad there for a minute."

I shook my head. "You saw the whole thing?"

"Yeah. I was lookin' right at 'em."

"Any idea what made him want to jump ahead like that?"

Duckworth shook his head. "The only thing I can figure is that he wanted to make the plane ride last longer. Gettin' in the back give him more time in the air."

I shook my head slowly. It was almost too much to believe. This kid was dead because he got out of kindergarten without learning that you don't cut in line.

Will and I both attended the autopsy of Tony Evans on Tuesday morning. He did, in fact, have a skull fracture. The cause of death was blunt force trauma and stupidity, the doctor said.

We made the decision to Grand Jury the case; however, I for one wasn't going to push hard for an indictment. We left the morgue in a hurry as Will had to get to the courthouse. It was right at lunch time.

I dropped him off at the west side entrance, across the street from the pool at the back side of the neighboring hotel. He said for me not to wait, to go on back to the office, that he'd catch a ride back out west with someone from Warrants.

Turning on Church Street, I made the block and then turned back west on Government from the head of the Bankhead Tunnel. There was a considerable amount of traffic on the road, it being lunch time, and I satisfied myself that it was going to take a while to get back to headquarters.

I got into the middle of the three westbound lanes – a mistake I knew better than to make – and we stopped for every light the six or seven blocks between the courthouse and Broad Street.

The Broad Street light always seemed to me to be interminable. There were turning lanes on Broad, long lines of traffic to empty out in two directions. Broad Street ran north and south, hooking up with the I-165 spur to the north and Interstate 10 to the south.

Traffic in all three west bound lanes was backed up for a block and a half on Government. I was about the fifth car from the light. The police radio was squawking and the AM/FM was playing on the all seventies station. Then I saw it.

A dingy red Nova, probably the only one in the whole city, drove through the intersection, on Broad, southbound. I looked hard to see who was behind the wheel, but the vehicle was moving too fast, and all I could make out was the head of what looked like a man. I turned down the AM/FM and picked up the police radio.

"SO 27."

'SO 27."

"See if there are any cars around Broad and Government."

"10-4. Any unit near Government and Broad acknowledge."

Traffic stood still as the Nova vanished. The Carpenters finished their song, and I looked around for ways to get out of the line of traffic. It was impossible, so I just

202

had to sit there and hope that the car had a flat or something.

"SO 27, no response."

"27, 10-4."

Well, at least I knew that our suspect, or someone in a car like his, was in town, and he had a reason to be around Broad Street. Either he lived in the area, was visiting, or he worked there.

When the light changed, I made it through the intersection and, as quickly as I could, got over into the left hand lane. I turned south on Marine Street, then made the block and got back on South Broad.

I rode the area for twenty or thirty minutes but saw no sign of the car. I picked up the radio microphone.

"SO 27."

"SO 27."

"Copy a short lookout?"

"Go ahead."

"Ask units in the downtown area to be on the lookout for a 1974 or 75 Chevrolet Nova; four door; faded red in color; possibly occupied by a white male. Any contact, hold and notify myself or SO 21; and give that to the PD, also."

The radio operator acknowledged, and I hung up the mic. With any luck, someone would run up on the car and at least get us a name.

Chapter 28

Three days later, on Friday the eighth of July, just for grins, Will and I decided to pay a visit to Zoe Woods's sister.

Neither of us expected to get anything from her, but, well, it was a base and it needed to be touched.

Laurie Woods-Tillman was a forty-two year old socialite who lived very proudly in the old moneyed neighborhood of Spring Hill. When I called her on the phone to set up the appointment, she allowed as to how her cardiologist husband would be home soon after taking the day off to make sure the engine of the family's boat had been serviced.

Spring Hill, located on a rise about ten miles west of downtown Mobile, sprang up in the 1820's shortly before the construction of Spring Hill College, the oldest Jesuit institution of higher learning in Alabama. It became a summer vacation destination for Mobilians; and, later, a point of refuge during the malaria epidemic that broke out in the city around the turn of the twentieth century. Various types of architecture lined narrow, oak-shaded streets that made up the approximately eight square mile community that was arguably the city's most desirable zip code.

We found Zoe's sister's home on Tuthill Lane, about half way between Old Shell Road and Spring Hill Avenue. It was a three story brick Federal with a Florida room off the south side. It was into that room that the Hispanic housekeeper ushered us and told us to wait, that someone would be with us shortly.

Three minutes later, a blonde woman with a slim build stepped through the screen door and paused to look us over. She wore a pastel print, midi length dress, baby blue heels, and a disgusted look. Her hair was short, kind of Jackie Kennedy-esque, and she had one of those flexible hair bands around it to hold her bangs out of her eyes.

"Good afternoon, gentlemen," she said.

She took a seat on a cushioned outdoor chair. Will and I sat on both ends of a matching couch. A clear glass coffee table sat between us. A vase of daisies with a dash of baby's breath sat right in the middle of the table.

"My name is Eubanks, ma'am. This is Mr. Faulkner. I think he called you earlier."

"Yes, yes, of course."

Her voice had a pronounced southern accent. Even if she was no longer a belle or a deb, she clearly continued to remind herself of what it was like to be one.

"We'd like to ask you a few questions about your sister, Zoe."

"Well, certainly, I'll do anything I can to help. But, honestly, she was nine years younger than I, and I really didn't know her that well."

"When's the last time you talked to her?"

"I believe it was last Christmas. To the best of my recollection, she was at Mother's and Daddy's on Christmas Day. She had that horrible man with her; the one that she lived with."

"You two didn't get along?"

"Well, it wasn't really that. He was just so, so . . ."

"Common?"

"Yes. That's a good word for him. Common."

"Did you speak to Zoe?"

"Well, only in passing. She and I were never close."

"Any particular reason for that?"

"I guess it was because of her mental state. I'm sure you know that she was retarded."

"We'd heard she was a little slow."

"A little slow? My baby sister couldn't conduct business. She was six before she spoke. She was ten before she could get dressed. She had to have special schooling just to get her where she was." She paused. "But you know the worst thing about her?"

Will raised his eyebrows.

"She never knew it. She never believed for a second that she had any limitations. She thought she could do anything; and the older she got, the more she believed that she was just as smart and as capable as anyone."

"That was a good thing, right?"

205

"For a normal child, yes. But for someone with her mental capacity, it was a disaster. She wandered off at the Plaza shopping center when she was ten and was lost for two hours. Once, on vacation in Orlando, she strayed out of the hotel and marched right into the Disney Park and spent the whole day. Mother was apoplectic when we couldn't find her. They called her name over the PA system, but she refused to answer. Security had to fight her to give her back to Mother and Daddy."

"Assertive, fearless?"

"Sure."

"What was her diagnosis?"

She took a deep breath and exhaled. "I don't know. Thirty-five years ago, they just called it mental retardation. Now, I think it's a learning disability, or something."

"No disease?"

"Oh, no."

"Tell me about when she left home."

She looked off, out the southside window. The slats were open and a breeze was blowing in through the screen. Then she looked at Will.

"Well, I wasn't there, but Mother told me that it was just heartbreaking. Zoe came in one day about five years ago and told her that she wanted to go live in Mobile with one of our cousins, that she was big enough. Mother tried to tell her that she shouldn't, that she couldn't, but that just made her mad. They argued about it, but Mother knew if she didn't let her, she'd just run off anyway, and she might never see her again. So . . ."

"How'd she hook up with this old man of hers?"

She raised her eyebrows and shrugged. "I don't know. When she left, Daddy contacted a lawyer and had him hire an investigator to follow her around and watch her for a few weeks. Daddy said he reported back that Zoe had moved into this apartment down off Michigan Avenue, and this Neal character had just kind of materialized one day. We never found out where he came from."

I cleared my throat and looked up from my notes. Will glanced my way.

"I understand Zoe had a goodly amount of money coming to her. Do you know anything about that?"

She looked at me suspiciously. It was funny how the subject of money could change the tone of an otherwise cordial conversation.

"She had the contents of a trust fund that had either come to her, or was coming to her in the future. I really don't know anything about it. Daddy can tell you all about that."

Will spoke. "You have any reason to believe that Albert Neal might be involved in hurting Zoe?"

"Well, I wouldn't be surprised, except for one thing. The only time I met him he appeared as if he was just as slow as she was. My heart tells me he could, but my mind tells me he wouldn't have the brains."

"Did Zoe ever mention The Society Lounge?"

"Once or twice. The last time I saw her I asked her what she was doing with herself. She said she was going to The Society. Mother told me that it was a bar down near where she lived. I guess that investigator told her that. Anyway, Zoe said that all her friends were there."

"She mention anyone in particular?"

"One woman; Gretel, or Gretta, or something."

"She ever mention any men?"

She shook her head. "Oh, no. Of course, I never talked to her in any depth, especially in the last few years." She paused. "You have to realize our family dynamics. Because of her condition, she always got all the attention. My brother and sister and I had to grow up taking care of ourselves." She took a deep breath and exhaled. "I suppose we resented her." She paused. "I'm not proud of that fact."

Will nodded. He looked at me.

I was pretty well convinced that while Laurie Woods-Tillman probably carried around a fair amount of jealousy for her sister, she probably didn't have her killed. In fact, it was my guess that she wanted to stay as far away from Zoe as possible. Spending time with her, even at family gatherings, had to have been very uncomfortable for everyone.

"Ms Tillman, do you have any knowledge of who killed your sister?"

She shook her head again. "None, whatsoever."

"Do you know of anyone who had anything to gain from her death?"

"Unless, it was that Neal character, no. He was the closest person to her. No telling what deals they had between them. Like I said, he was just as slow as she. I don't know how he could have talked her out of any of her money.

"Mister, Faulkner was it? Zoe's life was very uncomplicated. She was paid a monthly stipend from an attorney my father employs, and out of that she paid for her necessities and, I'm told, very little else."

I closed by asking about the private investigator who followed Zoe Woods around right after she left home. Laurie Tillman left the room and called her father, and afterwards she supplied us with the name of Erk Ressler. I knew Ressler. He was not the best PI in town, but he did have the biggest reputation.

We said our goodbyes to Laurie Tillman and rose. As we started for the door, I stopped, turned, and looked at her.

"I missed you at Zoe's funeral."

She looked back at me with hard eyes under raised brows. "I was otherwise engaged."

Erk Ressler's number was in my rolodex back at the office, so I called Denise Allenbach and had her get it. Will said let's talk to him if we could, and get it out of the way. It was four o'clock on a Friday. I knew where he'd be.

"Sure, fellas. Come on by. I'll be here 'til, oh, nine, at least," Ressler said over the phone.

We met at Crocker's, off the lobby of the Albright Building at Dauphin and Royal. It was a popular watering hole for lawyers and other professionals who worked downtown. On Friday nights they had a live band, and later in the evening the place would be packed. When we arrived, the crowd was sparse and things were quiet.

"Sit down, guys. Let me get'cha something."

Ressler had taken a booth in the back, and I could tell that he'd already had a couple. He was grinning broadly.

Erk, short for Erskine, had made his name in the city by taking every domestic peep job he could get for the first five years he was in business. He graduated up from following spouses to homicide defense after kissing up to just about every lawyer in town. Erk was an affable man who was clearly trying to live up to an image he had in his mind. He drove a Camaro, wore tweed sport coats with open necked shirts, and was not above telling a whopper to get what he wanted. He had a full head of blonde hair, a mustache, and a flat stomach.

"Nothing for us, we're still working," I said.

I knew Erk better than Will, having dealt with him on a couple of prowler calls back when I was a slick sleeve in a patrol car.

Erk took a swig from a beer and then exhaled loudly. He set the frosty mug on the table and took out a cigarette and lit it.

"Well, what can I do you guys for?"

I nodded toward Will. "You know my partner, Will Eubanks?"

He smiled and nodded. "Just by reputation. Erk Ressler. Nice to meet'cha." He stuck out his hand.

Will shook it. "Good to meet you, Buddy."

"We'd like to talk to you about Zoe Woods." I said. "That name ring a bell?"

He blew smoke into the air, furrowed his brow, and pursed his lips. "Refresh me."

209

"Young, retarded girl from Citronelle; daddy hired you to follow her around about four or five years ago; did I say retarded?"

The light came on and he nodded. "Oh, yeah, yeah. They were worried she'd get raped and killed, or somethin'. I watched her for a couple'a weeks, saw that she was gettin' settled, and told her daddy that it looked like she was gettin' along fine."

"Remember anything about where she went or who she saw?"

"What's this all about? She in trouble?"

"Not anymore. She's dead."

He looked genuinely surprised. "Get the fuck outta here. How?"

"Somebody killed her."

"Son of a bitch." He took a long drag on the cigarette and looked up. "Man, I don't know. That's been a while ago. I didn't keep too many notes. Her daddy just said, 'watch her,' and let him know."

"Anything you could tell us would be a help," I said. It was a lie, but it was something you said to get people to put their heart into it.

"Well, let me see. I remember I caught up to her at an apartment over off Michigan Avenue. I watched her a couple'a days, and a couple'a nights. She spent her days at home and her nights at some little dive around the corner. Man, that place was a dump. 'The Society,' I think it was called. The shitter was filthy; writin' all over the wall, sticky floor, you know the kind. I watched her for about a week then broke it off after she hooked up with some dude. That was all, really."

"Ever follow her inside the lounge?"

"Yeah, once. I stuck out like a sore thumb in there, so I made up some story about being a bar critic at one of these local artsy fartsy tabloids and left after about thirty minutes."

210

I had to hand it to him. I didn't know that I could have thought that fast.

"Any of the local color in there catch your eye?"

"You mean, any kooks hangin' around?"

"Yeah. Anybody else look like they didn't belong?"

He took another taste from the mug and shook his head. "You know, those people in there looked just exactly like who they were; a bunch'a folks looking to forget for a while that they had drawn the short straw."

"Do you know where she met her old man?"

"No, but he did go to the bar with her when she went, so I'm assuming it was there." He flicked the ashes off from the end of his cigarette into a clear glass tray on the table. "But, you know, I'd watch'em walk home, and they really looked like they belonged together. They'd hold hands, and they even looked each other in the eye a couple'a times; now, that's unusual for slow people. I know. I got a cousin that's a little off. He'll look anywhere but right at'cha."

"What made her daddy call it off?"

"I don't know. I think when I told him she had a man, he probably decided that at least somebody was lookin' out for her, and maybe she wouldn't get in trouble right away. So, after a couple'a weeks, he pulled the plug."

So far, we'd learned nothing. I looked over at Will.

"Buddy, you ever see anything of a red Chevy Nova around that neighborhood over there?" he said.

Ressler looked down at the table and fiddled with a diamond pinky ring on his left little finger. "Red Chevy Nova? No, not that I can remember. I may have written down some tag numbers, though. If you want, I'll check back."

"That'd be a help."

"I didn't give Woods a formal report, but I'm sure I took some notes."

"Did the name, 'Mike' or 'Mikey,' come up?"

He looked down again. "No. Hey, I didn't find out what her old man's name was until two weeks later." He

211

paused. "No, the only guy who was even halfway suspicious was a middle aged fella that sat over in the corner drinking the night I sat in with'em. He was a big thick dude with brown hair and a hooked nose. I think the waitress called him, 'Jerry' or 'Harry,' or somethin'. He didn't do nothin' but drink."

He was describing Jerry Painter. I looked at Will with a 'let's get outta here' look. He gave me one back.

"Well, Mr. Ressler, it was nice meetin' you. We better get gone. If you think of anything else, would you give Mr. Faulkner a call?"

"Sure," he said.

We rose, shook hands, and walked outside. In the car, Will spoke.

"Well, that was a complete waste'a time. That son of a bitch didn't know nothin'. No wonder Zoe's old man quit payin' him after two weeks."

"Oh, he's an okay sort. He doesn't really have to work, you know. He inherited quite a bit of money when his mama died. Now, he gets to run around and play Jim Rockford on somebody else's dime and have a beer at night to boot. I think he's got a pretty good life."

Will snorted. "Well, shit, Son. I'd have a good life too, if it didn't matter whether I solved a case or not. When you're freeloadin', life is good."

Chapter 29

The end of July rolled past and there was nothing new on the case. We had been unable to locate the red Chevy Nova moving about in Mobile, and thus had been unable to identify its driver.

At the same time, I'd also been unable to learn the whereabouts of Michael Tolliver. North Carolina had not provided us with a current address, and they'd been either unable or unwilling to forward me a mugshot. It seemed that Tolliver's criminal history consisted entirely of misdemeanor arrests and at most small departments in North Carolina a mugshot was not taken in cases of misdemeanors and violations. I did receive a copy of his driver's license photo, however. It was small, but I could see that it depicted Tolliver with light brown hair.

Had I a mugshot, I would have been an easy matter to put Tolliver's photo in a lineup and show it to a couple of people at The Society, namely Sis and Larry. They would probably be the only two that we could count on as having been sober enough on the night of the attack to either target him or eliminate him as a suspect. But with a different hair color than the one that they described, I was reticent to try a photo ID.

So, I was left with waiting for a lead to break. Robert Woods called the Sheriff every so often, and every so often the Sheriff called the Captain, who called either Will or me. It was certainly true that 'shit rolls downhill.'

One day, in the early part of August, Will and I were in the office discussing the case when the Department's Chaplain knocked on the frame of our open office door.

"You two tied up?" Arthur Wolfe said smiling.

"Not at all, Chaplain. Come on in," I said.

Wolfe, a rotund man with wavy brown hair, a big smile, and a collar, shook my hand, then Will's, and took a seat at the joint of our two desks. He was Episcopal by training, but he once told me that he had gotten 'saved' at the largest Baptist church in the city. Wolfe led a non-denominational fellowship on the west side of town, a congregation that had decidedly Protestant fundamentalist leanings.

Wolfe's daughter had drowned a few years back, an incident that had put him in close contact with the Sheriff's Flotilla for nearly three full days. In the midst of her death and his grief, he had gotten interested in the law enforcement community and was thereafter hired by the last Sheriff as a chaplain. He was paid a small stipend to be on call for retiree deaths, officer involved shootings, and some light counseling for staff that seemed to be hitting the bottle a little too hard. Will didn't think much of chaplains in general and this one in particular. He always said that he thought Wolfe was a spy for the Sheriff who came around every so often – especially close to Election Day – to find out who was sounding disloyal.

You see, Will believed in God, he just didn't believe that God was very concerned about what went on in his day to day life. His philosophy could most aptly be termed fatalistic; a product of over twenty years of looking at death and not being able to make any sense of why it occurred, when it occurred, or whom it victimized.

The Chaplain made it a point to stop by each of the detective offices once a month. Will usually made up some excuse to get up and leave. Today, he hung around.

"What brings you up our way, Preacher?" Will said.

"Oh, just my regular rounds. How's the exciting world of homicide and major crimes?"

"Not so exciting," I said. "You know, life is a grind; a slow and steady marathon, not a sprint."

"Well, I know that. There's nothing exciting about what you guys do, just depressing."

"I agree," I said.

"Is there anything I can do for you two?"

"Not unless you gotta a special prayer for a hot lead on the Zoe Woods case," I said.

"Zoe Woods?"

"She was a crazy girl that hooked up with an old boy at a bar and ended up gettin' her throat cut," Will said.

Wolfe made a face. "That's terrible. Any suspects?"

"A couple. If you happen to run across an old, red Nova, give us a call," I said.

"A Nova? One of those old Chevys?"

I nodded. "Yep."

He nodded also. "Okay. I sure will."

"What'chu think about this old gal, Preacher," Will said. "Everybody says she was retarded, and the Lord just let this old boy kill her."

"Will, you've been around a lot longer than I have, what do you think?"

"I think the Lord didn't really care. He just set things in motion a long time ago and what happened, happened." He paused. "You see it different?"

"A little. I think you're partly right. It's clear He didn't intervene to save the life of this woman. But I think you're wrong about God not caring. He cares. But in this case, from what you've told me, this woman was living her life a little on the dangerous side; hooking up at bars with men she didn't know. Chances are she wasn't a child of God, and if that was true, she may not have even called on God for help. God doesn't intrude into the lives of people who don't want Him, and those who don't respect His direction."

"Yeah, but she was retarded."

"That might make it a little harder to understand, however, God has a way of meeting each person on their own particular level. My belief is that God had spoken to her, somehow. If she had accepted Him – and she may have, I don't know – but then had disrespected His direction, she might have been at the mercy of the free will of the man she was with, and would therefore have to live with the consequences."

"So God cared, He just would'a cared more if she had cared back, is that it?"

"That's one way to put it. God will meet you more than halfway if you just express an interest in Him and His ways. But everybody has free will, even somebody that's

215

slow. That's one of the ways that God shows His love to mankind."

Will looked down at the floor and shook his head. "But still, you got to admit that she got a raw deal in life; tumor in her head, retardation, now murder. Why do bad things happen to 'all God's chillun'?"

It surprised me to hear Will so sympathetic to a woman for whom he had earlier expressed so much contempt. The Chaplain nodded and smiled.

"Oh, no doubt about it. But, first of all, she may not have been His child. Nowhere in Scripture, does it teach the fatherhood of God and the brotherhood of man. In fact, it says that the devil is the prince of this world. And, second, her retardation and murder are both results of original sin; the consequences of which I don't really think we've gotten to the bottom of yet."

He paused and looked back and forth at the two of us. "This Zoe no doubt made some wrong choices. It's sad, but it happens." He paused again. "But, what's important for you two is to repent of your sins and believe that Jesus is the Son of God who rose from the dead. Then your soul will be saved from hell and Father God can work for you, instead of Prince Satan working against you."

Will shifted in his chair and looked uncomfortable. Every time the Chaplain came in, he always ended our meetings with an altar call. I had made my peace, whatever that meant, with God a long time ago.

The Chaplain rose, gave us two free tickets for a church bar-b-que dinner, told us to call if we needed anything, and left. I cleared my throat.

"Well, you learn anything?" Will said.

I chuckled. "Yeah. I learned that Zoe was a kook, and we still don't have a real good lead on who killed her."

"Well, I agree with that, Son. But I still think that the Lord ain't really worried about what goes on down here ever'day."

216

I pursed my lips and shrugged. "Maybe, He is. Maybe she's in a better place now. Maybe He just took this opportunity to get her outta all this mess down here; to free her from her mental state."

Our musings were broken by Will's telephone. He lifted the receiver and took out a pen.

"Okay . . . okay . . . okay." He hung up.

I raised my brows.

"Two dead in Mount Vernon."

"How?"

"Drowned."

On the way, Will filled me in. Two females, thought to be patients at the local mental hospital, had been found, and were in the process of being recovered from Deer Lick Branch, a small creek just south of town. Apparently, the two had been missing for three or four days. Come to think of it, I had heard their names and descriptions over the police radio myself.

The tiny town of Mount Vernon, population about eight hundred, straddled US Highway 43 about five miles inside the county line on the north side. It was home to a state mental hospital, a grocery store, a couple of boat landings, and little else.

The institution, Stearns Hospital, was constructed as a military arsenal in the early 1800's. It was, of course, captured by the Confederates in the Civil War, but it reverted back to the US Army in 1865. It later became a military prison that housed, among other celebrities, Geronimo. The government deeded the land back to Alabama right before the turn of the twentieth century and it became what it is today, an eleven hundred bed mental hospital, with a special wing dedicated to females who are criminally insane.

I stopped the car in the parking lot at a Shell station on Highway 43, a few yards from Deer Lick Branch. Several vehicles, five or six four wheel drive pickups and a couple of fire trucks bearing markings identifying them as belonging to the Mount Vernon Volunteer Fire Department, were also parked in the lot. A knot of men with deadpan looks on their faces stood near a small boat landing. It was a beautiful day with just a slight breeze off the Mobile River, about three miles to the east.

Deer Lick Branch snaked its way from the River westward along the south side of town, under the four-lane, for about two miles, where it forked. It was no more than ten feet deep, but was said to be home to the largest catfish in the region. Some noodlers from Mississippi had even begun coming to the area to investigate the size of the fish and try their hands at catching them without the benefit of net or hook.

Will and I got out and walked across the gravel parking lot toward the knot. One of the men, the one who wore a red ball cap embossed with the word 'Chief' on the front, turned toward us and smiled.

"Snuffy, you old buzzard, how in the world are you?"

"Chief. I'm good." He nodded at me. "Do you know Mister Faulkner?"

The Chief, who had gray hair and a barrel chest pushed his glasses up on his nose and extended his hand to me. "Harold Martin. How ya doin'?"

I shook his hand. "Fine, Chief. I see ya got yourself a mess."

"Oh, just a little'un."

He looked back at Will. It was plain he wanted to deal with him. I took out my pad and began to write.

"I guess you heard about the two women that got over the wall at the hospital."

Will nodded. "Yeah."

"Well, we think these two are the birds that flew away."

"Who found'em?"

218

"A couple'a teenage boys paddlin' up the creek, goin' fishin'. They'll be coming out with the divers in a few minutes."

"You know anything about these gals?"

"Well, not much. The hospital said that they'd been committed, in two separate cases. One was from Birmingham and the other from Dothan."

"What were their crimes?"

"The people at the hospital wouldn't say; somethin' about patient privacy. I don't understand it. Seems to me, if you been committed for having done a crime, then it's ever'body's business. But I guess you boys'd know more about that than me."

It was true that a medical history was confidential. And in the case of these two women, if they'd merely been found incompetent to stand trial, then it meant that they hadn't actually been convicted of anything.

"Has anyone called the state lab?" The state lab is what Will called the Medical Examiner's office.

"They're here. They rode down in the boat to supervise the recovery. It's that nice lookin' young girl."

I was sure he was talking about Angie McDowell.

We stood under an oak tree and waited for ten minutes for the search and rescue personnel to make it back to the highway. Will and Harold Martin talked about people they knew and had known, and I got myself a Pepsi and some peanut butter M&Ms from inside the Shell.

As I walked back outside, into the bright sun light, I heard the sound of boat motors puttering up the creek from the west. I walked past Will and the Chief toward the landing.

When the vessels came into view, I could see that there were four. One, the one in the lead, carried two men and Angie McDowell. She was sitting in the middle wearing a life jacket.

The next two boats each carried one man and a large lump, a black body bag. The final boat carried two

219

young boys and one of the rescue personnel manning the small trolling motor. I thought about how it was a neat trick to get the two women, who had been in the water for who knows how long, into the body bags while in the boats.

The first small skiff came to a stop, and Angie stood up. The Chief extended his hand toward her, and she stepped gingerly onto shore. She was a carrying a metal clip board under her arm and a sour look on her face.

"You look like you just ate a lemon," I said as she walked up the ramp and turned around. "What happened, you get sick?"

She shook her head disgustedly. "No. I think it was the smell of that gasoline, or burning oil, or something. It nauseated me."

I unbuckled the side strap of her PFD and helped it over her head. She took two steps toward her car then bolted for the tree line to the west, and in a second was vomiting silently. I walked toward her, but she saw me and motioned with her hand to stay away. I had intended only to hold back her hair; that's what women seem to need and want the most at a time like that.

Turning back toward the ramp, I could see that the divers were lifting both of the body bags out of the boats and laying them on the concrete. I pulled out a pair of gloves and knelt down next to the one closest to the water. Will and the Chief walked over and stood just behind my shoulder.

When I unzipped the bag, I was not shocked by the bloating, only by the amount of animal corruption to the face. I had never seen a body in the water for that short a period of time, have that much maltreatment; though I shouldn't have been surprised. This part of the county was well known for its fishing. Still and all, right then, I made up my mind never to eat catfish again.

The woman looked to be about thirty. She was heavy set and had what was once a very dark complexion before it started turning green from the body gases. She was wearing a white t-shirt, a white brassiere, and jeans, but no shoes. Her long finger and toe nails were painted a bright pink. Nail art is one of the privileges that are allowed in prison, even crazy jail – that is if the patients demonstrate that they won't eat or drink the polish, or use their long nails as a weapon.

I looked specifically for something that could have once been a bullet hole or some other type of intrusion. The trouble with that idea was that a fish or some other type of animal would generally go right for a ready-made hole in a person's body first, and often these holes were unrecognizable as pre-mortem wounds.

Looking around at the group above me, I found Will's eyes. "Seen enough," I said.

"Yeah. Take a look at the other one."

I swiveled on my haunches and unzipped the other bag. The woman inside was black also, however she was of a lighter complexion, closer to chocolate, and had shorter hair. She wore a light blue, button up shirt and jeans. She had one cross trainer shoe on her right foot, but the other was bare. She too had nail polish on her fingers and toes, but the color was a dark crimson.

The mutilation of the second woman was not quite as extensive as the first. I looked at her face and open mouth and saw that her lips, surrounding the two gold teeth in her upper bridge, were still intact. I lifted her right arm and looked at it. The skin slipped off and stuck to my hand. I shook it off and laid the arm back down.

"Do we have an ID on these women yet?" I said.

Angie McDowell, having recovered from whatever it was that made her ill, had returned to the group and was writing. She spoke up.

"The hospital has fingerprints. If these are the two from there, we'll have them identified by this afternoon."

"If not?"

"If not, well . . ."

221

I stood up and looked at Will. He had said nothing. I could tell that he was thoroughly disinterested in the case, and I couldn't blame him. Apparently, a couple of crazies trying to get away from the only place that would have them tried to cross the creek and either thought they could swim and couldn't, or thought the creek was more shallow than it was.

Really, it was surprising to me to find them dead in this muddy branch. A black detective once told me that an African-American wouldn't get into any water that he or she couldn't see the bottom of.

Looking away, my eyes fell on Willie Anderson. Anderson was the only investigator at the Mount Vernon Police Department. The deaths were about a quarter mile outside the city limits, but I was glad he was there. He would know something about the escapees and would have contacts at the hospital.

"Willie. Good to see ya." I walked toward him and shook his hand.

Willie was a young man of medium height and proportionate weight. In my mind, at least, he bore an uncanny resemblance to Richard Roundtree. He was a good investigator, but was clearly not so much at home amongst all these older, white men.

"Hey, man. Good to see you, too."

I walked over and stood next to him and nodded toward the body bags.

"Did you get a look at those two females over there?"

He nodded. "From a distance." He shook his head. "I don't like dead bodies."

"Me, neither. Did you take the initial report from the hospital? You think they're the two from up there?"

"Looks like'em. The one with the teeth looks like Wilhelmina Atkins. The other, the heavy set, dark-skinned one, I think she's LaTonya Watson."

"You know what they were in for?"

222

"Watson tried to burn her house down with her two children in it, up in Birmingham; not guilty by reason of insanity. Atkins, cut off her old man's thing, and then tried to kill herself. She wasn't prosecuted, but she was committed."

I chuckled and shook my head. "Man, what a couple'a winners. Do they know how they got out?"

"They think they used a ladder to get over the brick wall. Watson was in a secure room, but she had a trusty's job. Atkins had a little more freedom. They'd both been there for a while and were medicated. That may have been why they couldn't make the swim."

He could be right. I could see Atkins doing something suicidal like jumping into a creek when she couldn't swim. Watson, who was crazy, would be easily suggestible and therefore likely follow without question.

"They got any family around here?"

He shook his head. "No. But I've got numbers. You want me to call?"

"If you would. The only thing I wanna know is if they could swim."

My attention was captured by Will's waving arm. I walked over to where he was talking to one of the teenaged boys.

"Listen to this," Will said as he leaned over and spoke in a low tone. He had heard it all once, but he wanted me to hear it so I could write the report.

"Tell this deputy your name, son," Will said.

The boy looked sixteen, with sandy hair and a fat face. He had a stocky build and wore jeans and a 'ZZ Top' t-shirt.

"Danny Masterson."

"Tell him what you boys was doin'."

The boy cleared his throat, swallowed and shifted his weight. He was clearly unnerved.

"Well, me and Terry was gonna go fishin' up at the fork. We put in here at the ramp and started paddlin' that

223

way." He paused and swallowed again. "We was windin'
down the creek and just paddlin' by, when I looked up and
saw a body hangin' on a limb about half way out of the
water."

"What did you do?" I said.

"Nothin'. I looked over at Terry, and he looked
back at me, and we just kept on paddlin'."

"You say anything to Terry?"

He shook his head. "I, I wasn't sure I saw what I
thought I saw, you know?"

"You didn't want him to think you were crazy?"

"Well, yeah, I guess. Anyway, we kept on paddlin',
and we went around another bend in the creek and, well, I
saw another body laid part way up the creek bank. This one
was hung up by her shirt. She was more in the water than
out."

"Did you say anything to Terry?"

He shook his head. "No. I just looked at him. He
looked really, really, kinda surprised, you know? We just kept
on paddlin' around the bend. Finally, I just couldn't stand it
no more, and I says, 'Hey, did you see what I saw?'"

"What did he say?"

"He didn't say nothin'. He just nodded. His eyes got
real big, you know?"

"Then, I says, 'You see that other one, too?' And he
just nods again."

I bowed my head to keep from laughing. "Then
what?"

"Then we just turned around and paddled back by
'em, to the ramp, and got out; and I run inside and called the
law."

"Okay, son." Will said. "I think that's enough for
now. Tell Terry we'll talk to him in a few minutes."

The boy walked away with the same sheepish
manner that he had when I met him. I looked at Will and
chuckled.

"Can you imagine them two out on that creek?" he said chuckling. "One says, 'Holy shit, did I just see what I thought I saw?' All the while the other one was thinkin' the very same thing. I can just picture their popeyes lookin' at each other."

I shook my head and walked back toward the bodies.

Willie Anderson called the next day and confirmed the identities of the two women. He also said that he had made contact with their families and that, as far as they knew, neither of the women could swim. When the preliminary autopsy report came back with drowning as the cause, Will and I called the deaths accidents and officially closed the cases.

We never did figure out how the two mental patients wound up hanging on the side of Deer Lick Branch, but for several years thereafter, whenever I thought of the two teenaged boys looking at each other, wide eyed, and finally asking each other, 'Did you see what I saw?' I had a good laugh at their expense.

Chapter 30

The month of August turned out to be an especially violent one in Mobile County. The first six months of the year had been relatively quiet, so it appeared as if the population was trying to catch up.

It started on a Friday night in the first weekend. About two AM, I received a call to meet Neely and Zane at

Springdale Hospital. They had been called to check out the shooting death of a teenager on his way home from the midnight movies.

The Hartwell, a fifteen screen multiplex located on Blue Star Parkway near the city limits, had been the scene of a number of shootings and a couple of robberies in the past five years. It was famous for its dollar nights on Fridays in the summer and the choices of aggressive films that it previewed. Rambunctious teenagers, some from the inner city, often ventured west to catch a movie and cause trouble.

I arrived at the emergency room at about two twenty in response to a page from the on-call detective supervisor, Blake Houston. Houston told me that he was still trying to locate additional help, notably, Alvin 'Bootsie' Warren, a notoriously heavy sleeper that supervisors had been unable to arouse on several other callout attempts in the past. There was no doubt in my mind that Warren, who was close to retirement, either turned off his phone or deliberately ignored the calls.

In the ER parking lot, next to a small pickup truck, Neely filled me in. He told me that Zane had gone to Theodore in an attempt to locate a crime scene.

"It looks like the victim, a fifteen year old kid, was on his way home from the midnight movie with a couple of his buddies. The dead kid was riding in the middle of the cab of that pickup over there." He nodded toward a Toyota.

"When they passed through Theodore, they got to the Bellingrath Road intersection, and the boy driving the truck says that he heard glass breaking over his right shoulder; and then he sees the dead kid fall forward. He gets a quarter of a mile down the highway and pulls over, and that's when he saw the blood, and he thinks that the boy's been shot in the back of the head.

"Well, he loses it and starts makin' it for the hospital. The boy in the middle was dead when they got here."

"They see anyone?"

226

"Nobody."

"Did they have to stop for the light at Bellingrath?"

"Nope. It was green. They drove right on through."

"Any reason to believe that it had anything to do with the movie theatre?"

"Not that we know of. I called the city police. They said there were no calls from the theatre tonight, and the boys say nothin' happened up there."

"Is the doctor sure he's been shot?"

"He says, yes. There's a small hole about three inches above the top of his spine, and the x-rays confirm a bullet inside."

"And the two boys with him aren't suspects?"

He shook his head. "I don't think so. One of'em is ballin' his eyes out, and the other had to be sedated. He's passed out on a gurney in the ER." He paused. "I checked the truck for a gun and couldn't find one. And there's a hole in the rear window glass that looks like it was made from outside. Rogers is on the way to make pictures."

I nodded. Will had not been called because he was out of town for the weekend. Neely and Zane would run things until the Lieutenant arrived.

"Okay. What do you want me to do?" I said.

Neely took a deep breath. He was an experienced detective, but this was a sure fire 'whodunit.'

"I need you to go down to Theodore and get up with Lonnie. See if you can find out where our suspect was when he shot at the truck. It coulda' been a roof, a balcony, the north side'a the road, the south side, anywhere. Just look around and see if you can get me something. When the sun comes up, we'll get together for a debriefing at the substation."

"Okay. I'm on my way."

In ten minutes, I was parking my car at the corner of Blue Star Parkway and Bellingrath Road. Except for an occasional eighteen wheeler, the street was deserted.

227

The 'downtown' portion of Theodore, Alabama, was two or three convenience stores, a couple of fast food joints, one bank, and one used car dealer; businesses that lined both sides of the highway. The town was just a crossroads near where the Parkway bisected Interstate 10 as they both ran north and south before turning west and bearing down on the Mississippi Gulf Coast.

Just to the south, was the black section of Theodore. Don't get me wrong, African-Americans lived anywhere they wanted, however most seemed to congregate on both sides of Bellingrath Road, a half mile south of the Parkway, in an area that people of both races called 'The Plantation.' The homes were old, the roads were just barely paved, and the drainage was inadequate; nevertheless, the families had hung onto their properties there for generations.

At the intersection, a hardware store sat on the northeast corner, woods on the southeast, a convenience store and motel on the northwest, and a broken down 'serve yourself' car wash on the southwest corner.

I parked in front of the motel office. There were two other cars visible – an old red Pontiac in front of room six, and a tan GMC pickup in front of what looked like room 20. I walked toward the highway, my head swiveling back and forth looking for Zane.

He was on the east side of the four-lane walking back and forth along the parking lot in front of the hardware store. His flashlight was trained on the ground, and his head was down.

My flashing light got his attention, and he looked up. Then he yelled across the road for me to check my side of the street.

That was fine with me. If the boys' truck was traveling south, they'd be on the right or west side of the highway. If they were in the far right lane, any shooter on that side of the road would be almost directly behind them as they went by. If the shooter was on the other side of the

228

street, he'd be shooting at the boys from a pretty severe angle, across three lanes of traffic. He would have most likely hit the boy in the driver's seat, not the one in the middle. Wherever he was standing, it was a devil of a good shot – the kind only a drunk could make.

I began to walk back and forth over the parking lot in long strips, starting at the corner next to the convenience store, and walking all the way to the end of the motel parking lot, about a hundred yards to the north. It was dark, but there were streetlights, and I had a flashlight, so, while I might miss something very small, I thought I could see anything as large as a shell casing.

Zane and I worked our respective sides for about thirty minutes. There was no obvious crime scene to be found. The night was hot, and very humid, and I was getting dehydrated. I felt the sweat begin to seep through my shirt in back. I stopped and looked all around.

It was obvious that there were going to be few or no eye witnesses to the shooting. There were just not that many people moving about at that time of the morning. Finding someone who had any knowledge of the crime was going to take resourcefulness and more than a little luck.

I waved at Zane across the street. He walked toward me while continuing to shine his light at the ground. When he arrived on my side of the street, I spoke.

"See anything?"

"Nope. You?"

I shook my head. "Nothing."

Zane looked around. "We'll get Rogers or his people out here to look the place over as soon as it gets light."

"How you guys wanna handle it?"

He looked in all four directions. "I think we've got to canvass the area just as soon as it gets five. I wouldn't want to bang on any doors until then."

I looked all around. There was one apartment complex directly to the west. And there were the two

229

vehicles in the parking lot of the motel; not to mention the motel clerk in the office. Other than that, there didn't seem to be too many places to canvass.

The complex had two buildings with a direct line of sight onto the intersection. And from what I could tell, the windows and doors of the motel were also within eyeshot of the highway. I took a deep breath and let it out. At least there was some place to start.

My cogitations were disturbed by the lights of a departmental SUV coming to a stop on the gravel of the motel parking lot. Hernandez extinguished the engine and then exited the driver's door. He stopped, stretched, and let out a long yawn. Zane and I walked toward him.

"Hey, what's up?" the affable Hispanic said.

Zane seemed disgusted. "Roy not comin'?"

"He'll be here shortly. He's gonna stop by the hospital first. He said to come and get the photography started."

"Fill him in," Zane said to me.

I motioned toward the highway. "Come on, I'll show you what we've got." We walked out to the edge of the highway.

"Apparently," I said, "three boys were traveling south on the Parkway in a pickup truck. At some point, and we don't know exactly where, as they were driving by they were shot at by an assailant standing, we think, on the side of the road. The victim slumped over when they were about a quarter of mile down the road, so the shooting could have happened anywhere from here in front of the motel, to just on the other side of the intersection.

"I've seen the truck, and it looks as if the flight of the bullet was from almost directly behind." I paused again. "Now, directly behind would be out in the street. So, as close to that as possible would be on this, the west side of the road."

Hernandez nodded.

230

"So, start from about here, in front of the motel, and work your way south, on both sides of the highway. Just get all angles. Then, when Roy gets here, you both go over the ground pretty good. We've looked, but we can't see anything."

Hernandez nodded again and started to walk back toward his vehicle. I held out my arm.

"Oh, and one more thing. When you finish, walk back to the apartments back here and get some shots from ground level back this direction. Get as wide a perspective as you can."

"Right."

As he began to reach into his truck, Zane walked up. He held up his radio.

"Scott and the Lieutenant want to have a meeting at office in ten minutes."

"Let's go."

In fifteen minutes, I parked in front of the Sheriff's Department's Theodore substation on the Blue Star Parkway, about two miles north of the crime scene.

The building was a single story, brick, converted office, that had been modified to accommodate a handful of desks and chairs in a great room. There were also a couple of offices, an interrogation room, and a small kitchen. It was just a place to bring suspects, witnesses, and victims so as not to have to cart them all the way to Headquarters back in the city.

When I walked in the unlocked front door, I found Neely and Zane seated with Houston in a semicircle. I pulled up a chair and joined them. They had coffee, I did not.

"Hey, Henry. Come on in. Scotty was just saying that he finally got the other two boys in the car calmed down, and they said they thought they saw a tall, thin, black male standing on the side of the road when they drove by."

Houston was fifty and thin. He had delicate features and wore glasses over his hazel eyes. His black hair had tinges of gray in it, and his oxford shirt and penny loafers gave him the appearance of an accountant or a businessman rather than a law enforcement officer. He looked tiredly at Neely.

"Okay, what's your game plan?"

Neely looked down at his notebook. "Well, we don't really have anything to go on. When the sun comes up, everybody put the word out with your informants."

Neely came from Burglary where informants were knowledgeable and helpful. Zane had worked in Narcotics, but many years ago. His contacts would be no good. I'd found that informants were not that common in homicide cases.

I spoke up. "Have you ruled out the two boys completely?"

"Yes. Judging from the damage, the shots had to come from outside the truck. I suppose one of them could have been riding in the bed, but from the way the two of them are acting, they don't strike me as having just committed murder."

"Do we know anything about the victim?"

"Just a kid, fifteen; went to a private school up in west Mobile, played football."

"No enemies?"

"None we know of." He shrugged. "How many enemies can you make in the tenth grade?"

Even if he had enemies, the chances that they would be capable of murder, and be capable of pulling off the shot like this, were slim.

"Right now, things look pretty random, to me."

"So," Houston said, "what we've got so far is somebody standing on the side of the highway, randomly shooting at a truck as it goes by, hitting a kid in the back of the head, and killing him."

Neely chuckled. "That's about the size of it."

Houston looked at Zane. "You got anything to add?"

It was plain from the look on Zane's face that he did not want to be there. "No. I think that's about it."

I looked at my watch and pointed to it. "It'll be sunrise soon. We better get down to the apartments if we're gonna catch everybody before they get out and gone on Saturday morning."

"I'll take the motel," Zane said.

"Well, that leaves the apartments to me," I said.

"I'm gonna stop and talk to Rogers, but I'll catch up to you later," Neely said to me.

"Let's go."

In fifteen minutes, after a short stop for coffee at the Waffle Hut, I was driving quietly, or as quietly as an automobile can, into the west side parking lot of the Peterson Oaks Apartments, located at the corner of Blue Star Parkway and Plantation Road.

The complex, a collection of fifteen buildings laid out in five groups of three, was a Section 8 project operated by a local property management company. The buildings were wood framed with tan siding and had seen better days. The parking lot was dirty and trashy, the courtyard's grass had long since been worn away into sand, and the sidewalks were cracked. If it had been located in the city, it would have been called a slum. We'd had quite a bit of trouble out of the residents over the years. I myself had worked on two homicides there. As it was, I wasn't so sure that our shooter might just answer one of the doors upon which I was about to knock.

When I got out of the car, a blast of hot humid air hit me and immediately began to dampen the shirt that had just dried while inside the office, and under the air conditioner inside the car. I stopped and looked all four directions paying special attention to the windows that were in view.

Since only two of the buildings, numbers 13 and 14, had clear lines of sight to the highway, I decided to start there. The rear windows, presumably the bedroom windows of the units, and the balconies and patios both faced the roadway through a space in between the motel office and the convenience store. I walked that direction and was accompanied by a mangy dog that sniffed my butt and then followed slowly behind me.

The bottom floor apartments yielded nothing. There was no answer at two of them, and in four others sleepy residents shielded their eyes from the harsh light of my flashlight and said that they had neither seen nor heard anything. I couldn't tell if they were lying or not.

Upstairs, it was different story. In the far corner, at 13C, a man answered. He was about five ten, medium build, wearing blue undershorts and a t-shirt. He had a medium length Afro, a close-cropped mustache, and a surprisingly alert face for five in the morning.

"Yes, sir. My name is Faulkner, and I'm with the Metro Sheriff's Office." I showed him my badge.

"Come on in. I don't want the neighbors to see me talking to you."

I stepped inside a clean but sparingly furnished living space. A brown recliner sat within five feet of a large screen television at one end of the room. There was only one other chair, one of those white, plastic outdoor pieces that you get at a discount department store. He motioned to that chair, and I sat down. He took his place in the recliner in front of the muted television set.

"I got insomnia. I hadn't got more'n two hours sleep in the past month."

His voice was not the common ebonic slang of the neighborhood. It was more precise, more polished. He sounded as if he was from the Midwest.

"I'm sorry to hear that. You know what's causing it?"

He shook his head. "No. I'm scheduled for the clinic up at Springdale Hospital next week. It'll be none too soon."

I nodded as a silent segway. "What is your name, sir?"

"William Raspberry."

"Mr. Raspberry, you may or may not know, but we had a homicide a couple of hours ago, out on the Parkway."

I knew by the look on his face that he knew something had happened, and I knew that he had seen something. I also knew that he intended to tell me what it was otherwise he wouldn't have asked me in.

"Did you see or hear anything between the hours of twelve and three this morning?"

"You mean anything, 'unusual'?"

"Well, not necessarily. What may have appeared usual to you might be quite important to me. So, I always ask, 'did you see anything at all?'"

"Well, I think it's unusual, but you can be the judge. About two this morning, I was out on the balcony smoking a cigarette." He nodded. "I know, I know, they're bad for me, but I use'em to try to relax."

He paused, as if expecting a reaction out of me. I gave him none.

"Anyway, I hear this pop, like a fire cracker and then a few seconds later I see this boy come runnin' across the parkin' lot, between the motel and the store."

"About two you say?"

"Yeah. He was a black kid; tall and thin, wearin' jeans and a t-shirt."

"What kind'a shoes?" Always look at a suspect's shoes was an admonition from an older more experienced partner from my past.

"All I know is white; just a bright white. I assume they were some type of 'tennis'," he said using the 1970's inner city vernacular for basketball or other athletic shoes.

"Anything else?"

"Yeah, one other thing. He was carrying a gun in his hand."

The words caught me off guard. "Really."

235

He nodded. "I don't know guns, but it was blue or black."

"It was a handgun, right? It wasn't a long gun."

"No. It wasn't a long gun. I do know that much about'em."

"Did you see where he ran?"

"No. He just ran toward this building, then veered off to his left and went between these two buildings." He gesticulated that direction.

"Did he see you?"

"I don't think so. He was running pretty fast, and I remember he stumbled and almost fell on his face, but he caught his balance and kept on running."

"Was he alone?"

"There was nobody running with him. If there was somebody with him out on the highway, he probably ran another direction."

"Do you remember seeing any other cars or trucks around or going by on the highway?"

He looked up at the ceiling as if thinking. I knew he had not, that his sight had been riveted on the running man.

He shook his head. "No."

It was time for the money question. "Have you ever seen the guy before?"

He nodded affirmatively.

"What is his name?"

"That, I don't know."

I ended our conversation by gathering pertinent information about Raspberry and by finding out whether or not he would be able to identify the suspect from a photo lineup. He assured me that there was no doubt in his mind that he could. When I left, I thanked him for his willingness to assist, all the while believing that he had been much too confident in his ability to identify the shooter. Most witnesses tend to equivocate and are more hesitant. The more I thought about it, the more I was sure: William Raspberry knew the shooter – or, at the very least, his name.

I checked the last four apartments in those two buildings with negative results. The sun was up now, and I found Neely walking from Building 2 to Building 3. He had hit almost all the complex with no results. I filled him in on Raspberry's story. He was elated.

"You think he knows the boy's name?" he said.

"I think he does. He was much too sure he could identify him from a photo. I think maybe he's a little afraid."

"Okay, if we need to, we'll lean on him some. Zane can finish up here. The boss just called and said there's a witness at the office with some information. Follow me up there."

In ten minutes, we were back at the office. Houston directed us to the interrogation room where we found a woman seated alone. She was looking nervously from side to side when we walked in.

Clattie Knox was about sixty. Her dark hair was streaked with gray, and she looked as if she was of mixed heritage. A mole rested on her smooth right cheek, and her lips were painted a bright red. She wore a print dress; black, patent leather low heel shoes; and she carried a matching patent leather purse. She was dressed up as far as she was, either for coming or going.

"Ms Knox, my name is Neely, and this is Henry Faulkner. I understand you have some information about a case." We took seats across the table from her.

"I sho do." Her speech was strictly country.

"What can you tell us?"

"Well, dis mawnin' I was comin' home from da boats, and I was stopped up at da light at Bellingraf Road, uhm, hum. All I seen was dis boy standin' on da side of da road wid a gun in his han'."

The 'boats' were the gambling casinos that lined the coast of Mississippi some fifty miles to the west. By statute, they could not locate in the state. They could, however, float in six feet of water ten feet from shore and be quite legal. Consequently, it was not uncommon for older people from

Alabama, where gambling was limited to bingo, to spend all night feeding their social security checks into the slot machines on, 'the boats.'

"What did this boy look like?"

"He was tall and skinny, and he were wearin' jeans and a white shut."

"And what was the boy doing?"

"He was jus' standin' dere wid dat gun in his han'."

"Did you see anyone else around?"

"No, suh."

"Did you see any other cars?"

"No, suh. Da road was quiet."

I couldn't wait any longer. "Ms Knox, what was the boy's name?"

Neely shot a look at me; a look that said that he believed that the question was premature or had no chance of being answered.

"I 'on't know his name." She paused. "But I know his mama."

"What is his mama's name?"

"Althea Washington. I thank her boy's name, it might be, I thank it's Ricardo."

"Ricardo Washington?"

"Um, hmm. I thank so."

I nodded. Neely looked shocked. I knew that if he was from her neighborhood Clattie Knox would know who he was. Black folks have a very close knit community, an almost communal attitude. It's a practice that dates from slavery and later during the 'Movement.' They thought by knowing everyone in the community they could somehow ensure each other's safety.

Excusing myself, I stepped out and called Roy Rogers on the police radio. He told me he was just finishing up the scene work on the Parkway. I gave him the ID on the shooter and told him to get a photo line up together, ostensibly to show William Raspberry.

238

Back in the interrogation room, Neely was just finishing firming up the ID from Clattie Knox. He had gathered contact information and was filling her in on why her information was so important.

"How well do you know Ricardo, Ms Knox?" Neely said.

"Not too good. I know he been in some trouble." She paused. "What'chu thank he done?"

"He may have shot someone this morning; some boys in a truck just ridin' down the road."

Clattie Knox put her hand over her mouth in shock. I couldn't tell if she was surprised or was just acting that way to impress us.

"Do you think he's capable of it?" I said.

She looked at me as if a war was going on in her mind. On the one hand, she didn't want to believe the worst about her friend's son. But on the other, her sense of morality told her that from what she knew of him, he very well could have done what we said.

"I 'on know." She shook her head.

Neely looked at me. I didn't know what was in his head, but I thought he might be finished. I decided to wrap it up, at least from my point of view.

"By the way, Ms Knox, how'd you do at the boats?"

Chapter 31

Two hours later, Neely was working on an affidavit to go with the warrant for the arrest of Ricardo Washington, and I was composing the narrative that would accompany a search warrant for wherever it was that Washington lived.

Zane had shown William Raspberry a photo lineup containing photos of six similar appearing males, one of whom – number 4 – was Ricardo Washington. He had also located one more witness that could put Washington in the area shortly before the shooting, a fact that I regarded as more than circumstantial considering the time of the day we were talking about. All that was left was to locate Ricardo, find the gun, and see if we couldn't extract a confession from him.

We had all been up since early in the morning, and I for one was exhausted. That's why when the Lieutenant called I wasn't overjoyed to hear his next directive.

"Channel Six will be here in about thirty minutes. Greg Wilcott is out of town, Neely's tied up, and Zane . . . well Lonnie just doesn't belong in front of a camera, so the Sheriff wants you to hold a press briefing," Houston said.

Gregory Wilcott was a former disc jockey that the Sheriff had plucked out of commercial radio to handle press relations for his last campaign. After the Sheriff's fifteen point victory, Wilcott was rewarded with a high-paying job as the department's Public Information Officer. When he was around, he talked to the media. When he was not, it was catch as catch can.

I cleared my throat. "Channel 6, huh. I look terrible, and I feel worse." I pause. "Who is it?"

"Dorothy Wallace, I think. That's who was on the phone."

"Oh," I said. Wallace was an attractive blonde; an up and comer around the city, obviously destined for larger markets.

"Just give her the basics; nothing that'll spook old Ricardo. If he knows we're lookin' for him, he's sure to bug out."

I hated to tell the Lieutenant but Ricardo knew we were looking for him since before Clattie Knox came into the office. My guess is that Knox had called the boy's mother just as soon as she could after she saw him standing on the side of the road with a gun.

His mama had probably told Knox to let her conscience be her guide, which meant that Washington's mother was fed up with him. She would never sanction handing him over to the police, but she understood that what he had done was wrong and that, on this one at least, she wouldn't feel right about protecting him.

"I'll take care of it. Maybe I can get this Wallace woman's number," I said ever on the lookout for love.

"One can only hope."

Twenty minutes later, after a cup of coffee, a quick shave, and a sharecropper's bath in the bathroom at the end of the hall, there was a knock on the office door. I answered and found the Channel 6 news crew standing there; Dorothy Wallace smiling broadly, her overweight cameraman behind her with a deadpan look on his face.

"Are you Detective Faulkner?" the woman said.

She was a slim woman who truly was, as they say, 'dressed for the cameras' in a short-sleeved white blouse, navy miniskirt, and blue pumps. Her apple cheeked face sat under a head of pixie cut blonde hair, and her face was covered with a thick pancake.

"I am. Come on in."

I ushered them into the best office in the building, the one the Sheriff used whenever he came west. It was paneled and had a bookcase directly behind the leather chair that was mated with the executive-sized desk.

The cameraman, whom she called Andre, set up a heavy tripod in the corner opposite the door and began to take a light reading. He also took the microphone out of a black leather case, affixed the cord to the camera, and laid it on the desk.

Wallace took a compact out of her purse, peered into the small mirror, and began to smooth her hair. She also took the pinky finger of her right hand and dabbed at the lipstick on her crimson-colored lips. After running her tongue over her upper bridge, she sat down in an upholstered club chair opposite the desk, and crossed her legs. I took my place in front of the bookcase and arranged some papers on the desk blotter. They were only there for show. I intended to speak extemporaneously.

Dorothy Wallace looked around at Andre, and he nodded his head. She took the microphone and adjusted it to a location where the head was between the two of us.

"Rolling," Andre said.

Dorothy Wallace cleared her throat. "Detective Faulkner, what can you tell us about the homicide that happened this morning?"

It was my turn to expulse the phlegm from my throat. "Well, very little, really. About two AM this morning, detectives responded to Springdale Hospital to investigate a shooting that had occurred in the Theodore area. When they arrived, they found the victim deceased. At this time, the investigation is continuing."

"Can you identify the victim?"

"We have, however at this time we are not releasing his name."

"Why not?"

"I'm not going to comment on why."

The kid was a juvenile. I didn't want Ricardo knowing that. That fact might be helpful in an interrogation.

Dorothy Wallace held her jaw in a tight line. She expected more, I could tell.

"Do you have any suspects?"

"We are searching for a person of interest."

"Who is?"

"I can't comment on who he or she is."

I heard her snort. She clearly had a curiosity for information, something that one day might make her a good reporter, but not today.

"How was he killed?"

242

"I'm not going to comment on how he was killed. I'll refer you to the medical examiner's office for a cause of death."

"Do you know where he was killed?"

"We have an approximate location, but I don't want to release it at this time."

People have a morbid curiosity. We didn't need 'looky lous' tramping all over the place until we knew we had found all the evidence that might possibly be there.

"Have you recovered a weapon?"

"I can't comment on whether we have or have not recovered a weapon, or on what that weapon is."

"Do you expect to make an arrest soon?"

That was one of the oldest traps in the books. Many a detective had told the press that 'an arrest is imminent,' only to have to eat those words when a case dragged on for days, weeks, or even months.

"I'm sorry, I can't comment on when we may or may not make an arrest."

She snorted. "Well, is there anything you can comment on?"

I looked her dead in the eye and gave her a crooked smile. "We had a homicide in Theodore last night."

That afternoon, I met Zane and Neely back in the Theodore area. We had an impromptu meeting at a fast food restaurant so as to go over what we had and to make a plan on where to go next.

What we had was a circumstantial case of murder against Ricardo Washington. Clattie Knox put him standing on the corner with a gun in his hand; William Raspberry saw him running away from the area with a gun in his hand after hearing a shot; and Zane's witness saw him hanging out in the apartment complex shortly before the shooting.

In addition, Houston had fielded an anonymous phone call from someone who said that Ricardo had stashed his gun over at his mother's place; specifically, in her flower bed.

The search warrant had been prepared, Judge Herbert Thompson had signed it, and Neely had made the decision to serve it just before dark.

Ricardo's mother lived on Old Military Road, off Bellingrath, two streets south of the railroad tracks. It was a paved road, but very narrow, with ditches on either shoulder. The area was rural in that it was in an unincorporated part of the county and therefore not subject to zoning laws. Dogs roamed freely, goats grazed in a couple of the yards, and junk cars were a common sight.

The Washington residence was located about a quarter of a mile down on the right side. It was a clapboard house that once was white but had seen better days. Mildew was prominent at the joints, and several of the boards had been replaced by untreated planks. The home's only redeeming value was that it was shelter and that it sat on what looked like a three acre lot.

We parked out front behind a marked patrol car. I was in my car, Neely and Zane rode together, and Hernandez followed with an SUV full of evidence gathering equipment.

Neely, Zane, and a young uniformed deputy that I did not know took the front, and I went to the back door. Hernandez stayed back at his truck and made ready his camera.

At the rear, I listened closely. I could hear Zane's knock at the front door, a knock that shook the entire house. I heard heavy feet walk across the floor. Then I heard the door open and muffled voices speaking.

But more importantly was what I did not hear: running inside the house. In two minutes, Neely opened the rear door and jerked his head toward the inside. I walked up two steps and into the kitchen.

The smell of greens assailed me. I looked toward the stove and saw steam rising from two pots sitting on grates over natural gas flames. There was a small table inside four chairs sitting in the middle of the room. On the table sat one clean plate and an empty glass.

I nodded toward the table. "Somebody's about to eat," I said in low tones.

Neely nodded. "They're checking the house. My gut tells me he's not here, but you may be right about him being on the way."

We walked into the living room to find Althea Washington seated on a couch over against the south wall wringing out a lace handkerchief. She was a heavyset woman with black hair who wore navy stretch pants and a pink pullover shirt. She was barefoot.

The room was dark. The overhead light was turned on, but the bulb looked as if it barely registered forty watts. There was some item of furniture, mostly chairs, all of them old, against every wall, and a bureau near the front door. On that bureau sat photographs of Martin Luther King and John Kennedy. On the wall above the couch was a family portrait. I recognized Althea's smiling face; however, an older man and a young male – presumably Ricardo – in the photo wore sour expressions.

Neely took a seat on the couch next to her and took out a pen and a small pad. I stood by the front door and folded my arms.

"Ms. Washington, as I said, we have a warrant to search your property. We're looking for your son and also for a hand gun of any caliber. You can save us and yourself some aggravation if you'll say where both are."

She said nothing as she shook her head back and forth while rocking briskly.

There's no way I could put myself in her position and know the anguish that this woman felt, though I've often tried. Her son, maybe her only son, was being hunted by the police. He would be taken in irons into captivity – like a slave – tried, and convicted of murder. Then he would be taken away. He would be gone for many years; he might

245

even die in prison. She would probably only be able to afford to visit him once or twice for the rest of her life. He would never marry, unless he had already. He would never give her grandchildren, unless he had done so, and there was a better than even chance he might predecease her.

He had brought the government into her home, to invade it. They were empowered to look into her underwear drawer, go through her bureaus, and take apart anywhere a gun might possibly be. They could stay as long as they wanted, and they could question her until they were satisfied that she knew nothing about where her son was or what he had done.

She might very well have been touched by murder in the past, and the thought of her only son killing another person was hateful to her. But she had seen it coming; the late nights, the eyes red-rimmed with drug and alcohol abuse, the minor and sometimes major incursions of the law. She knew this day would come and it gnawed at her stomach. She didn't know if her son would be the killer or the killed, but she knew that this day would come.

She was, at once, hugely depressed and insanely angry. If he was next to her, she would ring his neck. Then she would throw her arms around him and hug him to death. As it was, she sat and stared at the floor and shredded her handkerchief.

"Do you know where your son is?" Neely said.

She looked up, tears filling her eyes. "No, suh."

"When's the last time you saw him?"

"It's been two days, I guess."

"How about a gun?"

"If he has one here, it's prob'ly out in the shed. I told him not to bring no gun into dis house."

Zane had returned to the living space, and he heard her assessment. He nodded at Neely and stepped past me, out of the front door, and into the yard. I looked around and could see him wave Hernandez around toward the backyard.

Neely made notes on his pad while Washington leaned back on the couch. She shut her eyes and began to rock back and forth again. I didn't know if she was praying or if she had fallen into some type of trance.

Neely asked a couple more questions but got no responses. He called the uniformed deputy over to replace him on the couch. Then he rose and motioned for me to join him in the kitchen.

"If you need to go, we can take it from here," he said. "I'm just going to take a look around the house and then out in the yard. We'll probably be here another hour or so."

I nodded and looked around. "Do you have any idea where this guy is?"

"We think he's downtown in the projects at Lemon Grove. The known associates file lists names of three guys that he hangs with. All three live down there."

"Are you going to try to pick him up?"

"Not without a good location. You could ride around that place for days and not see anything but a few kids playin' in the street."

He was right. It was easy to vanish in a housing project. There's always an open door for anyone running from the police.

"Okay, well, if you don't need me, I guess I'll run over to the office and see what's happening."

I looked past Neely, through the rear window, and into the backyard. It was nearly dark, but I could see Hernandez using a probe to punch down into the soft dirt of the flower garden. My gaze was broken by the squawk of Neely's police walkie-talkie. It was Houston.

"SO 30," Neely responded.

"That subject that you're looking for is at HQ."

I looked at Neely, and he looked at me. "10-4. We'll be enroute."

247

Chapter 32

Thirty minutes later, I was parking in the west side lot at the office. Neely, who had remained at Althea Washington's to direct the final stages of the search, was about twenty minutes behind me.

The weekend entrance to the department was a southside door guarded by a magnetic lock. I punched my code, the month and day of my birth, and was inside, up the elevator, and on the seventh floor in five minutes.

As I walked through the double, glass doors of the Major Crimes Office, three detectives were standing around a single man seated in a chair next to a desk. The young investigators, all of whom I recognized as working in the Property Bureau, wore sidearms and handcuffs.

"Are you Ricardo?" I said standing in front of the young man.

"Yeah."

I could tell by that one word that he didn't realize the gravity of his situation. He was tall and slim, just as William Raspberry had described him. He wore a white t-shirt stained with red clay, jeans, and white athletic shoes.

His face was completely smooth, not a mark or wrinkle anywhere. The whites of his brown eyes were red and bloodshot, and his nose was flat and broad. There was a soul patch under his bottom lip.

I looked at the two detectives. "He been searched?"

One of them nodded. "Yes, sir."

"Why don't you come with me," I said to Ricardo.

Ricardo rose and followed me toward one of the interrogation rooms. Two of the detectives trailed him and watched as we entered, and Washington sat down at a metal table in the middle of the room; a table that was bolted to the floor and featured a curved iron bar the ends of which were welded to the surface of the piece.

The room was paneled and had a black and white checked tile floor. There was one large mirror in the wall across from where Ricardo was seated. Unbeknownst to him, there was a small microphone imbedded in the hanging light that fell from the ceiling to a location about five feet above his head.

I nodded at the detectives, and they closed the door.

"You want something to eat or drink?" I said.

The young man shook his head. He closed his eyes tightly and rubbed his face with both hands.

"When's the last time you slept?"

He looked at me as if he hadn't heard me. I had a feeling that he was coming down off something, and I didn't know how long we were going to be able to work with him.

"Are you sure I couldn't interest you in a cup of coffee or a soft drink?"

He shook his head. "Naw, man."

I paused and looked at him. "What brings you to the office today, Mr. Washington?"

The question seemed to animate him. His jaw tightened and he licked his lips.

"Man, ya'll out'ere messin' wi' my mama."

"We were looking for you."

"Hey, my mama ain't know where I was. Ya'll shouldn'a messed wi' her."

"Who told you we were there?"

He said nothing.

"Okay, well, we gotta wait for Mr. Neely. He's the main one that wants to talk to you." I paused and looked at him. "You sure you don't want something?"

He folded his arms and looked at the floor. He was the perfect picture of the angry, young black man. I got up and walked out, closing the door behind me. One of the investigators, who had been watching through the one way mirror from the room next door, a tall man with a blonde crew cut, stepped out and spoke to me.

"You think you'll be able to get anything out of him?"

I looked back at the door and nodded. "Oh, sure. Something. He came down here because he wants to talk; he wouldn't have come otherwise. That business about his mother was just a cover. If he was worried about making life miserable for her, he'd've changed his ways a long time ago."

The young detective was obviously trying to learn. "How would you approach him?"

I thought for a minute. "I'd just probe until I found something that made him aggressive; maybe talk about his mother. I'd just keep him talking then sprinkle in a few questions about the shooting. He'll deny it at first, but how he denies it will nail him."

"How so?"

"He'll either deny he was there, something we can easily refute; or deny firing the shot, a fact that we can't prove, but we have a strong circumstantial case for."

"And, if that doesn't work?"

I smiled. He didn't.

"We'll tune him up." I was joking of course, but he didn't know it.

The two cases had absolutely no similarities at all, however, at that moment, my mind drifted over to Zoe Woods. It didn't seem fair, really. Ricardo Washington, who had no connection to his victim at all, in a seemingly random manner, took a shot at a person and killed him, and then waltzed into headquarters in what looked to be a desperate effort to confess. Meanwhile, Zoe Woods' killer, a man who apparently developed a relationship with her, spent time with her, drank with her, even saw her naked, remained on the run.

The disparity in how people – perpetrators – perceive the crime of murder at once fascinated then angered me. The circumstances led me to believe that Zoe Woods' killer, this mysterious black haired man, may have killed before. Could Ricardo Washington care more about a victim that he did not know than the black haired man did about one that he did know? Or did Washington simply care less about himself? In my mind it could go either way.

My reflections ceased when Neely walked into the office. He walked with purpose toward me and the blonde haired detective. I looked at his face. It was beginning to show the wear of what was now going on eighteen hours of non-stop movement.

"Is he in there?" Neely said as he nodded toward the interrogation room.

"Yeah," I said. "He's declined food or drink. I haven't talked to him otherwise." I paused. "Are you up to getting something out of him?"

He knitted his brows. "You mean am I too tired to get a confession from this son of a bitch?" He shook his head. "Nope," he said walking past me toward the door. "I just got my second wind."

Neely took his place across from Ricardo Washington, and I sat down in a chair in the far corner. Then I gave the high sign to the blonde detective in the adjacent room to turn on the recording equipment.

"Mr. Washington," Neely began. "My name is Detective Neely, but you can call me 'Scott' if you want." He smiled at the young man across from him who yawned and slumped in his chair.

"Before we start talking, I want you know that you're not under arrest. You're free to leave at any time. And, as I'm sure you know, you don't have to talk. If you do say anything, it might be repeated in a legal proceeding. If, and I really can't understand why you would want to, but if you for any reason want to talk to a lawyer, well, you can." He paused and looked at him. "You understand?"

251

The man shrugged his shoulders. "Yeah."

It was as skillful a rights notification as I had heard. Ricardo seemed to be completely at ease.

Neely cleared his throat. "Why did you come here tonight?"

"I want ya'll to leave my mama alone. She ain't done nothin'."

"Have you talked to your mother?"

"I talked to her dis afternoon. She say ya'll goin' thru her house."

I tried to remember seeing Althea Washington make or receive a phone call while we were there. It may have been before we got inside. She must have seen us drive up and called him. A better bet was that one of the neighbors had tipped him off, and Ricardo didn't want to finger them.

"Okay, we'll leave your mother alone." He paused. "But you've got to do something for me."

Ricardo tilted his head.

"You gotta tell me what happened this morning out on Blue Star Parkway."

Ricardo shifted in his chair and looked away. He said nothing.

"'Cause that's what we're all wonderin' about. I mean, I know you had a pretty good reason for what happened. I just need to know what it is."

Ricardo still said nothing. He took a deep breath and exhaled. Hyperventilation: a sure sign of stress.

"Come on, man. Otherwise, you know, well, we'll just have to keep looking at your mother's house."

He looked away again. "I ain't on the Parkway dis mawnin'."

Neely had him, and he knew it. "Well, now we know that's not true. I got three eyewitnesses that saw you there. Maybe you misunderstood me. I'm talkin' about early in the morning. Maybe two, three o'clock. It was last night, really."

"Las' night, I was drinkin'"

"Where?"

"At the club?"

"Which one?"

"Mr. T's."

"Over on Bellingrath Road?"

He nodded.

"What time did you leave?"

"When dey closed."

Just about all the bars – except for private clubs – closed at two AM; a rule that was not strictly enforced. Mr. T's was within a quarter mile from the highway, but it was also about a quarter mile from his home.

"Where did you go then?"

"I went home?"

Neely sat back and rubbed his mouth. "Well, like I said, we know that isn't true. Your mama said she ain't seen you in two days; and people saw you up on the Parkway."

"Who?" He didn't deny being there. He just wanted to know who saw him.

"People."

"Dey ain't seen me."

Up to now, he had been relatively undemonstrative, however, now he raised his arm and pointed in disgust.

"They said you had a gun," Neely said.

"Gun? What gun?"

Still, no denial.

"People saw you with a gun."

"Man, I aks you, what peoples?" His voice went up and he was getting emotional.

"People. Your neighbors. You know I can't tell you who they are . . . just yet."

I was sure Ricardo already knew about Clattie Knox. He could have seen William Raspberry as he was running, but I doubted it. As for Zane's witness, I didn't know what he had seen or how he had seen it.

"Let's just get down to it, Ricardo. You were up on Blue Star Parkway this morning at about two or two thirty, and you took a shot at a truck as it was driving by. Now, people saw you do it."

"Man, I ain't shot nobody."

It was another non-denial. He was guilty alright. It was just a matter of proving it.

"What about your gun? Where is it?"

"What gun?"

"Man, a player like you? I know you got a gun."

"I ain't got no gun."

"Well, I know you ain't got one, now. Where's the one you had this morning?"

He said nothing.

"Man, that means I just gotta keep looking at your mama's."

"Man, who is dis dat say dey saw me shoot some dude on the Parkway?"

Ricardo was getting louder; a good sign. His emotions would eventually betray him. Already, he had dug his hole. Neely never told him a person was shot, only a truck.

"I can't tell you that. Not yet. But people saw you shoot the truck." He paused. "The only thing I want to know is, why."

"I ain't shot nobody." He raised his hand and pointed and spoke loudly.

"Well, some people saw you. Are you calling them liars?"

He took a deep breath and calmed dramatically, almost in resignation. It looked as if he was trying to take the pressure off.

"Man, I guess if somebody say they saw me shoot, well, I guess I shoot."

Ricardo pointed his hand at Neely, index finger and thumb extended, other three fingers folded under, the back of his hand turned up; the way the gang bangers hold a pistol. That was enough. He had acted out his crime. He admitted shooting. Neely had seen it, and he stood up. He took out his silver cuffs and handcuffed the startled man to the iron bar.

"Okay, Ricardo, you're under arrest for murder – capital murder."

"What that mean?"

"It means when you shoot into a moving vehicle and kill somebody, you're eligible for the death penalty." Ricardo's eyes widened, and he fell silent.

Neely repeated the rights waiver, this time more formally. Washington said he understood and didn't want to say anything more until he talked to a lawyer.

In my opinion, Neely had moved too soon. I thought he could have gotten a better idea of where the gun was stashed if he'd just worked him a little longer. But his case was solid; not rock solid, but it was a winner.

At that point there was a knock on the door. The blonde detective put his head in the door and looked at me.

"Mr. Faulkner, you have a phone call."

At my office, I picked up the receiver. Immediately I recognized the voice of my younger brother, Luke.

"Henry," he said. I could hear the emotion in his voice. "Daddy, died."

Chapter 33

My brother's words surprised, but did not shock or stun me. I knew this day was coming and, after all, I had in the past received many death notifications. My father was old. He had suffered two heart attacks and a stroke, and his last years had not been what I would call fulfilling. His speech

255

was impaired, his movements labored, and he suffered from a malaise that oftentimes seemed to border on full blown depression.

"Where is he?" I said.

"He's at home. Mother found him. The coroner and the police are here."

"What happened?"

I didn't mean for it to sound as if I was giving him the third degree, but with the lack of sleep and the stress that I had been under, I was operating from instinct. Besides, my brother was a tax attorney, and he understood the reasons for all of the questions.

"He went to the bedroom to take a nap," I could hear his voice catch, "and when Mother went to call him for supper, he wouldn't wake up."

He was upset. I was calm; calm and tired. I'd often wondered what I would be like at this moment. I had often wondered how my siblings would view me. Would they understand that I had given up all of my emotions a long time ago, or would they be offended that I was not appropriately moved or grieved?

"Do you know why the police are here?" he asked.

"Don't worry about that. They roll on all calls that the paramedics do. Is there any sign that he died anyway but naturally?"

It was an odd question, and I knew the light that it cast upon my mother, but it had to be asked. I wasn't necessarily intimating homicide. He could have fallen, hit his head, and had a delayed reaction; or even have taken his own life. There would be outward manifestations of both circumstances.

"No. It looks like he just went to sleep and died." He paused. "He looks pretty peaceful, really."

"Well, then gather up all his meds; give the coroner the name of his doctor, the one who's been treating him for his heart; and have them send him along to the funeral home. What is it? Greenlawn?"

"Yeah, yeah. Okay." His tone sounded as if he had suddenly drifted away into another place.

"Have you called Sister?"

"Not yet."

I took a deep breath and exhaled. My father was dead. There was nothing I could do for him now. The weight that I had been under for the last eighteen to twenty hours seemed to hit me all at once.

"Okay, look. I've been working since about two this morning. I've got to get a few hours of sleep first, before I get on the road."

I paused, knowing that what I had said would surely rub my mother the wrong way. But I said it because I saw that there was no other way to keep myself from driving off a bridge in the middle of the night while enroute to them.

"I'll drive up there first thing in the morning. Can you handle it until I get there?"

"Sure." His tone was confident once again. "I got it."

I was on the road by six, enroute to my parent's home in Prattville, Alabama, a city with which I was intimately familiar, but which I did not like.

Right outside of Atmore, I called Will. He was sympathetic yet unmoved.

"I'm sorry to hear that, Son. How old was he?"

"Eighty. He would have been eighty-one in September."

"Well, he lived a long life; surely longer than what he thought he would."

It was an odd thing to say, but I didn't take it wrongly. "He was sick, and I'm sure life wasn't what he thought it should be any more. He's in a better place."

"How do you know?"

"Well, you know. He believed in Jesus."

"Is that all it takes? Didn't he have to be good?"

It was a discussion I didn't want to be having right then, on the side of the highway, with a cup of coffee in my hand. People confuse religion – the religion of good works – with salvation by grace. Will was no different, and I certainly wasn't going to change his mind about it from a hundred miles away. I said nothing in response.

"When'll you be back?" Will said.

"Oh, I don't know; three or four days."

"Anything you need me to do?"

"Just get me a lead on Zoe Woods' case."

"It's as good as got, Son."

I spent the rest of the trip immersed in my memories of my father and engaged in what I thought was an honest assessment of our relationship. It wasn't a complicated endeavor.

My father was a gentle man, given occasionally to considerable displays of anger. I had exactly two good memories of him; one when I was four, and one when I was ten. Oddly, both involved eating. Otherwise, I saw him as one who was distant and unaffectionate, but one who did his duty. He fed me, clothed me, and, in his own way, I'm sure he loved me; but he just didn't show it, and I always wondered if it was true. I saw myself as an intrusion upon his life, incapable of pleasing him or making him proud of me; unable to bring him any joy whatsoever. Whether it was at the ball park or at report card time, he always looked bored, as if he wished he was someplace else. He just never seemed to me to act as if he cared.

I'm sure it was something that I had said or done that was disrespectful and hurtful to him that caused him to place a wall between us. Kids always hurt their parents. Once, when I was a teenager, I went to him and tried to apologize to him for the things that I thought I had done to hurt him. He just looked up from the book he was reading, listened to me, and then looked back down without ever having said a word. It was as if nothing had happened. I was devastated; not knowing what I had done to alienate him, and certainly of a mind that I didn't know how to fix it.

The miles clicked off, and the memories came and went. The closer I got to Prattville, the more I found that my own father's death meant very little, if anything to me; and that, frankly, I was quite peaceful with that thought. In fact, the farther I drove, the more I wished I could turn around and just go home and let the entire proceeding continue on without me.

In two hours and forty-five minutes I exited Interstate 65 and drove west on what the city called the Cobbs Ford Road, but what was actually an amalgamation of Alabama Highway 14 and US Highway 82 West.

My parent's home was located south of the main road. It was a plain, middle class neighborhood of single and two story brick homes set on half acre lots that were, for the most part, well-manicured.

I parked my car on the street in front of the metal mailbox that my father had erected ten years previous, before his first heart attack, and got out of my car. Looking around, I saw that vehicles belonging to both my sister and brother were in the driveway. I took a deep breath and started to the door.

The 'ding-dong' of the front door bell seemed out of tune and a little forlorn, not the spritely greeting that I remembered from times past. I had a key to my mother's home, for emergencies, but whenever I visited – which was not that often – I always called at the front door so as not to startle anyone.

My brother Luke answered the door. He smiled, but I could tell that he'd been up all night and the redness around his eyes said that he had cried. I didn't realize that he was that close to our father.

"Hey, come on in," he said.

I stepped through the door and into the foyer then paused. I did not want to be where I was.

"Well, how are things?"

"If you're asking about Mother, she's bearing up pretty well. Sister is in a little bit of shock."

She had been 'Sister' since we were kids. I, the middle child, couldn't say her real name, Elizabeth, so Mother just told me to call her 'Sister.' When my brother Luke came along, he followed suit.

"Are they in there?" I nodded down a short hall toward the den.

"Yeah. Come on in."

I walked through the doorway and into a pall that I had seen and felt at so many death scenes before. The room was just as it had been when I was a child; the familiar fireplace to the left, the sliding glass doors ahead, and a twenty-seven inch television against the far wall.

Mother was seated on the couch, her legs crossed at the knee, dressed in jeans and a light blue, cotton blouse, with socks and tennis shoes on her feet. She looked up and took a deep breath, but she didn't rise.

"Well, hey. I see you finally got here."

It was as I expected. "Yeah. I was a little wiped yesterday, so I decided not to chance driving last night." I paused, standing in the doorway. "How are you doing?"

She shrugged and pursed her lips. I stood silently and took a good look at her thin face. It looked like a road map. I never remembered it being that lined before. Her eyes were red, as was the tip of her nose, and her jaw was set in a tight line. She looked disgusted and afraid.

Sister, on the other hand, was nervous and fidgety. She sat on the couch wearing loose fitting jeans and a red t-shirt. Her eyes were red also, and she kept wiping her nose with the Kleenex in her right hand.

At that moment it occurred to me that I was the only person in the family that had not been crying. I believed everyone was staring at me and, for that reason, I felt hugely out of place.

My brother moved from around me to take a seat in one of two club chairs at the end of the room opposite the television. I parked next to him.

No one spoke for what seemed like several minutes. I looked all around the room once, and then began to stare at a small spot in one of the bricks – the third from the end closest to the floor – in the hearth. A clock on the mantle made an almost imperceptible hum.

Finally, Luke spoke. "Daddy's at the funeral home. We've got an appointment at one."

I nodded and looked toward my mother. "Have you made any decisions, yet?"

She shrugged again and looked away. "I don't know."

I knew better than to start making suggestions, but somehow one just slipped out. "Well, how about the funeral on Friday?"

"Friday? I don't want him out of the ground that long." She was all at once reanimated and angry. "He's not black," she said referring to the traditional African-American practice of not interring family until a week or ten days had gone by after death.

"Well, Wednesday, then."

She looked away and said nothing. I saw then how it was going to be. She was obviously angry, yet still clinging to control with all her might.

She and my father had been married for over fifty years. They had grown up within ten miles of each other in rural Alabama – outside of Union Springs – and had known each other since childhood. He was three years her senior, and they had married after my father's short stint in the Navy and my mother's high school graduation.

Their marriage had been dutiful, enduring, and, at times, remorseful. She had been in complete control of it and the whole family from as far back as I could remember. She passed judgment on everything. She was even critical

261

with the way I'd lived my life, spent my money, and fashioned my career. I didn't expect her to stop now.

"How was your trip, Sister?" Luke said.

Elizabeth looked around the room and took a deep breath. I couldn't tell if she was trying to hold back tears or merely trying to think of something to say. She was seldom at a loss for words so it must have been the former.

According to my mother, Sister had been my father's favorite. He had doted on her from the day she was born and had appeased her every whim. She and mother weren't the best of friends.

"It was fine."

The room was silent once again. "One o'clock, huh," I said looking at my brother.

He nodded and mouthed the word, 'yes.'

Three hours later we were in the office of Raymond Wilson at Greenlawn Mortuary and Cemetery. Wilson was thirty, with blonde hair parted in the middle. He had blue eyes, and a dark blue suit hung on his slim frame.

It was a little irregular to meet with the salesman on a Sunday, though it was not unheard of. My guess was that Wilson was new, and he was looking for a big sale.

"I realize his death was sudden, but had you given any thought at all to his arrangements?" His voice was a tenor and not too loud.

I sat next to Wilson who was at the head of the conference table. Luke was across from me, and Mother was next to Luke. Sister was at the other end of the table. We all looked toward Mother. The look on her face was pure confusion. She blinked twice and spoke.

"We just want to get him buried by Wednesday."

Wilson opened up a loose leaf binder and turned to the middle. "Might I suggest the 'Memorial' package? With it, comes the casket of your choice; the deluxe spray of roses, with baby's breath; embalming, of course; and a two hour wake the evening before the funeral. In addition, we'll take care of the death certificate as well as the obituary announcement in the newspaper." He looked up at Mother with his brows raised.

She looked at me and Luke. "What's the price of that one?"

Wilson looked down at the book. "It's thirteen five."

"Is that a metal or a wood casket?" she said.

"Metal."

"Does that include a vault?" I said.

"It does."

Luke spoke up. "Does it include the plot?"

Wilson shook his head. "No. Plots start at five thousand depending on the location. If your choice is under one of the oaks, it's slightly more."

"How about a stone?" I said.

"We'll help you get one; however, it's not part of our service."

No one spoke. Wilson took the open binder and slid it toward me.

"Of course, if you choose, the components are interchangeable; sort of an a la carte arrangement."

"What?" Mother said.

Luke looked at her. "It means you can pick and choose from a group of each of the different parts: the casket, the flowers, and the rest."

I turned the pages of the binder and looked at photos of flowers and coffins under sheet protectors. For my mother to decide on what exactly she wanted would take hours, if she even could. I thought about trying to do it, but I knew deep down that it was unlikely she would ever relinquish control long enough for anyone, especially me, to make those decisions for her.

Sliding the binder toward her, I looked at her face. She was staring at the table, looking lost. For a second, I felt sorry for her. The most important person in her life for the past fifty some odd years – I didn't even know how long

263

they'd been married – was dead. Everything that he had done for her she would now have to do for herself; and everything she had done for him she would now have no reason to do. It's no wonder that there's a better than even chance that a surviving spouse is likely to decease within a year.

At that moment, I was once again conscious of my feelings, or lack of them. I felt absolutely nothing; no pity, no grief, no nothing. It was as if the people with whom I was enmeshed in this tragedy were no more special to me than the players in the latest homicide in which I was involved. I was at once glad and ashamed; glad that I wasn't going to pieces emotionally, and ashamed that my work had effectively removed me from any sense of intimacy that I could ever have with anyone, especially my family; intimacy that would allow me to experience and to show grief.

My mother took a deep breath and began to thumb through the binder as my brother and I sat silently. Wilson asked if we wanted a soft drink. Everyone else declined, but I said, 'yes,' just so I could have a reason to get up and leave. Outside in the hall, I spoke.

"Well, how's business?"

"Unfortunately, pretty good. I've got two families coming in; one tonight and another tomorrow morning."

"Bummer having to work on Sunday, huh."

He smiled and shook his head. "I don't really mind."

Nodding back toward the conference room as he took a drink of soda, he said:

"She looks like she's taking it pretty hard."

"She is. They were all they had for the last ten or fifteen years." I paused and took a sip. "I think she'll get over it, though, eventually."

"How about you?"

"Oh, well, I'm kind of in the business. Law enforcement."

"This isn't your first rodeo."

"Not by a long shot; that and the fact that I and my father weren't close. Heck, this is my first trip back to Prattville in two or three years."

"I understand."

I looked away, a little ashamed of what I had just said. It was the truth, but it was none of his business, and it was nothing of which to be proud.

"How much is all this gonna cost? Ballpark, I mean."

Wilson shrugged his shoulders. "Oh, I don't know; as much as you want, really. If you throw in a plot, fifteen and up. The plots are pretty expensive."

"We're gonna need a plot. I don't think she wants to take him back to the country where they're from."

He nodded; no doubt pleased that he was going to get a cut of that sale, also.

We walked back toward the conference room. Mother was staring absently at the binder. Luke was standing over her shoulder looking at the pages. Sister had moved to that side and was leaning over, looking also. Wilson and I sat back down.

"Well," he said. "How's it looking?"

She looked up. "I'd like to see the caskets."

"Right this way."

We repaired to a paneled showroom at the end of the hall and began to walk down rows of wooden and metal coffins. Mother stopped and looked at each one, feeling the satin liners, knocking on the wood and metal. She walked down each of the three aisles and then stopped. She took a deep breath, exhaled, then looked at me and my brother.

"Which one do y'all want?"

We looked at each other. Luke's brows went up in surprise. He looked around the room quickly, and his eyes settled on a metal box in the corner. The sign on it read eleven hundred dollars. It was silver and had a white lining. The handles on the outside swiveled out and up.

"I like this one," he said.

I nodded. "I do, too."

Mother looked at us both. There was contempt in her eyes, but also resignation. In this instance, at least, she had given up.

An hour later, the contracts had been signed, and we were getting ready to leave. Wilson was putting papers into a folder when I walked over next to him.

"I'd like to see him," I said, "if it's possible."

I saw a sadness in his eyes that I'm sure he didn't ordinarily betray for other clients.

"Sure."

He directed me out the side door to an annex about fifty yards from the main building. In five minutes one of the embalmers was showing me into the room where my father's body lay on a steel gurney, under a sheet. He said to close the door on the way out and then left me alone.

I stood and stared into my father's face. He was made up to look about fifteen years younger than he was; a condition that made him appear as if he should still be alive. I took two deep breaths and paused as a sob began to well up in my throat, the first sign of any emotion in me. Inexplicably, I choked it off.

"I love you, Daddy. I'm sorry I wasn't a better son," was all I could say.

Chapter 34

On Wednesday morning, I rose early. I had spent the night in a motel on the east side, right off Interstate 65. I told my mother that with Sister's husband and children coming in, as well as Luke's family, it would simply be more convenient for me to get lodging elsewhere. My mother made a remark about me not wanting to be around her when she needed me the most, but it didn't matter to me. I'd been called a lot worse things than unsympathetic and inconsiderate.

After I showered and shaved, I put on my best dark gray pinstripe suit. I rubbed the dust off of a pair of black shoes that I hardly ever wore and knotted a red and silver paisley tie. I checked out and drove over to Greenlawn Cemetery at nine thirty for a ten AM service.

Luke had worked with mother to handle the rest of the arrangements; all except the headstone and the plot. I picked those out. He would close the estate also. And only because Mother had allowed it, did we all take a part. Sister had planned for a graveside service only and had written the eulogy. The work was shared, and mother was able to relax only somewhat, though I could see it was a strain for her to do so.

It was a beautiful day for a funeral, all except the temperature. The plot that I had chosen was under a spreading oak, a location that, unbeknownst to her, had cost my mother an extra two grand. I wasn't worried. She could afford it.

Walking up to the gravesite, I looked around at the assorted family members who had made the trip into town. There was my father's surviving sister who I hadn't seen in over five years. Aunt Juliette was a frail woman who nevertheless possessed a sophisticated look.

Several older men with gray hair, all wearing dark suits that hung loosely on them, milled about out from under the green tent that covered over the grave. These were no doubt former co-workers of my father who had spent nearly forty years as a civil servant.

I walked toward my mother who was standing with Sister and Luke. She wore a plain black dress and short black heels. My sister was in a navy blue dress. Elizabeth's husband was talking to their three children. When I reached the group, I stopped and put my hands in my pockets.

"How are you holding up?" I said to Mother.

She gave me the stink eye and said: "Fine."

I got the message and moved over under the tent and sat down. The pastor of my parents' church walked over, bent at the waist, and offered me his hand. He was a middle aged man with a receding hair line, a chubby face, and piercing blue eyes.

"I'm Brother Ted. I'm your father's pastor. You must be Henry from Mobile."

"Yes, sir, Pastor. Thanks for coming."

He sat down in the vacant chair next to me and spoke in low tones. "I'm sorry I missed you at the wake last night. I came over to find out if there was anything special you wanted the group here to know about your father."

His question bored into my brain. Many things came immediately to my mind that would describe my father. A few of them were complimentary.

"Just tell them my father was a good provider and that he loved his family. Tell them he was a follower of Jesus Christ."

He jotted my contribution down on a small white card and put it inside the huge Schofield Reference Bible with a burgundy-colored, leather cover that rested on his leg.

"I'll certainly let everyone know that." He paused. "Would you let me pray for you? I got to pray for everyone else last night."

If there's one thing I've learned about police work, it's that God is in charge. I've seen people shot in the face and live, and shot in the foot and die; so whenever anyone offers to pray for me, I never turn it down.

The pastor bowed his head, as did I, and began to pray. I didn't concentrate on every word, but picked up bits and pieces as my mind wandered.

"Lord, be with Henry in this time of grief . . . be with him in his work . . . help him to overcome those things that are besetting him . . ."

I wondered what he meant by that. Undoubtedly, my mother had told him that I was not right.

". . . and Lord, we pray that you would make Yourself real to Henry and show him Your grace; in Jesus' name we pray, Amen."

He raised his head, smiled at me and rose from the chair. He looked at his watch.

"Well, it's about time to get started. It was good talking to you."

After that, Pastor Ted gave some unseen 'high' sign to the funeral home personnel who began to gather the onlookers under the tent. I stood and watched as six elderly men whom I did not know walked toward the rear of a white Cadillac hearse, stood, and waited, three on either side of the rear door. I watched as the back door opened and the men pulled the silver casket out of the back of the vehicle. They took hold of the coffin by the handles, and when it was all the way out, began walking from the road toward the open grave, under the tent.

Prior to sitting down, I had looked into the six foot hole. As I stood and peered downward, a mild panic began to overtake me. I stepped back off the mound of dirt and onto the grass. The fact that I would one day be lowered into a hole not unlike that one had suddenly given me pause. My heart rate began to rise, and I felt flushed. All I could think of was my father's faith in Jesus and whether or not there was a heaven. I sat down hard on the chair.

Mother, Sister, and Luke took their places with me on the front row of two rows of chairs. The rest – my aunt, one or two of my mother's sisters, and my brother's and sister's families – filled in the back row and stood close by. The sun was getting hotter, but there was a breeze out of the south, and things were not as of yet unbearable.

The preacher took his place at the front of the group, at the head end of the casket, and opened his Bible. He looked from one end of the rows to the other, and a kind of solemn smirk crossed his mouth.

"We are gathered here today to celebrate the homegoing of John David Faulkner, born 80 years ago in

Bullock County, Alabama, and deceased this past Saturday here in Prattville.

"John was a veteran of the US Navy, a retired civil servant, a brother, a father, and a husband.

"But he was much more. He was a believer in Jesus Christ, and at this hour he is no doubt beginning to praise the Lord; an activity that will last him throughout eternity.

"At this hour, he is seeing through a glass clearly. He is finding out the answers to all of the questions over which he has pondered all of his life. He is wearing his glorified body and walking the streets of gold, and he is admiring the mansion that God has prepared for him."

As the preacher began a litany of my father's virtues: his loyalty, his charity, his love of music, his acumen for gardening, I bowed my head and pretended I was praying. The pastor was right: my father did live a life that was admirable. And he was not unlike any other man in that he was less than perfect. It was unfortunate that his lack of perfection had such a profound effect on me.

"John loved playing the banjo and guitar, and he used his talent at the church, until he was no longer able."

That statement brought me back to another of my failures. My father had tried without success for several years to teach me to play the guitar. My small fingers were just too short to encircle the large neck of the instrument; and the tips of my fingers were not tough enough to press down on the strings.

"John loved working in the yard and took much pride in the way his lawn looked."

Never, in all my youth was I ever able to mow the grass just the way he wanted it. I clenched my eyes shut and tried to push out the memories.

"John loved to read. He often spent many nights alone in his study engrossed in a good book."

I wished he would stop. If I was scolded once for disturbing my father while he was reading, I was scolded a hundred times.

"He was a fan of old movies; good ones."

It seemed as if every one of my father's virtues shined a light on a fault of mine. It was plain, the more I listened, the more I realized what a disappointment I was to him.

As the pastor continued, my mind wandered back to a time when I was a child; to a time when things were simpler, when nothing seemed to matter except when summer arrived and how soon it would be Christmas. At the final, 'amen,' I was devastated and thoroughly depressed.

Chapter 35

Back at work on Thursday morning, I met Will in the office. It was foggy outside, but the county was otherwise unchanged. Will had his feet on his desk and was blowing on his coffee when I walked in.

"How are you holding up, Son?" He looked at me with a deadpan expression – his way of exhibiting sympathy.

"I'm good. Everything went off without a hitch. He's gone; life goes on."

I wiped my face with both hands and looked toward the unclothed window closest to my desk. The dull of the fog was just beginning to burn off; nevertheless, the environment still matched my mood.

I had made up my mind that I was going to keep the events and the feelings of the preceding days inside me. There was no way I was going to share anything about my family or my past with Will, or anyone else. Police officers have no head, nor heart, for details like that and should never be entrusted with them. I was certain that if I opened up about my life, that one day one of my co-workers would find a way to use it against me. It would take several hours of meditation, some long walks, a couple of bottles of wine, and maybe a phone call to an old high school buddy who was now a therapist to get whatever was inside of me out; but it would happen. I would be cleansed. I still hadn't cried or grieved in any other way.

"Is there anything I can do for ya?"

"Not a thing. Unless you got that lead I asked you to get."

"Oh, on that Woods case?"

"Yeah."

He nodded and pushed some papers around on the top of his cluttered desk. He picked up a teletype and flipped it across the desk at me.

"This came in yesterday."

The print out was from Rufus Greenbaum. It said that he had gained some intelligence that Michael Tolliver was living in New Orleans. He provided an address and said he hoped the information was a help.

"You want to go to New Orleans?" I said.

"I thought you'd never ask."

Will and I spent the rest of the day filling the Captain and the Sheriff in on what we had learned, requisitioning a credit card, and getting the car serviced.

The Sheriff was very interested in the information and was therefore very supportive of our trip. We met him in his office. I noticed a new golfing trophy on the table next to his desk. The plate affixed to the base said that he had finished second in a charity four ball.

"So, you think this Tolliver might be the man that Zoe Woods was last seen with?" the Sheriff said.

Will spoke. He had a long relationship with the Sheriff, and he did all of the talking when we were with him. I spoke only when spoken to.

"Tolliver has or had a connection with a woman named Myrtice Abercrombie who worked with the Woods woman. Tolliver was her ex – either married or common law. She cut him pretty bad a few years ago. We think maybe he followed her down here to either get her back, or at least make her jealous."

"Does he meet the physical description?"

"Not that we know of." Will looked at me.

"We've only got a picture from a few years ago, and he didn't have black hair then," I said.

"How about the car?"

"Don't know about that either," Will said. "This trip is just to make contact with him, if we can; maybe see if we can get the police over there to help us get a photograph and some prints from him. We're just gonna spend some time with him and see what we can find out." He paused. "Except for a few eyewitnesses that saw them together, we really don't have much."

"Okay, well, call me at home if you need anything."

The County Garage was a brick and aluminum structure located on Vernon Street just off Interstate 10. It featured four gas pumps, four service bays, three body and fender bays, a small warehouse for tires and batteries, and an office with a phone and a television that county employees could enjoy during the wait while their vehicles were being serviced.

I pulled into the lot and parked the car next to the pumps. Josh, the gas attendant, filled my tank. I stood outside the car and made small talk while he cleaned the windshield.

"How's everything going, Sir?"

Josh talked kind of mush mouthed, but he was a very amiable sort who always had an encouraging word. He wore his hair in a military-style buzz cut, and his strong forearms worked the squeegee back and forth over the windshield with authority. His blue coveralls were still clean though it was nearly two in the afternoon.

He was the garage's unofficial greeter, and he was also responsible for pumping gas, a task that he took quite seriously. If you tried to pump your own gas, Josh got very, very angry, and you heard about it.

"Oh, I guess I'll get by. We gotta go outta town tomorrow, so I need to get the car serviced."

"I heard your daddy died, Sir."

I nodded. "Yep."

"My daddy died, too." He spoke wistfully. Josh was in his forties. "He's up in heaven."

"How long ago?"

"About ten years ago, sir."

"How'd you do with it?"

"I cried." He paused and looked hard at the windshield. "I'll go see if they can change your oil now."

We pulled out of Mobile the next morning about five. Will wanted to get to downtown New Orleans before the morning rush hour. I drove with a heavy foot, and we were in Gulfport at six fifteen, and crossing the Lake Ponchatrain Bridge at a little after seven.

New Orleans is not my favorite city. To me, it has a number of flaws. Besides perennially being the murder capital of the south – and occasionally even America – it's a town that sits below sea level, in a bowl. It stinks, the streets aren't well maintained; and, as for the 'entertainment' district, I've always thought that a city that based its tourism income on alcohol consumption and nude dancing – leading inevitably to prostitution and drug abuse – was asking for trouble crime-wise. For every decent restaurant, there's a bar or clip joint where drug addled women dance naked and visitors drink themselves into a stupor. Not my idea of how to spend a vacation. True, there is the river, the zoo, and a couple of interesting museums, but all in all, in my mind at least, New Orleans is a city to be avoided.

We crossed the river and rolled into town about eight; passed the 610 cutoff and made it to the St. Bernard Avenue exit shortly after. Traveling to New Orleans, I always got off there so we could drive part of the way through town and just kind of get the feel of the place anew.

I rolled down the window and got a whiff of the fish, creosote, and raw sewage coming in off the waterfront. The humidity felt as if was in the nineties, and the breeze that carried the noxious odors into town was out of the south at about ten miles per hour.

Will rolled down his window and took a deep breath. He looked at me and smiled.

"This town has its own unique smell, don't it, Son?"

"It stinks."

He chuckled. "You never did like this place, did'ja."

We had worked on one other homicide, the murder of a low level drug dealer who was shot and stabbed and then dumped in Mobile County, and had spent a couple of days in the city talking to his family and trying to run down a suspect. At that time, I had expressed my disdain for New Orleans.

"Not even a little bit."

"Well, we shouldn't be here that long. We'll just dig up a detective to go with us over to this address, knock this old boy around a little, and, hopefully, we'll be back home by tonight."

I turned west on Orleans Avenue, away from the Vieux Carre, and headed toward Broad. When we reached Broad, I turned back south, and in about ten or twelve blocks, I found the Police Building, on the corner of Broad and Tulane – US Highways 90 and 61. I parked on the Broad Street side. What looked like city-owned fleet cars filled up every space on the Tulane Avenue side. The last time we came to town, the city was in such bad financial shape that detectives were riding three and four to a car. I wondered if things had gotten any better.

The Police Building was vintage late fifties and early sixties architecture; lots of metal and glass, and not too much stone. The structure also served as the courts building, so there was a steady stream of people coming in and going out of the front door, paying fines, attending legal proceedings, and swearing warrants. The Detective Division – specifically Homicide – was on the fourth floor. We took the elevator up and met the receptionist, a not too attractive thirty year old who was poured into her pants.

"Yes, ma'am, we're from the Sheriff's Office in Mobile," Will said. I presented the woman my star, as Will continued. "And we was wonderin' if we could talk to someone about a homicide we're working on."

The young woman smiled. "Well, you're a little early. The detectives don't usually get here 'fore eight thirty."

I supposed that's why they call it the 'Big Easy.'

She consulted a list on her desk. "But, I think Remy's in the back." She picked up the phone. "I'll check. Why don't ya'll have a seat."

What looked like a wooden church pew sat along the wall across from her desk. We sat down, and Will crossed his legs. I looked around.

There were photos on the light blue plaster wall of what looked like executive officers in uniform. The area was dark and the tile floor was black. The place had kind of a tired air about it, like, 'work be hanged,' no one was going to worry too much about anything.

The woman hung up the telephone and smiled our direction. "Go on back," she said pointing to the hallway to our left. "He's the third door on your right."

Will nodded at the woman, and we started down the dimly lit hall. When we reached the third office, I knocked on the open door and got the attention of the older man behind the desk. He looked up and smiled.

"How ya'll doin'?"

He looked about fifty, with gray hair over a puffy and tanned face. His paunch and the strain that it was placing on the buttons on his shirt said that he had eaten one too many crawfish pies. He rose and extended his hand.

"Fine, sir." Will said. "Yourself?"

"Fine as frog's hair." He nodded toward two chairs. "Remy Boudreau. Ya'll have a seat." His accent was that familiar south Louisiana brogue that I had heard for many years listening to radio station WWL.

We parked in two metal chairs in front of his desk. Aside from the desk and chair, a couple of filing cabinets filled out the space.

Will made the introductions and got right to it. "I'm sorry we didn't call first, but our trip was kinda last minute. We got some information about a suspect we've been looking for in a homicide. A pretty good source said that he's livin' over here on Telemachus Street. Wonder if you could ride up there with us and let us talk to him?"

"Telemachus. That's only a few blocks from here. How good's your information?"

"It come from a detective supervisor at the PD up in North Charlotte, North Carolina. We don't know where he got it."

"I guess that's a pretty good source. What'chu got on this old boy?"

"Not much, really. He's got a connection to a woman who knew our victim. He's got the same name as our suspect; and he roughly fits the description." He paused. "We don't have enough to pick him up and hold him. We was just hopin' that he would talk to us and let some things slip that might either implicate him or clear him."

"What's his name?"

Will looked over at me. I filled in the blanks.

"Michael or Mike Tolliver; about five ten, stocky build." I supplied his birthdate.

"He got a record?"

"Nothing major. He got cut by his old lady pretty bad about five or six years ago. We don't know where he's been since then." Will spoke slowly and kept looking at me to verify the information.

"I'll call and see if we want him." Boudreau picked up the phone and dialed a three digit extension.

While he waited, I looked around at the pale blue walls. There were a couple of commendations, one photo of what appeared to be a younger Boudreau in a powder blue uniform shirt, and a promotion certificate announcing that Remy Boudreau had been elevated to the rank of sergeant.

In three minutes, Boudreau hung up the receiver and shook his head. "Well, we don't want him. Not even a parkin' ticket."

Will nodded. "Hey, we don't mind talking to him out at his house."

"You expectin' any trouble out of him?"

Will shook his head. "Not unless he's our man. Then, all bets are off."

Boudreau looked at the pile of papers on his desk and leaned back. He looked at us and then at the pile, then back at us. Then he smiled broadly.

"Le's go."

When we got out front, Boudreau started to get into the back of our Crown Victoria.

"Don't you want to take your car?" I said. "In case you need to leave in a hurry?"

He shook his head. "I share a car with three other guys. It'll have to stay here in case there's a murder."

I said, okay, and we all piled in. Boudreau directed me west on Tulane and in ten minutes we were in the two hundred block of South Telemachus.

It was a neighborhood of forties and fifties-era, single and two story shotgun homes, made of wood, and worn by the rains of too many hurricanes. They had small front yards and shell driveways up the sides, some of which terminated in leaning and nearly broken down garages.

"I didn't ask ya, but is your man white?" Boudreau said.

"Yeah, he is," Will said.

"Okay. This is a mixed neighborhood, but it's mostly black."

We found the house on the right hand side almost to the end of the block. There was no vehicle in the driveway, and no immediate sign of life. I parked on the curb.

The temperature was in the low nineties, and I began sweating almost immediately after we exited the car.

Taking one step up on the porch, I felt the timber give slightly. Will and Boudreau saw my hesitation and stepped carefully onto the slats. I rang the bell, then bladed myself to the door.

Footsteps sounded as one person walked toward the entrance. A dead bolt unlocked and the door opened. A man stood there, his brows raised but his hands empty.

"Mr. Tolliver? Michael Tolliver?" Boudreau said.

"Yes."

"My name is Boudreau, from the NOPD." He held up a badge. "These men are from Mobile. We'd like to talk to you."

Tolliver was as Will described him and with blue eyes and dark brown hair. He wore a blue and white striped pajama shirt, blue jeans, and his feet were bare. His face was smooth and puffy, his nose wide, and his lips were thick and pink. He had the look of a man who had never seen hard work.

When he spoke, his voice was a definite tenor. I didn't recognize his drawl immediately, but it wasn't from the east coast. I sounded more, deep south.

He looked from my face to Will's, then to Boudreau's. "Sure. Come on in. I was just fixin' to get breakfast. Ya'll want some?"

"No, thanks, Buddy. Just some conversation," Will said.

Tolliver stood to the side, and we walked in. Directly in front of us and slightly to the left was a stair case. Immediately ahead was a hall down which I could see all the way to the back door. To the left was a small room meant to be a receiving parlor. We followed Tolliver into that room, and he sat down in a ratty old chair that looked as if the seat was about to fall through. Will and Boudreau took seats on the couch that was in just as bad a shape. I stood.

"What's this all about?"

Will spoke first. "Buddy, we're working on a case over in Mobile, a murder case. We think you might have some information about it."

"A murder, in Mobile?" He sat up straight in the chair. "It wadn't me."

"How long have you been livin' here? In New Orleans, I mean?"

"Oh, 'bout eight or nine months, I guess. I come here from South Carolina."

"Any particular reason?"

"To get work. I got a job down at the docks unloadin' ships."

"Who do you work for?"

He supplied the name of some container company I'd never heard of. I looked at Boudreau. He nodded.

"I see. When's the last time you was in Mobile?"

"Well, I ain't never been there."

"Never been there? At all?"

"No, sir. Well, maybe I passed through there on my way somewheres else; but to light awhile, well, no sir."

"Where were you on the nineteenth of February?"

He chuckled. "Man, I don't know. Here, I guess. What day was that on?"

"That was on a Friday."

"Well, if it was on Friday, I'd'a been at work. I get off at three on Fridays, but I prob'ly come home. I'm usually pretty dog tired after work."

"Ever work any overtime?"

"Some." He shrugged.

"When's the last time you seen your ex-wife?"

"My ex-wife?" He chuckled again. "Which one?"

"There's more than one?"

280

"I got two. Doris is in North Carolina where I come from. Myrtice is . . . well, I don't where she's at. She tried ta kill me, so I steer clear'a her." He paused. "Is either of'em dead?"

Will looked at the floor. He took a deep breath and exhaled. I could tell that he thought this lead had expired.

He shook his head and moved on. "Do you own a car, Mr. Tolliver?"

"Well, yeah. It's out in the garage."

"You mind if we take a look at it?"

"No, not at all. Sure."

We all got up and walked back into the foyer and down the hall toward the back door. Tolliver exited first and led the way to the side entrance of the non-contiguous wood garage. He opened the door, and we all walked inside.

It looked to be about a '75 model Mercury, four-door, lime green. The roof was a little darker than the rest of the car. There were dents and rust spots at several different locations on the body, and there was a long crack in the front windshield.

I wanted to see two things: one was the tires, the other was the registration. I walked around the driver's side to the rear wheel and stooped down. I took out a short ruler and measured the depth of the treads. They were about a quarter inch deep. Then I drew out a quick sketch of its design.

There was a South Carolina tag on the vehicle; white with black lettering – three letters and three numbers – and a bird, something like a wren, in the middle. I copied down the number and stood up. Then I went up to the front, under the windshield, near the driver's door, and wrote down the identification number.

"How long you had this car?" Will said.

"About five years."

"Where'd you buy it?"

"In Charlotte. I got the papers right here." He started for the passenger side and the glove box.

I watched closely as he pulled papers out and handed them to me. The title was listed in the name of Michael Tolliver. It was five years old.

"You ever owned a Chevy?" Will said.

He shook his head. "No. I'm a Ford man. When me and my last ole lady broke up, she got the trailer, and I got this old car." He looked the vehicle over. "It ain't much, but it got me down here."

Will looked over at me. I only had two questions.

"Mr. Tolliver, is your hair dyed?"

He chuckled. "Dyed? No, sir."

"What about your family. Any brothers and sisters?"

"I got a brother in North Charlotte, North Carolina, and a sister in Beaufort, South Carolina."

"What are their names?"

"My brother is Rhett; my sister is Bonnie."

"Mother was a *Gone with the Wind* fan?" I said.

"Saw the movie fifteen times; read the book cover to cover every other year."

"So, how'd you get by with 'Michael'?"

He smiled. "Michael Ashley."

Tolliver agreed to accompany us to the Police Department in order to let us a get a mugshot and take his fingerprints. He was an amiable sort and took everything with good humor. We let him call his boss and tell him that he might be late for work. I asked him if he'd be willing to come to Mobile if we needed him, and he said, yes, if we'd ride him over.

When we finished at the Headquarters Building, we dropped Tolliver off back at his house, and Boudreau took us to lunch. It was eleven o'clock when we stopped at a little hole in the wall café right off St. Charles Avenue called, 'Marie's'.

"They got the best gumbo," Boudreau said as we took our seats in the middle of the dimly lit interior.

The place was mostly wood, but it had a tile floor and the tables were Formica-topped. Zydeco music, at a low volume, emanated from overhead speakers, and only a small amount of light found its way through the smoky windows.

"You think this Tolliver guy is your man?" he said.

I was thankful that Boudreau hadn't tried to horn in on our investigation while over at Tolliver's house. Will and I had made several trips out of town to interview suspects and witnesses in the past, and on a couple of occasions local detectives – even an FBI agent – had interjected themselves into the questioning and had divulged information that they shouldn't have; information that only the killer would know.

There's really nothing you can do to stop them because you're playing on their turf, but it still makes you mad. They talk and they know nothing about the case, so they don't know what to say or not to say. All you really want is to have someone there who knows the streets and who can show a local badge and put the people a little at ease, not blow up everything.

"Oh, I don't think so, Buddy. He don't fit the description, and his alibi's pretty easy to check."

"Who got killed?"

"Some old crazy girl met a man in a bar; he took her out and cut her throat, and she died a couple'a days later."

Boudreau nodded and was about to speak when a waitress walked up. I decided to live dangerously and try the gumbo. Boudreau did the same, and Will ordered a hamburger, well done, with French fries. When the young woman left, Boudreau continued.

"This ain't some kinda serial killer operatin' over there is it?"

"I don't really think so, Buddy." Will looked away.

It was obviously a thought that had yet to cross his mind. He and I'd always just assumed that our guy had lost his temper in the midst of amorous behavior. I never thought that he might have been killing for the fun of it.

I guess the first reason that I dismissed it was that the bar was kind of off the beaten path. If you didn't know where The Society was, you wouldn't just run up on it. Second, the black haired man let a lot of people see him with the victim. No respectable serial killer would be that conspicuous.

"No," Will said, "this was just a pick up that went sour; a one night stand gone wrong."

The waitress brought our food, and while we ate, Boudreau regaled us with stories of heads that he had cracked during Mardi Gras past; the time that as a patrol sergeant he had appeared on 'Cops' the television show; and the few months he spent undercover trying unsuccessfully to infiltrate the Dixie Mafia.

He was talking a mile a minute right up until the time that Will glanced at his watch. I looked at mine and realized it was getting on close to two.

"Well, Buddy, we really appreciate your help, but we better be gettin' back to Mobile."

"Sure. Yeah. Well, I hope you guys done some good."

"Well, I think we have."

I left a couple of dollars on the table for a tip, but Boudreau flashed his badge at the cashier as we walked out the front door, and no other funds changed hands.

We dropped Boudreau off at his office and, armed with Tolliver's fingerprints, got back on Interstate 10 just before three. I turned on the cruise control, and Will leaned back in his seat, ostensibly to nap.

"How about that Boudreau, huh. He looks like he walked out of a James Lee Burke novel," I said.

"Well, Son, that might mean more to me if I knew who James Lee Burke was."

I nodded. "What do you think about that serial killer remark he made?"

"I think he's been smokin' some bad crawdads."

"But, you know, he might have something. A new guy rolls into town, nobody knows him. He hits a random bar, picks out the stupidest chick there; talks her into leaving with him so he can kill her; then hits the road. Maybe it's not as goofy as it sounds."

Will shut his eyes, and I could tell he was thinking. I knew for a fact that Will had arrested one serial killer, and he would have some insight about it.

"No," he said. "I don't think so. It just don't have the feel of it."

"How so?"

"Well, first thing is, there's no evidence that he's killed anyone else, at least not here in our area. That's the definition of a 'serial killer.' There's got to be more than one body. Second, our man is just too big a slob to even be called 'disorganized.' I mean, tracks everywhere and panties up her snatch, and all them witnesses that saw him. And third, there's the fact that he didn't kill her. Killers kill. I feel like if he did this sort of thing often, or had done it before, we'd've see a few more wounds on her; enough to make sure she was dead."

I nodded. "That's kind of the way I had it figured."

Will scrunched down in the seat and adjusted his head against the headrest. "Just be patient, Son. We'll run across this bird, some time or another."

In ten minutes, I could hear Will snoring. I settled in and the miles began to click off. When we passed over into Mississippi, I set the radio on an oldies station out of Ocean Springs. I always listen to old music. As far as I'm concerned, anyone over thirty-five who listens to modern music has a Peter Pan complex. Will didn't listen to anything.

I was tired but not uncomfortable, until we got to the Grand Bay exit, exit four off Interstate 10. Will was gone to nappy's house, oblivious to the music and the ride.

Just as we passed the ramp, completely without warning, a flushed feeling began to come over me. My temperature rose quickly, and I began to see stars. With the rise of my blood pressure came an accompanying rise in heart rate. I gripped the steering wheel tightly and tried to concentrate on the music.

There was no apparent reason for my symptoms. The only thing I'd eaten out of the ordinary was the gumbo, and I hadn't been sick in over a year. I had no idea of what could have brought on all of this.

I took deep breaths and exhaled. My heart rate was somewhere around one hundred and thirty beats a minute. I started to believe that I was going to black out. I glanced at Will. He was sound asleep, incognizant of my situation.

Believing that if I passed out I would most assuredly run off the road, I got into the right hand lane and began to slow down. Cars and large eighteen wheeled trucks raced past us on the left. The thought that I might be dying of a heart attack began to assault my mind.

Then, just as quickly as it came, the attack left. My heart relaxed, and my breathing slowed. The flushed feeling went away, and by the time we reached the Tillman's Corner exit, nine miles away, I was back to normal, driving slightly under the speed limit just to be on the safe side.

I never told Will, and I only mentioned it to my doctor once, a year later when I went to see him to get an antibiotic to help clear up a rhinovirus. He told me it was probably a panic attack and wrote me a prescription for a depressant, for the future, if it ever happened again. I took two of them once, just to see what they were like. I got a buzz, about like a half a bottle of wine, then dropped off to sleep pretty quickly. When I woke up, I had a bad hangover. The high was pretty good; the crash not so much.

The doctor said it was all about stress. But I never understood how my body could just take over for a few minutes and me not have any control over it. I guess it was like Will said, only God knows.

Chapter 36

The next morning, I stopped at the Captain's office on the way to my own. Will, cup of coffee in hand, was already there filling the Boss in on our trip to New Orleans. I knocked on the open door.

"Come in, come in," the bald headed man said. "Sit down, Henry. Snuffy was just tellin' me about your trip."

I took the empty seat next to Will and crossed my right leg over my left. I had in the past learned that in these sessions I should just keep my mouth shut. Agnew and Will would talk a little about the case; the Captain would remark about what a tough one it was turning out to be; and then he, Agnew, would break into a recitation of one of his most memorable cases from years past. It had happened before.

"So, you don't think this cat over in New Orleans is gonna be involved, hunh."

Will shook his head. "We've got the detective over there checking his alibi; his car don't match, his description don't match, and he claimed not to even know where his ex lives."

The old man looked out the window. "So, it was a wasted trip."

"Not really. He was a lead; we had to run him down." He took another sip of coffee.

"This one's turning out to be a real stumper, ain't it."

It wasn't a question. I knew what was coming next.

"It's like old 'Jose in the tomato patch', thirty-five years ago."

I nodded but had to put my hand over my mouth to keep from chuckling. Knowing that Will had heard the story before, he turned his eyes to me and continued.

"Jose was a migrant farm worker. Him and his ole lady showed up every year to work in the watermelon fields down in Grand Bay. Well, one day old Jose just quit showin' up for work, and we got a call from old man Henson that owned all them fields down there. He sent us over to the trailers that the workers lived in when they come to town.

"Well, we got over there and talked to his wife, Maria, I think her name was, and man, was she sweatin' bullets. Ha, ha," he chuckled. "I knew she'd killed him. She told us he'd run off with one of them senoritas down there, but I knew better.

"Well, we checked all over the house for blood, but couldn't find a drop. I talked to her for a good long time; she spoke good English. I finally told her that I knew she killed him." He shook his head. "She never denied it.

"So, I just kept comin' over there every few days to see her. Every time I'd show up, she'd just get real nervous. I went over there two or three times a week for the whole summer, until finally one day she broke down and told me he was dead. She'd hit him over the head with a skillet and then had gotten some'a them boys to drag him out to the garden in the backyard. She'd buried him in the tomato patch out there." He paused. "I guess she just couldn't stand it no more."

Will nodded, like he was interested. I tried to keep a straight face. I almost couldn't stand it.

Back in our office, I closed the door and started laughing. Will snorted.

"Have you ever heard that story before?" I said while wiping away the tears.

"Only about fifty fuckin' times, Son. 'Old Jose in the tomater patch' gets more play than the Beatles." He was deadpan as he shook his head. "I think it's the only case that lazy old bastard ever made."

I continued to chuckle. "I just got a picture in my mind of about a thousand cartoons that I ever saw where a fat Mexican woman brains her Speedy Gonzales-looking husband with a skillet."

Will snorted. "To hear him tell it, it was the crime of the fuckin' century; but it was just some old wetback bitch whoppin' her old man over the noggin."

Our amusement was interrupted by the telephone. Will picked it up and reached for a pen.

"Natural?" He said. "Well, ain't there somebody else that can go?" He paused and wrote. "Alright." He put down the receiver.

"Shit." He looked at me. "Natural death on the south side."

Wiping my eyes, I reached for my notebook.

The call was to a rundown, rural area off the Blue Star Parkway, east of Grand Bay, on Lutie Tilson Road. It was a tree shaded dirt trail, a little wider than one lane, made of fine, red sand that ran north off the highway, up a hill, and through some pasture land.

It was a beautiful day; a cloudless sky with a slight breeze out of the south. It would be hot on the inside of the house, but outside, it was still pleasant.

The residence in question was wood framed with a steeply pitched roof and a tall porch, a house that looked as if it had been built in the nineteen twenties. The wood was weather beaten, and any speck of paint that had once adorned it had long since flaked away.

Two marked patrol cars, one in the dirt driveway, the other blocking one half of the road, as well as a patrol supervisor's car, distinguishable by its lack of overhead lights, were already on scene.

There was a small knot of people milling about in the front yard. Two young females in their twenties, and three teenaged males, all very tall, wearing shorts and basketball shoes, were talking and looking around. Two young children stood on the ground, one of whom clung to the pant leg of the largest of the females.

I stopped the car behind the patrol car in the road. As we stepped out, the coroner's vehicle stopped behind us, and Angie McDowell got out. I stood by the driver's door of my car and watched as she walked toward me. She'd cut her hair since I'd seen her last, and, in my opinion, it was unattractively short. She was carrying a camera bag and a clipboard, and she was not smiling.

"So," she said, "what have we got?"

"Don't know; haven't been inside yet." I looked her up and down. "You look terrible."

"Gee, thanks. I've had a bad week. I got called out last night for a murder in Prichard; the night before for one in Saraland; and I haven't gotten more than two hours of sleep in the last four days. So, keep it to yourself."

I smiled and made a gentlemanly gesture of a sweep of my right arm showing her the way toward the front yard. We looked ahead and saw Will talking to Terry Scarborough. Megan Crenshaw was standing next to them with a notepad in her hand. As we got closer, I heard one of the women sniff and saw her wipe her eyes.

"Looks natural to me," Scarborough said. "Megan's got all the information." He nodded toward the house. "He's in the bathroom."

When he looked back at Will, a slight smile crossed his lips. Crenshaw grinned.

"What the fuck's going on?" Will said. He spoke in low tones so the family couldn't hear.

"Nothin'. He's in the bathroom," Scarborough said.

Will smirked and started toward the door. I was five feet behind him. McDowell stayed in the yard to get information from Crenshaw.

In two long steps we were on the rickety old porch, and in three more we were over the threshold and into the dark living room. Will stopped and looked both ways before deciding to turn right down a long hallway.

The bathroom was the second room on the left. Will stopped in the threshold, and I stepped up beside him. The pungent odor of feces and urine was outstanding.

The man was lying on his left side, between the tan commode and a matching bathtub. His gray, cloth pants and his white boxer shorts were down around his ankles, just above a pair of scuffed, black oxfords. His shirt was plaid and long sleeved. There was a copy of the *Examiner* newspaper, open and turned to the sports page, lying across the lip of the tub.

The old gentleman appeared to be in his seventies. Gray hair covered the sides of his head, but had deserted his crown. His beard was gray also. He looked to be of average height, but his pot belly hung down, effectively obscuring his genitalia.

Will stopped and surveyed the scene. "That son of a bitch."

I looked around Will's shoulder. My gaze started at the old man's head and worked its way down until it reached his bare buttocks. There, protruding from his anus, was a nearly eight inch clump of feces, about the circumference of a banana and curved at just about the same arc.

The sight made me chuckle to myself. I had long since stopped laughing on crime scenes – but this was funny.

Will was disgusted. "Look at that shit hangin' out his ass."

Apparently, in the middle of his morning constitutional, the old man's heart had given way in mid-strain, or mid-grunt as it were. He had fallen over onto the floor before gravity could do its job and put the waste into the bowl.

I chuckled. "Man, that's ugly."

"I'm gonna kick the shit outta that Scarborough." He stepped back out of the threshold. "Go call that woman from the Lab in here. This is her job."

291

Outside, McDowell had finished talking to Crenshaw and was conversing with the older of the two women in the yard, the one with the child hanging onto her pant leg. The males had walked away and were just meandering about, throwing a basketball back and forth.

I walked slowly to McDowell and leaned over next to her ear. Her perfume was fantastic.

"Will says to get in here."

She looked at me with wide eyes. "What's up?"

"Just come inside," I whispered. "The murder weapon is still in him."

She said 'excuse me' to the woman and followed me into the house, down the hall, and to the door of the john. Will had stepped away from the doorway and was leaning against the frame, his arms folded.

"I think you can take custody of the body now," he said.

McDowell was looking at Will, her eyes wide with anticipation. She turned and looked into the room and froze. It took her a second to the digest the scene, but when she did, her face wrinkled up like a raison and all she could say was:

"Eeeuuuu. What's that?"

"It's a turd, sweetheart," Will said lightly but softly.

He and I started back down the hall toward the living room. "Let us know what the doctor says," I yelled over my shoulder. "And keep it slick."

Chapter 37

We got back to the office after lunch and finally got to sit for a few minutes and once again reflect on what we had on the Zoe Woods case.

In my mind we had effectively eliminated Michael Tolliver as a suspect in Zoe's murder. I just didn't get a murder vibe from him. He had an alibi, and nothing matched; not the hair, the car, nothing. I called down to Roy Rogers' office and made sure that he compared Tolliver's fingerprints to the one found on the two dollar bill that we'd gotten from Sis. I didn't expect a hit.

There was no reason to believe that Tolliver had anything to do with the case, except for one thing. In his garage, when I leaned over and looked at the South Carolina tag on his car, something caught my eye.

The tag was white with black characters. There were three numbers and three letters. In between the numbers and letters was a picture of a wren. Then it had hit me. It was a bird; a 'bur'; the syllable that Zoe Woods had been unable to articulate but had repeated several times to us in the hospital. It was a stretch, but I brought it up to Will. He was intrigued.

"So, what are you thinkin'?"

"Well, maybe the brother. He's from up that way. Maybe he's got a car with a South Carolina tag on it."

Will paused. "What do we know about this brother? And what connection does he have to this area? I mean, why does he come to Alabama, pick up a woman, and cut her throat?"

"Well, he does know Myrtice, his brother's ex-wife. And, it is on the way to and from New Orleans. Maybe he hits town, can't find Myrtice, so he goes to a bar; and then it's just like we talked about. He takes out Zoe, something goes wrong, and he goes off on her."

Will put his hands behind his head and shut his eyes. He didn't speak for a couple of minutes. When he did, he was not as dismissive as he sometimes was of my other ideas.

"Okay, I'll buy that. Just what do we know about Tolliver's brother?"

I flipped through my notebook. "Tolliver said his name was 'Rhett.'"

Will took a deep breath and exhaled. "Alright, see what you can work up on him."

I nodded. One thing was for sure: we could find out everything about him, but if we couldn't find him, none of it meant a thing.

My first call was to Rufus Greenbaum in North Charlotte. He said he'd get back to me with what he could, but the name Rhett Tolliver didn't ring a bell to him.

I also called Rogers down in ID and gave him the name of Rhett Tolliver and told him to see if he couldn't dig up some prints on him from the FBI, or anywhere else. Then I suggested to Will that we take a run out to the chicken plant to see Myrtice Abercrombie and ask her what she knew about our new suspect, Rhett Tolliver.

Before we could leave, Neely sidled into the office. Will was still in his thinking position, and I was making notes about the case of the old man on the commode. Neely sat down in the chair next to my desk and smiled.

"Hey, what's up?" he said looking from Will to me.

I looked at him suspiciously. "Nothin'. What's up with you?"

"Condolences about your dad. You get all that squared away?"

"Yeah, thanks. Sorry I had to bug out on you and your case."

"Don't worry about it. We found the gun at a crack house down in the Village. It was a revolver, by the way. He gave us that half assed confession, and we talked to the guy that drove him out of Theodore. We've got a pretty good case."

I nodded.

"Oh, and that old woman at the stoplight? She picked him out of live line up. And the man on the balcony, the one that you found, well, you were right, he knew the boy's name all along. He just didn't want to say it."

"That son of a . . ."

Neely leaned back in his chair with a self-satisfied look on his face. He was really a good detective; energetic, and persistent. I got the feeling on several occasions that he wanted to work with Will. He reached in his pocket and took out a piece of paper.

"Hey, you wanna hear somethin' funny?"

"We were actually on the way out."

"It'll only take a second." He reached and punched the speaker function on the phone and dialed the dispatcher's extension.

"Metro Sheriff's Office."

It was Cathy, the most prim and proper sounding of all the dispatchers. Her voice was high, and she spoke with exaggerated articulation.

"Yeah, this is Neely. I need you to run a tag. Can you copy?"

"Go ahead."

"It's a Florida passenger car." He supplied the numbers.

"Hold on." She put the call on hold, and we sat in silence.

She returned in two minutes. "Can you copy?"

"Go ahead." Neely was smiling broadly.

She repeated the number. "It's registered to Won Long Dong, on Heritage Road in Pensacola; it should be displayed on a 1990 Toyota, four door, white in color; warrant check is negative."

Her voice only slightly betrayed the obvious humor of the Asian name that she had just read. We heard what sounded like laughter from other female voices in the background.

"Thanks," Neely said as he hung up the phone.

After he did, he burst into hilarity and slapped his leg. I smiled. Will didn't move.

"Is that what you came over here to do?" I said.

"That and to tell you that the Captain's lookin' for ya."

"What for?"

"He said he had a special detail for you."

My heart sank. When the Captain had a special detail for me it usually involved some sort of personal security; picking someone up at the airport and riding them around; or worse yet, a trip out of town.

"You know what it is?"

Neely shook his head. "Nope, but he had me get the Harden file for him this morning."

That probably meant that somebody, one of the Sheriff's political cronies perhaps, had called in a lead that he wanted run down.

"Well, that was Will's case. He should take this detail."

Will's eyes shot open and bored a hole in me. "Not a chance."

Carl Harden was a biker in the Las Ratas (The Rats) motorcycle gang. He had come through town on I-10 with his mob about five years ago making the annual run to Daytona for Bike Week. A farmer found Harden in the bed of an old pickup truck parked in his pasture, through a gate and about a quarter mile off the main road, one Sunday morning. Carl, or 'Cal' as the other bikers called him, had been shot in the chest, and he was minus his boots and leathers. I had been the ID officer assigned to the case and had photographed the scene, as well as processed the truck.

"You know as much about that case as I do," Will said.

I was just about to argue with him when the phone rang. It was the Captain summoning me to his office.

When I hung up, Neely rose and turned to the door. He walked out chuckling.

296

"You come on, too," I said to Will. "He wants us both."

Upstairs, the Captain's door was open. Things were the way we left them that morning.

"Sit down," he said.

Will and I took our assigned seats. The Captain slid a case file across the desk toward me. I reached and picked it up.

"You remember the Harden case?"

"Yes, sir; the biker that was killed out near the state line a few years ago."

"Right. Well, the Sheriff wants you to go over to Jacksonville and present it at that Robbery-Homicide Convention that they have over there every year."

I was familiar with the annual Robbery-Homicide Convention, though I never knew who put it on. It had been held in Mobile a few years previous, but I heard that it had lost money.

"When's it going to be?"

"It's in October. Just get ready for it. According to the literature, you get up to a fifteen minute presentation if you need it. Take some slides, or get Rogers to blow some photos up for ya. Just give them an overview and maybe somebody will call in with a lead."

Will sat silently. I didn't know if he was insulted at not being asked to take on this responsibility, or if he was relieved at not having to make the trip and the public speech. The Captain handed me the brochure with all the information.

I picked up the paper and glanced at it. It was the same week as my high school reunion. I wondered if I could get back in time.

"Anything in particular that you want me to leave out of the talk?"

"Ahh, don't mention about them taking his boots and his leathers. You can tell them where he was shot and found, and all that. Just hold back that we know it was a biker thing. If they're not smart enough to figure that out, then they won't send us anything anyway."

I nodded. "Can Will come?"

Will's eyes opened widely. "Oh, no. The Sheriff wants you." He pointed his finger at me like Uncle Sam.

"But," Will said, looking at the Captain, "we need you to keep some of the small stuff off of us if we're gonna get anything done on this crazy girl case."

The Captain nodded, not knowing what Will was talking about. I knew for a fact he made it a practice to stay detached from the day to day calls unless the Sheriff got involved.

"This morning we had to go out and take a look at an old man that blew his heart out while he was sittin' on the shitter. It was somethin' that somebody else could'a handled; like the patrol sergeant."

Agnew nodded. "I'll look into it."

Will got a disgusted look on his face because he knew that nothing would come of his complaint. He had worked for Linus Agnew too long.

Forty-five minutes later, Will and I caught up with Myrtice Abercrombie just as she was punching the time clock to leave the chicken plant. She still had a clear, plastic hair cover on her head and white boots on her feet when we stopped her, in the parking lot, about fifteen feet from her car, the Ford with the South Carolina tag.

"Myrtice," Will said as we walked toward her. She looked surprised at first, but then she shrugged with recognition.

"Hey. What'ch'all want?"

"We want to ask you about your ex-brother in law, Rhett."

"Rhett? I ain't seen him in five years."

"Where was he when you saw him?"

"Back in Charleston. Seems like I run into him in a bar."

Will stood by the driver's side wheel well. I stood four feet away, toward the driver's rear door, while Myrtice leaned against the car door and wiped off her hair cover. It was cloudy and the wind was blowing out of the west.

"Me and Rhett are okay. I mean, I stabbed his brother and all, but he don't hold it against me."

"Have you talked to him?"

"I think he called me a few years ago."

"What for?"

"I don't know, just to talk."

I could tell she was lying. First, she saw him in Charleston; then she talked to him on the phone.

"Something I want to know," I said. "Are you guys from North Carolina or South Carolina?"

"We all grew up right outside'a Charlotte. That's where I married Mikey. Then, when we had our troubles, after I got out, I moved to Charleston. Rhett, he come down there to see me a couple'a times, and he gotta job at a furniture company. Mikey was in and outta there, too. Their sister lives near the coast, I think."

"Could you describe Rhett?" Will said.

"Uh, oh, I ain't seen him in a while, but last time I did, he had black hair, about five ten, kinda husky."

"What was he driving?"

"Some little red car. I don't know what kind."

I looked at Will. His expression was deadpan. "You think you could meet with our artist and help us get a drawin' of him?"

She was hesitant. "Well, yeah, I guess so. I mean, it's been a while. It may not be so good."

"That's not a problem."

"Rhett done somethin'?"

"We just wanna talk to'im."

Will told her to come in on her first off day, which, that week, she said, would be Thursday. We let her go, but I didn't expect to see her again.

In the car on the way to the office, Will wanted to talk. He seemed wired.

"I think we might be onto somethin', Son. This old girl gives us a good drawing, and we show it around, or get it on television, and we could come up with somethin'. We just have to be careful and not run him outta town."

"If he's in town."

"If he ain't, he'll be back. My guess is that he's fuckin' Myrtice." He looked at me. "She couldn't make it work with one brother, so she's givin' the other one a try. You've seen her. It ain't like she's gotta whole lotta choices. If he's gone, he'll be back in town soon enough."

Chapter 38

Two days later, Myrtice, contrary to my suspicions, did show up at the office to help Roy Rogers create a composite drawing of Rhett Tolliver. I remarked to Will that we could guess that Rhett probably wasn't as good a lover as we thought he was, else she would have protected him better.

Will took her downstairs, and Rogers used the Identi-Kit system to create a drawing of a man with a square head; a flat, thick nose; and thin lips. The lips and the coal black, possibly dyed hair were the only things that matched the descriptions we received from our other witnesses.

We probably should have gotten Sis and Larry Flynt and maybe some of the others from The Society to do the same thing, but, frankly, I didn't trust drunks to create a likeness in which we could have confidence. At least Myrtice had spent a reasonable length of time with Rhett Tolliver and could honestly say what he looked like – if she was being honest. I intended to save Sis and Larry for a potential live line up, if we ever caught the guy.

I took copies of the drawing and passed them out to every detective in the division, and also to all the deputies in patrol. I also sent a raft of copies over to the Police Department for distribution to their patrolmen, especially the officers in the First Precinct, which covered downtown Mobile and the area around The Society.

Will and I talked it over and decided that while he worked on administrative tasks, I would take the drawings around to show them at some of the other bars, the white ones at least, in the area to see if anyone might recognize Tolliver's face. I could tell Will thought it was a waste of time, but he often indulged me in the 'busy-ness' of detective work – the bases that had to be touched, the doors that had to be knocked on – that he could often skip because he had much more experience than I.

My first stop was a dive called the 'Right Hip Pocket' on Duval Street, two blocks from Dauphin Island Parkway. I stopped in at about two PM the Monday after Myrtice came in. It was cloudy and threatening rain outside. There were two cars and a beer truck in the shell parking lot.

The building was a gray cinderblock with a hand painted sign. It didn't look professionally done, which is probably why the name was as long as it was. A real sign painter would have charged by the word. It would have looked better, but it would have cost more.

Inside, it was dark, but not pitch. A blade of light flashed across the interior when I opened the door and walked in. There was a woman behind the bar, next to the beer guy who was unloading a case into the cooler. He had six more on his hand cart.

It was the kind of place to which full blown alcoholics come to get drunk fast. There was no pretense about a place like this; none of that neighborhood meeting house thing goin' on. The whiskey was watered down, the beer was common, and the people didn't bother you when you sat on the stool and kept your mouth shut.

I walked toward the end of the bar and stood under a Pabst Blue Ribbon clock that in the dark seemed to put out an abnormally large amount of light. The chubby, middle aged woman with dishwater blonde hair walked toward me and stopped. She gave me a half grin, and I could see that she had a gold tooth in front.

"Can I hep ya?" she said smiling while wiping her hands on a multi-colored (pink and blue) dress that draped her thick body. Her voice was high and soft; not the hoarse, raspy speech of a smoker.

"Yes, ma'am. My name is Faulkner, and I'm with the Metro Sheriff's Department." I held up my star and watched for a reaction.

Her brows went up. "Oh, okay," was all she said.

I seemed to catch her by surprise. It was hard to believe that I was the only officer ever to have enquired within her bar.

"And you are?" I said.

"Gladys Burton. I run the place."

I nodded while noticing that she didn't say 'own.'

"I want to show you a drawing and see if you might recognize this man." I opened my padfolio and removed the likeness of Rhett Tolliver that I had encased in plastic.

"Have you ever seen this guy?"

She took the plastic and held it up to the light from the clock. She knitted her brows in what I thought at the time was feigned concentration.

"Well, let me see here."

She reached in the pocket of her dress and pulled out a pair of those drugstore brand, off-the-rack reading glasses, after which she put them on and pulled the bridge down toward the tip end of her nose.

"You know, he does look familiar."

I didn't believe her. "How so?"

"Well, I mean, he may have been in here before."

"Are you sure?"

"Well, not a hun'ert per cent positive, but he does look familiar."

"Any idea when he came in?"

She shook her head. "Oh, now, I wouldn't know that. See, we have a lot of people come in an' outta here."

"Any idea what he was drinking?"

She pursed her lips and stared at the photo. "You know, I think it was bourbon."

I nodded. "You happen to see what he was driving?"

She shook her head hard. "Oh, no. I wouldn't have seen him come or go."

"How about a bouncer? Someone workin' the door maybe?"

"No, we don't have nobody like that."

"What do you do when you have problems?"

"Oh, we don't have a lotta problems here, but when we do, we call you fellas."

"Are any of your regulars here that I could talk to?"

"Nobody here but me and ole Tommy there," she smiled and motioned toward the beer guy, a thirtyish man with brown hair and a gut. He was bent over, putting cans into the cooler.

I took back the composite and handed her a paper copy. "Okay, well, if you see this guy again," I handed her my business card, "be sure and give me a call."

She took the card and stared at it. "How come you want this guy?"

"He's wanted for murder."

I love to tell those people who think they're being cute, trying to jerk me around, that the person I'm looking for has killed someone. They think it's all a big game until they find out someone's dead.

"Oh." Her response had a surprised lilt on the end of it.

"Thank you for your time."

The next establishment was called the 'Trick Knee.' The name was not quite indicative of the type of place it was. Don't get me wrong, it was no Studio 54, but it was nicer than the 'Hip Pocket,' and the parking lot was paved.

The place was located on Barkus Street, about halfway between the old Brookley Air Force Base and Interstate 10. It was a wood frame structure with an attached, covered patio, and a large neon sign above the front door. The building itself was painted blue, and there were two old growth oaks, one at each of the front corners. When I got there, a metallic blue, tricked out F-250 was the only vehicle in the lot.

On the inside, it was not dark, and my eyes were acclimated to the interior in no time. I looked both directions and saw no one.

"Hello? Anybody here?"

There was no response except the sound of ice falling out of the maker, behind the bar, into the aluminum bin below. The atmosphere was eerie. I put my notebook down on a Formica topped table, reached down to my ankle holster and extracted my pistol, and then held it behind my right leg as I cautiously walked to a location where I could see behind the bar. It was clear.

There was a sense of apprehension within me. An officer tries to prepare himself for walking in on a robbery, or finding a clerk shot behind a counter, by practicing in his mind what he will do if that one in a million chance occurs; but it's not the same as when the real thing happens.

Behind the bar, I looked through the small pane of glass up near the top of the swinging door that led to the back of the building. I expected to see a kitchen, but what I saw was a short hall with one door on the left and two on the right.

From what I could observe, the door on the left looked sturdier, so I supposed it to be the office. I pushed through the swinging door, checked the two doors on the right and found them both locked.

As quietly as I could, I tried the knob on the door on the other side and felt it turn under my hand. I pushed it forward about an inch to see if it squeaked. It did not. I stood to the side of the frame, brought my pistol up, and used my left hand to push the door open slightly. My heart was beating hard.

What I saw didn't register for a second. I pushed the door open no wider than was needed to see who or what was inside and then stopped. There, leaned back in his overstuffed leather chair, was a fat, bald man who I guessed was the owner of the truck outside. His eyes were closed, and he looked as if he was asleep.

Kneeling in front of him, with her back to me, was a female wearing a pair of jean shorts and a blue tank top. Her bare feet were dirty. I couldn't see all of what she was doing, but I could tell that her head was moving up and down rapidly in the unmistakable posture and action of fellatio. I slowly and silently pulled the door closed and stepped back.

When I'd bent down and replaced the pistol in its holster, I pulled out my star from my left hip pocket and, as hard as I could, banged on the door about six or eight times with my fist.

"This is the Metro Sheriff's Office! Everything okay in there!?"

I couldn't see what was happening, but it sounded as if a tornado had struck. Pushing the door open again, I found the fat man supine on the floor, the woman sprawled on her back, and the leather chair turned over on its side. Papers and a couple of books were on the floor and the phone was off its cradle, the base assembly lying across the arm of the chair.

"Is everything okay?" I said holding my badge out in front of me and stifling a laugh.

305

"Uh, ah, yeah, ah, yeah, ahhhhh, shit," the man said, while holding his exposed penis in his right hand. The woman was wiping her mouth.

Knowing that now any conversation with the man about Rhett Tolliver and the composite would be totally useless, I stood and took in the scene in detail so that I could recount it fully to Will. He would be sorry he missed it.

I wasn't sure, but I thought I saw blood on his organ.

Chapter 39

About a week later, toward the end of August, Neely, who usually worked Sunday, asked if I would switch off days with him. I reluctantly agreed; reluctantly, because whenever I did that sort of thing – working when I should be off – something out of the ordinary always happened. This Sunday would be no different.

Standing in the checkout line at the drug store with a pint of milk and a cinnamon roll in hand, I received a radio call to contact the dispatcher. I found the first phone I could and called. It was about nine o'clock in the morning.

"Hey, what's up?" I said.

"Look," Mary one of the senior dispatchers said. Her tone was strained. "We just got a call from a deputy in Jacks County, Florida. He said he had two males and two females in custody." She paused. "One of the girls said that the boys had killed a man named 'Larry' in Mobile . . . and that this 'Larry' was somehow affiliated with the Sheriff's Department."

"Oh, no." I thought quickly. "Did she say where this happened?"

"She said that they met him at a bar on the Blue Star Parkway, and that they went to his house; she said he had a farm not far from the bar."

I took a deep breath. My mind quickly ran down the roster of 'Larrys' that I knew in the department. There was only one, an older civil deputy that worked in evictions. In the picture of him that I had in my mind, he didn't strike me as a guy who would run bars; he was fifty-five and had a fat face. However, everyone has a secret life, so I didn't dismiss him immediately.

"You think they're talking about Larry in Civil?" I said.

"I was thinkin' it was more like Larry Stinson, in the Posse."

I paused. "Now, that is very likely."

Larry Wayne Stinson was born in the northeast, on a farm in upstate Vermont. He came from an affluent family and was headed for an Ivy League education and a career on Wall Street until an unfortunate accident changed everything. When he was about fifteen, Larry was thrown from a horse and struck his head on a wagon tongue. He fell into a coma and didn't wake up for more than a month.

Afterwards, Larry just wasn't right. He lost interest in school, fell into severe substance abuse, and just generally became what a lay person would call 'touched.' His parents, after enduring several years of erratic behavior, shipped him south to be near extended family. They bought him a fifty acre farm, including a house, in south Mobile County, and he began to live the life of a country gentleman more or less quietly on what was believed to be a sizeable trust fund.

Linus Agnew met Larry when the Sheriff's Substation was located up on the Old Pascagoula Road in Theodore. Larry had wandered in one day, with a knot on

307

his head, claiming that he had been hit with a flat iron by a woman who had stolen three hundred dollars from him. The Captain recognized his helplessness and decided to take him under his wing.

It was not unusual for Larry to pick up fallen women and bring them home with him for sex, then awaken the next morning to find that they had robbed him and more often than not left him tied to his bed. Larry had a serious drinking problem and that, coupled with the residuals from his injury, made him susceptible to commit acts that were not rational. That he might have picked up two females at a local bar, brought them home, and thereafter wound up dead would not be at all out of the realm of possibility.

One of the things the Captain tried to do for Larry was to get him involved in the 'Posse,' a forty year old social and service organization made up of some of the Sheriff's political cronies who met once a month over at the county-owned horse arena for a beer swill and bull session. Each year, they wore ornate, Wild West-looking uniforms while riding on horseback in the local Mardi Gras parades. But their biggest claim to fame was that they had ridden in John Kennedy's inaugural. The two females had undoubtedly seen a uniform or a photograph in Larry's home and that had led them to believe that Stinson was affiliated with the Sheriff's Department.

"Go ahead and check the Posse roster," I told Mary, "and get me Larry Stinson's address."

"10-4."

I called Chuck Hernandez and told him to meet me in Theodore. Mary radioed me to say that Stinson's house was located off Marsh Road about two miles from the Parkway. Marsh Road was a paved, two lane, county road that wound through rural farmland from the main highway to Hamilton Road about six miles to the north.

Hernandez, working his normal shift, met me at a convenience store at Marsh and Old Pascagoula Roads. I shared with him what I knew and admonished him to be careful, after which we drove south, cautiously, toward Larry Stinson's farm.

We turned off the main road and onto Larry's one hundred and fifty yard long driveway about ten minutes later. The drive ended in a circular roundabout with a dry fountain in the center. We parked on either side of the statue – Lady Godiva on horseback – and exited our vehicles. It was a beautiful day, not a cloud in the sky.

The residence was a two story, Japanese pagoda with a bamboo-looking veneer. It was an odd choice of architecture for its location, but that was Larry – odd. The trim was painted brown and there was a short porch in front of the main door.

I motioned for Hernandez to check the rear, and I walked to the front door. It was locked. There were windows on either side, so I stood to one side and looked in.

There, in the front living space, seated in one of four club chairs arranged in a semi-circle in front of the television set, was Larry Stinson, in the end chair on the right; fingers interlaced and resting on his belly, legs crossed at the ankles, and his head down. He wore jeans, but no shirt or shoes. I saw what looked like dried blood that had communicated from his head, across his face, and down the middle of his chest and onto his abdomen.

I stood and looked at the scene for several seconds, as if not quite certain of what I saw. I shouldn't have been surprised; we had the call, there was blood, and homicides do happen. I guess it was the fact that this was someone that I knew, though not at all well, and had talked to, and now he was gone. Somehow, at that moment, he seemed as close, yet as distant, to me as my own father had been on that steel table at the funeral home. It all seemed surreal.

My gaze was broken by the sight of Hernandez as he walked forward from the back door, through the kitchen, and into the wide living room. He stopped to check Larry's pulse, then continued on, flipped the deadbolt on the front door, and opened it.

I stepped inside and reached to my ankle for my pistol. Hernandez, who was in uniform, drew his also, and I motioned to him that we should search the rest of the house.

The ground floor contained the kitchen and an 'L' shaped living space. We checked the closets near the back of the room and then went upstairs.

There were two bedrooms on the second floor. We checked the bathroom first, and then looked in both bedrooms. The master bedroom was unremarkable except for the clutter that covered the floor.

Downstairs, I used Hernandez's radio to call the dispatcher. I told her to get in touch with Will, the Captain, and the Sheriff. Then I looked at the body.

Funny how he was 'Larry' a couple of months ago when I saw him last. Now, he was 'the body.'

I, too, checked for a carotid pulse. He was in full rigor, and his skin was cold. Without moving him, I tried to find the source of the bleeding. The best I could tell, it was coming from the crown of his head.

Larry was forty, five ten, with a husky build, which is to say that his stomach was full, but not rotund. He had a brown mustache, but sandy blond hair that was thinning on top. It was through the thin hair on his crown that I could see four, one inch long lacerations on the top of his head. It was clear that he had been beaten to death with a blunt object.

"Did you know him?" I said.

Hernandez looked at the dead man and shook his head. "Not really, no. I mean, I saw him around, but I don't think I ever talked to him."

"He was a kook; but he was a lovable kook." I paused and hyperventilated. "I have a feeling the Captain is going to take this one hard."

There was nothing to do then but wait. I stepped back, took out my notepad, and began to document what I had seen and done since the dispatcher had called me earlier; all the while silently cursing Neely.

The Captain was on scene in thirty minutes, Will in thirty-five, and the Coroner in an hour. Meanwhile, Hernandez was making his self useful by photographing the house. I pointed out a couple of items that I wanted him to seize and print, but we both agreed that until we knew more from the boys and girls in Florida, there wasn't much need in gathering up the whole house and taking it down to the evidence office. We would just see that the house was sealed until we could get back, and then we could take what we wanted.

"He's got a sister over in Pensacola," Agnew said. "I'll have to find her number."

I was only partially right. Agnew was affected, but not in an emotional way. His look and his words conveyed more of a sense of disappointment rather than shock or grief.

When Will arrived at the house he immediately got on the phone with the people in Jacks County to find out exactly what happened. He talked for fifteen minutes and hung up. His look was calm.

"Well, I've worked harder cases," he said.

Agnew looked at him with inquisitive eyes. I took out my pad.

"This Lieutenant Robertson says that one of his boys was ridin' through the I-10 rest area early this morning when he saw a car with some people sleepin' in it. He stopped and looked in the window, and apparently, one of the girls was awake.

"She got out and told the deputy that the two boys in the front seat had killed a man in Mobile, Alabama. She said the dead man's name was 'Larry,' and he worked for the sheriff's department.

311

"The deputy got some help, canned'em all on suspicion, and when they got'em apart, both girls spilled it. They witnessed it all."

"Did they say why?" Agnew said.

"This Robertson says he didn't ask'em, but the boys had some liquor and a couple'a hundred dollars on'em, so he thinks it was robbery."

Agnew stood and looked at Larry while slowly shaking his head. "He sure didn't deserve this."

A pall settled over the room. Had it been anybody else, we'd be serious, yet lighthearted. We'd be looking for unusual things to chuckle about; things that might lighten the stress. Instead, we all wore somber looks and realized that our usual demeanor might not seem so funny to the Captain.

Everyone stood around staring, saying nothing for what seemed like several minutes but what was only about two or three. The silence was broken by a knock in the front door.

I walked over to the window and motioned for Danny Leftwich to come around to the back. I could see that one of the pathologists, George Walters, was with him.

Walters was a free-spirited Californian who had spent time in the South during a short stint in the Navy. He wore wire-rimmed, granny glasses, and his scraggily beard and gaunt face caused him to bear a striking resemblance to Abraham Lincoln. He was tall, thin, and bony, and on this day, he wore jeans, a t-shirt, and leather sandals.

"Does everyone know Dr. Walters?" Leftwich said.

Himself a transplanted Nevadan, Leftwich knew that the doctor, with his flower child looks and laid back manner, might have a hard time assimilating into the Deep South, so he did all he could to help him fit in, including making all the right introductions.

We all nodded at the physician who looked at us with tired eyes. If I hadn't known better, I'd've said he was high.

"Thanks for coming, Doctor," Agnew said. He pointed toward the dead man in the chair. "We all knew him," he said. "He was in the Posse."

I was sure that Walters didn't know what the Posse was. Perhaps Leftwich, if he knew, would explain it to him.

The Doctor nodded and walked toward him. He reached around to his back pocket and took out rubber gloves. Leftwich produced a camera and began snapping photos.

Walters started at Larry's head and began to work his way down. He studied the four lacerations closely then took a good look at his chest. I could see that he had found something we'd missed.

"It looks like he was stabbed in the heart," Walters said spreading the wound with his fingers, "though I can't see how deep." He paused. "I guess you noticed the strikes to the head. I can't tell you what killed him until I get him to the office, but you can bet it was one of the two." He looked up at the Captain's face.

"Can I note you as confirming his identity?"

Agnew nodded. "I've known him about fifteen years." He looked around. "I've been in this house many times." He paused. "But his fingerprints are on file from when he joined the Posse, if you need'em."

"Does anyone know how he got this way?" Walters said.

Will spoke up. "He was at a bar, and that's where he picked up these two girls and two boys, teenagers. He brought'em home, and apparently somethin' set the boys off." He paused. "Bringin' strangers home was somethin' that was not unusual for Larry to do."

"Kind of a reckless person, was he?"

Agnew spoke up. "He fell and hit his head when he was young. He wasn't right after that. If you see anything in the autopsy that might explain it, I for one would certainly appreciate knowing it."

"I'll take a look."

313

The room was silent. I wrote. Leftwich wrote. Hernandez photographed the rest of the house. Will walked and looked. Walters continued examining the body, and the Captain just stood aside and stared at Larry.

"It looks like they was watchin' a movie," Will said. "There's a tape in the machine, and it says. . ." he looked closely at the label, ". . . *birthday*."

"It looks like they may have taken some food, too," Hernandez said. "And, the kitchen phone's missing."

I noted all the information as it came in. While the girls would no doubt exchange their testimony for immunity, we would still have to put the boys in the house forensically.

"When do you expect to examine him?" Agnew said to Walters.

"I'll look at him as soon as we can get him downtown."

Will looked at me. "Go on down there with'im. I'll call Florida and tell'em we'll be there late this afternoon."

Leftwich opened the front door and let in two ambulance attendants and a gurney. They carried a black body bag.

I laid down my pad and helped Leftwich wrap Larry in a clean white sheet then zip him closed inside the bag. Before we secured it, I found his wallet in his left hip pocket. It contained four hundred and fifty dollars in cash.

"If robbery was the motive, they certainly didn't do a very good job of it."

"I'll take his wallet," Agnew said.

I took out Larry's driver's license and glanced at Will as I handed the leather billfold over to the Captain. At that moment, I didn't know whether to make the amount of money in it a matter of evidence or not. I'd ask Will about it later.

The attendants loaded the body into the back of the ambulance and closed the door. The thud of the van's doors closing had a sound of finality that I'd never noticed before.

An hour later I was at the morgue. I'd left Will and Hernandez at the house to see if they couldn't come up with some reasonable cause for what appeared to be a senseless crime.

Motive is not necessary to prove in a criminal case. The state has only to prove the victim was a human being and that the defendant had caused his death. Law Enforcement was left with trying to find out if the defendant had the intent and the means to commit the crime; and to the exclusion of the rest of the population, no other person had a better opportunity. But, people being who they are, for the most part rational beings, if you can't show them the 'why' that someone was killed they sometimes get very reluctant to convict. Even if you make it up, if the defense can't refute it, a jury'll accept whatever it is, as long as it makes a little sense.

I parked in front and walked around to the rear service doors, those being the only ones open on Sunday. During weekend days, there are two pathology technicians – 'dieners' they're called; from the German, meaning: 'servant of the corpse' – available for autopsy assistance when necessary. The most senior, a large woman named Gussie, met my ring and opened the swinging doors. She had a huge smile on her face.

"Hey, Mr. Faulkner, how you doin'?" she said loudly.

"Just fine, Gussie, and you?"

"I couldn't be better. God is *so* good."

"I know He is. He solved this case for me." I smiled myself.

"I know that's right."

Walking past her, up the ramp and past the cooler door, I turned the corner into the autopsy suite. It was abuzz with activity on the far end of the room. A man who looked from a distance like Walters was gloved and gowned and standing next to a shiny steel table on which lay the nude body of a man. Another diener, Demetrius, a young man with huge hands and a slender build, was flitting about the table quickly, arranging test tubes, cleaning the saw, changing out instruments, and generally catering to the Doctor's needs.

I strode across the room and stood at the head of the body. Walters looked up, and I could see his eyes crinkle around the corners indicating that he was smiling under his mask.

"We're just getting started." He spoke to Demetrius: "Let's roll him over."

The two of them took hold of the body and flipped him, backside up. Walters picked up a thirty-five millimeter camera and began snapping pictures while standing on a rolling ladder.

"This is interesting," he said.

"What?"

"His tattoo." He pointed to the superior confluence of the two gluteus muscles – the top of the crack of his buttocks.

There, in 'Times New Roman' font were the words, 'One Way. Do Not Enter,' in two neat lines. There was also an arrow pointing toward his anus.

"I guess the man was a confirmed heterosexual," Walters said.

"I never knew to him to be otherwise."

Walters finished his photography, and I stepped back to make notes. The door bell rang loudly, and in forty-five seconds Roy Rogers walked into the room.

I looked at Rogers then back over at the naked body on the gurney, and then back at Rogers. "Hurry up. Get a shot of Larry's butt."

Rogers put down his bag and pulled out his camera. He walked over to the corpse and looked. He smiled broadly and then took several photos of the tattoo.

He stepped away and paused. "How'd this happen?"

I shrugged. "I don't know. Looks like he went on a spree, picked up a couple'a kids, brought'em home, and one of'em beat the piss out of'im."

"Motive?"

"Well, it doesn't look like love or sex. And, it doesn't look like robbery. If they took anything at all it was only a telephone. They left over four hundred bucks in his wallet."

"That leaves only one thing."

I raised my eyebrows.

"R-E-V-E-N-G." He deliberately misspelled the word.

I smiled because I got the joke. "Did you know him?"

"Didn't everybody? Yeah, I knew him, but not well, though. The Captain had him pretty well wrapped up."

"What do you think his will says?"

"What, are you trying to hang this on Agnew?"

"Noooo. We know who killed him. But, I mean, you said it yourself: 'the Captain had him pretty well wrapped up.'"

"Oh, you think he was takin' care of him to get a line on his money."

"I heard he was pretty well fixed."

"It would stand to reason; the house, the farm. He had horses too, didn't he?"

"I think so."

"But, the Captain? You think he's *that* mercenary?"

I shrugged.

Chapter 40

Three hours later, after a trip home to get a 'go' bag, I met Will at the office, and we started for Florida. Jacks County was about a hundred and seventy-five miles to the east, past Crestview. The way I figured it, we'd be there around five.

Will was usually pretty sedate on trips like these. This day he was keyed up.

"When we get there, we'll talk to them girls first. That lieutenant over there said that one of 'em was especially cooperative; said she had green hair."

I chuckled. "So, these kids are in their twenties?"

"He indicated that the boys are both twenty-two."

"Local?"

"Nope; traveling through town on their way from Louisiana to Jacksonville."

"They must have had some connection to Mobile."

"I guess we'll find that out when we get there."

I pulled off the interstate in Daphne, Alabama, to get something to drink from a convenience store. As I was walking back to the car, I noticed a female dog at the back corner of the building. I knew she was female by her unmistakable posture when urinating. In the car, I pointed her out to Will.

"You think human females learned how to squat from dogs, or the other way around?" I said.

"Only God knows that, Son. Only God knows that."

It took us two and a half hours to get to Marion, the county seat of Jacks County, what with the rain coming down as hard as it was. Marion was a small community of about five thousand located fifteen miles north of Interstate 10. The area appeared largely rural. We saw horse farms and what looked like soybean fields on either side of the county road that we took after we exited the highway.

The combination Sheriff's Department and County Jail was easy to find. Lonnie Zane always said that to find the sheriff's office you had only to look for a large radio antenna, and in Jacks County a massive one sprouted from the headquarters building. It was a modern structure: steel framed, covered in stucco, two stories high, with an adjoining four story jail. There was a chain link enclosure on the east side that served as an exercise yard for prisoners. I noticed a weight bench and some pull up bars near one of the standards on the basketball court.

It was the early evening, however they knew we were coming, and Robertson, one of only four investigators in their department, told Will that he'd be happy to wait. He allowed as to the fact that he was in the process of getting a divorce, and he didn't really want to go home anyhow.

A fat deputy in a green uniform, who looked like he was about to fall asleep, was manning the main desk when we walked in the front door. We told him who we were, and he dialed a four digit extension and told someone we were waiting. In five minutes, Scotty Robertson appeared in the doorway and beckoned us into the tan cinderblock hallway.

He was well over six feet tall, with a slim build, blond hair, and a suntanned complexion. His thick mustache was black and it hung down over his top lip, thereby giving the term 'soup strainer' a graphic meaning. A Sig Sauer pistol was prominent on his right hip, as was a police walkie talkie on his left. He extended a huge hand in a welcoming shake.

"You fellas have a good trip?" he said. His voice was a baritone.

"Fine, sir. A little wet, but fine," Will said.

"The boys are in jail – they invoked their right to counsel – but I've got both the girls upstairs. They've had their supper, so you can talk to them as long as you want."

"How are they?"

"Just the way you might think. They're young, a little ditzy."

"What kind'a witnesses are they gonna make?"

"They'll do. I've seen worse."

We rode the elevator to the second floor, exited, then turned right and walked to the end of another cinderblock hall. When we reached the door to the last room on the left, Robertson took the lead and walked in first, then Will, then me.

There they were, two teenaged girls, in all their young, modern, female essence. For some reason, their looks surprised me. I was never around young people, as I hadn't worked a juvenile crime in several years, and I rarely had personal contact with young females through friends or family. Will, however, was the father of one daughter who had a baby granddaughter.

They were seated in chairs in the middle of the floor. One, presumably our best witness – the one with the green hair – was sitting with her leg tucked under her. She looked to be in her late teens, with a peaches and cream complexion. The young girl still had her baby fat; by that I mean her arms and legs were round and full, and her cheeks looked as if they contained a whole winter's nuts.

The aforementioned green – kind of a shiny emerald – hair was parted in the middle and hung down in an arc on either side of her head, thereby framing her face and making it appear fuller than it actually was. Her dark brown eyes were set off by dark lashes and thick, almost black brows, and her pug nose sat on top of thick lips painted a bright crimson. She wore jean shorts, a tank top, and pink 'flip flops.'

Her companion looked appreciably more normal. For one thing, her hair was a natural sandy blonde. It hung straight down to her shoulders. Her complexion was also flawless, and her facial features were soft. She had blue eyes and a small mouth under a small, inconspicuous nose. She wore jean shorts also, as well as a white t-shirt, but no shoes.

Both girls could be called classically attractive. Both had waists smaller than their hips; both had small hands and feet; and both were unblemished. Almost.

Green hair had six earrings through her left ear. She also had a small tattoo of some Chinese alphabetic symbol on the side of her neck under her right ear.

Blondie had a ring through her nose and tattoos on both arms. From where I was standing, I couldn't make out exactly what they were, but they appeared to be garish representations of horses.

Robertson stopped in front of them and spoke.

"Gentlemen, this is Amy Ludlow," he said pointing at green hair. "And this is Lisa Harrell." He pointed to the blonde.

Both of the girls nodded but looked at the floor. They appeared as if they were about to get shots from a doctor.

"Hello, there, young ladies," Will said. "Mr. Robertson here tells me you're from Louisiana. Whereabouts?"

Ludlow looked at Lisa Harrell. Then she spoke up for the both of them.

"Slidell. We're from Slidell." Her voice was soft and high toned.

I pegged green hair as the leader of the two. If she spilled it, the other girl would also.

Slidell was right off I-10 not far from New Orleans. I'd been there once, but only to stop at Schwegmann's, a big box discount store that sold items, especially liquor, at wholesale.

"Have you two ladies had supper, yet?"

Once again, Amy Ludlow spoke up. "Yeah. Mr. Robertson brought us some hamburgers."

"Good." Will looked at Robertson. "Where can we talk?"

Robertson nodded toward the back of the room. "There's a small office over there."

"Okay. Ms Ludlow, why don't you come on with us, and we'll chat a few minutes over here."

Ludlow rose and walked slowly toward the room, looking over her shoulder at the other girl in the process. I followed her into the room, and Will closed the door behind us.

She sat in a chair on one side of a wooden table. Will sat on the other side, and I sat on the end, the ready stenographer. I took out my pad and pen, sat a tape recorder on the table in front of us, and turned it on.

Amy Ludlow wrung her hands and occasionally bit the nail of her right thumb. She shifted her weight back and forth from her right hip to her left and looked all around the room. If I didn't know better, I'd've thought she was about to lie.

"Young lady, my name is Eubanks, and this is Mr. Faulkner. We're detectives from Mobile. Mr. Robertson has you here in his office, and I guess he had to arrest you to get you here. If that's so, I'm gonna read you your rights. It's not 'cause I think you did anything wrong, but only 'cause I don't want you to leave until I hear your story."

She nodded. Will recited the rights and waiver.

"Tell me what happened in Mobile."

She looked down and acted as if she didn't know where to start. Will told her to just start at the beginning.

"Well, me and John, that's my boyfriend, we decided we was gonna take a trip over to Jacksonville 'cause John wants to join the Navy, and he said they had a bunch'a ships over there. I told Lisa, and she said she wanted to go too, so she called her boyfriend, Jason, and we left on Saturday afternoon.

"We got to Mobile about five or so, I think, and John says he knows a place where we can get some beers, even though me and Lisa was too young. So, we stopped at this bar and went inside. That's where we met Larry."

"You know the name of the bar?"

"No, sir. I think it had a animal in the name; jaguar, zebra, or something, some kinda jungle name."

I knew it. She was talking about the Puma Bar and Grill on the Blue Star Parkway, about three miles outside of Theodore. They wouldn't have been able to find it if one of them hadn't been there before.

"Go on," Will said.

"So, we stopped, and when we got inside, John and Jason went to the bar to get us some drinks. Well, there was this guy playin' pool, and he walked over to Lisa and me where we was sittin' and was tellin' us his name was Larry and it was his birthday, and did we want to come to his house to party. About that time, John and Jason come back with the beers, and we all just sat around and drank beer. John and Jason played some pool, and me and Lisa, we just sat at the table and talked to Larry."

"What did you think of Larry?"

"Nothin' really, just that he was old. He acted okay."

"What did John and Jason think about you talkin' to him?" I said.

She looked at me. "I, I don't know. I mean, they didn't say nothin'."

"Go ahead," Will said, a little annoyed that I had broken into her story.

"So, we drank and talked, and I played some pool with John, and Larry kept sayin' let's go back to his house and party; he had some horses, and he had food, too. So, John said, okay, for just a little while."

"So?"

She shrugged. "So, we went over there. We followed him."

"What did you do then?"

"When we got there, we ate and watched TV."

"What did you watch?"

"We watched a couple'a movies, and then he had a movie of his birthday from last year, so we watched that."

323

"So, what then?"

"So, John said he wanted to go see his mama. She lives out in some place called Semmes, I think."

"Did you know that before?"

She shook her head. "No. I met him at home, and I thought he was from there."

"What happened then?"

"So, John leaves and Jason goes with him, and they're gone awhile."

"Whose car was you in?"

"We come over there in Jason's car, 'cause it was bigger. They left in his car."

"What happened while they were gone?"

"We just watched TV and had some more beer. I don't usually drink too much. Larry said did we want to go out and feed the horses, so I said, yeah, sure, so he starts to take off his shirt. Lisa says, 'wait, what are you doin'?' And Larry says you have to feed the horses in the nude or they won't eat."

I smiled. That sounded like one of Larry's pickup lines.

"Well, did you?" Will said.

The young girl looked shocked. "No. All we did was watch some TV and eat." She paused and then spoke wistfully. "I guess them horses never did get fed."

"What happened then?"

"Well, it wadn't long 'fore John and Jason got back. We was still eatin' popcorn and watchin' TV." She paused again and shrugged. "Then, that's when it happened."

"Tell me about it."

"Well, I was sittin' in a chair watchin' TV, and I heard something, and I looked around, and I saw John hittin' him."

"John was hitting who?"

"Larry."

"With what?"

"One of them iron bars; like what you use to change a tire."

"How many times did he hit him?"

She closed her eyes tight as if to see into the past. "Two or three. I only saw two."

"You said you heard a noise, what did you hear?"

"I don't know. Kind of a 'bump' or a 'thump.'"

The noise that she was describing was probably the boy pounding on Larry's skull. It would have made a very distinctive sound.

The room fell silent for a few seconds as if Amy Ludlow had just realized that it was at that moment that Larry had died. She blinked and took a deep breath.

Will broke the pause. "What did Jason do?"

"I stood up and moved back. Then he walked around to the front of Larry's chair and punched him in the chest."

"When you say 'he,' do you mean Jason?"

"Yeah."

"Did he have anything in his hand?"

"I don't know. I don't think so, but I couldn't see."

"Okay, what happened next?"

"Lisa yelled, or screamed, really, and I hollered at John, 'What are you doin'?!' And he just hollered back to come on, we was leavin'. I, I was kinda, I don't know, in shock, I guess. I just stood there, so he come over and grabbed my arm and started pullin' me to the door. I remember Lisa ran past us and out the back door, that's where John had parked, and we jumped in the car. We was gone in like thirty seconds."

The location of the parked car was significant. By putting it in the back and not out front, it showed that the boys were trying to hide it. It was evidence of premeditation.

Will paused to collect his thoughts. I was writing as fast as I could trying to keep up with the phrases: 'stood there'; 'grabbed my arm'; 'Lisa ran'; 'jumped in car'; 'gone in 30 seconds.'

325

"Did anybody take anything from the house?" Will said.

She stopped to think. I knew then that she had picked up something.

"Jason reached in Larry's pocket." She pointed to her front pants pocket. "He pulled out some bills, but I don't think it was very much; maybe forty or fifty dollars. We had to steal some gas a little later on down the road."

I don't suppose it would've have mattered to her if I told her that in their haste the boys had passed up over four hundred.

"Did John take anything from the house?"

"I didn't see him get anything."

"Lisa?"

She chuckled once. "She was runnin' too fast."

"I guess she was. So, did you talk about what happened on the way over here? You and John, I mean."

"Me and Lisa was in the back, and we just lay down. I went to sleep for a little while, but I heard John and Jason talkin' about what happened."

"What did they say?"

"I don't know, I couldn't hear much. Just, like, John said, 'did you see me thump'im'? And Jason was like, 'yeah, I got him, too.'"

She mimicked the young boys' voices in kind of a sarcastic way. It didn't sound believable.

"Do you know why they did it?"

She shook her head. "No. They shouldn't have. Larry was nice; kinda crazy, but not a bad person. I mean, he kept tryin' to get me and Lisa to go to bed with him, but other than that, he was okay; kinda funny, really. He wasn't pushy at all."

Will looked over at me and nodded. It was my turn to ask a couple of questions while he got his second wind.

"Did you or Lisa have intercourse with Larry?" I said.

She turned to me quickly. "No! Ewwww!"

326

"Did either or you perform fellatio on Larry?"

She looked at me with the knitted brows of ignorance.

"Did either of you give him a blow job?"

"No."

Funny, intercourse rated a 'ewwww,' however fellatio was apparently more palatable to think about. It's a crazy world.

"What did you take from the house?"

She paused as if she didn't want to admit anything, but she was afraid of lying. "I mighta' grabbed a bottle of bourbon on the way out. It was sittin' on the counter."

I looked at her closely, wanting to catch her first words when I asked her my next question. It would make me the bad guy, but one of us had to be.

"How many times did you hit Larry?"

"I didn't hit him," she said. Her words were clipped and her teeth were clenched. Sometimes, those were symptoms of lying.

I nodded to calm her down. She denied hitting him. That's all I wanted to hear.

"Did you stab Larry?"

"No."

"Do you think the guys were jealous of Larry hitting on you two? You and Lisa, I mean."

She looked away, and I thought I saw the beginnings of a smile cross her lips. Could it be that the fact that John was jealous of Larry was something that was flattering to her? Did it prove that he loved her? Was she aroused thinking that the boys would kill for her? Seriously, would we be able to keep her on our reservation when it came court time? I decided to let Will and the DA worry about that. My job was to take notes.

"I don't think so," she said.

"Do you know where they went when they left the house?"

She shook her head.

"You'll have to say, 'yes' or 'no' for the tape."

"Uh, no. Just to John's Mama's. I don't know where that is."

I thought I had a handle on what took place. When these two young females walked into the Puma, Larry saw the makings of an orgy; no matter that the girls had partners, the more the merrier. Back at the house, the girls weren't interested, but my guess is that Larry was fine with that. The boys left but came back mad. They probably went looking for money and couldn't get any.

I looked back at Will signaling the end of my questioning. My character in this little interrogation drama came off looking mean and accusatory. That was fine with me.

"Young lady, is everything you told us the truth?" Will said.

She nodded. "Yes, sir."

"Will you testify in court to the truth of what you've told us?"

She nodded and cleared her throat. "Yes, sir."

"Okay. That's all for now, but this is not going to be the last time anybody questions you about what happened. You understand that, right?"

She nodded again. "Uh, what happens if I decide not to testify?"

Will stopped suddenly in the middle of rising from his chair and sat back down. "You'll be charged with murder, and every statement that you just made will be used against you in court." He paused. "Now, I don't wanna hear no more about not testifyin'."

She bowed her head and mouthed the word 'okay.' I turned off the recorder.

Out in the squad room, Lisa Harrell was seated at one of the desks writing on a pad. Robertson was at his desk doing the same. Amy Ludlow exited the room first, then me, then Will. Amy went immediately to Lisa and stood next to her, real close. The two looked each other in the eye but did not speak; possibly communicating with one another in some unspoken adolescent female language. Will stepped over to Robertson's desk. I sat down near them to clean up my notes.

"How 'bout the boys, did they indicate they were willing to talk?" Will said.

Robertson shook his head. "I talked to them this morning. They both invoked, but you're welcome to try'em again if you want."

I could see by the look on Will's face that he wished Robertson would have waited. I, on the other hand, was glad he didn't.

"How about extradition?"

"We didn't get that far." He chuckled. "I don't think the boys know the meaning of the word."

"Not too swift, huh."

"One of'em asked if he could have an orange jumpsuit; wanted to know, when was the 'perp walk.'" He grinned.

"Where's the car?"

"It's in the impound yard, out back."

"Did you look through it?"

"I just opened the trunk. Your murder weapon is back there – a tire tool sittin' on top of the spare. It's got blood and hair on it."

"Will it be okay here until my man can get over and go through it?"

He nodded. "Sure. It'll be there when you want it."

Will looked around the room. The two girls were talking in low tones. I was sitting close enough to hear most of what they were saying. They were talking about where they were going to sleep that night, and did they think they could get their clothes.

"Okay, we'll talk to the other one and then spend a minute with the boys."

Will gave the high sign to Lisa, and she got up from her chair and walked toward the same interrogation room. She carried her pad and pen with her.

When we were seated, Will began. "What'cha writin' there, young lady?"

She looked down at the pad as if embarrassed. "Just a poem."

"Mind if I see it?"

She slid the pad across to him. He read it quickly and slid it toward me. I had a hard time making out the young girl's cursive writing, what with all the curly ques and loops, but it went something like this:

> *Like pounding sand*
> *He hit the man,*
> *His time was up*
> *He took a big gulp,*
> *It was his last gasp*
> *He lost his grasp, on his life.*

It wasn't much, but it put the girl in the room when the murder was committed, if she would testify to it.

"Young lady why don't you tell us what happened to Larry," Will said after reciting the rights and waiver to her.

She shrugged her shoulders and stared at the table. "Didn't Amy tell you?"

"We need to hear it from you, too."

She took a deep breath. "Well, we met Larry in this bar, and he wanted us to come home with him and party. So, we went home and then the guys left and when they come back, John hit him with a steel rod. That's about it."

"Did you see him do it?"

She nodded. "Yeah."

"Did you see Jason stab him?"

She nodded again. "Yeah."

"Okay, so we got the important part out of the way. Why don't you start at the beginning and tell us all about it."

It was like pulling teeth, but Will coaxed a narrative out of her, from the time that Amy Ludlow had called her on the phone and told her she was going to Jacksonville, to when the deputy woke her up in the back of the car at the rest stop. Her story differed from Amy Ludlow's only in small details.

I asked her the same questions I asked Amy: Did you sleep with Larry? No. What did you take from the house? Nothing. And how many times did you hit Larry? None. She said she watched the entire attack, and wouldn't admit to running out the back door when it all started. She said she didn't hear the boys talk about the assault, and while the attack bothered her somewhat, it really hadn't sunk in that another person was dead.

Her attitude was not unusual for a person of her age. Most young people have no concept of death, even when they see it. The finality of it escapes them. They don't believe it can happen to them, so they can't perceive of it happening to others. They have no opinion at all about an afterlife. They only know that if at a point in time someone is present, moving, and speaking, when they are dead, they are present, not moving, and not speaking. And, if they have little or no history with the dead person, it's as if that person never existed at all.

"We're going to need you to testify in court," Will told her.

She seemed confused as to what that meant, but she also seemed willing to be led to do whatever she was told. She ended up nodding assent to Will's direction.

I could tell that Will was getting tired and wanted to get things wrapped up. We stepped out of the room, and he went immediately to a phone. I heard his end of the conversation as he talked to one of the assistant district attorneys back in Mobile.

331

"Yeah, we've got two eyewitnesses, and I think we're gonna be able to get some of the stolen property out of the car."

Pause.

"Yeah, the two girls know they're gonna have to testify. We got statements from both of'em, and they told it all."

Pause.

"No, we don't know why yet. We're gonna try to talk to the boys, but the officer over here says they invoked."

Pause.

"Yeah, maybe we can get something out of them about why."

Pause.

"Yeah, okay."

Pause.

"I'll call you tomorrow, after we get back to town." Pause. "All right."

He hung up and turned to Robertson.

"If you'll just take us to the jail, and let us spend a little time with them two boys, then we'll take the girls off your hands, back to Mobile, and get'em set up."

"Sure. Just go down the hall and turn left and go across the catwalk. I'll call the sergeant, and he'll be waitin' for you there. He'll have the boys out and in the interrogation rooms."

We thanked Robertson for his help and walked back down the cinderblock hall to the catwalk. When we got to the door, we were met by a tall man with a bald head, wearing a green uniform. He spoke in a very deep voice.

"You gentlemen here to see our two desperados? Just step this way."

"Thank you, sir." Will paused. "Have they been hard cases?"

"Well, they was at first, but we've gotten'em calmed down. We fed'em and give'em some clothes and they've had

332

a nap. They're better now." He motioned toward a door. "Step right through here."

He led us down a short hall to the attorney's rooms. He identified John Christopher Tompkins in the first one. We thanked him again and stepped inside.

The boy looked like a thousand others his age. He was rail-thin, tow-headed, and had kind of a blank look on his face. His eyes had that 'thousand yard stare' that said he had no clue, and no conscience. His fingers were long and thin and, surprisingly, his nails appeared to be manicured. He had no visible body art and no piercings, and he wore the orange jumpsuit that he had so coveted.

Will and I both took seats across the table from the boy. I set up my tape recorder in full view. The boy shifted in his chair nervously.

"Son, we're from Alabama. My name is Eubanks and this is Detective Faulkner." Will recited the rights waiver.

Tompkins had a baritone voice. "I told the other man I didn't wanna to make a statement."

"That's fine, son. We just wanted to make contact with you and see if you were gonna fight extradition back to Alabama."

"What does that mean?"

"It means that if you're not willing, we can't take you back across the state line into Alabama without a judge says it's alright."

He looked at Will, then down at the table. "Is Alabama close to Louisiana?"

"It is."

"Well, I wanna get back home as soon as I can. So, I guess I'm willin'."

"Good. I'll tell the Lieutenant." He paused and looked at the boy. "You have anything you wanna ask?"

He looked up then he shrugged his shoulders. "You think I could get home tomorrow?"

"It may be a little longer than that, Son. You'll have to see a judge and ask'im about it. He'll get you a lawyer, and he'll help you get back in touch with your family."

The boy nodded. I looked up from my notepad and stared at him. He was just a kid, but not a kid. He was big enough and old enough to do a man's crime, but obviously not big or old enough to understand what he had done nor why. Had we raised up a generation that had no understanding that life was precious and something to be guarded and preserved? That the rights of others were at least as important as our own? That some desires are to be delayed and not instantly gratified? That murder was wrong?

Will looked at the boy. "There's just one more question and then we'll go."

The boy raised his eyebrows.

"Why'd you do it?"

He pursed his lips, in that 'I don't know' look. Then, the beginnings of a smiled creeped across his lips as he said, "I guess I just wanted to see what it feels like."

It was the wee hours of the morning when Will and I, and the two girls, got back to Mobile. The girls slept the whole way, as did Will. I drank two cups of coffee and steeled myself to make the drive without running off the road.

Prior to leaving Florida, we talked to Jason Allen. He was as clueless as his partner, but he knew enough to keep his mouth shut. We also took a look at Jason's four-door, brown Ford Granada, a piece of junk with a broken headlight and a large dent in the right front fender. I shined my flashlight in the back seat and saw a bottle of bourbon and a cordless telephone. Will hit the trunk and saw the bloody tire tool that Robertson had mentioned. Will also removed the girls' two small suitcases.

Will woke Roy Rogers up at home and told him to make arrangements to get some people over to Florida on Monday. Rogers would know what to do about the search warrant and getting the car towed back to Alabama.

As we rode back, the hum of the highway, Will's snoring, and the girls' heavy breathing all sang a soothing tune. I nearly fell asleep twice, so I turned on the radio and played it with a low volume.

Thinking about it all, I realized that at that time death was so common in my life, that life carried no special meaning any more. In some ways, I was in the same position as those stupid kids with whom I had just spent the day; life no longer held the same sanctity that it once had. I was looking at about seventy-five or a hundred dead bodies a year of one sort or the other; all races and sexes, all ages and sizes. They were all alive one minute and dead the next; and how had the world changed because of their removal? For that matter, how had the world changed because of their arrival?

We hit town at two, and Will registered the girls at the General Jackson Hotel, next to the courthouse. When he got them settled, I took him to the office to pick up his car, and then headed home. It would take me a while, but I would think up a way to get even with Scott Neely.

Chapter 41

It took about a week to wrap up the Larry Stinson murder. We spent one whole day walking both sides of Marsh Rd south to the Blue Star Parkway looking for the small pen knife that Jason Allen had thrown out of the window on the way out of town. The girls tried to show us the location, however it was dark when they left Larry's house, and they weren't familiar with the area, so pinpointing the exact location was impossible.

Roy Rogers and his crew went to Florida on Monday, processed the vehicle, and brought it back to Mobile that evening. We met him when he pulled in the back parking lot with the Granada on a roll back wrecker. He was wiping his face as he stepped out of the departmental SUV driven by Hernandez.

"Whew, man it's hot."

Will was in no mood for small talk. "What'd you find?"

"Just the stuff you told us about, the tire tool, the bourbon, and what I think was Larry's telephone. There was no evidence that he was ever in the car. Aside from that, it was just an old car with some clothes in it."

"Anything on the tire tool?"

"Some blood, one small hair; but if you're talking about prints, then no. The surface is too rough."

I could see Will's mind working. He could put the boys in the house by the girls' testimony. He could put the boys in constructive possession of Larry's property, as well as the murder weapon. And he could put the murder weapon in John Tompkins' hand by the girls' testimony. But proving that Jason had been a willing participant in the murder was going to be difficult. We didn't have his weapon and only the girls could say he had anything to do with the crime. If his lawyer was smart, he would say that Jason was just a bystander like the girls and was no more a part of the murder than they were. The only thing we had going for us was that there were two different kinds of wounds on the body. It was unlikely that a jury would believe that the same man would use two different weapons; they were more likely to believe that the more timid of the two killers just wanted to get in his lick in order to show his criminal mettle also.

The boys didn't fight extradition and came back to Mobile on Wednesday after the murder. John Tompkins' mother came to see us that afternoon, and we met her in our office. She was a rough thirty-five, which meant that she had given birth to her son in her mid-teens. Even so, she appeared as if she had once been an attractive woman. She had light brown hair streaked blonde, brown eyes, and a thin figure, and only a few wrinkles showed through her olive complexion.

"Thank you for seein' me," she said. Her southern accent was heavy and the rasp in her throat indicated that she was a smoker.

"Certainly, Ms Tompkins. We're glad ya came," Will said.

"We was in court this mornin'," she said as she sat down. "My boy Johnny didn't get to talk to me like I wanted." She looked away out of the window wistfully.

"Ms Tompkins, did John come to see you last Sunday?"

She nodded. "Yeah, he did. He come by the house with that other boy, Jason, I think was his name."

"What did he want?"

She snorted. "What do you think? Money. I didn't have any to give'im, and a'course he got mad."

"Who does John live with in Louisiana?"

"Oh, he don't stay with nobody, really. His daddy's over there, and that's where he sleeps, but he don't look after'im. I think they both just run the streets."

"Did he say what he was doin' in town?"

"He said him an' Jason was drivin' to Jacksonville; that he was thinkin' about joinin' the Navy."

"How'd you feel about that?"

"Well, I don't know, I guess it's alright. I mean, it might get him to turn his life around. But I don't really think he could stick it out."

"Turn his life around? Tell me about that."

"Well, you know, he takes drugs; and I think he drinks pretty heavy, too."

After that, Cathy Tompkins started at the beginning and told us how she had gotten pregnant young; gone on welfare and food stamps; tried to raise her boy by herself, and did, until he got older and she just couldn't handle him anymore. The next thirty minutes were kind of an unhappy intersection of an Oprah program, a Dr. Phil therapy session, and a plain old hen party gabfest. She seemed to want us to know that what had happened and what her son had done was in no way her fault.

"Did he mention anything about Larry Stinson when he was at your house?" Will said.

"No, he just said he needed money, and when I didn't have any, he just went off."

"Does he usually have a bad temper?"

"Well, I don't know. I know his daddy does. He prob'ly gets what he does have from him."

Will looked over at me. I cleared my throat.

"Ms Tompkins, did your son say why he killed that man?"

It was a trick question designed to test her; first to find out if she had talked to him. Then I was hoping that she'd go ahead and answer the question and in a roundabout way admit that he had confessed to her.

"He said the man was a pervert."

"I see."

"He said the man wanted to have sex with his two little friends, them girls he was with. He said he . . ." She paused.

She looked at Will and began to tear up.

"Is my boy gonna get the chair?"

Will looked at her in as sympathetic a way as Will could, and said, "I don't know, Ms Tompkins. Don't you think he deserves it?"

She paused and thought then shook her head. "No."

The next Friday morning, I was sitting in my office putting the finishing touches on a scene report when the phone rang.

338

"Hey, Henry."

The voice was familiar, but it took me a half second to process it. When I did, my heart jumped. It was Lynn Glass, the last serious girlfriend I'd had.

"Yeah, Lynn. How are you?"

I tried not to sound too excited. Lynn and I had met at an aerobics class, back in the 80's when that kinda thing was popular. She was recently out of college and had taken a job as an accountant for the employer tax division at the Department of Industrial Relations. I noticed her instantly. She was petite and pretty, with wedge-cut blonde hair and a small nose over a small mouth. Her blue eyes were pale, almost gray; and she had small hands and feet, but the muscled legs of a dancer.

"How are *you* doing?" she said.

That had been almost ten years ago. I was a rookie police officer doing rotating shift work. We would meet together for lunch when I was on nights and evenings, and we saved our night dates for when I was on the day shift.

"Good, good. Yourself?"

We had good times together. She once told me that, 'you're all I could ever want in a boyfriend.' I didn't know at the time that I had just gotten the kiss of death. I cared deeply for her and intended to ask her to marry me.

"Oh, fine. I've got my kids here. We're just in town to go the Exploreum. There's some exhibit about bugs that they just had to see."

Kids. That was new.

"Kids? How many?"

"Two boys, and a girl so tomboyish that she should'a been a boy. The twins are seven, and little Sally is five."

"Sounds like an armload."

"You know it. How about you?"

"Well, you tracked me down. This is what I do."

"The lady who answered said 'Investigations.' Which part are you in?"

"Homicide."

"Oh, yeah? How long?"

"Close to five years now."

"Well, that's where you always wanted to be."

"Yep. That's right."

There was an awkward pause. Then it hit me – why she called.

"Married?" she said.

"Married to murder."

Another awkward pause.

"So, how about your old man? You still married?"

"Oh, yes. We're still in the Army, too. We've been in Hawaii at Schofield Barracks for about five years. We just got sent to Fort Benning. That's what we're doing down here, visiting family before we have to report."

"Right. I guess he's a major now? Or a light Colonel?"

"Lieutenant Colonel. Yeah, he just got promoted before we came back stateside."

I should have seen it coming. Ten years ago, Lynn had dropped me and my pittance of a salary, and my shift work, for a prosperous military officer, travel, and all the exotic stations. The last time I saw her, she was kissing him on the front stoop of her apartment as I rode by in my patrol car one Friday night at eleven, just as I was coming on shift. The shock was startling. I was young then, and it was the sickest I'd ever been in my whole life.

"So, how do you like military life?"

"Oh, it's good, I suppose. You've got a readymade group of friends; you never have to worry about a place to live; and you've always got a knot in your stomach."

"He's been to some hot spots?"

"Oh, yes. But I never know anything about where or when. It's . . . . "

I was silent. She may have gotten a lot of perks in her marriage, but she had gotten a lot of stress, too.

340

"Well, hey, you gotta take the good with the bad, right?" I said.

"I suppose so."

I paused. "So, you wanna get a cup'a coffee?"

The question seemed to catch her off guard. "Oh, well, no, I really can't. The kids'll be done here soon, and we've got to get back to Mom's."

"You sure?"

"Yeah, thanks, but I can't."

"Okay. Well, tell your mother I said hello."

"Sure."

There was silence on the phone. I debated about whether to call her hand. She really had no business contacting me and bringing up all these memories the way she had. I was at once angry and, then, strangely, apathetic.

"Well, look, I better go," she said. "It was good talkin' to you."

"Yeah, you too." I paused. "And, hey . . . it's okay."

"What?"

"You made the right choice."

She was speechless for a second. "Bye."

Chapter 42

August turned into September and life – and death – rocked on at the Metro Sheriff's Department. There was about one natural death each week that had to be looked into, and add to that the random suicide and the accidental death cases, all of which had to be ruled out as murders, and Will and I – or I, at least – was kept busy with police reports, autopsy attendance, and consultations with doctors, hospitals, and the state pathologists.

But always, always, the Zoe Woods case hung over my head. Like a dirty shirt hanging in my closet, it was there, staring me in the face, waiting to be taken out and washed.

Roy Rogers notified us the he had gotten a copy of Rhett Tolliver's ten print card from Charlotte and that the print on the two dollar bill that we had recovered from Susy Weaver was a match. That print put him in the bar the night of the murder, and in my mind made him the killer. Will was not quite so certain.

"Well, think about it, Son. Susy Weaver's a barmaid. She takes in money all the time, and while it's likely that she got the bill from Tolliver, her standin' up under cross examination is gonna be tough. First, you can expect that a jury'd believe that she'd take a drink while she's on the job, even if she don't. Second, for her to say that she got that bill on the specific night of the week that Tolliver was in the bar with our victim is somethin' that she's gonna have to go a long way to convince a jury of; maybe if she'd brought it to us sooner, a day or two after the murder, maybe, it would be easier. And, finally, oh, I don't know, she's a barmaid."

"Well, I think he did it."

"Me, too, Son. Now, we gotta find him."

I thought about calling his brother and getting him to hunt him up, but Will said don't do that, that he'd tell him what we wanted him for, and then we'd never find him.

"You think we got enough to get even a probable cause warrant?"

"No. All we got is the bill, and a composite that nobody's ID'd yet. Let's just try to hunt'im down."

I called Greenbaum in North Carolina and told him what we had and to keep an eye out for Rhett Tolliver. He said he would, and he'd send us everything he had on him, including a mugshot if he could find one.

A couple of days later I got a Grand Jury subpoena to testify in the Patridge case. I was scheduled for Tuesday morning, the day after Labor Day.

Alabama, unlike most other states, uses the Grand Jury system as the second probable cause filter, rather than just an investigative body, in cases of felony crimes; the preliminary hearing being the first. By using the Grand Jury to indict felons, police officers and the DA's Office can insulate themselves from any charges of false arrest and/or malicious prosecution.

I got to the waiting area a little after nine thirty. My case was scheduled to be called at ten. I signed in at the desk that was staffed by one of the court police officers, a gray haired man with a mustache, wearing a blue uniform and Corfam gun leather. I sat down next to a window and picked up a five year old Newsweek with a picture of an atom on the cover, laid my case file down on the seat next to me, and thumbed the pages. The officer interlaced his fingers over his expansive abdomen and in a few minutes his chin began bouncing off his chest. There was no one else in the room, and *my* chin was also beginning to do a dance, that is until a young woman entered and sat down without speaking to the officer.

I looked up from my magazine and watched her as she plopped into one of the armchairs. She had on a pink blouse and a white skirt; but she carried no purse, only a white handkerchief that she twisted in her hands.

"Ma'am?" I said. "You're supposed to sign in at the desk."

She looked over at the policeman who was still lounging in his chair.

"Are you a policeman?" she said. Her voice was high and squeaky.

"Deputy Sheriff. Is something wrong?"

She took a deep breath, exhaled, and changed her chair from across the room to within two seats of me.

343

"My old man's lookin' for me. We was down in court, and I ran out. I had to get away from'im."

"Which court?"

"Domestic relations."

She was close enough so that I could smell the beer on her breath. I looked into her face and tried to gauge from which part of the county she hailed. I finally concluded it was probably from the west, near Wilmer, Alabama, a rural community four miles from the Mississippi state line. She had stringy blonde hair, a thin nose, pale skin, and freckles. Her fingers were long and thin, her nails were bitten to the quick, and her knuckles were scratched. I also noticed that the toes of her flat shoes were scuffed.

The uninitiated might have felt sympathy for her, a woman running from an abusive man. But, having been around the block a few times, I knew that her troubles had probably been caused as much by her own actions and choices as by anyone else's, and jumping to run to her aid was something that would simply be a waste of time. She was the kind of female that when you came to her house to break up a fight between her and her old man would, if you tried to arrest him, be just as likely to jump on your own back. I'd seen her kind a few times before, and frankly, I wanted no part of her.

"I suggest you have a talk with that officer over there, ma'am. He can make sure you get out of the building safely."

She looked at me with raised brows, as if she expected me to solve her problem. But what she didn't realize was that she was not my problem. We stared at each other for about a minute.

The silence was broken when an attractive blonde woman opened the door to the Grand Jury room and looked out.

"We're ready, Detective Faulkner."

The blonde smiled and stood out of the way as I rose and walked through the door. I didn't look back at the

344

girl from the country, and frankly, I really hoped that she'd be gone when I returned.

The Grand Jury room at the courthouse was located on the fifth floor, just down the hall from the DA's own office. The room was paneled and had no windows, which made it unusually dark. There was a wood carving of two tablets of Commandments hanging on the wall above the platform.

The assistant who ran the show was Judy Dean, a middle aged woman with a fair complexion and a plump build. The clerks varied, but on this day it was Gloria Easley, the woman who had called me in; an attractive twenty-five year old with whom I wouldn't mind spending some time if the opportunity arose.

I walked quickly toward the platform in the front of the room and took one of three chairs, the one next to Dean. Usually, the DA asked a beginning question, and I would break into a short narrative and tell what I expected the evidence to show.

What is unique about the Grand Jury was the fact that the jurors, as well as the prosecutor, can ask questions of any witness. Defendants generally decline the opportunity to testify because lawyers aren't allowed to sit in; and because defendant's statements can be used against them later, in court.

Settling into the straight-backed wooden chair, I arranged my file in front of me and turned toward Dean. Without being told, I raised my right hand. She looked at me and smiled.

"Do you solemnly swear that the testimony that you are about to give is the truth, the whole truth, and nothing but the truth, so help you God?"

"I do."

I swung around and took a quick gander at the group. There appeared to be about a sixty-forty mix of white and black; old predominated over young; and females took the measure of males.

345

Three people jumped out at me. The first was on the far left hand side on the front row. It was an older black man with glasses. The hairline of his processed hair had receded back to his crown, and his mustache was pencil thin. He looked like a refugee from the Cotton Club.

The second was a middle aged white woman seated in the middle of the back row. I pegged her as a Junior Leaguer; thin, with a dark suntan on skin that shouldn't have had that much sun, blonde hair from a bottle, and a patrician nose under soft features. She struck me as a doctor's wife who usually spent her days on the tennis court, but was on this occasion very happy to do her civic duty.

Lastly, was a black female on the front row. She was middle aged also, with jet black hair, glasses on a chain, and a garish pink and green print frock. The scowl on her face and the smirk on her lips reminded me for all the world of Sapphire Stephens.

All three had steno pads in their laps and pens poised. Of the three, I half expected trouble from the older black female. In the past, I had found that women with her look possessed an abiding lack of faith in law enforcement.

"State you name and occupation for the record."

"Henry Faulkner; Deputy Sheriff, Mobile Metro Sheriff's Department."

"And what is your current assignment?"

"I am currently assigned to the Major Crimes Bureau of the Criminal Investigation Division."

"And how long have you been so assigned?"

"Approximately five years."

"Were you so assigned in March of this year?"

"I was."

"Tell us what occurred on the night of March 17th."

I cleared my throat and let my eyes run over the group in front of me. The majority of them looked bored. One young girl yawned.

"I received a call from the dispatcher to go to the K-Bar Lounge on Airport Boulevard in West Mobile

County. I responded to find uniformed deputies on scene and one man in custody."

"That would be the defendant?" Newsome said.

"Yes, Stanley Simpson Patridge."

"Continue."

I nodded. "I spoke with Deputy Barry Parsons, and then I spoke with Rassie Ireland, the bartender."

"And did you determine what had happened?"

"Yes. I learned from my investigation that apparently, the victim, Justin Daigle, came into the bar and began to play pool. The defendant entered the bar, without a shirt and shoes. The victim then made a remark, about the defendant's attire, or lack of it, that he considered humorous. The defendant was not amused. He produced a knife, began chasing the victim, first inside the bar, then outside, where he ultimately cut him. The defendant then got into his truck and drove away."

"How badly was the victim hurt?"

"He was cut from the top of his shoulder to the top of his buttocks." I gestured as best I could. "The doctor estimated over a hundred stitches."

"Whom do you expect to testify?"

"The victim will testify as to his injuries and also to the identification of the perpetrator; Rassie Ireland will testify to the identity of the perpetrator, and he also witnessed the crime; Mr. Hernandez of the Sheriff's office will testify to the recovery of the knife; the physical evidence, including a pair of bloody jeans that the defendant was wearing; and to the photographs of the scene."

Dean paused and looked at the pages in front of her. Then she looked up out at the jury.

"Are there any questions?"

My eyes scanned back and forth, and I tried to meet all eighteen faces. Most looked tired and wished they were someplace else. Then the black woman on the front row raised her hand.

"Yes, ma'am," I said as politely as possible.

"Was this 'perpetrator' injured in any way?"

"Not to my knowledge. When I arrived, he was asleep in the backseat of the patrol car. At no time did he complain of any injuries."

She paused. "How did you arrive at him as a suspect?"

"Mr. Patridge is known to the department and to the people in the bar. They identified him to the deputies that arrived, and he was arrested not far from the scene."

"Did you find any prints on the knife?"

"None. If there *had* been fingerprints on the weapon, it would be an anomaly."

She apparently didn't know what 'anomaly' meant because she didn't ask anything else. After that we heard a loud bump out in the waiting room, a bump that caused everyone to look around.

Then a twenty-ish looking female with brown hair wearing a conservative, navy colored, business suit raised her hand. I acknowledged.

"Were you ever able to establish a motive for the crime?"

She had an innocent face; soft brown eyes, a fair complexion, shoulder length blonde hair. She looked, in some ways, angelic.

I paused. In my mind it wouldn't be wise to just come right out and tell this group of laymen that there were those who walk among us who are sociopaths, or even psychopaths, capable at any time of the worst forms of aberrant behavior. That would be too much for her and for them to swallow. They might not believe me; or, it might cause a panic.

In the meantime, what, I thought, should I tell this young woman? Someone who had probably not experienced too much of the evil that this world had to offer.

"Well, let's just say it was a perfect storm."

Dean looked at me with knitted brows.

"It was a perfect storm of alcohol, sociopathy, bad luck, and lack of oral temperance."

The woman looked confused for a moment then smiled as she finally got the joke.

Dean finished the presentation by publishing photos to the jurors. If they hadn't made up their minds to indict before then, the pictures would surely make their choice clear. I walked out of the room confident of at least a charge of Assault 1st degree, if not attempted murder.

Out in the waiting room, the scene surprised me. The young woman who was waiting earlier, and who had expressed some measure of fear of her husband, was standing over next to the window where I had been seated. Three court police officers, in addition to the older officer who worked the room, were standing around a young man lying prone on the floor, handcuffed, with his long, brown hair disheveled, and his nose mashed into the carpet.

"What happened here?" I said.

The older officer looked at me and shook his head. "Oh, this jackass comes bustin' in here, yellin' at the girl over there. I had to use the pepper spray on him."

I nodded and smiled, and looked over at the girl who had her arms folded across her lap in the way that young females do. I always thought it was an inherent defense posture used by women to protect their bellies when pregnant, but a woman once told me it was just because young girls didn't know what else to do with their arms. I watched her for a second and thought I saw a smile cross her lips.

A couple of days later, in the early morning, Will and I were in the office discussing what we could do to locate Rhett Tolliver and get the Zoe Woods case wrapped. I wanted to insert him into NCIC (the national crime computer) and let everyone in the country start looking for him. Will was against it. He said that if anyone stopped him they'd want good cause to hold him, and a two dollar bill with his print on it, and a questionable sketch was just not enough. He said we'd just have to wait until somebody ran up on him and could call us and let us know where we could find him.

We didn't have long to wait. Rufus Greenbaum called on Thursday of that same week.

"Are you still looking for Rhett Tolliver?"

My pulse went up. "We are."

"Well look, I've got an informant here in town. He's on the shady side, of course, but he's friends with the Tolliver family. He says that Rhett is in Birmingham, working at a restaurant up there. He says he lives in Five Points. Does that mean anything to you?"

It did. I'd been through Five Points many times. "Yeah. Yeah, it does. Does he know which restaurant?"

"He said, O Henry's; there in Five Points."

I knew it. I'd even eaten there a couple of times. "Does he have a home address?"

"No. But I guess you can get it from the restaurant manager."

"Right." I tried to think of something else to ask him. "Did he say whether or not he was still in the Nova?"

"No, he didn't say."

"Okay. Well, thanks."

We said our goodbyes, and I hung up. Will had just walked back into the office and sat down with a cup of coffee. I filled him in.

"What do you think?" I said.

"I think it's worth a trip up there. Greenbaum's information has been pretty good so far."

"You think we can get up there an' back in a day?"

"Sure. Four hours up there; four hours to hunt him down; four hours back; and four hours overtime. If we find him, we can get the Birmingham boys to hold him until we can get a warrant." Will took a deep breath and exhaled. "I'll get the credit card."

Chapter 43

I gassed up the car that afternoon, packed my ditty bag, just in case, and met Will at the office at seven the next morning. He sat his coffee in the cup holder in the console of the Crown Victoria and rubbed his face hard with both hands. Then he yawned and cleared his throat.

"I hope this does some good, Son."

I shrugged. "Well, even if we don't catch him, maybe we'll get some intelligence about where he's been and where he's going." I paused. "If we can just put him in Mobile at the time of the killin' . . ."

Three and a half hours later we pulled off Interstate 65 at the University Boulevard/6th Avenue exit, and started heading east, past the University of Alabama at Birmingham's urban campus. Will had slept most of the way, including during a near accident north of the Evergreen exit. An eighteen wheeler had attempted to change lanes in front of me, and I had to take the shoulder to avoid it. I was glad that he was asleep. If he had been awake, I know exactly what he would have said: 'Shit, Son! Look out!'

We turned south on 20th Street, and went up about five blocks to the area called Five Points; past the yuppie coffee houses, tea rooms, bookstores, and specialty shops frequented by the physicians and PhD's from the campus. It was one of those Bohemian districts common to college neighborhoods; all brick with trees sprouting up out of the sidewalks around metal tables and chairs. O Henry's was on the left, about halfway up the large hill that climbed the side of Red Mountain.

There were only a few spaces of short term parking in the lot on the north side of the building. That meant that

351

the majority of the patrons at the business had to park on the street and feed the meters that lined both sides of the four-laned boulevard.

We parked in the empty lot and waited. It was ten o'clock and the restaurant didn't open until eleven. Will leaned back and shut his eyes.

"Ten bucks says he's already blown town," he said.

"What makes you say that?"

"This guy's a drifter. He's spent time in Mobile, New Orleans, Carolina. He's not gonna stay in one place for too long."

I stared out the windshield and exhaled deeply. His description jogged my memory.

"I had an uncle that was like that – Uncle Abner, my mother's brother. He was an alcoholic who just went from place to place. He'd hit town, get a job in a garment factory – back when they were common around the south – work three or four weeks until he got a check, then go on a drunk, get thrown in jail, and lose his job. He'd barely have enough in his pocket to get him to the next town, the next job, the next party; then he'd start it all over again." I paused and shook my head. "He always smelled like whiskey and cigarettes." I smiled. "He used to roll his own; Prince Albert in a can, or Bugler."

"He still livin'?"

"Nope. Died in a car wreck. But get this: he was stone cold sober when it happened."

Will chuckled. "Well, I bet he did exactly what he wanted to do all his life."

"Yeah, I guess. But what makes a man just drift like that?"

Will thought for a minute. "A couple of things: fear; anger, maybe; some sense of self destruction."

Will's thoughtfulness surprised me. He was usually too pragmatic to think philosophically. I closed my eyes and tried to think about what could have happened to old Uncle Ab. His father, the grandfather that I never knew, died of a heart attack at a young age. I wondered if that could have been the source of Ab's pain.

"Then again, sometimes somebody just gets a taste of the drink and it grabs'em, and they spend the whole rest'a their life tryin' to break free." He paused. "What kind'a jobs did'ju say he had?"

"He always said he was an expert cloth cutter. You know, cuttin' shirt and trouser patterns. He said he could cut more cloth quicker'n anybody around."

"Well, at least he was smart enough to learn a trade; one that could get'im a job whenever he needed one."

Abner was tall with an angular build, a sun baked complexion, and coal black hair. He could swear with the best of them and never ran from a fight. And when he'd had a few, he loved to recount the battles he'd fought in bars and roadhouses throughout the South; battles fought over the slightest of remarks and disagreements.

Once my father took Ab to downtown Montgomery and got him a room at a pretty nice boarding house on Herron Street. He helped him get a job, referenced for him on a couple deals around town, and even facilitated him getting a car. True to form, Ab was gone in a month, leaving the car to be repossessed and the boarding house to eat a week's lodging. My father took it all with a grain of salt. He knew it was coming. It was mother that was hurt.

I glanced down at my wrist watch and saw that it was five minutes to eleven. The silence had awakened Will, and he looked ahead and noticed when the front door of the restaurant opened and someone stuck their head out.

"Let's go," he said.

Will walked in first, and I followed while finding a clean page in my notebook. He spoke to the greeter at the front with what sounded like exaggerated politeness, but was really just his 'way'.

"Hello, there, young lady. We'd like to speak to the manager, please."

The woman, girl really, a petite brunette with dark brown eyes, wearing all black, smiled nervously while looking up at Will. The thought occurred to me that she may have believed that we were there to hold up the place. She turned and walked with quick, choppy steps toward the bar directly behind her station.

In three minutes, she returned with a short, chubby man with brown hair and a mustache. His smile was tentative also. Will stuck out his hand.

"Good morning, sir. My name is Eubanks and this is Mr. Faulkner, and we're with the Sheriff's Office down in Mobile."

I showed my star and replaced it in my hip pocket. The manager relaxed noticeably.

"Ron Franklin. How do you do?"

Franklin had slicked back hair and glasses. He wore a white shirt, black tie, and black trousers; and his black oxfords were scuffed and worn.

"Fine, sir. We wonder if we can talk to you about a case we're working on."

Franklin nodded. "Sure, step this way."

He led us past the bar and past the kitchen, to an office at the far end of the building. It was a small room, filled with stacks of papers and loose leaf binders. He cleared spaces for us and then parked himself in a swivel chair behind a paper-choked desk.

"How can I help you?"

"Do you have an employee by the name of Rhett Tolliver?" Will said.

Franklin chuckled. "Well, I had a Tolliver, but his name wasn't Rhett. His first name was Mike; but he called himself 'Mikey.' And, yes, he did work here."

Will looked at me. "Is this 'Mikey'?" Will reached for and I handed him the composite.

Franklin took it and nodded. "Well, it's not *exactly* like him, but it's close enough."

"How long has he been gone?"

354

"About a week or ten days, I think. He just didn't show up one day and . . . ." He shrugged.

"Where did you send his pay?"

"Oh, I got a call a couple'a days ago. It was Mikey telling me to send his check to an address in Tallahassee."

"Do you still have that address?"

He turned toward the desk and looked. "I think so." He rummaged through some papers, culled a scrap from the pile, and handed it to Will.

"I think that's it."

Will took the paper, looked at it, and handed it to me. I read the address and recognized it as being on the east side of Tallahassee, not far from downtown. It was an address with a unit number. It could have been an apartment or a motel.

"What did he do for ya?"

"He was a busboy and dishwasher. He couldn't cook, and really, I didn't feel like he would be good with the customers, so he just cleaned up the dishes."

"Was he a good worker?"

"If you mean was he here on time and did he do his job, and all that, I'd say yes. He was older than most of the other employees."

"Did he ever give you any problems with the waitresses? With the girls, I mean."

"Well, no. Like I say he's a lot older than they are. Most of the girls here are college age. I don't really think they ever had much contact with him."

"Did you ever see him with a woman, or hear him talk about a girlfriend?"

He shook his head. "No, he just kinda came and went."

Will looked over at me. I looked down at my notes. "Can you give us his address?"

Franklin looked back around at the desk. It was hard to believe that he could find anything in that mess, but find it he did. He handed me a job application.

A quick examination of the paper told me that Rhett Tolliver aka 'Mikey' was almost illiterate. I looked up at Franklin.

"May I keep this?"

"Ahhh, okay. But let me make a copy, just in case. You never know when somebody's gonna wanna come back and sue me."

He got up, left the room, and in a minute returned with a duplicate of the paper. I took the original.

My eyes went first to the address. It looked like an apartment or rooming house. Then I glanced at the work history. I don't know if I was expecting lies or the truth, but there it was. Starting in December of last year, Rhett Tolliver stated that he had worked for Tyndall Poultry in Mobile, Alabama. He left a week after the assault, in early March. I took out my pen and pointed to the notation as I handed it to Will, who was making small talk with Franklin.

Will looked down at the page, and then looked at me and nodded. He handed it back to me, and I folded it for travel. Will spoke to Franklin.

"Did he ever go by any name besides 'Mikey'?"

"Nope. You say his name was Rhett?"

"Did he ever say who 'Mikey' or Mike was?"

"No; just said to call him, 'Mikey.'"

Will looked at me again. I thought fast.

"Did you ever notice that he had an unusually quick temper?"

Franklin closed his eyes and looked up. "You know, there was one time. I don't know if this means anything, but he kinda lost it one day when one of the cooks said something about how slow he was gettin' the tables cleared. I wasn't here at the time, but I was told that the cook said something about him 'movin' like a woman.' Then Mikey threw a dish down on the floor and broke it, deliberately."

I jotted the information down in my notebook. There was really only one more question.

"What kind of car did Tolliver drive?"

"Well, he walked to work most of the time, I think; but once I saw him leave in an old Chevy. It was red, possibly a Nova. I know it was a Chevy. I remember it 'cause one of the girls left with'im."

Will's head turned quickly. "Is that girl workin' today?"

"I think so. Let me see." Franklin turned to the messy desk and picked up what looked like a schedule and stared at it. "Yeah, it was Laurie. She should be out front. You wanna talk to her?"

Will nodded. "We do, if it's okay with you."

"Sure. I'll get her." He rose from his chair and walked out of the office.

I looked at Will. "I bet this girl don't know how lucky she is."

"Well, let's don't tell her, Son; at least, not too quick."

In three minutes, the door to the office opened slowly and in peeked a curly head of hair.

"Come on in, Laurie," Will said. "Sit down."

She was thirty or more; blonde and rail thin. She looked the complete opposite from the other waitresses in the restaurant. She had on the same black shirt and pants as the others, but she was having a hard time filling them out.

Her face was lined and tan, her eyes were sunk back in their sockets, and her nose was long and thin. She was either a drug user or a chain smoker because women her age just weren't that thin without help.

"Laurie, my name is Eubanks, and this is Detective Faulkner."

She nodded but said nothing. She had taken Franklin's seat at the desk and was leaning forward. She clasped her bony fingers together and gripped them tightly.

"Laurie what's your last name?"

"Singleton."

"And your birthdate?"

"Two, 1, of 65."

357

"What we wanted to talk about was Mikey Tolliver. We understand you spent some time with him, away from work." We showed her the composite, and she identified it.

She shrugged her shoulders and pursed her lips. "We went out a couple'a times. It wadn't no big thing."

"Tell us about him."

"Well, nothin' to tell, really. We just went to a movie once and then got a hamburger. The other time, we went back to his place and looked at TV."

"What kind of person was he?"

"He was alright. I mean, it was pretty plain that he wadn't gonna be around here long, 'cause he said so right up front. But he was nice, most'a the time."

"Not all the time?"

"Well, a couple'a times he got mad. It seemed like he could fly off the handle quick if things didn't go his way."

"Tell us about it."

"Well, the one time, at the movies, there was some kids in front of us talkin'. He stood up and told'em he was gonna kick their asses if they didn't shut up."

"How'd they take it?"

"I guess they thought he meant it, 'cause they quit. I could hear'em whisperin' about it afterwards, but they didn't do nothin'." She paused. "Mikey in some kinda trouble?"

"Well, we don't know yet. We'd like to talk to him. Do you know how to get in touch with him?"

She shook her head. "No. He said he'd call me when he got set up, but I knew he wouldn't. Why do men say that?"

I felt a little sorry for Laurie Singleton. Without even delving into her past, I could tell she'd had a hard life. Rhett Tolliver was probably the best she could do, and he had run off and left her.

Will cleared his throat. It was my understanding that, before he was married, Will was a love'em and leave'em kind'a guy.

"Laurie, did he say anything to you about him bein' in any trouble anywhere?"

She shook her head. "He just said he had a brother in New Orleans, and he was from Atlanta. Did you guys know he was one of the founding members of Lynrd Skynrd?" She nodded. "Yeah, unh hunh. He left the group when he found out they wanted to go another direction musically."

"He got turned down for the astronaut program, too. They said he was too short." Her face was deadpan.

Will looked at me. I couldn't tell whether she believed any of the stuff that she was telling us or not.

"What else?" I said.

"Well, he was in the TCB band; you know, Elvis's band. He took over when the reg'lar guitar player got sick."

"Why didn't he stick with it?" I said with a straight face.

"Oh, when the guitar player heard how good he was, he come back real quick."

"Anything else?"

"Well, he said his mama and daddy owned a rubber factory over in Georgia, but I didn't believe him. He said that rubber come from trees. I told him he was pullin' my leg."

That she didn't believe? I decided to get her back to earth.

"Laurie," I said, "if you don't mind kind of a delicate question, we heard that Mikey was a pretty violent lover. Did you get that impression?"

"You know, now that you mention it, I do see where you might could'a heard that. When things didn't go his way, he got a little rough."

"Well, how was it?"

She shrugged. "Just so-so."

"The 'gettin' rough' part, was that when he was drinkin'?"

"Oh, no. He didn't drink when we did it. He said he didn't care if I did, but he never had more than a beer around me."

She didn't seem the least bit self-conscious when disclosing the fact that they had been intimate. My guess was she was proud to let everyone know that someone had wanted to make love to her, if only for a short time.

"He ever drink around ya?"

"Not really. He said he only drank one kinda' drink and that was a Black Russian. When we went to his house, he said he didn't have the fixin's to make one, so we just had beer."

We spent the rest of our conversation finding out more about Laurie Singleton in an effort to gauge her fitness as a witness, should she be needed. Just as I suspected, she was a semi-recovering drug abuser.

"I used to do a lot of heroin, but I'm gettin' my life back together now."

That's how they all said it: 'I'm gettin' my life back together.'

"So, how was Mikey with you 'gettin' your life together'?" Will said.

"Well, he didn't know about my past. I told'ja that he said he didn't want no strings."

"You have any reason to believe that Mikey was into anything shady?"

She looked down at the floor. "I don't think so. I mean, he talked about his brother a lot, you know, the one in New Orleans; and I kinda thought he might'a been into somethin'. But, hey, it was just a thing, you know? We had some fun, and that was it."

We left her with a card and told her to call us if she heard from Mikey again. She said she would, but she really didn't expect to. I told her that if she spent any more time with him, just to be careful.

"I don't know what this is all about, but," she shrugged, "okay."

360

Before we left Birmingham, we checked out Tolliver's room not far from the restaurant, in Forest Park. It was a second floor, weekly rental at a place called Oakwood Apartments.

The landlord was on site and told us that Rhett, or Mikey, or whatever he wanted to be called, was a model tenant. He never made noise, paid his rent on time, and when he moved out, he gave a week's notice, just like he was supposed to.

In forty-five minutes, we were on the road heading back to Mobile. Will closed his eyes, but I made up my mind that I wasn't going to let him off that easy.

"So, what do you make of Tolliver now?" I said.

"Well, he's pretty much what I thought. He's a drifter, a loner, a man with no idea on how to live life. He's just tryin' a little bit'a everything until he finds somethin' that works."

I thought about what he said. Will was partly right. Tolliver did move about looking for something, and he did seem to have no purpose. But I think Will's view of him was a little too complicated. He had him pegged as a seeker; someone who was searching for meaning in life. Tolliver wasn't looking for anything. He was just surviving.

"How about those stories; you know, that stuff about Lynrd Skynrd, and all that. You think he told all that to Zoe Woods?"

"Prob'ly not. He was prob'ly just tryin' that shit out on this ole gal." He paused. "Besides, even if he did, old koo-koo wouldn't'a cared. She was just too stupid. She prob'ly told him: 'hey, just shut up and show me your dick.'"

I laughed. Will was deadpan.

"Okay," I said. "We can put Rhett Tolliver in Mobile at the time of the assault; we gotta witness that identifies his favorite drink as a Black Russian; and we know that every now and then he's got a temper. We also know he drives a red Chevy, probably a Nova. We got his fingerprint on a two dollar bill passed at the bar the night of the assault,

361

and we got a composite of a guy that's Rhett Tolliver, but who calls himself, 'Mikey.'" I paused. "You think that's enough to get him put on NCIC?"

Will sat and thought in silence for about a half mile. "You know what, Son? It is."

Chapter 44

Monday morning, back at the office, Will and I discussed whether or not to go to Tallahassee to look for Rhett Tolliver. Will was against it, and frankly, so was I. Another day-long drive like the one I had just made would do me no good physically, especially if there was only a slight chance we'd be successful. We ended up deciding to enter Tolliver into NCIC and then contacting the Police Department over there and asking them to check the address that we had gotten from Franklin up in Birmingham.

"Make sure you add in his alias, 'Mikey,'" Will said.

"Wonder what makes him use his brother's name like that? You think that's part of a dodge, or is there another reason."

"Most likely it's the easiest name he can think of when he gets in a pinch. I don't think there's anything else goin' on, in his head."

I paused. "I disagree, for two reasons. One is how he's kept in contact with his brother's ex, Myrtice; followed her down to South Carolina, and all. I think he's got a thing for her, and he might have something against his brother for breaking up with her. I think she likes Rhett, too. You know, she didn't rat him out when she knew he was in town

362

working at the chicken plant. He may be trying to get brother Mikey out of the picture."

"Mikey's already outta the picture, Son. And, by the way, you need to confirm his employment with the chicken people," Will said.

I said nothing.

Will looked disgusted. "What's the other reason?"

"The other is that he's jealous of his brother and wants to be him. He wants his old lady, his job, and whatever else. It's clear that he has delusions of grandeur. This guy has a lot of self-hate, or self-love."

Will shook his head. He had never been a proponent of psychobabble. He believed that people acted for the basest of reasons – to meet one of Maslow's needs. I, on the other hand, saw actions as symptoms of deeper problems.

"Son, this Tolliver is just trying to get some pussy, and he's gonna say whatever it takes to get it." He paused. "And, hey, he may have the hots for Myrtice, but that just makes it clear to me that the boy, likes, pussy."

I smiled. "Okay. Okay. You're right."

Will picked up the phone and was talking to the dispatcher when Denise the secretary knocked on the opened door facing. I looked up and admired her. She was wearing a blue miniskirt and a white blouse, and she was holding a small slip of paper.

"You guys busy?" she said.

I nodded toward Will. "He's talking with the dispatcher."

She looked at him and made a face. Denise liked Will. It was just that sometimes she could be disgusted by him. Somewhere, in the deepest darkest recesses of my mind, I had a sneaking suspicion about the two.

"I see you got your hookin' skirt on today," I said with a smile on my face. "Who're you trying to impress?"

She stuck out her tongue at me and thrust the paper my direction.

363

"Well, if you're gonna be nasty, you can take this call."

I chuckled and took the paper out of her hand. Meanwhile, Will got off the phone and looked at both of us.

"What are you two jawin' about?"

"He was nasty to me, so I gave him some work." She wrinkled her nose at me, and I smiled again.

"You're sexy when you're mad," I said.

She growled in the back of her throat and whirled toward the door. In a second, she was gone. Will scowled at me.

"You know you could tap that if you wanted to. There wadn't no reason to run her off."

I chuckled again. "Maybe." I looked at the paper. "But first we got a call." I read the words and looked up.

"It's a possible suicide, up in Eight Mile."

"Shit."

We were on the road in ten minutes and in Eight Mile in twenty-five. Eight Mile, Alabama, was the largest suburb of Prichard, the second largest city in the county. It hugged Highway 45 from Interstate 65, north, to the small community of Kushla, and also extended north on Lott Road to the county jurisdiction line.

It was basically the white suburb of Prichard, a predominately black city run by black leadership. White flight in the sixties had sent many families north, into what was, at that time, the county, away from the crime that had overtaken the downtown area. Mobile home parks, a few stand-alone trailers, and single family brick homes on slightly larger than normal lots dotted each side of Lott Road – County Road 217 – as it wound its way from Highway 45, north to the outskirts of the recently incorporated Semmes, Alabama.

It was to one of these brick homes, in a new neighborhood, that we were called. The Ashland subdivision was a small development of about twenty, three and four

364

bedroom homes on tree shaded lots on the east side of Lott Road, not far from the Spice Pond Road intersection. It was a picturesque area with lots of greenery and new, white concrete. Fifty-one twenty-five was on the left side of Ashland Drive, about two hundred yards off Lott Road.

When we arrived, it looked like a Fraternal Order of Police convention. There were two vehicles from Prichard, one from the newly created Semmes Police Department, three cars from the county – including the crime scene SUV – the coroner's wagon, and me and Will.

We stepped out into the morning air, and I took a deep breath. The temperature was in the high seventies, and there was a breeze out of the north. The clouds above looked as if there might be a chance of rain in the afternoon.

The home was a red brick ranch with a white railing around the front porch. The newly landscaped yard said that the house had only recently been constructed. Tiles of winter rye grass in the front yard had not yet completely melded together.

Two Prichard officers, one a sergeant, were standing on the porch talking with Megan Crenshaw. The Semmes officer was standing back listening. Crenshaw had a map in her hand and was gesturing to it. It appeared to me as if the three were discussing just exactly under whose jurisdiction this particular case had fallen.

As we walked toward the door, Will looked at me.

"Let me handle this," he said.

We stepped onto the porch, and Will inserted himself into the discussion. The Prichard officers, a black sergeant named Brown, and a white patrolman named Wilson, immediately looked at Will.

"Good morning, sir," Will said.

Sergeant Brown stuck out his hand. "Good morning."

"We were just lookin' on the map . . ." Will said as he shook the hand.

365

"I know just what you're gonna to say," Brown said. "We've checked the map also, and this subdivision is fifty feet outside the police jurisdiction line. We're certainly happy to relinquish the case to you." He looked around at the white officer. "Come on Mr. Wilson." The two smiled and in less than ten seconds they were at the street getting into their patrol cars.

Will stood there, dumbfounded.

"Is that the way that was supposed to go?" I said smiling.

Will looked at me and scowled. Then he looked at Crenshaw.

"Were you trying to take this call?"

"No, no. I was just checkin' the map." Her brows went up, and she took a defensive posture.

Will shook his head, and he and I walked through the front door and into the foyer of the residence. I stopped, turned around, and spoke to Crenshaw.

"What's in here?" I nodded toward the interior of the house.

"You'll have to see it to believe it. It looks horrible." She made a face.

In the foyer, Chuck Briley was standing, camera hanging around his neck, writing on a pad. He looked up and pointed down the hallway.

The house was immaculate. The anteroom was bright and airish, and the tile floor sparkled. The walls were painted white and there was a gold-colored hanging light right in the middle of the ceiling.

"What's it look like back there?" I said.

"You'll just have to see it," Briley said.

Looking down a hall, I could see Will standing in the threshold of the last door on the left, hands on his hips, looking all around the room. He found a clear place on the floor just inside the door and stepped in. I walked up and took his place just outside in the hall.

366

It was the master bedroom; a space about sixteen by twenty and furnished normally: carpeted floor, queen sized bed, dresser, bureau, and night tables. The head of the bed was on the opposite end of the room. I noticed that the room was cool and that a ceiling fan was in operation.

The victim was lying on the floor between the foot of the bed and the dresser. He wore white briefs, but was otherwise nude. He was a white man, and judging by what I could see of his face as well as his complexion was about thirty-five years old. A shotgun lay next to him, on the floor, muzzle end toward his head.

My eyes immediately gravitated to that location. There was a thick groove starting at his chin and progressing upward to the crown of his head. As it neared his forehead it widened until it mushroomed out the top of his skull. His eyes dangled crazily on either side of his head, and his nose was missing. He lay in a wide pool of blood.

But it was what I saw next that surprised me. My eyes left the body and began to scan the room. There were red splotches on all four of the walls, starting at about halfway up from the floor, all the way to the ceiling. The ceiling itself was covered by the same red stains. I looked closely and could see that all the marks were made by blood and what looked to be brain matter.

"What happened here?" I said.

Will had moved to a location next to the body and was kneeling. He reached and got a pair of gloves from his back pocket and put them on. Then he began to manipulate the man's face and try to pull it back into some semblance of a visage. It was something that Will did, oftentimes, to help him think.

"This old boy shot his self, Son."

I looked around the room. "This place looks like a Wes Craven movie."

Will stopped and looked up at me. "Who's Wes Craven?"

"He makes scary movies."

"Shit, Son. This ain't no movie. This is real life – or real death."

Walking over to the wall, I looked closely at the matter that was stuck to it. It was clearly brains, with some small shards of bone mixed in.

I was quiet, trying to figure out how the detritus that was once this man's mind had come to be painted all over the four walls and the ceiling of this room. I was stumped until I looked down at my pad. The top page kept flipping forward as a result of a breeze that was coming from somewhere. Then I looked up. The ceiling fan went around and around at a brisk clip.

Apparently, while standing beneath the fan, the man had put the muzzle of the shotgun under his chin and pulled the trigger. The fan had then broadcast his brains all over the room, thereby redecorating it and ensuring that whoever lived in the home would sell it as quickly and as cheaply as possible. I wondered if that was the dead man's plan all along.

Will was still kneeling down by the dead body when Leftwich of the Coroner's Office walked in. He sat his camera bag down on the floor and looked around.

"Man, is this a mess," he said. "I talked with his family only briefly. Have you?"

I looked up from my pad. "As a matter of fact, we haven't. And you know, I didn't even think of askin' about'em."

Talking to this dead man's family was a conversation that I'd just as soon not have. Any man that was angry enough to commit suicide in this manner, had to have been miserable and was very likely making everyone around him miserable; or they had made him that way.

My experience has been that suicide is another perfect storm. It occurs when a person who has such ideations procures a means, usually a gun, a rope, or pills; they ingest some kind of inhibition reducing substance, usually alcohol; after which a precipitating event occurs.

Sometimes, the perpetrator will plan it in advance. Sometimes, it happens on the spur of the moment. I'm convinced that a little voice – the devil, maybe? – goes off in his or her head, saying: 'do it.' If they're weak and suggestible, they will.

"Look how he's screwed up this room. Whoever lives with him has got to be angry," I said.

Leftwich reached into his camera bag, but stopped short when Will spoke.

"Here's what you're lookin' for," he said. He threw something toward Leftwich's nylon bag.

"What?" Leftwich asked.

"The shotgun wadding. It was under his tongue."

Leftwich looked at Will with a smirk on his face. I'm sure he was thinking about having to pick up the remains of this anonymous man and putting them into a body bag. It would be dirty, stinking, filthy work.

He said softly and calmly: "Whoopee."

Chapter 45

When the first week in October arrived, I happened to look at the calendar and I noticed that in two days I would have to leave to attend the Robbery-Homicide convention, something about which I was not necessarily excited. It was an eight hour drive from Mobile to Jacksonville; I was not scheduled to speak until the second day; and I would be alone.

Will said that he had been to those things in the past, and I should just enjoy myself. He said it would be a vacation. I asked him if he had ever presented at any of these kinds of meetings. He said that he had not, but the only thing that might give me any trouble was the questions, and if I would familiarize myself with the case file, that wouldn't be a problem. After all, he said, the people at the convention – drunk policemen, mostly – if they did care at all, wouldn't know anything about the case.

On Monday, I went to the Records Section and saw Jean Adler. She was a full figured woman who wore her uniform shirt tightly across her massive breasts. Her blonde hair was almost yellow, and she had a dark complexion. Bright, crimson, lipstick-painted lips encircled her gleaming white teeth. She smiled.

"Well, what can I do for you, Henry?"

"I need to get an old case. Carl Harden is the victim." I gave her the case number.

"Neely got that case out a couple'a months ago, didn't he?"

"Yeah. I read it and turned it back in. Now, I need it again."

"I wish you boys would make up your minds." Her tone was one of playful disgust. "Come on in." She stood aside and opened the bottom half of the Dutch door not ordinarily opened to persons not assigned to that section.

I walked into a great room full of desks manned by women whose job it was to keep the journal of crime in Mobile County. I followed her to a section of large rolling shelves that contained reports and case files for the past seven years. Anything earlier had been taken out and copied to microfiche and was stored off site.

Jean used a crank to roll two of the shelves aside, after which she walked down a long aisle and returned in twenty seconds with the large accordion style envelope stuffed to overflowing with papers. It took two hands to carry it.

"Here you go. You get a break on it?"

I chuckled. "Nooo. I gotta go to a conference and give a presentation."

370

"Where at?"

"Jacksonville," I said as I turned and started walking off.

"Nice." She paused. "I got a sister there. Can I go?"

I chuckled again. "Sweetie, if you can talk the Sheriff into it, I'll take ya."

"You'd love it. I guarantee it."

I smiled and walked out, wanting no part of Jean Adler. She was way too much woman for me.

Upstairs, I opened the file and laid out its contents on my desk. But before I began reading, I sat back in my chair and closed my eyes.

I was at the office when Carl Harden was found. I remembered that it was a beautiful spring day, the sun was shining, and there wasn't a cloud anywhere. The dispatcher told me that there was a murder on the second dirt trail off Newman Road south of Airport Boulevard, about five miles north of Grand Bay. I knew the place.

Newman Road was a two lane, paved road that ran from Airport Boulevard south to Interstate 10. It was farming country, and fields and pastureland lined the roadway. Most of the houses in the area were well off the road.

The second dirt road was on the Clyde Newman property. It was a farm road only, had no name, and was made of that fine red sand common to the area. It ran west off Newman Road about two hundred yards, to a point where the path was arrested by a pasture gate. The clearing outside the gate was about the size of a baseball infield.

I arrived at around three o'clock. The sun was still above the tall pines to the west. Will and Lonnie Zane were there, with the Captain and one patrol deputy. Old Man Newman was there, too. I recognized him from answering his house alarm as a patrol deputy.

The truck was an old International Harvester, about a nineteen fifty model. It was white, but badly rusted. The nose of the truck was facing the fence and the tail gate was down. I remember getting out of my car with my camera around my neck.

Will told me that Old Man Newman had found the truck and the victim in the bed of it when he was out riding his fence line, something he did about once a month. Will also said that the dead man had a driver's license identifying him as Carl Harden. He told me to take some pictures of the victim and see if I couldn't get any prints off the truck.

I walked up to the open tailgate and looked in. The victim was white, gray haired, and scruffy. He wore a white t-shirt and blue jeans.

His arms were cartooned with tattoos from his wrists to his shoulders. His hair was thinning on top, but shaggy on the sides, and his beard and mustache were gray and full.

There were two unusual things about him. The first was the large hole in his chest at the bottom edge of his sternum, a hole about the size of a half dollar; a hole that had soaked his t-shirt in blood. The second was that fact that he was barefooted.

"Where are his boots?" I had asked.

"They're missing," Zane said.

I had eyed him up and down and looked up. "He's a biker?"

"It would appear so," Will said.

I opened my eyes and started looking at the file. It revealed a list of facts learned from the investigation.

Carl – he was called Cal – was a member of the 'Las Ratas' biker gang; he made the run to Daytona, Florida, every spring for 'Bike Week'; he was from Houston, Texas; and his family had refused to claim his body.

I closed my eyes. It would be a short speech.

The next morning, I was on the road early and in Panama City, Florida, by nine AM. The stretch of interstate between Pensacola and Panama City was particularly barren – flat land full of scrub forests. Except for the tall signs identifying the gas stations at each exit, there was no evidence of humanity, and the landscape was devoid of anything to look at. I stopped at Tallahassee for lunch, and was back on the road and pulling into Jacksonville right at five o'clock that afternoon.

There was a slight breeze in the air, wind from off the St Johns River, when I got out of the car in the parking lot of the Chamberlin Hotel, a four-star resort on the east bank of the river, just off I-95, across the bridge from the Central Business District.

It was a ten story building made of glass and steel. It looked green from a distance, but standing on the pavement and looking up, it changed colors and was blue; slightly darker than the cloudless sky above it, more of a royal blue.

I parked six rows from the front door, though there were blue-vested valets manning the canopied driveway. Truth was, I didn't have any bills to give them. I got my bags out of the trunk and lugged them up a slight grade, past the attendants, and through the automatic front door.

The front desk was to the right. Two young women wearing identical blue vests smiled at me as I approached the counter. I identified myself.

"Yes, sir, Mr. Faulkner, we have your reservation right here."

One of the desk clerks, the one with long brown hair and green eyes, typed some things on a keyboard, swiped my card, then programmed a couple of card keys and handed them to me.

"Take the elevator to the ninth floor, exit and turn left. You're about halfway to the end of the hall."

Thanking her, I took the cards. On my way through the lobby, I saw the convention check-in desk and decided to go ahead and get that chore out of the way.

I noticed her immediately as I walked toward the tables. She had a look about her that was too glamorous to be a police officer. Her hair was shoulder length and blonde, her blue eyes large and set widely apart, and her lipsticked lips framed straight white teeth. The sleeves of her blue sweater were pushed up, and she had a small gold crucifix around her neck. Her name badge identified her as Missy Padgett from the Jacksonville Sheriff's Office.

She was thirty, or that was my best guess. The hands and neck always tell the tale. Her fingers were short and thin, and her neck was smooth and tight. Her nails were painted with polish that matched her lips.

"Yes, ma'am," I said. "My name is Faulkner, from Mobile County, Alabama."

She smiled and thumbed through a box with papers standing on end until she found one with my name on a card inside a clear plastic cover.

"Here we are, Mr. Faulkner. And, I see that you're also scheduled to present." When she spoke, her voice was airy and there was a hint of a drawl.

"That's right, uh, Missy," I said cocking my head and eyeing her own name badge, "and you may call me Henry."

"Okay, Henry," she smiled again and looked down at some papers in front of her. "Looks like you're speaking the day after tomorrow, at one thirty."

"Beautiful."

I said it the way Robert Wagner used to, with a little bit of disgust in my voice. My time slot meant that I'd have to spend a day and a half listening to a bunch of scientists and theorists pontificate about cases on which they'd never worked and about which they knew very little.

She grinned, as if she knew how I felt. "Well, you know, there's the heated indoor pool, the exercise room, and, of course, the bar."

"Oh, don't worry. I'll make do." I paused. "And just how long have you been assigned to homicide at the Jacksonville Sheriff's Office?"

"About a year."

"Well, may I say that you're the best looking murder cop I've ever seen."

374

"Well, thank you. Perhaps that's what my husband saw in me."

I tried to keep the disappointment I felt inside from showing on my face. I looked back at her hands expecting to find a ring, but saw none.

"Well, may I say, he's a very lucky man."

"I think so, too."

I nodded, unsure of what else to say. She seemed to sense it.

"Look, there's a reception tonight. Look me up, and we'll have a drink," she said.

"That would be fine."

She nodded and smiled. I picked up the papers detailing the speakers and the vendors, a small swag bag, my own luggage, my chagrin, and walked toward the elevator.

That evening, I dropped in at the convention reception in the Ponce de Leon Room, a large space with wall paper that depicted the explorer drinking from the fountain of youth in nearby St Augustine. It had a tapestry carpet and a large, very dim, hanging light in the middle of the ceiling. The bar was a tall wood table in the corner, and two other tables with white table cloths were along the wall near the large open double doors. I ordered a small bottle of ginger ale from the bar and checked out the hors d'oeurves on the tables.

There were about fifty people in the room when I arrived. We were all dressed casually in sport shirts and slacks. No weapons were visible; however, I was certain that the majority of the room was packing.

As I popped a deviled egg into my mouth, my eyes surveilled the area. Most of the crowd was male; however, there were three or four females, short women in dresses and heels that I was sure were sales people, who stood amongst the much taller men while laughing and acting interested in the war stories they were spinning.

375

I was only slightly startled when she tapped me on the shoulder. I turned quickly and came face to face with Missy Padgett.

"I see you made it."

"Wouldn't have missed it."

She wore a silk blouse and a miniskirt over muscled and tanned legs and black pumps. I also noticed a plain gold band on her left hand.

She smiled. "What'cha drinking?"

"Oh, ginger ale. I do my drinking at home, where I can be depressed and not bother anyone."

She smiled. "Oh, I see. And you're not depressed tonight?"

"Actually, no." I nodded at her hand. "How about you?"

"Bourbon and branch," she said holding up her glass.

"Just like J.R."

"Who?"

"I guess you're too young to remember."

"You flatter me."

"It's an obscure reference."

She nodded her head toward one of five round tables along the wall opposite the food. I followed her over, taking in the view as she walked.

When she sat down, I took a seat across from and not next to her. She seemed disappointed.

"So, 'Missy,' is that short for Melissa?"

She shook her head. "Millicent; named after my grandmother."

I raised my eyebrows. "Classy." I took a drink. "Sounds rich."

"Somewhat."

"Your husband a cop, too?"

"Oh, no," she said in the middle of a swig. "Navy. Pilot."

"Oh, Top Gun."

"Kinda. He changed over from jets to larger planes a while ago. He's out on a carrier."

"Where?"

She put her finger up to her mouth. "Shhhh. I don't know. It's all 'hush, hush' whenever he leaves."

There was a lull. "So, homicide, huh. What did you say, a year?"

She nodded. "I love it."

"How long you been with the department?"

"Three years."

"Wow, you must be pretty good."

I didn't really believe that. Her career sounded for all the world like a social experiment – or a political payoff.

"Oh, not really. I just caught a lucky break."

"Anything interesting, yet?"

"Well, they've got me working on a couple of cold cases right now. I'm getting into the day to day stuff gradually." She paused and took a drink. "How about you?"

"Five years, or thereabouts. I'm already into the day to day stuff." I don't know if she could tell that I was being just slightly condescending – but I was.

"What case are you presenting?"

"Oh, uh, a dead biker found out in a rural part of the county. It's a yawner, really. I don't know why the Sheriff sent me over here with it."

She raised her eyebrows. "Maybe he just wanted to get you out of town for a few days."

I actually hadn't thought of that. If the Sheriff had some nefarious motive, he could've just done what he was going to do right in front of me. I would have respected him more. If he thought I was working too hard, he could've just told me to take some time off. I wouldn't have bucked him on that account either.

I smiled. "Perhaps."

There was silence for five seconds as she looked around.

"So, is there a Mrs. Faulkner?"

377

I chuckled. "Oh, no."

"Why not? You're a good-looking guy; you've got a really cool job. I'd think the girls would be falling over you."

I smiled, not really knowing where she was going with this. Her assessment of my life was a little comical. I was beginning to think she was some kind of uniform groupie herself; one who had trumped all the rest and had made it to the inner sanctum, so to speak.

The truth was that the women I had spent time with over the years had no taste for the late hours, ruined dinners and movies, and long nights working on homicide cases. When they found out what I did, and quickly realized where my hands had been, they usually wrinkled up their noses and said, 'Ewwww.' And when it hit them that I worked in civil service, and that the job really didn't pay that much, they most often decided that they could do better.

"Well, you're too kind. But, alas, it seems that I've taken another bride."

Her brows went up again. "Oh?"

"I'm married to murder."

She laughed out loud. It was a nice laugh, not one of those obnoxious female laughs that can be heard across the room.

"Tell me about Mobile," she said looking directly into my eyes.

I knew then what she was after. No woman would ask such an inane question of a man unless she wanted to sleep with him.

"Well, it's not as big as Jacksonville; it's got a small urban area, but a pretty large rural component. We have about seventy or so murders a year, both in and out of the city." I smiled. "But, all in all, it's not a bad town."

She smiled, showing her teeth. She was leaning forward and her eyes were locked onto mine.

"Well, that's the first time I ever asked anyone about their home town and got a sociological description of the murder rate."

"I gotta be me."

"You're really into this stuff, aren't you."

"Death is my life."

She laughed again. "Do you always speak in cliches?"

"I have a lot time on my hands." I paused and looked at her. "How about you?"

"How about me, what?"

"What's a nice girl like you doing in a place like this?"

She laughed again and took a sip of her drink. Then she broke into a short biography. Born in Jacksonville, her uncle was the Sheriff. After college at Florida State – Sociology – she came back home and started work, first in patrol for a year, then in Internal Affairs. It was clear to me that this woman was being fast tracked by her family for, if not a career in politics, at least a steady job in a not too dangerous part of civil service. I guess they hadn't counted on her marrying into the military.

When she finished, there was an awkward silence. I looked into her eyes, but I got the feeling that she thought it was my turn to talk. To tell you the truth, I had nothing else to say.

"So many clichés. Are you a writer?"

"Well," I said, "if I am, I'm a pretty bad one. You're not supposed to write in clichés." I paused. "Nope. Just police reports."

She sat back and looked around the room. I could see that she was preparing to go.

"Well, I guess I better mingle a bit; you understand."

"Sure." I nodded.

She paused. "Hey, you have a business card or something?"

"I do."

I reached into my back pocket and took out an engraved silver card case that my brother had given me two Christmases ago. I extracted one and handed it to her.

She took it and looked down at the printing. "Mobile Metro S.O. Homicide Bureau. 'Our day begins when your day ends.'"

She threw her head back and laughed out loud again. Then she rose and took two steps away. When she stopped, it surprised me, just a little. I rose also.

"Say, I've gotta be down here for a little while longer, but . . . maybe we could go upstairs for a drink?"

I smiled slightly. She looked good. It was tempting.

"You know, it's a thought," I paused, "but I couldn't stab a service man in the back like that." I shook my head. "I don't want what's not mine."

She nodded. "I understand. It's nice to see a guy with some scruples."

"Hey, maybe I'll see you around." My tone was cordial, but, frankly, I hoped I never saw her again.

"Sure."

She started to walk off, but I stopped her. Our eyes met once again.

"By the way," I said. "If you wanted to go upstairs, why did you ever tell me you were married?"

She shrugged. "I don't know. I spoke too soon, I guess. You grew on me."

As she turned away, she shook her head and smiled. "Ha, 'married to murder.' I gotta remember that one."

That night, my sleep was troubled; but not as troubled as it would've been had I spent the night with Missy Padgett. I tossed and turned and finally had to get up and turn on the television. I don't know whether it was the strangeness of the environment, or something else, but it wasn't until somewhere around three thirty that I finally dropped off, right in the middle of an old *Naked City* rerun.

The next morning, I was up early and hit the gym. After breakfast, I went to the lobby and took a tour of the vendors who lined the halls from the front desk to the restaurant at the end of the hall. There looked to be more than fifty booths, all of which contained the latest in technology designed to identify, locate, and apprehend people who commit murder.

The hall was long and the ceiling high. About halfway to the restaurant, the double doors of the meeting room were open wide. The day's events had not yet begun, and the hallway was just beginning to fill up with police types standing in front of each of the displays.

I walked slowly, looking at the booths on both sides. There was a laser designed to locate fingerprints on any surface; three vendors were selling a variety of computer programs that managed leads for any type of major case; and there were several companies that offered polygraph and voice stress analysis services.

A place called 'Infacticon' caught my eye. It was a software company that manufactured a half a dozen different programs for law enforcement. The booth featured red, white, and blue bunting and print, as well as photographs of officers from a department that I thought I recognized: the Montgomery, Alabama, Department of Police.

"Does Montgomery's Department use your product?" I said to the young woman seated at the table.

She looked up from the magazine in front of her and smiled. "They do. They have a lead management program, a computer aided dispatch system, as well as a traffic accident reconstruction program."

I nodded and looked up at the wall behind her, but my eyes soon fell back to her face. She was young, petite, and blonde. Her eyes were cornflower blue and set widely apart. Her small nose sat above a small mouth that when she smiled looked twice as large.

"Infacticon. Is that short for something?"

"It stands for informational confluence of facts." She smiled.

"I see. So, what does one of these lead management programs cost?"

She reached for a catalogue. "Well, it depends on which one you get." She paused. "Are you the decision maker at your department for this type of purchase?"

I looked at her and chuckled. "Wow. That's the first time I've ever been asked that question. But I guess the best answer is, yes and no. The boss usually says, 'hey, whatever you need, we'll get it for you.'" I looked into her eyes. "But, do I sign the checks? The answer is, no."

"You sound like you're close enough. The lead management program is twenty-five hundred with installation, training, and tech support."

I raised my eyebrows. "Hmm. Well, let's see what it can do."

She smiled and stood up. It was then that I noticed the gold name badge on her navy blue tunic that identified her as Janet Sylvester. She took two steps toward the end of the six foot long table and lifted the cover of a laptop computer. I could see her shape under a matching blue skirt.

"Take a look," she said punching the enter key on the machine.

A man's voice, over violin music, began to describe how that information is the most vital tool in criminal investigation. The voice, a deep baritone, spoke precisely and with no accent. The first scene of the video was of an obviously staged homicide crime scene. The second was of a detective seated in front of a computer, inputting information. The five minute presentation played out with the detective looking at papers, then talking to another detective, after which they walked a handcuffed man into a jail cell. It ended with a soft sell pitch that said my clearance rate would rise as much as fifty percent were I to purchase this program. I really didn't pay much attention to the words. I was thinking about Janet Sylvester.

When it was over, she retook her seat. I walked back over in front of her and stood.

"You guys have a flyer or something I can show the boss?"

"Sure." She reached behind her into a sample case and brought out two full color brochures and handed them to me. "All the contact information is on here."

"Are you guys local, or what?"

"Des Moines, Iowa. We're part of a larger technology firm there."

I nodded. It's something I do quite often when I talking to women. It helps me think before I speak; it keeps me from saying something stupid.

"By the way, I'm Henry Faulkner, Mobile, Alabama, Metro Sheriff."

"Janet Sylvester." She smiled again. It was a nice smile.

"You from Des Moines, too?"

"Oh, no. Fort Worth, Texas."

"Oh, really. I spent a week there one night."

She knitted her brows and tilted her head like the RCA Victor dog, but broke into a chuckle when I smiled.

"It's really a nice town," she said.

"I know it is. I was just joshin'."

There was a short, awkward pause. "So," I said, "are you manning the home front here by yourself?"

She looked both ways down the hall. "Oh, no. Arthur is here with me. He went to the restaurant to get breakfast." She smiled and looked both ways.

I was hoping this would go somewhere, but things weren't progressing well. For now, she knew that I was with the Sheriff's Department. But that was all she knew, and she had made no other inquiries about me. I snuck a peek at her left hand and found the third finger bare. I couldn't figure it out. I was witty, engaged, attentive . . .

I pulled out a business card from the case in my hip pocket and handed it to her. She took it and looked down.

"I'll show the brochure to the boss, and if he says go, I'll give you a call."

"I'll be expecting it." She paused. "Here, take this also." She handed me a compact disc.

I looked down at the disc and then up at her. "Thanks." I took two steps away and then stopped. "Hey, can I interest you in lunch?"

She smiled but shook her head. "Oh, no, thanks. I'm kind of working."

I nodded and said, "Okay, well, see ya 'round."

Fat chance.

That afternoon, I spent my time in the meeting. The list of speakers was long and boring.

There was an older psychologist from the northeast who expounded on the mindset of Charles Manson and other manipulative serial killers; a couple of forensic scientists from California who presented on some mass murder in LA; and two detectives from Las Vegas talked about how to use forensic nonverbal communication analysis when interrogating a suspect.

But the most interesting talk was about content analysis in written and oral statements. I had heard about this before, but I had only just begun to practice it.

The theory is based upon the fact that every person wants to reveal the truth linguistically – either written or spoken – and will usually do so, in his or her own way. The words and syntax both indicate whether a person is telling the truth, or at least, 'their' truth.

There were some aspects of speech content that I had begun to notice, the most interesting of which was the 'non-denial.' At the heart of it was the theory that a guilty man would always answer a question about his involvement in a crime with something other than a flat denial. The speaker was a professor of communications at some university in the Midwest who claimed to have done some consulting work for the FBI. He spoke for thirty minutes and, frankly, I learned nothing new.

That night I sat in my room and wished I was home. I'd gotten a come on from a married woman, and the cold shoulder from an unmarried one. I'd learned little from the lectures, and my own talk was going to be a snoozer. As it was, I had a half a mind to pack up and go home that night; and if they hadn't signed me up to speak, I would have. I supposed I could always feign some type of illness. Depressed, I spent the evening with a paperback and a drink from the mini bar.

The next afternoon, I had lunch, and, dressed in slacks and a blazer, reported to the meeting room, to a man wearing a badge that identified him as Terrance Faircloth, of the Jacksonville, Florida, Sheriff's Office. He was standing at the front of the room near one of the side exits. He was a round man with gray hair and a mustache who wore a blue polo shirt with his department's logo embroidered over the left breast. When I introduced myself, he stretched out his hand.

"Nice to meet'cha, sir."

"How long before my short talk?" I said looking around.

"You go on next. Are you ready?"

I nodded and held up my three by five cards.

"Okay, have a seat over there on the front row, and when it's time, I'll introduce you. You'll have fifteen minutes."

"Can I take Q and A?"

"Sure, if you want."

"I'm counting on it."

Looking around at the crowd, I could see that there were less than a hundred people in a room designed to hold two hundred and fifty. My guess was that most were either at the buffet line at a strip club, or drinking their way through eighteen holes on a golf course.

In five minutes, Faircloth called my name, and I stood up. I buttoned my jacket, walked to the podium, and laid my cards on the lectern. I cleared my throat and looked over the crowd. Completely at random, my eyes fell upon Missy Padgett, seated on the second row, to the left. She smiled.

There were about ten or twelve people in the first two rows, and the rest were spread out over the other ten or twenty. When I spoke, the echo was loud.

"This is the case of the homicide of Carl 'Cal' Harden, who was found deceased in the bed of his pickup off a remote dirt road in rural Mobile County, Alabama."

Continuing on, I described his injuries, what we knew about his affiliation with the Las Ratas motorcycle gang, and the last twenty-four hours of his life, or actually the last forty-eight. We couldn't track him after he was seen at a swap meet over in south Mississippi. I looked out over the crowd and saw two men yawning and another nod his head.

I finished as fast as I could and called for questions. No one spoke, so I said thank you, left the podium, and started for the door. Frankly, I couldn't get home fast enough.

Three steps out of the double doors on the hall side, I heard someone call my name. I looked around and saw a woman walking toward me.

"Mr. Faulkner."

Her voice was high and soft. She didn't sound much like a police officer.

"Yes, ma'am."

She shuffled to a stop. "I want to talk to you about your case."

She was not unattractive, but had a clean and clear quality about her. She was barely five feet tall, thin boned, with sandy hair that was straight and hung just below her ears. The glasses that sat in front of her blue, almost gray eyes were the very thin, wire-framed type, giving her kind of a bookish air; not unlike a female Ben Franklin. Her fair skin, and the freckles that were sprinkled across her nose, made her look rather delicate, and about thirteen years old. She wore a red polo shirt, and tan khakis, and she took two large breaths before she spoke.

"I'm Sandy Winston with the of Sheriff's Office over in Jackson County, Mississippi."

Her twang made her origin obvious. It was a nice drawl, not obnoxious or uneducated. Jackson was the first county west of Mobile, on the Mississippi Gulf Coast.

"Henry Faulkner."

"I think I might have some information about your case."

My brows went up. "Really?"

"Can we step down to the coffee shop?"

It was going to put a crimp in my departure plans, but never let it be said that Henry Faulkner turned down a lead in a murder case.

"Sure."

We walked the twenty-five yards to the small restaurant at the end of the hall opposite another meeting room and took a seat two booths from the cash register. I ordered coffee and she a glass of lemonade.

"My mother always told me that coffee would stunt my growth." She chuckled.

"She was right," I said as I sipped from a thick institutional-type mug.

She smiled. It was an innocent smile that revealed straight teeth.

"So, are you a detective over in Jackson County?"

"Oh, no. I'm a civilian crime scene tech. But that's how I know about your case. I was going through some old fingerprints in the office about a month ago, and I remembered some taken from an assault case over at a swap meet, in Kiln, Mississippi. When you said that about the swap meet, it reminded me of the prints."

"Tell me more."

387

"Well, I don't know much more, really, I mean without looking at the stuff we got. I think it was about five years ago. They still have that swap meet over there every Saturday you know. We had three latents that I think were taken off a baseball bat. I remember that the card said it was in March, about the time of your murder. I was supposed to go through those old prints and if they were on cases where the statute of limitations had run out, I was supposed to destroy'em."

"How come you hung onto these?"

She shrugged. "I don't know. I just had a feelin'."

"Did you ever get a look at the case file?"

She shook her head. "No. I just looked at'em, then put'em back in the file. But I know right where they are."

I was encouraged for only one reason. It was just crazy enough to drive five hundred miles to meet someone from twenty-five miles away who would have information about a murder that our office had almost forgotten. I was not encouraged by the fact that with a bunch of rednecks and bikers at a swap meet the potential was there for at least a dozen fights every weekend. Still, the time frame – five years ago – fit. And, even if it didn't have anything to do with Cal, maybe the names of those involved would give us some people with whom we could talk.

"I take it you weren't with the department then," I said.

"Oh, no. I just got out of school; Southern Miss."

"CJ major?"

She nodded as she sipped her lemonade through a straw. "Double with Forensic Sciences. I'm working on my masters at University of Alabama, Birmingham."

I shook my head. "Gee whiz, why would a cute young girl like you want to join the cops?" I said cute before I realized it. She smiled.

"I'm a 'CSI baby.' I've been hooked on mysteries and crime shows all my life. The first book I ever read all the way through was a Nancy Drew."

"I see. Well, don't let it ruin you."

"Oh, I won't. I love my work. All the guys are like big brothers. They take good care'a me. I'd'a been an officer, but I don't meet the height requirement."

"How did you wind up here?"

She slurped the last of her lemonade. "I saw it in *Police Chief* Magazine, so I just walked in and asked the boss. He told me to go see the Sheriff. I did, and here I am."

"Having fun?"

"Absolutely. I've learned a bunch; especially from that guy that talked about Charles Manson. I never heard'a him before. Do you remember him?"

I smiled. "How old do you think I am?"

She smiled.

"Sadly, yes, I do," I said.

"I just love that stuff. It is sooo interesting to me."

"I'm glad. Just remember, murder is a crime, not entertainment."

"Oh, well, yeah, sure. I know that. But the puzzle of it, you know."

I nodded. "I know."

We sat and talked for what seemed like hours but what was really only about forty-five more minutes. She had a vivacious and effusive personality, almost too animated to be a good ID officer.

She told me about her family – farmers near Petal, Mississippi; her siblings – two older sisters who picked on her as a child, now, both married; and her dog – a chocolate lab named Andy.

"Andy and Sandy?"

She smiled. "I know. It's kinda dumb, but he just looks like a 'Andy.'"

I nodded and smiled. Then I looked at my watch.

"Well, look, I was gonna cut out for home this afternoon. Maybe I better get moving."

"Oh, no, don't. Stay, and I'll buy you dinner."

This was crazy. I was nearly twenty years older than she. I looked at her for a minute.

"Sure."

Chapter 46

By ten the next morning I was on the road back to Mobile. There was still one more day left in the conference, but I felt no obligation to hang around. None of the speakers on the program piqued my interest, and even if they had, I didn't want to hear their war stories. I had enough of my own.

Dinner with Sandy Winston had been pleasant enough. I had the surf and turf at a local place, Dr. Bill's, who promised to cure any appetite with his ten ounce steak. The bill was in the fifty dollar range, but I didn't feel bad about it because her sheriff was paying.

I left her my business card and told her that either I or Will would call her in a few days, and we'd come to take a look at her file and those unknown latents. I had in the past learned not to get too hopeful in matters such as this; however, stranger things had happened.

Sandy Winston and I had a good talk. She picked my brain about cases and methods and history. Then she rattled on about how she was going to be a homicide detective one day, when she got stronger and gained a little weight. I told her that investigators were a dime a dozen, but crime scene techs and fingerprint analysts were pretty highly skilled and usually in high demand at any department in America, and she should stick with prints. As Roy Rogers always said, 'Not just anybody can tell the difference between a fingerprint and a picture of a zebra's ass.' Anyway, looking at her bone structure, I had my doubts as to whether she could ever gain enough muscle to do even one push up, let alone the twenty-five necessary to qualify for somebody's police academy.

The next morning was Friday. I could have taken the day off work, but I wanted to get in and see who had called and what was on my desk. I got there at seven forty-five. Will was already at his desk drinking coffee.

"What the fuck are you doin' here, Son?"

"I got back last night. I wanted to come in and see what was on my desk."

"Well, shit. You're about a dumbass."

I smirked and sat down in front of about eight phone messages. There were two from the ME's office; two from the higher-ups; one from Sandy Winston; one from the DA's office; two from people I didn't recognize; and one from Greenbaum in North Carolina.

"I see I got a message here from Greenbaum. Anything new on the Zoe Woods thing?"

"If there is, I hadn't heard it." He paused and took a sip. "You learn anything over there?"

"Not really.

"Get laid?"

I chuckled and shook my head. "I had one woman come on to me, but she turned out to be married – to a Navy pilot."

"Did that matter?"

I shook my head. "I couldn't cuckold a service man. Besides, I've seen people shot for less."

"That's why God give you a pistol, Son."

I shook my head again. "Nope, won't do it. Besides, I got dinner out of another young girl."

"Now, you're talkin'. Where's she from?"

"Now, don't get excited, but she's from over in Pascagoula. As a matter of fact, she thinks she's got some information that might help out on our Harden thing."

"How so?"

"She said that when I mentioned that he was last seen at the swap meet in Kiln, she remembered running across a couple of old latents in their files over there. She said she they were from March, five years ago, and that they came off a baseball bat found after a fight. She was gonna look up the file and call me next week." I held up a pink sheet from one of those message pads. "In fact, this is her right here."

"Sounds thin."

"I said the same thing, but it's worth checking out. It might be good for finding a witness, if nothing else." I picked up the phone. "But first, I'm gonna call Greenbaum."

After three rings and a secretary, I finally got him on the line.

"What can I do for you, sir?" I said.

"Have you found Rhett Tolliver, yet?" he said.

"We have not. We checked out that lead in Birmingham, but he'd already split town. They put us onto Tallahassee, but the PD over there said the address was bogus. So, right now, we're still suckin' wind."

"Well, I've got another lead, if you're interested."

I picked up a pen and prepared to write. "Shoot."

"I got a call from an informant up here who said that Tolliver was somewhere in north Mississippi, working at a Christmas tree farm."

"He say where?"

"No, but he's trying to nail it down. I just thought you might have some other information to put with it. When he gets more, I'll call you back."

"Thanks. Christmas tree farm, huh. You know, they use those hook bill knives there."

"That fits your case?"

"It could."

We said our goodbyes. I hung up and relayed the information to Will. He was unimpressed.

392

"Well, shit, Son, you don't know any more now'n you did ten minutes ago." He paused. "That ole boy could be anywhere."

"You're right. But at least he thought enough to call."

"It's a longshot." He paused. "But I'm more interested in that thing over in Mississippi. Go ahead and call that woman."

"She's probably not home from Jacksonville, yet."

"Well, she's got somethin' to tell ya."

I nodded. "Okay." I picked up the phone.

She answered after three rings. Her voice was high and squeaky. I identified myself.

"Hey, I'm glad you called," she said.

"Yeah, what's up?"

"I just wanted to tell you what a good time I had the other night."

"Uh, well, uh, yeah, sure. Me, too."

"It was great hearing about your career, and stuff."

"Yeah. Look, I thought you might have something on our case; you know, with the fingerprints and all."

She seemed surprised. "Oh, sure. I'll be back home tomorrow, and I'll go into the office this weekend. Let's plan on meeting on Monday, or, uh, Tuesday. Monday's a holiday. How's that?"

"Okay. We'll come over about ten Tuesday morning. Are you at the courthouse?"

"Sure am. In the basement."

"See you then."

I hung up and told Will about our plans. Then I sat down in my chair and contemplated what I was going to do about my groupie.

That weekend, I was on call. My guess was that it was some sort of payback from the Captain for me getting a week out of town in a nice hotel on the Sheriff's dime. At least

Monday was Columbus Day, and I'd have an extra day to recuperate.

Saturday night, the phone rang at about eleven.

"This is the Sheriff's Office. We have a call."

I had just dropped off to sleep and it hurt to wake up. I wiped my face and ran my fingers through my hair. At no time in my career did I ever expect to get used to being awakened out of a sound sleep. Someone once reminded me that it was a common method of torture in prison camps to awaken prisoners just after they'd fallen asleep.

"What'cha got?"

"A homicide on Creek Court off Old Pascagoula Road."

I knew the place. It was a small, private dirt trail that ran north off Old Pascagoula, about halfway between McDonald and Theodore-Dawes roads. It was about a quarter mile long, and there were three or four small cottages on one side of the road and half a dozen mobile homes on the other.

"Okay. Any other details?"

"Ahh, one dead. Suspect on scene and in custody."

I took a deep breath and exhaled. "Okay. I'll be there in about twenty minutes."

She hung up, and I replaced the receiver in its cradle. Even with someone in handcuffs, it would be well into the morning before I got back in bed. It was times like this that I very badly wanted another job.

In ten minutes, I had showered and shaved and was in my car. I took the back way, south on Sollie Road, where the traffic would be lighter. There were no businesses, only houses in the area.

On Creek Court, there were four patrol cars lined up end to end in front of the only building that was lit. I stopped my car across the street from what looked like a vacant double wide. I notified the dispatcher, looked around, and then got out of the car with my notebook in hand.

The air was crisp and there was a peacefulness about the neighborhood that was almost eerie. I got the sense that everyone who lived along the court had shut off their lights and was looking out of their windows at me as I went to work.

The first deputy I saw was Sergeant Paul Fraley. He had curly red hair and wore his sidearm low on his right leg in one of those swivel holsters, like the motorman he once was for the city police some fifteen years ago. He smiled as I walked toward him, revealing the fact that he was missing his upper left canine, a casualty of his last wreck on a Harley. After that accident, his wife had laid down the law: no more motorcycles. Shortly thereafter he was hired by the county, an agency that had no traffic division and therefore no motorcycles.

"Hey, Henry. Sorry to get you out."

"That's what I'm here for." I flipped open my notebook. "What'chu got?"

"Well, looks like this guy in the car over here," he pointed to a marked patrol car, "shot the dead fellow inside. My man found him sittin' in the bedroom. The gun's in my car, and the dead man's in the hall."

"Motive?"

"All we've been able to get out of the suspect is that it's domestic."

"Woman?"

"There's one inside."

"Coroner?"

"I called him first thing. He shoulda been here by now."

"ID?"

"Roy Rogers called and said he's five minutes out."

As I stood and made notes, half of me wanted to get in the car and drive away. The other half was so curious to find out what had taken place inside the house that, even as tired as I was, I was busting to get in and take a look.

I suppose it's like that about most calamities. It's why people drive slowly by a wreck and look to see if there are any injuries. People want to see if the misfortune of others is worse than their own; if other people's lots in life are somehow more insufferable than the hand that they've been dealt. I guess, they're really looking to see how fortunate they are. In my own way, I was no different.

Walking toward the house, I looked around and saw Rogers' SUV drive slowly down the lane. He parked behind me and got out, camera in hand.

Rogers carried a twelve thousand dollar Leica brand, thirty five millimeter camera. It was a small piece that sat on a frame with a detachable flash. He was the only person in his unit who had one. He claimed that it made better photographs than any other camera on the market.

When he got within three feet, he stopped and sniffed. "Ahh. This is where I belong. Welcome to the Jungle."

"Alright, alright," I chuckled. "Calm down." I paused and nodded over my shoulder. "I haven't been inside, yet. But apparently that man over there in the back seat of the patrol car shot some other man, over a woman."

"Could it be anything else?"

"I guess not."

The house was a small structure, no more than a thousand square feet. It was wood framed, with what looked, in the dark, like light blue-colored aluminum siding. The front door was dirty white and sat under a small porch, illuminated by what was probably a forty watt bulb. There were two windows in front, one on either side of the door.

Inside, just over the threshold, we were immediately in the living room. There was a uniformed deputy standing just to our left, through a door, in a small kitchen. Straight ahead was a hall. In the hall lay a dead body, a male with a large pool of blood under his head that because the floor was not level had communicated back toward the living space. In fact, the dark red liquid and the body had

396

effectively blocked the hall and were so large that we couldn't step over it or him.

"I wonder if there's a door this way," Rogers said.

He walked past me into the kitchen while I stood and drew a quick sketch of the scene. I still hadn't seen any signs of a woman.

In thirty seconds, I noticed Rogers standing in the hall opposite the body. "The kitchen door leads to the bedroom."

I nodded and walked into the kitchen, turned to my right, and exited that room into a bedroom. There was a woman sitting on the bed, cross legged, with a stunned look on her face.

Passing her, I walked into the hall next to Rogers. He was busy snapping photos of the dead man. The corpse had not yet begun to smell.

He was a white man, of what looked to be average height and weight. His coal black hair was oiled heavily and combed straight back, and his mustache was waxed and curled on the end. He wore a long sleeved plaid shirt, blue jeans with a wide leather belt, and saddle-type cowboy boots. Oddly, his shirt was tucked in and his boots were shined. The boots appeared to be of some exotic leather; alligator or lizard skin, perhaps. He was lying on his right side in something akin to the fetal position, but his right hand was extended above his head and his left rested on his chest.

I knelt down and tried to see where the wound was. I couldn't tell for sure, but it looked like it was in the middle of his chest. It also looked like a shotgun pattern that was about twelve to twenty inches wide. I wondered where the coroner was.

"He looks like a drugstore cowboy." I spoke keeping my voice low so I couldn't be heard by woman in the next room.

"He looks like James Best."

I smiled. "Okay, shotgun to the chest. That's all I need to know." I stood up and looked around. "Be sure and get a good record of the bedroom. Somethin' tells me that most of the action took place in there. I'm gonna go talk to this woman."

Rogers nodded. I turned and walked that way.

The bedroom was small and appeared smaller because of the clutter. There seemed to be a piece of furniture in every nook, however the queen sized bed took up most of the space. It sat in the corner next to the door that led into the kitchen. There was a bureau, a vanity, and, although there was no closet, there was a clothes rack, made of metal and painted black, and it was chock full of male and female garments. I stopped and looked all around before turning my attention to the woman.

She was not classically beautiful by any measure, but to a man who could look past a woman's face, she had an earthy quality that made her look sensual and therefore serviceable. She had a flawless olive complexion and a thick muscular build, with heavy breasts, but a flat stomach and wide hips. Her hands and feet were small, with blue painted nails. She wore one of those short nightgowns, pink and not transparent, but thin enough.

I looked into her face. Her cheek bones were wide, as was her mouth, and she had a strong Roman nose. Her long hair was jet black with a slight frizz, and I couldn't tell if she was of Mediterranean or American Indian descent.

"Ma'am," I said. "My name is Faulkner. I'm with the Metro Sheriff's Department. What's your name?"

She seemed to be in a trance. She looked straight ahead and rocked back and forth, and I had to speak to her again and snap my fingers in front of her face to get her attention.

"Oh, ah, Mary. Mary Weatherford."

That settled it for me. She was most likely Indian; or, what is it they're called now? 'Native American?'

"Can you tell me what happened?"

"He shot my husband."

"Who?"

"Tommy."

"Why don't you start at the beginning."

She took a deep breath and looked straight ahead as she spoke. Her voice was a lazy alto, with a drawl that I didn't recognize.

"Tommy and me was, was in bed. I heard a knock at the door, and I got up to see who it was." She paused. "It was Bill."

"Bill is the dead man?"

"Yeah."

"Are the two of you related?"

"Yeah," she nodded. "He's my husband."

She paused as if to let the information sink in. I supposed that she was trying to gauge my reaction, but this was a familiar story.

"So, I let him in," she continued, "and we talked there in the livin' room. I guess he must'a heard somethin', 'cause he stepped over to the door and looked in and saw Tommy. I said, hey, baby, come back in the livin' room and let me go and get dressed, and we can talk things over. So, he come back in and sat down in the chair in there. I went back in here to get dressed and the next thing I know Bill was at the door yellin' at Tommy. Then I don't know what happened. I got in the bed and put my head under the covers." She paused.

"What happened then?"

She swallowed. "Then I heard a loud boom."

"Where is the gun now?"

She looked at me, then around the room. Her head stopped and she pointed over in the corner between the bureau and the vanity.

"It was right over there. I don't know where it is now."

"Whose gun is it?"

"Mine. Well, Bill's."

399

Killed with his own shotgun. Marvelous.

"What happened then?"

"I, I looked up from the covers, and saw Tommy standin' there with the gun and . . ."

"Who called the law?"

"He must have. I didn't."

"Did Tommy say what happened?"

"He just said, 'I thought he was gonna kill me.'"

I nodded. I was beginning to get the picture. Mama and new boyfriend are at home getting it on; husband shows up; new boyfriend sees the opportunity and offs the husband. It was a pretty old story.

"How long have you lived here?"

"About six months." She sniffed.

"And how long have you and Tommy been seein' each other?"

"About six weeks."

She had moved to Mobile County from Enid, Oklahoma, which explained the dead man's attire. She claimed that Bill had been physically abusive, and that's why she left him. She cleaned out the bank account, came to town, took a job as a waitress at the Trackside Lounge, over by the greyhound park, and intended to start a new life. This Tommy was a compulsive gambler who had been a patron at the lounge. He lived in his car on some land off Highway 90 in Irvington, that is, until Mary Weatherford took him in. She bought him drinks, they got to know each other, and three days later they were roommates.

As she sat and stared, I quizzed her about the names and addresses and birthdays of the principles. She gave me as much as she could about Tommy Sullivan, who grew up in north Mobile County and was once a logger.

I walked to the kitchen door and signaled to the deputy standing near the refrigerator. He walked over.

"Go tell her to get a change of clothes, then put her in the car and take her to the big office. When you get there, call you a female deputy and get her dressed, save what she's

400

got on in a bag, and then set her to work writin' her statement. I'll be down there in a few minutes. Don't let her wash." I paused. "Oh, and get Rogers to take a picture of her before she leaves."

The deputy, who I didn't know, and who looked as if he lifted weights for a living, nodded and stepped into the bedroom to break the news to Mary Weatherford. I looked for Roy Rogers.

Rogers was at the end of the hall, near the back door. He was talking to someone just outside. I called to him.

"Go outside and come around back," he said. I waved an arm in response.

In two minutes, I was at the west side of the house. I was surprised to find Larry Ridgeway, the on call medical examiner standing under the porch light talking to Rogers and another uniformed deputy. Bugs swirled about the exposed bulb.

I smiled. "Well, if you can't get here when you should, get here when you can," I said.

Ridgeway mopped his brow and cleaned his glasses, which had fogged, even in the cool night air. He looked around.

"I went to the Creek Road out near the state line. I went up and down that road twice before I figured out I was in the wrong place."

Ridgeway was an affable man with a southern drawl, educated in Nashville, and trained in forensic pathology in New Mexico. He had sandy hair, a fair, sunburned complexion, and he carried a black leather bag.

"Them dispatchers, they could fuck up a wet dream," Rogers said, naturally ascribing Ridgeway's mistake to the ladies giving him the directions.

I looked down and smiled. Rogers did know how to turn a phrase.

"Did you fill him in?" I said nodding at the doctor.
"Not really."

I turned Ridgeway's direction. "Doc, looks like the dead man was married to the woman who lives here. She claims that she ran away from him because he beat her. The shooter is the new boyfriend who was in bed with the wife when the husband walked in. The cause and manner are not in question. What we need for you to do is to render an opinion as to whether or not this shooting could or could not possibly have been self-defense."

"How close was he standing when he was shot."

"Right."

At that point the big deputy and Mary Weatherford stepped out from around the corner of the house. She was carrying a paper bag, ostensibly containing a change of clothes. I stopped her.

"Roy, get a photograph of this woman."

Rogers directed her to a spot five feet away near the clothesline. We watched as the flash from the camera illuminated the night. Rogers took full size photos of her, back and front, and both hands and feet. When he was finished, she left with the deputy, and I turned back to Ridgeway.

"Just take a look and see if self-defense is an option."

"You think the woman might have done the shooting?"

"I didn't get that impression. But it wouldn't be the first time that a wife murdered her husband."

After I got Ridgeway situated inside, I got Rogers to photograph Sullivan; after which I sent him to the office by one of Fraley's deputies. In a little over an hour, Sullivan and I had adjourned to the interrogation room at the Major Crimes office.

He sat before me in navy blue briefs and a white t-shirt, what I assumed were his sleeping clothes. Sullivan was slightly over five and a half feet tall, and looked to weigh in at a little less than a hundred and forty. His skin was dark, his hair was black, and he had a mole on the left side of his neck. His nails were dirty and a small jailhouse tattoo altered the back of his right hand. His left hand was cuffed to the iron bar attached to the table.

I turned on the recorders and got situated. His eyes were wide, and he fidgeted nervously.

"Have you ever been arrested, Tommy?"

"Yes, sir." His drawl was noticeable.

"Well, then, you know your Constitutional rights." I recited the familiar spiel.

I never understood why the police should have remind a person who has committed a crime of the fact that it would not be in his or her best interest to confess. To me, if a scumbag was too stupid not to have learned about the Bill of Rights in fourth grade, then he, or she, deserved to incriminate themselves as much as possible. Heck, even immigrants – legal ones, that is – learn the about the Fifth Amendment when they apply for citizenship.

He nodded when I asked him if he understood.

"You'll have to say, yes, Tommy, so I'll know you understand."

He cleared his throat. "Yes, uh huh, yes."

I opened my steno pad and turned to a clean page. "Why don't you tell me what happened. Start at the beginning."

He took a deep breath and exhaled. "Well, I met Mary a few weeks ago at the bar where she works. We started, you know, seein' each other, an' she, you know, she, we been seein' each other ever since then."

"She ever tell you she was married?"

"Well, yeah, but, you know, she said it was over 'cause her ole man beat her." He paused and waited for me to talk. I didn't, so he continued. "So, like tonight, we went out and had a few drinks an' come back home, I mean to her house."

"You livin' there?"

"Well, you know, I got some clothes there, but no, not really."

403

"Where are you living?"

He paused to think. "Well, my mama is . . . I don't know. In my car, I guess."

I looked him in the eye. "Are you married, Tommy?"

"No, sir." I believed him.

"So, what happened next?"

"So, we was, was in the bed together, and we heard a knock at the door. She says, Mary says, 'I wonder who that is?' and she gets up and goes to the door."

"What happened then?"

"She comes runnin' back in and says, 'Oh, shit, it's my husband.'"

I stared at him. He continued.

"So, I jumped up and started runnin' around. I didn't know whether to run, or stay there, or what, 'cause she said he beat her. So, she says, 'just stay here, and I'll get rid of'im.'"

He paused. Whenever a suspect pauses it usually means that either, he's lying, and he wants to see if I'm buying it; or he's buying time to make up something; or he is trying to say what he thinks I want to hear.

"So, I stayed there in the bedroom, lookin' for ma shoes, and then I look up and he's there standin' in the door. He says 'What are you doin' here, son of a bitch?'"

"What did you say?"

"Well, nothin'. I was too scared."

"What happened then?"

"Well, Mary comes to the door and grabs him by the arm and says, 'Come on back in here, Billy.' So he turns and walks back into the livin' room.

"Well, I started lookin' for my shoes again, and in a few minutes, he come back to the door. He says, 'I'm gonna kill you, you wormy little bastard.' So then he started chasin' me around the room, and that's when I grabbed up the shotgun. Then, well, you know the rest. I thought he was gonna kill me. He said he was. I was afraid."

404

There were some holes in his story. One was the part about running around. I didn't believe that happened. For one thing, the girl didn't say anything about it; and for another was her location when the shooting took place. He didn't mention her coming back into the room to get dressed and subsequently hiding under the covers. Third, was the fact that the room was much too small for one man to chase another without catching him rather quickly.

"Where were you standing when the shooting took place?"

"I'd say," a sure sign of a lie, "about three feet away from the door. He was about to grab me."

"Where was Mary when the shooting happened?"

He looked up. "I don't remember. I don't remember seein' her."

That might be true. If she was hiding under the bed clothes, he might not remember seeing her. Still, he said nothing about her coming in to get dressed. I had pretty much made up my mind to put him in jail.

"Where was the gun?"

"In the corner."

"How did you know that?"

"It's my gun. I put it there."

He said that not realizing how guilty it made him look. If he brought a weapon and put it in the house, he was undoubtedly planning for the day when her old man came calling, and it indicated that he didn't intend to give her up; that is, if it was really his gun. My guess was that it was not. First, Mary said it was hers, or her husband's, and she no doubt brought it with her when she moved from Oklahoma. Second, if Sullivan was the gambler that Mary said he was, and he was truly living in his car, he would have long since pawned anything of value, like a shotgun, for gambling money.

"Where are you from, Mr. Sullivan?"

"I was born and raised in Citronelle."

"Ever been to Oklahoma?"

405

"Yeah, I mean, no, I mean, not to do more than to just pass through."

By his answer, I knew there was more to this than what I'd heard so far. I talked to him a while longer, then decided to wind it up.

"Tommy, I'm gonna put you in jail. You might think this is a self-defense case, but the evidence doesn't support it. I don't want you to skip town, I don't believe you were three feet away when you shot him, and I don't believe he chased you around the room." I looked at him. "Would you care to revise your statement?"

He looked down at the table and took a deep breath. When he blew it out, I felt the wind on my arm. When he spoke, it was a whisper.

"No."

It was after five on Sunday morning before I got away from the office. I went home and caught a couple of hours sleep, and came back in at about ten.

The first thing I did was call Ridgeway. He said he had looked at the wound and the victim's shirt, and estimated that the victim had been shot from six to eight feet away.

William Weatherford, the dead man, had a minor history of persons crimes back in Oklahoma. However, he had never done time, and his only serious offense had been an Arson 3rd degree – burning an unoccupied building.

A quick check of Tommy Sullivan's criminal history told me that he had a couple of arrests for burglary, a few more for theft, and one, inexplicably, for abuse of corpse. I also found that he had once had his driver's license suspended . . . in Enid, Oklahoma.

Chapter 47

On Tuesday morning, I attended the early morning bond hearing at the Metro Jail. I recommended to the judge that Tommy Sullivan's bond be at least twenty-five thousand dollars. He concurred, and I went back to the office to finish up the paperwork. Will was seated in his chair, leaned back, blowing on a cup of coffee.

"Heard you had a little somethin' over the weekend."

"Yeah. A man busted in on his wife and her new boyfriend. The boyfriend shot the husband, so I stuck him in jail."

"What'd'you that for? He was just givin' the old gal what she wanted." His tone was sarcastic; however, I knew from his past that Will had a passing knowledge of what cases like this were all about.

"Well, he lied to me. So, that was the tipping point."

"Well, don't make puttin' these boyfriends in jail a habit, Son."

I chuckled. "I won't."

While I shuffled papers, Will slurped coffee. There were other things to do, and I knew it.

"When do you want to go over to Jackson County and look at that file?"

I caught him in mid slurp. "Call her first," he swallowed, "when you're done."

I nodded and finished putting together the file in front of me and locked it in the cabinet in the corner. Then I picked up the phone, read the number off her business card, and called Sandy Winston. She answered on the third ring.

"Hey." Her voice was cheery.

"Hey. So, what about the case file? You pull it?"

"Yep. It's waitin' whenever you get here." She paused. "I think you'll be pleased."

407

"See ya, shortly."

We were in the car in twenty minutes, and in an hour we were on US Highway 90 in Pascagoula, Mississippi.

Pascagoula was once, and still is today, built on the shipbuilding industry. It was a town of twenty-five thousand, mostly generations-old Mississippians. The town folded around Highway 90 to the south and Interstate 10 to the north. On the south side, there were beach homes; on the north, rural scrub land and middle and lower class residences.

The Sheriff's Office was located in the south wing of the county courthouse, a Greek revival-styled, marble building with four large pillars in front. The ID section was located in the basement, the entrance to which was under the front stone staircase. Shell parking lots were located on the south and east sides of the building, and I put our car under a pecan tree as close to the front door as possible.

"Well, let's go meet this super cop," Will said.

"I told you, she's a civilian crime scene tech."

"Right."

We walked in the building through the double glass doors under the staircase. We found the ID office on the right hand side, near the north side exit.

An Identification Unit differs from a Crime Scene Unit in that ID deals only with the methods of positively identifying a suspect, by his fingerprints and/or his actual face, or some facsimile. Therefore, ID only handles mugshots and fingerprint or ridged impression evidence. Crime scene investigators gather all types of evidence and fully document the appearance of a crime scene. In most departments, the two functions are interchangeable. That was apparently the case in the Jackson County Sheriff's Office.

Through the wooden door, we were immediately in front of a civilian receptionist. The large woman was about thirty-five, wearing a gray uniform shirt, green uniform trousers, and glasses on the end of her nose. She looked up and smiled.

"Ya'll here to see Sandy?"

"Yes, ma'am," I said. "She's expecting us."

"You must be Mr. Faulkner. Sandy mentioned you." She smiled knowingly as she stood up. "I'll get her."

Will looked at me and smirked. I cleared my throat.

In ten seconds, Sandy Winston walked through the door behind the receptionist's desk.

"Hey, you guys. Wow, you got here fast."

"Yeah, well, we were anxious. Sandy, this is my partner, Will Eubanks."

She smiled and nodded at Will. Will said, "Well, hello there, young lady."

Before Will could say something to embarrass me, I spoke up. "You got that case file down here?"

"I sure do. Come on in here to my desk."

We followed her through the door back into a combination laboratory/workroom. Half the room contained two long lab counters with sinks and faucets; the other half was full of desks and filing cabinets. Sandy Winston's desk was the one in the farthest corner.

"Here's the file." She handed me what looked like a copy. "Apparently, there was a female who got into a fight with a man at the swap meet. It escalated and she picked up a baseball bat and hit the man with it." She paused. "The man was Carl Harden."

I looked at Will, then at Winston. "Any blood on the bat?"

"None was noted, but at that time, nobody submitted it for testing. They only dusted the bat for prints."

"Did you get a name on the woman?" I said. Will took the file from me and began to peruse it.

"No one was mentioned in the file. Back then, of course, there was no AFIS, and nobody sent it off to the FBI for a search . . . especially since Carl wasn't there to prosecute."

I glanced at Will and saw his brows fly up. My guess was that he had a line on who this woman might have been.

"Well, since the victim is now deceased, I guess you can close this case, right?" I said.

"Well, yeah, I guess."

"Since the victim is dead, you'll have no need of the prints, will you?"

"No."

"We'd like to take them with us."

She was hesitant. "I guess so. I'll have to check with the Sheriff or the Captain." She rose from her desk. "Let me run upstairs. Just make yourselves ta home."

When she'd left, I sat in a vacant chair. Will did the same.

"This female. I think I know who she is." He paused and looked down at the report. "I think it was Cal's girlfriend. I don't remember her name, but it's in the file."

"Tabitha Higgins."

"Tabitha, that's right. That was her name. We never could find her at the time. I bet her prints are on file, though."

"You think she could've shot Carl?"

"I don't know, Son."

In five minutes, Sandy was back in the office. She was carrying papers.

"Sheriff says go for it with the prints. You just have to sign this release of custody." She laid the papers on the desk in front of me.

I signed two copies of the same page and gave her one. I took the other and dropped it in my pad folio, then picked up the small envelope containing the prints.

"Now," I said, "two things: one, could you see if you have a ten print card for a Tabitha Higgins."

"Sure, I'll look. What's the other?"

"Just her address."

"Be back in a jif."

410

She rose and bounced out of the office, through the door, and into the reception area. Will and I sat in silence. Finally, I spoke.

"If she's close by, you want to stop and see if she's home on our way back east?" I said.

"We can do that, Son."

In another two minutes, Sandy returned. She walked to a filing cabinet six feet from her desk, opened it, and after thumbing through a few of the thousands of cards, extracted three print cards and walked toward me.

"Three arrests, three cards. Her last known address is on this one with a new name: Tabitha Higgins McElroy." She pointed to the first one in the stack.

I took the card, opened the envelope with the latents, and set them on the desk. "You got a glass?"

"Sure."

She opened her desk drawer and took out a three power magnifier. I took it and set it on top of the latent prints.

The first two were smudges. But the third was a large print, apparently a thumb. It was clear and distinct. I looked closely at it, then moved my glass to the inked impressions and found the thumbprints.

Comparing prints is not difficult, but it can be tricky. You have to find a particular reference point, like an unusual ridge formation, on the latent print, then you work your way from that point on to other distinctive points not far from it. Then you find the same points on the inked print. When you've found eight complementary points – ten if you're the FBI – on both, you've got the same digit.

Looking closely, both the latent and the inked thumbs were whorls. I concentrated and started counting the ridge distinctions on the latent print. There was a ridge ending; one ridge down and to the right was a bifurcation. I found these two on the right inked thumb. Back on the latent, I picked up where I left off and found another ridge ending, two bifurcations and an island. They were at the

411

exact same locations on the inked print. I continued on until I found ten points of similarity. No doubt about it, the latent lifted from the baseball bat was made by Tabitha Higgins McElroy's right thumb. I looked up and smiled.

"Got a hit."

"Hey, great," Sandy said smiling. Will leaned forward in his chair.

"Is the old boy that got these latents still at the department?" Will said.

"He just retired, but he's still around town and available."

Will nodded. "We may need him. Can you give him a call?"

"Sure. You have a card?"

Will nodded to me.

I looked at Sandy. "You've got one'a mine."

She nodded.

I took the latents, put them back in the small manila envelope, and put them in my shirt pocket. I handed Sandy the newest print card, the one with the address.

"Can I get a copy of this?"

"Sure." She took the card, left, and in thirty seconds was back with three clear, detailed copies of the prints.

"I've got to keep the originals, you understand."

"I know."

I rose. Will did also.

"Hey, don't rush off," Sandy said. "You guys stay for lunch." She looked me in the eyes and raised her brows.

"No, we gotta run and see if we can find this McElroy woman." I paused and made sure I had everything. "Look, we really do appreciate your help."

"No problem. I'll give you a call, right?"

I didn't know what to say. "Yeah, sure."

Sandy followed us out of the office and into the hall. We were out the courthouse door and into the parking lot when Will spoke.

"You could get'cha some'a that if you wanted."

412

"Are you kidding? She's half my age."

"I saw the way she looked at'cha. It'd only take one drink."

I shook my head. "Big as I am, I'd break'er in half." I paused. "Besides, I wonder if she's old enough to drink."

"Okay, but it's yours if you want it."

"I'll think about it."

"I'm just sayin'."

Chapter 48

Tabitha Higgins McElroy's residence turned out to be a ranch-style brick home on ten acres off Highway 631 in the north part of Jackson County. The home was actually on a private road, Parsons Trail, and we had to get directions from a friendly general store manager who I was sure wouldn't have spoken to us had anyone else been in the business at the same time that we were.

Will talked to the old man, who knew Tabitha and didn't like her. He said she had shoplifted from his store on a regular basis, and he didn't mind putting the law onto her for whatever reason.

The area was part of the coastal plain; flat, with tall, thin southern pines about every thirty or forty feet; the stands having been thinned out by the semi-regular hurricanes that had pounded the coast over the years. The house was at the end of a long shell drive. Actually, the place was not more than four or five miles as the crow flies from the crime scene. We parked about half way up the drive and walked the rest of the way.

Using the brass knocker, Will rapped on the red door three times. The woman who answered looked like she was forty, with a dumpy figure and long, straight brown hair. Her face was one of those hard ones with lines; not a lot of them, but deep vertical creases on both cheeks and across her forehead. Her green eyes were tired, and she held her mouth in a tight line.

"Yes, ma'am, we're looking for Ms McElroy," Will said.

"Which one?" The woman's voice was as tired as her eyes.

"Tabitha McElroy."

"That'd be me."

"Ma'am, we're with the Sheriff's Office over in Mobile. We need to talk to you for a minute about a case we're working on."

She looked at us both. I showed her my star and replaced it my pocket.

"Is this about Cal?"

"It is."

"Sure, come on in."

I looked at Will. It wasn't exactly the attitude of a suspect. She stepped out of the way and waved us into the foyer.

In the living room, she motioned us toward two leather upholstered chairs against a hard wall across from the front bay windows. Then she took a seat in a cloth covered chair near the fireplace. The room was paneled and there was a tapestry rug on the hardwood floor under a glass coffee table.

"Ms McElroy is my husband's mother. She's at the doctor. I'm just plain ole Tabitha, or Tabby around here," she said.

Tabby, like a cat. She didn't remind me very much of a cat.

"So, what's this about Cal? Did you guys catch somebody?"

414

"Not exactly. How did you know Carl?" Will said.

"Cal and me used to be together, when he was with the Las Ratas. I rode with'im." She looked away out the window. "We was together nearly five years."

"Where'd you meet him?"

"In Dallas. That's where I'm from. He was from Houston."

"Did Cal have any other women?"

"At first, yeah, but after we'd been together for a while, there wadn't nobody but me. We rode all over the country together."

"When's the last time you saw him?"

She closed her eyes and lifted her head to the ceiling. "I guess it was at the swap meet up in Kiln. We had a fight. I wanted Cal to buy me one'a them spray painted shirts."

Will looked at her and said nothing.

"I was drunk; he wadn't quite as drunk. He wouldn't buy me the shirt, so I picked up a bat and took a swing at him."

"You hit him?"

"On the shoulder." She didn't mention any blood.

Will nodded. "What happened then?"

"He got mad, jumped on his bike and took off. I caught a ride back to the camp with a guy that rode with us, and I didn't see him again. I think somebody called the law – prob'ly the folks that run the swap meet – but I was gone when they got there."

"Where'd you spend the night?"

"Here. I knew Jimmy McElroy from way back. We met when he was a trucker for Allied. He knew Cal, too. He told me if we was ever in town to look him up. I didn't really wanna spend the night at the campsite, so I got one'a the guys to drop me here. I slep' it off, and when I heard that Cal was dead, I never left." She paused. "Jimmy's been good to me."

415

I could see on Will's face that a new suspect had just emerged. Too bad Tabitha was going to alibi for him.

"Did Cal own a truck?"

She frowned. "I think so. I'm not sure. If he did, he probably parked it at Bryson's Garage, over in Ocean Springs. He always worked on his bike over there. See, Pascagoula was a regular stop when was on our way to Daytona every year."

"So, how'd you hear about Cal?"

"Jimmy told me. He said he was at the grocery store up on the corner and heard about it on Tuesday. I got a paper and read about it."

Will nodded again. Then he turned to me.

"Do you know of anyone who wanted to kill Cal?" I said.

She shrugged and smiled slightly. "Hey, who didn't. Cal had a temper, and he got on the wrong side'a people pretty easy. When he got tight, he could be really mean."

"Well, let's narrow it down a little. Was there anyone in the Las Ratas that had it in for him?"

"You know, I'd have to think about that. Usually, if there was bad blood in the bunch, they'd have it out; you know, fight, right then. Nobody really held a grudge. In fact . . ."

I paused and looked at her. "Yes?"

"Well, I mean, there was this time in Kansas . . ." She paused, and I could see that she didn't know whether to continue.

Will looked at her. "You witnessed a murder, didn't you."

She shrugged her shoulders. "Well, I was pretty high that night, so I don't remember much about it."

At that point, I was of the opinion that we should leave the Kansas thing alone. If she had information about a murder, I'd just as soon it be ours than anyone else's. I was for letting that one lie until ours was taken care of, or if we needed her.

We continued to talk to her for another hour or so. Will tried to narrow down the suspect list, including who all might have been present at Bryson's Garage when Cal went to get his truck. Tabitha threw out a couple of names and then clammed up. Apparently, they still lived close by, and she didn't want to cross anyone she reasonably felt might try to burn her house down. And, as if to read my mind, she volunteered that Jimmy McElroy was home all night with her while Cal was missing.

"By the way, what was your name back then?" I said.

"Higgins. Tabitha Higgins."

"Do you know who got Cal's ashes? We heard somebody picked'em up a month or so after he was killed," Will said.

Will knew who had gotten them. He had told me it was Cal's girlfriend. He just wanted to see her reaction.

Her eyes sprang open wide, and she put her hand over her mouth. "Oh, shit." She paused. "I'm glad you reminded me'a that. They been out in the garage in that cheap ole urn sittin' up on a shelf. Jimmy ain't noticed it, yet; at least, he ain't said nothin'. I've been meanin' to sprinkle them over at the swap meet, in the pond. Cal liked to sit over there and feed the ducks."

Will and I looked at each other, and I had to stifle a smile. Cal fed the ducks, and now Tabitha was going to feed Cal to the ducks.

Chapter 49

It was late in the afternoon when we got back to the office. Will had spent the trip back making a new suspect list in the Harden murder.

In my mind, that was 'his' case; though technically, we were a team. But I wasn't in homicide when he caught Cal Harden's murder, and it was generally considered that if you responded to a case initially – though we operated by the 'team' concept and everyone was obligated to assist – it was 'your' case, and unless you quit, retired, got fired, or transferred out, it was your 'baby' until there was a conviction, the suspect died, or there were no more leads.

Of course, my baby, for better or for worse, was Zoe Woods. I had done little in the last few weeks to locate her killer. In my mind, Rhett Tolliver was the perpetrator. He had the means and, at least, a made up motive. The opportunity was kind of iffy, but it was certainly possible that he was in Mobile last February.

His name was in NCIC, his hometown police department was aware of his situation, and everyone who knew him in Mobile had knowledge that we were looking for him. As far as I was concerned, it was just a matter of time. However, the longer it took, the less likely our case would come together. By now, he'd had time to dispose of evidence, establish an alibi, and ensure that witnesses, especially habitually drunk ones, would have a hard time remembering him.

The fact that he was a rolling stone was the biggest obstacle to his arrest. As long as he had a car – the beat up old Nova – and the money to fuel it, he could keep moving, and only his willingness to remain in one place for a period of time would allow us to finally get a handle on him.

In the meantime, life went on. So far that year, the Major Crimes Unit had handled six homicides and twelve suicides. And with the natural and accidental deaths that we had to run on also, each investigator had a load of about twelve or thirteen cases to resolve. It was not an unmanageable burden, but a steady one. The only way that one got bounced out of the unit was if he was an obviously incompetent investigator, his paperwork was unreadable, or he did something to make the boss mad. It certainly wasn't because he didn't solve a case.

Will had always been philosophical about clearing cases. He believed that the community was as much responsible for solving murders as he was. In his mind, someone knew something about a case, and their unwillingness to help put a killer behind bars was directly related to the attitude that they had toward their community, the victim, or their own lives. Someone, he reasoned, who took pride in him or her self also took pride in their community and did what he or she could to keep it a safe place to live. If they didn't, then they wouldn't, and frankly, they were just as likely to be one of the perpetrators.

My opinion didn't stray far from this. I felt that the quality of law enforcement in a community was directly related to the morality of the community as a whole. Of course, there were things that government officials could do to make solving crimes more of a certainty, however, if the community was against the idea, or the number of crimes overwhelmed the ability of law enforcement to handle them, then, frankly, the whole system was mostly doomed. Until the day that the forensic sciences catch up to the theories that had given rise to them, and policing agencies could begin to identify perpetrators without the help of human witnesses, then the populace would always have a part in the process. In my mind they should always get the most of the credit or shoulder most of the blame for a safe community.

Effective policing will always be a question of just whose ox is getting gored. A citizen will call and complain if his driveway is blocked by a parked car, or if the kids are racing through his neighborhood, however, let an officer stop that same citizen for his own breach of the traffic code and suddenly the police are only out to generate revenue in the form of fines; and by the way, why aren't they out looking for real criminals like robbers or murderers.

The bottom line is that laws and police are the best that *men* can do to keep the peace. If they're willing to submit to governments and laws, then the system works. If they aren't, it doesn't.

So, I say all that to say this: Will was always on the lookout for the 'magic phone call.'

The magic phone call was the telephone conversation that gives us the name of the perpetrator. It was the quickest and easiest way for a case to be solved, and it only happened when someone with actual knowledge of a murder, usually by being directly related to the case, either grew a conscience, or got scared, or just wanted to get the heat off themselves. When the circumstances were right, they picked up the phone, and an arrest was usually not far away.

Chapter 50

October turned into November and things got a bit airish weather-wise. The patrolmen went to long sleeved shirts, and I broke out my Polo jacket – a waistcoat, really – that was red and could be spotted anywhere in a crowd, especially on television. It was 100 per cent cotton and zipped up the front, and I bought it with my first clothing expense check. It was the pride of my wardrobe. I got it one size too large so that if I gained weight I could still wear it. It had two large pockets, big enough for a tape recorder and my notebook, and it was just heavy enough to knock off the chill, but still light enough not to cause a sweat when the sun came out. I loved that jacket. I wore it to nearly every dead body in the fall and spring, and many in the winter, and I could always spot myself on television when the press came on scene to cover one of our cases.

I was wearing that jacket when, in the second week in November, Will and I got a call to look at a dead female in a house on Old Military Road in Theodore. It was shortly after eight, and it had rained the night before, so there had been a ten or fifteen degree temperature drop behind the cold front that had passed through Mobile on its way to Florida.

Will had a favorite jacket also. It was an old M-65, US Army field jacket. He had purchased it while on the occasion of a trip to Nebraska six years previous. He and Zane had gone there to talk a murder suspect. It had been warm when they departed Mobile, however when they reached the Midwest, it was thirty degrees with snow flurries. Will and Lonnie were rushed by the locals to the nearest Army-Navy store where they both purchased heavier coats; Will this M-65, and Zane an old Navy peacoat.

We were away and on I-10 fifteen minutes after the dispatcher's phone call. Marissa, one of the newer radio operators had told us that an elderly black female had been found dead in her home. She said that the patrol deputies on scene had requested detectives because of what they called 'unexplained circumstances.'

Despite the impending mystery, I drove at a leisurely pace toward Theodore. There was a moderate amount of traffic on the highway, the sky was clear, and the sun shone brightly. Will was silent and the radio was playing softly in the background. The sun was warm on my face, and it would not have taken much for me to have fallen asleep at the wheel, the early hour of the morning notwithstanding.

We were in Theodore in thirty minutes and on Old Military Road in ten more. This particular part of 'The

Plantation' was known as 'Slack Jaw' for a reason that no one seemed to remember.

The house in question was a brick cottage located on Old Military, about a mile and a half off Bellingrath Road, the main north south artery from the Blue Star Parkway to Bayou La Batre, along the coast. It appeared to be one of the nicest homes in the area. There was a well-kept Buick of 1970's vintage parked next to the house at the head of a shell driveway. Red shutters accented the two burglar-barred windows in the front, and there was a black wrought iron fence around two sides of the short porch.

Three patrol cars, an SUV from the Crime Scene Unit, and the state vehicle from the coroner's office marked the location. I parked ten yards from the house on the paved road that was just wide enough for two cars, and which had no shoulder to speak of. Three feet from the pavement was a ditch meant to catch and remove rainwater. Will, whose arthritis was flaring up, struggled from the car and walked stiff-legged toward the front yard.

Sergeant Terry Scarborough was standing in the yard, near the street, talking to Megan Crenshaw who had a clipboard in her hand. He was gesticulating back toward the house. As we neared his location, he stopped and looked our way.

"Good morning," Scarborough said. "Good to see both of you. Mr. Faulkner, I haven't seen you in a while."

I nodded. "I've been up to my ears, so to speak."

Crenshaw smiled. Remembering the 'turd case,' Will jammed his hands in his pockets and said nothing.

"Well, we got a weird one. This little old lady is dead in the living room of her house; which in and of itself is not unusual. But she's got some wounds on her that I can't and the coroner's investigator can't explain."

Will cleared his throat. "Any sign of forced entry?"

"None that we can see."

That was a good thing. It meant that if she was murdered, it was likely by someone she knew, and not a random burglar.

"Who found her?"

"Her daughter. She came over to take her to the doctor."

"Medical history?"

"Heart trouble."

Will nodded, and I quickly jotted down the pertinents off Crenshaw's incident report. He watched until I finished, then we both turned toward the front door.

The concrete sidewalk from the street to the small porch was lined with annuals of different colors in full bloom. Purple, yellow, and red blossoms were surrounded by green foliage. I made sure not to step on them as I followed Will up the sidewalk, over the threshold, and through the wooden door.

The room was small and warm. We stood in the foyer and oversaw the scene. The temperature felt like eighty degrees, and I reached down and unzipped my jacket. Will stood still and looked to our right at the woman lying on the floor. Angie McDowell was standing next to her, as was Chuck Hernandez. Hernandez carried a thirty-five millimeter camera, McDowell a clipboard.

The room was full. There were chairs in every crevice and a coffee table in the middle. The couch was early American; two of the chairs looked French; the rug was Persian; the coffee table was modern – metal framed with a glass pane on top. One of the lamps was a weird looking hippie piece, with long metal tubes, and the other was a Buddah with a bulb and a shade coming out of his head. There were photos on the walls of a number of different families, but oddly, there was no television.

The woman was black with coarse gray hair. She was not real black, but she was the black of an older African when their skin pigment has faded and age spots have appeared. The hue is actually something akin to hot chocolate.

She was supine, her arms extended, and her head turned to the right. She lay length-wise on the floor about a foot from a gas space heater. Her red and white checked blouse was in place, but it was the bottom half of her was what was unusual.

Her white underpants, what the kids call 'granny panties,' were down at her ankles, and she was otherwise nude from the waist down. Her stout legs were spread about a foot apart and her bare feet were turned out.

What was unusual was what looked like second and third degree burns on the tops and insides of both thighs starting from her groin and finishing at a location almost to her knees, on both legs.

Will looked at McDowell. "Well, Doc, you know what happened?"

Angie raised her eyebrows and smirked. "Well, no, not really. Other than these burns, she's got no other wounds on her that I can see. I can't tell if she's been raped right now, but I don't see any vaginal tearing, and there are no scratches or cuts to her legs. Her underpants aren't bloody or torn, and her shirt's in place. There are no defense wounds on her arms and hands and no marks on her face." She knelt down and used a gloved hand to run it over the burns. "I just can't figure out how she got these."

Will looked at me. "You got any ideas?'

I took a deep breath and exhaled. I said nothing at first. Then I looked at the heater.

"Not unless she was burnt by the heater."

Will looked over at Hernandez. "How 'bout you, Pedro. Anything?"

Hernandez shook his head. "Not me. I just take pictures."

Will nodded. "Okay, well, let's look at it reasonably. After all, that's how it's supposed to be done." He turned his head and coughed, loudly, into the sleeve of his jacket.

"What do you take your pants off for?" he said looking around.

No one spoke.

"You take your pants off to change clothes, go to bed, fuck, or go to the bathroom." He looked at us with raised eyebrows. "So?"

No one spoke.

"So, she wet herself. Those burns are from uric acid. She's got a bad case'a diaper rash. My guess is she was probably trying to dry off or somethin' in front of the heater when her heart give out. She mighta' died from embarrassment."

"So, where's her pants?" I said.

"Who knows, take a look in her bedroom. If we'd gotten here sooner, her drawers would'a been wet. As it is, I think you'll find urine stains on'em." He looked around. "Nobody broke in, she hadn't been raped, nobody knocked her in the head. I'd say she pissed on herself and for some unknown reason, probably 'cause of the cool snap last night, she tried to dry herself off rather than take a bath. The heart attack was just bad timin' designed to give us some shit."

We all looked at each other. I didn't have anything better. No one said anything. A minute went by. Angie McDowell spoke first.

"Well, we'll get her downtown for an autopsy and see. I don't know what else to do."

Will turned to me and said, "Let's go."

Outside, Will stopped where Scarborough and Crenshaw stood. Both uniformed deputies turned with questioning faces.

"Make sure the woman's daughter checks the house and sees that nothing's been stolen. And make sure there's no sign of forced entry."

"Will do," Scarborough said. "What happened?'

"She pissed on herself and had a heart attack, probably because it's too hot in there. They'll do an autopsy, but I think that's what they'll find."

"That's where the burns came from?"

"Diaper rash."

"Well, I'll be." He paused. "You're not gonna hang around?"

He shook his head. "Absent the burns on her legs, any reason to believe that she was murdered?"

Scarborough shrugged his shoulders. "No, I guess not."

"Then nothin' for me to do here."

With that, Will turned and started toward the car. I followed, after saying goodbye to Crenshaw.

In the vehicle, I put the key in the ignition but did not turn it. I looked at Will who was in the passenger seat.

"How'd you know?"

He spoke while looking straight ahead. "I've seen it before. If she wadn't fuckin' nobody, and she wadn't changin' clothes or sittin' on the shitter, there's no other explanation. I recognized the burns, their location and degree. I've seen'em before."

I nodded. "I guess that's why you're the boss."

"That is a true statement, Son."

We left out of 'Slack Jaw' headed north on Bellingrath to the Blue Star Parkway. I continued through the light and onto Plantation then to Theodore-Dawes Road. It was just a short jump to Interstate 10. We turned east and prepared to go back to the office.

We'd been on the highway for less than a minute when I saw it. There was an old, red Chevy Nova, four door, west bound on the interstate.

"Look at that," I said pointing at the car.

"What is it?" Will said opening his eyes and sitting up in his seat.

"The red Nova. I gotta get turned around."

I started scanning the median for one of those dirt crossovers that the state troopers use. There was one about two miles up, but I needed one right then.

"Be lookin' for a place to cross over," I said.

426

"I didn't see it. Are you sure?"

"How many old Novas do you see on the road?"

I slowed down in the inside emergency lane and looked. The rain the night previous had left the grass wet, and I knew that crossing at a place other than a dirt median would be treacherous. When I saw no suitable location, I looked up and found we were at the Blue Star exit. I got off, turned left at the light, went under the bridge, and in two minutes we were heading westbound.

"He's long gone by now, Son. Might as well slow down."

"Yeah, I know."

We drove two miles, and Will looked at me. "Why don't you take a run down toward Myrtice's place. If he's in town and down this way, chances are he's goin' to see her, if she's home."

It was a thought and a good one. The chances of running into the Nova on I-10 were pretty slim. But he had to be going somewhere; maybe to the south part of the county to see his ex-sister in law, maybe west to New Orleans to see his brother, or maybe he was just making another leg to another town.

"You got anywhere else you need to be?"

Will leaned back in his seat and jammed his hands in his pockets. He closed his eyes and said:

"I get paid for eight hours, Son; no matter where it is."

It took twenty minutes to reach Myrtice's trailer park. I turned off Highway 188 into the almost deserted neighborhood and drove slowly toward her home. There were a couple of Asian children, offspring of the boat people working in the seafood industry, as well as two black kids, a male, and a female with strings in her hair, playing in the community playground. They stopped their work – for play is the work of children – and watched us as we rode by.

At Myrtice's trailer the driveway was empty. I parked, got out, and walked around to the rear to make sure

427

that the Nova wasn't parked in back, out of sight. I got back in the car and Will was yawning.

"Anything?" he said.

"No. It was clean."

"It probably wadn't the right car no way."

"Maybe not, but the chances were good."

"Shit, Son, you're probably gonna start seein' Chevy Novas everywhere; even in your sleep."

"It's my white whale."

He looked at me, and I wondered if he got the reference. I started the car and slowly began to negotiate the bumpy road as it made a wide circle around the park. The community appeared desolate. There was an occasional vehicle parked in front of a trailer, and there was even a Big Wheel toy in front of one of the homes, but no other signs of life.

About three quarters of the way around, I looked to my left and spotted a man walking around from the back side of one of the mobile homes.

"You see that guy?" I said.

Will lifted his head. "Yeah."

"Wonder what he was doin' around the back side'a that trailer?"

The home was a mint green-colored double wide parked on the outside of the circle. The rear of it backed up to a stand of trees. It was the perfect victim home: close to the entrance, the back side was camouflaged, and the home was large enough and nice enough so as to indicate that there might be some items of value within.

I brought the car to a stop, geared it into park, and opened the door. The man stopped abruptly. I thought he was going to run. He didn't.

Will opened his car door. I reached into my back pocket and pulled out my badge and held it in my hand. I took two steps toward the man, who was frozen near the front corner of the building.

428

He was short, with a medium Afro that needed to be picked, and long arms. His slim and bony frame gave him the look of a druggie, making burglar the perfect avocation. He wore a black, short sleeve, pullover shirt, dirty blue jeans, and dirty white tennis shoes.

Will walked around the front of the car, put his foot up on the bumper, and leaned on his knee. I raised my badge then made a motion for the man to come toward the car.

"Deputy Sheriff, Buddy. Come on over here."

He walked slowly toward us, acting as if he didn't know what to do with his hands. He ended up shoving them into his back pockets, but quickly pulled them out again.

I motioned him to the driver's front quarter of the county car, and he stepped close to the fender. Will was four feet away.

"Put your hands on the car, Buddy, and let me pat your pockets."

He complied, and I gave him a quick pat down. There were lumps in the two back pockets of his jeans.

"What'chu got in your back pockets?"

"Who me?"

I reached in one of them and pulled out a dirty sock. Then I knew what we had.

"What's your name, friend?" I said.

"Who me? Martavius."

"Martavius what?"

"Frazier." His voice was deep, yet soft.

I took out my pad and pen and jotted the information down. He had no identification on him, so I wrote down the no doubt bogus birthdate and address that he gave me. He said he was twenty-two years old.

"You gotta nickname?"

He shrugged. "Dey calls me, 'Mule Dick'."

Will chuckled. I did also as I wrote the words down in the notebook.

"Mule dick? Is that what you said?" Will said taking over the questioning.

"Yes, suh."

"Son of a bitch. As little as you are?"

He shrugged his shoulders and grinned.

Will nodded and smiled slightly, then reached in his pants pocket, removed a small folding knife, and opened the blade.

"Well, shit." He paused. "I'll tell you what, Mr. Mule Dick. You lay your shit out here, and if it ain't six inches longer than mine, I'm gonna take this here knife and whack that bastard off."

Will looked at him hard, expressionless, for four or five seconds. Frazier shifted nervously. The look on his face was pure fright. Unbelievably, he reached for his belt.

Will strung him along for a couple more seconds then broke into a big grin. The man began laughing nervously, and he smiled also.

"Aw, man," Frazier said.

"Where you comin' from, around the back side of that house trailer?" I said.

"Who me?"

"You heard me."

"I's jus walkin'."

"What were you in jail for the last time you were in?"

"Who me? Oh, uh, non-suppote."

"Whose trailer is that?"

"I 'on't know."

If he had just hit that house, or any other one in the neighborhood, I felt sure he would have run when he first saw us. The fact that he had socks in his pocket indicated that he was a burglar. I believed that we caught him just prior to the act.

I looked at Will. "You wanna check, or shall I?"

He took his foot off the bumper and walked toward the back side of the home. I looked at Martavius and spoke.

430

"If there's anything you need to tell me, now's the time."

"No, suh."

I picked up the radio microphone and radioed in his name, date of birth, and address. In four minutes the dispatcher called to say that Martavius Frazier was wanted by the Bayou La Batre Police Department for a couple of unpaid traffic tickets. I told her to call them and ask them if they wanted to come get him.

When I looked up, Will was ambling back toward the car. He looked at me and shook his head. As he got closer, I reached in the car and got a pair of handcuffs.

"Bayou PD has a warrant on Martavius. He's gonna have to go with them."

The young man looked stunned as I put first his right hand and then his left behind his back and snapped the cuffs shut. We stood next to the car, and Will and I chatted for about ten minutes until the black and white PD vehicle arrived. Martavius had nothing more to say. My guess was that he thought he was being jailed, not for what he had done, but for what he was thinking of doing.

Chapter 51

In short order it was Thanksgiving. The hurricane season ended; daylight savings time ended and gave us five o'clock sunsets; the gray winter pall began to fall over the county; and the low temperatures of an early winter began to chill me on workday mornings.

Everything was up to date on my case log – except the Zoe Woods case. Rhett Tolliver was who knows where in the southeast. We had heard nothing from Greenbaum up in North Charlotte for a while, and nothing from the NCIC machine. Two calls to Myrtice's hometown PD in South Carolina had also yielded nothing. I had taken several trips out to the Bayou to keep a watch on her trailer on the off chance that Rhett Tolliver might show up, but had come up dry every time.

I spent a considerable amount of time thinking about him. The only things I really knew about him were: he was named after a character in *Gone with the Wind*; he drank Black Russians, with chocolate sauce if he could get it; he was a hobo who drifted from town to town; he was known to go by his brother's name; he drove an old car; and he liked the ladies.

The thing that struck me in the midst of all my musings was the fact that with all the traveling that he was doing, he must have some sort of income, more than just casual labor in whatever town in which he happened to land. Moving about that much would take real money; money for gas to get from town to town, money to get set up in an apartment or rooming house; or at least money enough for buying all the drinks that he would need to talk all the women into his bed – or his old red Nova.

What this all meant relative to locating him was a mystery to me. He was still in the southeast, I was sure, but in the meantime, he could be anywhere there was a redneck dive with damaged women, and where there was a bartender who knew how to mix vodka and coffee liqueur with a dash of chocolate sauce.

The day after Thanksgiving, Will and I were both off – the County Commission usually declared the day a holiday, and this year was no different. I wasn't on call, but I was at home watching football when the phone rang. It was two o'clock in the afternoon, and it was the office.

"Mr. Faulkner, can you help out with a murder?" It was a dispatcher whose voice I did not recognize.

"You know, I'm not on call."

"Yes, sir, but the Captain said to see if you can help."

I took a deep breath and exhaled. "Where do you need me to go?"

"Meet Detective Neely at Headquarters."

"I'm on my way."

Remembering my generosity towards Neely that resulted in the Stinson murder case, I was in no hurry to get to the office, so I took my time and stopped and got a burger on the way in. I arrived thirty minutes after the call, and got off the elevator to a strange sight.

From one end of the seventh floor hallway to the other, the space was covered with the dirtiest, grungiest, grimiest-looking men I had seen since I rode a patrol car and my beat was the waterfront along the Alabama River in downtown Montgomery, Alabama. The men were being guarded by two uniform deputies, one of whom was Megan Crenshaw.

Neely was standing in the middle of the squad room when I walked through the glass double doors. His fair skin was red, beads of sweat glistened on his forehead, and he looked out of breath. Apparently, rounding up all of the bums had been a huge undertaking.

"Good," he said, "I'm glad you're here."

"Have you got this thing by yourself?"

"For now. I've got Zane and also Reynolds and Carter from Narcotics coming in."

"Okay, fill me in."

"I get a call this morning that there's a homeless man beaten to death down where they hang out in the woods behind the J-Mart in Tillman's Corner. When I got there, we rounded up everybody we could find and brought'em here." He shook his head. "We had a devil of a time trying to identify the dead guy."

The wooded area behind the J-Mart, not far from Interstate 10, was a common hangout for homeless transients; so much so that the federal government had even

433

sent enumerators out to their permanent colony in order to count them during the last census.

"Did you get an ID?"

"Herman Caldwell Johansson, from Gainesville, Florida."

"What a mouthful. Any leads?"

"Actually, yes. One of the bums told us that our victim was arguing with one of the other bums last night."

"Over what?"

"Mouthwash."

Mouthwash was a cheap, common substitute for normal drinking whiskey. If a homeless man could scare up a dollar or two, usually by picking up bottles and cans, he could get an inexpensive ethanol fix from the over the counter pharmaceutical aisle at a nearby drug or general store

"So, which one of the bums did it?"

"That's what we can't figure out. Nobody'll tell; not even a description."

"Some kind of 'code of the bum'?"

"I don't know. Maybe." He chuckled.

"How many of them have your interviewed?"

"Oh, about half. That's why I called you. I want to go ahead and knock out the other half as quick as we can." He looked toward the door. "Crenshaw says they're beginning to stink up the hall."

"I did notice that it was gettin' a little gamey out there." I looked over my shoulder. "Okay, I'll get one of'em and get started."

Walking toward the door, I steeled myself against the stench that I knew would hit me when I opened the glass doors, which were beginning to fog up, by the way. I opened the door, pointed at the first dirty face I saw, and crooked my right index finger. The man pointed at himself with his brows raised, then stood and walked toward me.

He was different from the rest, this man. He had a beard, but it was cleaner and appeared to be neatly trimmed.

His clothes, while garish and inappropriate, fit him better. Finally, I looked at his feet and noticed that he had on shoes rather than boots, and that they had, under the scuff marks on top, what could pass for a shine. Also, when he opened his mouth, his teeth looked as if they had been polished. Either this man had just become a bum last week, or something else was going on.

I motioned him toward interrogation room three on the west side of the squad room. I closed the door behind us, laid my notebook on the table, and took a seat across from him.

He was white, but dark complected and about thirty. He wore a 'CAT' hat over his dark brown hair, a brown cloth fleece jacket, a purple shirt, and tan slacks. His brown eyes were tired, and he had two small vertical lines on his forehead between his brows. He spoke first.

"Whew, I thought you guys were never going to call me in here. What took you so long? It reeks out there."

"Hey, I just got here." I paused. "You got somethin' to say?"

He grinned. "You haven't figured it out yet?"

I looked at him. "Well, there's definitely something different about you, I can tell that. Are you some kind of philanthropist slumming for the sake of your conscience?"

"I wish. I'm undercover with State Police. My name's Humphrey, Sergeant Mark Humphrey."

It was my turn to grin. "Henry Faulkner. That was my next guess. You know of course, I'll need to verify your ID."

"Sure."

I wasn't overly skeptical. No one just walks up and confesses to being a police officer. And, an undercover officer embedded anywhere is not that unusual. I mean, stranger things have happened than to find that a law enforcement officer had witnessed a murder that you were investigating. But until I verified it, the information exchange would be decidedly one way.

435

"Sure. Call Captain Howard Watters in Montgomery. He's my section chief. He'll ID me." He supplied a telephone number.

"Why would the state police want to infiltrate a bunch of hobos in Mobile, Alabama?"

"I'm in the Intelligence Section. We've been getting reports that a large number of homeless are really illegals passing through on their way to safe houses in Birmingham and Montgomery; kind of an underground railroad of sorts. We wanted to find out who's takin'em in, hidin'em, and then gettin'em acclimated into society."

"How are they getting in?"

"We think they're coming across in Texas, then catching fishing boats and coming ashore down near Brookley Field, at that college campus down there."

I knew exactly where he was talking about. It was a shallow part of Mobile Bay where at low tide anyone could walk to shore from the middle of the channel. The state had just passed a tough immigration law and enforcement was a priority of the new governor.

"Okay, well, that's all well and good, but we got a murder on our hands. You know anything about it?"

"Oh, sure. But, well, listen, I'd like to keep my cover if at all possible."

He paused and looked at me. I said nothing.

He continued. "The guy that did it is called 'Chet.' He's the black guy out in the hall wearin' a . . ." he looked up at the ceiling and thought, "a red shirt and jeans." He's got on wing tip shoes."

"What'd he kill him with?"

"A tree limb; about yeah long." He held his hands about four feet apart. "It should still be out there, and it's probably got blood on it. I think he hit him two or three times, although I only saw him hit him once; but it was a really good lick. When this 'Chet' guy laid back down, a couple of us looked at the dead guy. He'd had it."

"Who called the police?"

"Well, it happened this morning before light. Then about sunup, before I could get away to a phone, one of the illegals ran up and got the guy at the gas station to call. Then he took off."

"Okay, you take a break while I make a phone call or two." I stood and walked toward the door. Then I stopped and turned back. "You want some coffee?"

He shook his head. "No, I'm just gonna chill. Hurry back, will ya?"

"Sure."

Out in the squad room, I found Neely wolfing down a sandwich. I told him what I'd found out and how we had an eyewitness who was a police officer. He was euphoric. I gave him the phone number for the Watters guy up in Montgomery.

I sat down and waited while Neely made the call and verified Humphrey's identity. He was off the phone in ten minutes and was smiling through his tuna salad.

"Whew. This is good." He paused and took another bite. "Reynolds just walked in. I think I'll have him talk to our suspect."

"Humphrey says the weapon was a tree limb."

"Okay. We picked up the mouthwash bottle. Let's hope our suspect's prints are on it. That, the limb, and the investigator's ID should be enough."

"Humphrey wants us to keep him out of it, if we can."

He took a deep breath and exhaled. "What's he working on?"

"Some kind of illegal immigration thing. He looks Hispanic. I think he's just tryin' to gather some intel on where and how they're gettin' in, and where they go once they do."

He took another deep breath. "Well, I'm not makin' no promises. I suppose if what's his name out there confesses, we can do without him." He took another bite of

437

sandwich. "Can you go in there and babysit him until we see what happens?"

I rose from the chair. "Sure." It was overtime, and I could use it.

Back in the interrogation room, I sat back down across from Humphrey who was leaned back with his eyes closed. He sat up straight when he heard the door open.

"Well, I've got some good news. We got in touch with Watters in Montgomery, and he verifies you and your assignment."

"Good. How did he take it?"

"Well, I didn't talk to him, one of the other guys did. But there was a lot of smiling and it didn't seem like anyone was angry. He said for you to be of help if you could." The last part wasn't entirely the truth.

He nodded. "Okay, but you told your partner I'd like to keep up my dodge, right?"

"Yeah, I told him. He's getting the suspect in the box and they're gonna hit him up pretty hard for a confession. Reynolds, the detective who's with him, is pretty good. They'll get him to cop to something. If that happens, then the other bums outside will probably roll, and you can fall right back into your act."

He nodded and closed his eyes again. He wanted to rest, but I wanted to find out more about his operation.

"So, have you gotten very far into this immigrant thing?"

He opened his eyes. "Not too far. I've ID'd a couple of illegals that are on their way out of town. I was tryin' to get one of em to hook me up, but so far, I haven't gotten any takers."

"Any idea whose funding all this?"

"Not, yet. We think money is being routed through one of the large banks in Charlotte. But which one, we don't know."

"You speak Spanish?"

438

"Yeah. My mother's from Costa Rica. It took a while to get the Mexican dialect straight, but a couple'a trips down there with the DEA did the trick."

I nodded. I didn't have an immediate follow up, so he took the opportunity and jumped in.

"What are you guys working on? I mean, aside from 'bumicide'?"

"Well, not much. I've got one open murder case. We're looking for a guy named Rhett Tolliver who picked up a woman at a bar and tried to cut her head off."

"Ouch. What did he do that for?"

"Who knows. Why do any of these jackasses do anything they do. We've got to find him to know for sure."

Will said that one time he found a dead body out by the Causeway, ten feet from the waterfront. All the bosses came out and stood around, and they all wanted to know why the killer had dumped the body *there*. Will said he thought about it, but all he could come up with was that he didn't know. Nobody knew except the person who did it, and even then, they didn't always know. Sometimes, you just don't know.

He nodded. "Interesting." Then, I had an idea.

"You think this Intelligence Department up in Montgomery might check and see if they have something on Rhett Tolliver?"

"Well, sure. I could give them a call and see."

"You know, just a run down on where he's been in Alabama and where he's worked."

"Yeah. We call it a dossier."

I hadn't heard that word since the sixties. Humphrey was in, or at least he thought he was in, the spy game.

Why I hadn't thought of it earlier, I don't know. There were intelligence departments in every state police agency in the southeast. Surely, one of them would have a 'dossier' on Rhett Tolliver; a field interview card or a traffic ticket, or something, for Pete's sake.

439

"I'd sure appreciate it. We've had him on NCIC for a couple of months now, and no one's bumped him yet," I said.

"I'll call them first thing Monday."

"Good. All I need is just a thread. Once I lay hands on him, I'm sure I can get him indicted."

He nodded. "Just do your best to keep me out of this murder."

I rose from the table. "I'll check on that right now."

Outside, in the squad room, I slipped into the viewing room adjacent to Interrogation One. Inside, Neely was sipping a coke while listening to the speakers.

"Anything?" I whispered.

"Jerry's just about to get him to come off it."

An older black man was slumped in the seat across from Reynolds. He had a medium afro that hadn't been picked in a year, a scraggly beard, decaying teeth, and eyes that looked as if they were about to pour out of their sockets. He was fifty or sixty, I couldn't tell which, and his eyes said he was in another world – the planet dipsomania. With Reynolds' clear head, it really wasn't a fair fight.

"Chet, we got your prints off the tree limb," Reynolds said. "You just can't beat that. I can understand why you did it; you needed that drink."

"I sho' did."

"So, tell me. How many times did you hit him?"

He paused and looked at the table. The old man seemed so out of it, I doubted that he knew he was about to confess to murder.

"Two, I thank."

"Well, he'll get over it. Did you take anything from him besides the bottle?"

"No, suh. Jes' the bottle."

"We got your prints off that, too."

Neely reached up and turned off the speakers. "Never fails."

"Hey, this old man wasn't much of a challenge."

440

I left the viewing room and walked back inside with Humphrey. He sat up straight when I sat down.

"Good news," I said.

"He confessed?"

"Sang like the wasted canary that he is. You're off the hook."

"Good. That means that the last ten days won't go to waste."

About that time, Neely knocked on the door. He thanked Humphrey for his cooperation and finished getting contact information from him. I gave him my card and told him to call me the next week. I didn't expect to hear from him.

Humphrey didn't call on Monday, but he did call on the next Wednesday. Will was in the office with me when the phone rang.

"Okay, this Rhett Tolliver that you're looking for. We actually have a sheet on him, or a guy that I think is him. We have him as Michael Tolliver," Humphrey said.

I picked up my pen. "Really."

"Oh, yeah. His name has come up in relation to what I'm working on."

"Go on."

"One of our informants told us that Tolliver goes around the southeast settin' up safe houses for illegals. He's been to Birmingham; Tallahassee; Jackson, Mississippi; and New Orleans. Apparently, he blows into town, rents a house or a large apartment then hits the road. He mails the key back to the people who are behind it and then hits the next town."

"Any idea who these people are?"

"We've got some ideas, but we don't wanna say just yet."

"Does he use his own name when he rents the apartments?"

441

"We don't think so; at least we haven't been able to find his name anywhere. All this comes from a snitch that may or may not know what he's talking about."

I was writing everything down while looking across at Will. Wouldn't he be surprised.

"Anything else?" I said.

"That's about it. I hope it sells."

"We'll see."

I hung up and filled Will in on what happened the Friday previous; about the murder, Humphrey the undercover investigator, and Humphrey's investigation of illegals coming into this country.

"So, whoever wants these illegals in the country is payin' Tolliver to set up these safe houses?" Will said.

"That's what he said."

He shook his head. "Bullshit. Somebody wantin' a bunch'a illegals to flood this country is somebody with a lotta fuckin' resources to throw around. First of all, they won't waste'em on a jackass like Tolliver; and second, Tolliver don't get his hands on that kind'a money without it affectin' him in some way that people can see. He'd've gotten a new car, someplace nice and steady to live, and he'd just be throwin' it around. Remember, this is a guy that hangs out with people like the dead woman, at a bar called 'The Society.' There's no way he's hidin' anything big like this. He hasn't told Myrtice, his brother, that Lieutenant up in Charlotte's informant, or that bitch in Birmingham. Even if he lied about where he got it, he'd've still let'em know he was in the pink." He shook his head. "I don't buy it."

"Well, just for the sake of argument, who would pay for some big operation like this?"

Will closed his eyes. "Large industrial farmers would, for the cheap labor; the hospitality industry, for the same reason." He paused. "If you really wanted to get crazy about it all, maybe the Cubans or the Mexicans."

"Why the Cubans?"

442

"To destabilize the borders; bankrupt the country; just like what's happ'nen'. And, it'd make it easier to infiltrate the country with agents and spies."

"But you don't think so."

"Shit, no. Who'd give that much money to a two bit dumbass like Tolliver?"

Chapter 52

In the next few days, I tried to digest what both Humphrey and Will had said. Birmingham, New Orleans, Jackson, Mobile, Tallahassee, and who knows where else Tolliver had traveled, were all big cities where illegals would blend into the workforce.

If Tolliver wasn't paid to do it, where did he get the money to go from place to place like that? And where would he meet someone with enough power and money to want to do something like what the government thought was going on? And why choose him? Will was right. From what we knew about him, he didn't seem to be the brightest bulb.

But, on the off chance that the state had something, I decided to try to anticipate his next move. We could put him in Birmingham, Tallahassee, Mobile, and New Orleans with his brother. What other large city on the coast might he go to set up shop? There was Pensacola, but that was too close to the Gulf. Montgomery wasn't large enough. Memphis, Nashville? They were large touristy towns close to the farm belt. And of course, there was Atlanta. A Hispanic family could easily get lost in Atlanta.

I tried to think of what more we could do to locate him. He was already on NCIC, just waiting for some motorman (motorcycle cop) to pull him over. Frankly, his car wouldn't be hard to spot if anyone was looking for it. The only other way we were going to find him was if someone wanted to turn him. I had almost forgotten about the reward. How much was it? Ten thousand?

The best way to go about finding him, I finally decided, was to put out a supplemental NCIC broadcast asking all stations, especially those in large southern cities, and those with Hispanic populations, to check in those areas for the car. If we couldn't run across him that way, the only other way was for the feds or the state police to find him.

Rhett Tolliver, aka Mike Tolliver, aka Mikey Tolliver, the white whale, was still running, and hiding, from me - Ahab.

But life went on. On Tuesday of the last week in November, I had a subpoena for the grits case that was finally coming to trial. I came to the courthouse a day early to meet the new assistant DA who had inherited the file.

Perry McCoy was a rotund man with an almost bald head and a thick black beard. Think Sebastian Cabot with a little less on top and no accent. He motioned me to the hard backed chair across the desk from him.

His seventh floor office had a large picture window on the north side that overlooked downtown Mobile. The sun-drenched vista gave the space an expansive, airish feel. It was outfitted with cheap wood furniture stained to look like cherry: a desk, credenza, and bookcase. His law degree from the University of Georgia and a certificate entitling him to practice law in front of the Alabama Supreme Court hung on the wall behind him. His desk was covered with files and papers, as well as a couple of open volumes of the *Southern Reporter.*

"So, grits in the face, huh?" McCoy said. His voice was a low range tenor.

"That's right. It's a picture no artist could paint, Mr. McCoy." What?

"Call me Mason. Everybody does."

444

It took a minute, but it finally sunk in. His first name was Perry, he was a lawyer, and his girth was a definite nod to Raymond Burr.

"How long have you carried that flag?"

"Since law school."

"Well, okay, Mason."

"So, tell me about the case."

"Not much to it, really. The victim hired a PI to follow his wife because he thought she was screwin' around on him. The PI watched her for three or four nights and caught her over at the boats in Biloxi with an older man who looked like he had a few dollars. The PI then met his client, the victim in this case, at home, and he was there when the client confronted the wife. She didn't take the news too well, ran to the kitchen, got a pot of grits off the stove and threw them on her husband." I paused to think. "That's it."

"So, what do we have?"

"We've got the PI, MacArthur Penn, who witnessed the whole thing; we've got her statement, she admitted it; and, of course, we've got the guy's face."

"He's black, isn't he?"

"He is."

"So, his face looks all splotchy white, right?"

"Well, I haven't seen him since the domestic relations trial, and he was still pretty bandaged up in a couple of places, but, yeah, I think you're probably right."

"They got a divorce?"

I chuckled. "Wouldn't you?"

He grinned. "Yeah, I guess I would."

I took a deep breath and exhaled. "Has she come lookin' for a deal?"

"Yes, actually. Her lawyer offered Assault 3rd with probation."

"What a joke. The man's disfigured, for cryin' out loud."

445

"I know, I know. I countered with a plea to Assualt 2nd with a recommendation of five years split to serve three. He said he'd take it to his client. That was three days ago."

"Who's her lawyer?'

"Jeff Mathers."

I knew him. He was pretty high priced. I wondered who was paying for him, her new sugar daddy or her old husband.

"Well, lunch says that the husband drops the charges," I said.

"Ha, ha. That's a fool's wager. He's already called and made noises about that very thing."

"What are you gonna do?"

He used his hand to wipe his beard. "I'm gonna ask the judge for a recess, get'em both in here in the office, hand him a mirror, and make sure he knows just exactly what he's got to live with for the rest of his life. My guess is all that won't happen until after we strike a jury and she sees that it's all for real. Then they'll both want to stop it."

I shook my head. "I thought otherwise when it all started, but now I'm convinced. It won't take that long."

"At any rate," he shuffled through some files on his desk, "I think you and I have another one coming up," He looked at the file, "uh, Stanley Simpson Patridge."

"Right. Simp Patridge. I want it on the record that I am opposed to any deals with Mr. Patridge. He needs to spend a few years in prison."

"Tell me about his case."

"Oh, well, he was a bar one night, and this boy from out of town, who didn't know him, made the wrong comment. Simp chased him around the parking lot with a hook billed knife, and when he caught him, he cut him from his shoulder to his butt. It was one of the worst things I ever saw."

McCoy made a face.

"The only thing that has been comparable was one night when I saw an old boy that was cut from his temple to

446

the corner of his mouth; all the way through to his teeth. He stumbled out from between two parked cars and fell against the hood of our patrol car early one morning about three. That one bled much more."

"Really."

"It was like a bad horror movie; nearly scared me to death."

He leaned back. "So, this Patridge is a bad dude?"

"Complete psycho. Well, you've got his record there. What does he have, thirty-five arrests?"

"About twenty I think."

"He's incapable of living amongst civilized people."

McCoy smiled, as if I was exaggerating. I was not.

"He once set a litter of puppies on fire. Another time he stole an ambulance and a drove it through a plate glass window. And, I can't count the number of fights he's had in which no prosecution ever resulted."

"Why not?"

"Intimidation. Victims have either been bought off or threatened into dropping the cases. The only reason this one works is because the victim is not from around here."

McCoy nodded. He picked up his pen and turned a page within the file.

"Okay," he said as he wrote, "officer, opposes, plea, bargain."

"You got it."

"Anything else?"

I shook my head. "I guess not. The woman and the grits thing is a family matter. They've got a right to settle that amongst themselves. 'You only hurt the one you love,' you know? But this Patridge, he's a menace. We all need to be protected from him."

The next morning, true to my prediction, the man with the face like a polled Hereford showed up at the courthouse, marched into McCoy's office, and said he wanted to drop

447

the charges. He had gotten his divorce, he said, and he just wanted it all to go away.

And, true to his word also, McCoy pulled out a small mirror, handed it to him and told him to take a good look at himself. He refused. He had seen himself, he said, and he knew how he looked. But the truth was, he loved his wife (not ex-wife) and was willing to let her do what she needed to do to be happy. If she wanted another man, she should have one.

Later, as I listened to McCoy recount the story, I wondered whether this victim was a masochist, had a Cinderella complex (are those two the same thing?) or did he merely hate himself so much that he felt that someone – anyone – else had the right to treat him the way that she had treated him.

I'm firmly convinced that ninety percent of the people in the world, because of how they were raised, grow up with a neurosis that makes them accept the absolute worst in life. Parents, a child's first authority figure, usually pass down to their children their insecurities, faults, and fears. A child sees them, figures that's the way you live, will do anything to please them – their meal ticket – and they mature the same way. It's a cycle so insidious as to create a world that has no hope of survival. Suicide is its ultimate end.

After trying to convince him otherwise, McCoy finally acquiesced and agreed to a motion to dismiss. The victim and his ex were last seen walking hand in hand toward the seventh floor elevators.

Chapter 53

In December it turned cool. Will, who loves it when the temperature falls, took the first two weeks off on vacation. I took call the second week, and the Captain said that if I had anything major, to let him know, and he would get someone to assist me.

I took the occasion of Will's time off to take a trip out to Myrtice Abercrombie's trailer and ask her once again about Rhett Tolliver. It was a Thursday afternoon, and she looked as if she had just gotten up. She opened the door wearing a flimsy bathrobe and tan mules. Her odor almost knocked me flat. It was the smell of dead skin, feet, and unwashed groin.

"Not at work today?" I said.

She held the two halves of her housecoat together with her left hand at her waist and her right hand at her throat, and turned her back on me, ostensibly to let me in the front door.

"I got fired."

"Fired? How come?" I said as I stepped just inside the front door.

Myrtice walked toward the kitchen. I heard her cough twice and clear her throat.

"They said I come in late too often. It ain't true."

She paused and coughed again, after which she relieved herself of the phlegm and spittle and walked back into the living space carrying a cup of coffee.

"Besides, the boss called today and said to come on back in tomorrow." She looked away.

"Well, all's well that ends well," I said knowing that she didn't know what I meant. "I just stopped by to see if you'd heard from Rhett."

"Oh."

Her face told me that I had caught her completely off guard by the question. Her brows went up, and she looked at the floor. It also told me that she'd heard from him.

"Well, I, uh, I, yeah, once. He told me he was in New Orleans to see his brother."

Probably a lie made up on the spur of the moment. "How long ago?"

"A week or so." She took a seat on the couch. I stood by the door.

"What else did he say?"

"Nothin'; just that he was gonna stop by when he could."

"Did you tell him we were lookin' for him?"

"No."

I looked around the room while trying to decide what to ask next. My eyes fell on a small table at the end of the couch opposite Myrtice.

The phone was one of those old Western Electric models, black, with a rotary dial. But what was interesting was the answering machine that was hooked up to it. It was newer than the phone; an AT&T brand, the kind with a micro-cassette tape inside. I had one like it about five years ago. The light was blinking.

"By the way, Myrtice, what is your phone number? In case I need to get in touch with you for court."

She supplied me with her exchange. She got the first three numbers quickly, but had to look up to the ceiling and shut her eyes to remember the rest.

"I don't never call my own number."

My mind stopped for a second. There could be a way . . . .

"So, goin' back to work tomorrow, huh?"

She nodded. "Yep. I'm the best plucker they got. I knew they couldn't do without me."

"Rhett say anything about where he was or what he was doin'?"

450

The uncomfortable look came back to her face. She was trying to remember the lie that she just told. Then she shook her head; another sign of deception.

I reached into my back pocket and pulled a business card out of the silver case. I handed it to her.

"Well, if you hear from him, be sure and call me."

She looked at the card. "I will. I really will."

The next morning, I detoured by the Tyndall Chicken Plant on my way in. I turned into the parking lot and slowly drove through looking for Myrtice Abercrombie's white Ford with the South Carolina tag. It was on the fourth row, near the fence, close to the street, indicating that she had once again arrived late for work.

Her vehicle safely tucked away for the next eight hours, I drove onto headquarters forthwith. I went immediately to my office, closed the door, and plopped into my chair.

It was going to be tricky. Actually, I didn't know if what I was about to do would work, or if it was entirely legal. But, it's easier to ask forgiveness than to ask for permission, and it wasn't like I was going to base any of my prosecution of Zoe Woods' case on it. I just wanted to get my hands on Rhett Tolliver.

I picked up my phone and dialed Myrtice's number. It rang four times, after which the answering machine picked up.

"When you hear the beep, you know what to do," the high pitched female voice said.

After the beep, I took a chance. I pressed *49, the old factory installed code that I had in the past used to remotely check my messages, and then waited.

"Hey, Myrt," a female voice came on. "Good to hear you got your job back. Now you can buy me lunch. Call me."

There was another beep. "Hey, hun. Call me about Saturday. I'm gonna bring the young'uns. Bye."

451

Another beep. The next voice was male, a baritone. "Hey, babe, this is 'Tink.' I'm gonna be in town soon, and I want to get up wi' ya'. It'll be around the first of the year. I'll call ya."

That was him. Something in my gut told me that 'Tink' was Rhett Tolliver. I hung up the phone and leaned back in my chair.

First, I was right. Rhett Tolliver was making it with his brother's ex-wife. Second, she hadn't lied to me, she had heard from him, although it was most certainly on more than the one occasion to which she had confessed. Third, it was a cinch that I had just violated about three different federal statutes. But, in my mind it was worth it. Now, I had a way to keep tabs on Tolliver and at least have an idea of where he was or where he was going to be.

Chapter 54

Will was back from vacation the next week, the third week in December. He and his wife had taken a trip to the mountains of Tennessee and had spent some time in a cabin up there.

"Anything happen while I was gone?" he said in between puffs on his coffee

"Not really. The grits case got settled. This new ADA, McCoy, has got Simp Patridge's file. I told him not to make any efforts whatsoever to settle it."

"That son of a bitch."

"Patridge, or the lawyer?"

He chuckled. "Both."

I smiled. "And, I took a trip out to see Myrtice."

"That boy in New Orleans' ex old lady?"

"Yeah. I'm thinkin' there might be some movement on that thing just shortly."

"What makes you think so?"

I paused and sucked my teeth. "I'll let you know if, or when, it happens."

He nodded and seemed satisfied. I'm sure he got my cryptic message. He was smart enough not to ask what I was up to. In a case like this, because I had done and was going to do something a little ethically questionable, then I wasn't going to involve him in it, unless he just made me.

"Okay," Will said, "what have you got on the front burner, right now?"

"Right now? Today? Nothin'."

"I want to do a couple of things on this Harden case."

"Let's go."

That afternoon we took a trip over to Bryson's Garage in Ocean Springs, Mississippi. The business turned out to be a blue metal building with three repair bays and a concrete parking lot. Shells filled in the large potholes that dotted the lot, and some large chunks of concrete that used to be in the holes had been carried over to a location underneath a large oak tree.

I stopped the car near the oak. Things seemed deserted. Will was out of the car and making a beeline straight for the office area on the left, or west side. Clearly, he was interested in this case. The building faced Highway 90 and was probably three miles from the Gulf.

The tinkle of a small bell greeted us when Will opened the glass front door. The interior was oblong and had paneled walls. There was a four foot high wood counter on the left. A beat up twenty-five inch color television, working off an antenna, inside a cruelly scratched wood cabinet, was airing a game show. A wooden door was over in the corner near the set.

Will stood in front of the counter. One of those punch bells was next to a phone, so he hit it hard with the flat of his hand. In ten seconds, we heard a flushing sound coming from behind the door next to the television.

The slightly underweight man who walked through the door had a brown beard with gray flecks and matching head hair that was long and tied in a ponytail. His dirty, blue, work shirt had the name 'Hoss' stitched over the left breast pocket, and his blue pants were equally as dirty and oily. He was wiping his almost black hands on a paper towel as he walked toward us with a half grin on his face.

"Sorry. I was conducting another kinda business. How ya'll doin'?"

"Fine, sir," Will said. "My name is Eubanks and this is Mr. Faulkner. We're with the Metro Sheriff's Office over in Mobile."

I held up my star as Hoss took his place behind the counter. His half smile turned into a guarded smirk. He threw the paper towel in the trash.

"How can I help you fellas?"

"Are you Mr. Bryson?"

"Nope. Bryson's dead. I bought the place from his daughter. I'm Hoss McElhaney."

Will nodded. "Well, Mr. McElhaney, we was wonderin' if you was the owner about five years ago."

"I was." He stopped. "Oh, you're here about Cal, I bet."

"Yes, sir. We are."

"Well, what can I do for ya?"

"We heard that Cal parked his truck over here, when he wadn't on his bike."

"That old, white International? Yeah, he left it out back. He give me five bucks whenever he come to town, just to watch it."

"You remember the last time you saw him?"

454

He wiped his chin with his dirty hands. "I guess it had to be the day before he died. He come and got his truck; said he had to go up to Pascagoula."

"He say what for?"

"Nope."

"Anything happen here before he left?"

"You mean, like some kinda fight or somethin'?"

"Anything."

"No. He just come by, got his truck, and took off."

"Was anybody else here?"

"Well, let me see. Seems like Sonny was here, and maybe Slim."

"You know how I can get in touch with them?"

He shook his head. "Naw. Slim used to come around some, but he quit. I hadn't seen Sonny here in years."

"Quit when?"

"I don't know, about two, three years ago."

"You know their names?"

I quickly got out my pad and pen. "Seems like Sonny's name might'a been Grimes. I don't know about Slim."

"They both in the Las Ratas?"

His brows went up, like we weren't supposed to know anything about the gang. He cleared his throat.

"Yeah. Sonny wore his colors all the time, but Slim didn't. He may'a been workin' or somethin', I don't know.

Not many, but a few of the members would hold down regular jobs to make money and contribute it to the group. This Slim may have just ridden when he could, and the others would pass him sex and dope to compensate him for living the straight life.

"Tell me about the day Cal came and got his truck."

He shrugged. "Well, I can't remember much. It was just a reg'lar day. The only thing I remember was that I was rebuildin' a carburetor, and when he come in, I hardly noticed him." He paused. "I always felt bad about that. He

455

come in, said he needed his truck, and when I looked up, he was gone." He closed his eyes and looked at the ceiling. "I think Sonny was here. I remember him standin' out in the bay drinkin' a beer."

"He say anything to Carl, uh Cal?"

He closed his eyes again to think. "I think, he asked him, 'where ya goin'?' and that's when Cal said, 'Pascagoula.'"

"How'd he seem? Cal, I mean. He seem agitated? In a hurry? Or what?"

"He wasn't runnin' ner nothin', but he didn't stop to talk. He just walked in, said, 'I'm takin' my truck,' and he was gone."

Will looked at me. I cleared my throat.

"Who got his bike?" I said.

"You know, I don't know. I come in a day or two later and it was gone."

"You report it stolen?"

"Why? Whoever took it had a key. For all I knew, Cal come back and got it. I didn't hear about him gettin' killed 'til later."

"You know anybody that wanted him dead?"

He chuckled. "Hey, them guys piss off a lotta people. It could'a been anybody."

"Anybody in particular stickin' in your head?"

He shook his head, but I saw a twitch; a slight one, but a twitch nevertheless. My guess was he knew, but he was afraid.

"Nope."

I looked back at Will. He asked Hoss for his personal information, and I copied it down. Will stuck out his hand and shook Hoss's dirty one.

"We thank ya for your time, sir," he said as he turned to me. "If you think of anything else, give us a call."

I took my cue and gave Hoss a business card. We turned and walked out the front door, once again awakening the tinkling bell in the process.

456

Outside in the car, on the way back to the office, Will was pensive. He closed his eyes.

"Okay, we found out where he was within the last twenty-four hours of his life. He said he was going to Pascagoula. We also know his bike is missin'. If we can run it down, then we've got a suspect. All we need is the VIN."

"If it's not in fifty thousand pieces."

"It won't be. People don't do that to Hogs. They appreciate with age. They're worth more together than apart, especially if the numbers match. No, if we can find it, we've got somebody. Maybe this Sonny Grimes."

"He killed him for his bike?"

"Sure. If these bikers want somethin', they take it. Hey, he could'a been killed for any reason; a woman, a slight, anything."

We rode a half mile in silence. "What's the weirdest reason you ever heard of for killing a man?" I said smiling.

Will paused to think. "Well, I heard about a man killin' his ole lady 'cause she peed in a pot'a greens she was cookin' for'im. He beat her over the head with a ball bat."

I immediately burst out laughing. The image of a woman, with her dress hiked up, squatting over a steaming pot of collards that she intended to serve to her old man came suddenly to my mind, and it was more than I could stand. I laughed until I cried. Will stared at me curiously.

"Be careful with your drivin' there, Son." He paused. "And, I heard of a man bein' killed over a ham sandwich," he continued. "Another man was killed 'cause he wouldn't change the TV channel; and one old boy got killed 'cause'a the size of his dick."

"Too long or too short?" I said through my tears.

He looked at me with a deadpan expression. "Well, shit, Son. Does it matter?"

457

Chapter 55

For the next week and a half, until Christmas, I periodically checked Myrtice Abercrombie's answering machine, waiting for a call from Rhett Tolliver. The man 'Tink' hadn't left any other messages, and while I wasn't completely sure that it was Tolliver, my gut told me it was.

In the meantime, we had a couple of shootings around Christmas time. One was at the Shade Tree Lounge on the Blue Star Parkway. Will and I were called out on Christmas Eve. The dispatcher told us that a woman had shot her husband.

The Shade Tree was the last tenant on the south end of the strip-type shopping complex, located at the northwest corner of the Parkway and Theodore-Dawes Road. It had one door in the front and one in the back, and no windows.

I met Will at the office, and we drove out there together, arriving a little after one AM on Christmas morning. All the lights in the parking lot were out.

We entered the wood front door, which was ringed with multi-colored Christmas lights, and stood for a moment to survey the scene. The inside wasn't much brighter than the outside, so my eyes adjusted quickly. They were soon diverted to the bar on the right side of the room. The rest of the space was deserted.

A uniformed deputy with a clipboard, and Chuck Briley with a camera, stood over a motionless man lying supine on the concrete floor, his left arm hanging over the foot rail. I could see a large pool of blood under his head, and owing to the floor's slant, the liquid had progressed away from the wound to a location approximately four feet from his head, out onto what was supposed to be the dance floor, a tile space surrounded by metal tables and folding chairs. Briley looked up and smiled.

"Ho, ho, ho," he said.

Will and I walked up to the three men and stood. Will spoke with a disgusted tone.

"Well, what the fuck happened?"

The deputy, who I did not recognize, but whose name badge identified him as Glen Whitman, spoke. He was a muscular man of medium height with blond hair and a blonde mustache, and his accented voice was decidedly southern.

"Well, this here is our victim. He was drinkin' alone at the bar when his wife, or a woman who identified herself as his wife, arrived. She produced a revolver and shot him one time in the head."

"You got the gun?"

"Briley secured it in his car."

"What is it?"

"A little Colt Detective Special."

"Where is she?"

"She's at the Theodore substation. Meg Crenshaw's with her."

"Well, shit," Will said.

I couldn't tell exactly why Will was so disgruntled. Was it the fact that he had to be out working on Christmas Eve? That couldn't be it. Will's daughter was grown, he wasn't religious, and holidays usually held no special place for him.

Was it the fact that this murder was particularly senseless? It couldn't be that either. Will had seen senseless murders before, and they had never bothered him.

My mind ran down all the other reasons that might have put him in a foul mood: loss of sleep, a problem with his wife, hunger, thirst. I finally decided that the most plausible conclusion was the fact that this case was solved. There was no puzzle here, nothing to put together, nothing to exercise his brain. Therefore, to him, this murder was a complete waste of his time.

He stepped back away from the body and began to walk around the room. He stopped and studied a painting of Confederate General Stonewall Jackson hanging next to an illuminated Bud Light sign. I took out my pad and decided that I would take the lead on this one. The sooner I got enough facts to write it all up, the sooner we could get home. I looked at Whitman.

"Any witnesses?"

"They're in the backroom with McDermott. He's gettin' their names."

"The owner? Bartender?"

"Owner's off site. The bartender's in the back. It liked to have scared the shit outta him when she clicked the ole boy off."

"Ya think?" I said smiling.

I took rubber gloves out of my back pocket and knelt down by the body, making sure not to step into the blood. I looked up at Briley.

"You got your photos?"

He nodded. "Yeah. About ten or twenty. I'm good until you move'im."

I started at the top of his head and began to scan down his body. He was a white man, about thirty-five, with brown curly hair that just barely crept over his ears. His round face was only slightly lined, just a few crow's feet at the corners of his eyes, and his cheeks were puffy. He had a one, maybe two days growth of beard on his face, and a cleft in his chin. He wore a blue flannel shirt with the sleeves rolled up, a long sleeved undershirt, blue jeans, and saddle boots made of some type of textured leather. He looked just like who he was: a good ole boy out on the town.

Running the backs of my hands across his pockets, I felt what I thought was a wallet on his right hip. I lifted that side of his body just enough to slip it out.

"Hey, get your hands off my body."

460

It was the voice of Angie McDowell who had exited the back room and was walking toward us. I looked up.

"You wish," I said.

"*You* wish," she said back.

She wore a formfitting blue jumpsuit, her hair was pulled back in a ponytail, and she had even taken time to put on perfume – Chanel, I thought – before coming to the scene of a dead man lying on a barroom floor. The irony was almost laughable; her taking the time to doll herself up just to look at a man who two hours earlier wouldn't have gotten ten seconds of the attractive woman's attention when he was alive, but now, in death, he had it all.

I opened the wallet and pulled out his driver's license. After making notes about his full name, address, and vitals, I handed the card to McDowell. His DL photo looked exactly like him, though Briley knew a fingerprint ID would be have to be made.

Angie looked at the license. "Billy Claude Thompson, thirty-three years of age," she said to no one in particular.

I looked around at the group that had formed around the man, a group that once again included Will.

"Anybody know anything about this guy?" I said.

McDowell spoke up. "According to the barkeep, he was a regular; came in once or twice a week. Never caused any trouble; never got outta hand."

"Women?"

"You mean did he flirt? Bartender said he'd buy a drink for somebody, occasionally, but he doesn't ever remember seeing him leave with anyone."

"Anything else in his pockets?"

It was Will that spoke, trying to re-engage. Why this man was dead was apparently enough of a mystery to get him back in the game.

I patted his two front pockets and then ran my hands into them both. In the left was a lid of marijuana. In the right, a small scrap of paper with a phone number on it,

461

and his keys. For no reason, a possible scenario popped into my head.

"Anybody know anything about this wife?"

Whitman shook his head. "We walked in, Meg Crenshaw and me, and she was sittin' on the floor with the gun in front of her. We handcuffed her, the bartender hollered that she had killed him, and Meg took her to the office."

"What was she wearing?" Will said.

Whitman flipped through pages of his report. "A nightgown, slippers, and a leather bomber jacket."

I looked at Will. He seemed to know what I was thinking. Could it be that this woman was sleeping and had just decided to get up out of the bed and go shoot her husband?

The wound was in his head. I found it on the right side, hidden by his curls. There was also what appeared to be a through and through hole in his right hand – a defense wound.

I took a deep breath, exhaled, stood up and peeled off the gloves.

"Okay, I've seen enough. Where's the barkeep?"

Whitman nodded his head toward a door in the back. I looked at Will, and we started that way.

The room in which the bartender and two other witnesses sat was a combination office and stockroom. It was sixteen by twenty but looked smaller. Cases of liquor – Cutty Sark; Old Forrester; Jack Daniels; and beer, lots and lots of beer – lined three of the walls, effectively shrinking the size of the space by two thirds. A small wooden desk sat right next to the door. Three of the metal chairs from out of the barroom had been drawn in and placed in a semi-circle. Light was provided by one nude, forty watt bulb in the middle of the ceiling.

Two women and one man occupied the three chairs. The man was forty, with a balding head and a mustache. He wore jeans and a pullover shirt. The women, one of whom wore an apron, were similarly attired. McDermott, a muscular man with a crew cut, stood silently in the corner, presumably to ensure that the witnesses didn't talk and compare stories. I nodded at him when we walked in. Will walked McDermott's direction and stood next to him.

Looking at the man, I spoke. "Are you the bartender?"

He nodded. "Walter McKenzie."

"Are you the owner also?"

"No, sir. The owner ain't here. I just run the place for'im."

I walked over to him. "Tell me what happened."

The man rubbed his hands together and licked his lips. When he spoke, his voice was a sober tenor.

"Well, it all happened really fast. Billy Claude was standin' at the bar drinkin' a Heineken. We was talkin' about the ball game and this, that, and the other, when the door opens and this woman walks in. I don't know how he knew her, or who she is, or what, but she's got on this leather jacket and slippers. It was the craziest thing. She just walks up to him and shoots him in the head."

"What'd you do?"

He kind of chuckled. "Shit my pants?" He paused. "Man, I hit the floor, 'til I didn't hear no more shots. Then I raised up a little, and I didn't see nobody. I figure she'd left, so I stood straight up. Then I see her squattin' down next to him and goin' through his pockets."

"Did she get anything out of them?"

"If she did, I didn't see it."

"Did she say anything to him before she shot?"

"She may have, but I don't remember. All I 'member was that shot."

"Then what happened?"

"While she's down on her knees, I grabbed the phone and called you guys."

"She do anything?"

463

"No, she just kinda falls over off her haunches and sits down on the floor and starts squallin'. That's where she was when Glen and that girl deputy got here."

I nodded. He'd have to be interviewed more fully, but I didn't hear anything that I thought could shake his story in court. I looked at the women.

"Either of you see anything?"

The two women looked at each other as if to decide who should talk first. The dark haired woman with the apron, who looked about fifty, spoke first. She had a deep, tobacco-conditioned voice.

"I didn't see nothin'. I was back in here gettin' some napkins. I heard the shot, and I thought the place was gettin' held up, so I just stayed back here. That's what we was told to do; if we think the place is gettin' robbed, we're supposed to get to a safe place."

"What's your name ma'am?"

"Uh, Alice, Alice Webster."

"Okay, Ms Webster." I looked at the other woman. "And you would be?"

She seemed surprised that I would call on her. "Oh, uh, Candy Albritton." She was younger than the others, in her twenties, plump, with blonde hair and cheeks like a squirrel.

"Tell me what you saw and heard."

"Oh, nothin'. I was in the restroom."

"Didn't see anything?"

"Not 'til I come out. She was sittin' on the floor. It looked like she was cryin' to me."

I looked over at Will. He shook his head.

"Ya'll all have to come and give statements," I said.

All three nodded. "Can I call the owner now?" McKenzie said.

"Sure. Tell'im you've got to lock the place up until we get through."

464

He nodded then reached for the two line phone on the desk. He cleared his throat, exhaled deeply, and dialed the number.

I parked in front of the substation, in the spot closest to the front door. From the outside, everything was dark. Will yawned obnoxiously.

Inside, Megan Crenshaw and our suspect were in the large squad room. Crenshaw was at a desk near the front and the woman, who had her head down on folded arms, was seated against the far wall. I could see that her left hand was cuffed to the chair arm. When we walked in, she raised her head.

She looked to be in her fifties, thin and gaunt, with dark circles under her eyes. Her clavicles were pronounced under pale skin, and her brown hair was cut short, very short; a buzz cut. It seemed as if she had been a wreck long before she shot her husband. Under the jacket, her nightgown was white with little pink flowers across the front collar, and her slippers were pink and shaggy. I saw her shiver once and noticed goose bumps on her neck.

"Let's turn up the heat just a little, in here," I said. I found the thermostat and set it for seventy-five.

Will took a chair next to Crenshaw, unzipped his jacket, leaned back, and interlaced his fingers behind his head. I sat down across from the suspect.

"What is your name, ma'am?"

The woman rubbed her face with her right hand. "Angela Thompson." Her voice was high and weak, almost a whisper.

"Ma'am, my name is Faulkner and this is Sergeant Eubanks. We're looking into the death of your husband."

She stared at me with vacant eyes and heavy lids. I recited the rights and waiver spiel, and she acknowledged it with a nod.

"You're gonna have to say you understand, ma'am."

465

"Yes, I understand." There was no fight in her tone at all.

"Why did you shoot your husband, ma'am?"

She shrugged, and her head fell over on her shoulder. She looked weak, tired, and listless.

"Did he hurt you?"

She said nothing.

"Was he seein' another woman?"

She remained silent. I had run down the main motives. Will spoke up.

"Are you sick, Ms Thompson? Do you have cancer?"

Her head shot off her shoulder as she turned his direction. There was still no animation, but at least she was more alert. He had obviously struck a nerve.

"Did he take the marijuana?" he continued. "Is that why you come to the bar? You take marijuana for the pain? He had it, and you come to get it?"

Will's voice was more sympathetic than I'd ever heard it. It was softer, quieter. I wondered if he'd had experience with cancer previously.

"He took it all," she said. Her voice was as weak as her face looked. "He even took the number of the dude we buy from." She paused. "I was so mad."

"You use it medicinally?"

She nodded. "I was hurtin' tonight. The pain comes in waves, one after the other. It gets so bad I can't sleep, can't do nothin'."

"So, did you try to call him?"

She exhaled loudly. "I looked around the house first, to see if we had some medicine here. I was just hurtin' so bad." She paused and rubbed her brow. "I was gonna call the guy I get it from, but I couldn't find his number. I didn't know where Billy Claude was. I just got in the car and started ridin'. I checked over at the Shade Tree 'cause he's goes there, sometimes. When I saw his truck, well, it just made me so . . . to think he was in there drinkin' when . . . ."

"Why did you have the gun?"

"'Cause I always carry it with me; 'specially if I'm goin' over to get medicine."

"What did you say to him? When you walked in, I mean."

"I said, 'you're off down here drinkin' when I need my medicine.' I was so mad."

"Why'd you take the gun in the bar?"

She paused to think. It was plain she was measuring her words.

"I was just goin' to scare him. I pointed the gun at him, and it went off. It was an accident."

The old 'the gun just went off by accident,' defense. It hadn't worked yet, but that didn't mean it wouldn't the next time a prosecutor neglected to remind a jury that a trigger had to be pulled before a gun will discharge. If he didn't, his case would be in trouble. Personally, if it was me, I'd have used the 'temporary insanity due to physical pain' defense.

Will said nothing while I wrote. He cleared his throat to let me know he was about to ask another question.

"What kinda cancer do you have?"

"Lung; stage three."

Well, there it was. There were more serious cases, but the fact that she: a) had killed her husband, and b) the state would have to foot the bill for her treatment, I was convinced that if she pled guilty, the judge would very likely place her on probation. I was certain that with her being sick, and her old man out on a toot instead of staying at home to take care of her, that no jury in Mobile would convict her.

Will looked at me. "You heard enough?"

I nodded, "if she'll give me a written statement."

"You'll write it up, ma'am?"

She nodded and laid her head back down on her shoulder.

467

"If you'll do that, ma'am, we'll send this case to the Grand Jury."

His words shocked me. At no time, since we'd begun working together, had we not incarcerated someone after they had confessed to murder. I looked at Will with brows raised. Then I relaxed, reached into the desk drawer, and pulled out a blank statement sheet. I mated the form with a ball point pen and handed both to her.

Thirty minutes later, Angela Thompson, in a slow and smooth hand, had laid down her version of events at the Shade Tree Lounge shortly after midnight on Christmas Day. It was a quick statement, to the point, and I made sure it contained the words, 'I shot him,' at least twice. Will told Crenshaw to take her home, and we locked up the office and went to pick up Will's car.

"I was a little surprised to hear you Grand Jury this case," I said when we were on the road.

"Aw, there ain't no need to arrest her, Son. She'll probably be dead 'fore the trial anyway. If she was in the kinda pain that she said, and if a doctor had told her that marijuana was the only thing that could make her feel better – and they do say that when it's hopeless like that – then she ain't goin' nowhere."

"But she said it was stage three."

"That's somethin' else doctors do. They never tell ya how bad it is. They think if you give up hope you'll stop comin' back for treatment, and they'll lose all that insurance and medicaid money. If they say three, you can count on it being four, or worse."

These were things I did not know. It was apparent to me that cancer had touched Will – hard - but it was neither the time nor the place to delve into it.

"Anyway," he said looking at me, "that's one more different motive for killin'; your ole man stole the medical marijuana."

468

Chapter 56

I spent Christmas in my apartment, asleep. I awoke at three and walked across the street to the convenience store to get a bag of chips and I don't remember what else. It was the only business open, and I kept no food in my home. My obsessiveness didn't allow me to keep anything in the refrigerator or the cabinets. If I did, I'd be as broad as a barn.

The next day was Friday. I went to the office early. Many of the other detectives had taken several days off to be with their families, so the place was deserted.

Will came in also. He made coffee, and I had a cup. It was awful, but I didn't let on.

He told me that he had briefed the Captain, by telephone, the day before, regarding the Billy Claude Thompson homicide. He told me the Captain wasn't pleased.

"But, what does he know," Will said. "He hadn't made a case in twenty-five years. That woman didn't deserve jail."

"Well, he's the boss."

"In name only."

I paused and took a sip. "So, you know somebody that had cancer?"

He was silent as he looked out the window. I took another drink while he took a deep breath.

"Yeah, my daddy had it."

"What kind?"

"Lung. He was a smoker for thirty or forty years. He got it when I started in the Bureau." He shook his head. "It was an ugly thing to watch."

I said nothing.

"He would'a done anything to get some relief from the pain, but there wadn't nothin' nobody could do for'im." He paused. "So, that's why I cut that woman some slack the other night. I could tell she was sick, and if a toke on a joint could help her feel better, then I wadn't gonna put her in jail. Besides, the county would'a had to look after her and get her to her treatment, at least until she made bond; and she'd'a been stupid to do that."

I said nothing.

He shook his head and looked out the window. "It's a sorry thing to watch, Son." He paused. "That cancer is some damnable stuff."

The next Monday, I checked the parking lot of the chicken plant on my way in and confirmed that Myrtice Abercrombie was at work. When I got to the office, Will was away from his desk, so I took the opportunity to check her answering machine. The voice told me she had three messages. I was only interested in the first.

"Hey, Babe, it's Tink. I just talked to Mikey, an' I told him I'd be in to see him on New Year's Day. That means I'll stop and see you on New Year's Eve. I'll be in about eight. Keep the peas warm."

That cinched it for me. 'Tink' was Rhett Tolliver and the peas to which he was referring were the black eyed peas that were served on New Year's Day, an old southern tradition. He also talked with that Tidewater brogue when he said 'wam' for warm and 'awn' for on, and 'ye ahs' for years. It was him, I knew it. The other two calls were from friends.

I was just hanging up the receiver when in walked Will. He was blowing on a steaming cup of coffee.

"Who ya talkin' to, Son?"

I cleared my throat. "An informant. I got a line on Rhett Tolliver."

"Who is this informant?"

470

I paused and looked at my desk. There was no time like the present.

"I did something."

He looked at me with a deadpan face.

"I went out to see Myrtice while you were on vacation, and while I was there, I noticed that she had an answering machine like the one I used to have. I called it from the office, put in my old factory code, and I've been checking her messages periodically for the past two or three weeks. Tolliver just called Myrtice, and he's gonna be at her place on New Year's Eve."

I stopped and waited for his reaction. It surprised me.

He grinned and chuckled. "Well, Son, that's just about the most ingenious thing I ever heard."

"Well, when we saw him on the interstate that day, I figured he was either going to or coming from seein' Myrtice. I just believe he's screwin' his brother's ex old lady."

Will took a deep breath and exhaled. Then he leaned back and looked out of the window.

I gave him a minute before I spoke. "Did I do wrong?"

He shook his head. "No, but we can't use anything you heard. Let me think a minute."

The room was silent until the phone rang. It was the dispatcher forwarding me a message from Briley. I told her I'd call him.

Briley answered on the third ring and told me that he ran down the phone number that Billy Claude Thompson had in his pocket and found that it was that of a small time dope dealer out in Grand Bay. Briley also said that the gun Angela Thompson used was stolen in the burglary of a house in Prichard ten years previous. I was surprised, but not much.

"Okay, send a message to Prichard confirming it and then call'em. Let'em know their suspect has cancer."

471

"All right. You want'em to lay off her?"

"They can talk to her, but if she admits to anything, have'em get up with me. We'll bundle their case with ours and present it to the Grand Jury at the same time. And, let'em know that the weapon is gonna be at the Forensic Lab."

I hung up and looked at Will. He cleared his throat and sat up in the chair. I told him what Briley had said. He concurred. We both thought that Billy Claude was probably going to go buy her some marijuana – after he'd finished a couple'a drinks first.

"You come up with anything?" I said.

"Well, I figure we got three choices. One, we go back out and see Myrtice and lean on her; tell her we believe she knows where he is, or that at least she's had contact with him. Two, we see if we can get a subpoena for her phone records and approach it from that end. Or, three, we feed a line to the patrolmen and tell them be to hangin' out down there on New Year's Eve when he's supposed to come in. They'll spot the car – if he's still in it – and pull him over. They'll call us and we've got him."

"Which'll be the easiest?"

"The easiest would be to drop something on the patrolmen. But if we do that, we still might have to explain where our information came from. The best way is to fall on Myrtice; let her turn him in. If we remind her of the ten grand reward, she might even set him up for us."

"Okay. Where do we approach her? At work, or at home?"

He paused and took a deep breath.

"I think we better hit her at work. She won't be on her turf. The unspoken message will be that if she don't cooperate it could go bad for her on the job. We'll have her in that place at the plant, that room that looks like an interrogation room. She'll think she has to help."

"But how do we start things off?"

"Watch and learn, Son."

The next day, we went to the Tyndall plant and met the HR manager in his office. Will told him what we wanted.

"I hate to get her off the line, but we got some information that we've got to move on pretty quick, and she needs to confirm it," Will said.

Frank Smoot nodded. He looked skeptical; however, he didn't want to appear uncooperative. His mouth was in a smirk when he picked up the telephone and dialed a three digit extension. When he finished talking and hung up the phone, he directed us to the room down the hall that we had used previously.

When Myrtice walked in, I closed the door behind her. Will gestured toward the empty wooden chair at the table. She sat down with a thud and wiped the clear plastic cover off her head. I sat, Will stood. He spoke.

"Myrtice, we're here 'cause we been doin' some thinkin'. Mr. Faulkner and I been talkin' it over, and we think you been holdin' out on us."

Her eyes opened wide, and she looked directly at him.

"We think you been talkin' to Rhett Tolliver; as a matter of fact, we're sure you been talkin' to him, and on a regular basis."

I could see what Will was doing, and I knew her first words would be the most important. My pen was at the ready.

When she spoke, her voice quivered. "You're crazy." She looked down at the table, and I saw her tighten her grip on the plastic cap.

There it was: a value judgment on Will's mental health, but not a denial.

When Will spoke, his words were soothing. "Now, see, Myrtice, I know you're lyin'. I been doing this for a long time, and I can tell. Now, we want to know when you saw him last, when you talked to him, and when you're gonna to see him again."

Silence fell on the room. Myrtice stared at the table and shifted her weight from one hip to the other. She licked her lips and even bit her lower lip once. Her tough girl persona had wilted under the slight pressure that Will had applied.

"Tell it, Myrtice. If you do, maybe you'll be in line for the ten grand reward. If you don't, maybe we charge you with hindering prosecution."

She took a deep breath. "Look, I've talked to him a couple'a times, but I don't know where he is."

"When did you last hear from him?"

"Two, maybe three weeks ago." Her voice was almost a mumble.

"Now, Myrtice, see, that's a lie. Don't do that anymore."

She swallowed visibly. "Okay. I heard from him the other day."

"What did he say?"

She seemed to relax. She took a deep breath and exhaled, apparently having decided to go ahead and come clean.

"He's comin' to town on New Year's Eve. He's gonna come to my trailer." She bowed her head.

Will paused. "Now, see, that wadn't so bad. Anyway, why protect him, Myrtice? You know he killed a woman. Is that okay by you?"

"He told me he didn't hurt her. He said that they had a fight, but he didn't hurt her. He left her on the side of the road. He didn't know she died 'til later."

Fantastic. I scribbled the words quickly. Now, we knew his defense. He took her out; they did or did not have sex; they had a fight of questionable seriousness; and then he left her on the side of the road for someone else to assault and kill. Heck, he'd probably say she wanted out of the car.

"You an' Rhett fuckin'?" Will said.

474

She nodded. "Um, hmm. We been seein' each other for a little while."

"Well, if she was alive when he left her, then he's got nothin' to hide then, has he. We'll just come on by for the party on New Year's Eve and let him tell his side, and then you and him can get back to doin' what'ch'all gonna do; celebratin' the new year."

She nodded. "I guess so."

Will looked at me. I shook my head.

"Okay, Myrtice, we'll let you get back to work." He paused. "Oh, and by the way, if he don't show up on Wednesday night, I'm gonna put you in jail for Hindering Prosecution, 'cause I'll know you tipped him."

She looked at him as if the thought hadn't crossed her mind; not that it wouldn't have, but it hadn't yet. She rose, put the plastic cap back on her head, then started toward the door. She reached for the handle but stopped.

"So, I get the money, right?"

Like Ahab, I knew we were close. With my surreptitious wiretapping, I had made things, in some ways easier, and at the same time harder. We knew Tolliver was coming and where he'd be, but we'd had to tell Myrtice that we were on to the both of them, and only time would tell if Will's threat or Myrtice's greed would somehow trump true love and keep her from warning him away.

In the next two days, Will and I spent time cooking up a strategy for taking Tolliver down. That afternoon, I took a trip down to the area around Highway 188 and the entrance to the Bayou Waters Mobile Home Park to reconnoiter.

At the office, Will and I discussed it and just on the off chance that Tolliver might want to start trouble, we didn't want things to go down inside Myrtice's trailer. First, we wanted to arrest him inside his car so we could tow it without any problems. Second, we wanted to keep from burning Myrtice.

By my count, it would take three patrol cars, as well as Will and I, to get him hemmed in. That particular stretch of highway was level and straight; however, about a mile down the road to the west, the pavement took a sharp dogleg left. The entrance to the park was a two lane road with a grass median. The community's mailboxes sat in that median about halfway between the main highway and where the entrance turned into Bayou Waters Circle.

My plan was to put a patrol car west of the entrance, in the curve, since that was the route from which Tolliver was the most likely to approach – the interstate exit being closer that direction. Once the Nova passed the first patrol car, we would wait for him to turn into the complex, and onto the divided road. Our car would block him from the front, and a patrol car would block him in from the back just as he turned off the highway. The other marked car would be held in reserve in case he decided to rabbit. After he was stopped, we would remove him from the car and transport him quickly to the office. One of the patrol deputies would stay and tow the Nova.

On the off chance that he was no longer driving the older red car, we would just have to try to spot him as he turned into the park. If we couldn't, then we'd have to knock on Myrtice's door and take our chances.

I ran my plans by Will at the office on the morning of the thirtieth. Overall, he was pleased.

"What are you gonna do if he tries to run?"

"You mean on foot?"

"On foot, or in the car."

"Well, you know, I'll chase him on foot. In the car, we can put one of the marked cars after him and trail'em."

Will shook his head. "Why don't you make arrangements to get one of the dogs out there? He can run him down if he happens to get out of the car."

"Good thinkin'."

476

"Lester Houseman has the best one."

Houseman had a Doberman named Cesar, who was generally considered to be the craziest canine in the department. The dog could often be seen chasing his tail while waiting at the scene of an open building or a burglary. He once chased, caught, and bit an armed robber in the scrotum. Another time, at an elementary school demonstration, Cesar jumped on the teacher's desk and barked uncontrollably. He had clean white teeth and a bobbed tail, and his coat was so black it was blue.

"Cesar? Are you sure?"

"Absolutely. He's fast, he'll bite, and his size is intimidatin'. He's an okay tracker, too."

I nodded. "I'll call Lester."

"Make sure your blue light's workin'."

I nodded again. "Okay. I think it's in the trunk, though. I'll have to get it out and make sure."

Will got into his thinking position.

"How you gonna handle the interview?" he said.

"I thought I'd start by getting him to admit he was in Mobile last February. I'm gonna tell him we know he was here. If I have to, I confront him with that Birmingham job application. Then I'll try to run down where he hung out while he was here.

"Then I'll shift gears a little and talk about what he's been doin' runnin' around the southeast. Maybe we can get him to talk about that immigration thing, if there's anything to that.

"Finally, I'll get him to admit to drinking Black Russians; callin' hisself Mikey; and see if he will admit to recognizing Zoe Woods' picture; then, I'll bring up the knife."

"What if he denies it all?"

"I'll offer him a polygraph."

Detectives are usually ambivalent about the polygraph. Will, however, was a huge proponent. He believed that the intimidation factor was so high that a suspect would always end up admitting something. Herman Caine, a man of considerable size, with a deep voice, was the department's polygraphist. He had a quiet disposition when asking the questions but could get animated when a suspect was obviously lying.

"He's gonna deny it."

"He may, but I think we've got enough to hold him. We've got his print on the two dollar bill that puts him in the bar that night; if he brings the Nova, we can use that; when we get a picture, we can show a photo lineup; he was using his brother Mikey's name; and, of course, the jet black hair and the bird on his tag."

But even as I said it aloud, I knew it all sounded pretty thin. So much of it depended on what he still had in his possession, what other people could identify, and what he would admit to. Anybody, with half a brain, that is, who had committed murder, would have long ago done a thorough job of disposing of the evidence, changing his appearance, and trying to get his self as far away from the scene as possible. Perhaps, just the fact that he was willing to come back to Mobile to see Myrtice indicated that he either believed that he had beaten the odds and was not going to get caught, was oblivious to the fact that he done something wrong, or, perhaps, he really didn't have half a brain. All of the choices worked in our favor.

Chapter 57

New Year's Eve came and with it our prospective confrontation with Rhett Tolliver. The weather had turned much cooler, and the days right after Christmas were overcast and dreary.

I met Will at the office at four o'clock in the afternoon. We both had the day off as a holiday and were a bit more refreshed than we would have been had we worked all day. I had a thermos full of coffee for both of us, lightly creamed, just the way Will liked it. I also reminded him to bring his pistol, just in case.

We left the office at four thirty and drove south toward the mobile home park. I wanted to take a run by Myrtice's trailer before we set up our stakeout just to be sure he wasn't already there. When we got there, the driveway was empty, except for Myrtice's Ford; in fact the whole park seemed deserted, which was not unusual for a New Year's Eve when people could reasonably be expected to be out partying.

At five thirty, I picked up the radio and called Scarborough, the patrol sergeant on duty. We had prearranged with him our need for two deputies. He told me that he would be involved in the stakeout also. We met at the Fernland Grocery on Highway 188, about a mile from the Bayou Waters entrance. Scarborough was there along with Larry Dodson and Graham 'Gray' Suits, both deputies with whom I had worked and in whom I had a reasonable amount of confidence.

Suits and I went way back. We rode together at the police department before I moved over to the SO. He followed five years later. Our beat was up in north Mobile, in the area of the Roger Williams Housing project.

One of our favorite pastimes was to roll silently up on crap games in progress. When the gamblers saw us and ran, we appropriated the abandoned bills left lying on the ground, and, back then, it was usually enough for a couple of steak dinners at Shoney's.

"Okay," I said while handing out copies of the Identi-Kit drawing of the man thought to be Tolliver, "here is what we think he looks like. He'll probably have dyed,

479

black hair, but we don't think he'll have any facial hair. We believe, and we hope, he'll be in a red Chevy Nova, four door, about a 74 or a 75 model. The paint job is probably faded, at least we haven't been told otherwise; unknown about body damage, but it probably has a South Carolina tag on it." I looked everyone in the eye. "Any questions?"

Suits spoke. He was a big boned man of medium height with a receding hair line. "What's this guy wanted for?"

"Right now, we've got him entered in NCIC as 'suspicion of murder.' But he cut a woman's throat and left her for dead over on Lauderdale Road almost a year ago."

"Armed?"

"Don't know. He cut her with a knife. He may have a gun, but I wouldn't suspect it." I paused and looked at Will. "Personally, I don't think this guy is too swift."

"You think he'll run?" The speaker was Dodson, a young deputy who was a former Marine."

At that moment, Lester Houseman drove into the parking lot. His vehicle was a Chevy Caprice painted flat black with grates on the two rear door windows. I could hear his dog barking loudly as he stopped the car and got out.

Houseman was tall and rail thin, perfect for chasing a dog through the woods. His uniform was a black fatigue type, and his Corcoran jump boots were shined to a high gloss.

"What'd I miss?" he said as he neared the group.

I handed him the composite and pointed to the vehicle description at the bottom of the page. I continued.

"Now, Gray, I want you to set up down at the dog leg on 188." I motioned southwest.

"Larry, you take the old boat warehouse about a quarter of a mile north of the trailer park entrance. Will and I, and Lester, will be inside the park near the entrance, behind a vacant trailer that we found. We'll be near the

480

mailboxes. Sergeant Scarborough, you get where you think you can do the most good."

My eyes roamed to each man. "Okay, now if you see him, or a car that you think is him, sing out. We don't know when he'll be coming, but it's already dark, so I don't think it'll be too long. If you get behind him, wait 'til you see another marked car and then put the lights on him. Try to stop him as close to the park's entrance as you can. He'll either rabbit or turn in and pull over. I really don't know which. The important thing is that we get him, and his car."

Everyone nodded. "If you need a relief, call one of us, and we'll come take your position. We'll be working off channel three. I've already notified the dispatcher."

"If he runs, how bad do you want him?" Dodson said.

I knew what he meant. Dodson was a champion pistol shot who carried a nickel silver Colt .45 on his hip and wore competition ribbons on his chest.

"All rules regarding pursuit and use of force apply," Will said.

He was leaning against the car while sipping coffee. All heads turned toward him.

"Any other questions?" I said.

Everyone shook their heads. "Okay, let's go." It was six thirty, and dark.

In ten minutes, we were in position. Suits and Dodson called in from either end of the Highway 188 window, and Will and I, and Houseman, took up a position just inside the mobile home park, behind a vacant trailer not far from the mailboxes. We could see the highway from our vantage point; however, we were invisible to traffic unless it turned onto the property.

I backed our car in and Houseman put his black Chevy next to us. He opened the driver's rear door, took Cesar out of his run, and put him onto a leather lead. The dog heeled obediently until Housman spoke to him in German and unhooked the leash. Then the black dog ran a

481

short distance away and promptly urinated at the base of an oak tree.

"He's trained in German?" I said.

"Yeah. Spanish too. If you hear me say 'fuego,' then freeze. It means I've let him go, he's chasin' whoever's runnin', and he's lookin' for a bite."

Will got out of the car, and he and I leaned against the driver's front fender. We were silent as we watched the dog frolic around the cars and venture around the back side of the vacant trailer.

"How long you been trailin' this guy?" Houseman said. His voice was deep and raspy, worn from yelling at his dog.

"Nearly a year. It's been a busy year," I said.

"Well, how's it feel to be closing in?"

"Ask me again if we lay hands on him."

His question was a good one, however apprehending a murderer never really gave me much sense of satisfaction. The interrogation, the grand jury, the trial, none of it gave me any sense of success – except maybe the verdict. When we had identified a suspect, and the evidence, in my mind, proved his guilt, that's when it happened for me. That's when I could relax. It didn't take a jury verdict to affirm or validate my judgment.

"That's right," Will said. "Let's see how the night goes."

We stood and talked for the next hour about the weather, retirement, politics, dogs, and people from the department who were long gone, retired, or onto other endeavors. Will and Houseman were partners from years ago and knew a lot of the same people. I listened as they talked of how things used to be and how they'd changed. Houseman put the dog back into the rear seat, and the animal rested on his short, plyboard run. Twice I heard him lapping from his water dish.

The air was coolish but not cold. The breeze that usually came off the water had turned around and was now hitting us in the face from out of the north. I looked up and tried to find the big dipper in the southern sky.

It was a little before eight when Suits radioed in. I jumped into the driver's seat of my car.

"118 to 27."

"27"

"I'm behind a red Nova headed your way."

"License?"

"It's white with black letters. I haven't gotten close enough to see yet."

Will and Houseman moved quickly.

"Speed?"

"Normal right now. He hasn't made me yet."

"27 to 119."

"119."

"Are you at the warehouse?"

"10-4."

"Start inching up toward the entrance. 118, when you get to the entrance, light him up. If he doesn't suspect anything, he'll pull over close by."

"10-4."

"27 to 105, did you copy?" I was calling Scarborough.

"105, 10-4. I'm down in Grand Bay. I'm heading that way."

"10-4."

I hung up the radio and looked at Will. He was in the process of putting on his seatbelt. "You ready?"

"Are you?"

I nodded. "I guess so. I just hope he pulls over."

"We'll know in a minute."

"118 to 27."

"Go ahead."

"I see 119."

"What's your location?"

"I'm about a fifty yards from the entrance to the trailer park. I'm gonna light him up now."

483

"10-4."

I started the engine of our car and waited. My hands were moist so I wiped them on my pants. The AM/FM radio was playing, and I reached and turned it off.

"118, he's startin' to run."

I dropped the car in gear and picked up the mike.

"Switch over to channel 1 and call the dispatcher," I said. "105, did you copy?"

"105, 10-4."

I reached and switched over to channel one and heard Gray Suits. His tone was calm and his voice seemed to have deepened.

"Let's go," Will said. He was leaned back in his seat with his hands jammed in his jacket pockets.

I pulled out onto the park's access road. In five seconds, we were at Highway 188. Houseman and his dog were behind us. I looked to the northeast and saw blue lights. The chase was on.

On channel one, Suits was telling the operator that traffic was light, the streets were dry, and visibility was 100%. He also told her that the suspect was wanted for homicide and that speeds were around eighty miles per hour. She relayed the information to Scarborough. Putting these facts on tape was all part of covering everyone's exposure in case something bad happened. Now that it was done, we could all concentrate on the drive ahead.

My guess was that Tolliver had little idea of where he was. Unless at some point he had lived in the area, or had at least spent a great deal of time there with Myrtice, then he would have only a rudimentary knowledge of how to get back to the interstate. He probably knew how to get to Myrtice's trailer and that was all. He would have to turn completely around to go back down the highway the same way he had come, and in a chase, changing directions dramatically like that was unlikely. In my mind, he would drive until he saw a well-used main road that turned north,

484

at which time he would go that way and hope that it took him back to I-10.

In five minutes, we were at the outskirts of Bayou La Batre. The Nova was followed closely by the two patrol cars. Will and I, as well as Houseman, were less than a quarter mile back. There was no sign of Scarborough.

In the dark, I could see the tail lights of the Nova as it slowed down at the Irvington-Bayou Highway intersection. The vehicle took the turn in the oncoming lane and shimmied just a little before righting itself and moving on. Both patrol cars, with heavy duty suspensions, smoothly changed direction and started north.

I had been in car chases before. Once, while in uniform, I took over the pursuit of a narcotics dealer from some undercover cars and chased him to Mississippi where he flipped while making a sharp curve on Old Pascagoula Road.

Another time, my partner and I rolled up on a man beating a woman with a broomstick handle in the middle of Decatur Street, downtown. The man saw us and jumped in his car and took off. After going round and round in an adjacent neighborhood, we stopped in the driveway of a house where the driver bailed and then hit the front door. I chased him into the house and almost didn't get him back out, having to push my way past family and friends. The driver ended up sporting a nice little knot and fifty or so stiches on his forehead after that one.

I say all that to say that the adrenaline rush when chasing someone is sometimes too much to manage. Emotions rise to an almost uncontrollable level, and can shift from anger to fear and back to anger in a millisecond. It's no wonder that when it's over the pursued usually has to make a stop at a hospital, accident or no accident.

"118, north on Bayou Highway," Suits said, his siren wailing in the background.

Will and I stayed the requisite quarter mile behind as we made the turn and started north also. Will had put the

485

portable blue light on the dash and plugged it into the cigarette lighter. It rotated slowly and the light flashed throughout the interior of the car. He left the siren off.

Suits provided location updates at every other intersection. In addition, he called out the traffic violations the Nova committed as it made its way past Four Mile Road, Two Mile Road, and Half Mile Road. Surprisingly, on New Year's Eve, traffic was light. Only three vehicles passed us in a five mile stretch.

When we reached the Half Mile Road stop light, I slowed to run the red light. Out of nowhere, an old pickup truck with a headlight missing came into the intersection from the west. I swerved to avoid him, and continued on. Will didn't take the event as casually as I did.

"Son of a bitch!" he yelled. "Look out!" He reached for the dash. "Shit, Son, be careful."

"I got it."

In three minutes, we were on our way west on Highway 90, and in ten more we were at the Interstate 10 interchange in Grand Bay. The Nova had to slow as it made the curve onto the west bound ramp. I picked up the radio mike.

"27 to dispatch."

"27."

"Notify Alabama State and the Mississippi Highway Patrol of our location and direction."

"10-4."

Traffic on the interstate was slightly heavier. We moved over to the left lane and kept the two marked cars in sight as the Nova weaved in and out of traffic.

In three minutes, we were at the Mississippi state line. One Alabama trooper had joined the chase. We passed the Welcome Center and were in Mississippi without incident. Remarkably, speeds were still only around eighty or eighty-five miles per hour. My guess was that the old Nova wouldn't go any faster.

486

As we neared the first exit, I could see three Mississippi Patrol vehicles, lights flashing, on the sides of the road. I slowed down. Will looked over at me.

"Spike strips."

"Yeah. I see'em."

I could see Suits' and Dodson's brake lights coming on in anticipation of the trap. Evidently, Tolliver saw it coming also because, without warning, he turned his car almost ninety degrees and drove it off the road bed and down into the ditch on the north side of the highway. Unfortunately for him, the incline was close to the thirty degrees, and the speed at which he took the hill caused the Nova to slide in the grass and flip over twice before coming to rest on its side at the bottom of the grade.

I skidded to a stop on the opposite shoulder and dropped the car into park. I took a deep breath and exhaled. Will looked at me.

"Well, Son, you managed to get outta that one without gettin' me killed."

"You're welcome."

"If you'd killed me, I'd'a shot ya."

I smirked and hit the seatbelt button. "Hey, I had it all under control. You're just gettin' soft in your old age."

"Yeah, and I intend on gettin' a whole lot softer."

Houseman had stopped also, but had not gotten out of his car. He waved at Will, made a u-turn in the median, and started back toward Alabama. The Alabama trooper did the same.

After looking both ways and waiting for three or four cars to speed by, we crossed the two west bound lanes, stopped on the interstate's gravel shoulder, and waited while Suits and Dodson ran down the steep bank to join two Mississippi troopers down at the Nova. The vehicle was resting precariously on its passenger side, and though the engine had stopped, the front wheels were still spinning. The Mississippi troopers had trained their spotlights down the hill and the area was illuminated as well as it could be.

"Hey!" came a voice from inside the car. We could hear it at the top of the hill some thirty or forty feet away.

"Hey!" one of the troopers said.

"Help me! I'm hurt!"

"Can you wait on a wrecker?"

There was resignation in the voice when it said, "Yeah, I guess so."

"There's one on the way. Where you hurt?"

"I think my arm's broke."

Up the hill, I looked at Will. "Hear that? I'm 'hut'; I think my 'ahms bwoke.' That's our man."

Will nodded. I had my doubts as to whether he had gained any more enthusiasm about the case. He would be there, but it was clear that he had little or no emotional investment in it.

I stepped gingerly down the hill, trying to keep from sliding into the rainwater that filled the shallow ditch at the bottom, and walked up to Suits and Dodson.

"You guys okay?"

Suits nodded. "We never really got that fast. I think Larry had one close call when we tried to merge onto the interstate, but other than that, things went off pretty good."

"Larry?" I said.

"Some bitch in a BMW wouldn't move over."

"No damage?"

He shook his head. "Nope."

I looked around. "Anybody know where Scarborough is?"

Suits and Dodson started looking around also. Just then Scarborough's patrol car stopped on the shoulder of the highway behind the others. He stepped out of his car and walked over to Will who was still observing the proceedings from the shoulder of the highway.

"I wonder where he was?" I said.

"It's not generally known," Dodson said, "but he's got a girlfriend out in Grand Bay. He was probably knockin' boots."

I nodded. That was why he wanted to be a part of this detail, so he could be close to his lover. Well, we didn't need him.

One of the troopers, a large red haired man with a name tag that identified him as 'Meriwether,' walked over to me just as the ambulance skidded to a stop on the highway. His gray and blue uniform and patent leather gear were perfect.

"You the detective?" he said in a decidedly southern accent.

"I am. Henry Faulkner, Mobile Metro SO."

"Ken Meriwether. He's prob'ly gonna need to go to the hospital. What all you got on'im?"

"If he's the man I think he is, he's wanted for Suspicion of Murder. We've got him entered in NCIC."

"Well, let's just find out if he's the man you think he is."

He stepped around to the roof of the car then motioned for me to do the same. We both looked in through the broken windshield.

"That him?"

Crumpled behind the steering wheel was a black haired man, short, with a stocky build.

"Hey, Rhett," I said.

"Hey," he answered back.

"You got your driver's license on ya?"

"Yeah, but I can't get at it right now. My arm's broke."

"Okay. Just hang on. The wrecker'll have you hooked up in a minute."

I looked at Meriwether. "He answered to his name; he's got that tidewater accent; and it looks like him. It's him."

"Okay, when he gets outta the hospital, we'll put him in the Jackson County Jail. I want to hold him on something to cover ourselves for runnin' him off the road. You understand."

I nodded. "Sure." I paused. "When you think he'll see the judge over here?"

"Well, we got a memo that said that bond hearings would be held every day, as normal. But I'd guess there wouldn't be an extradition hearing 'til next week, after the first."

Shortly thereafter a wrecker driver walked by, tugging on a thick wire cable with a hook on the end. He found a place on the frame of the car, at the bottom of the driver's door, where he secured it. Then he walked back up the hill and stood at the back of the truck, next to the controls. Suits, Dodson, Meriwether, and I, and the other trooper stood back about twenty feet as he turned on the winch. Slowly at first, then with a thud, the Nova flopped over onto its belly and rocked back and forth twice. From the inside, we could hear Tolliver yell.

Meriwether waved the ambulance crew down the hill, and a man, a woman, and a gurney slowly worked their way down to the car. By the time they arrived, Meriwether and his partner had the driver's door open and were helping Tolliver out of his vehicle.

"Which pocket's your license in, Rhett?" I said.

"My back. Owww."

I reached in his right hip pocket and took out one of those cheap, faux leather wallets. A North Carolina license in the name of 'Rhett Hampton Tolliver' was in the front pocket, the one with the clear plastic window. I slipped it out, copied down his personal information, and handed it to the trooper with whom I had not yet spoken. Then I looked up the hill and gave the thumbs up to Will who was still talking to Scarborough.

The attendants strapped Tolliver onto the gurney and began working to splint his right arm. Meriwether took out his handcuffs and affixed one cuff to his left arm and the other to the bar on the gurney.

"What are you doin'?" one of attendants said. She was an overweight female with brown hair.

"This guy's under arrest."

She looked at him with a smirk and went back to her work on the fractured limb. Tolliver hollered as she wrapped gauze around a plastic splint.

"Where they takin' him?" I said to Meriwether.

"Singing River Hospital in Pascagoula. The car'll be towed to the Public Safety lot in Gulfport. It'll be there for your man to come and do what he needs to do," he looked toward the somewhat mangled vehicle, "though I don't know how much good it's gonna do for ya now."

"It's good enough. You don't see a lot of '74 or 5 Novas runnin' around. And the tag; just don't let anybody monkey with the tag."

He nodded. "It'll be just like it is." He reached in his shirt pocket. "Here's my card. Have your man call me when he's ready."

I took it and nodded. What I really wanted to do was talk to Tolliver, but any statement he made right then would be considered under duress and not useful. I'd have to wait until he got to jail.

As the EMTs worked on Tolliver and the wrecker driver struggled with the car, I walked back up the hill toward Will. Scarborough had left, and Will was standing with his hands in his pockets rocking from side to side.

"Well, did he confess?"

"No, but he did break his arm."

"Serves him right."

"But it's what he didn't say that helped us. He didn't ask why we were chasin' him; he didn't ask why he was under arrest; and he didn't ask who I was."

"You think he'll crack?"

"I couldn't tell. He's going to the hospital first, then to jail. I want to get to him tomorrow before he gets a lawyer."

"Let's hope he don't get smart."

491

Chapter 58

The next morning at eight thirty, Will and I parked in the gravel parking lot at the County Courthouse in Pascagoula in order to the see if the Sheriff was in before heading over to the county jail for a bond hearing. We were there to wave the flag for our own Sheriff. He'd told us to stop by and say 'hello.'

In our possession was a copy of the probable cause warrant for the arrest of Rhett Tolliver. We didn't expect to find the County Sheriff in on New Year's Day. We were surprised.

"You boys think you got a pretty good case?" Sheriff Tim Powers said. He was a short, rotund man with a round face, a perpetual smile, and no hair. He met us at the door to his office and laughed as he slapped Will, a man that he had never met, on the back.

"We think so, sir," Will said. I could tell he was disgusted.

"Well, good, good. Glad to hear it."

Powers talked like every other southern sheriff I'd ever met, part politician, part salesman, part good ole boy from down the road, and part law enforcement officer.

The sheriff had three main duties: run the jail, service legal process, and provide courthouse security. Law enforcement for unincorporated areas was a secondary concern in most counties as any cities or towns of any size and consequence within the county were usually more than willing to trade police service for the increased tax revenue that would come to them with incorporation. The state police have the real responsibility for enforcing laws out in

492

the rural areas. Running the jail and serving process could best be farmed out to private enterprise, and judges would rather have their own police forces anyway; therefore, in my opinion, the sheriff could effectively be put out to pasture. But he never would be. The office was a political entity and people love politics, for whatever reason.

"How's ole Andy doing?" He was talking about our own sheriff.

"Doin' good, doin' good," Will said.

"I met him at a convention up in Memphis a few years ago; a real nice guy. I liked him a lot. When does he stand again?" I didn't know what he meant, but Will did.

"Next November."

"I got another year myself. Any opposition?"

"Not really. I've heard a couple'a names, but nobody's made anything public yet."

We had both heard that one of the circuit judges, a prominent local defense attorney, and a very popular ex-district attorney, had all expressed, for who knows what reasons, a desire to run for sheriff. Why these three would give up legal careers to take on the headaches of the sheriff's office was beyond me, but Will had heard that the Sheriff had rubbed them all the wrong way at one time or another, especially when it came to bail bonds and the bonding process. My guess was that the judge and the DA were both being courted, and would be backed, by outside interests.

"Well, you tell ole Andy that if he needs any help at all, to just pick up the phone and call me. I'll be right there."

"I will, sir. I will." Will looked at me. I took the cue and looked at my watch.

"Well, we better be moving along if we're gonna meet that hearing," I said.

"I understand. You boys take care. And stop by and see me when you're back in town."

Will shook his hand. I stood away from him and nodded. There was something kind of smarmy about the guy, and I didn't really want to touch him. We turned and walked out the doorway, down the hall, and back outside.

The county jail was newly built; a modern-looking structure, made of brick, and surrounded on three sides by chain link fencing with serpentine razor wire along the top.

It looked like a thousand other jails, but it was a monument to the sheriff's political acumen that he was able to talk the county out of the several million dollars needed to construct the five hundred bed facility, which featured a kitchen, law library, and exercise yard complete with weight benches. It had always puzzled me why sheriffs provided physical fitness equipment to inmates, equipment that allowed criminals, while in jail, to get bigger and stronger. In my mind, the sheriff was taking a big chance that they would, when they went back out on the street, be able to best his deputies in hand to hand combat.

We were directed by the docket room intake officer through a thick, steel door on the east side of the building, which opened into a large room populated by two rows of about ten plastic chairs each, all bolted to the floor. A desk, out of which sprouted a thin microphone, sat directly in front of a large picture window. The same kind of plastic chairs, as well as another steel door, was on the other side of the glass. Will and I were alone in the room. I looked at my watch. It was ten to nine.

"This room smells," I said. I couldn't quite put my finger on it, but I think urine was in the mix.

"Well, I guess so, Son. Ever' jail I ever been in stinks."

I smirked and shook my head. "Hey, they've got prisoners and they've got bleach. What's the big deal?"

"You know them boys don't have to work, unless they want to."

"Well, still, I don't know why the judge puts up with it."

We sat in silence for the next five minutes. My eyes ran around the bare, yellow walls and across the hard

494

concrete floor. It was all very stark and cold. I had made up my mind long ago after working a short time in the jail that I never wanted to be incarcerated for any reason. In fact, my worst nightmares always included being jailed.

At two minutes to nine, a tall, distinguished-looking man wearing an overcoat and tasseled loafers, followed by two green shirted corrections officers, walked into the room. He had an orange suntan, no doubt honed by hours on the golf course. One of the jailers was carrying a plastic file box and sat the box down on the desk. The gray haired man took off his coat and laid it on the back of the leather chair. He was wearing a pink polo and navy slacks underneath. He sat down and began to situate the files and papers that he removed from the box. Then he looked at us and smiled.

"Which case are you here about?" the judge said.

"State of Alabama versus Rhett Tolliver, Judge," Will replied looking alternately at me and then back at the man.

"What's the charge?"

"Murder, sir."

"Oh." He sounded surprised, as if he never had to deal with anything more than drunks and wife beaters.

"Do you have a warrant?"

"A copy, yes sir."

"Let me see it."

I handed the certified copy to Will who handed it to the judge. He looked at it.

"Okay, well, we'll try to get to him close to the front."

He moved some more files around and then looked at the male corrections officer. "Call'em."

The officer went over to the intercom on the wall and pushed the button. "Bring'em in."

At that moment, the large door behind the glass opened and six prisoners, all wearing orange jumpsuits, white socks, and slides shuffled into the room. Tolliver was the third in line, easily recognizable by the cast on his right arm and a limp that slowed his gait. His face was expressionless, though I thought I saw a smile cross his lips, for just a millisecond.

The judge cleared his throat and leaned forward to speak into the microphone.

"Be seated." The five men and one woman behind the glass all took seats in the chairs.

"I'm Judge Johnstone. I'll be setting bonds this morning." He looked at the first file in his stack. "Rhett Hampton Tolliver."

At the corrections officer's direction, Tolliver rose and walked toward the glass. He took his good arm and smoothed back his black hair, which I could now see was dyed – and not a very good job of it.

"You're charged with Eluding Police, Reckless Endangerment, and Reckless Driving. I'll set your bond at five hundred dollars per offense." He shuffled the papers again. "Ah, there are some gentlemen here from Alabama, and . . . they want you for Murder over there." He looked up at Tolliver who stood motionless, with a blank look on his face.

"So, unfortunately, that's going to force me to hold you without a bond pending an extradition hearing next week." He paused. "Do you have a lawyer?"

Tolliver shuffled his feet. "No."

"Okay, well, they'll deal with that on Monday. For now, have a nice weekend."

"Hey." It was Tolliver. He raised his good arm. "Could I speak?"

"Go ahead."

"Look, I don't need no lawyer. I hadn't killed nobody in Alabama."

"Well, Mr. Tolliver, that's why we have court, to decide these things."

"Well, can't I go ahead back over there and get this thing cleared up?"

496

I could see the judge pondering. "So, you want to waive and forego an extradition hearing and go back with these men today? Is that right?"

"Yeah."

"What about these charges that the Mississippi people have on you?"

"Well, can I plead guilty to'em and be done with it?"

The judge looked at us. I really couldn't believe what I was hearing. He either didn't know that Zoe Woods, if he ever knew her name, was dead – an unlikely circumstance – or he was supremely confident that he could beat the charge. I stared at his body language and tried to get a read.

"If he wants to come, and it's all right with you, Judge, we can take'im," Will said.

The judge smirked and raised his brows. He realized that he was only jumping the gun by one court appearance and giving the defendant what he wanted anyway. But I think the thing that bothered him the most was that Tolliver was doing all of this without benefit of an attorney. Somehow, in the judge's mind, I think he not only thought that it was a bad move legally, but it was also an affront to the profession itself that somehow Rhett Tolliver might not see the value in retaining counsel.

He looked back at the glass. "Are you sure you don't want a lawyer, sir?"

"I ain't done nothin', Judge."

"Okay. I'll have the paperwork sent over from the courthouse. You sign it and have the jail get it back to me before noon, and I'll release you into the custody of these two gentlemen here." He paused and looked at him hard. "But I think you're making a huge mistake."

"I just wanna get outta here, Judge."

497

Two and a half hours later, after several cups of coffee and a drive around town, we were back in the intake room of the Jackson County Jail waiting for Rhett Tolliver to be released.

Will yawned and closed his eyes as we sat on the same kind of plastic chairs as earlier. I was wide awake from the coffee, but anxious to get home.

"So, what about that Tolliver, huh? You think he thinks he can beat this case, or is he just dumb enough to only be thinking about getting out of *this* jail, not realizing he's just gonna get put back into another one?"

Will spoke with his eyes closed. "Prob'ly a little bit'a both. He prob'ly can only see about twenty minutes ahead."

At that moment, a female corrections officer walked Rhett Tolliver through the jail doors and into the waiting room. He was wearing the same long sleeved, red and blue flannel shirt and jeans as he had at the accident site, albeit the shirt was stained with a couple of drops of blood, and the right sleeve was cut to accommodate the cast. His brown Brahma brand steel-toed boots were scuffed on the toes and also had a couple of drops of blood on them.

The corrections officer handed me a clip board and indicated with her finger where she wanted me to sign. I scribbled my name quickly and handed it back to her.

Then I looked at Tolliver and thought. His arm in a cast gave him a ready-made weapon, so I took a handcuff and cuffed his left wrist and took the other cuff and put the swing arm underneath the part of the cast that ran over the palm of his right hand. It was awkward, but his arms were secured together and his cast couldn't be used to brain me.

"Let's go, Mr. Tolliver," I said as we started to the door.

"This don't feel too good."

"Well, I'm sorry. We'll be back in Mobile in about twenty-five miles. Until then, you're under arrest for Murder, and you gotta be handcuffed in the car."

He said nothing. I looked at Will.

"You wanna drive, or you want me to?"

498

He fished in his pocket for a set of keys. "I'll drive. Maybe it'll keep me awake."

Thus began our journey to try to get justice for Zoe Woods.

Chapter 59

When we arrived back in Mobile, it was shortly after two. We went immediately to the Metro Jail and had Rhett Tolliver booked in under an open count of 'Murder'; a kind of catch-all charge that meant it could be straight Murder, Capital Murder, or even Manslaughter or Negligent Homicide, depending on what the circumstances were, and which could be changed at arraignment by the prosecutor. I asked the supervisor, Logan, a woman who had worked there for over twenty years and who was there when I spent my short nine month stint on the midnight shift, to expedite things. She had Tolliver photographed and fingerprinted within fifteen minutes.

While we waited, I got on the phone to the dispatcher and had her contact Roy Rogers. He called back in five minutes.

"Roy?" I said.

"Yeah."

"I need you to go to Gulfport, to the trooper's impound lot, and work up that red Chevy Nova over there. This is in the Zoe Woods homicide. It's been wrecked, but get what pictures you can; and make sure you take the tag off." I paused. "When do you think you can do it?"

"Prob'ly, Monday."

"Okay. When you finish the outside, have it towed over here, and I'll have a search warrant ready. Then you can give it a good going over. I'm looking for blood, women's clothes, any kind of cutting tool, the victim's prints, and, oh, yeah, the tires. Get enough to make a comparison of the tires."

"Sure."

"You know what to do."

"Sure." His tone was not cheery.

Will and I checked Tolliver out immediately and took him to the office for a talk. We settled into interrogation room one and started at a little before three.

I made sure the recording devices were in operation when Will read him his rights. Tolliver said again that he had done nothing wrong and just wanted to get it all cleared up.

"Mr. Tolliver – can I call ya 'Mikey'?" Will said.

He had told me to let him go first at interrogating Tolliver. I wasn't wild about the idea, but he was the boss. My guess was that he wanted to find out what he needed to know and get out of the way before he lost interest.

Tolliver looked at him with a curious face. He sat up straight at the table with his left hand cuffed to the iron bar. I looked closely and thought I saw a couple of signatures already on the cast, names he had probably gotten while at the hospital. If they were nurse's names, I'd eat my hat.

He had a confident look about him; by that I mean that he held his head erect, and at times, lifted his jaw and cocked it back slightly while pursing his lips. He looked prepared to answer whatever question he was asked, or deny whatever he was being accused of. It seemed almost as if that he believed that no one should have the audacity to question him, his actions, or his motives.

Wide and expressive blue eyes sat under brows that were in such a position on his face as to give him a permanent look of surprise. His thin lips were drawn in a tight line and they contributed to his arrogant look. His ears and nose were oversized, too large for his age, but not grotesquely so. His hair was parted on the right side, combed over, and it looked as if it had been plastered in place by hairspray. Large and calloused hands at the end of muscular forearms sat motionless on the table. His large Romanesque head and olive complexion gave him an appearance that your normal, average, everyday, garden variety, dyed in the wool barroom bimbo would most assuredly go apeshit over.

"Yeah, sure, if you want," Tolliver said.

Will started off by asking him questions about his hometown, his family, his prior police record, and what he liked to do for fun. He was just trying to get a feel for his personality and gain his trust. Tolliver was guarded but not obstinate.

"You call yourself 'Mikey' sometimes, don't you?" Will said.

He nodded. "Sometimes."

"Does Myrtice know you as Rhett or 'Mikey'?"

"She calls me Rhett, or 'Hamp.' That's my middle name. Sometimes, 'Tink.'"

"Why do you call yourself 'Mikey'?"

He shrugged. "I don't know. I never liked my name. My mama said she got it outta some book. What'd I care about a name from some book. None of the other kids had a name like that." He seemed disgusted but not angry.

"Well, 'Mikey' is your brother's name, right?"

"Yeah, well, Michael. Some people call him 'Mikey', I guess."

I was taking notes off to the side. Will had gotten him to acknowledge that he had, or could have, told Zoe Woods his name was 'Mikey.'

"Before last night, when's the last time you were in Mobile County?"

He looked up to the ceiling. "Oh, I don't know. A month or so, I guess."

"How about before that?"

He shook his head. "I don't remember, really; in the summer, maybe?"

"When did you ever live here?"

"Live here? Well, I hadn't really lived here. I just stayed a while with Myrtice."

"Were you here last Christmas?"

"No."

"New Year's?"

"No, I don't think so."

"After?"

"Well, maybe." He shrugged.

"January?"

"I don't know."

"February?"

"I don't know."

"Well, we know you were."

"Okay, maybe I was."

Tolliver had told the people in Birmingham that he had worked at Tyndall Poultry, but I had checked and they had no record of him in their employ. Will was just bluffing him; we couldn't prove it, but he had taken the bait.

Will took a deep breath and leaned back. Tolliver wasn't gonna come off of this quickly, or easily. His body language was tight; by that I mean that his hands were clasped in front of him, his feet were crossed at the ankles, and his head was held straight, eyes forward.

"What do you do when you come to town?"

"Nothin' much. I just hang out with Myrtice and, you know."

"Are you two lovers?"

"Well, yeah."

"For how long?"

"Since the summer."

"So, last year you'd'a been lookin' for somebody when you were in town."

"Well, you know," he chuckled, "a man's gotta do what a man's gotta do."

502

"Have you ever been to a bar called, The Society?"

"The Society? I don't know."

"We know you've been there."

He looked at Will with a short but hard stare. "Maybe so. I been to a lotta places in town."

"What do you like to do when you go out?"

"Oh, have a few drinks, dance a little, you know."

"Dance?"

"Yeah, sir. I can shore cut a rug." He chuckled.

"Drink?"

"Well, yeah. Don't ever'body?"

"I guess. What's your poison?"

"Black Russians, with a dab'a chocolate sauce."

I took a deep breath and exhaled. With Myrtice hearing his confession, and now his own admissions, we were close. I just didn't know how we were going to get him to come off his defense.

"Let's talk more about The Society. You met a woman there."

"I talk to a lotta women wherever I go. Women like me."

"But there was one special one. Zoe Woods. You met her last February at The Society."

He looked up at the ceiling. "Hey, maybe. Like I say . . ."

"You bought her a few drinks; took her out."

He shook his head. "Sorry. I don't remember her."

Will looked at the floor. "What kind of work do you do, Mikey?"

"Oh, I've done a bunch'a jobs. I move around a lot."

"What specifically?"

"Well, you know, restaurant work. I'm a chef, and I've worked in the hotel industry."

He washed dishes and cleaned the grounds of hotels, was my guess. Will's patience, I could tell, was

503

beginning to wear a little. He would get to the meat of it all, shortly.

"You remember a woman named Laurie Singleton, Mikey?"

He looked down at the table and thought for a minute. "Oh, sure, that chick up in Birmingham. Yeah, nice gal. I really liked her."

He remembered the woman that he didn't kill, but not the one he did. Interesting.

"How long have you had that old Nova?"

"My car?" He paused and waited, trying to figure out our angle. "Oh, for years. It was a good car. Never give me a bit of trouble."

"Why did you run from us?"

"Well, you know, I got spooked."

"About what?"

"Well, nothin'. I just get blue light fever, sometimes."

"Well, you ruined a good car."

He shrugged. "I'll get another one."

Will took a deep breath, and I could tell he was about to get going.

"Mikey, we know what you did. You met this Zoe woman at The Society Lounge, had a few drinks, danced a little, and then took her out. You cut her throat and left her on the side of the road." He paused. "Why'd you do that?"

"No, sir. No, sir. That's crazy." His eyes widened slightly.

He was right. It was crazy.

"Be careful, Mikey. You don't know what we know," Will said.

"No, no, no. This is ridiculous. I didn't kill nobody."

"You didn't do it?"

"No."

"Will you take a polygraph?"

"A what?"

He knew exactly what.

"A lie detector."

He paused and looked at the table. I could see him wondering if he could beat it.

"Well, yeah. I want to clear my name."

"I'll set it up for Monday."

We put Rhett Tolliver back in jail and got back to the office about six. Will made a pot of coffee, and we sat around and went over what we had. I started typing out the search warrant for Tolliver's car.

"I think our case is better," I said. "He admits to using the name 'Mikey'; he admits to drinking Black Russians – with chocolate sauce; and he volunteered that he 'hadn't killed nobody'; which means that he killed 'somebody.'" I paused. "And we still don't know what we're gonna get from the car."

Will slurped loudly. "It's good, Son, but there are still a lotta holes." He took another drink and continued.

"Let's look at what we can prove and how we can prove it. One, we can put him in the bar by a fingerprint on a two dollar bill from the waitress. But a good lawyer will cast some doubt on when she got that bill. He never said he wadn't never in the bar, or how many times.

"Two, we got the ID of the car at the bar on the night Zoe Woods was there. But the witness is a convicted 'weenie wagger.' How good is he gonna be in court?

"Three, we got Mrytice hearing him confess, but is she gonna be willing to put the finger on the one that's been givin' her the dick?

"Four, we got a tentative ID from his boss in Birmingham namin' him as 'Mikey'; but gettin' him ID'd by the drunks in The Society, if we can find'em, is gonna be the devil. What kind of witnesses are they gonna make?"

He paused and took another drink. "The only thing we got going for us is that tire track, Son, and you know as well as I do except for the fact that they're bald, they're not

505

alike." He looked out the window. "That's the only thing that puts him at the scene. Unless there's some blood or somethin' in that car, we might be suckin' wind."

"You sound like some of those weak-kneed prosecutors over at the DA's office."

"Well, we're gonna hear it all from'em sooner or later, anyway. We might as well try to get all their objections out of the way right now."

"He's guilty. I know it."

"It ain't what you know, Son, it's what you can prove."

Chapter 60

Two days later on Monday, I had to get the oil changed in the county car. I got there at seven thirty, so there was one ahead of me.

I parked in front of one of the empty bays and left the key in the ignition with the window down. Two or three cars, one of them a county commissioner's red Ford truck, were at the pumps being fueled when I walked into the office and picked up a blank work order from the tray on the table. I filled it out with a request for a service job and walked outside to lay it on the dash of my own vehicle.

Back in the garage's office, I settled in with a magazine and the television. The room was warm, and I was about ready to sack out when Josh came in.

"How ya doin', sir?" he said.

"Good, Josh."

"You here for a oil change?"

"Yes, sir."

Josh called everyone 'sir,' so I called him 'sir.' He sat down behind the desk and took off his green, county-issue ball cap, after which he took out a red kerchief and wiped his brow.

"You look pretty tired for a man that just came to work a half hour ago," I said.

"Whew, this is hard work, sir."

"You shouldn't take it so seriously, Josh."

"It's my work, sir. I gotta do it."

"Yeah, but you can't let it kill you."

"It's my work, sir. I gotta do it as hard as I can."

I nodded. "I understand."

"What'chu working on, sir?"

"Murder, Josh. Murder."

"That's bad, sir."

Josh had a way of passing judgment quickly, and getting to the heart of things.

"You know who did it, sir?"

"Yes, I do, Josh, but puttin' him in jail is gonna be tough."

"He belongs in jail, sir."

"I know it. But he may not end up there."

"He will, sir."

"How do you know?"

"'Cause he killed somebody, sir."

If it were only that simple.

At nine, I met Will at the office. He had just returned from Metro Jail where he had attended Rhett Tolliver's bond hearing. It was a task I had to talk him into. He was seated at his desk when I arrived.

"So," I said as I arranged myself in my seat. "What about Tolliver."

"No bond. I told the judge he'd been hard to find, and when we did, he ran. He said he agreed."

507

"Good. At least we don't have to worry about hunting him down anymore." I paused. "So, what do we do next?"

Will took a deep breath and exhaled. "We better go ahead and get him in a live line up before he gets a lawyer."

"Who should we invite?"

"Let's invite the barmaid . . ."

"Sis,"

". . . and Larry. They're the most likely to have been sober that night."

"What about Jerry Painter?"

"The weenie wagger? I don't know."

"Lincoln Hayes, the truck driver?"

He was silent. "Not yet. Let's see how it goes with Larry and, uh, Sis. If they can pick him out, then maybe we'll move onto the others. If they can't, we may have to. Besides, our problem is not puttin' him in the bar, he admits to that. It's puttin' him out there where they found the girl."

I nodded then picked up the phone. The jail said they could have a line up together for us by two that afternoon. I hung up and told Will.

"We want to be sure and get a look at the group they pick before we show'em to the witnesses," he said. "I wouldn't put it past them bastards at the jail to run a couple'a tall black boys in on us and call it a good group."

I chuckled when I thought of a motley looking group of jail inmates, all different from Tolliver, marching into the lineup room.

Next, I picked up the phone and called Sis at home. She was just waking up. I told her we needed her at the jail by two that afternoon. She said okay and said she would get word to Larry Flynn. My guess was that he was lying right next to her in the bed. I cringed as I thought of their two naked bodies entwined.

Then I called Rogers and told him to have Hernandez or somebody meet us there with a camera. He said he would.

"What'chu wannna bet they both bug out on us."

Will shook his head. "Not the waitress. She'll step up. But the bartender, he'll say he don't recognize him. He'll say he was too far away, even though he wadn't no more'n fifteen feet. I never thought he was with us. The woman though, she's got gonads."

At a quarter past two that afternoon, Hernandez and I met Susy Weaver and Larry Flynn outside the visitor's entrance to the jail. They arrived in Flynn's pickup, an older, rusty red GMC with shiny mag wheels that seemed out of place.

Sis stepped out of the passenger seat wearing jeans that looked like they were painted on. Her white blouse was translucent, and her red brassiere was clearly visible underneath. Red heels rounded out her ensemble. I wondered if she was trolling for a new man amongst the inmates in the lineup. I didn't have the heart to tell her the men wouldn't be able see her through the one way glass. Larry wore a white t-shirt and dirty jeans. It was clear he was looking for no one.

"Glad you came," I said.

Sis smiled and put her red hand bag under her arm. Larry nodded and looked uncomfortable.

"Ya'll got'im?" Sis said.

"Well, I don't know," I said. "If you see him, let us know."

Larry was silent. I looked from one to the other. Sis was wide eyed and excited and clearly had no clue what she was being asked to do. Flynn was nervous, and his eyes shifted from one side of the asphalt parking lot to the other.

Will stepped out of the door two minutes later. All eyes turned to him.

"Hey. How ya'll doin?" he said smiling. He looked at Sis. "Dern, woman, you're lookin' good."

Sis smiled wide. "Is he in there?" She pointed toward the door.

509

"Well, you tell me." He looked at Sis and Larry. "What we've got in there is six similar appearing men; one of whom may or may not be the man that you saw drinkin' with Zoe Woods. What I want you to do is walk in, take a look at these men, and let me know if any of them are familiar to you; and if they are, you tell me how." He paused. "Any questions?"

Sis shook her head. Larry was stonefaced.

"Okay," he said, "Sis, why don't you go first. Larry, wait outside." Will nodded at me, and the two of us, and Hernandez, followed Sis into the lineup room.

It was a small space, with cinderblock walls painted a dark brown. A one way mirror of thick, ballistic glass separated the space from a larger room where the prisoners were, and an intercom was on the wall next to the glass. On the other side of the glass were six men, all illuminated by footlights.

The men were all white, all between five foot five and six feet, and all about the same weight. They all wore the orange jumpsuits that are issued to felony inmates. In addition, the corrections officers had to wrap each of their right arms in a heavy layer of gauze to simulate Tolliver's cast. I stood back and surveyed the men who stood in a line and held placards with numbers from one to six. Tolliver held placard number four. Hernandez snapped three photos of the group, then turned and walked out.

Sis stood directly in front of the window. "Can they see me?"

"No," Will said.

She looked at Will and then back at the group. I could see her eyes moving from one to the other. She stopped on number four and then moved on. I watched as number one, a young man with a dark tan, moved the placard to his right hand and scratched his nose with the middle finger of his left, effectively giving us the 'bird.'

Number six, grabbed his crotch and then smiled. Number two looked at the floor, then took his left hand and shielded his eyes from the light.

"Do you see anyone you recognize?" Will said.

"I think so." She paused. "Number four looks like him."

"Number four looks like who?"

"He looks like the man that was drinkin' with Zoe."

"Can you say for sure?"

She paused and took two steps toward the glass. She nodded.

"Yeah. That's him."

"Okay, fine." Will looked at me. "Take her outside and bring Larry in."

I escorted Sis outside the room and walked Larry Flynn in. He took two steps in the room and stopped. Will spoke.

"Okay, Larry, take a look and see if you recognize anyone here."

His eyes went from one end of the group to the other in ten seconds. Then he looked at Will and shook his head. He said softly and with no conviction at all.

"No."

Chapter 61

An hour later, Rhett Tolliver, wearing leg irons, was in the back seat of my car, and Will and I were escorting him to the small Sheriff's Department Investigative Annex in the Albright Building at Dauphin and Royal Streets in downtown Mobile. We parked on the Royal Street side of the fourteen-story, early 1900's era structure in one of two spaces reserved for law enforcement vehicles. A vintage elevator in the lobby carried us laboriously to the ninth floor.

Brass doors slid open, and we stepped out onto shiny tiled floors. Will and I walked, and Tolliver shuffled down the hall, made a right hand turn, and then stopped in front of the of the Polygrah office. Herman Caine answered our knock.

Herman was a tall, muscular man with a wide smile and a short Afro haircut. His ebony skin made his teeth look like pearls. He was impeccably dressed in a starched white shirt, a red and blue striped tie, and dark gray suit pants over shiny, black loafers.

He had come to the Sheriff's Office ten years ago and after a short stint as a patrol deputy, was promoted and transferred to the jail as a supervisor. He was soon bored with that – as anyone would be – and went to the Sheriff. He wanted a new assignment, as a polygraph examiner. Then, for the next seven years, he immersed himself in the art of deception detection. He became a muckety-muck in the national association, lobbied the legislature to pass laws about it, and did a lot of work in the area of speech and writing content analysis. He prided himself in eliciting the truth from suspects by no other means than mental persuasion.

The room was small and sparse. There was a small couch and two wooden chairs on a checkerboard tile floor. A wooden door opened into the inner office where the examinations were performed. Next to it was a one way mirror.

"Come in, come in," Caine said smiling.

Tolliver went first. Will and I followed.

"Sit here on the couch, Mr. Tolliver."

Caine motioned to an old vinyl piece across from the door. Tolliver moved over and sat down with a thud.

Caine looked at me. "Do you have the questions?"

I nodded and took three typewritten sheets from the leather padfolio I carried. Included in the papers was a copy of the police report and the first supplement.

Whenever a suspect submits to a polygraph examination, the case agent has to supply the examiner with a set of ten questions with which to query the examinee. They contain strike questions that indicate guilt or innocence. I had written them the night before.

1. Is your name Rhett Tolliver?
2. Did you cut a woman's throat in Mobile, Alabama?
3. Are you from North Charlotte, North Carolina? . . .

And so on. I handed the list to Caine and watched as he glanced down the page. After his initial interview, he usually changed the wording in a few of the questions.

"Mr. Tolliver, are you ready?"

I looked over at Tolliver on the couch. Immediately, I noticed something different about him. The confidence that he had displayed earlier, both at the hearing in Mississippi and at our own interrogation, that chin in the air, hands on the table, smirk on his face kind of confidence, was now gone. In contrast, he was rubbing his uninjured hand on the leg of his jail clothes, his eyes were wide, and he kept looking around the room. I thought that we might finally have found something of which he was afraid.

Tolliver rose from the couch and began trundling toward the door, and the inner office. Caine followed him, and we watched through the window as he sat down in a black vinyl armchair. Caine quickly affixed the device to his body: the blood pressure cuff to his good arm, the basal skin indicators to his good hand, and the sensor across his chest to measure breathing. In two minutes, Tolliver was trussed up and ready to go. Caine took his place in a chair behind the instrument.

Will and I stood at the window and watched. He reached and hit the intercom button, and Caine's deep voice, in the middle of explaining the process to his subject, was distinctly audible.

"Now, we're gonna chat for a few minutes, then I'm gonna ask you the questions twice. The third time I'll be recording your responses with the instrument." Caine recited the constitutional rights. Tolliver waived.

He still looked nervous. I wondered why he agreed to this if he knew he couldn't handle it. Maybe he didn't know.

"What is your name?"

"Rhett Hampton Tolliver."

"Do you sometimes call yourself 'Mikey'?"

"Sometimes."

"Why?"

"I don't like my name."

"Who named you?"

"My mama."

"Where are you from?'

"Charlotte, North Carolina."

"Did you cut a woman's throat in Mobile?"

"Yeah, I mean, no. No."

"Well, which is it?"

He was silent. I couldn't believe he was folding this fast.

"No, it's no. I didn't kill nobody."

"Nobody said anything about killing anybody. I said did you cut a woman's throat in Mobile, Alabama."

He was silent. Caine's voice was slow, deep, and even.

"Did you meet a woman in a bar and cut her throat?"

He hesitated. "Well, yeah."

"How did it happen?"

He paused and swallowed. "We was drinkin' at this bar, and she said she wanted to go somewhere and fuck, so we got in the car and started drivin'. She told me where to go, so we went out to this field or somethin'. It looked like a

514

field. So, we was talkin', and I started tryin' to kiss her. Well, then she pulls this knife and says she wants my wallet. Well, I tried to take the knife away from her, and when we was fightin' over it, she got a cut on the neck. I reached across't her and opened the car door, and I kicked her out."

"Why didn't you call the police?"

"I was scared. I'm new in town, ya know. Nobody was gonna believe me."

"Did you have sexual intercourse with the woman?"

"Well, no, I mean, she took her pants off, but we didn't."

"Why not?"

"Well, 'cause she tried to rob me."

"What kind of pants were they?"

"What? Oh, jeans, I think."

"Did she take off her underpants?"

"Well, I don't know . . ." He paused. Then his eyes opened wide. "You know, she must have been on the rag 'cause her drawers was inside her."

"Inside her?"

"Yeah, you know; up her twat."

"You mean her vagina?"

"Yeah."

"Did you put them there?"

"Are you kiddin'? I think she must have been on her period."

"Where was the knife?"

"The knife?"

"The one she tried to rob you with."

"Uh, in the pocket of her jeans. I told you she took it out and told me she wanted my wallet."

"How did you get it from her?"

"I grabbed her arm and just took it from her."

"What kind of knife was it?"

"A, uh, a pocket knife."

"How big?"

He shut his eyes. "About two inches long; a foldin' knife."

"Did you have sex with her?"

"No."

"Did she ask you to?"

"What? Did she ask me to?"

"Yes."

"No, I mean she wanted to, but I wouldn't do it with her."

"Why not?"

"What? 'Cause she was sloppy drunk and nasty, and she acted like a bitch."

Slowly but surely, without ever having to turn on the polygraph machine, Caine led Tolliver through their meeting at The Society, their drinking party, and their fateful trip. Most of the first part of the story was true. It only turned unbelievable when Tolliver and his victim got out to the field and the so-called robbery was supposed to have taken place. He even mentioned another key piece of evidence.

"How did you tip the waitress?"

"I give her a two dollar bill; that's kinda' my trademark."

"So, what was she doing the last time you saw her?" Caine said.

"The last time I saw her?" He paused. "She was on the side of the road. I just drove off. I didn't wanna have nothin' to do with her."

He was right about that. She was on the side of the road. He just neglected to mention that she was flat on her back and surrounded by dogs.

I looked at Will. He was deadpan.

"We got enough?" I said.

He cleared his throat and shook his head. "It ain't never enough, Son." He paused. "But we're close."

About that time, Caine walked out of the interior room into the waiting area. He was smiling broadly.

"How about that. Record time."

"Thanks, Herman," Will said. "You'll get a transcript for us?"

"Sure." He paused and looked around. "Man, I was juiced in there. It was like whatever he said, I was gonna slice'im up with it."

"Great job, Herman," Will said.

"Thanks, Herman," I said. "You got all you need?"

"I do, if you do."

"Okay, we'll take him back to jail."

We finally got back to the office about six. I sat at my desk and rubbed my face with my hands. Will closed his eyes and put his feet up on the corner.

After a time, Will spoke. "Well, Son, now comes the hard part."

"What do you mean? Court?"

"Convincing twelve folks off the street that, not only did Tolliver cut that girl's throat, but that the crazy girl didn't deserve it. I mean, we can't prove she didn't try to rob him."

"Yeah, I know." I paused. Then I chuckled. "What about that story, huh. Her underpants in her vagina 'cause she was on her period."

"Well, the doctor can tell us about her cycle. No, what we gotta worry about is the fact that she was a 'b-girl' and that's what b-girls do, they roll drunks."

"I know that, but his story of how it happened is just so implausible. She's got to get a folding knife out of her pocket, get it opened, threaten him for his money, and then fight over the knife; all while her pants are down. That's all a little over the top. Especially, since she was the size she was. And did you see his forearms? Like Popeye. Heck, it shouldn't have taken him more than three seconds to disarm her."

"Yeah, but still, she's gonna be on trial as much as he is."

"That's what a prosecutor is for."

We sat in silence for several minutes. A huge weight, for me at least, had been lifted off my shoulders. In my mind, this case was over. We had investigated, gathered evidence, and identified the killer. There was no doubt about who had killed Zoe Woods. It didn't matter to me what some court or jury said. He was the man. My work was done. For me, it was all over but the paperwork.

Unfortunately, the Sheriff and the prosecutors didn't think so. Neither did the public. In order for this case to be considered solved, someone had to be convicted and sent to prison.

But that was their problem.

Chapter 62

The next day Will and I heard from Rogers about his examination of Tolliver's car. I took the call in the office.

"What'd'ja find out, Roy?" I said.

"Well, basically, nothing. I got some good photographs, although the car's a little mashed in on top. I went over the inside pretty good, but there weren't any latents worth lifting. I found a pocket knife, but a presumptive test for blood was negative."

"Save it anyway. Maybe the doctor'll at least be able to say that the wounds *could* have been made by it."

"No blood anywhere, no women's clothing, no nothing."

"Okay. How 'bout the tire print?"

"All four are bald; but no identifying marks."

"Okay, thanks for your help. Just bag the knife."

"10-4."

I gave Will the news as he walked in with a coffee cup. "Well, shit, Son, it's been a year. Did you think there'd still be somethin' in there?"

"We could always hope."

He shook his head. "This old boy probably hosed down that piece'a shit car the next day." He paused. "The first thing we need to do is put that ole boy in Mobile at the time of the killin'."

"How do we do that?"

"Well, we can call a little ole organization called the IRS."

Will made two phone calls and had someone on the line at the local office of the Internal Revenue Service. He put the call on speaker.

"Hey, Dave. This is Will Eubanks over at the Sheriff's Office in Mobile. How you doin'?"

"Good, Snuffy. I hadn't heard from you in years."

"I been layin' low. I got Henry Faulkner on the speaker with me. He works here too."

"How are you doin', sir?" I said.

"Good, good. What can I do for you, Snuffy?"

"Listen, we got an ole boy in jail for murder, and we're tryin' to shore up our case a little. Could you look and see if he was workin' here in Mobile in February'a last year."

"What's his name?"

Will supplied his name, birthdate, and social security number.

"I'll have to get back to you."

"That's fine. Mr. Faulkner will type up a subpoena and get it to you."

"Okay, good. Hey, Snuff, you remember me and you up in Washington that time?"

"No, sir. My memory's faded with age." His tone was guarded.

"Aw, sure ya do. We had us a time."

519

"Look, Dave, we gotta go. Call me when you have that information."

Before he could speak again, Will had disengaged the phone and was leaning back in his chair. His past was clearly a topic that was off limits.

"What was that all about?" I said.

"What's that?"

"That business about Washington?"

"That's somethin' that happened a long time ago that don't concern you, Son."

I held my hands up in surrender. My guess was that Will in no way wanted anything that he may have done in his past to make its way back to his wife, and that was fine with me. I knew that he had a checkered interpersonal history. He had even let a little of it slip to me on one or two occasions. I just didn't want it to affect our working relationship.

"Okay, okay. But if there's anything from that IRS agent that can help us, I'd sure like to get it."

"That will not be a problem, Son." He paused. "See, I know about *his* past."

Three days later, on Friday, Rhett Tolliver's arraignment was held in courtroom 4200 at the Judicial Plaza. I was there early to see who his lawyer was going to be.

Judge Anthony Kenny was perched high on the bench when I snuck in the back door and slid onto the second bench from the back on the right side. There were three other people in the gallery; two old women and a middle aged man both of whom sat stone still. All three looked stressed and beaten.

Kenny had a pencil thin mustache and a short Afro. He was in his late forties and had been appointed to the bench by the last Democrat governor of Alabama. He had been a defense attorney for fifteen years and was generally considered by all to have a decidedly pro-defendant lean.

520

Joyce Ritchie was the assistant from the DA's office standing at the front table behind a large tub of files. She was wearing a gray jacket and matching skirt that was stretched tightly across her bottom. When I sat down, she was gesticulating toward one of the lawyers standing next to a jumpsuit-wearing defendant, a young black man who kept looking over his shoulder at the older African American woman seated up front.

"Mr. King, you're charged with Rape in the First degree. How do you plead?" Kenny said.

"Not guilty," the young boy mumbled.

"Is there a bail recommendation?"

"Yes, Your Honor. State asks for no bail, for the safety of the community," Ritchie said.

"Any other compelling interest?"

Ritchie was stunned. I could see her wanting to make a remark about what other compelling interest there might otherwise be than public safety, but she didn't.

"No, Your Honor."

"Bail set at fifty thousand dollars." He banged his gavel. "Next case."

The door immediately to the judge's left that led to the holding cells opened in response to the bailiff's knock, and Rhett Tolliver shuffled, while a corrections officer walked, into the room.

The clerk called the case. "State vs. Rhett Hampton Tolliver, the charge is Murder."

"Mr. Tolliver, how do you plead?"

"Not guilty."

"Do you have legal representation?"

"No, sir."

Kenny looked down at his desk and moved pages. "I'm going to appoint Gregory Harper to represent you. Make no statements to the police until you talk to him. Do you understand?"

"Yes, sir."

I knew Harper. He had about ten years experience handling murder cases. I had dealt with him in one other case. He was an enthusiastic user of alcohol, and as I recalled, he could be creative with his choice of defenses.

"Ms. Ritchie, do you have a bail recommendation?"

"Your honor, the defendant was on the run for a year. We consider him a decided flight risk. The people ask for no bond."

Kenny snorted. "Is that true Mr. Tolliver?"

"I didn't know they was lookin' for me, Judge."

"Ms Ritchie, do you have any other factors?"

"Judge, he's from Charlotte, North Carolina; he has ties to South Carolina and New Orleans; and deputies chased him to Birmingham as well as Tallahassee. Add to that the heinous nature of this offense . . ."

Kenny didn't speak. I could tell it was causing him pain to agree with Ritchie.

"Okay. Mr. Tolliver, I hereby order that you be held without bond. Your attorney can revisit this issue in the future."

Kenny banged his gavel again. The corrections officer motioned toward the door and escorted Tolliver out of the room. Ritchie turned around to face the gallery and gave me the 'high' sign, apparently so as to meet her after the docket was completed. I acknowledged her with a wave and leaned back against the pew.

Court can be the most boring venue one minute, and the most exciting the next, depending on the circumstances. Recitations of law, procedure, and verbal housekeeping can almost put you to sleep, but introduce a human life into the equation, with all its emotions and passions, and it can get interesting very quickly. A dusty, dry, status hearing at which a trial date is set or changed is one thing. The jury announcement of guilt or innocence is quite another. One usually elicits yawns, coughs, or sighs; the other, groans, shrieks, or a paroxysm loud enough to elicit a response from the judge and the court police. The right case in the right court, in the hands of the right judge can really wake up your day.

I watched as six more felony defendants entered from the door to the judge's left and stood before him. A couple had lawyers, most did not. Will and I had reflected the night after his confession how lucky we were that Tolliver had not seen fit to, at any time, ask for legal counsel.

When he had called the last case, Kenny banged his gavel – something he was fond of doing that other judges were not – stood, and without comment exited the court through the door to his immediate right. Ritchie put files in her tub, took off her glasses, and turned toward me. I watched as she walked quickly down the aisle and slid into the pew next, but not too close, to me.

"So," she said, "this Tolliver case is yours?"

"Yep."

"Okay. It's going to be mine, also. I'll have it all the way to Circuit Court."

I nodded. "Good. Did you get a chance to read my report?"

"I skimmed it. Your case is pretty much circumstantial, isn't it?"

"It was. Two days ago, he confessed."

Her eyes widened. "Out of the goodness of his heart?"

"We sicced Herman Caine on him. He came clean in the polygraph office."

"Really. What made the difference?"

I shook my head. "I don't know if it was the wires and the machine, or the large black man running it all."

She grinned. "Can you anticipate his defense?"

"Sure. He said she tried to rob him with a knife. He wrestled it away from her, and in the process her throat was cut. He pushed her out and left her on the side of the road."

"Is it plausible?"

523

"Not to me. We've got pictures of her, and he could easily have taken the knife out of her hand without cutting her. She was found with her pants off, but he tells some inconsistent story of her wanting to have intercourse and him turning her down. How he plans to work that into the robbery angle, I don't know."

She looked away toward the front. "Okay. Well, put it all together and send it to me."

I nodded. "Herman's getting it typed up as we speak." I paused. "So, Greg Harper, huh?"

"What? Oh, yeah."

"Pretty tough?"

"Ah, well, he's not much on the law, but I think we can count on him for some theatrics."

"Smart?"

"I don't know. Let's hope he's dumb enough to put his client on the stand."

"Well, he's implicated himself twice: with his girlfriend and with us. If he doesn't testify, he doesn't have much else."

Back at the office, I filled Will in on developments. He didn't seem into it.

"You know this Greg Harper?" I said. Will had gone up against most every criminal defense attorney in town.

"Yeah. That little shit. When he gets to court, he's liable to jump up on the table and dance a jig."

I chuckled. Will could always keep a poker face when making his comments or telling a story; that was half the humor in them.

"I remember one time he was defendin' an old boy for rape. When the victim got on the stand he tried to get his client to whip out his pecker, for identification purposes, he said. The judge cut that short."

I chuckled. "Get outta here," I said in mock disbelief.

524

"Oh, yeah."

"Well, at least we know he'll try anything." I paused. "You ever hear back from your buddy at the IRS?"

Will cleared his throat. "Yeah, I did. He said that they had no record of Tolliver paying any federal income tax in that time period."

"Great."

We sat in silence. Finally, I spoke.

"You think we got a chance with this one?"

"Son, you always got a chance."

Chapter 63

Two months past. In the meantime, I finished the paperwork on Zoe Woods' murder and sent it over to the DA's office. Any investigative work necessary after they got the case would fall within the purview of Tommy Neill and his staff.

Will and I caught two murders before March 1st. One, a day-old newborn found in a creek off Old Pascagoula Road, was cleared quickly. We interviewed the guidance counselor at the local high school and learned the identity of a young girl who had gained weight then, all of a sudden, had miraculously gotten back her figure. We picked her up, and she quickly ratted out the baby's daddy. He was there when the child was born; then he dropped the male infant into the creek on his way home. The boy confessed, and we identified the child with a blood match.

The second happened on Martin Luther King Day in January. A young kid was found shot, stabbed, and tied to a tree in the woods near Interstate 10, at the last Mobile exit west. We identified him by his dental work – gold dollar signs inlaid in his front teeth – and spent two whole days in

Pensacola, Florida, talking to his family. He was a drug dealer, which meant that he could have been killed by anyone. His family claimed not to know anything about his dealings, and really, seemed to care little if his killer was found. Well, Will said, if they didn't care, he wasn't going to lose any sleep over it either. We exhausted all the leads and then shelved it. I made up my mind that when things got slow, I'd take another look at it. I always did.

We also did some work on the Harden case. Will checked with the feds and located information on Forrest "Sonny" Grimes, from Houston, Texas. The ATF had a file on him as a member of the Las Ratas motorcycle gang. A message put out on the southeast net located him in the Escambia County, Florida, Jail charged with possession of a sawed-off shotgun. We visited him the last week in February.

Deputies brought Grimes to a cinderblock interrogation room in the basement of the jail on West Leonard Avenue. It had none of the recording devices we were used to, so I had to get my writing hand ready.

"Mr. Grimes, my name is Eubanks." Will introduced me and I nodded.

"Good to meet'cha." His voice was a raspy tenor.

Grimes was fat. Rolls of it spilled over the belly chain that was around his waist. He appeared to be about fifty years old with graying hair pulled back in a ponytail. His mustache was long and thin, and if I didn't know better, I'd've said it was waxed; although I knew that mustache wax wasn't, as a rule, available in jail commissaries.

His face was round and full, and he had the obligatory scar on his right cheek giving him that thuggish look that he was so obviously seeking. The beard on his face was a day or two old, and added to his look, though his cobalt blue eyes didn't seem to fit.

Will reminded him of his constitutional rights, and he waived. Why do they do that?

"They call you 'Sonny,' right?"

"Yeah."

"When is the last time you saw Cal Harden?"

"Cal Harden?" He knitted his brows as if trying to remember. I made a note of his answer.

"Yeah; average height, a little chunky like you, rode with Las Ratas."

He said nothing. I could see him trying to decide if he should lie or not. That's what we were waiting for: a lie with which we could ensnare him.

"Tell us about your relationship with him. Did you two get along?" Will said.

"Well, sure. Yeah."

That was good. With that statement, he admitted knowing him.

"So, when's the last time you talked to him?'

"Uh, I don't really remember. It's been so long ago."

"You remember seeing him at the garage?"

"The garage?"

"Bryson's. Where he used to park his truck."

"Well, yeah, I mean, maybe. If you say so."

It was clear to me that he wasn't going to admit anything. I'm quite sure this wasn't his first ball game.

"Well, look, Mr. Grimes. Cal's dead. He was killed five years ago." He paused. "Did you kill him?"

The question seemed to catch him off guard. He pulled back visibly.

"I didn't kill anybody."

It was a telling answer, and I wrote quickly to get his exact words. Will jumped on him.

"Did you shoot Cal Harden?"

"I said, I didn't shoot anybody."

That's not what he said. For a tough guy, he was visibly shaken.

Will stopped to think. "Well, who killed him?"

Grimes shook his head. "I don't know."

Will looked at me. I cleared my throat.

527

"Sonny," my tone was smoother, "where were you when you heard Cal was dead?"

He looked at me. "Well, that's been a long time ago. I might'a been at the garage. I remember I used to hang out there a lot."

"You never did say how you and Cal got along."

"We was okay, I mean, as best as I remember."

I decided to take another tack. "So, possession of a sawed-off shotgun, hunh? Tell me about that."

"Nothin' to tell, really. I was in a car with some dudes, and they pulled us over. The gun was in the back. It didn't belong to me, but they hung it on me anyway."

Maybe that was our hole. Will saw it also and climbed in.

"These guys in the car," he said, "they ride with you?"

"No. Well, one of'em does."

He was trying to appear co-operative.

"Who were these guys?"

"Uh, 'Slim' and Tony. 'Slim' rides, Tony don't."

We spent the next ten minutes probing Grimes about his two friends. 'Slim' was one of the men at the garage in Ocean Springs the day that Cal was last seen alive. Could they have been some type of 'hit team'? Were they going to do a job the night they were stopped? The shotgun that was in Grimes' possession when he was busted suddenly became our key piece of evidence.

"What's 'Slim's' real name?" Will said.

"What? His real name?"

Will stared at him.

"You know, I don't really know. I've known him for ten years, and I just call him 'Slim',"

We spent ten more minutes with him and then left. In the car, I looked at Will.

"Well, what do you think?"

"At least we've got something to work on now. We can make sure that shotgun is tested and traced. And, we can run down this 'Slim.' You never know, maybe he's got a conscience now. And, this 'Tony'; we can run him down, too. It's enough to keep us busy for a few days."

Chapter 64

The first week in March was Rhett Tolliver's preliminary hearing. I called Joyce Ritchie the day before and filled her in on Tolliver's confession. She said she didn't anticipate any problems getting him bound over to the grand jury.

We met the next morning, a Tuesday, in a sixth floor courtroom. The room was full with misdemeanor cases and felony hearings. I walked forward and took a seat in the jury box with four or five police officers, none of whom I recognized.

Ritchie was seated on the first row. A younger, less experienced state's attorney was busy handling the misdemeanants. He was a thin, bespectacled man with a head of brush cut brown hair who was obviously nervous. He kept picking up files, opening and closing them, then putting them down. His eyes darted back and forth from the judge to the defense table, then back to the files. At one point he reached up and wiped his brow.

I held a manila folder in my lap; a folder that contained a short list of pertinent points I wanted to make about Zoe Woods' murder, and a narrative of what I believed had happened to her – some of which I could prove, most of which I could not.

Scanning the gallery, I saw Robert and Evelyn Woods sitting about three rows back on the prosecution side. Their presence surprised me. It shouldn't have. Even if I was finished with Zoe Woods, they weren't.

Tolliver's case was called about thirty minutes in. Two drunk drivers and one domestic abuser provided the drama before the shackled and orange clad Tolliver was ushered in front of Judge Melissa Davis, a plump, middle aged woman with straight, dark hair. Davis had been appointed to the bench six years ago and had since won election on a platform of 'protecting the children.'

As Tolliver reached the defense table, Gregory Harper rose and almost ran to meet him. Ritchie and I met at the lectern at the end of the state's table.

Harper was forty but looked older because of a spread around his middle. He was of average height but looked shorter for the same reason. But his most noticeable feature was his shiny bald dome and the two inch long tufts of brown hair on both sides and in the back of his head. At first glance, it kind of made him look, to me, like a buzzard.

"Who is here for the prosecution?" Judge Davis said. Her voice was high and very feminine.

"Joyce Ritchie, ma'am."

"And, the defense?"

He cleared his throat. "Greg Harper, Judge."

"Mr. Tolliver, you're charged with murder. Has your lawyer explained your rights to you?"

"Yes, sir, uh, ma'am."

"Ms Ritchie, call your first witness."

"State calls, Henry Faulkner."

I stepped forward and raised my right hand. Davis asked me if I swore to tell the truth, and I said I did. I laid my manila folder on the table in front of me and waited.

"Mr. Faulkner, how are you employed?"

"As a detective for the Sheriff of Mobile County."

"And what is your principle assignment?"

"Major Crimes involving death and homicide investigation."

"Did you have the occasion to investigate the death of Zoe Woods?"

"I did."

"And what did your investigation reveal?"

"It revealed that on the night of February 19th of this past year, Ms Woods was in The Society Lounge located on Duval Street in Mobile. At that location, she met and spent some time socializing with the defendant, after which they left the bar, and the defendant drove to a remote location off Lauderdale Road. At some point, while they were parked there, the defendant used a knife or some other cutting tool to cut the victim's throat. He then raped her with her underpants, after which he left her on the side of the road. She died later."

I paused and looked at Tolliver who I noticed was without the cast on his arm. Harper was writing.

"The defendant was arrested after being sought for a year," I finished.

"Did you locate any witnesses that saw the two together?"

"I located one, a bar employee, who positively identified the defendant in a live line up as being with the victim on the night in question."

"What about his car?"

"I located one witness, a bar patron, who described the defendant's vehicle."

"Has the defendant made any statements to you?"

"The defendant confessed, in my presence, to drinking with the victim at the lounge; to leaving the lounge with the victim; to driving the victim to the location on Lauderdale Road; to fighting with the victim; and to cutting her, thereby causing the injuries that ultimately led to her death."

Ritchie paused. Then she said, "Is Lauderdale Road within the confines of Mobile County?"

"It is."

"Pass the witness."

Harper looked up. "Judge at this time, we would move for a summary acquittal of the defendant on the grounds that the state has used hearsay and supposition to make this case."

Davis leaned back in her chair. "Denied."

Harper looked at his legal pad. "Mr. Faulkner, was the victim found deceased on Lauderdale Road?"

"She was not. My investigation revealed that she was picked up by a passing ambulance and taken to the hospital."

"So, she was alive when she was found, is that correct?"

"Yes."

"Where did she die?"

"In Springdale Hospital."

"Now, regarding these statements made by the defendant, did he have any attorney present when he made these statements?"

"He did not."

"Mr. Faulkner, are you aware that the defendant was recently treated for a broken arm?"

"I am."

"How did he come by that injury?"

"He was injured in an automobile accident."

"In fact, his injury occurred at the time of his arrest, did it not?"

I could see where he was going with this, and I didn't like it. "It did not. It occurred prior to his arrest."

Harper looked down at his legal pad. He had no bullets to shoot and he knew it. He could keep this hearing going for hours if he wanted to, but there was no need.

"Now, you testified that the defendant was identified as being with the victim by a lounge employee, is that correct?"

"Yes."

"What is her name?"

Ritchie spoke up. "Judge, in the interest of time, the names of all the people interviewed in this case will be available in a full discovery."

"Is that good enough, Mr. Harper?"

He smirked. I could tell he was looking for something on which to jump but could find nothing.

"I suppose so, Judge, if the court will make available funds for a private investigator."

"I think we can scare up some money for that. How about a thousand dollars?"

"That's a start."

"Okay, anything further?"

"No, Your Honor."

Davis sat up straight. "After hearing the evidence presented, I rule that there is probable cause to bind this case over to the grand jury for further investigation." She paused and wrote, then looked up. "Anything on bail?"

"Judge, the state would ask that the defendant would be held remanded as at present," Ritchie said.

"Your honor, everyone is innocent until proven guilty," Harper said.

"Judge, it took a whole year to locate the defendant; he is from North Carolina and has no ties to this community; and this is a violent felony."

Davis nodded. "The no bond order stands." She looked at Harper. "We can revisit this issue at a later time if additional evidence surfaces."

I looked at Ritchie as I picked up my folder. She picked up her file. The Woods family rose and followed us out of the courtroom.

Back at the office, Will was talking on the phone. I fell into my chair and rubbed my face. Will hung up.

"How'd it go?" he said.

"Smooth."

"You pick up on their defense?"

"Looks like they're gonna claim we beat the confession out of him."

"Well, he's just lawyer'n, Son."

"I know. But it's disgusting to me."

Will laughed out loud.

"What's funny?'

"Of all the things you've seen and heard, and the places where you've put your hands, *this* is what's disgusting to you?"

Chapter 65

Spring turned to summer, and Rhett Tolliver was going on six months in jail. Will and I kept busy with whatever happened, including spending time on the Harden case.

It took until May, but Will finally located 'Slim.' Wayne Harris 'Slim' Stillman, a mechanic, was living in Hattiesburg, Mississippi. Will had gotten the information from a Mississippi Bureau of Narcotics agent who put the touch on an informant in nearby Star, Mississippi.

We caught Stillman at home, one afternoon, at about six o'clock, just as he was getting in from work. Home, for him, was a seventy-two foot double wide with a metal outbuilding, in a park off US 11 on the west side of town. My guess was that the outbuilding housed his Harley. He pulled up in a beat up old, white, GMC just as we were knocking on his front door. I remarked to Will how much the old truck looked like Cal's International.

"Howdy," Slim said with a suspicious look on his face.

He was just like his name; six feet six and rawboned. He had sandy hair, long arms, and the boots on his feet had to be size fifteens. His nickname, stitched above the pocket of his blue work shirt, identified him.

"Good evenin', sir," Will said.

Slim stopped at the bottom of the wooden steps that provided access to the front door. "What can I do for ya'll?"

"We're with the Sheriff's office over in Mobile, Buddy. My name's Eubanks and this is Mister Faulkner. We was wonderin' if we could talk to you about a case we're working on."

I held up my star. Slim tensed noticeably. He wasn't expecting us – but, in a way, he was.

"Yeah, uh, sure. Come on in."

Slim walked as heavily as a thin man can up the steps and unlocked the door. We followed him up onto the little platform that functioned as a porch, and then inside the home. The large living room had a musty smell, which fit in well with the musty couch, the stained chair, and the dirty carpet.

"Sit down," Slim said.

Will and I took seats on the musty couch, and Slim put his metal lunch box down on a counter and parked himself in the stained chair. I prepared to write.

"We wanted to talk to you about Cal Harden."

He tensed noticeably, again, and his face went white. I noted his symptoms and thought about how I had never seen a man blanch that thoroughly, that quickly, in my life.

"Mr. Stillman, I can tell that this all means somethin' to you. What do you want to tell me?"

He swallowed hard and rubbed his hands. His head turned right, then left, then he looked at the floor.

"Go ahead and tell it. You'll feel better."

He looked Will right in the eye. "Look, I didn't kill Cal."

535

"Who did?"

He swallowed again. "Sonny."

"Why?"

"Over Cal's woman. He wanted her."

"Tabitha?"

"Is that her name? I didn't know her. Sonny just said they argued about it."

"He confessed to you?"

He nodded. "Yeah."

"What did he say, exactly?"

He took a deep breath and exhaled. "Man, this feels good. I been holdin' this shit in for a while now." He paused. "He said he saw Cal at the garage where Cal used to park his truck, and they had a argument. When Cal left in the truck, Sonny followed him and got him to pull over. Sonny walked up, and when Cal got out, Sonny shot him."

I wrote fast. Someone was holding out on us; Tabitha, or maybe McElhaney, the garage guy.

"Where'd this happen?" Will said.

"It was on Highway 90, close to the state line in Mississippi; over near The Red Barn. There's a wide spot in the road just past it, and that's where he pulled over."

I knew the place. The Red Barn was an old, rather infamous combination bar and liquor store located on US 90 a couple of hundred yards west of the Alabama state line. It was closed now, but in its heyday, every under aged teenager in Mobile made at least one trip there to purchase a forty ounce bottle of beer from the proprietors who were somewhat lax in their due diligence when it came to checking IDs.

"How'd the body, wind up off where we found it?"

He looked down. "Look, I don't know the area real well, but Sonny said he left his bike down at The Red Barn. He put Cal in the bed of the truck and drove him north. He left him next to a pasture, walked to a general store, and called me at Bryson's. I come and got him."

"Where'd you pick him up?"

"Uh, it was a general store up on the Airport Boulevard in Mobile County."

"Did you know what he'd done when you came and got him?"

"No. I mean, when I took him to his bike, I figured he'd done somethin'. But he never told me."

"When did he tell you what he'd done?"

"It wadn't until, I don't know, six months later."

"Why didn't you come forward?"

His eyes widened. "Are you kiddin'? He done killed Cal. He'd'a killed me, too." He paused. "I heard he's in the federal joint now. Ya'll, just don't let him out."

We spent the next hour firming up his story. Sonny had mentioned the murder only once since that time five years ago. That was one time when he was drunk, down in Florida. Slim had asked him about it later, and Sonny denied mentioning it.

"Tell me, that gun that Sonny had over in Pensacola. Was that the shotgun he used on Cal?"

"I don't know. But I know 'fore we was picked up, Sonny used to carry that thing ever'where."

Will looked at me, as he did whenever there was a lull in the conversation. I cleared my throat.

"Did Sonny ever make it with Tabitha?

"Not that I ever heard or saw."

"What were you and Tony doin' with Sonny over in Pensacola?"

He looked surprised again. "We was just out joy ridin; smokin' some weed and drinkin'."

He was lying, and I knew it. Judging by his expression, Will knew it too. It was something that would have to be ironed out later. My guess was that they were looking for some place to rob.

"Who is Tony?"

"Tony is somebody Sonny knows. That was the first time I'd met him."

"His last name?"

He shook his head. "Don't know it."

It wasn't finished yet, and it would take a good bit of work to put it together, but in my mind, the case of what happened to Cal Harden was solved. We had to eliminate Slim as the shooter, and try to habilitate him as a witness, but it was possible. The trip to Jacksonville, a trip that at the time I thought was a waste, turned out to be worth it after all.

Chapter 66

The summer was a hot one in Mobile that year. The temperature crept up toward a hundred a couple of days, and it was close to it the day I was called back to the courthouse on Zoe Woods' murder.

The second week in July, on Wednesday, I starred in another performance in front of the Mobile County Grand Jury, sharing with them the story of Rhett Tolliver and Zoe Woods. Joyce Ritchie was the defacto master of ceremonies; the audience, the grand jurors themselves.

As I settled into my seat on the raised platform – the stage – I took a look at the group. It looked the same as always: fifty per cent retirees; twenty per cent female professionals; twenty per cent working men; and ten per cent who looked unemployed, who looked as if they were there just to get off the street.

"State your name, please."

"Henry Faulkner."

"And how are you employed?"

"Mobile Metro Sheriff's detective, assigned to the Major Crimes Bureau."

"On February 19th of last year, did you have occasion to investigate the death of Zoe Woods?"

"I did."

"Have you made a probable cause arrest in that case?"

"I have."

"And who have you arrested?"

"Rhett Hampton Tolliver."

"And how did you arrive at his identity?"

I began slowly, by telling about seeing Zoe at the hospital, a description of the crime scene, her injuries, and what we got from the scene. I moved on to what we got from Sis at The Society – the lineup ID, the description, and the two dollar bill with Tolliver's print; the red Nova from Jerry Painter; the 'bur' or bird – a Carolina wren – on the South Carolina tag; Tolliver's own admissions regarding his alias, 'Mikey,' and his favorite drink; Tolliver's confession to Myrtice; and finally, his confession to Herman Caine, including the admission about the underpants. It took about twenty minutes and two sips of water. When I was done, I looked at Ritchie.

"Are there any questions?"

A woman in a print dress, on the back row right, raised her hand. "You say, he confessed?"

"Not exactly. He told us that he was in the car with her, and at some point she produced a knife and attempted to rob him."

"Did she?" the same woman said.

"I don't believe so. The victim was a wealthy woman. She would have no need to rob him."

A blonde junior leaguer in slacks and a cotton blouse spoke up. "What were they doing out there on that road?"

The group giggled softly. The woman looked around, embarrassed.

"Presumably, they went to the area to have sexual intercourse," I said. "The defendant said that the act was never consummated."

There was silence. Then a scruffy looking man in dark slacks and a white shirt raised his hand.

"What kind'a drunk was she?"

He had obviously had some experience with barflies before. I couldn't let my answer taint the group.

"I think that testimony from the waitress and perhaps some others at the bar will show that the victim was a boisterous personality when she was under the influence of alcohol. But there was no indication that she had ever been violent with anyone that she met."

"Did she carry a knife?" the same man said.

"We found no witnesses that will testify to that fact."

The man nodded. Then an older woman with silver hair, in white slacks and a blue top, raised her hand.

"You mentioned something about her underpants earlier. What was that?"

"I'm glad you brought that up," I said. "When the victim came to the emergency room, nurses found her underpants inside her vagina. This is a fact that only the killer would know, and Tolliver mentioned it in his confession to Sergeant Caine."

"How did he explain it?" The older woman had a sick look in her face, as did several of the women, both young and old.

"He said that the victim was on her period and the underpants were absorbing her discharge."

Several female 'oo's and 'yuks' could be heard throughout the group. At that point, I thought I had them.

"Have you recovered the knife?" The speaker was an older gentleman with suspenders.

"No, sir."

"So, basically, you just have his confession, is that right?"

"Absolutely, not. We have witnesses that can put the two of them together on the night of her assault; we have a witness that puts his car at the bar on that same night; we have a tire print of a bald tire at the scene, the defendant's car bares bald tires. And, the defendant confessed to his girlfriend." I paused. "And, we have the decedent. She had to die somehow."

It sounded like a lot more than it was. In fact, when I recited the facts out loud, I almost agreed with the juror. It was a circumstantial case to be sure; but circumstances could be very powerful. And, there was nothing like a confession.

Ritchie looked around the room. "Anything else?"

When no one spoke, she turned to me and said, thank you. I gathered my file and rose.

"Oh, I have one more question."

The questioner was a young woman, about twenty-five, wearing a thin, white, pullover shirt and jeans. Her hair had blonde highlights.

I looked at Ritchie and sat back down. The woman continued.

"Do you know at all why he did that to her?"

"Well, I know what he said, and that it was to stop a robbery."

"Is that what you think happened?"

"Anything that I say would be pure conjecture."

"Yes, but what do *you* think?"

I looked at Ritchie. She shrugged as if to say, 'sure, why not.'

I took a deep breath and exhaled. "I think they went out there to have intercourse, and for some reason – probably too much alcohol – he was unable to achieve an erection. I think she ridiculed him for it, and when she did, he raped her with her underpants and did his best to try to kill her."

I heard a few 'ohs' and also a feminine chuckle.

"Well, I guess he showed her, hunh," the young woman said.

541

I wanted to answer, but I didn't.

When I walked out into the waiting room, I saw Susy Weaver seated in the corner reading a magazine. She was what passed for dressed up in yellow slacks and a white blouse. She smiled when she saw me.

"How's it going?" I said.

"Oh, you know, nervous as a cat. How was it in there?"

"Just answer the questions they ask you and don't volunteer anything. The DA'll get you to say what she wants you to say."

She nodded and looked down at her magazine. "You know, things just haven't been the same since all this happened; at the bar, I mean."

"How so?"

"Well, the reg'lars don't come in no more, not like they used to. We get a different crowd ever'night. Sometimes, I think they heard what happened and they're just there sightseein'." She paused. "Larry's thinking about sellin' the place."

"Get outta here. Why?"

"He thinks it's haunted. He says it's got bad mojo."

I thought of the cinderblock building and the wood floors, the bad lighting, and the stinking toilet and smiled to myself. The place had bad mojo long before Zoe Woods ever had a problem there.

"What do you think?'

She shrugged. "I don't know."

"Well, are your tips slowin' down?"

"Not really. Not yet, anyway. Larry thinks that things are really gonna get bad after the trial when everybody kinda forgets about the place. He says he's gonna put it up for sale before the trial starts and maybe he can get rid of it by the time it's over."

"So, what are you gonna do?"

She shrugged again. "I don't know. I guess I'll find another place to waitress. It's all I know."

542

"Wait, I thought you and Larry had something goin'?"

She frowned. "Are you kiddin'? Well, a long time ago, yeah, but," she shook her head, "not in years. He's just the boss. We been together a long time, but," she shook her head again, "we ain't together, you know?"

I nodded. "Well, you'll land on your feet."

"I hope so." She looked toward the door. "I just need to get through this, first."

"Hey, piece'a cake. All they'll ask you about is the lineup, maybe the two dollar bill. Just tell'em what you saw and heard."

About that time the grand jury room door opened and the foreperson, a middle aged man that sat on the front row left, stuck his head out and called Sis's name. She stood up.

"Hey, good seein' ya. Look me up, hunh?"

"Sure."

I watched as she wiggled past the foreperson and through the door. In her dreams I'd look her up.

Chapter 67

Rhett Tolliver's case was true billed by the Grand Jury, and he was indicted for straight Murder. I didn't expect anything else, really, and Will told me it was a foregone conclusion; but still, I was a little anxious until I got the word. I kinda hoped they'd throw in a Manslaughter charge, as a lesser included, just in case.

Joyce Ritchie called me the last week in July after the grand jury had reported out. She told me that the case was on the docket for September.

"That's pretty fast," I said.

"It is, but since he's been in jail almost nine months with no bond, his lawyer has filed a speedy trial motion."

"Who's the judge?"

"Hartsfield."

"Okay, I can live with that," I said.

"He'll be fair, and he won't do anything crazy like grant a motion to dismiss." She paused. "Look, we need to have a meeting."

"Okay, name it."

"Next week in my office."

"I'll be there. You want me to bring Will?"

She laughed. "Yeah, bring him. I love him. He's hilarious."

The next Monday, at three, Will and I met Ritchie at the DA's Investigative office. She caught us in the hallway and motioned us into a conference room at the end of the hall. We walked into a space outfitted like the situation room at the White House: a long conference table, overstuffed leather chairs, video screens, and a huge eraser board on the wall. Files and photos covered the table from one end to the other.

"This is some spread," I said.

"Yeah. Turns out your victim's family is kind of connected up in the north part of the county. The boss wants to make sure we nail this one. All this," she waved her arm around, "is to impress anyone that cares."

We took seats at the long table, Will and me on one side, Ritchie on the other. I spoke first.

"Joyce Ritchie, do you know Will Eubanks?"

"I think we've met once or twice."

"Hello, there, young lady." Will's voice boomed.

"Hello."

She smiled broadly. I could tell she was stifling a chuckle.

"So, what can we do for you?" I said.

"I just wanted to go over the case and make sure I have it all straight in my head." She looked at us with brows raised. "If I don't understand it, I can't sell it to a jury."

"Sure."

"Why don't I start and you correct me as I go along."

I nodded. Will leaned back in his chair and folded his arms.

"Apparently, Zoe Woods, our victim, lived on Lewis Circle about two blocks from this bar – what was it? The Society?"

"Correct."

"From your description, this place sounds like a real palace."

"It's an outhouse," Will said, "one step above a shithole, honey."

Ritchie chuckled. Will seemed to want to perform.

"Anyway," she said smiling and looking down at a legal pad, "Zoe comes to the bar often; apparently, she's kind of a fixture there. The employees know her and know she's slow. By the way, do we have a diagnosis on her?"

"We do not," I said. "Her family can provide that."

"She was crazy," Will said. He labeled everyone he found abnormal as, 'crazy.'

"So, on the Friday night in question, Zoe comes to the bar as usual and meets up with Rhett Tolliver. We know this because the bar maid picked him out of a live line up as being there, and she also supplied us with a two dollar bill that she says was given to her, by him, that night, as a tip."

"With his fingerprint on it."

"With his fingerprint on it." She paused. "They drink Black Russians, and dance, until at some point in time, and we don't know what time, the two of them leave. They go to a location on Lauderdale Road, and we know this because of a bald tire track at the scene, and the fact that his tires are bald."

"What are the chances, hunh?" Will said.

"Right," Ritchie said glancing at him with a smile. "Zoe Woods is found the next morning on the side of a little dirt trail off Lauderdale . . . by an ambulance?"

"How's that for luck," I said.

"I know, right? They take her to the hospital where she codes twice before being stabilized. She dies a week or so later from an infection." She looked at us both. "Good so far?"

"Well, you forgot his confession."

"We'll get into that in a minute." She studied her pad. "Do we have the knife?"

"No. It's been a year; it could be anywhere."

"Any evidence she ever carried a knife?"

I shook my head. "She was a b-girl, but no one ever talked about her rolling drunks. She didn't have to. She had money any time she needed it."

"Yeah, what about that? Why is she living in the projects, hanging out in dives, when she's got money?"

"She's crazy," Will said. Ritchie looked at him as if waiting for a further explanation. "She had a tumor and it made her all screwy," Will said a bit more diplomatically. "How it affects us is that if her mental state gets in, what she told us – basically, only the business about the 'bird' on the tag – is called into question. And, it also confirms why she acted so erratically.

"How it helps us is that she becomes a slightly more sympathetic victim. She goes from being just a barfly to a woman who was incapable of appreciating the consequences of her actions, includin' gettin' into a car with a man she barely knew."

Ritchie was transfixed by his evaluation. I wasn't. Will was an experienced, intuitive, competent, albeit rough around the edges police investigator who had seen and heard more than the two of us put together.

"Well," she said, "I think I get the picture." She cleared her throat and looked back down at her pad. "So, how about this confession?"

"Well, there are two. He confessed to his girlfriend, who is his brother's ex-wife, by the way."

"Sounds incestuous," she said."

"It does. She told us that he said that the two had fought, but that he didn't kill her; and she was alive on the side of the road when he saw her last." I paused. "Which is the truth, actually."

"Will she testify?"

"She's got to," I said. "But, you need to know they're lovers."

"Oh, okay. Well, what did he tell you?"

"He said they were in the car preparing to have intercourse, at which time she pulled a knife and tried to rob him."

"She was mad 'cause he didn't pay her for the pussy," Will said. "She just wanted her money up front."

Ritchie burst out laughing. I shook my head.

"What's funny? I know I've paid for it every single day'a my life," Will said with a deadpan expression.

Ritchie bowed her head. I knew her, and I knew she wasn't at all embarrassed.

When she'd composed herself, she continued. "Now, this business about the underpants, you say only the killer knew it?"

"Right," I said. "Early on, we made the decision that this would be our strike fact. Only the person that cut her would know about it."

She nodded. "Okay, let's go over the witness list. The doctor will testify to her injuries and the panties. Susy Weaver?"

"She's the bar maid who picked him out of the lineup; who'll testify to the two dollar bill that he left as a tip; and can name him as, 'Mikey', Tolliver's brother's name."

"Jerry Painter?"

Will looked at me. "That the weenie wagger?"

I nodded and looked at Ritchie. "He puts the car at the bar on the night of the incident. He's the one that gave us the vehicle description and approximate year."

"I've gotten a look at his rap sheet. It's pretty terrible. They're all misdemeanors, but still . . . ."

"We know. But everyone else that was there was drinking and pretty all over the map when it came to what day, and what description and all."

"Okay. Myrtice Abercrombie."

"That's the girl friend and the ex-wife of his brother."

"Tell me about the arrest?"

Will spoke up. "We found out from Myrtice that he was coming to town around the end of the year, so we staked out the trailer park where she lives. A couple of marked cars jumped him, and we followed him over into Mississippi. When they set up a roadblock, he took the ditch."

I didn't know what effect, if any, my surreptitious interruption of Myrtice's phone messages would have on the case. Apparently, Will saw no need to mention it, so I didn't bring it up, either.

"Was he hurt?"

"The car flipped, and he broke his arm in the crash." I paused as she wrote. "Why, what does his lawyer say?"

"He says you guys beat a confession out of him."

I looked at Will. "Herman Caine won't think much'a that."

"I don't think I know Herman Caine," Ritchie said.

"Polygraph examiner; his office is in the Albright Building."

"No chance he broke Tolliver's arm."

I shook my head. "We were watching the whole thing. The only thing he didn't tell us was where the knife was, and my guess is he doesn't remember himself."

"He remembers," Will said. "Didn't Rogers say he found a couple of knives in the car?"

"Yeah, but I don't know the lab results."

"I'll look into that," Ritchie said. "Otherwise, what else do we have? Physical evidence-wise?"

"Well, we've got a print on the two-dollar bill that Tolliver said was his 'trademark' tip; we've got the imprint of a bald tire found at the scene."

"Did it match the ones on his car?"

"Only in the sense that both are bald," I said.

"Of course, that in and of itself is unique, but you have to factor in that he's been drivin' the car around for nearly a year," Will said. "You can't make a tire bald in a year with normal wear and tear, but you better believe his lawyer is gonna try to make the jury think he can."

I looked at Will and back at Ritchie. "That's about it; a photo of his car, maybe, and the car tag."

Ritchie leaned back, took a deep breath, an act that caused her breasts to strain against her white blouse.

"Well, that's all pretty thin." She paused and looked at her pad. We were silent.

She looked up. "What do you guys say to a deal?"

My eyes widened. Will was deadpan. Finally, he spoke.

"What did you have in mind?"

"A blind plea to Manslaughter; or, Manslaughter, with a sentencing recommendation."

"What does her family say?" Will said.

"I haven't approached them yet. I wanted to see what you guys thought first."

Ritchie looked at me.

"Well, I think we can get a conviction," I said. "But, she was *their* daughter. If they don't want to go through a trial, I don't suppose you should make'em." I looked at Will.

When he didn't speak, Ritchie started again. "Well, I won't keep you. There is one other thing . . ." She looked through her notes.

"Here it is, a young woman in Birmingham. Does she have any relevance?"

"Just that fact that she went out with Tolliver; can testify to him identifying himself as 'Mikey'; maybe recognizing the car."

"I think we'll just give her a call." She paused. "And this State Police investigator. Does he know anything?"

"He just told us that Tolliver might be involved in immigrant smuggling."

"Was he?"

"I don't think so," Will said. "I think he's too fuckin' stupid for anybody to trust him with the kind of money that this old boy was talkin' about."

"Okay, well, maybe we'll just call him also."

She leaned back in the chair and thrust out her breasts once again. Then she took her hand and brushed back the shock of blonde hair on her forehead. She really was good looking woman. I could tell Will thought so too.

"I guess that's all I can think of. You guys got any questions?"

We both shook our heads.

"Well, okay. Let's just hope everything goes smoothly."

We rose, said our goodbyes, and left the room. Outside, I looked at Will.

"So, what did you think of that deal? You never said anything."

"Oh, that Manslaughter thing?"

"Yeah."

"I think gettin' shed of a crazy woman and the old boy that killed her is a good deal anytime, Son."

Chapter 68

Joyce Ritchie called the last week in August and told us that the Tolliver trial had been postponed until the first week in October due to scheduling conflict. I asked if it was hers or Greg Harper's. She said it was his.

Until then, Will and I made it through each day, waiting for something to happen, me more than him. He took it all in stride, while I was constantly sitting on the edge; that edge that would send me from a state of calm to a place of panic and distress in the course of one phone call.

Each night on call was its own special kind of misery for me. I didn't see the phone calls as adventures or quests but as trips into a type of purgatory; a journey into the lower regions to see man's inhumanity to man, only to return after a time of being repulsed, horrified, yet in some ways intoxicated. Sleep was impossible, for to sleep meant to relax and lose the edge. Being asleep meant eventually being awakened and feeling the pain of having been snatched from a place of serenity and sent to a place of torment. To this day I don't know why I did it.

Every morning Will and I met in the office to plan our day; he blowing on his ubiquitous cup of coffee and me wiping the sleep from my eyes. It was a morning ritual. Then Will would visit the Captain while I scanned the jail log to see who had been incarcerated overnight. Usually, the names meant nothing to me. Monday, the second week in August was different.

About halfway down on the second page I saw a name I recognized: Lucy Santos.

Lucy was an old acquaintance of mine from back about four years ago; a medical intern that I had dated a few times right after I had gotten assigned to homicide. I scanned across to her date of birth. She was about the right age. I followed over to the charge in the right hand column: Murder – hold for pertinent jurisdiction.

I was at once invigorated, shocked, and heartsick. I can't say that I loved this woman, but she was someone for whom I had no small amount of affection. Our relationship had ended with a whimper instead of a bang. Our lives just didn't seem to be able to mesh, what with her and her work and me and mine.

When Will got back to the office, I told him I had a detail to take care of, to call me on the radio if he needed me. He must have had things on his mind, because he didn't quiz me on it. I was grateful.

When I got to the jail it was just before ten AM. The prisoners had finished breakfast and were just beginning to move about. Attorneys usually met with their clients in the afternoons, after court, so investigators came in the mornings. I didn't even know if Lucy would still be there, but if she was, I wanted to see her; partly out of curiosity, partly out of a sense of nostalgia, and, in a small way, out of concern.

I stepped inside at the investigator's entrance, then through two additional magnetically-locked doors. I walked around the corner to the female corrections officer who was seated at a small table near the control room. She directed me to visiting room number four and told me Lucy would be there as soon as they could notify the control pod on her block – that is, if she wanted to come.

Ten minutes later, I looked down the short hall and saw Lucy walking toward me wearing a brown jumpsuit, socks, and slides. I stood up and opened the glass door.

It had been close to four years since I'd seen her, but she hadn't changed. Lucy had always been a knockout and still was. She was five foot three, a hundred and ten pounds, with dark brown hair, cut shoulder length, and a perfectly unblemished latte-colored complexion. Her face was an egg-shaped oval with a small nose and a bottom lip that protruded slightly under a small mouth. Her dark lashes and brows brought your eyes immediately to hers, and she had small hands and feet. I noticed a ring on her married finger as she seated and situated herself. She looked at me and said nothing.

As I studied her face a warm feeling of peace came over me. Memories that I thought had been drained from my head slowly began to seep back in and first her eyes, then her lips and mouth began to remind me of times past.

"Hey. You remember me?" I said.

She smiled slightly. "Yeah, Henry, I do. How are you?"

"How are *you*?"

She looked at the floor and then the ceiling. "Well, I'm in kind of a pickle right now." Her voice was the same smooth and sexy tone that I remembered, though she sounded tired.

"Look, I didn't come to ask about your case. Really, I don't want to know. I just came to see how you were and if there's anything I can do for you."

"Well," she paused, "I don't suppose there is. My mother is helping me get a lawyer. That's what I need right now more than anything."

I nodded. "So, what have you been up to? Where are you living?"

"I'm in Tampa. I was up here visiting family over in Baldwin County when they picked me up." She paused again. "My husband is dead."

"I'm sorry."

"Don't be. He was a bastard." She looked away, then back at me. "Are you still in homicide?"

I nodded. "Yeah, going on six years now."

"Well, you were good at that."

"Are you still practicing medicine?"

"Yeah. I'm in the emergency room of the county hospital down there. I've been there about three years."

"Good, I'm glad to hear it."

"After this, I may not be there much longer."

"Oh, everything's gonna work out. I know you. You're a survivor."

She smiled at his description of her. "You always did know the right thing to say."

"Well, I can't say I was in love, but I cared for you a lot, Lucy."

"I know you did. Just like right there, the way you said my name." She looked at me wistfully. "I was just too wrapped up in my work."

"I know. You wanted to be a doctor since you were a little girl. That was fine. I understood. I never held it against you."

She looked off out through the glass. "You know, I didn't realize what a great guy you are. We fell apart, and I hooked up with my husband. He turned out to be a real jackass."

"Is that what this is about?"

She nodded but said nothing more.

I took a deep breath. "Do you ever miss me?"

She looked me right in the eye, and I could see her shoulders relax. "Yes."

"You don't have to say it if it's not true."

"No, I mean it."

I didn't believe her. Women have an annoying way of trying to manipulate men by telling lies they think they want to hear. I could tell that even in her dire straits she was trying to pile up some points in case she needed them in the future.

"Well, regardless, I missed you. I mean, I wasn't debilitated, but, you know, there was a hole there for a while." I paused. "I wish it could have worked."

"Yeah, I know."

"So, this stuff you're here on, will it take you back to Tampa?"

"Yeah, yeah, it will." She looked me in the eye. "Thanks for not asking me about it."

"Sure."

"What I did, I did for a good reason."

"I'm sure you did."

"And, I think that everybody that hears about it will agree with me."

I nodded.

She said nothing for thirty seconds. Then she looked up to the ceiling. I thought I saw her eyes tearing up.

"I miss the old days. Things were much simpler then. I knew exactly what I wanted. Then, just a couple of wrong decisions, and . . ." she said.

"I understand."

We looked at each other for another minute. Then I leaned forward and decided that it was time to go. I reached and put my hand on hers.

"I guess I just wanted to see you and say, 'I'm sorry.' I hope you didn't think I came here to gloat or anything. I saw your name and remembered some good times we had." I paused and chuckled. "You remember going to the beach that time, and I put sun screen on all over – all except the bottoms of my feet. Man, I couldn't walk for two weeks."

She smiled. "I do."

"And that time we went to the fair and rode the Ferris wheel. Man, I was so nervous."

She nodded and smiled. "I couldn't understand why you were so afraid."

"Hey, I've seen what happens when people fall outta the sky. It's not a pretty sight."

I looked at her directly in the eye. "We saw a few movies, ate some meals. It was good, wasn't it?"

"It was. Very good."

I rose, and she did too. I took her by the hand and squeezed it. Then I opened the door and pointed her back toward the corrections officer. Before she walked off, I handed her my card.

"When you put all this behind you, if you want, call me. There's nothing I can do for you now, but, you know, later."

She looked down at the card and nodded. "Yeah, later." Her voice was soft, and I thought I heard it crack just a bit.

I watched her walk off and then turned to leave the visiting area.

Chapter 69

It started raining along about September fifteenth. Not a hard rain, but a steady one. It happened right as Hurricane Darrell came ashore at Pascagoula, Mississippi. It wasn't a bad storm, nor was it a large one, as storms go, but it was a very wet one, and Will and I did have to work two, twelve hour shifts at the Theodore office. We were on call to take a look at anybody that died during the storm, had there been. Thankfully, there were no fatalities.

But back to the rain. Mobile is the rainiest city in America, but most of it falls in the spring and in the afternoons in the summer. A series of fall rains, while not unheard of, was not as common as rain at other times. Not downpours, just steady, soaking precipitation that keeps everything moist and the ground so saturated there always seemed to be a puddle.

It was in the midst of this deluge that the trial of State of Alabama v. Rhett Hampton Tolliver was called in Mobile County Cicuit Court, Judge George Hartsfield presiding.

Subpoenas for Will and me had come out a week earlier, and I called Joyce Ritchie to see if there was anything last minute that she wanted to do, or discuss. She said no, she thought she had it put together. We mutually decided that I would sit at the prosecution table. Will said, that was fine with him, that I could testify to everything he could, probably more. I spent the weekend before the trial reading over my notes and generally thinking about how things would go.

On Monday, in the first week in October, it was raining. I picked up Will, and we left the office and headed downtown. I parallel parked on Church Street, in the first block east of the Judicial Plaza and notified the radio dispatcher that Will and I would be out of service until further notice. I grabbed the accordion style, faux leather wallet that contained all my notes and reports, slid into my raincoat, and we walked toward the south entrance. The rain tapped lightly on my bare head, not enough to be uncomfortable, but enough to know that my hair would be matted.

"Looks like it's gonna rain all fuckin' month," Will said.

"That's fine with me."

I liked rain. I always slept better in the rain, it normally drove most crime indoors, and the world always seemed to me to be a cleaner and a more sedate place when it rained.

We walked across Church Street, past the front door of Christ Episcopal Church, up the sidewalk, and into the east entrance of the courthouse. I almost slipped twice, first on the oily city street, then on the sidewalk. Will chuckled at my acrobatics.

This particular part of Church Street was lined by large, thick, old-growth oak trees, whose limbs extended over the pavement and spread a huge canopy over the south side of the plaza next to the east end of the courthouse. One tree in particular, near the east or rear entrance of the church, had particularly thick limbs that hung low overhead, one no more than twenty or so feet above the street. A sign had to remind trucks of the hazard.

557

Inside the atrium of the building, I stopped to take off my raincoat, and Will closed his umbrella. Will was wearing a dark gray suit and white shirt over his dirty shoes. His tie was a sedate maroon and gray stripe.

I was in my regular court uniform: blazer, khakis and starched shirt. I had worn it or a variation of it since I started in police work ten years previous.

As we walked toward the elevators, Will had to stop and speak to at least four people, attorneys mostly, who accosted him. Will had been around for many years and had made a lot of friends, and I'm sure some enemies, at the courthouse. Most respected him for his ability and his nerve; the nerve he had to look at all those dead bodies, for all those years.

We bypassed the metal detector and went around to the officer's entrance on the north side of the lobby. There was a large crowd of people, mostly the jury pool, waiting to ride the elevators up to the seventh floor where they would muster for eventual dispersion to each of the trials that would be called that week. Will and I waited against the glass wall until the doors opened and the majority of the civilians flooded the four elevators. By the time the group was out of the lobby and upstairs, we had waited fifteen minutes.

We rode elevator number four to the sixth floor and stepped off. Turning to the left, we made our way to number 6200, Hartsfield's courtroom. There were three or four people that I did not recognize milling about outside the double doors. I followed Will through the entrance and up the aisle toward the front. Joyce Ritchie was standing with her back to the door arranging files in front of her, on the prosecutor's table.

"Good morning, there, madam," Will said.

Ritchie turned and smiled. "Well, hey. You two ready?"

"Mr. Faulkner is, ma'am. I'm gonna be in and out."

"I understand." She looked at me. "We've got a couple of motions to reconcile before the venire comes in."

She paused. "One's about an illegal wiretap on Myrtice Abercrombie's telephone. You know anything about that?"

I looked at Will and smiled. "Wiretap? No."

She saw us smiling. "What?"

"You better tell her," Will said.

I cleared my throat. "I went to visit Myrtice, and when I got out there, I noticed that she had an answering machine that was just like mine. I remembered the factory code for checking messages remotely, and afterward, I periodically checked her machine while she was at work. When I heard that Tolliver was coming to town on New Year's Eve, we went and talked to her. We told her that we suspected that she knew where he was and when he was going to be around town again. She folded and told us he was coming in on New Year's Eve. We staked out the road and got after him as he came her way." I paused. "We didn't wiretap anything; we certainly didn't wiretap Tolliver's phone; and the information that we got that we used to catch up to him was provided by Myrtice."

Ritchie smirked. "You should have told me about this earlier."

"Why? Myrtice is not on trial. We didn't tap her phone. We told her about the reward, and she gave Tolliver up. All we had was the knowledge that he was on his way to town."

There was nothing to think about really. All she had to do was ask the defense to offer proof of their allegations. Even if they had phone records, all it would show is that I called Myrtice three or four times over the month of December, during the day, while she happened to be at work.

"Don't worry about it," I said. "They don't have a thing."

"You'd better be right."

We milled around and talked about nothing in particular for a few minutes before Will excused himself to, in his words, 'go check some things.' I took a seat on the front row and shut my eyes until I heard a noise to my left. When I opened my eyes, Ritchie was gone, and Robert and Evelyn Woods were standing there.

He was in a dark tweed suit and she a black dress. I noticed that she had a wadded up handkerchief in her hands and that her eyes were red.

"Detective Faulkner, how are you?" Zoe's father said.

I rose and shook his hand. "Fine, sir. How are you two doing?"

"We're getting along. We have our good days and our bad days."

We three looked around at the empty courtroom and stood in awkward silence for what was only about five seconds, but what seemed like two or three minutes.

"How are things up in Citronelle?" I said.

"Good. We just got a new police chief, and the library's expanding."

"How 'bout that."

"Yes, we're really growing." He paused. "So, you think we're gonna get what we hope for here?"

I looked away. "Mr. Woods, I learned a long time ago not to try to predict what juries will do. I think we've got all we can get, and it'll come down to what they think."

"Well," he said, his eyes blinking, "I know you did the best you could."

I felt about three feet tall right then. Had I done the best I could? Had I given this case a hundred percent? Had I put as much into it as I could to get a solution and make an arrest as quickly as possible? Deciding what was right, my feelings or his opinion, would take time to sort out, and right then was certainly not the time, nor the place, to try to do it.

I said, "Well," because I didn't know what else to say.

Evelyn Woods looked at me. "Would you mind praying with us, Detective Faulkner?"

560

It was the first time I'd ever been asked that. It didn't make me feel uncomfortable, but I tended to believe that the end of the trial, if God intended to take a hand in its resolution, was already a foregone conclusion.

The truth is that laws, police, and the like are the best that man can do to keep order in society. I am of the opinion that civil law is in many ways antithetical to the grace of God. The morality and the effectiveness of the law, or civil justice as it were, are only as good as the players who inhabit it: the judges, lawyers, detectives, wardens, jurors, citizens in general, even jail guards. When they become less moral, the system falls apart. That's why I think God will, in the end, have to balance the books.

"Sure, Ms Woods."

They bowed their heads and closed their eyes as I looked around the room. Then I bowed my head, but kept my eyes open, more as a matter of safety than anything else.

Woods' baritone voice began. "Father, God in heaven; hallowed be Thy name. Thy kingdom come, and Thy will be done. You told us in all things to give thanks. We thank You that today is the beginning of the end of this ordeal. We pray that You would rule these proceedings, and we are confident that justice will be done. We thank You for the work that Detective Faulkner has done." He paused. "Amen."

The Woods opened their eyes and looked at me. At that moment, I felt at once humbled and fearful. Had I done enough? Was my work something of which, at the end, I would not be ashamed?

"Thank you, sir. We may or may not get the verdict that we want," I said, "but, whatever happens . . ."

They nodded, turned away, and then walked to the second row and sat down. I turned back toward the front of the courtroom and the judge's bench. Ritchie walked through the door immediately to the right. She was smiling.

"Good news. We're going right to our case. Judge's canceling all the cases on the status docket."

I rubbed my hands together. "Let's get this show on the road."

Chapter 70

It was fifteen minutes later, right at nine o'clock when a dapper-looking Gregory Harper walked through the double doors at the back of the courtroom and strode confidently to the defense table in front. Everyone else, anyone who had any interest in the case, like Susy Weaver, Jerry Painter, and Myrtice, was being held in a witness room right off the hall, near the back door. Consequently, the courtroom was almost empty.

Harper wore a three piece, double breasted, light gray pinstriped suit, over a pink shirt. A pink and gray tie hung around his neck and was tied in a large Windsor knot. His white leather, tasseled, wing tipped loafers barely peeked out from under the cuffs of his pants. It was the perfect late seventies discoing outfit.

He smiled broadly as he walked toward Ritchie and stuck out his hand. She held out her hand, as women do, with her fingers together and her hand turned downward at the wrist; as if she expected it to be kissed.

"You look really sexy today, Joyce," he said.

"Don't give me that."

"Don't give me what?"

"That trying to get in my head thing. I'm gonna beat the pants off you."

Harper looked at me and smiled. "Notice how they always go for the pants."

I smelled the whiskey on his breath.

"Oh, you." She smiled slightly and looked embarrassed. "Judge says we're gonna get right to it. He's cancelled his status docket."

"Well, good." He looked around. "I'm thinking three days at the most. How 'bout you?"

"That sounds about right to me."

Their conversation was interrupted by the entrance of Judge Hartsfield into the courtroom by way of the door to the right of the bench. He coughed once as he took his seat and shuffled papers in front of him. His clerk, a woman I knew only as Becky, a female in her late middle age, sat down in the box immediately in front of the bench. She was followed by the reporter, a young, blond haired woman wearing all black, who sat next to Becky, back to back, in the same box.

Hartsfield rubbed his red nose and looked down at Ritchie. Then he cleared his throat.

"Ms Ritchie, are we ready?"

"The prosecution's ready, your honor."

"How about you Mr. Harper?"

"Ready also, Judge."

"Becky, bring in the defendant."

Becky rose from her seat and walked to the door to the judge's right. She opened the door, put her head just inside, and I saw her nod. She stepped away, and Rhett Tolliver was escorted into the room by a large, male corrections officer.

The look on Tolliver's face was apprehensive. He took two stiff legged steps into the room, stopped, and looked around. Then, after a shove from the corrections officer, he stumbled over to the defense table.

His hair was wet and plastered to his head. Since he'd been in jail and unable to get it dyed, it was now a dirty blond.

He wore a white, long sleeved shirt that was buttoned to the collar, and navy blue slacks over black oxford shoes. The stiff legged walk was due to the two braces on his legs under his trousers. They were an invention by a company in Massachusetts; if the defendant tries to run away, he can't; and if he tries walk off, he is easily spotted by his unusual gait.

He sat down at the table and leaned over and said something to Harper. Then he adjusted himself in the wooden chair and folded his hands.

"Julie," Hartsfield said to the reporter, "we're ready to go on the record."

The young blonde girl nodded and punched the record button on her tape recorder. Then she poised her fingers over the keys of her stenotype writer.

"Okay, we're here in the matter of State v. Rhett Tolliver. Present is counsel for the state, Joyce Ritchie, and for the defendant, Gregory Harper. The defendant is present also. I see there are a few motions to dispose of first." He shuffled papers in front of him. "One is a motion to dismiss from Mr. Harper."

Harper rose. "Yes, sir."

"Okay, make your case."

"Well, Judge, we maintain that the Sheriff's Department wire tapped the home of Myrtice Abercrombie and therefore the arrest of my client occurred as a result of the information gained by listening in on her phone calls. Other than Ms Abercrombie, no one else knew that the defendant was coming to Mobile."

"Any evidence of that? Bugs, wires, recorders, that sort of thing?"

"None, your honor. We just know that the sheriff's detectives knew things that my client only told Ms Abercrombie."

Hartsfield looked at Ritchie. "Ms Ritchie?"

"Preposterous."

"Mr. Harper, are you prepared to offer testimony?"

"Only Detective Faulkner."

I got very nervous very quickly. If I told the truth about how I came to know Tolliver's movements, I might just get myself sued by Myrtice Abercrombie. If I lied, it would be the first time I had ever done so on the witness stand.

Ritchie rose. "Judge, we object. The defense just wants to try to impugn this officer and his partner, and he hasn't laid any kind of a predicate for this, anywhere. And, besides, this sounds as if it has something to do with his arrest, not the case in chief against the defendant."

The judge looked at Harper. "Mr. Harper, is this a fishing expedition? What does it have to do with the case?"

"No, Judge. The defense thinks that the detectives got information about the case from defendant's phone calls to Ms Abercrombie. If I may be granted a little latitude . . ."

"All right, I'll allow a short voir dire, but get right to whatever it is that you're driving at."

I felt better that Ritchie was fighting for me. I just hoped Harper didn't stumble upon the right question. I stood up from my place at the prosecutor's table.

"Raise your right hand." Hartsfield said.

I did so. He administered the oath. Harper spoke.

"Detective Faulkner, how did you determine that my client would be in Mobile County on New Year's Eve?"

I cleared my throat. "Myself and my partner, Sergeant Eubanks, interviewed Myrtice Abercrombie, and she divulged the information."

He looked shocked. Apparently, he either didn't remember or hadn't read the report of our interview at the chicken plant.

"Did you at any time install any electronic listening device to intercept any of my client's calls?"

"No." He still hadn't asked the right question.

"Did you listen in while my client was in conversation with Ms Abercrombie?"

"No." Maybe there was something to this prayer business.

565

Harper looked down at his pad. "I guess I have nothing further, Judge."

I sat down and tried to calm my heart.

"Okay. Motion denied." He shuffled more papers. "All right, I have here another motion to suppress the defendant's statement to police on the grounds that it was obtained under duress." He looked up. "Just exactly what kind of duress?"

"My client was beaten by the detectives, Judge," Harper said.

"And you offer as evidence . . ."

"His broken arm."

"Ms Ritchie?"

"Judge, the defendant broke his arm in an automobile accident while attempting to elude police. We can offer medical records to that effect, given time."

"Your honor, the defendant is prepared to offer testimony that the detectives used pain and intimidation to extract a confession from him."

"Your honor . . ."

Hartsfield held up his hand stopping Ritchie. "Hold on, Ms Ritchie. I'll allow the confession to be entered, but if the defendant wants to dispute how it was obtained, I can't stop him – when the time comes." He looked at Harper. "But, Mr. Harper, there'll be no suborning perjury in my courtroom."

"I understand, Judge."

"Okay, I'll take this motion under advisement and rule on it when or if the confession is offered."

Hartsfield looked down at the papers in front of him. "Okay, here's a motion for a change of venue." He looked at Harper and smirked. "Really, Mr. Harper?"

"Judge, my client is from out of state. He has no friends here, and he's accused of killing a Mobile County woman. We feel the jury pool will display a level of regional prejudice against him, and we'd have a better chance of getting an impartial jury in another city."

Hartsfield, who had been looking at him while resting his chin on his hand, took a deep breath and exhaled.

"Well, we can't leave the state of Alabama, Mr. Harper. We'll still be in the same region, won't we?"

"I guess that's true, Judge."

"Denied."

"All right," Hartsfield said, "we have another motion here to sequester the jury. Mr. Harper?"

"Your honor, the defense thinks that any publicity at all, especially about the victim's mental state, if the jury is exposed to it, will prejudice them against my client; and her mental state is sure to be mentioned in any news reports about the trial."

Hartsfield raised his eyebrows. "Interesting. What say you, Ms Ritchie?"

"Judge, I haven't read the first story about this case in the local newspaper, nor have I seen any reports of it on the television news. The government feels that instructions from Your Honor to the jury, admonishing them to stay away from newspapers and television, will be sufficient in this case. As for her mental state, well," she shrugged, "it's sure to come up when the medical examiner testifies."

"I feel that way also. Mr. Harper, I myself hadn't heard of this case prior to it coming across my desk, and if the jury is going to hear about her mental state anyway, then . . . motion is denied." He looked around. "Anything else before we get started?"

Both lawyers shook their heads. "No, Judge," they said in unison. Hartsfield looked at Becky.

"Okay, bring in the jurors."

Becky stood up and walked around the bench, after which she disappeared through the door and into the judge's chambers.

"Anybody see that Alabama game, Saturday?" Hartsfield said.

The judge was an alumnus, both undergrad and law school, and was once the president of the state alumni association.

Harper was an Alabama grad also. "I did, Judge. I won a grand . . . uh, oh, I mean, I waaas in the grandstand for the game." He grinned broadly.

Hartsfield smiled and held up his hand. "I understand. We'll say no more about it."

Becky walked back through the door and announced that the venire would be there in five minutes. I picked up my case file and walked around the prosecutor's table to a location with my back to the bench. I was situating myself when the first of the fifty potential jurors walked through the back double doors escorted by two court police officers. The Woods were escorted out of the room by one of the officers and the jurors filled in the first four rows on both sides of the aisle.

Ritchie sat down next to me. I got a whiff of her fragrance and made a mental note to compliment her on it.

To say the group was diverse was not true. They were of primarily two races (I saw only one Asian); they were of primarily the same age (they seemed to range in age from thirty to sixty); and they were mostly women (just a handful of men). Juries were usually made up of older people who had either retired or were wealthy enough to be away from their jobs.

In the past, I'd always been afraid of two groups. The first was women, some of whom seemed to have a problem understanding 'reasonable doubt.' The other group was blacks. They could sometimes be inclined to believe the worst about police.

With fifty jurors, both sides would have eighteen strikes. Fourteen jurors would remain: twelve jurors and two alternates. The alternates were necessary in order to keep from having a declared mistrial if one of the primary jurors got sick or otherwise had to be released.

568

Hartsfield cleared his throat. "Ladies and gentlemen, you have been chosen as potential jurors for a murder case. It is not, I repeat, not a capital case; that is, a case for which, upon conviction, the defendant could be sentenced to death. The maximum sentence that can be imposed upon conviction in *this* case is life in the state penitentiary. The prosecutor is Ms Joyce Ritchie of the District Attorney's Office. The defense attorney is Mr. Gregory Harper of the firm of Harper and Daniels."

He continued on with his spiel about the questioning process, the ability to be objective, any reason why someone could not serve – surprisingly, no one raised their hand – and whether or not they had for religious reasons any conflict with sitting in judgment of another human being. Then he turned the proceedings over to Ritchie who walked to a lectern next to the table.

"Ladies and gentlemen, I'm Joyce Ritchie of the District Attorney's office. We expect to call the following witnesses." She listed everyone, starting with me, and including all our old friends: Sis; Painter; Flynn; Myrtice; Harris from the ER; as well as Roy Rogers; Hernandez; Crenshaw; the ME, Martin Goldberg; and the two ambulance drivers. Then she asked if any of the jurors had any relationship to anyone she had mentioned.

One of the jurors, a black female, raised her hand and said that Goldberg had performed an autopsy on her son, who had been murdered.

"Do you believe that will have any bearing on whether or not you can reach a fair verdict," Ritchie said.

"No, ma'am. I can be fair."

"And what is your number?"

"Panel 2, number fifteen."

When she reached the question about criminal history, four people raised their hands. The judge motioned them to the bench, and within earshot of only Ritchie and Harper, they confessed their particular crime or crimes.

Ritchie wrote them down and their panel numbers, then stepped back to the podium with a smile on her face.

She continued on with questioning regarding those who had been crime victims, those who had family members that were crime victims, and those who had any dealings with the Metro Sheriff's Department – favorable or unfavorable. After each question, each juror who raised their hand stood, said their panel number, and recited how they had been so affected. Then they sat down. After the last, I snuck a peak at Tolliver. He was pointing at different members of the pool and then whispering in Harper's ear.

Finally, Ritchie finished and passed the pool onto the Harper. He rose, walked deliberately to the lectern on his side of the room, and stopped. He looked at his legal pad, cleared his throat, and began.

"How many of you believe that the detectives would lie in order to make an arrest?"

Ritchie sprang up. "Objection."

"Overruled. Mr. Harper, be civil."

"Yes, Judge." Harper turned back toward the venire.

Three or four jurors raised their hands, explained, and recited their numbers.

"How many people believe that just because a person is indicted, he is therefore, automatically, guilty of a crime?"

Four people raised their hands. That was eight people who had given themselves a reason to be struck. I looked at Ritchie. She was busily writing down the numbers of the offending panel members.

As for my own list, I preferred to judge by sight and add or subtract those who I felt didn't belong based on their answers. Just because someone said they didn't trust the police didn't, in my mind, automatically disqualify them. If they were, say, a male with a responsible profession, then I could live with them being on the jury and trust them to make the right decision. A female who in the past felt she had been wronged, however, might hold a grudge and vote against us, regardless of the facts.

Harper continued on with his incendiary questioning: Do you believe law enforcement will make an arrest regardless of the facts, just to clear a case? And, would an officer plant evidence to assure a conviction? I'd heard it all before, so it didn't bother me. I just wished he would hurry up. Finally, Hartsfield spoke.

"Mr. Harper, can we wind this up?"

Harper looked around at the judge. "Yes, sir. That's all."

"All right. Ladies and gentlemen, we thank you for your candor. You may retire to the lobby, but please stay on the sixth floor. We will reconvene in, say," he looked at his watch rather than the clock on the wall, "oh, thirty minutes."

We kept our seats as the jury filed out. I looked over at Ritchie who was looking at the list of jurors.

"By the way," I said, "when you met those arrestees up at the bench, you came away smiling. What was that all about?"

She smiled again. "That older man that was up there said he had been arrested once, by a policeman. He said that he was drunk, but the officer told him he was being charged with hibachery. He didn't know what that was, but he thought it was pretty bad."

Thirty minutes later, I slipped back into my seat just as the jurors were coming back into the courtroom. I slid my list of juror recommendations across to Ritchie as the last of the panel was settling into their seats.

It wasn't hard picking this jury. I tried to get every man and every old person that I could. There was, among others, a college professor, a female doctor, two grandmothers, a mechanic, three homemakers, an unemployed engineer, and a retired postal carrier. Ritchie took my list and compared it to her own.

Fifteen minutes later, the jury was struck and seated in the box. We didn't get everyone, but we did get the college professor and the retired postal worker, two that I considered critical. Both were men, and both were white. We also got one of the grandmothers, who Ritchie wanted, and Harper took a musician who we did not want.

When they were all ensconced in the jury box, I scanned their faces. They all looked bored, tired, or sleepy. None seemed too delighted to be there. I guess if I didn't have to be, I wouldn't have wanted to be there either.

After instructing the jurors not to discuss the case, Judge Hartsfield adjourned for lunch with instructions to be back at one PM.

Will was seated in a chair in the hall, with his legs crossed, his back to a large picture window, when I walked out. He had his umbrella next to him and his pant legs were wet. I stood next to him.

"Well, how'd it go, Son?" he said.

"Pretty good so far. We got about half the jurors we wanted. The judge is gonna let his confession in, but he's gonna say we beat it out of him."

"Well, he's just lawyerin'." He paused. "How about that lady DA? You talk you up some pussy, yet?"

I smiled. "Not yet. I don't want to distract her."

He shook his head. "That's one good lookin' broad."

"You're all class, Will."

Chapter 71

It was raining when we walked across the street to the General Jackson Hotel for lunch. The hotel, one of the oldest in the city, served an excellent buffet daily. It was also a meeting place for lawyers, judges, and public officials of all stripes, many of whom take their lunch in the lounge across the hall from the restaurant. They feature, among other things, mutton, a meat that I happen to like very much.

"Does the Captain know where we are?" I said before forking up a bite of potato.

"I called him and told him."

"Any words of wisdom?"

Will smiled. "Yeah. He said to bring him somethin'."

"Gee whiz. I'm not on vacation."

"That's Linus for ya."

We watched as Judge Hartsfield walked into the restaurant, picked up a plate, and helped his self to the choices on the buffet table. He was in front of the vegetable courses when a waitress walked up to him holding a mixed drink. He took the glass and nodded in thanks.

When he'd left the room, I looked at Will.

"I think there's somethin' wrong with him."

"How so?"

"Why would he be drinkin' at lunch when he has a trial in progress?"

"Don't worry about it, Son. They all do it. Them bastards live on alcohol. They believe what they do is so fuckin' important and serious that they gotta have somethin' to get'em through it all; and in the end they think theirselves right into alcoholism. They gotta get shitfaced 'fore they can take a dump in the morning."

"Stress?"

Will looked at me. "I guess."

Back in court, Hartsfield explained to the jury about opening arguments. None of what the lawyers say is evidence, he told them. They're just going to give you an overview of what they intend to show, or what *they* believe the evidence will prove.

I looked over my shoulder at the gallery. The Woods were on the front row holding hands. Al Neal was absent, as were Zoe's sisters and her brother. Everyone else familiar with the case was outside in the witness room.

Ritchie began with a short profile of Zoe Woods. She described her as having a psychological defect, the effects of a tumor, which made her slow. Slow. I was getting tired of hearing the word. It was a good thing we didn't have to prove that, or to what level she was inhibited, for no one could. Ritchie moved on to The Society Lounge and Zoe's place in that culture. Then she talked about Rhett Tolliver, his predator mindset, and his flight when approached by law enforcement.

She said she expected the evidence to show that Tolliver was the last person to be with Zoe before she left the bar, that he drove her away in a red car, and that he admitted to two people that he had hurt her and left her dying on the side of the road. Ritchie painted a picture of her injuries and her ultimate cause of death. When she finished, the sparsely populated courtroom, was silent.

Gregory Harper rose and walked toward the jury. He adjusted his vest.

"Ladies and gentlemen of the jury don't be fooled. This case is not about a man and a woman having a couple of drinks in a bar, for that is all the prosecution is going to offer you. Mr. Tolliver doesn't deny that. He met and bought drinks for Ms Woods. Afterwards, he spent some time with her. But he didn't kill her. When he last saw Ms Woods, she was alive and standing on the side of Lauderdale Road, having decided she didn't want to share an interpersonal relationship with the Mr. Tolliver.

"Now, the prosecution is going to regale you with supposed confessions from my client. Well, the information in those statements is false, and was extracted from Mr. Tolliver by . . . well, let's just say, less than ethical means."

"Objection," Ritchie said.

"Overruled, but let's just stick to what you know, Mr. Harper," Hartsfield.

Harper began again. "Ladies and gentlemen, my client was looking for some female companionship and found a, well, for lack of a better term, a shrew of a woman who said, 'yes, yes, yes,' when apparently she meant 'no, no, no.' Not only that, after she said, 'no,' she then tried to relieve my client of his wallet by threatening him with a knife. He disarmed her, kicked her out of his car, and then left her alone, where she obviously wanted to be."

He looked around at the jury. "This case is not about my client. Ladies and gentlemen, it's about the Metro Sheriff's Department that is trying to frame an innocent man. When this case is over, we know that you'll find the defendant not guilty."

He turned, walked back to the table and sat down. The room was quiet. I scanned the juror's faces, a few of whom, oddly enough, were looking at me. I got a bad feeling in my stomach.

"Call your first witness, Ms Ritchie," the judge said.

"State calls, Robert Woods."

Woods rose from his place and walked slowly to the front. He was sworn and took his place in the witness chair.

"State you name, Sir," Ritchie said.

"Robert Woods."

"How are you related to Zoe Woods?"

"She's my daughter."

"I show you a photograph of the victim in this case. Do you recognize the person depicted in this photograph?"

Woods took an eight by ten photo of Zoe Woods, looked at it, and handed it back to Ritchie. "Yes."

"And who is this person?"

"It's my daughter, Zoe."

I recognized it as an autopsy photo of Zoe Woods. Robert Woods had a sick look on his face.

"May I publish, Your Honor?"

"Any objections?" Hartsfield said.

"None, Judge," Harper said. Ritchie handed the photograph to the juror on the end of the front row.

Then, in painstaking detail, Ritchie began constructing a profile of Zoe Woods. Robert Woods spoke in detail about her childhood, when they first noticed that she was different, her schooling, and later, her emancipation. He also talked about her finances.

"What could Zoe do?"

"Zoe could function as a normal person however, her decision-making skills were sorely lacking. She oftentimes had difficulty appreciating situations that were dangerous. She was unable to navigate the logical reasoning process; when she observed factors that could cause her harm, she was unable to appreciate their significance."

"Objection," Harper said.

"Grounds, Mr. Harper?"

"He sounds more like a psychologist than a father, Judge. He's drawing some psychological conclusions that he is not qualified to make."

"He can testify to what he saw in her," Ritchie said.

Hartsfield paused then took a deep breath. "It did sound a little like he was making a diagnosis. I'm going to sustain the objection." He turned to Woods. "Just limit your answers to what you saw and heard, sir." He glanced at the jury. "The jury will disregard the witness' last statement."

Ritchie began again. "Why did she leave home?"

Woods took a deep breath and exhaled. "She said she wanted to live independently. We tried to tell her that there were going to be situations that she would encounter with which she would be unable to cope, situations that might cause her problems, but that wasn't important to her. Zoe, well, she wanted to be just like anyone else."

"Tell us about Zoe's financial situation."

"Zoe was taken care of. She inherited a trust from her grandmother that matured when she turned twenty-one."

"Without being specific, what was the size of that trust?"

"It was in the low seven figures."

I could see the jury shift in their seats.

"Would it be fair to say that she had plenty of money?"

"As long as she could get to a bank, yes."

"Would it be fair to say that she would have no need to rob anyone of their money?"

"Objection."

"Overruled."

"Yes. That would be more than fair to say."

"Pass the witness."

Harper rose. He clearly had not made up his mind whether he wanted to ask Zoe's family any questions. He knew there was a danger that he'd come off looking heartless and hateful, or at the very least, unsympathetic.

"Mr. Woods, my condolences on the loss of your daughter."

Woods nodded.

Harper looked at him for what seemed like three or four seconds. Then he said:

"No questions."

Ritchie rose and looked down at her legal pad. "State calls, Martin Goldberg."

Goldberg marched up the aisle and stood next to the witness box to the right of the judge. He wore a blue blazer and white pants, and with his red hair, he looked very patriotic.

The judge swore him, and Goldberg took the seat in the witness box. He held in his hand a manila folder containing a copy of the autopsy report, a report that Ritchie had received weeks earlier.

577

Ritchie rose and walked to the lectern. "Sir, state your name and occupation."

"I'm Martin Goldberg, and I'm the medical examiner for Mobile County."

"Are you a medical doctor?"

"I am."

"As a medical examiner, what are your duties?"

"I investigate other than natural deaths of citizens of Mobile County and then render opinions as to the causes and manners of those deaths."

"And how do you render those opinions?"

"Normally, I evaluate information gathered through the performance of a medical procedure called an autopsy. I also consider facts gathered in the course of a death investigation."

"And when you say 'manner of death,' what do you mean."

Goldberg turned and looked at the jury. "Each death is classified in one of five ways: 'natural,' 'homicide,' 'suicide,' 'accident,' or, in the case in which a death cannot be classified, 'undetermined.'"

She continued qualifying him with regards to education – Yale Med School; experience – twenty-five years in practice; and number of autopsies – close to ten thousand.

"Judge, we would offer Dr. Goldberg as an expert in the field of forensic pathology," Ritchie said.

"Any objections, Mr. Harper?"

"None, Judge."

Ritchie continued. "And did you have occasion to perform an autopsy on the body of Zoe Woods?"

"Yes, I did."

"And what was her manner of death?"

"Ms Woods was the victim of a homicide."

"And in the course of that autopsy, did you produce any photographs of Zoe Woods' body?"

"I did."

Ritchie then turned off the lights and turned on a slide machine that projected photographs of Zoe Woods five feet high on a white screen.

"Dr. Goldberg, tell the jury what you discovered at that autopsy."

Goldberg stood up, walked over next to the screen and prepared to use a laser pointer to indicate her injuries. He cleared his throat.

"As you can see, she sustained a laceration laterally across her throat, rending her esophagus."

"Did she die as a result of the wound?"

"Actually, the cause of death was of an infection that resulted from the injury; however, but for the injury, she would not have gotten the infection, and therefore she would not have died."

"By the way, Doctor, what was Zoe Woods' height and weight?"

The doctor looked at his notes. "At autopsy, she was five four, and she weighed around a hundred and six pounds."

Ritchie led the doctor through a description of the injuries to Zoe Woods' pudenda, the fact that she was not menstruating, as well as the defensive wound she sustained on her hands. She also asked him about the tumor in her head.

"Was this tumor benign or malignant?"

"I would say it was benign; however, that is not to say that she wasn't affected by it."

"What would have been the effects of this tumor?"

"She would have had a reduced mental function; her decision-making ability would have been compromised. There would also have been some effect on her personality."

Then she said, "Pass the witness."

Harper rose and asked that the lights be turned on and the slide machine turned off. Goldberg returned to his place in the witness box. It was a good move. The less the jury saw of the injuries the better off his client was.

"Dr. Goldberg, you testified that the victim was cut, is that correct?"

"Yes."

"With what?"

"In my opinion, it was a small, sharp-edged instrument of some type."

"Have you been shown that instrument?"

"Not to my knowledge."

He paused. "Now, doctor, describe this benign tumor in the victim's head, please." He didn't use her name.

Doing this, I knew, would be a mistake. The jury would never hear anything after benign tumor.

Goldberg went into detail in describing Zoe Woods' tumor, its location and size.

"Do you think that tumor could have affected her personality?" Harper asked.

The doctor nodded. "I do."

"How so?"

"It has been my experience that she could have been subject to manic swings in mood or personality."

"Could these swings have had the potential to turn violent?"

"Possibly."

"No further."

"Any redirect, Ms Ritchie?" Hartsfield said.

Ritchie wanted to get him down as soon as possible. "No, your honor."

"Witness may step down."

Harper had done a little damage; not much, but a little.

Ritchie called the ambulance attendant, Bill Thomas, next. He told how they found Zoe Woods on the side of the road and of getting her to the hospital.

Next was the ER doctor, Julia Harris. She described Zoe's injuries and got in the fact that she had been raped with her underpants. Harper had only one question.

"What was her blood alcohol level, Doctor?"

580

Harris looked at her notes. "It was point two, two."

"Over twice the legal limit, is that right?"

"Well, I'm not an attorney, so I can't comment on what the legal limit is."

Harper looked disgusted. "In your opinion as a medical doctor, would it be fair to say that Zoe Woods' judgment was impaired due to alcohol usage?"

"It would be fair to say that, yes."

It was part of the ongoing saga of lawyer vs doctor in the courtroom. Lawyers, with less education, generally feel slightly inferior to doctors; however, they have, unofficially, as a group, resolved to give no quarter in their own arena. Therefore, you can always count on witnessing small battles of will whenever a doctor gets on a witness stand.

Meanwhile, Harris got off with no real damage. Zoe was drunk and everyone knew it. Ritchie looked down at the pad on her desk. Then she looked up.

"State calls, Henry Faulkner."

I rose from my seat, walked to the jury box, and was sworn. I took my place and laid out copies of all my police reports on the ledge in front of me. Then, I stated my name and occupation and told how I came to be involved in the investigation of the death of Zoe Woods.

"Did Ms Woods make any statement to you regarding who may have cut her?" Ritchie said.

"No."

"Did she offer you any help at all of identifying the man who did it?"

"Objection, leading the witness," Harper said.

"Excuse me, 'the person,' who did it."

"Objection, calls for hearsay."

"Judge, he can interview the victim of a crime, can't he?"

"I'll allow it."

"She gave me a clue in the form of the word, 'bird.'"

"And did you determine what if any was the value to that clue?"

"Objection, calls for speculation."

"He can tell us what he thinks the clue means," Hartsfield said.

"When the defendant was arrested, his automobile bore a South Carolina license plate; a plate that bears the likeness of a bird on it."

"Did you have occasion to visit the location of the victim's assault?"

"I did."

"Where was that location?"

"It was off Lauderdale Road, about equidistant between Bellingrath Road and Dauphin Island Parkway."

"Now, in the course of your investigation, did you develop a suspect?"

"Yes, I did."

"And who was that suspect?"

"Rhett Tolliver."

There was very little I could add without being peppered with hearsay objections. Susy Weaver would put him in the bar with a two dollar bill; Jerry Painter would put his car at the bar; Rogers would put his car at the scene and the print on the two dollar bill; Myrtice would hear his confession; and Herman Caine would hear his confession. It was thin, but it was there.

Harper asked me only about other tags with birds on them. I said I didn't know of any. He asked me if I had ever looked for a suspect by the name of 'Mikey.'

"Yes."

"Did you find him?"

"Yes."

"And who was it?"

"Michael Tolliver."

"Why was he not arrested?"

I couldn't believe that an experienced lawyer had asked such a dumb question. I cleared my throat and turned to the jury.

"Because it was Rhett Tolliver who was driving a car like the one observed at The Society Lounge; because he was picked out of a live line up as being with the victim; . . ."

"Objection, your honor."

"You opened the door, Mr. Harper," Hartsfield said. "Overruled."

I continued quickly. " . . . he was put with the victim by his fingerprints on a two dollar bill, a tip he admitted was his 'trademark'; he admitted to calling himself 'Mikey,' his brother's name; he admitted to cutting the victim with a knife; and he alone knew that she had been raped with her underpants, a fact that only the killer would know."

It was a once in lifetime opportunity. I thought fast to try to remember if there was anything else. When I couldn't, I stopped and took a breath.

"Nothing further," Harper said quickly before I could begin again.

Hartsfield looked at his watch. "I see it's three thirty. We're going to adjourn for today, as I have another matter to entertain this afternoon. We will reconvene tomorrow morning at nine AM." He turned to the jury. "My previous instructions regarding talking to anyone or having any contact with media in relation to this trial still stand." Hartsfield banged his gavel.

I stood up as the jury walked into the jury room and closed the door. Ritchie turned around and spoke to Robert and Evelyn Woods and shook their hands. I heard Evelyn Woods sniff twice before their meeting broke up.

"Well, how'd it go?" I said when she turned back to the table.

"That was some coup, getting all the evidence in at once."

I nodded and smiled. "That's happened to me only once before. I couldn't believe it.'

583

We both looked up and watched as Will walked up the aisle. He still had his umbrella, and his shoes were still wet.

"Raining?" I asked.

"It is; coming down hard, too." He looked at Ritchie. "How you doin' there, young lady?"

"Fine, Will. Your protégé knocked it out of the park."

He looked at me then glanced over at Harper. "Did you kick his ass, Son? Well, he deserves it."

"I guess it's going pretty well. We may need you, though," I said.

"What for?"

"He's gonna say we beat the confession out of him."

Will looked at Ritchie. "You gonna call Herman?"

She nodded. "Yes, but we may need you, also."

He took a deep breath and exhaled. "All right. Just let me at that needle dick little bastard. I'll cut him down to size."

I looked at Ritchie, and she burst out laughing.

Chapter 72

The next morning, it was raining, as usual, and we were to reconvene in courtroom 6200 at nine. I arrived earlier, at eight thirty, for coffee up in Ritchie's office. She was obsessing over Myrtice's testimony.

"Look," I said, "just get her to admit that she was involved with Tolliver, and then if she doesn't say what she told us, treat her as hostile witness."

"Oh, I know that, but it may not be that simple. I can tell you, a woman like Myrtice won't give up her man that easy."

She was probably right, though Myrtice was not as hard up as one might've thought. Rhett Tolliver was at least her second lover, after his brother.

"I guess ole Myrtice puts a stink on them Tolliver men that just don't wash off," I said.

Ritchie smiled. "I wonder what her technique is?"

"Have you seen Myrtice?"

She shook her head.

"She just grabs'em in a leg lock and don't let go until one of'em comes."

In court, Ritchie called Susy Weaver. Sis strode toward the witness box in a short sleeved black dress and matching pumps. Her hair was pulled back in a bun that was held in place, oddly, by a thick rubber band.

"Ms Weaver, what is your occupation?"

"I'm a waitress at The Society Lounge."

Slowly, Ritchie led Sis through the duties of her job; her relationship with Zoe Woods; her presence at the bar on the Friday night of the assault; and finally, the identification of the defendant.

"And do you see the man that Zoe was with in the courtroom today?"

"Yes."

"Point him out please."

Susy Weaver stood and pointed right at Tolliver who bowed his head and looked at the table.

"Let the record show that the witness has pointed to the defendant." She continued. "And did he give you a tip that night?"

"Yes."

585

"And what was it?"

"A two dollar bill."

"And what did you do with it?"

"I give it to Mr. Faulkner and his partner."

Ritchie showed her the two dollar bill enclosed in plastic. "Is this the bill?"

"Yes, ma'am. I remember the serial number ended with '911.'"

"Judge, the state would offer this exhibit into evidence."

"Any objections, Mr. Harper."

"None."

Ritchie turned away then turned back to Sis. "One more thing, did you ever know Zoe Woods to carry a knife?"

"No, ma'am."

"Nothing further."

Greg Harper rose from the defense table and walked to toward the witness box. When he got next to it, he stopped.

"Ms Weaver, do you serve alcoholic beverages at The Society Lounge?"

"Yes, sir."

"In fact, that's what you do more of than anything else, is that right?"

"Yes."

"You're around intoxicating drink every night, are you not?

"Yes, sir."

"Do you ever drink yourself?"

"No, sir."

"Surely you must take a drink every now and then, don't you?"

"Well, once in a great while. Larry, he says don't drink up the profits."

"Could you have been drinking on the night that Mr. Tolliver was in the bar?"

"No, sir."

"Are you sure?"

Sis hesitated, and when she did, her whole testimony went out the window; the ID, the bill, everything. I could see it on the juror's faces.

Ritchie was on her feet quickly, but not quick enough. "Objection. Asked and answered, Judge."

"Well, uh, no. I don't think so," Sis said.

"Wait a minute, wait a minute," Hartsfield said. "The objection is sustained. Jury will disregard that last answer."

"Now, you said that you knew the victim, is that correct?"

"Yes, sir."

"How would you describe her personality?"

"Oh, she was a nice enough person."

"When she was sober?"

"Right."

"What about when she was drinking?"

Sis hesitated. "Well, she could get a little surly."

"Like how?"

"Objection. The victim's personality is not on trial here. Relevance, Judge."

"It goes to prove our defense, Judge."

"I'll allow it."

"Continue, Ms Weaver," Harper said.

"You know, insulting, sarcastic; maybe a little mean."

Harper looked at the jury. "No more questions."

The next witness was Jerry Painter. Ritchie had told Will and me that she was reluctant to put him on the stand due to his criminal history, but she had decided to go ahead because of his identification of the car.

"Mr. Painter, what is you occupation?"

"I'm a mechanic. I work on cars."

"Would you say that you can recognize the makes and models of automobiles with some expertise?"

"Well, yeah."

"On the night in question, the night you were at The Society, did you notice a vehicle that you had never seen there before?"

"Yes."

"Describe that automobile for me."

"It was a nineteen seventy-four or seventy-five Chevy Nova, four door, red."

"Do you see a lot of that kind of car in your shop?"

"No. Not anymore."

Ritchie picked up a photo of Tolliver's car. "Is this the automobile you saw?"

Painter took the photograph. "It looks like it, but the one I saw wadn't tore up like this one."

Ritchie took back the picture and walked away. "Pass the witness."

Harper stood at the table. "Mr. Painter, have you ever been arrested?"

"Objection," Ritchie said.

"Goes to credibility, Judge."

"What does his arrest record have to do with whether or not he recognizes different makes of cars?" Ritchie said.

"Just allow me one more question, Judge?"

"Overruled, for now."

"Are you the same Jerry Painter who has been arrested four times for Indecent Exposure?"

Ritchie was on her feet again. "Objection. That question was completely improper. That's not a felony offense, Judge. And by the way, Mr. Harper knows it's not."

"She's right, Mr. Harper. Jury will disregard counsel's last question." He looked at Harper. "Play by the rules, Mr. Harper."

"The State would request sanctions, Judge," Ritchie said. Hartsfield waved her off.

Harper nodded and looked at the jury. "No further questions."

Ritchie called Roy Rogers and got the photographs of the crime scene and the car into evidence. Rogers also testified about the three knives found in the car as well as the license plate. In addition, Ritchie got him qualified as 'expert' in fingerprint comparison, and he put Tolliver's print on the two dollar bill. On cross, Harper brought out the fact that blood was not present on the knives.

Minutes later, Hernandez took the stand and testified as to plaster cast of the tire tracks at the scene and the comparison to the tires found on Tolliver's car. On cross, Harper got Hernandez to say that he found no identifying points that would match the tires to the cast. On redirect Ritchie made sure that the jury knew that the baldness was, in and of itself, an identifying anomaly. Harper, on re-cross got Hernandez to admit that there might possibly be more than one car on the road with bald tires.

By the time all of the truculence was concluded, Hartsfield broke everyone for lunch. I contented myself with a tuna salad sandwich in the luncheonette down in the lobby of the courthouse.

As I chewed, I thought about the case. Ritchie still hadn't done anything with our strongest piece of evidence, Tolliver's confession. Normally, you put your most compelling evidence on first. Why she was waiting was lost on me.

We had put Tolliver with Zoe the night she was cut, and we had almost put his vehicle where she was found. But, if we didn't get that confession into evidence, or if the jury somehow believed that it was obtained under duress, there was a real chance that he could be acquitted.

The jury hadn't let on that they would be that hard to handle. Most appeared bored and looked as if they wished it was all over. Even when the photos of the victim were shown, none of them flinched. They looked like the perfect jury: dispassionate, reasonably attentive, and bored; therefore, willing to convict someone just to get out and be gone.

I swigged a cup of tea and looked out the plate glass window at the rain as it fell. What was it the weatherman had said – the twenty-fifth straight day of rain? The drops hit the glass and rolled slowly down to the concrete sidewalk. Pedestrians stepped in puddles as they walked by, but the puddles remained, they just refilled with water.

The scene reminded me of me and my world. I walk through mud and filthy standing water every day. I step in the puddles, and the water splashes out, but it never goes away. It just stands there. If you make an about face and walk back through it, it still stands there. It remains. The puddles, like the dead bodies, never seem to dry up.

Back in court, Ritchie called Myrtice Abercrombie to the stand. This was the witness I'd been waiting for. If she talked, we had our case. If she didn't, the jury was left with the confession that we had elicited, and the lie that Tolliver would tell about how it was obtained.

Myrtice was wearing what I was sure was her Sunday best. She was sworn and laboriously climbed into the witness box wearing a multi-colored, tent dress with, oddly, a lace collar. Her hair was set and sprayed, and it stood out around her face making her head look like the center of an oddly colored sunflower.

"Ms Abercrombie, do you know the defendant?"

"Yeah."

"How long have you known him?"

"A long time; since me and my first husband was married."

"In fact, he's your former brother in law, is that right?"

"Yeah."

"And, you two have a relationship, is that correct?"

"We know each other."

"I mean, are you two lovers?"

She shook her head, a sure sign of deception.

"You'll have to answer aloud."

590

She cleared her throat, another sign of deception. "Uh, no."

I wasn't surprised, but I was disappointed. But the worst part of it was that if she would lie about that, she was going to lie about what she said.

"Do you recall telling Detective Faulkner that you and Rhett Tolliver were lovers?"

"No."

"Permission to treat as a hostile witness, your honor?"

"Go ahead."

Ritchie reached back and picked up a typewritten page off the prosecution table. "Ms Abercrombie, I have here a record of a conversation that you and Mr. Faulkner had the last week in December of last year." She paused. "Do you recall that conversation?"

"Not really, no."

"Didn't you tell Detective Faulkner that you and Mr. Tolliver were lovers?"

"I don't remember."

"And didn't you tell him that the defendant would be coming to town on New Year's Eve?"

"I don't know; maybe."

"Well, you must have. They were waiting for him when he got to your trailer park. And didn't you tell them that the defendant had told you what he had done to Zoe Woods?"

"I don't remember."

"Didn't you tell Detective Faulkner and Sergeant Eubanks that Rhett Tolliver told you what happened to Zoe Woods?"

"I don't know."

"Didn't Mr. Tolliver tell you that he and Zoe Woods fought?"

"I don't know."

"Didn't the defendant tell you that he cut her neck and put her out of the car?"

"No, no, I don't remember."

Ritchie stopped and looked at her. She smirked.

"Well, it's a good thing that Mr. Faulkner wrote it all down."

"Objection," Harper said.

"Sustained. Don't testify, Ms Ritchie."

"Yes, Your Honor. Pass the witness."

Harper walked toward the witness box. "Did the defendant tell you he killed the victim?"

"No."

"Did he tell you how she was when he left her?"

"He said she was fine."

"No further."

Myrtice Abercrombie had just ensured that I would have to testify again as a rebuttal witness. Well, at least the jury had heard what she told us, even if it hadn't come out of her mouth.

"State calls Herman Caine."

Herman walked with a determined stride to the witness box. His three piece suit was immaculate and his loafers bore a perfect spit shine.

"Sergeant Caine, what is your occupation?"

"I am a sergeant of deputies for the Sheriff of Mobile County." His deep bass boomed across the courtroom.

"And what is your current assignment?"

"I am the department's polygraphist. I also work as a Crimes Against Persons investigator in the Criminal Investigation Division."

"Now, regarding the Zoe Woods murder case, did you have an occasion to speak with the defendant, Rhett Tolliver?"

"I did."

"How did that come to be?"

"Sergeant Eubanks contacted me and told me that he had a subject who had agreed to undergo a polygraph examination. He provided me with pertinent questions, and then I met him and Detective Faulkner, along with the defendant, at the polygraph office."

"Did you, in fact, conduct that examination?"

"No."

"What happened?"

"I connected the proper sensors to Mr. Tolliver, and then, as per normal protocol, prior to turning on the instrument, I began asking the questions. At that time, Mr. Tolliver confessed to the crime."

"What exactly did he say?"

Herman looked down at his notes and began to read. "He said that he and Ms Woods met at the bar, and he bought her several drinks; specifically, Black Russians, an alcoholic mixed drink. After spending some time with each other, they subsequently left the bar and the victim directed him to drive to a remote location. When they stopped, he said that she produced a knife and tried to rob him. He defended himself, and in the process, she was injured. He then opened the car door and left her on the side of the road. He said he did not call authorities because he was from out of town and he thought that no one would believe that he was defending himself."

"Did he mention having sexual intercourse with the victim?"

"He did. He said that she had prepared for intercourse by pulling down her pants, but he declined; after which she produced the knife and tried to use it on him."

"Did he mention her underpants at all?"

"Yes, he said that she was menstruating and that she had used her underpants to stanch the flow by putting them into her vagina."

Ritchie turned to the jury as if to say, can you believe it? She then offered Herman's transcript of the interview as evidence.

"Pass the witness."

Harper rose. "Mr. Caine, was the defendant injured when you talked to him?"

"He said he had a broken arm."

"A broken arm. Now, you say you hooked up the sensors to him, but you had not turned on the machine, is that right?"

"We call it an instrument, but, yes, sir."

"Did you electrocute Mr. Tolliver?"

Ritchie was on her feet. "Objection. There's been no predicate for such a question."

"Judge, he just said there were wires hooked up to my client."

Hartsfield exhaled. "I'll allow it."

Caine smiled. "No, sir. These were sensors; wires to measure heart rate, blood pressure, perspiration. They had no electricity running through them."

"I see. Did you strike Mr. Tolliver?"

"Objection. He's not laid a predicate for that question either, Judge."

"We already know he had a broken arm, Your Honor. That's predicate enough."

"Overruled."

"Mr. Caine?" Harper said.

"Absolutely not." Caine was clearly insulted.

"So, if Mr. Tolliver said that he proffered that statement to you under duress, is he mistaken?"

"He is deceptive."

Harper looked at the jury. "No further."

"Redirect, Judge," Ritchie said rising. "Sergeant Caine, how did you know the defendant had a broken arm?"

"He had a cast on his arm."

"Did the defendant ever complain of any pain during the interview?"

"No, ma'am."

"Nothing further."

Hartsfield looked at his watch. "I see it is getting along toward three o'clock. Are we at a stopping place, Ms Ritchie?"

Ritchie looked at her notes. "I think so, Your Honor."

"Okay, let's recess for today. I have previous appointment that I have to get to. We'll return at nine AM."

I rose and looked at Ritchie. She was busy putting papers into a file box.

"He quits at three every day. What's he got going on?"

"I don't know, but there's a rumor going around the courthouse that he's getting some kind of medical treatment; for cancer, maybe."

I nodded and said nothing. More pain, more suffering.

Chapter 73

The next morning it rained (what else), and I once again met Ritchie in her office for coffee at eight. She was wearing another one of her tight skirts, a wardrobe choice that drew my seal of approval.

I blew on my coffee as Ritchie pored over her notes. "I don't think Myrtice hurt us too badly."

"She sure didn't help," she said.

"Hey, we got everything in, and you can use me to rebut. The jury'll know." I took a swig. "How do you feel about Herman's testimony?"

"It was fine. Herman comes off as such a high toned guy that there's no way the jury gets him working Tolliver over. He's just too . . ."

"Too what?"

"Too dignified."

"I think they teach that at polygraph school."

In court, at nine, the jury was seated and the judge gaveled the proceedings to order. I looked over at the jury box and saw an older white man yawning.

"Ms Ritchie?"

"Yes, Your Honor."

"You may begin."

"The prosecution rests, Judge."

Hartsfield nodded. "Okay. Mr. Harper?"

Harper rose. He had made another interesting wardrobe choice, this time a brown suit with a lime green shirt and a Jerry Garcia tie.

"Your honor, at this time we would renew our motion for a dismissal. The state has not proven that the defendant has committed any crime."

"Denied. Move on, Mr. Harper."

Harper cleared his throat and looked around the room. "Defense calls Rhett Tolliver."

Tolliver, wearing what looked like the same white shirt and dark slacks as the first day of the trial, rose from his seat and walked, stiff legged, around the table toward the witness box. He held his head high and looked straight ahead, noticeably avoiding eye contact with the jury. His hair was perfect. How he got Brylcreem in the jail was the real mystery.

He stopped at the corner of the judge's bench, in front of the court reporter and raised his right hand. The judge administered the oath and Tolliver said, "I do," hoarsely. Then he climbed in the witness chair.

"Before we start," Hartsfield said, "ladies and gentlemen of the jury I would like to tell you that the defendant's willingness to testify in his own behalf should not be given any more or less weight, one way or the other, than any other witness."

596

Harper came and stood in front of him so that the jury would have a full view of both of them. Tolliver kind of slumped his shoulders and leaned back in his chair.

"Rhett, tell the jury your name."

"Rhett Hampton Tolliver."

"And where are you from?"

"North Charlotte, North Carolina." He pronounced the word 'Chawlette,' with no 'r.'

"And what is your occupation?"

"I'm a poultry farmer."

"Are you married?"

"No."

"Do you have children?"

"Not that I know of." He grinned and looked at the jury.

Harper seemed disgusted, but just for a second. "Rhett, do you have any brothers and sisters?"

"One brother, and one sister."

"Have you ever lived in Mobile, Alabama?"

"No."

"When is the last time you visited here?"

He looked at the ceiling. "Oh, prob'ly about a year and a half ago."

"What were you doing here?"

"I was passing through, on my way to see my brother in New Orleans."

"How long did you stay?"

"I don't know, maybe a day or two."

"Rhett, did you at any time go to The Society Lounge?"

"Sure. I was out driving around, looking for a place to get a drink, and I ran up on it, not far from the highway, uh, the interstate, I mean."

"Did you meet anyone there?"

"Well, yeah. I met this woman there, she called herself Zelda."

"What happened then?"

597

"We had some drinks and talked."

"Then what?"

"Then she says she wants to go somewhere and do it."

"Do it?"

"You know, have sex." Oddly, he seemed embarrassed at the revelation.

"Go ahead."

"So, I says, let's go. So, we got up and left."

"Then what."

"Well, we start drivin', and I says, 'Hey, I'm not from around here, so you'll have to tell me where to go.' And she says, 'just go down there to the highway.'"

"Which highway?"

"The interstate, right up the street, there. So, we drove out to somewhere in the middle'a no place. I don't know where we was, and I couldn't find my way back."

"Rhett, tell the jury what happened when you stopped."

"Well, we started kissin', an' then she undid her pants and pulled'em down." I looked over at the jury. Some of the women had averted their eyes.

He continued. "Then I was about to, you know, but she reached in her pocket and pulled out a knife and opened it."

"What happened then?"

"Then she says, 'gimme your money,' and I says, 'I done spent it all on you.' So, she says, 'I'm gonna cut you,' and she leans in with the knife."

"Go on."

"So, I grabbed her by the arms and then we start wrestlin'; you know, wrestlin' over the knife."

"Then what happened?"

"Well, she, you know, she was cut."

"What did you do then?"

"I kinda reached across the front seat and opened the door. Then I just pushed her out the car, and then I started the engine and got outta there."

"Why did you not call for help?"

"Well, you know, I'm new, and I figgered that nobody would believe me; that she was tryin' to rob me. I thought she wadn't hurt that bad and could get herself home."

Harper paused and then looked over at the jury. They were awake. A couple wore smirks, and three or four were leaned slightly forward with intense looks on their faces. Harper acted as though he had more to say, but he was afraid of opening the door for the prosecutor. In the end, he looked back at Ritchie and said:

"Your witness."

Ritchie rose from the table and walked behind the lectern. The unspoken message to the jury was, 'this is a slime ball, and I don't want to get too close to him.' She folded two or three pages over her legal pad and paused.

"Mr. Tolliver, do you go by any other names?"

"No."

"Are you sure? Don't you sometimes go by the name of 'Mikey'?"

"Oh, no, Mikey's my brother's name."

"Didn't you tell Zoe Woods that your name was, Mikey?"

"Maybe, I could have. I don't remember."

"Why would you not want to use your own name?" She didn't have to spell it out to the jury – or did she?

"I don't remember tellin' her I was Mikey."

"Okay, let's try something else. Are you the same Rhett Tolliver that was convicted of assault with a knife eight years ago?"

"Now, that was in self-defense."

"Yes or no, Mr. Tolliver."

"Well, yeah."

"Now, on the night in question, you testified that Zoe, or Zelda, as you knew her, suggested that the two of you leave, is that correct?"

"Yeah."

"And she directed you to the place on Lauderdale Road, right?"

"Yeah."

"Where did you go when you left Lauderdale Road?"

"I went on to New Orleans."

"Now, you say when you stopped, you started kissing."

"Yeah."

"And then she undid her pants."

"Yeah."

"Was she wearing underpants?'

"Uh, no, her underpants was, uh, you know, they was inside her."

"Did you find that unusual?"

"Well, hey, you know, I don't know nothin' about that."

"Did you put her underpants inside her?"

"Uh, no, not me."

Ritchie glared at the jury then back at Tolliver. "Now, let's talk about the knife. How many times did you cut her with it?"

"Objection. Judge, he's testified that they fought over the knife; that's how she got cut."

"Judge, if they were fighting over the knife, then he had his hands on it also; so, if she was cut, he must have cut her. She certainly didn't cut herself," Ritchie said.

"I'll allow it. Overruled."

Tolliver looked from the judge to Ritchie. "Once, I think. We was fightin' over it."

"Tell me again how you pushed her out of the car, and left her there."

Ritchie was getting angry at him and it showed. He hadn't lied completely, but neither had he told the complete truth. He had bolstered reasonable doubt – his best defense – and if for some reason they should happen to believe his story, then we could be in for a rough time.

"I just reached across the seat and hit the handle then I pushed her out with my right hand."

"Just pushed her out onto the ground."

"She was tryin' to cut me."

Ritchie stopped and checked her notes. "Now, you testified that she undid her pants. How far did her pants come down?"

"Uh, well, not far. They was just unsnapped and unzipped and down around her legs."

"When the ambulance found her, her pants were off. Did you take them off?"

"No."

"You told the officers her underpants were inside her because she was having her period, did you not?"

"I don't think I said that."

Ritchie flipped through Tolliver's statement. "Well, let's just take a look at your statement." She walked to up to the side of the witness box. "Read right there, Mr. Tolliver, in the part highlighted in yellow."

Tolliver took the sheath of papers and held them in both hands. "'You know, she must'a been on her period 'cause her underpants was inside her.'" He looked up.

"Are you telling this jury that those are not your words?"

"Well, I said that, but that was when they was hittin' me."

It wasn't a huge mistake, but so far, Harper had not gotten into Tolliver's confession in depth. Had he mentioned it on direct, he would have only succeeded in mentioning one more time that there was one. Ritchie had just opened the door for him to talk about the duress but not the confession. She quickly got off the subject.

601

"Now, Mr. Tolliver, on the New Year's Eve of last year, you came to Mobile County, did you not?"

"Yeah."

"And when you got to Ms Abercrombie's neighborhood, the deputies got behind you didn't they?"

"Yeah."

"What happened after that?"

"They chased me."

"Why didn't you stop?"

"I was scared. I thought they was tryin' to shoot me."

"Did you know you were wanted for murder?"

"No."

"Isn't it true that you did know you were wanted, and that's why you ran?"

He was silent for several seconds. "Well, no. I mean, I thought they was gonna shoot me."

Ritchie took her legal pad and flipped the pages. Hartsfield took that opportunity to speak.

"Ms Ritchie, how much longer do you anticipate needing?"

"Not too long, Judge."

"Okay, let's break for lunch." He looked over at the jury. "Let's be back at one thirty."

Everyone rose as he vacated the bench. I stood next to Ritchie and watched as the panel filed out of the box and into the jury room. Then I turned and looked at the Woods.

Both looked chagrinned at what they had heard and seen. After the judge left, they sat back down on the front pew. Evelyn had a blank look on her face, and Robert's shoulders slumped noticeably.

"I'm sorry you had to hear all that. It wasn't the truth," I said.

Robert Woods' mouth was in a tight line. "I could kill that . . ."

I didn't know what else to say. Handling grief was not my strong suit. And when a family had to keep reliving a death over and over again, I *really* didn't know what to say.

That's the most insidious part of the criminal justice system. Hearing a family member was dead was bad enough; hearing he or she was murdered was worse; hearing how it happened was excruciating; but hearing it time and time again was . . ."

"I understand," was all I could say.

After lunch, we reconvened. We were in the home stretch, and I was getting a little tense. I knew I was going to have to get on the stand once more.

When the jury was seated and Tolliver was back in the witness box, Hartsfield looked at Ritchie.

"Continue, Ms Ritchie."

"Mr. Tolliver, what was the last thing the victim said to you?"

He looked up – a sure sign of deception – presumably to remember, but actually to think up an answer.

"I think she said, 'give me your money,' no, 'give me your fuckin' money."

"Did she happen to mention her injury?"

"No, she just wanted to get some money."

"When you saw her last, how was she laying?"

"Oh, no. She was standin' up."

It seemed to be getting worse for us the longer she went on. As implausible as his story sounded, he seemed, somehow, to be selling it to the jury. Ritchie must have heard my thoughts because she looked down at her notes and said:

"Nothing further."

"Mr. Harper?"

"Yes, Judge. I just have a couple of questions on redirect." He walked to the jury box. "Mr. Tolliver, you said that the deputies were beating on you when you made that confession. How were they beating you?"

"That big black man was twistin' my arm; and he had them wires in me, and I could feel a shock."

"Was what you told the detectives true?"

He paused and looked down. "Most of it wadn't. I mean, I took her out there, but she tried to rob me. We fought over her knife, and she got hurt. Now, I'm sorry about that, but she was okay when I left her. Somebody else must'a kilt her." He looked toward the Woods.

Harper nodded. He looked at the jury and said nothing else, undoubtedly figuring that Tolliver's answer could not be improved upon.

After that the defense rested. Ritchie called me to rebut Myrtice's reluctance to recall her boyfriend's confession and also to watching what occurred in the polygraph office. That took about five minutes, and Harper waived any cross. And with that, it was over.

Hartsfield called for a twenty minute jury recess to give the lawyers time to present their jury charges. It was a simple matter. The state wanted Murder, and the defense wanted an acquittal.

I would have preferred that the state include a charge of Manslaughter, especially after I heard what their final defense was. But Ritchie said, no. He murdered her and that's all there was to it. As far as the defense, I fully expected for Harper to move for another dismissal when court reconvened.

Harper also wanted a jury explanation of the self-defense doctrine. In my mind, it all boiled down to whether or not the jury believed that Zoe Woods had pulled out a knife and threatened Rhett Tolliver with his life if he didn't give her all the money he had in his pocket. If they didn't, they'd convict. If they did, they'd acquit.

Hartsfield looked at the papers in front of him and nodded. "Yes, this all looks in order. Anything else before we call'em back?"

Both lawyers looked at each other and shook their heads. "All right, head'em up."

Chapter 74

When the jury was back, Hartsfield told them that it was time for closing summations. He told them that the prosecution would go first, then the defense, then the prosecution once again. He told them that the prosecution got two opportunities to speak because they had the burden of proof.

When he finished, Joyce Ritchie rose. "Ladies and gentlemen of the jury, first, I would like to thank you for your service. But there is one more duty on your agenda. I would urge you to convict the defendant of the crime of Murder.

"You have heard testimony placing the defendant in the company of the victim, Zoe Woods; you have heard testimony that they left the bar together and went to a remote area of the county; you have heard testimony that a knife was produced and that Ms Woods' throat was cut, ultimately leading to her death.

"You have heard testimony that the defendant had the knife in his possession; that in his presence and by his hand Ms Woods was injured; and that the defendant pushed her out of the car and left her.

"Now, you will hear that the defendant's actions were exclusively in self-defense. That is not true. Look at the defendant's height and weight, and look at that of Ms Woods. The defendant could have easily subdued Ms Woods without any harm to either of them. You have also heard the Ms Woods tried to rob the defendant. That is not true also. Ms Woods was a wealthy woman and had no need of money. She had her own, in abundance.

"Then, when the defendant was finally located and approached by officers, what did he do? He ran. Ladies and gentlemen, innocent people don't run.

"Now, you can believe the defendant's account of what took place on Lauderdale Road, or you can believe your eyes, your ears, and the facts."

She took the jury through a recitation of what each prosecution witness said and also of Zoe Woods's injuries. Then she reiterated that fact Zoe Woods had money and no reason to rob anyone. Then she fed them her own conclusions about what happened.

"Consider this: consider that the two of them went to Lauderdale Road to have sexual intercourse. For some reason, probably because the defendant was impotent after so much alcohol, the victim began to deride him. I submit to you that the defendant became enraged, produced a knife, and cut Ms Woods from ear to ear." She took her hand and made the throat slashing motion. "After that, he pulled off her jeans, removed her underpants, and then raped her using those underpants as his tool. Raped her in a fit of anger, as if to say, 'I'll show you how impotent I am.' Then he left her; left her for dead on the side of the road. That's what happened, ladies and gentlemen, and that's why you must find the defendant guilty."

Ritchie sat down, and we looked at each other. I could see beads of sweat on her brow and on her upper lip, and it struck me right then that what she was doing was real work. Will often ridiculed lawyers for the fact that they read, wrote, and talked, but didn't actually do any work. I wish he could have seen her at that moment.

Quickly, as if to blunt the passion of her argument, Harper rose from his seat and almost ran toward the jury box. He stood in their line of sight, so they couldn't see the defendant; as if to take him out of their minds.

"Ladies and gentlemen, I, too, want to thank you for your service. The victim's death was an unfortunate incident; nevertheless, it was an incident that could have been avoided.

"My time with you will be short. I have just one thing to say: every human being has the right to defend themselves. Mr. Tolliver included.

"Mr. Tolliver was with the victim, yes. He went with her to Lauderdale Road, yes. But, Ms Ritchie's fantasy about impotence on the part of my client is just conjecture; pure speculation; her own imagination. The truth is that the victim tried to rob my client of his money and possessions, and Mr. Tolliver defended himself.

"Ladies and gentlemen of the jury, there was an eyewitness to this crime, and he testified in open court. My client has nothing to hide, and he got on the witness stand and swore to tell the truth. That's it. Had you been in his position, would you not have tried to save your own life?

"Mr. Tolliver was guilty of bad judgment for leaving the bar with a woman he hardly knew. He was guilty of bad judgment for not notifying the police agency that a crime had been committed, attempted robbery. He was guilty of bad judgment for not seeing that Ms Woods got home safely. And he was guilty of running from the police. But he is not, ladies and gentlemen, guilty of murder."

He paused and looked at each jury member. "The right of each person to defend him or herself is a fundamental natural right – not a constitutional right, for it is a much higher law than that. If you can't defend yourself, how can you live and work, and love?" I thought that was an odd way to put it.

"The state will try to tell you that since the victim had defense wounds, she must have been fending off an attack. You can get defense wounds by fending off a counterattack, also. They will say that since the victim was so much smaller than my client, he somehow could have disarmed her. Try disarming a person attempting to cut you with a knife."

He was right about that. It's a hard thing to do; certainly not like on TV or in fiction.

"And, by the way, Ms Woods' weight at autopsy was considerably smaller than when she was admitted to the hospital.

"The state will try to say that Ms Woods had no need of money, therefore she could not possibly have robbed Mr. Tolliver. Well, I submit to you that Ms Woods was living a life of erratic and reckless behavior and robbing Mr. Tolliver was just one more reckless act. She was, for lack of a better term, 'touched.' I don't even think she knew how much money she had."

He stopped. "Finally, let me mention the actions of the police when questioning my client. When he was questioned, my client was suffering from a broken arm that he sustained in an automobile accident. The fact that officers would use that injury to inflict more pain upon him and coerce him into giving a statement that he did not want to make without counsel is, well, despicable. Do not condone their actions."

He turned away from the jury and walked slowly back to his table. Tolliver, who had been sitting with his eyes down, sat up straight and confidently looked ahead. The jury was alternately looking at him, then at me. There was distaste on their faces.

Ritchie stood and went over it all again. She brought up the fact that it wasn't until the polygraph session that the defendant had mentioned the alleged robbery. She added the fact that nowhere was there any evidence to indicate that there had been any coercion on the part of Herman, Will, or I to get a statement from him. She also elaborated on the severity of Zoe Woods' injuries and also about the 'panties in the vagina' phenomenon – something that I had not seen before, nor have I seen since.

"Ladies and gentlemen, Rhett Tolliver took advantage of a woman who was slow of mind. Then, when he didn't get what he wanted, he killed her. That's it. You must find him guilty."

When she finished, she sat down, and everyone coughed, sneezed and cleared their throats. All that was left was the jury charge, and then the deliberation. Hartsfield spoke.

"Ladies and gentlemen of the jury, we are at the conclusion of the testimony phase and we are now beginning the deliberation phase. It will be your duty to look at the evidence, weigh the evidence as to its veracity and validity, then render a unanimous verdict as to the guilt or innocence of the defendant.

"You have heard the testimony of all the witnesses. You should not give any more value to one as opposed to another. And as I mentioned you should give no more value to the fact that defendant testified than you would had he not testified; and no more value than you would give to any other witness. If you determine that a witness has been untruthful at any point, you may disregard all of that witness's testimony."

Hartsfield picked up some papers in front of him. "Ladies and gentlemen of the jury the defendant is charged with Murder. Murder, by statute, occurs, when, with the intent to cause the death of another human being, he or she causes the death of another human being.

"Now, if you find the defendant guilty, you must find him guilty beyond a reasonable doubt. Reasonable doubt is doubt for which you have a reason. You do not need to find him guilty beyond a shadow of a doubt. That is not the standard. If you doubt he is guilty, but you have no reason for that doubt, then you have not necessarily met the standard for acquittal. It is only if you have a reason for your doubt. Now, keep in mind that there must be unanimous agreement in either guilt or acquittal." He paused and laid the papers aside.

"Now, ladies and gentlemen, your first duty is to elect a foreperson. After you do that, notify me, and we will recess for today. You will reconvene tomorrow morning at nine o'clock."

Hartsfield concluded his instructions and the jury rose. We did also. Tolliver was escorted out by a corrections officer. The members were ushered into the jury room by Becky, who was carrying the tire impression, the two dollar bill, the photographs, the license plate, and a copy of Tolliver's confession. The door closed behind them, and that was it.

Ritchie and I turned to the Woods. I noticed George Malloy standing in back with a pad and a tape recorder at the ready. Malloy was the courthouse reporter for the Examiner newspaper who had slipped in sometime after lunch. He was a pudgy man with half moon glasses whose white shirt, frayed necktie, and wrinkled khakis confirmed his low salary; a fact of which he continually reminded me. I liked George and gave him the high sign.

Ritchie was shaking hands with the Woods when I looked back at them. I couldn't help but wonder how their lives had changed, ultimately, by the death of their daughter; or by how it would change by the expression of this verdict. After all, she wasn't living with them; she had been a disappointment to them by leaving home; and she had become estranged from them, something to which they had resigned themselves a long time ago.

"Well, Detective Faulkner, what do you think?" Robert Woods said.

I shrugged. "Mr. Woods, I'm confident that the man who killed your daughter was sitting at that table over there. I really don't have any control over any other part of it all." I paused and nodded to Ritchie. "Ms Ritchie knows that juries can and will do anything. It's a flaw in our system."

"Well, I just want to thank you both for all you've done," Evelyn Woods said. "I . . ."

I could see her choking up. Other detectives might have put an arm around her and tried to comfort her, but that wasn't my way. When you do that, you let those people

610

inside your head, and that's when you start to do yourself harm.

Robert Woods put his arm around his wife – the exact right thing for him to do, at the exact right time. They held each other, and I knew then that they would be okay. Homicide has a way of tearing families apart, but when murder affects a family, they must run to and not away from each other. They must identify different aspects of their grief and then learn to meet each other's needs.

We said our goodbyes, and Ritchie and I gathered our belongings and walked toward the back of the room. Malloy approached us and asked for a quote. Ritchie put down her file box and thought for a minute.

"We're confident we have arrested and tried the perpetrator of the crime in this case. We are also confident that the evidence was presented in a clear and complete manner, and we believe the jury will agree with us."

Malloy held out his tape recorder at me, but I declined, citing departmental policy on unauthorized press releases. Malloy nodded, and we walked past him out of the door.

When we got to the elevator, Ritchie looked at me. "Are you going to be here tomorrow?"

"I'll have to go by the office first. If or when they come back, give me a call, and I'll rush right down. If I haven't heard from you by lunch, I'll stop by."

"Okay."

"It's been real," I said, beginning a well-worn saying.

"But not real fun?"

"We'll see tomorrow."

Chapter 75

That night I met Peggy Matthews for dinner and drinks at Alfredo's on Airport. I sidestepped puddles and ducked a heavy shower to get in and get us a table before she arrived.

Peggy was a copier salesperson that I had met a year ago when she came to the office to re-lease our copiers for another two years. She was a short blonde with a ready smile. I bought her a cup of coffee in the break room, and we became fast friends. I talked to her often on the telephone, and she was always interested in what I was doing for many reasons, but one main one.

Peggy's favorite aunt had been murdered. It happened in Montgomery on the east side of town. A burglar broke into her house and bludgeoned the elderly woman to death. I learned of it when we talked about another woman who'd been killed in a similar way.

She told me that the case had devastated everyone in her family. Her cousins were particularly guilt-ridden that they had not been with their mother in the days before she died, and had not found her sooner. The resulting conflict between the old woman's siblings left everyone angry. I told her that there was no way I could understand what her family had gone through . . . but I almost could.

The auburn-haired waitress at the restaurant took our drink order and left us each with a menu and ten minutes to peruse it. Alfredo's was a quiet place, dark, and with atmosphere; by that I mean that the walls were covered in a dark-colored, hanging velvet fabric, to absorb the sound of people talking, thereby quieting the room. Each table also had one of those wine bottles with a candle stuck in the neck and dried wax running over the sides. Peggy and I ate lunch or dinner once or twice a month, and Alfredo's was one of our favorite haunts.

The waitress brought our drinks – white wine for her and red for me – and I ordered a large bowl of soup.

Peggy ordered the pasta with Alfredo sauce, the house specialty. I leaned back, took a deep breath, and exhaled.

"Man, what a week," I said.

"That's right. You were in trial this week."

"Just wrapped it up today."

"Verdict?" she said with a piece of breadstick in her mouth.

"Not, yet. The jury's got it; they start deliberating tomorrow."

"Now, which case was this?"

"I told you about it, the woman meets a guy at a bar and they go to the country. He can't get it up, and she lets him hear about it, so he cut her throat."

"Oooo. Yeah, I remember." She paused and took a drink. "So, what do you think?"

I shrugged. "We made as good a case as we could. But you never know."

"So, how are you doing?" She asked. Her brows were raised in understanding sympathy.

I hyperventilated again. "I don't know." I looked her directly in the eyes. "Sometimes, it all seems like a game. I know something has to be done with people that kill, but we caught the guy," I shrugged, "so what. Nobody's going to kill him for taking her life. He'll go off to jail for a while and live his life there, eating and drinking and exercising, watching television and reading a few books, all at somebody else's expense; that is, if he's convicted."

"Well, while he's there, he's not out trying to kill me or you, right?"

"Oh, he's a sociopath, and he'll kill again if he gets mad enough, or if he doesn't get his way; either in jail or out of jail. But really, will a similar set of circumstances like this ever come up again in his life?"

"Who knows? But we're all still better off with him in jail, rather than out."

The waitress brought our food, and I saw Peggy bow her head in a quick and silent blessing. It was a side of

613

her I had not seen. I should have waited, but I went ahead and dug in, and soup was dribbling down my chin when she looked up.

"So, what about the woman's family? The dead girl, I mean," she said.

"Oh, I guess they're bearing up all right. Her common law old man has put it in the wind. Her parents are the only ones who showed up. They've got money, and money always takes your mind off your troubles."

"I bet they were devastated, though."

"I suppose. She wasn't exactly daughter of the year, but they say you should never outlive your children."

"Didn't you tell me she was a little slow?"

"She was, though I never really figured out what 'slow' meant, or how slow she was. She may have been slightly autistic, or a little retarded, but I really don't know. She could function. She ate, dressed herself, worked, and was smart enough to hustle a drink. I think, at the end of the day, she just talked before she spoke. Most of us learn how to control it. She had something in her head – the doctor says a tumor – that never let her."

"So, what does Will think about all this?"

"Will was never really into this thing. First, he said that if she lived, we'd've been better off if she died. Then when she died, and she wasn't around anymore to push the thing along, and we knew who did it, he had no reason to get after it. It fell to me to put all the energy toward making a case.

"I think Will just believed it was all her fault, that she did it to herself; when you lie down with dogs, you know . . ."

"Yeah, but you can't look at it like that."

"Hey, I'm not sayin' he's right. But you've got to admit that when a person puts their self in a position where they're more likely to get burned, it's hard to have much sympathy for'em."

"Well, hey, everybody makes mistakes."

"Sure, they do. You just have to limit your mistakes and make sure that when you're committin'em you're not doing it with the dregs of society."

"Is that what he is?"

I nodded and took a spoonful of soup. "If he's not, he's pretty close. The state thinks he's involved in some kind of immigration dodge. As it is, we know he roams the countryside taking menial jobs, meeting women, and just spreading his seed." I blew on the spoon to cool the soup. "He's sleeping with his brother's ex-wife, for Pete's sake."

"So, what have you learned?"

I chuckled. "Ask me when the verdict comes in."

"Oh, come on. You've had a chance to digest it already."

I thought for a minute. "I'm not sure I learned anything that I didn't already know. Like I said, let's wait until the verdict comes back. What I'm afraid of is that Will is right: some cases are not meant to be solved – or are not worth being solved – no matter how much effort and time you put into'em."

"I just don't believe that's true."

"I'm not saying you're wrong. I know in my career, I've seen cases where we have plenty of evidence and witnesses, and they just never come together. At the same time, I've seen cases where I told the victims or victim's families that we had nothing to go on, and I was doubtful that anything positive would ever happen, and in those cases we made an arrest – and got convictions." I took a drink. "It's the same with injuries."

"How so?"

"Well, take the victim in this case. She had her throat cut, true enough, and she even coded twice in the ambulance and at the ER, but she was gonna make it. She died from an infection. Bacteria killed her. It was almost as if you could say, 'it was her time.'"

"You know, I'm not sure that's true. Aunt Marilyn shouldn't have died."

615

She looked at her plate and moved noodles around with her fork. I could tell the pain was still in her mind, even two years later.

"Well, I'm sure I don't know," I said. "Who knows, if she hadn't've been killed, she might've died from a heart attack or something.

"I just know homicide is a horrible thing. And yet people use it for entertainment purposes; books, television, and all that," I said.

"Now, you're right about that. I don't think I've seen one of those cop shows in years."

We ate in silence, listening to Frank Sinatra (who else at an Italian restaurant) over Muzak. Finally, Peggy spoke.

"So, just exactly how disappointed will you be if the verdict is not guilty?"

"Well, first of all, I don't think that's going to happen. But, if it does, I'll sit and talk to Ritchie and Will and try to figure out what went wrong, and then move on. If there's one thing I've learned from police work, it's that you have very little control over anything. No use in me losing sleep over something I've got no say in.

"Now, Will, he's another story. Something like a wrong verdict, or a case we couldn't solve, will work on him for days. He'll be calling me every night for a week. Maybe that's why he hasn't been so interested in this case." I took the last swig from my wine glass and looked away. "He couldn't take the disappointment of losing it."

Chapter 76

The next morning, I met Will at the office. It was still raining, and I shook out my raincoat before sitting down. He was sitting at his desk with the Harden file in front of him, going over his notes.

Will didn't keep notes in a notebook. He took notes on a legal pad, then tore the pages off the pad and made them a part of the case file. We called them 'Snuffy sheets.'

I came in and sat down and rubbed my temples. I should never drink wine at dinner. Even a little always gives me a headache in the morning.

"Well, it's about time you cut that shit out over at the courthouse and got back to work," he said.

I knew he was joking, though he didn't look it. I think he thought he was keeping me humble.

"You get you any of that lady lawyer's pussy?"

I chuckled. "No, no. She's much too bitchy for me."

"Hey, you can't see bitchy with the lights off."

"No, but you can hear it. And that's worse."

I paused and thought of Joyce Ritchie, her muscular legs and the skirt pulled tight across her bottom.

"What are you working on?" I said.

"I'm just trying to figure out a way get old Slim over in Hattiesburg to help us get Sonny to admit what he done." He looked up. "What time are you due back in court?"

"Ah, the jury's out right now. She said they'd call me when they were back."

"So, you've got the morning, at least."

"Probably."

At that moment, Denise Allenbach knocked on the open door and strolled in. She looked fantastic in a red pullover and gray miniskirt. Her hair was pulled back over her ears and there was a red ribbon in it.

"Hey, Henry. How'd it go?"

"Good. The jury's out. We're just waiting for a call."

"The reason I ask is that the Captain wants to know."

"Tell him, I'll have something for him this afternoon, hopefully."

She nodded. "He wants to be able to tell the Sheriff that it's a win."

"I understand."

"Just let me know, huh?" She smiled at me and then looked at Will. "Nice to see you, too," she said in exaggerated politeness.

Will looked up and grunted. Denise turned her back quickly and walked out in a huff.

We spent the rest of the morning on the telephone. Will talked with the Mississippi Bureau of Investigation about getting a wire put on Slim. I called Escambia County, Florida, and made preparations to take custody of the shotgun that they had taken off of Sonny.

I stopped by to see the Captain before we went to lunch. He was leaned back in his chair asleep when I knocked on his door.

"Captain, are you busy?"

"No, Henry, come on in."

I took two steps in the door. "I just wanted to let you know that it looks good over at the courthouse. I think the Sheriff's going to be happy."

"Good. Good. You know that family is big up in Citronelle. They could be of help to the Sheriff."

"I know. I think we made a good case, but . . . now, you never can tell what a jury'll do."

"I know, but you think you made your case."

"I believe we did. As well as we could."

"Good."

At that moment, his phone rang. The Captain picked up the receiver. "Um, hmm. Okay, I'll tell him." He hung up the phone.

"The jury's back."

Will and I made it to the courthouse in fifteen minutes. It was raining harder, but fortunately traffic on the interstate was sparse. I got off at Canal Street, and Will cursed as I slid through the stoplight at the foot of the ramp. We found a place on Church Street and walked quickly across the courtyard to the doors of the atrium.

The sixth floor lobby was almost deserted. We walked from the elevator to 6200, and I looked through the window before entering. The jury was not yet in the box. I walked in and strode quickly to the prosecution table where Joyce Ritchie was fidgeting with papers. The judge was on the bench, Harper and Tolliver were at the defense table, the clerk and the reporter were in their places, and Robert and Evelyn Woods were seated directly behind us on the first row. Thomas Neill was standing in the back, and Will took a place next to him. George Malloy was seated on the back row, and the only other new people in the room were a female corrections officer and a court policeman, an older man with gray hair. Apparently, I was the last piece of the puzzle.

"Becky, bring in the jury," Hartsfield said.

Becky got up and walked to the jury room and opened the door. In a minute the fourteen people were back in the jury box. I watched their eyes. Some looked at Tolliver, some looked away.

The room was almost completely silent. The only sound was the clicking of the court reporter's keyboard. When the jury was seated, Hartsfield spoke.

"Okay, the first order of business is the two alternates." Becky handed him a paper. "Jurors number twelve and six you may be dismissed. You can wait in the jury room, and Becky will have a little monetary something for you. Thank you for your service.

"Next, I want to remind everyone that there will not be, and this should not be a problem, any emotional outbursts. Please control yourselves."

Hartsfield looked at Ritchie and Harper. "Can you two think of anything we need to do before the verdict?"

"No, Judge," Ritchie said.

"No, Your Honor," Harper replied.

He looked around, then back at the jury. "Okay. Ladies and gentlemen of the jury, have you reached a verdict?"

A tall, thin white man with wire rimmed glasses, a tweed sport coat with patches on the sleeves, and an oxford shirt stood up.

"We have, Your Honor."

"Will the defendant rise." Tolliver and Harper stood.

Hartsfield looked at the jury. "What say you?"

He looked around the room, and then down at the verdict form in front of him. He cleared his throat.

"In the matter of the state of Alabama vs Rhett Hampton Tolliver, we find the defendant . . . not guilty."

"Oh," Evelyn Woods said.

There was a titter in the back of the room. Ritchie threw down her pencil. Tolliver clapped his hands once and smiled at Harper.

Immediately my blood pressure spiked, and I got a flushed feeling throughout my body. For a second, a sob rose in my throat. Ritchie was on her feet quickly.

"Judge, the state requests a poll of the jury."

Hartsfield then called each juror by number and asked them what their verdict was. Each looked at the judge and said, "Not Guilty."

When he was finished, Ritchie spoke again. "Judge, we would ask for a directed verdict. The evidence warrants nullification in this case."

Hartsfield looked at her hard. Clearly, he had prepared himself for this eventuality.

"Denied.

Ritchie sat down.

"Rhett Tolliver, the jury having found you not guilty, I hereby declare you to be not guilty. You are free to go. Ms Fletcher," he said to the corrections officer, "take Mr. Tolliver and get those braces off his legs."

The corrections officer came forward and took Tolliver back to the holding cell. I heard Harper tell him he would take him back to the Metro Jail for his belongings.

Hartsfield dismissed the jury with thanks and sent them back to the jury room. I didn't want to, but I turned back to the Woods. I shook my head.

"I'm sorry," was all I could say.

Both of them nodded, but said nothing. They just sat there, silently, without moving.

I looked at Ritchie. She appeared on the verge of tears. I raised my brows and shrugged.

Will walked up to the front and stood. I was afraid of what he was going to say, but, thankfully, he did not speak.

Twenty minutes later Will and I were standing on the sidewalk on the south, or Church Street side of the courthouse under Will's umbrella waiting for traffic to clear so we could cross the street.

We had stepped out of the courtroom and into the hall, and tried to debrief, just for a minute, with Ritchie. She wasn't distraught, but she was clearly stunned. I told her we would meet with her in a couple of days. Then we left.

Standing on the sidewalk, I looked east, and Will looked west, and we waited for the lunchtime traffic to lighten. It was still raining.

It surprised me just a little, but when I looked down the street, I saw Tolliver standing on the sidewalk next to Harper, under his umbrella. He was close to the Episcopal Church, underneath two oak trees. Tolliver was smiling broadly and at one point he threw his head back and laughed. I was at once, infuriated, then calm – wondering just exactly how I could exact justice. Will could see it on my face.

"Forget about it, Son. He ain't worth it."

"How'd you know what I was thinking?"

"'Cause, I've thought the same thing a hundred times."

I was thankful that the Woods were not nearby. It would have hurt them to see him laughing and joking, knowing that he was going free while they were still in the bondage of their grief. I looked away, across the interstate, and up at the cloudy sky.

When I first heard it, I thought the 'crack' sounded like lightning. Then I thought it was the report of a rifle shot, but it lasted much too long. Then I looked in the direction of the sound and saw what was happening.

One of the limbs from a tree, a large one that appeared about eighteen inches in diameter, had broken off and fallen – right on Rhett Tolliver. Will said:

"Son of a bitch!" and we both walked fast in that direction.

When we got there, I could see that the limb had fallen on the Tolliver's head. He appeared unconscious.

Harper was getting up off the ground and wiping the leaves and debris off of his burnt orange colored suit and cursing to himself.

I yelled to a police officer to call for a fire department rescue truck. Then I tried to step between branches to check on Tolliver. The way was almost impassable, but when I got within three feet, I stretched as far as I could and managed to get two fingers on his neck trying to locate a carotid pulse. I found none.

The medical examiner's ruling was 'accidental death by an act of God.' A forensic biologist ruled that nearly thirty straight days of rain had so heavily saturated the tree that the limb just couldn't stand the strain any longer and broke.

Imagine that.

The End

Epilogue

I spoke to Robert and Evelyn Woods a week or two after Rhett Tolliver's death. They were shaken but satisfied. They said that they believed that God was just righting an injustice that had happened in court. I'm not certain they were wrong.

True to Susy Weaver's prediction, The Society closed about six months after the trial. I drove by recently and saw that weeds were growing up through the oyster shell parking lot and the place had an even more run down and desolate look than it had when Will and I first drove onto the property shortly after Zoe Woods was found. Thereafter, I lost track of Sis and Larry Flynn.

Al Neal faded into the woodwork. I never saw or heard from him again. My guess is that he got his disability judgement – everyone does – and found another woman to shack up with. Wouldn't it be funny if it was Gretta Jones?

Myrtice Abercrombie continued working at the Tyndall Chicken Plant. Last I heard, she had become the supervisor of the plucking and cleaning department and eventually moved out of the trailer park. She never found out that I had listened to her answering machine to learn when Rhett Tolliver was coming to town.

After six years and five more months, we finally made a case and Sonny Grimes ended up pleading guilty to killing Cal Harden. He was sentenced to life, or thirty years in prison, whichever comes first; which just goes to show you that the answers to some of life's hardest and most perplexing questions are oftentimes right around the corner.

The two boys that killed Larry Stinson got life in prison without parole. When it came time for the two girls to testify in court, Amy Ludlow had given birth to John Tompkins child, a baby boy, and Lisa Harrell had herself enlisted in the US Navy.

Simp Patridge got seven years for cutting the Cajun from Louisiana; Ricardo Washington, a repeat offender, got life without for shooting into the truck and killing the fifteen year old kid going home from the movies; Alphonso Middleton got twenty years in the federal prison for robbing the Commerce Bank at Government and Espejo. And Tommy Sullivan, the man who shot his lover's husband, well, his case was no billed at the grand jury, and he and Mary Weatherford moved back to Oklahoma where they no doubt lived happily ever after.

Will said it. The dead bodies were there before he and I got there, and they would be there long after we left. Well, I didn't leave, but Will did. When a new sheriff was elected, Will took retirement after thirty-seven years service and moved to the hill country of Kentucky to get away from it all.

It was a somewhat acrimonious departure. Will and the new sheriff didn't get along so well; something about a disagreement over how to handle a murder case. I guess you could say that Will and the Metro Sheriff's Department went through a divorce. After all those years, I guess their relationship *was* kind of like a marriage.

I, however, soldiered on. I was ultimately promoted to lieutenant and made a supervisor in the Major Crimes Bureau. Megan Crenshaw became my new partner, and we became the primary team.

And, what of all the women? McDowell, Allenbach, Ritchie, Sandy Winston, Lucy Santos, and the others? Well, let's just say that I'm still alone – married to murder.

Fin

Caleb Lott, who was once a homicide detective, is the pseudonym for the author who lives and writes in Alabama.